MILE END

To Dorothy & Tom Donoghue —
I hope you like my tome.

Alan Grayson

Alan Grayson

Ragged Sky Press

Library of Congress Catalog Number: 2003112184

ISBN: 1-58961-092-X

Cover design: FoosRowntree

Printed in the United States of America

"Never forget that in this world, proctologists

earn more than philosophers."

— *Uncle Sid*

Acknowledgements

I gratefully acknowledge the years of support and encouragement from author and chief librarian Jinny Baekler and members of her Plainsboro Literary Group. I am equally indebted to Jane Marchetti, Barbara Johnstone, Deborah Kaple, and Michael Bruner. Also author Rose Marie Burwell, poet Dick Greene, Hilda Barry, and Jane Buchanan. Wilma Grayson suggested the title, and in 2002 our son Marlowe accompanied me to Mile End — fifty years later — where the old house, far from being the anticipated mound of rubble, had actually been beautifully rebuilt!

Thanks to the New Jersey State Council on the Arts for its confidence in awarding this novel a grant towards completion.

Most of all I am indebted to Ellen Foos of Princeton University Press, without whose loving care and hard work this manuscript would not have blossomed. What began as occasional editorial assistance deepened, over ten years, into a life-long friendship and a monumental debt of gratitude.

–1–

"Sieg heil!"

"Fu–uck orf up there!" My father cursed the shouted commands and the shuffling feet that threatened to bring the ceiling plaster down onto our heads. Mrs. Woodbridge, the hard-faced widow who lived with her pimply teen-aged son in the flat above us, had made their living room the gathering place for the local Nazi youth movement, and we'd hear them *Sieg heil*-ing into the evening hours. The snapping of fascist boots tormented my Jewish-atheist father Abraham. He cursed them through the ceiling with an exuberance that elevated his declamations to an art form, serenading the street — exchanges often punctuated by Abie rushing upstairs in an apoplectic rage to hammer on their door so violently that in innocent surprise the acned troupe would fall to a stunned and besieged quiet.

This particular night his massive fist went right through their door, and he later described with salivating glee how, through the splintered hole, he saw them jump up from the table and back away in terror against the far wall. His disembodied, bloodied hand gesticulated fearsomely through the rent: "You fu–ucking barsteds you... eee, uh'll show you!" Inside, a stricken silence. Finally he withdrew and backed down the stairs, jubilantly purple-faced. "Eee, that'll show 'em," he exulted. "Eee, they won't forget that... twenty years from now they'll remember that!"

"*Oy*, quick, quick your hand it's all bleeding, your suit, come outside to the tap." In the dark yard at the only running water for the entire house, a faucet secured by a looped wire nailed into the sooted brick garden wall, my perpetually anxious mother turned the tap handle: "Put your hand under the water, *schvunce*, before you ruin your jacket."

●   ●   ●

In November of 1930 during the depths of the Great Depression, my mother had brought me, Zachary Grossman, home fresh from London hospital to two sisters and an out-of-work father. Home, on Bloomfield Road up the street from Burdett Road in Bow, was the rented lower floor of a two-story row-house, a gas-lamp mounted on the cracked and peeling wall in each of two rooms, one tiny fireplace for cooking and heating, and outside down the garden steps a frequently-bunged-up outhouse.

The recurring jousts with our upstairs neighbors marked for my father a more interminable battle, one that raged endlessly between him and anybody else unfortunate enough to engage his attention. To note that Abie never enjoyed a friendly exchange is rather to beg the point: he locked into combat with every living thing that ever, through inadvertence, misjudgment or folly, did more than simply pass him on the street. The spectacle of each engagement tended to camouflage its cumulative effect, which was to keep him battle-ready for the prime focus of his martial attentions — his family. In Abie's domiciliary warfare, his

arsenal consisted of any item of heft that came quickly to hand: crockery, a fireplace implement, a chair. Any one of us might be suddenly mustered to front line, but in retrospect the
children's were only preparatory skirmishes; his real quarry was his wife Lily, who as a result
sported a deep wound over her left eyebrow until the day he finally finished her off, fifty
battle-scarred years later, in New York City in 1982 — the most protracted murder in history.

We children spent much of our early years in hiding. Zilla, the eldest, bore the brunt of
Abie's paternal attentions, affording Rebecca, three years younger, some strategic latitude.
Both my sisters recognized that our household mode was unorthodox, that other families
along Bloomfield Road were not regularly obliged to dodge a barrage of flying furniture. I,
however, seemed to have had little grasp that the ruckus was untoward; I would run to the
window and, looking out, silently sing a song I'd learned from my sisters, albeit prudently
weaving and ducking. And should the sun have already crept around to the brick wall that
sided the garden, I would assume my post at the window and, between lyric phrases, observe the orderly manner in which shafts of sunlight slowly but predictably invaded the
sooted red, ocher and black crevices that surfaced the parallel rows of bricks and cement.

When Abie was away at work, a hysterical merriment sometimes pervaded the house,
proportionate to our fear and hatred of the old blue-nosed baboon: that was Rebecca's name
for him. Mum (née Leah Cohen, though Zilla and Rebecca addressed her as Lily), Mum and
Zilla would chortle with glee at Rebecca's imitation of him: "Lily, eee, uh'm 'ome, gimme me
dinner, er, er..." and here she'd mimic the odd thin smile — "they're not 'ungry... they're
kids, wha'd' *they* know."

·   ·   ·

Evening, and came the usual scraping of the massive key into its lock, the squeaking of
street door hinges, the shuffling in the dark outside passage: he was home from work. Lily's
face became lined, and we all were girded. The kitchen door began to open.

Lily hurried to the fireplace grate to fetch the enormous dinner bowl that had sat over a
saucepan of simmering water all evening awaiting his arrival. With a dish-towel she picked
up the steaming plate and its shiny dark brown cover chipped white at the edges, and hurried
it toward the table, a line of condensed water dripping along the worn and curling linoleum.

The door swung wide and there he stood, five feet ten, solidly proportioned, the smell of
sweat from his day's labors preceding him into the room. He shuffled guardedly through the
doorway, "Er, er, 'allo, eee, the kids." Laboriously he removed his heavy black overcoat and
piled it over the mass of clothes heaped on the brown ceramic hooks and knob of the
buckling door. Under his coat he wore an aging double-breasted suit that once could have
been grey herringbone, its wide and thinning lapels yellowed from nicotine, as was the collar
of his whitish shirt where he frequently pulled at the neck with two yellow-stained fingers; he
chain-smoked four packets of Woodbines a day.

An array of circumstances would influence what next transpired: the indignities and
insults, real and imagined, that had been visited on Abie that day at Lipman's, the ladies
garment factory where he labored ten hours a day at his sewing machine, six — and during
busy season seven — days a week. Two dozen men appended to as many machines spaced
across the planked floor and separated by heaped, creaking, wood-framed canvas work bins,
bare electric lightbulbs hanging on long fluff-covered wires from the ornate once-white
ceiling, grimy windows, the drone of foot treadles muffled by lint suspended chokingly in the
air; and the foreman checking seams, counting the work, rush, rush, never a word. A place

where survival meant to race, everyone bonded by a common fear of the sack, of destitution — everyone bonded but Abie, who never did see commonalities.

His arrival home from work meant he was primed to eat, and Lily was well advised to have his dinner served, at the right temperature, by the time his coat was off.

At an oddly apologetic angle he started across the room to the table, and with careful deliberation eased himself down before the plate, scraping the wooden chair into place. The blue protruding veins on the sides of his neck and the backs of his hands, his still-youngish face, and his black hair thinning perceptibly on top, radiated a handsome and fearful strength. The deep-set hazel eyes watered, and he rubbed them; he was coughing, always coughing, now into a dirty white handkerchief he fumbled ceremoniously from the depths of a trousers' pocket. He blew his nose, wiped it, sniffed, then lovingly restored the handkerchief to his pocket. Easing side to side, he settled more emphatically into the chair. He was now ready for food.

Lily leaned over the table, set his plate down and removed the hot cover. A redolent fog billowed to the ceiling. The plate was mounded with boiled potatoes and scraps of stewed meat, brown onion gravy soaking down through heaped rice and farfel. A few boiled beans slid onto the table, and with the dinner spoon she shoveled them back onto the plate. Her immediate duties discharged, she retreated a judicious distance and busied herself. She had learned soon enough to cook for him only exactly what he wanted, never a surprise. Perhaps tonight's offering would suffice to mitigate his precarious angers — but then, he might be looking for something, some pretext; perhaps his spoon had a blotch on it, maybe dinner had not been served at precisely the right temperature. This right-temperature business was a problem because we never knew what time he was coming home — it could be anywhere from six o'clock to one in the morning.

In our corner of the room we three kids began whispering deliberately among ourselves as though continuing some earlier conversation, a nonchalance to palliate our apprehension.

He leaned forward and sniffed at the plate, the probe of his mottled nose weaving a glancing track as it navigated from rice to farfel to beans. With his dinner spoon he shoveled a small piece of meat into his mouth and began to chew. Quickly his face twisted; he lurched forward in the chair, spitting the offending mouthful onto the torn oilcloth that covered the table, "Fah!" He sampled another scrap of beef, jerked in his chair, and with palpably rising fury spat that out too. Next he pushed beans, then rice through angry teeth, testing, spitting, his facial contortions purpling to crescendo.

Our focus was riveted to the ineluctably unfolding script, all pretense at disinterest forgotten, hearts slamming at unbearable and familiar pressure. Inevitably — and it would even come as some kind of relief — he leaped from the table, hurling the chair away behind him, flaring blue veins standing in high relief on his hated temples, "This fu–ucking rubbish, this, this... *drek,* this fu–ucking *shit,* that's what it is!"

And the loaded dinner plate sailed majestically high over the room to the far wall, smashing to the floor with barbarous dissonance, rice and beans riding tributaries of gravy meandering down the peppered surface; and Mum shouted through riven lips: "You barstard you, go back to your *farkakteh* mother, let her cook for you, maybe she'll make what you want."

And we kids huddled into the wall.

—o—O—o—

–2–

In October of 1932, Lily repeated her trek to London Hospital on Whitechapel Road, producing this time her third and last daughter, Katherine.

Two years following, the fifth and final child was due. Lily kept the older girls home from school that day. By midmorning when the contractions had become an imperative she caught the bus alone to hospital, leaving Zilla, now ten, and Rebecca, seven, at home to care for their younger brother and sister.

At Lipman's at the same hour, the frenetic pace stilled while the machinists each ate their sandwich. Hirshberg, at the next machine, commented that *he* wouldn't have to come to work if his wife was having a baby, they didn't need the money, he'd take her to hospital himself.

"The money? Oo cares about the money?" responded Abie. "So why should uh go to the 'ospital? Dogs 'ave puppies, women 'ave babies."

After work, at half past six, Abie stopped at his widowed mother's flat over Elgrod's jewelry shop in Black Lion Yard. He banged on the door; upstairs, his mother pried open the little window and called out, "Vat is it already, vat is it?"

"It's me, Abie."

"*Noch*, it's Abela, vait, I'll come down, I'll come down." A few moments later the door opened. He doused his cigarette and flicked the butt into the snow. "Abela, come in, quick it's cold, you're hungry." She beckoned him to precede her up the narrow stairway and thence into the kitchen. One grubby curtainless window, starved of light and air by an oppressive brick structure immediately adjacent, allowed muted designs to play on the bare floor. Across the room, beyond the small oilcloth-covered table and single chair, a coal fire burned in the grate. "Take your coat off, look, a nice *shisel* of chicken soup you'll have."

"Alright, eee, uh'm in a 'urry, gimme the *shisel.*"

Protecting her hands with a cloth, his mother grasped the handles of the iron pot that sat astride the fireplace and hoisted it onto a soot-impregnated pad on the table. From it she poured soup into a high-sided enamel bowl.

"The *shisel,* here, it's good, fresh today a fresh chicken I got, eat already." She handed him a huge spoon. As he sat eating, from the pot she added to his bowl more small pieces of chicken, undefined greens and several carrots. "Your father, he would have been in *shul* this time already. Abela, why you don't go to the synagogue, ashamed you should be, you not got no time for *shul?* Too busy with that woman and her *kinder,* you didn't should'a married her, I told you, *don't marry that woman* I said, you'll be sorry I said."

"Alright alright, uh'm in a 'urry, quick." Abie downed the soup. "Uh'm in a 'urry, uh'll... uh'll come 'round...." and he grabbed his coat, ran downstairs and continued on his way half a mile past London Hospital over the road, past Wickham's and on to the cinema, the Empire on Whitechapel Road, where in the foyer he surreptitiously picked up two discarded half-tickets from the floor. When his section of the queue reached the ticket-taker he displayed the two halves as a whole, then as a kindly accommodation seemingly tore the composite into two, handing over one half-ticket.

At the hospital, a nurse wiped Lily's forehead and neck; it was the beginning of twenty-two hours of labor, followed post delivery by copious bleeding. Two days later when she'd recovered sufficiently, Lily whispered to the nurse that her new-born son's name was to be Marius — this, after the tenderly romantic actor Marius Goring with whom she'd fallen in love that bright Sunday afternoon several weeks earlier when Abie had taken her to a matineé at the Empire. The nurse unbuttoned Lily's bodice, mopped her neck and handed her the child. Marius found the nipple and suckled furiously but began to cough, then choke. The nurse quickly took the baby from her, held him upside down, patted his back and chest until he breathed more easily, then returned him to Lily's breast. As he resumed suckling he began once more to cough, splutter, then gasp for air. The nurse rushed him from the room. Twenty minutes later she returned, alone, to tell Lily: "Seems to have a little bit of something, maybe it's with his lung, the doctor said."

"Lung? What is it, is it serious?"

"A touch of something, dearie, nothing to worry about, just lean him back over your knee and pat him real hard and he'll be alright."

The next day two doctors came by on their rounds. One of them asked Lily: "Anybody in your family had difficulty breathing — parents, uncles, aunts?"

"No, not that I remember." She thought further. "My husband said his father had trouble sometimes. In Russia it was. It was a pogrom, some men came. His family got him away in time but he died, he couldn't catch his breath they said."

One doctor rubbed his chin. "Hmm. You think bronchiectasis?"

"Could be complications," responded the other.

On succeeding days the nurse made a point of being present when Marius was breast-fed, and when he experienced difficulties she demonstrated to Lily how to restore his breathing.

And at home each evening, Abie told Zilla and Rebecca to stay home from school the next day and look after the younger children. He gave them sixpence and had them write up the list they were to buy in Lovich's grocery shop by the railway arches.

When Marius was sixteen days old, Abie arrived at the hospital to escort his wife and last-born son home on the bus.

•   •   •

Thus was our familial nest ensconced: five children, desperate Lily, jack-boots over-head, little money, and Abie.

When Lily bought groceries, to avoid Mrs. Lovich's supercilious glare, she waited outside until she saw Mr. Lovich alone behind the counter, then quickly entered and gathered her purchases before he could disappear back through the heavy curtain to their living quarters.

"I'll pay on Friday, alright? My husband gets his wages on Friday; also for the *challah* and milk from yesterday."

"Alright, alright already," mumbled Mr. Lovich, anticipating his wife's scowling disapproval. He pushed aside the loaf of bread she always stood on the counter by the till — he could hardly add *that* into the total, this time. He felt his wife's contemptuous gaze bore holes into his back.

When the Lovich's bill had run close to two shillings and sixpence, and Lily was too embarrassed to ask for more credit, she was impelled to range farther afield. This time she'd found a new shop, Dalton's, in the Roman Road Market, distant enough that she was not yet beholden. Before Abie left in the morning, she arranged to meet him at Dalton's after he'd finished work that day.

"Quick, quick," she insisted, "eat your breakfast, you'll be late, they'll take off from your wages."

"Alright, quick, gimme, gimme the sandwich, the bus, uh'll miss the bus, eee, uh'm late."

"Quick, go quick, you'll be there after, remember it's Dalton's, it's a new shop, you won't get mixed up?"

"Dalton's, shmalton's, uh'll come straight from work uh told you." He hurried out the door and ran toward the bus stop, disappearing under the railway arches.

Lily closed the street door and braced herself for the next round. She called toward the bedroom: "Rivka, it's late, get Zilly up, you'll be late for school."

"Alright Mum," a sleepy-voiced Rebecca responded.

"Wake Zilly up, she'll be late, you'll both be late, quick."

"Alright."

She put the kettle back on the grate and buttered two slices of bread for the girls' breakfast, hearing Zilla's grumbling from the bedroom, "Oh, leave me alone."

"It's school time, you won't be ready, I'll go by myself," Rebecca threatened her elder sister.

"Oh, alright, I'm getting up."

Lily called out again, "Your tea's on the table already, get dressed, *oy*, you'll both be late...."

Katherine and I shared the bedroom with our elder sisters, sleeping together on a mattress on the floor over in the corner, away from the window's drafts, from where I witnessed this routine every weekday morning.

After the big girls had finally left for school, in the kitchen Lily lifted back the bedclothes that had draped beyond the edge of the opened settee, grasped the iron rail at its foot and hoisted the lumbering frame up and over until it passed its mid-point and sank closed. She replaced the cushions, then checked Marius's cot standing alongside to see that his breathing was not obstructed by a wayward blanket. I caught her glancing into the bedroom to check on us; Katherine was still asleep, and I squeezed my eyes closed.

That afternoon at a quarter past four the older girls were returned from school. Lily called Katherine and me in from the garden and fed the four of us a supper of boiled potatoes and green peas in hot milk. While we ate, she roused Marius and breast-fed him. The repast completed, she had the four of us don our coats, and carrying Marius she shepherded us the two miles to Dalton's, in the Roman Road. There, for half an hour we helped her stock the canvas market bags with provisions.

Finally, Abie arrived in his black overcoat, flushed, not a word. She said something to him; whatever those few words were they must have been inopportune, because dark-faced, hands thrust into his pockets, he swirled around, strode out of the shop, and was quickly lost along the darkening street.

The shopkeeper hadn't noticed our small drama unfold, and he looked on disparagingly as we returned everything to the bins: "Can'chu make up your mind, dearie?"

Then the trek back home, shopping bags empty, Mum urging her brood before her along black streets punctuated by an occasional pool of yellow gaslight.

Abie didn't come home until after midnight. In his absence Lily sat sewing up holes in our socks. Marius's labored breathing echoed loud as he slept in his wooden cot alongside the settee. Light from the kitchen mantle seeped under the door into the bedroom where we four older children lay, Zilla and Rebecca sharing the dilapidated box spring mounted on its wood frame. Beside me Katherine was already asleep. I lay awake as usual, anxiously fearing I might wet the bed, that Mum would threaten to tell Abie if she found the mattress and covers soaked.

From the recesses of the other bed, Rebecca's sharp voice pierced the shadowed darkness: "Oh, shut up crying, he's not even home yet."

"Oo-er!" Zilla sobbed. "You shurrup also!"

•   •   •

"Quick, quick, eat your breakfast, you'll be late, they'll take off from your wages."

"Alright, quick, gimme, gimme the sandwich, the bus, uh'll miss the bus, eee, uh'm late."

"Quick, go quick, you'll be there after, remember it's Dalton's, it's a new shop, you won't get mixed up?"

"Dalton's, shmalton's, uh'll come straight from work uh told you."

Abie hurried out the door and ran toward the bus stop, disappearing into the darkness beneath the railway arches. He sprinted for the red bus as it juddered noisily away from the curb, and reached out for the vertical handrail worn to a bright metallic shine. Loped along by the bus's acceleration, he managed to get one foot up onto the ribbed boarding platform. The conductor gripped his coat sleeve and helped pull him aboard, "Tryin' a get y'self killed, guv?"

The bus was crowded downstairs, so Abie climbed the curved open stairway to the upper deck. He sat down in the only available seat, next to a flushed-faced middle-aged woman. Her plump torso bulged over the demarcation line that set off the two seats, and he gave her a push.

"'Ere 'ere, who do you think you're shovin'?" she cried.

"Move your fat arse, you bladdy...."

"Call the conductor I will, bladdy rude!"

"Sod orf, missus."

Abie got off the bus at Aldgate East and hurried along Wentworth Street to Lipman's. Approaching the factory, he found everyone milling around outside, and started toward the crowd, "What's going on, what's a matter?"

The foreman spotted him and called across: "'Ey, Grossman, come 'ere."

Abie elbowed through, his stomach grinding in familiar anticipation. "What's going on, what's a matter?"

The foreman checked off his list with the pencil from behind his ear. "'Ere, Grossman, four days this week" — he scribbled as he spoke — "and Friday last week." He pulled out of his coat pocket a ten-shilling note and counted one more silver shilling and one sixpence. "No work, you can go 'ome, we'll send someone 'round yer 'ouse when it picks up."

Abie stood there in the churning sea. In his trousers pocket he felt the two ha'pennies for his bus fare home, noticing that his newspaper-wrapped sandwich bulged out the line of his overcoat. He pushed the eleven-and-six deep into the watch pocket on the front of his trousers, and buttoned its little flap. Now Lily wouldn't be able to pay the rent when the barsted came 'round for it, she'd have to eke out the *gelt* for food. How long could they last, a week? He hated everybody standing there, like waiting, for what?, the foreman, the owner Lipman peering out from behind the doorway, the other machinists, the noise, everybody busy talking, talking.

Hirshberg, him from the next machine, he came over, with 'is twisted face. "'Ey, Abie, I'm going over to Cohen's, you know, Cambridge 'Eath Road? I don't need it really, we got enough to keep going, for months we got enough, Sarah, she's marvelous, she knows 'ow to manage bless 'er 'eart, we got plenty *gelt,* we'll be alright 'til it picks up."

Abie knew Hirshberg wasn't going to Cohen's — it was a trick. He was going to Adleman's on Commercial Road in Stepney; they sometimes had extra work at the end of the season. Abie had to get there first. He extricated himself from the crowd and deliberately strode off in the opposite direction to turn the corner. A horse and cart was approaching. Quickly he crossed the road, and trotting hidden behind the cart's large clattering wheels he passed down the other side of the street unobserved by the preoccupied machinists.

When he got to Commercial Road, Adleman's was already closed. He ran on to Dolphman's; then to Wunderman Brothers, then Collyer's on Bromley Street. By now exhausted, he strode on to Preiseler's.

No one was taking anybody on.

His hands were sweaty and cold. He bought a cup of tea for a ha'penny and sat on a bench at a wooden table, facing away and eating his sandwich under his coat so the proprietor wouldn't see. What should he do? The thought of again begging a few shillings from his sister Anya's husband Harry made him shrivel up inside. He asked a man with a draped gold watch-chain the time: quarter to three already, eee, the whole day looking, in just a few hours it would be getting dark.

The bus — he couldn't even think of the bus, he'd better save every farthing. The day now declining, he started to walk the several miles to the new grocery shop where he'd arranged to meet Lily, what was it, Dalton's, in the Roman Road.

As he entered the shop she was waiting there with all the kids and the swollen shopping bags. He was flushed, damp and sweated. He thrust his hands deep into his coat pockets; he felt ashamed that anyone should see he was old enough to have five kids.

"What took you so long?" asked Lily. "You said you'd be here by half-past-six, you said you'd come straight from work."

—o—O—o—

The two-room flat we lived in was old and rickety, and its heavings produced their own noises. Some nights the sounds were so loud they'd wake us — creakings, muffled groans as if ghosts were struggling to climb out of the walls. Katherine and I would lie on our mattress in deepening silence and wait for the clamor to begin, and this was when I discovered an interesting correlation: so long as we listened for noises, the walls were quiet; the moment our attention ranged elsewhere the mysterious cries would resume, seeping up through crevices between our words. And sometimes, in the middle of the night when all three of my sisters were asleep, in the yellow half-light the gas lamp across the road cast through the window onto the ambiguous contours that marked the walls, disparate shapes would swim together and assume a life of their own. I endured the grotesque drama until resolution collapsed, whereupon in the flagrant terror of night my sisters would waken and join in my screaming — an *a cappella* quartet.

The passageway to the back door was inky dark at evening, and unnameable monstrosities lurked beyond where the lavatory sat at the bottom of the wide broken stone steps that ran alongside the brick garden wall. Katherine and I shared an unspoken pact to go out to the lav together after dark.

I carried the candle. Along the passageway we walked in deliberate conjunction, my hand, protecting the flame, casting a huge trembling shadow on the walls. I felt for the latch and pulled open the back door. Against the moonlit silhouette of trees and roofs tracing the sky, we clambered down huge stone steps. I pulled ajar the slatted wooden door, and in the candle's murky flickerings confirmed that no unspeakable thing prowled inside the lav. A few drops of hot wax onto the high wooden perch anchored the candle. "You go first," I volunteered.

The garden outside, where I stood guard, was large — too large to divulge its secrets casually. I peered, turned, then methodically continued rotating so that no shadowed area went unexamined beyond a few seconds. Inevitably a first breath of wind stirred the requisite single leaf, and good intentions dissolved into panic. I rushed back toward the house; Katherine, abandoned, leaped shrieking from the seat, bloomers twisted around her ankles. She stumbled up the garden steps into the black passageway, and together we burst frantic and disheveled into the kitchen. Nobody paid particular attention; that was how Katherine and I normally returned from the lavatory.

· · ·

Zilla and Rebecca had been attending school for several years, and now it was time for me to begin. From their recountings of kids' chasing and punching, I anticipated school with dread. Abie had taught Zilla how to punch back — "Keep yer thumb outside yer fingers, not inside, nah! nah…" and he'd grab her hand, "an' like punch 'em, eee, punch 'em, straight in their face punch 'em."

And so I found myself attending morning prayers in a cavernous brown-paneled, dimly-lit hall, an assembly that commenced each day's schedule. Occasionally I caught a glimpse of Rebecca and Zilla, but they preferred to stay with their own group, disinclined to admit the embarrassment of a young brother. That first morning during prayers, and for an eternity of mornings afterwards, a large and particularly formidable girl clamped onto me. "Look left," she said in a commanding whisper. "Look right." "Look up." "Now look down." Then came the dreaded part: "Don't look anywhere, and don't close your eyes."

Our teacher, Miss Hutchins, had us recite poetry: *What are little boys made of?/ What are little boys made of?/ Snips and snails, and puppy-dogs' tails,/ And that's what little boys are made of.* That explained why Dad always shouted and hit us, because he was a boy — a big one — and boys were made of horrible things. Then the next stanza: *What are little girls made of?/ What are little girls made of?/ Sugar and spice, and all that's nice,/ And that's what little girls are made of.* Zilla and Rivka and Katya were so lucky to be girls; that was why I peed in the bed but they never did. School days soon homogenized into a fog of terror. Some pupils were brave enough to bring in odd possessions, so I brought in things I'd fabricated at home from brown gummed paper-tape — a motor car and a little scooter — in a small cardboard box. Along with other kids' belongings, Miss Hutchins put my box in the classroom closet for safe-keeping. After class, too fearful to respond when she asked whose box it was, my toys became the property of some unapproachable bully.

The boy sitting next to me, Donald, whispered: "Didn't you bring that box?"

"No," I quaked.

"I'll tell Miss Hutchins it's yours, if you like."

"No, it's not mine."

It was inevitable that my fear of asking permission to go to the lavatory reach precipitate proportions, and one day I defecated in my trousers. Returning home after school with Donald and another boy who lived in my direction, I calculated that if I skipped along the pavement keeping my left leg constantly in front to maintain tension in the elastic underwear seam, I might avoid a catastrophic humiliation. Of course it was also necessary to feign nonchalance, and so I danced home at unwieldy angles. Such formative incidents engendered an enduring interest in geometry, physics, and uninhabited planets.

•   •   •

1937 arrived, and Zilla, now twelve, and Rebecca, nine, were being regularly spat upon and punched by other pupils while on their way home from school. Lily went to see the headmistress.

"They're just children, they should leave them alone."

"It is regrettable, but what can we really do?"

"Well, tell them to stop!"

"I would tell them, Mrs. Grossman, but you must also try to bring some understanding to this situation."

"What is it to understand?"

"The… how shall we say… provocation?"

"Provocation?"

"Mrs. Grossman, you too have a responsibility, and that is to recognize how the other children feel. It is incumbent that you view the situation in the larger context."

"What are you talking about?"

"No one's *blaming* you, it's an unfortunate accident of birth, but you really must try to understand the other children's position."

"Position, accident of birth, what's going on here?"

"Since you're insisting that I be quite explicit, Mrs. Grossman, when you deliberately bring Jewish children into this world, you have to recognize it's not going to be a... shall we say, *normal* situation."

"Normal?"

"Now, my comment should not be taken as criticism of your children in any way...."

"Normal? You ought to be ashamed...."

"Well well, this outburst really doesn't help, does it."

"Normal, call yourself a headmistress?"

"I do not tolerate rudeness in my office, Mrs. Grossman!"

"Normal! A... a dirty thing to say...."

"Please control yourself! My goodness me! As I say, I shall continue to remain even-handed and do all I can to maintain tranquility among the children." She stood up. "And if you'll now excuse me I have important duties to which I must attend. Good day, madam!"

Also by 1937, Oswald Mosley's black-shirted Nazis were parading more and more openly in the streets. They marched in pairs along the pavement in high-booted step like well-scrubbed boy-scouts under their shiny peaked caps, except that you had better step out of their way to let them pass. We would have liked to move to a better section where Nazis' promenade might be less brazen, but the rental adverts in the *News of the World* called for more money, and usually included: "No Jews or dogs."

•　　•　　•

Abie's younger brother Joseph was a waiter. When Uncle Joe visited late one evening, Katherine and I crawled off our mattress, hid behind the door and listened. Uncle Joe told Dad he was sick of his life, waiting on customers all day long then going home to Aunt Muriel and her nagging. He said his friend Sol had gotten a waiter's job on a transatlantic liner, the *Aquitania*. The friend had described the fat tips he got from rich passengers, and the holiday atmosphere of a place called New York City where each voyage he could go ashore for one or two days while the ship's supplies were replenished. He said that Muriel did not approve of Sol.

When Aunt Muriel herself subsequently visited Lily, she confirmed everything Uncle Joe had said, noting it had been the worst shock of her life when she'd realized after all the talk that her husband longed to take such a job himself. Had she known beforehand he would leave her alone so many nights every week she would have happily remained a spinster.

And that, the family story went, was the reason Uncle Joe finally deserted Aunt Muriel.

Freed from the financial encumbrances of matrimony, Joe's wages and tips permitted him to rent a small two-bedroom house opposite an attractive little park in the Mile End section of the East End. He helped his (and Abie's) now-ailing mother to move out of her flat in Black Lion Yard and into his extra bedroom. *Bobbeh's* rent now covered most of the expenses for the whole house, and this additional freedom allowed him full rein to search for a job aboard ship himself. Shortly, he found himself a waiter on the *Aquitania* alongside his friend Sol. After several voyages, which included exciting forays into New York City, he decided to emigrate to America.

The legal immigration procedure was too protracted and cumbersome for Uncle Joe. So, encouraged by familiarity with his intended destination, he plotted a less formal process. In early May of 1937 when the *Aquitania* docked in New York harbor, he jumped ship. His plan went awry — but not disastrously so. He was apprehended by the New York authorities, who labeled him *WOP*, which meant *With Out Papers*. Brought before a judge, he was asked why he jumped ship.

"I want to have a new life, I want to work hard and make something of myself. That's the dream of America."

At that invocation the judge responded: "This heroic spirit is what makes America great."

"Thank you, your lordship."

Whereupon the judge opened his own wallet, took out a five dollar bill and handed it across to the bailiff. "Give this to the plaintiff, and let him go."

•   •   •

The very day after Abie found out from *Bobbeh* that Uncle Joe wasn't coming back, he returned home early from Lipman's. Lily put his dinner out, and without the usual melee he just sat down and started eating. He called Mum to the table, and as he ate they whispered. There came a knock on the door; Dad jumped up, opened the door and let in a man, a stranger. Mum removed all the clean cups and plates from the chest of drawers standing alongside the wall, and stacked them on the table. The man helped Dad carry the empty chest of drawers out to the street; I peeked, and saw they were hoisting it onto a barrow. The man eased the pole in front of the barrow upward to a horizontal position, buckled a leather harness around his waist and began pulling the barrow along the street, Dad steadying the chest so it wouldn't slide off onto the cobblestones.

Now we were left with an empty space along the kitchen wall.

"Why did the man take it away?" Katherine asked.

"Your father doesn't want it anymore," answered Mum.

"No, why did the man take it really?"

"Sshh sshh don't ask."

The next morning, while Rebecca and Zilla were getting ready for school, Mum put both Katherine's and my breakfast bread and jam together onto my plate.

"Where's Katya's plate?" I asked.

"Sshh eat your bread and jam, both of you." So my sister and I ate from one plate, and Mum had us also share tea from a single cup. "Go on, drink, drink, I'll make another cup when you're finished."

"Why are Zech and me drinking from the same cup?"

"In the night the other dishes broke, we had to throw them into the rubbish."

"Ta-ra, ta-ra!" trilled Rebecca and Zilla as they ran off to school.

"No, what happened really?" continued my little sister.

"They did, they broke, the little tyke she is with her questions! Hurry up, drink, Zech'll be late!"

But Katherine pursued the mystery: "They broke when they were by themselves?"

"Eat, eat, *oy*, leave me alone! When we have money we'll buy new ones."

Mum and Katherine walked me to school. When I returned home, Mum said we had to sleep in the opened settee in the kitchen instead of our usual place on the mattress in the corner of the other room.

"Why?" asked Katherine.

"Because... because that mattress is no good, your father's throwing it out."

"Then where will you and Dad sleep?" she continued.

"Oy... we're not tired, we don't have to sleep. Sshh, run away and play."

In this kind of conversation where I didn't quite know what was going on, I used to be afraid that Katherine's bluntness would get her smacked. If I wanted to find something out I was always careful to make up a first question related to what I wanted to know but still at the edge of it; then if the person's face seemed all right and they weren't going to hit me I could carefully ask the next question, a bit closer to what I really meant. Though, with this method I easily got mixed up because one part of my mind would have to line up words for the next question while the other part was trying to remember what I wanted to know in the first place; sometimes a person would look at me strangely because they didn't realize the complexity. But with Katherine, she wasn't yet old enough to understand these aspects of conversation. Right away she asked the question at the center of what she wanted to know without realizing the person could easily get wild and smack her.

Anyway, that night after supper she and I went to bed in the settee in the kitchen with all the smells of food, and with Zilla and Rebecca doing homework at the table. Mum turned the gas mantle lower, so we could sleep.

"Oo-er, it's dark!" said Zilla.

"It's light enough, you can see, sshh, the *kinder* let them go to sleep."

"How can I do my homework then?"

"Oh, stop grumbling," said Rebecca. "I can see to do mine, why can't you do yours?"

"Yours is different, you don't have to see so much."

"Sshh quiet, both of you, let them sleep."

It was exciting to go to bed in the same room with people still busy. I woke up to low voices, and thumping; it was nighttime, the window was dark. I peered over the top of the blanket, and that same man was back again. This time he and Dad were carrying out the street door Zilla's and Rebecca's bed from the other room. And, who should be lying on the other side of the settee in bed with Katherine and me, but Zilla and Rebecca!

"What's the matter, what's happening?" I asked.

"Shurrup, go to sleep," said Abie.

"Sshh, go to sleep, Dad's throwing that bed out, soon we'll buy nicer ones."

Katherine was awake.

"Katya, what do you think it is?" I whispered under the covers.

"Someone bought all our things so we could have some money," she whispered back.

Later I woke up again; the room was light but the gaslight was out — it was morning already. Dad and Mum were sitting on chairs with their heads resting on the table.

Suddenly Dad jerked: "Eee, Lily, it's late, uh'm late." He jumped up. "Uh'm late, eee, uh'll miss the bus uh'll miss."

In a moment Mum was up and over by the fireplace. "Your breakfast, quick, I'll get your breakfast, what time is it, my neck...."

"It's late, uh'm late."

Mum was already pouring water from the pot.

"Tea, uh don't 'ave time for tea...."

"What time will you be home, then?"

"'Ome! Uh told you, late uh'll be 'ome, Alf, 'e'll come late."

She finished buttering his bread. "Your sandwich, here's your sandwich." She tore off half a page of newspaper to wrap it.

"Alright, lemme go already." Suddenly he stopped, raised his nose and sniffed at the air. "The smell, what's that, like a... fah!, a terrible *stink!*"

"Smell? What smell? What can you smell?"

"Like *pischershs,* it smells!" His face was a deep scowl.

Immediately my heart was thumping. I felt the mattress under me — and it was soaked. Right away I'd made a mistake: I shouldn't have moved, I should have made out I was asleep. Now my heart was banging in my ears.

"What did 'e do..." began Abie.

Mum rushed around to the side of the settee where I was lying. She bent over Katherine and started feeling under me. She stopped, and for a moment was absolutely still. Then slowly she stood up, not saying anything.

"Wharris it, what did 'e do?"

Mum's voice was flat: "Nothing. It's not him."

Abie ran around to where I was trying to hide under the covers, and elbowed Mum aside. "What, what did you do, you barsted you?"

Mum tried to push him away, but he was too big. "Leave him, it's nothing, I'll dry it out, I'll put it out, in the sun I'll put it...."

He ripped the covers down. "You stinking little barsted you, you, you pished in the mattress you pished..." and grabbing both collars of my sleeping suit with one huge hand, he lifted me out of the settee, up in the air.

"Stop it! Stop it!" screamed Rebecca; everyone had woken up. Marius, who'd been asleep in the cot on the other side of the settee, started crying.

"*Oy a broch,* put him down already, it's nothing, I'll dry it out!" shouted Mum.

I was up in the air as his other hand swung out wide in a big circle. Somehow I heard it, like hitting wood, but I didn't feel anything; it just pushed my head all the way sideways and my ears were ringing. I didn't know where I was, then I realized it was Mum who was screaming at him: "Put him down, *oy a broch,* leave him alone...."

"Don't, don't, stop it... you're a murderer!" That was Katherine's voice, trying to shout.

Rebecca was sitting up in the bed. "You bullying barstard you, leave him alone!" Suddenly I was down on the settee again, on top of the covers, on top of a lot of bumps; it was Zilla under me, under the covers. Rebecca was still shouting at him: "You bullying barstard!"

Next came a loud crash somewhere, the whole room shook and china rattled. Zilla, who still seemed to be in the settee under me, sat up and started crying: "Ee, stop it, leave 'er alone, you *fucking bully,* leave 'er alone."

"*What!* Did you 'ear that, did you 'ear what she said to me, to 'er own father, *filthy* language, to 'er own father!"

I saw Mum getting up off the floor; she'd been on the floor.

It was Katherine's feet; Katherine was standing next to where I'd rolled down off Zilla, and she was shouting at him in her little voice: "You murderer, you're a murderer, you're murdering my brother and my mother!"

Mum had gotten up and was swaying, standing by our side of the settee, brushing herself off. Dad was now around by the bottom, leaning over the end where Zilla was crouched.

Zilla was both crying and shouting at him at the same time: "You *barstard,* you're a *fucking rotten* barstard, that's what you are!" She was trying to pull her legs up, away from where he was.

With both hands he yanked all the covers off the settee and flung them over the table right across to the other side of the room. He was grabbing at Zilla's legs; he got one ankle and was trying to pull her down off the bottom end of the settee.

"Oooow! Stop it, stop 'im, ow!, my leg!" she screamed, as Rebecca rolled on top of her to try to stop her being pulled away off the bottom. Marius was choking in his cot, gasping and coughing.

"The police, I'm going for the police, I swear on my life I'll get the police," shouted Mum, and she ran into the passage and out the street door.

Dad dropped Zilla's leg with a bang onto the iron rim at the bottom of the settee. He ran to the street door, leaned outside and shouted after Mum: "You bladdy fool you, come back 'ere the bladdy fool, the police she's getting!" And he turned around and stood there, his face all purple.

Zilla had gotten the covers back onto the settee and pulled them over us. Rebecca was up and holding Marius; he was gasping and struggling to breathe, and she slapped him on his back the way Mum did.

Katherine was holding my arm, both of us hiding under the covers. "You alright, Zech?" she whispered. Everything was all wet.

"It's all wet," I said.

Mum came back in through the door. "You *ponce* you, here's your sandwich, quick, you're late for work, they'll take off from your wages."

"Eee, uh'm so late already, they'll wonder what 'appened."

"Go already."

Dad just stood there. He started to giggle, and his voice went up high: "Eee, they'll wonder, what 'appened to Abie, they'll wonder!"

"Go already," said Mum.

He left, pulling the street door quietly closed behind him as though nothing had happened.

Mum took Marius from Rebecca. She sat down, lay him across her lap and began slapping him on his back, "Sshh, sshh, it's alright, it's alright."

"Ow, the barstard twisted my leg," said Zilla.

Marius's gasping and coughing were quieter now, the only sound. Then Mum looked at me: "If you didn't *pish* in the bed he wouldn't go mad." I realized my cheek felt stinging hot.

"What do you do it for?" asked Zilla angrily. "Why don't you go outside in the lav like everybody else?"

Mum put Marius on her shoulder and rocked him back and forth, back and forth. "What's done is done. Come on, it's finished already, get up, everybody's late for school. Zech, you'll stay home today, you'll help with the mattress." Marius was still jerking and breathing in little gasps. "Sshh, it's all over, go back to sleep, it's alright, it's over," and she lay him back in the cot. Then, to Katherine and me, "Go on both of you, lay on the dry side 'til I get the girls off."

After Zilla and Rebecca had left for school, Mum dragged the wet covers along the passage and outside to the garden. She washed me off from the tap outside, took me in and gave me dry clothes. Then Katherine and I helped her unhook the heavy mattress from the settee, lift it off and drag it outside. As we got it onto the stone steps, the upstairs window opened and Mrs. Woodbridge put her head out: "'E still pissin' in the old bed, Mrs. Grossman?"

"Sod off, mind your own business!" Mum shouted back.

"Real bladdy mad-'ouse this morning, weren't it dahn there!"

"Ugh!, sod off with your lousy Black-shirts up there, may you *gae in dreard,* all of you!"

"Why'n'cha speak the king's English, we're in England 'ere, you know."

"England! You know what you can do with your England, and your king, you can *gae in dreard* with him!"

"What?"

"Ugh, go to hell with your king there already! And keep your pimply Nazi nose out of other people's business!"

The window slammed shut.

Mum brought out the pail and filled it at the tap. She scrubbed the top of the mattress with a wooden brush, and we helped her drag it to where the sun would come around to dry it. Next she spread the two blankets on the steps and scrubbed them, too, pouring pails of water over them. Katherine and I together held one end of each blanket while Mum twisted the other around until most of the water had been squeezed out and run down the steps, pooling into curlicues on the stone slabs and into the crevices where tufts of grass grew. Segment by segment she hoisted the sodden blankets up onto the first washing line, then across until they bridged both lines.

"Sod her upstairs if she wants to hang up her washing today," said Mum.

That afternoon, when Rebecca and Zilla returned from school, Mum said the whole family had to go to sleep early. Katherine came outside to the lav with me, and I peed as much as I possibly could. My three sisters and I lay down in the settee by nine o'clock; it still felt a bit damp on our side. Just then we heard the door lock scraping, and Abie walked in. My heart banged so loud I was afraid he would hear it through the covers. But he seemed to have forgotten about the morning. Mum brought his dinner across from the fireplace, and this time he was even humming to himself as he ate! It was the second dinner in a row where he hadn't either shouted or thrown his plate.

In the night, something, a hand moving under me, woke me with a terrible fright, "What, who is it?"

"Sshh!" It was Mum. The room was fairly dark and everything was quiet. She was leaning down and feeling the mattress. Quickly I felt down also: a bit damp, but not from pee because my skin didn't sting. Mum stood up. "Come on, rise and shine, time to get up, time for school." Now she spoke in a loud voice, looking at me and Katherine to get up also.

"Is Katya starting school today?" I asked.

"No, we're all getting up, that's all."

Everything seemed shadowy and I realized it was still dark out, still nighttime, and the gaslight was on low.

"It's nighttime, we don't have to get up yet," said Katherine.

"It's a special surprise, we all have to get up."

Dad was sitting in the corner; I hadn't even realized he was there except for the smell of cigarette smoke. Zilla and Rebecca were already dressing, as though they normally got up in the dark.

"Don't cha know what's 'appening?" whispered Zilla.

"Shurrup, you big mouth!" Dad barked across the settee; then his voice dropped almost to a whisper: "Shurrup and get dressed already, eee, she'll tell 'em all she will, with 'er big mouth there." There came a subdued knocking outside, "Eee, 'e'll wake up the whole 'ouse!" Dad quickly went to open the street door — "Sshh, Alf," he giggled, "you mustn't wake 'em up, up there they'll wake up!" Alf came into the kitchen with Dad; he was the same man from the other times with the barrow.

"Quick, quick, get dressed, quick everyone," said Mum in a loud whisper as she began bundling up Marius. As I got up I realized the kitchen table wasn't there anymore. The whole room looked empty.

"What happened to the table...." Katherine began, but Dad glared at her.

As soon as we were all out of the settee, Dad pulled off the covers, picked up the bottom bar with just one hand and easily flipped it over closed. He and Alf tipped it backwards on two legs and began carrying it out the door. We were still dressing when Alf came back in alone and picked up Marius's cot and carried it outside also.

"Are we moving?" asked Katherine.

"Sshh sshh don't ask," said Mum.

"Course we are, wha'd'y' think?" whispered Zilla.

"Why must we be quiet?"

"Tsk!"

"Quick, your coats, everybody."

Dad ran back in, "They ready, you ready?" He collected all the cushions and hurried out with them, then came in again for the final things — all the sleeping suits and everything rolled up in a big blanket.

Mum herded us into the street. "Alright, come on, sshh, don't make any noise, everyone's sleeping...." It was nighttime and the street lamps were on. Our settee was on the barrow with the folded cot high up on top, and chair legs sticking up. Alf hooked the pole in front of the barrow to his leather harness as Dad pushed on a wheel spoke, trying to get everything moving. The stubborn wheel lifted out of a dip between the cobblestones and the barrow began riding, clicking, Dad trotting alongside, his raised arms holding the furniture in place.

"Quick, you didn't shut the street door!" Mum called in a loud whisper.

"Fu–uck 'em, with their *becuckter* street door there!"

Mum half trotted along the road, holding Marius on her shoulder with one arm. Katherine held her other hand, and I hung on to Katherine. Zilla and Rebecca were in front, talking as usual, and ahead of them rode the barrow, its iron-banded wheels' stark clatterings echoing off the buildings on both sides of the street.

I whispered to Katherine: "I wonder why we're moving in the middle of the night?"

"That's when people are supposed to move," she replied. "What time is it?" Her question was directed to Mum, already breathless with Marius bounding on her arm. "Is it exactly the middle of the night?"

"No, it's the morning," Mum gasped as she alternately walked, then trotted a few steps.

"What time is it?" Katherine repeated.

"It's four o'clock."

"Why is it cold?"

"It's always cold in the street at four o'clock at night."

"You said it's the morning."

"*Oy...* you'll be warm in a minute, we'll be there in a few minutes."

"Where are we moving to?"

"You'll see, sssh stop talking already."

Up ahead, the barrow's rhythms were becoming ever remote. I peered into the weight of darkness that lay over the roadway before us; I'd never imagined streets so empty, and sporadic blotches of yellow gaslight only accentuated our isolation. We strode on, intermittently falling into a brief trot, then actually running a few steps in a futile attempt to sustain the lagging tail of our nocturnal entourage. A little thing ran silently by our feet, an animal — "*Oy a broch!*" Mum caught herself — but it was only a cat.

She panted into the darkness: "Abie, carry the baby, I can't keep running."

In the black distance a voice returned: "Sshh, you want the bladdy furniture to fall all over the road?"

"Rivka, Rivka...." Rebecca materialized ahead of us, and took Marius.

"Careful, be careful with the baby, *oy*, I'm... I'm...." Then, suddenly louder: "The gas, we didn't turn it off, the light!"

A faint and disembodied chortle: "Heh, heh! Deliberately uh left the gas on, with their *drek* there, the whole bladdy place should burn down it should, with their stinking Blackshirts up there...."

We now barely heard the barrow's wheels tapping their disjointed rhythm against the cobblestones. "We're over half way," gasped Mum. The regular, even-spaced clickety clack of horseshoes drew up from behind, then the subdued thrumming of rubber tires, then rattling of glass bottles. As the big four-wheeled cart pulled around us, an oil lantern — white light at the sides, a red circle at its back — swung periodically from side to side. "The milkman," Mum said.

Finally, our little group gathered close and crossed the wide Mile End Road, then on down long streets, past tall iron gates. Diagonally across from us was a patch of dark trees and grass — and there on the corner across the road from the park, resting in the glow of a street light, stood the barrow, already empty, its pole in front lying on the edge of the pavement.

"I know that house!" I cried.

"Oo-er, 'course you do, it's Uncle Joe's," said Zilla's shadowy figure as she entered the yellowed circle.

Mum laid doubt to rest. "We're going to live in Uncle Joe's house from now on." She gathered herself. "Joe went to America, and *Bobbeh* lives upstairs now. Quick, give me the baby."

The street door was open wide. We filed up two high concrete steps into the passage, then to the right into the living room. We'd visited Uncle Joe's before, but now the desolation of empty streets carried into these rooms, deserted and alien with Uncle Joe's familiar furniture gone. A gaslight in the center of the ceiling cast its stark light, and over by the wall opposite the two big dark windows our settee sat askew, piled high with blankets and pillows. In the middle of the room stood our table and chairs. Dad and Alf were just coming down the stairs.

"The covers for upstairs, you didn't lose the covers?"

"They're upstairs, it's all upstairs Mrs. Grossman," said Alf.

"Come on then everybody, up the stairs, be careful!" Mum handed Marius to Dad, and we followed her along the passage to the stairway. The bottom three stairs turned sharply to the left, the rest continuing up and up alongside the wall to a little landing at the top. Up there, where I'd never been, were two doors and a little window. "Sshh don't make any noise," Mum pointed ahead, *"Bobbeh's* asleep in that room." Rebecca and Zilla filed to the left through the open door into the back bedroom, and we followed. A gaslight mounted on the wall at the left of a fireplace illuminated a dark brown closet that leaned outward, a broken mirror in its door reflecting multiple layers of unknown walls. Under the window stood Zilla's and Rebecca's bed; Katherine's and my mattress lay on the floor against the wall behind the door.

"Quick, help me." Mum retrieved covers and cushions from the big blanket in the middle of the floor and put them on our mattress. "Alright, quick, get undressed and go to bed." And down the stairs she went, leaving the four of us to make up our respective beds; Rebecca helped Katherine and me on the floor with our blanket and cushions.

As my little sister and I climbed onto our mattress, Mum came up again. "Sshh, don't talk, go to sleep, you'll be tired in the morning." Then, *"Oy* I forgot! Come down Zech, quick!" and she pulled me off the mattress, out to the landing and back down the stairs. She clicked a latch and the back door swung open. Stars laced the darkness above. She pulled my sleeping suit trousers down to my knees: *"Pish, pish* go on, quick." The stone slab we stood on was freezing cold to my bare feet, and by light that seeped out of an adjacent window on our right I could make out a large black cavity, a sort of open metal-lined bin to the left of the garden steps. The pee rattled as it found its mark in the bin. Upstairs once more, she again tucked Katherine and me in, then turned the gaslight out completely and quietly closed the door after her.

As her footsteps faded, I realized that the window was already brighter, definitely brighter than before! Through black branches immediately beyond the panes of glass, high in the distant sky I could make out a fleck of cloud reflecting a muted and diffused coral glow. "Look! It's getting light!"

"Oo-er, shurrup, go to sleep!"

—o—O—o—

4

Mile End was a nicer section of the East End, with clean, wide streets. Our new house, 27 Morgan Street, was on a corner diagonally across from Tredegar Square, a little park with curlicued wrought-iron railings and tall gates, neatly tended flower beds and several ornate loden-green benches scattered along the paths where, on warm days, old men sat and played Snakes and Ladders. The park was surrounded on three sides with elegant though deteriorating older homes, and on the fourth by row houses. Our house was of the cheaper row variety, its brick side wall bulging outward in a graceful curve — which explained why marbles rolled unassisted across the living room floor. Like our old flat in Bow, this house had neither electricity nor an inside tap, and again the lavatory was outdoors, down stone garden steps. But now we did have almost a whole house, and instead of Nazis upstairs we had *Bobbeh.* Mum said she didn't know which was worse.

The street door swung open all the way back until it hit the wall, exposing a dark stairwell that lead down to a moldering cellar, empty except for a sodden couch sitting in several inches of water. We soon realized that every person entering the house for the first time fell down those stairs. Kids only went down a couple of steps, but grown-ups would mostly go halfway down before catching themselves; workmen, if they were carrying tools, usually went all the way to the bottom.

The kitchen and the upstairs rooms had small enclosed fire grates with removable round iron lids. To save coal we never lit those fireplaces because the kitchen had a real gas stove for cooking and in winter a token quantity of warmth did percolate up the stairs from the wide fireplace in the living room. Mum would usually get up first, clean out the previous day's ashes, place crumpled newspaper and firewood in the grate, then add a few chunks of coal from the bin in the garden. This fireplace didn't provide a lot of warmth, as most of the heat went up the chimney — which frequently caught fire. "'Bout time," the helmeted firemen said every year after rushing over in their big red fire-engine to extinguish the fire in the flue, "'bout time you 'ad that bloody chimney swept." But sweeping the chimney cost sixpence, whereas the firemen would come for nothing.

When we finally did get the chimney swept, the soot-covered sweep arrived, pushing his black handbarrow riding atop wooden-spoked wheels banded with iron rims that, like Alf's barrow, clattered easily over the cobbled road. He screwed a long wooden handle into the middle of a circular brush and began working it up into the flue. As each section of handle disappeared he added another length, and with every twist an avalanche of soot belched into the living room. When the stack of handles had dwindled he asked me to go outside and check. News of his visit had spread among the neighborhood kids, who now congregated to watch. I edged my way through the crowd as a triumphal shout erupted: the brush had emerged, and soared victorious above our roof! Back inside again, too choked by emotion and soot to speak, I indicated that the brush had appeared. The sweep shoveled his sacks full of soot and loaded them onto his barrow, which finally clamored off. It would take Mum a full month's sweeping and dusting to get the house clean again.

The water supply consisted of an outdoor tap on the end of an undulating lead pipe secured to the brick garden wall we shared with Mr. and Mrs. Harney next door. Mr. and Mrs. Harney never argued nor raised their voices — because they were Protestant, Mum said. Toward the end of November the lead pipe froze, and during intermittent thaws we filled saucepans with water. Then the hard freeze set in, when we kept our feet close by the fire and got chilblains. Those months we'd have to get water from a neighbor a few houses along Morgan Street, Issa Cohen's mother who was born deaf, never learned to talk and could only utter strange howls, but who nevertheless boasted a tap and a sink inside her kitchen. For the duration of the winter we battled the unflushed newspaper stuffed in the bottom of the lavatory, breaking the ice with a special tree branch that leaned against the wall. Early April greeted us with a rainbowed arc spraying across the yard from the burst pipe, and Mum would have the plumber come and add one more bead to the string of silvery bulges. Just as one dates a tree by its growth rings, so I knew the age of this lead pipe by its beaded insinuations.

The high brick wall on the side of the house that faced Tredegar Terrace, the wall that curved outward, was apparently the neighborhood's most inviting surface for bouncing balls — particularly good for playing German Cricket. In German Cricket you threw the hard ball at a small wicket set up against the wall. The impact was pretty loud inside the house — and if the ball happened to miss the wicket and hit our street door, it was much louder. On Sunday afternoons when Abie was home he'd hide behind the door, then yank it open and leap outside to grab someone. The kids knew he was going to do that so they'd run away, then jeer at him. Sometimes from a safe distance they'd jump up and down to make him even more angry.

When Abie wasn't home, Mum carried a bucket of water upstairs to pour out the landing window over the kids. One day she was complaining about the noise, so I carried a bucket of water upstairs to hurl out over them, the way she did. I hid below the sill, then swung the bucket out the small window opening. But in the time it took the water to fall to the street below, Mum had rushed out the door. The kids retreated as my deluge landed squarely on her head. They all quieted in guarded jubilation as she stood drenched, gasping. My stomach knotted and I ran downstairs to explain it was an accident.

"We'll see what your father thinks about this, a son throwing water on his own mother."

That night I lay on the mattress in darkness behind the door listening for him to come home. Uncountable hours passed. Then I heard the living room door bang open, and they were both shouting. Blood pumping in my ears made everything go quiet, then loud, then quiet as I lay clenched for his mad rush along the passage, massive hands grabbing the banister to pull himself upstairs faster, shoes smashing against the risers. I tried taking slow deep breaths through my nose. Maybe she hadn't told him yet, maybe they were shouting about something else. The struggle to decipher their words was exhausting.

Then suddenly I was awake. It was dark, but now all was quiet and still, with no slivers of light from downstairs creeping under the door. Maybe they'd both fallen asleep without ever getting to the pail of water. Mum would be lying on one side of the settee, Dad snoring across the middle, and in the cot, Marius struggling to breathe.

•   •   •

"That's all he'll ever give you, babies," Lily's genteel triumvirate of spinster sisters, Rae, Zelda and Cissie had forewarned. My three aunts shared the top floor of their brother Harold's brick Tudor on the north side of London in Clapham Common, a tranquil middle-class residential section of winding streets and wrought-iron garden gates. Uncle Harold's wife Vera, when she wasn't nagging her husband, liked to stand at the bottom of the stairs and hurl insults up at her three sisters-in-law. They, in a huff, would slam their door and reflect on how their elder brother — intelligent but naïve and defenseless Harold — suffered such a shrew. They could always close their door, but poor Harold! Vera, *she* was the intruder all right, the way she'd purloined their brother, split the family.

My aunts were secretaries, daily riding the London Transport to their respective City offices. Zelda — tall, narrow, stooped-shouldered and invariably capped with a matronly hat that poorly concealed the glow of luminous scalp through thinning strands — Zelda consistently arrived home earliest from her office. This probity accrued to her the status — and, responsibility — of noting when the other sisters returned home.

Should Cissie or Rae walk in markedly later than normal, the immediate assumption was the intrusion of some male acquaintance, a conjecture that would prompt Zelda to a deluge of preemptive slights. And should the premise prove true and the interloper entertain presumptions to additional rendezvous, slighting blossomed into laceration.

Cissie, with deep blue eyes and curved black hair whose metallic sheen glinted against a pale skin — the only sister to wear lipstick — Cissie was clearly the most vulnerable of the three, her comings and goings demanding the closest scrutiny. For two consecutive mornings, through the window Zelda had observed Cissie in conversation at the bus stop below. The second evening, as Cissie walked in the door, the matter was addressed: "I saw you talking to that one again. He looks something like a lapdog, a *shmek tabik.*"

"He only said what nice weather we're having."

"And what's so nice about the weather?"

"Zelda, he was just being friendly."

"Friendly! Friendly? You must be going mad. I bet you thought he was *interested!* I always thought you were a bit mad."

Rae's disposition assigned her a less confrontational rôle. "That kind isn't good enough for you," she said. "Don't lower yourself."

Of the three aunts, Cissie was my favorite. When she visited us I felt particularly shy at the softness of her voice, her enunciation as faultless as that of *The Third Programme* classical music announcers on the wireless. In awed fascination I watched the pearled white rectangles that flashed behind those sumptuous red lips. But most important, she usually brought us a whole bar of Cadbury's Fruit and Nut. And always after she departed, Mum would lift up the heavy brass candlestick on the end of the mantelpiece; her face would flood dark, and in a quick confusion she would slide into her bag the ten-shilling note Cissie had invariably secreted beneath its base.

"Be nice to Cissie, her weak heart," Mum always said.

Occasionally Aunt Zelda came to visit. Zelda certainly didn't bring any chocolate. She arrived one Saturday morning while Rebecca and Zilla were still in bed, and promptly ordered Katherine and me out into the garden.

"What's the matter, what is it?" asked Mum.

Katherine and I ducked down by the open kitchen window to eavesdrop. From the living room, Marius coughed in his cot.

"What about Marius?"

"He's a baby, he doesn't understand," said Mum.

"Listen!" Zelda's voice dropped. "Cissie's come home late three times this month already."

"What do you think it is?"

"I'm sure it's the one from the Guards."

"What do you mean, do you think she's...."

"I don't know what to think."

"What about her heart?"

"She won't listen to me anymore. Last night Rae tried to speak to her, she said she was reading."

"Do you think...?"

"She said, 'Cissie, when you've finished the book — it's a thick book — when you've finished the book.... We're your sisters, everybody thinks you're making a fool of yourself.' 'I'm reading,' she said. 'Alright, when you've finished reading.'"

I didn't know what to make of this conversation, but Katherine, leaning forward to catch every nuance, pursed her lips as though she understood; by now I realized that that was because Katherine was a girl. It had become apparent in overhearing Zilla's and Rebecca's conversations that girls and women talked like that, talked in some kind of code that boys couldn't understand. One would say something strange and the other would nod and say something back, using real words but strung in sentences that didn't quite mean anything. They'd pause, squint their eyes knowingly, then continue as though they were actually having a normal conversation.

Other relatives would occasionally stop by, like Uncle Sid. Because Uncle Sid was a man he didn't talk in code, but the strange thing about him was he never got wild, even though his face looked exactly like Dad's. Mum said he was Dad's brother. Although he was thinner and wore a plaid jacket, his face looked so much like Dad's that after he'd been in our house a little while Katherine would test him to make sure he wasn't really Dad. She'd say: "The cat made number two on the table." Uncle Sid would look at her without getting wild, and Mum would jump up and say: *"Oy a broch,* where?"

Lastly, there was cousin Seymour. Seymour had a fountain pen with a gold nib, and Mum told us he was going to be an accountant one day. He always came on his bike, which he left in the area in front of the house behind our iron railings. Seymour only talked about important things, which meant he never talked to kids. I also didn't understand what *he* was talking about, but that was because whatever he said was so important. I knew I would never be able to say anything as important as what Seymour said. When something terrible happened, as when *Zaideh* choked from the chicken bone stuck in his throat, it was Seymour who delivered the news. Seymour's appearance at the door meant doom.

One evening Aunt Zelda came around and knocked, just after Mum had sent Katherine and me up to bed. "Sshh, quick, go to sleep," said Mum, and closed our door.

Katherine reopened the door a crack, and Zelda's voice downstairs was clear: "I went to the office, Cissie wasn't there, the manager said, How's your sister?"

"Really? What do you think?"

"The office manager, he told me she leaves early, she says she's feeling poorly."

"*Oy a broch,* her heart...."

"Tsk!, sshh, listen! So, Seymour waited by the office. She came out and she caught the bus, the number nineteen."

"...Nineteen."

"To Victoria Park, on his bicycle he followed the bus."

"To Victoria Park!"

"The soldier, the Guardsman, he was waiting there on the pavement, as she got off the bus he took her bag and they started walking away, they didn't even say anything!"

"So where did they go?"

"A skinny-faced *yock,* if someone should see her with a soldier!"

"Uh, well, I don't know...."

"You don't know?"

"So where did they go?"

"Did you say, you *don't know?*"

"Zelda, is it so terrible...?"

"*Is* it so terrible?"

"What's so terrible, to see someone, maybe enjoy a little bit...."

"*See* someone? A soldier? Who knows what diseases they've got!"

"So what else does she have?"

"What else? Tsk! She's got a comfortable home, she's got her sisters, Harold talks to her."

"It's not the same, a brother...."

"She'll kill herself she will, she'll kill all of us, with worry."

"Zelda, maybe it's not so terrible...."

"Tsk! I should have known, you're mad like Cissie you're mad, look what *you* did, you let him make you pregnant and now look how you live, like an *animal.* I knew I shouldn't come round."

•   •   •

Behind the abundance of flowers that closed off the far end of our garden, beyond the clumped dark green mosses, a low brick wall bore a small window where all sunlight and fresh air was halted at its grimy panes. Tall hollyhocks grew against this wall, their petals a flagrant yellow brilliant as the sun, in sharp contrast with the view through the glass into a low hut where all seemed dark and murky. Lead toys were cast in that hut — little lead soldiers, on foot and mounted on horseback. As I watched through the streaked glass, men poured scalding metal from a vat into an iron mold vise-locked to the edge of a big work bench. When the smoke from each pour cleared, with pliers they extracted a phalanx of gleaming soldiers, clipping off the connecting metal scraps to throw back, spattering into the vat. Sometimes the vat would ignite for an instant, the yellow flare illuminating the intense, blackened faces of a father and his two teenage sons. When the trio came outside into Tredegar Terrace and sat on the curb to eat their newspaper-wrapped sandwiches, their hands burnished silver with lead, ragged jackets laced with burn holes, I saw suggestions of more serious mishap: scarred hands, pockmarked faces, and particularly the father's ill-fitting eye patch covering a scary lid that curved inward over a vacant eye-socket.

Mum had said we mustn't talk to them because they were *yocks* and they hated Jews. But all *yocks* bad, all Jews good? What about Reuben Berger around the corner? He was always bullying, ready to hit us, and his father went to *shul.* From what I'd gathered so far at prayer assembly each morning in school, god's main concern seemed to be how many people he could frighten into believing how marvelous he was. If he were that marvelous, instead of terrifying people he'd pay our rent and give Mum some extra so she wouldn't always owe money to Lovich's grocery. Anyway, I'd already worked out my own categorization when it came to *yocks:* those who were looking to fight, and those who weren't. The *yocks* from the hut seemed nice to me, and so I secretly disobeyed Mum's admonition.

The three of them took me inside and showed me how they picked up the scalding pot from the gas burner with huge tongs and poured the radiant, sputtering metal into the mold. Where spilled lead went awry and hit the bench top, it would splash up and outward to form a ring of droplets; the amazing thing was it would set while still falling through the air, as though time had stopped. I got to hold the piece for close examination, a perfect reproduction of a liquid splash.

I realized that if they could lift a pot of cold water from beneath up around the mold to cool the hot lead faster, they wouldn't have to wait so long between pours. They tried it, and sure enough the lead did harden right away; I felt proud to have thought of a scientific way to help. But the next pour caused a little explosion, with dots of molten lead flung across the hut.

My arm stung. "You're christened now," the father said as he returned the vat to the burner. He was right, there was a burn hole in my shirt sleeve and my arm had a red spot. "That's alright, lad, some water must 'ave got inside the mold, but if you don't try something new you'll never know."

Outside again, I went back into the garden and climbed the tall plane tree that soared above their roof. From the little hut's chimney, smoke drifted up through the leaves toward me. High up, at an altitude safely remote from earthly discord, a thick branch beckoned and I climbed all the way up, leaned into a fork, and sang a song I'd learned from the wireless: *Under-neath the ar-ches,__ We'll dream our life a—way.__* Mrs. Harney from next door came over to her side of the garden wall to listen. I felt too shy to look her way, so I pretended I didn't know she was there, and just kept on singing for a long time. Her staying to listen to me was so exciting that my foot slipped; I grabbed at a branch, missed, and fell all the way down and out of the tree, through the hollyhocks and onto the mossy bed. A twig had caught in the burn hole and ripped my shirt sleeve right up to the seam. Inside, I managed to get the shirt off before Mum noticed, and hid it under the dirty clothes piled in the corner of the kitchen.

That night, even after Katherine came to bed, my mind was filled with Mrs. Harney, her smiling and listening to me sing. It made me feel light, as though I could hold my arms out like a paper glider and fly up and out of the window.

Pow! My head was lifted sideways off the pillow; it was daylight, it was morning. The side of my face was hot and stinging. He was looming over the mattress, holding the shirt. "You barsted, you... you... what did you do? You tore it, you gorrit all burnt with matches, the shirt...."

Mum came running upstairs: "Leave him alone, enough already, your breakfast it's on the table, you'll miss the bus, quick, they'll take off from your wages...."

At school that day I told my friend Manny Yanklewitz, who lived in Antill Road, that I fell out of a tree and tore my shirt.

"You're not supposed to climb trees," he responded.

"Why not?"

"My Mum said it's too dangerous."

"I was looking at the sky."

"You can see the sky from the ground."

"Well, it's... different up there, it's quiet."

After school I went to the library on Mile End Road and asked for books about music and about science. The librarian got me a book by someone named Cecil Forsyth that described all the different kinds of musical instruments. Then she asked me what kind of science. I said about stars and the moon, and she found *Modern Astronomy*. Back in the garden and holding the astronomy book I climbed the plane tree to read; despite what Manny said, I felt closer to the whole universe up there. I wondered how far away planets were, if one day people might go there — but actually go, not like in silly *Flash Gordon Conquers the Universe* pictures Manny and I saw at the La Bohéme cinema on the corner of Burdett Road where sometimes on Saturday morning, if someone hadn't locked the back door properly, we sneaked in.

As it got darker, then too dark to read, stars appeared one by one. If there were a patch of sky with no stars, I only had to look back to the same spot a minute later to make out one, two, three stars. Low over our house was the constellation Cassiopeia, like a big upside-down *W*, and Ursa Major through the leaves almost above my head — a saucepan with a crooked handle. According to *Modern Astronomy*, the star that aligned with the far edge of the saucepan was the one called Polaris, the North Star. The North Star! The star that gave guidance to ships in the lost reaches of the ocean — here I was, united with all mariners from the beginning of history, looking at that very same star winking mysteriously through the branches!

A gentle ruffle of wind moved the leaves, stirring my foothold, bringing me back to the present. I sucked in a deep, deep breath. The air was pure and fresh, and energy from the sky magnified the ripe scent of flowers that floated up from the garden. I would show that conceited god a lesson, how to *really* look after the world. When I grew up I was going to be powerful but very kind, and never shout at anybody, never frighten anyone and never, never fight. Maybe I'd have one fight one time only, with Reuben Berger, and I'd have him on the pavement in a headgrip; he'd scream for mercy and people would be watching. Mrs. Harney would come through the crowd to see and I'd let go the headgrip, put out my hand to help Reuben up, then tell him he'd better not be a bully anymore, and I'd smile at him and everybody would cheer, and Mrs. Harney would be proud of me.

A deep red hue had settled like a thinning blanket on the rooftops. Suddenly, above, a brilliant point of white light traversed an elliptic curve over my head, then down, down toward the north, disappearing in an irretrievable instant to nothing. A shooting star, just as the book said! That meant it had wandered millions and millions of miles, and by accident I'd witnessed its arrival. From now on it would stay with us on earth forever, a friendly visitor from space. The shooting star, the periodic flare of soft yellow light from the window below where the men threw metal back into the vat, the soft quietness, Polaris — it was all so beautiful I felt my chest would burst.

A quickening gust moved the leaves, rocking the branch where I stood, and the fork I leaned into oscillated back and forth in regularly diminishing cycles. The way everything worked together perfectly, because there was nothing else it could ever want to do, was all too stunning for some stupid god to have even understood, let alone invented.

It seemed I had been up there forever. I climbed down feeling too overwhelmed to talk to ordinary people, so inside the house I crept directly upstairs. A few steps from the top, the door to the front bedroom opened and *Bobbeh* came backing out of her room. She stood on the landing without speaking, the gaslight drifting from the open door behind her creating a halo.

"Hello, *Bobbeh,*" I said to her back.

She turned and stood there without saying a word, looking directly down the couple of stairs at me. Her face was little and so old, with tiny eyes and deep cracks in the shriveled skin. She had only a few scraggly hairs left on her head — that must be why she always wore a babushka. I'd never seen her face so close before. She stood there a full minute more, unspeaking. Then suddenly, as though I weren't even there, she did a long loud *fotz.* When she finished she turned and walked slowly back into her room, closing the door and leaving a terrible smell, and I wondered how someone could just *fotz* like that without being embarrassed. I went in our back bedroom, climbed onto Rebecca's and Zilla's bed on top of the covers and looked out the window at the gently bobbing branches of the tree outside. I would *never fotz* like that, even if I got old — I would live a noble life. I, and the leaves, which included the way they undulated so gracefully, and the plane tree at the end of the garden, and all the stars and planets and the hollyhocks and the lead soldiers and the good *yocks,* we were all a secret army that would conquer the whole world and let everybody be happy, and no one would be allowed to punch anybody or shout at anyone, ever.

The next afternoon while I was in school, *Bobbeh* died — Mum told me when I came home. She said men came and took her away already, and now we had another bedroom. Zilla and Rebecca would be sleeping in *Bobbeh's* bed tonight. Mum said *Bobbeh* had been Dad's mother, she supposed it was a shame, but anyway she was always making up terrible lies about us to everyone in the family.

"Mum, where's your mother?" I asked.

"My mother died when I was nine. The doctors didn't have medicine in those days. You'll be lucky if I'm still alive when you're nine."

I was seven. That meant I had two more years to have a mother.

"Help me lift the mattress up onto the box spring."

The way *Bobbeh* had done that long *fotz* last night, I wondered if people do that the day before they die. Maybe doctors could recognize that type of *fotz* — the death-*fotz* — and when someone did it they knew the person was going to die the next day. They'd look at the person's children standing there and wonder if it was better to tell them their mother was going to die the next day, or whether they should say nothing so the children could have one last day without being sad.

I undressed just by starlight without being afraid, and climbed up onto what was now Katherine's and my bed, under the covers this time. Lying on it felt very high up; I could actually see the top of the gas lamp on Tredegar Terrace, the one that threw soft yellow blotches onto the ceiling. I heard Katherine coming up.

"Hello," I said.

"Zech is in bed already," she called down.

In the very low light I watched her shape as she undressed. Every way she moved, as she bent to untie her shoes, then as she stood up and stretched her dress off over her head — every move seemed perfect, completely beautiful. *What are little girls made of? Sugar and spice, and all that's nice; and that's what little girls are made of, made of.*

"*Bobbeh* did a loud *fotz,* last night before she died," I said.

She climbed into bed next to me under the covers, and I felt an overwhelming urge to touch her, but I was careful not to. "Maybe she gassed herself to death," she said, then turned to face me. "Auntie Cissie is going to get married."

"Is she? Then... I wonder if she'll still bring chocolate?"

"If her husband lets her come round, she will."

"Her husband? Do we... know him already?"

"No. Mum said she's going to marry a soldier."

Downstairs there came a scraping and clicking, then the loud creaking of hinges *dut-dut-dut-dut-dut* as the street door opened. "...Tsk!... oil the bladdy door, why doesn't someone...."

"I hope he doesn't come upstairs."

"Don't worry, Zech."

5

Mum took us to hospital to see Cissie. I didn't even recognize my aunt in that white, muffled room. They had removed her lipstick, and she looked old. She smiled weakly at me; she could barely manage to tell me to come closer. I leaned over the starched, rigid sheet, and she whispered to me: *When I get big I should find a nice girl, even if she weren't Jewish it didn't matter, as long as I was faithful I would always be happy, even if I had to die.* I didn't know what it all meant, even though I understood the individual words — how could you be happy if you're already dead? It was like one of those conversations that girls have. I really wanted to talk about that and ask her exactly what she meant, but she seemed so tired it frightened me. How could anyone get that tired, especially lying in bed?

The following day cousin Seymour came to visit. Through the window Mum saw him riding his bike across Morgan Street, and her face went white. I hid outside the open back door and listened: Cissie had died right after we left hospital yesterday. I didn't really believe it; how could a person just die, where did they go? I didn't mean someone like *Bobbeh,* who *fotzed,* but Aunt Cissie, with her lovely white teeth and soft careful voice. Now who would give Mum money?

I scrambled down the broken stone steps into the garden, over to where the hollyhocks reached up so brilliant toward the blue cloudless sky. I climbed the plane tree, clambering up through the branches, scraping my hands until I leaned into my nook. Through the leaves the house seemed as remote as though it were on another planet. There was no wind. Everything was still.

·　　·　　·

A whole year passed, and it was August of 1939. Workmen came with oxyacetylene burners to cut down the wrought-iron railings that set off the front of our house, guarding the cellar's window well. They loaded the metal onto their lorry, then rolled slowly along the street, cutting down everybody's railings house by house. People came outside to watch. The men drove across to Tredegar Square and next cut away the lovely high ornate iron scrolls fencing off the park. I watched as the beautiful tall gates and posts crashed to the ground. Mum said the government needed the iron to make guns and bombs, because there was going to be a war.

Everything seemed so bare. People who previously had walked around the park or crossed from gate to gate on the diagonal flagstone paths now started cutting across the grass, and after a week or two even the flower beds were trampled despite the little green signs with *Please Keep Off the Grass* spelled out in white letters.

The slender bottle-green lamp posts whose luminance had swept Morgan Street with strands of soft yellows now no longer shone at night. Dad sewed large black opaque fabric covers for the windows. Each evening at dusk we nailed the covers up around the window frames with small tacks. Then we went outside to make sure no light leaked around the edges from the living room through to the now-blackened street. In the extreme of darkness the silent stars, lacking competition, blazed clear, round and unblinking above us, poised to witness the gravity of the coming war.

Workmen dug a big rectangular hole in our garden. They lifted large panels of corrugated iron over the wall, some sheets straight and some curved at one end, all with curlicued silvery swirls on their zinc-plated surfaces. Standing inside the excavation the men bolted the pieces together, erecting half below ground level a little iron room with a curved roof. The earth they'd quarried was then shoveled back over the top so that the structure was virtually buried, except for a three-foot-square opening at one end. They told us every house would be getting an Anderson shelter like ours for when the bombing began. Mum said she would never go down into it because of spiders, and if the Germans really did start dropping bombs she'd just stay in the house.

I played inside the Anderson shelter with Manny from Antill Road, and also sometimes with Jack Pristein who lived further away. The reason Manny was my best friend was because when Miss Ratchet asked me a question about history, Manny always wrote down the answer on a slip of paper and was ready to slide it onto my lap. Jack, who lived on the other side of Mile End Road, also knew all about history, but his desk was on the opposite side of the classroom; however I got the feeling that even if he sat next to me he wouldn't approve of just giving me the answers. Anyway, playing in our garden, Manny and I discovered that the earth the men had heaped over the Anderson made a perfect height for us to crouch on, hidden just below the top of the garden wall, with Manny's bicycle tire pump filled from a pail of water. When a grown-up passed by in the street he and I would silently stand and squirt cold water down onto their head. They'd jump and look around, but by the time they thought to check the top of the garden wall, we'd ducked down again. Once we even squirted rotten old Reuben Berger; he shouted out he knew who we were, he'd get us in school.

The workmen came back, this time erecting an eighteen-inch-high brick wall around the front of our house where the iron railings had stood, to prevent people falling through the grating into the cellar. They built it using beautiful new multi-hued bricks, constructing little battlements along the top, keeping everything straight by stretching white string from corner to corner to guide the selvages of cream-colored cement curling out in crisp, parallel rows. I loved this little wall. It was so direct and peaceful in its orderliness, quite unlike the miasma of our old crooked house with its bulging walls and sloped floors. The men told me that only corner houses would get these new little replacement walls; ours was a corner house. We were the lucky ones.

Only a couple of evenings later, when Richard Dimbleby was announcing the six o'clock news report on the wireless, he said that the Germans were invading Poland. At school the next day the rumor was that Hitler would soon begin dropping real bombs on London. After morning prayers the headmaster announced that we were all going to be evacuated. In class, Miss Ratchet distributed gas masks in brown cardboard carrying cases with string that went over your shoulder. We were instructed to try the masks on: the buckles were so strong and the black rubber straps so tight it felt as if your head was being crushed. Air entered through a fat metal tube beneath the one-piece celluloid visor, and when you exhaled it escaped under the rubber edges that lay flat in front of your ears. If you breathed out fast you could make the rubber vibrate and produce a loud sound like a *fotz*. Quickly I discovered the pitch of the *fotz* could be controlled by how you stretched the rubber sides against your face by pulling down on the fat metal tube: down and tight for high-pitched squeaky notes, up and loose for the heavy low ones that vibrated and fogged up the celluloid. I helped Manny and Jack get their correct notes, and we harmonized a trio. Miss Ratchet heard us; she said we were disgusting and made us stop.

Finally we finished our last day at Malmsebury Road school. That evening teachers came around to houses telling parents to accompany their children to school the next morning, and to bring for each child one bag of clothes plus their gas mask.

The next morning as soon as Abie left, Mum called upstairs: "Quick, get up everyone, the kettle's on. Rivka, wake Zilly up, quick, your clothes, both of you make sure you've got everything." Mum had packed Katherine's and my bags the previous evening, but my older sisters had insisted they pack their own. She hurried upstairs to our bedroom: "Did he *pish*, did you *pish?*"

"No," I said, but still she felt the sheets under me. At least for our last morning at home, my bed was dry. "Quick, get up, have your breakfast, you've all got to go on the bus."

After breakfast, all packed and accounted for, our entourage — Zilla, Rebecca, me, Katherine and our bags and gas masks, with Mum carrying Marius — walked the two streets to Malmesbury Road. A column of red double-decker buses was lined up by the curb. The playground was mobbed with kids and teachers. I saw Miss Ratchet, who said the four of us would be staying together, and she directed us to Zilla's teacher's queue.

In due time, amid bulging bags getting in everybody's way, my three sisters and I were herded onto a bus and given seats on the lower deck. Mum was calling through an open window, "Rivka, look after everybody, see Katya's alright." She elbowed closer: "And remind Zech to *pish* before he goes to bed!" My ears flared red; I should have handed her a megaphone so she could make sure everybody on the bus knew! "Zilly, you remind him!"

"Why doesn't 'e remember 'imself?" Zilla called back.

The bus was rolling away from the pavement, and though I tried to retain Mum and Marius in sight as long as possible, they both dissolved into the receding mayhem before the next vehicle came forward. The turmoil of a minute earlier was quickly transformed into a silent hush, with just engine sounds filling the vacuum. I held Katherine's hand as we rode along Mile End Road toward the city. At Victoria Station everybody was disembarked and funneled onto an already-teeming platform of screaming kids, the tumult amplified by the high domed roof that curved above us. In a few minutes, even that deafening racket was eclipsed by the roar of billowing steam as a train came slowly into the station, inched along the platform's edge then screeched to a stop. Porters shouted, compartment doors were flung open. Somehow hanging on to each other we clutched our belongings and were carried aboard by the frenzied mob, along a corridor that ran the length of the carriage, to find ourselves finally seated together in a single compartment, Katherine and me opposite our big sisters. Doors slammed closed and the riot subsided to a welter of good-byes, sobbing and last-minute admonitions to those kids whose parents had brought them directly to the station. Someone called "Aboard!" More doors banged shut and the train began to glide forward.

We were riding on a real steam train! Katherine and I sat on a giant cold leather bench seat with a hard high back, so different from the velvety fabric of the Underground. At the ends of the compartment were fixed windows, and in the door a vertically-opening sliding window supported by a wide leather belt with brass eyelets that hitched onto a hook. Near the ceiling opposite, above Rebecca's and Zilla's heads, were dark-stained slatted wooden racks with shiny brass supports where my sisters had deposited their belongings; I climbed up and placed Katherine's and my bags, plus our gas masks, on the racks above our own heads.

The train rolled slowly between dark buildings, which, after twenty minutes or so gradually opened up to rows of houses seated among flower gardens, and later still to expansive green fields. We clicked along faster, de-DU-du-du, de-DU-du-du. Zilla and Rebecca were busily conversing between themselves, as usual. Real cows stopped munching grass to look up as we whisked by, and Katherine and I lowered the window and called out to them.

"Oh, shut the window, it's all blowing," said Zilla.

The train's clattering wheels echoed sharply back off station walls: *Kings Sutton, Burnham, Pangbourne, Streatley,* as teachers, officials and crewmen in black jackets and peaked caps strode intently down the outside corridor.

"I wonder if they'll let us all go to the same house," I said.

"They have to keep us all in the same house," Katherine answered.

"How do you know?"

"Because if they don't we'll tell them they have to."

Two big boys had noticed Zilla and Rebecca, and came into the compartment to talk: "Where do you live then?"

Rebecca seemed inclined to respond, but Zilla looked angry and pulled at her arm. I continued my separate conversation with Katherine. "But supposing they still make us go to different houses?"

"We'll tell them our Mother is ill, and we all have to go to the same house or she'll die."

An hour and several deceptive retards later the train slowed to a crawl, rattled over a tangle of siding tracks and rolled into an open-air station, jerking to a stop amid a roar of hissing steam. People lined the platform, and above their heads the name *BANBURY* stood out in enormous black letters on a chipped white enamel panel. The carriage doors burst open and we were hustled out. Strange accents shouted names from lists. Anxious children were grouped together and marched off the platform to a big waiting area, a vast enclosure with no walls but topped with a high sheet-metal roof supported by pillars into the grass.

"Oi'll take that one, that one, there!" screamed a woman, pointing at Rebecca.

"What be your name, dearie?" asked another, holding sheets of papers.

"Grossman," said Rebecca.

"Grossman," the second one repeated, perusing her papers. *"Grose*-man?" She looked at Rebecca.

"No, it's pronounced Gross — like moss, Grossman."

"Gross-man; they 'as to stay together, Ethel," she called to the first woman. "Abbott, they's going to Mrs. Abbott, you 'as to speak to Mrs. Abbott if you wants one."

"Grose-man: Zilla, Rebecca, Zachary, Katherine!" called another woman's voice, again mispronouncing our surname. Hands pushed us through toward a small black car waiting on the grass. The driver, a middle-aged lady, told us to climb in and stand our bags on the floor, Zilla in front next to her, the rest of us in the back. Now we were riding inside a real motorcar! The seats were stiff and hard, and a detached panel hung on the inside door, swinging loosely back and forth on a silver handle in reaction to the car's motions.

We bumped out of the field and onto a paved road, and the lady stopped and looked again at her instructions. "You be going to stay with Mr. and Mrs. Abbott. They be wanting to take four children." She read on. "Oh, yes, Doris, they 'as a very nice daughter Doris, aged sixteen. Now you behave yourselves and Oi'm sure you'll be 'appy there."

The roadways twisted and the tires buzzed on cobblestones, rattling everything in the car. On the first couple of streets, adjacent houses were joined the way our house in London was to Mrs. Harney's, and set forward to meet the narrow pavement. On the next two streets houses were separate, individually situated further back behind little front gardens.

The car rolled to a stop, and this time as the lady switched off the engine, after a final tremor the shaking ceased. We climbed out and deposited our bags and gas masks by a rough unpainted wooden fence. A path led through the garden to the street door, which opened. A grey-haired woman stepped out: "Well now, so you be our new family!"

This had to be the one we were going to live with. We were ushered into the front room — the shiniest room I'd ever seen, everything reeking of being newly cleaned. The brown wooden arms of a sofa were burnished bright, and the low tabletop standing in front reflected a matching radiance. Under draped white sheets, singular shapes lurked mysteriously.

"You be waiting in that there kitchen now, you children," our foster mother said, pointing through to an adjacent room. We filed through to where, standing in front of a rough-hewn counter that ran along the wall beneath the only window, a fat girl in a shapeless grey woolen dress, her straight hair trimmed level with her earlobes, was busily stuffing the remains of a sandwich into her mouth. She interrupted her chewing for a moment to eye us warily, then without any semblance of acknowledgement resumed chewing.

The street door closed, and Mrs. Abbott came into the kitchen. "Oi be Mrs. Abbott. This 'ere be me young daughter Doris." *That's the ugly fat one!* "You can put your bags by the wall. Now you children must be right 'ungry. Doris, lay the table for our new family."

Doris, moving with a quickness that belied her bulk, set out plates and knives and spoons on an oblong wooden table in the kitchen's center."

"Now then, you Zilla sit there, Oi surely ain't 'eard no name like that Zilla before," she said, pointing at one of four chairs. "And Rebecca you sits next to your big sister" — she sat them along one side — "and you, Zachary, sits 'ere and little Katherine you sit next to your big brother."

Doris brought in two additional chairs and seated herself at the far end of the table. She didn't say anything, nor did her expressionless scrutiny change.

Mrs. Abbott served cabbage and potatoes from an iron pot. On my plate lay what seemed to be a two-inch-long green caterpillar; I touched it with my spoon to see if it were real. It didn't move but it really was a caterpillar, with rows of feet and little short hairs, so I pushed it to the rim and covered it with a bit of cabbage. Katherine lifted up a leaf of her cabbage; she also had a cooked caterpillar and she started to cry. Zilla and Rebecca said they weren't hungry, so I said I wasn't either.

Mrs. Abbott picked up Katherine's caterpillar on her fork. "That be-ain't no caterpillar, look," she said, and put it in her mouth. Looking at Doris with an equally stolid face, she chewed then swallowed the caterpillar, which made me feel sick. She seemed determined to continue eating, so the four of us had to just nibble little bits until she was finished.

She realized we weren't really eating. "Oi s'poses as 'ow you children be-ain't 'ungry, must be leaving your parents an' all that." Her own meal completed, she again addressed the daughter. "Doris, now you take these children upstairs and show them their bedrooms where what they be going to sleep." Bags and all, we followed Doris through the door, up cramped twisting stairs to a first landing, then up a further set of yet narrower steps to a tiny landing on the top floor, an attic divided into two rooms.

"You — wait 'ere," Doris said to me. With downturned palm and four pudgy fingers she gestured the girls to precede her into the front room, the brighter-looking of the two. I watched through the doorway as she pointed silently to the big bed, and to a high chest between two windows. Simply pointing at the bags my elder sisters still held in their hands apparently meant they were to be placed on the floor by the wall. Rebecca giggled for a moment, which caused Doris to look directly at her.

I peered into the other room, which I presumed would be for me. It was comparatively dark, and I was afraid to go in alone. Beyond the brown door was a sloping ceiling, with a high bed up against the wall where the ceiling was lowest; if I woke up in the night and sat up I'd hit my head on the ceiling unless I moved down to the middle first. Doris finally came out, brushed me into this dark room and bent down by a three-legged wooden stand. She twisted a knob which switched on a real electric light, but one whose dim glow barely penetrated the shadowy gloom. With the same pudgy fingers she pointed at my clothes bag, then at the massive dark closet leaning out from the wall.

That was it; not a word until she called back from the stairs: "My Mum'll be calling all you children down later, so you all be ready."

My room was frightening. After Doris was downstairs and out of earshot I called, "Can I come in there?" and even my voice sounded strange.

"Tsk, wait a minute!" Rebecca's spectral words echoed back.

Even if I did wake up in the night I'd be much too afraid to get out of bed to pee. And if in the morning I found I'd done it in the bed I knew I'd never be able to hide it from Mrs. Abbott. If I were a girl I wouldn't have this terrible curse; my sisters never wet the bed, and they didn't have to sleep in a frightening room by themselves.

"Is Mrs. Abbott a witch?" I heard Katherine ask.

"Oo-er! Don't be dopey!" That was Zilla.

"Is Mrs. Doris a witch?"

Rebecca settled the matter. "There're no such things as witches, only in stories."

"Can we go home?" Katherine asked.

"No, we have to stay here 'til the war finishes."

"When will it finish?"

"Nobody knows for sure, only Winston Churchill."

"Can you ask him?"

Zilla's voice: "Oo-er, don't be mad!"

Silence.

Then: "Won't he tell anybody?"

"No," Rebecca answered.

"Will he let us go home?"

"Tsk, no."

"Will he let us see Mum?"

"Oh, shut up, I dunno."

Mrs. Abbott called up the stairs: "You children come down now and play in the garden." We descended the almost vertical flights of stairs. "Now don't you be touching anything in that there front room, then!"

Outside, two boys came walking along the pavement, to stop by the fence. "You be new, be-ain't cha."

Rebecca told me and Katherine to go play somewhere else; it was a small garden so we went to the opposite corner.

"You be the new kids from London, be-ain't cha?" said the taller one.

Zilla bristled. "What's it got to do with you?"

"Yes, we are from London. We're evacuated," said Rebecca.

"We be living 'cross the street, in that there 'ouse." He pointed. "E's Ed, 'e be moi young brother, Ed Slattery. You gonna come out after tea?"

"Not just to talk to you," said Zilla.

I heard Rebecca's whisper: "Ssh, they seem alright."

The shorter one had put down his school bag. "You be going to Saint Leonard's?"

The street door burst open and Mrs. Abbott hurried out. Grasping at Zilla's and Rebecca's arms she hustled them back into the house. At the street door, she called to Katherine and me: "You two children come on inside also, now then." Over her shoulder she called back: "Now you go on 'ome there, you lads, don't want you 'anging around that there gate." The boys slunk off across the road.

Inside the house, she addressed my elder sisters. "Oi'm going to 'ave to report this to your parents. We can't 'ave neighbors talking. Tsk! What next, Oi don't know!"

"We were only talking...."

"This be-ain't London 'ere, you know.... Upstairs now the lot on you 'til Oi calls you down."

Up on the second landing, I asked Rebecca: "Can I come in your room?"

"Tsk, oh, maybe afterwards."

"What's the matter with 'er?" asked Zilla. "We can't even talk to anybody."

"They're different in the country."

"Can someone put my light on?" I asked.

"Don'cha know 'ow to switch a light on?"

I peered behind Zilla into my dreaded room as she switched on the light. In the shadows sat a dark wooden rocking chair I hadn't noticed before. It faced the bed, so that if something sat on it in the night it would be looking straight at me in bed. *In the night a ghost will start rocking that chair, and it'll do something to me from across the room and I'll be paralyzed so I can't scream, and Zilla and Rebecca will stay fast asleep and they won't even know what's happening.* I tried not to think anymore, just opening my bag and laying out clothes in the chest's drawers, hiding the two books I'd kept from the library, *Modern Astronomy* and *Orchestration,* about musical instruments, underneath the clothes in case Mrs. Abbott checked.

Later, downstairs, a little old man with bony fingers and wearing an outdoors cloth cap sat with a newspaper at one end of the table. Dinner was more cabbage and boiled potatoes, now with carrots and little pieces of white meat.

"Say 'Ello to our new family now, Tom," Mrs. Abbott chastised him.

He lowered the newspaper, grunted "'Ello, 'ow be you all?" then resumed reading. He had to be Mr. Abbott.

The boiled chicken tasted rubbery. "Mrs. Abbott, I can't eat all the chicken," I said.

"That be-ain't no chicken, that be rabbit, 'ealthier 'n chicken, tastier too. Mr. Abbott 'ere, 'e catches 'em 'imself, 'e does."

"And right fresh they be, young 'un," added the voice from behind the newspaper. Zilla stopped eating and gulped as if she were going to throw up.

"Fetch a bucket, Doris. These children 'ave 'ad a busy day, they must be right tired. Oi think a good night's sleep 'ould be right good for all 'n you. Finish up and up to bed now."

I lay in bed and listened to them talking in the next room. When they were quiet for more than a minute I called out "Good night" again, in case they'd fallen asleep.

Downstairs, Mrs. Abbott took out a pen and paper: *"Dear Mr. and Mrs. Grossman, Your two big girls was seen talking to boys by our fence. I wants you to know what your big girls is like, I shall do me best but I can't be held responsible for how them girls was brought up. This ain't London here...."*

•   •   •

The window — it was light — suddenly I realized the room, everything was light, it was the morning. I ran my hand around the sheet under me: dry!

After our cups of tea, porridge and a slice of bread and jam, Mrs. Abbott walked us over a canal bridge to school. The headmaster's office was crowded with kids from London. "Now you come straight 'ome at dinner time," said Mrs. Abbott, and grasped Katherine's hand to leave.

"I want to stay with you," Katherine yelled to Rebecca, struggling to free herself.

Zilla seemed embarrassed at the commotion Katherine was causing: "Oh shut up, you can't go to this school, this one's for big kids!"

"Now then you behave yourself," said Mrs. Abbott to Katherine, as the other kids looked on. "You're too little to go to Saint Leonard's."

"Mrs. Abbott, do you think Katherine should start school tomorrow instead of today?" asked Rebecca. "Maybe she could go home with you, and then we'd see her when we come home at dinner time."

Katherine was crying angrily. "I'm going to stay here, I don't want to go with her."

"Now you can't stay 'ere, young 'un, you be going to come 'ome with me," Mrs. Abbott said firmly.

"Can you come back also?" Katherine glared at Rebecca.

"Now then your big sister 'as to stay 'ere in school. You'll come 'ome and 'elp me in the kitchen, and don't you worry 'bout your sisters and brother; they'll be 'ome in no time at all." Katherine's mouth was tight as Mrs. Abbott pulled her out of the office.

In class, the Londoners were grouped on one side of the room. I didn't recognize any faces from Malmsebury Road. My desk top had girls' names carved into it: Eileen, Beryl, Caitlin loves Robin. The teacher taught us spelling, English grammar and pronunciation, but she did it with a strong accent like Mrs. Abbott's, which seemed like a contradiction. At twelve o'clock she took all of us Londoners to the hallway where other evacuees had been assembled, and we were all walked to the headmaster's office. Zilla and Rebecca were there already, and a teacher was giving them directions back to Mrs. Abbott's. Outside the building the three of us walked across the playground and through the gate into the street — the first time we'd been alone and free since we got off the train.

"I wish we could go home," I pleaded. "I hate it here. Can't we get on a bus or a train or something?"

"Oo-er, what about Katya?"

"Maybe Mum could come here the next day and take her home. We could write down the address."

Rebecca settled it. "We can't go home, and we have to go back to Mrs. Abbott's."

The very next morning I awoke to a pool of soaked sheets. I pulled the covers up high over them, straightened everything out as well as I could, and dressed. Though it made a strong smell in the room, I didn't tell anyone; maybe Mrs. Abbott wouldn't notice. While we were eating our porridge she started up the stairs. My heart was suddenly thumping and I could hardly breathe. She came down after a while, but didn't say anything. I didn't dare lift my eyes from the table, but I must have looked funny because Zilla said: "What's the matter with 'im?"

The three of us left for school, Katherine staying home this time without a fuss. When we returned at dinner time Mrs. Abbott still didn't say anything about the bed. Maybe she'd just tidied up and never felt the sheets.

When we came home again at the end of the afternoon, Katherine was peeping around the street door; it opened further and Mrs. Abbott stood right behind her. A big cardboard box tied with string, reeking of garlic, sat on the front room floor. In front of us, Mrs. Abbott dragged it across and into the kitchen.

"The postman, 'e brought this box, this afternoon," she said to Zilla. "'E were knocking on me front door, and 'e right said, 'Mrs. Abbott,' 'e said, 'Them Londoners what be staying with you,' 'e said, 'this box be addressed to them children,' 'e said." She paused. "Looks to me like that box it come all the way from London."

"What, your Mum be sending y's food so's you don't starve from not eating?" said Doris, standing by the table. "'S'pose our food ain't good enough for Londoners." It was the first time I'd heard her say whole sentences.

"Now then, Doris, we'll 'ave none of that talk in this 'ouse. Now you go on up to your room 'til Oi tells you you can come down."

"Aw, Mum, Oi didn't mean nothing."

"Now, Oi means what Oi says, you go on up 'til Oi says you can come down. Right now you go."

Doris dragged her bulk across the kitchen and up the stairs.

"Now then, you children, Oi don't know as 'ow what be in that there box of yourn, but Oi won't 'ave your parents sending you no food in my 'ouse. My family's been eating my cooking nigh on fifteen years and it ain't done 'em no 'arm. We eats good 'ealthy food in this 'ouse, we grows our own veggies, and we be-ain't needing no food from no fancy London. Oi won't as 'ow look in your box this time, so you be all taking it on upstairs."

Zilla and Rebecca hoisted the box between them and the four of us started up the stairs. On our way past the first landing, Doris hissed in a loud whisper from her room: "No Londoners be-ain't gonna get me in no trouble."

Halfway up the top flight, Mrs. Abbott called from below: "Doris, you come right on down now."

For the first time, Rebecca said I could come into their room. Its two windows made it bright and relatively cheerful, just as it had seemed through the door from the landing outside. One double bed faced the windows from an opposite wall, and a single bed stood at a right angle against the far side. My big sisters put the box on the double bed, and as Zilla carefully closed the door behind us Rebecca began untying the string. The cardboard flaps blossomed and the marvelous smell, like from the stalls in Petticoat Lane, made my mouth water. We lined up the contents in a row on the bedcovers — brown paper bags wrapped around other paper bags. The biggest bag contained a rye bread with seeds, even a knife to cut it! The next bag had a cellophane-encased *worsht.*

"Sssh, don't let 'em hear us, they'll kill us if they knew," said Zilla.

"Would they really kill us?" asked Katherine.

"No, she doesn't mean it, don't worry," said Rebecca as she cut slices of bread on the low chest of drawers, trying to keep the rustling paper sounds to a minimum. Real saltbeef sandwiches! Then *worsht* sandwiches, even pickled cucumbers, and — bread pudding with raisins! It was unbelievable to be eating such lovely food so soon after the caterpillars.

"Sssh! What's that?" choked Zilla. Nobody moved. Creaking sounds came from the stairs. "Ee, what should we do, Mrs. Abbott'll come in!"

"Quick," said Rebecca, "let's put it in the suitcase."

Zilla protested: "That one's my case, you'll make it all greasy inside."

"Oh come on, we don't have time to worry whose case it is. Quick, hurry, they're coming."

Rebecca shoveled the torn-open paper bags, crumbs, knife, and the rest of the wrappings into Zilla's case and snapped it closed, then lined it up with the other bags against the wall. In silence the four of us listened. Faint rustling movements came from immediately behind the closed door. Half a minute later, very quietly, Rebecca started across the room.

"Where you going?" gasped Zilla in surprise. Then in a horrified whisper: "No, don't open it!"

Rebecca stood grim-faced behind the door as we listened to the slow breathing outside. Her hand rose; suddenly she yanked the knob and flung open the door.

Outside on the small landing, Mrs. Abbott was on her knees facing into the room. Doris stood one step down, behind, peering over her mother's head. For a startled moment nobody moved. Doris broke first; she half turned, hesitated, then began clumping downstairs.

Mrs. Abbott was the first to speak. "Oi were... just cleaning up that spot that be on the floor, outside your door."

"Oh!" said Rebecca.

"Oi sees you got that there box what come from London there up on the bed. Don't want you dirtying up my spread! What... what be inside that box of yourn?"

Rebecca hesitated; then, "Nothing."

"Nothing?"

"Nothing. It was... empty."

A long pause. "You sure now that there box were empty? It didn't look like no empty box to me when our postman put it down on my front room floor."

Rebecca had colored a deep red. "Well, it was empty. I suppose someone sent it by mistake."

Mrs. Abbott stood up. "Well, now then! Oi never did see such a 'eavy box before what were empty."

"You can look in it, then."

Taken aback at the invitation, Mrs. Abbott edged a couple of feet into the room toward where the box sat in the middle of the big bed, its flaps drooping outward. "Doris," she called, "you come on back up, girl."

"Aw, Mum."

"Doris, now you come on back up 'ere, right now, girl." Her voice rising, she remained motionless as Doris lumbered to the top of the stairs; she then addressed her in the sharpest tone we'd yet heard: "Come on in this room, Oi say." Doris crept just inside the doorframe and stood beside her mother.

Mrs. Abbott spoke deliberately. "Now girl, you go on over and tell me what be in that there box."

"Oi don' wanna go over there," said Doris.

"Now, nothing's wrong, you do as Oi say, you tell me what be in that there box standing on that bed."

Gingerly, Doris approached the edge of the bed, looked around at each of us, then leaned over and peered into the box.

"They be-ain't nothing in there, Mum."

A lengthy silence, then: "Daughter, you be sure they be-ain't nothing in there?"

"Sure, Mum, Oi can tell if there be something in a box. Oi be-ain't stupid."

"Now Oi won't 'ave you speaking to your own mother like that! Tip that box up so's Oi can see for meself."

Beads of sweat on her forehead, Doris leaned the box over so the opening faced her mother.

A pause. "Doris, you look under that bed."

"Aw, Mum, Oi don't wanna get down on that floor."

"Now you'll do as Oi tells you, gel, or Oi'll 'ave your Dad take 'is belt to you when 'e gets 'ome. Think 'cause you go to work you're too big for the belt? Now, get you down on that floor this minute and tell your mother what be under that there bed."

Doris clambered down on her knees and eased her thick torso prone to the floor. She peered under the bed. "They be-ain't but nothing under there. Oi don't see nothing but where it ain't been cleaned."

Again, a long silence. "You sure, gel?"

"Oi'm sure, Mum."

"Alright. You can get yourself up now." Doris struggled up again, and backed toward the door. As she passed her mother she was dealt a stinging slap across the cheek, which caused her to gasp in surprise. "And don't you be telling your mother that that there floor under that bed be-ain't spotless. Royalty can eat dinner straight off the floors in my 'ouse, it can. More'n Oi can say for some people."

Doris lurched sobbing out to the landing and thudded down the stairs. Her bedroom door slammed shut.

Mrs. Abbott backed tight-lipped from the room, her eyes darting from each of us to the other. She pulled the door tightly closed, then called out from the other side: "Oi suppose as 'ow you Londoners won't be needing no supper tonight." Then, a final riposte: "And another thing: we don't want no bed-wetters in this 'ouse."

It was a knife into my chest. Zilla and Rebecca turned to look at me — the first time any of us had moved since the whole incident began. The clumping footsteps thumped to the lower landing.

Then, quietly: "Oo-er! Wha'd'ya do it for?" That was Zilla.

My ears were raging hot.

"You have to try to remember to go before you go to bed," said Rebecca.

"I...I did...."

"Will she come up in the middle of the night?" asked Katherine.

"No, it's alright. What can she do? We didn't do anything wrong." Rebecca's voice dropped even quieter. "We'll have to finish eating everything up."

I sat mortified on the edge of Katherine's bed.

"Zech, do you want another sandwich?" Katherine asked. She never got angry when I wet the bed, maybe because she was too little.

"I don't know…." It was hard to think about sandwiches.

"Well, at least we're having a proper dinner," insisted Rebecca. "I'm still hungry; come on, quick, let's eat."

"Don'cha think we better wait 'til after they've gone to bed?" Zilla was still alarmed. "Ee, supposing she caught us, after all that!"

"Let's forget about her, that part's over, she won't do anything."

"Do you think she really believed us the box was empty?" asked Zilla. "I suppose someone could have sent an empty box, by accident."

"I don't know what she thought," Rebecca responded.

"I hate it here," Katherine said. "Can't we go home?"

"I don't know, how can we?" said Rebecca.

Mrs. Abbott did not make supper for us that evening, but later on called us down and told us to sit at the kitchen table. Mugs were set out; she poured tea, then sat down herself.

"My 'usband an' Oi we been talking, and we think little Katherine 'ere's too young to be away from 'er parents like, so I've been over to Mrs. Carter's 'ouse — she be the billeting officer what's in charge of the Londoners, all you evacuees. She said as 'ow she'll 'ave little Katherine picked up tomorrow morning, and Miss Brindley, that lady what brought you 'ere Saturday, she'll be driving little Katherine right the way to London, right 'ome to your parents' 'ouse."

"Can Miss Brindley take us all home?" pleaded Katherine.

"No, dearie, your sisters and brother they 'as to stay 'ere."

"I want Miss Brindley to take all of us back to London in her motor car. There's enough space. I'll sit on the floor."

"No, dearie, they 'as to stay 'ere, 'til the war's over."

We went back upstairs, and Rebecca called me into their room to finish the last of the food. As we ate she bundled the paper wrappings into a ball and went to stuff them into Zilla's bag. Zilla didn't want the greasy paper in her bag; Rebecca said we couldn't put them in Katherine's bag because Mrs. Abbott would find them when she came up in the morning to see that Katherine was all packed for her return to London.

"Put 'em in your bag, then!" hissed Zilla.

"I can't put them in my bag. There's no room."

"That's 'cause you took the extra clothes. They said we shouldn't take extra clothes."

"They're not extra. I had to have them in case."

"Rivka," I interrupted, "can you turn on the light in my room?"

She came and turned on the light. "Make sure you go down and pee before you go to sleep."

I reached around under the blanket, and the sheets were completely dry; maybe Mrs. Abbott hadn't actually meant me when she spoke of bed-wetters in the house.

I kept waking up in the night. One time I really had to go. The moon was shining on the moving tree outside the window. I didn't want to force myself *not* to think about ghosts because that would be enough to start everything. I looked at the rocking chair, made myself get out of bed without calling Rebecca, lifted the window and peed through the opening into the night. It all went outside and down onto the grass, and I didn't have to clean anything up, and nobody would know.

Early morning, Mrs. Abbott came upstairs to pack Katherine's clothes. I woke up with a fright, my jaw and teeth aching. I hardly had to feel the sheets to know that again every-thing was soaking wet. I moved over to a dry part of the bed and pretended to be asleep, in case Mrs. Abbott came into the room. Luckily, she didn't. When it was time for me to get up, again I covered the sheets and the smell with the blanket.

While we were eating porridge in the kitchen, there came the knock on the street door. Mrs. Abbott opened it and Miss Brindley stood there; in the roadway beyond, the same little black car waited.

"Be careful," Rebecca said to Katherine.

I carried Katherine's bag outside so I could whisper to her privately: "Katya, tell Mum it's terrible here, I want to go home."

The engine started, the car vibrated and rattled. Miss Brindley didn't wait a moment — before I could say or do anything, the car was chugging along the street, away from me. I made a picture in my mind of thick elastic bands hooked onto the rear bumper so I could pull it back, but it just kept going. At the end of the street the vehicle easily turned the corner and disappeared. Gradually its various noises blurred together, becoming fainter and less distin-guishable, and in less than a minute, as I stood there, even they vanished.

The silence was absolute.

–6–

I must have been in a trance, hoping the car would come back around the corner, that Katherine would get out, I'd carry her bag, and we'd all remain together at Mrs. Abbott's. Suddenly the street door opened and Zilla and Rebecca were outside; it was time to go to school. I walked with them through the town, over the bridge. They were chattering all the way, without ever mentioning Katherine — as though they hardly noticed she were gone. When I found myself in my classroom, the kids, everything, seemed disconnected. The others would laugh if they saw my face, so I had to keep looking away.

By twelve o'clock I was so drained trying to pay attention to the lessons that I was glad to see my elder sisters, and even to walk back to the house with them. This time Mrs. Abbott met us at the door, and told us to come and sit at the kitchen table. She sounded extra polite, and my stomach roiled: something terrible was going to happen.

"Young Zachary 'ere 'e wet 'is bed last night, an' also 'e wet it a couple o' nights before, but Oi didn't say nothing." So she had found out! Zilla's and Rebecca's faces were looking straight at me, but from far away, disembodied, as though through a long tunnel. Mum had found out also, that time in Morgan Street when she came upstairs. The bedroom had been pitch dark and I was too frightened to go out into the murkiness of the stairway to the lavatory outside. There was a vase on the mantlepiece and I'd peed into it, intending to empty it as soon as it became light out. The vase was small and filled right up and still I needed to go more, but I was too frightened and just raced back into bed. Almost right away Mum came upstairs with a candle and started searching, looking everywhere as though she knew I'd done something disgusting, and in about three minutes she found the filled vase. I was so ashamed! She threatened to tell Dad when he came home, saying the words in an ordinary-sounding voice as though she were talking about something else, something that didn't matter. My stomach had still been clenched tight in the morning when I woke up, and all for nothing: she couldn't have told him because he didn't come smashing up the stairs.

Mrs. Abbott's voice drifted through again, the same flat tone: "…So Oi told Mrs. Carter Oi couldn't be taking no bed-wetter in this 'ouse, an' she said she didn't know as 'ow 'e were a bed-wetter, nothing weren't writ down. Mrs. Carter said as 'ow they 'as a special place for children as wets their beds, an' she'd make arrangements so 'e's in a proper place to look after 'im."

On the walk back to school, Zilla asked: "Why do you do it? Why don't you go to the lav? I know, you're too lazy so you just do it in bed deliberately."

"It'll be your birthday soon," said Rebecca, "try to make up your mind you won't do it anymore because you'll be nine."

That afternoon in school I still couldn't concentrate because I kept trying not to think about being sent to a special place. When the teacher asked me some question, my answer must have been wrong because she said "No, no...." and the kids laughed, the Londoners as well. She made them stop: "Now behave yourselves. We have to be kind."

After school, as we got back to the house, Doris walked in from her job in the munitions factory. The kettle was boiling on the gas stove, and Mrs. Abbott told her daughter to take off her coat and pour tea in the four cups on the table. Then she told the three of us to sit. Doris poured the tea, then retreated with the kettle to stand by the sink.

Mrs. Abbott's face was fixed in a half-smile as she sat down, and I tried to not think about anything at all. She began speaking: "Now then, while you children was in school this afternoon, Mrs. Carter she come over the 'ouse, and Oi showed 'er the bed. She said as 'ow we can't 'ave that, an' as 'ow she'd arrange for young Zachary 'ere to go to a special 'ome, for bed-wetters it is, in Whitney. Miss Brindley'll be 'ere tomorrow morning bright 'n' early with 'er motor car she will, to take 'im." One hand automatically brushed off her apron. "My, seems like you children surely is giving that Miss Brindley lots to do since you been 'ere!"

Over by the window, the enamel kettle stood silently on the stove, its white sides streaked with vertical brown blotches from the gas flame. Doris leaned against the sink, her dead hands wiping the same plate. When I stirred my tea the spoon made an extra loud clanking noise inside the cup.

Again I tried to imagine it was not me she'd been talking about, that it was somebody else who had nothing to do with me. "Mrs. Abbott, where is Whitney?" I asked as though I weren't really interested. "Is it a long way?"

"Miss Brindley'll be taking you in 'er motor car."

"Is Whitney near London?"

"Oi really don't know as 'ow just where it be. Doris, do you know where be Whitney?"

Doris continued wiping the plate, and spoke slowly: "Don't rightly know."

That evening, at supper, I addressed Mr. Abbott for the first time. "Mr. Abbott sir, do you know where Whitney is?"

He looked around the newspaper. "Whitney? Whitney.... Can't say as 'ow Oi does, young 'en."

The next morning I woke up early, because it was still dark. I felt around under me; the bed was dry. As I lay thinking about Whitney, beyond the window the tree branches began to emerge, first black, then their blanketing of leaves assuming yellows and browns as the sky brightened. Footsteps on the stairs, and Mrs. Abbott came into the room. I told her my bed was dry.

"Oh, you be a good young lad," she said. "It's them big sisters of yourn what's gonna be the problem. They'll be looking for trouble with them Slattery boys, mark my words."

But nothing I could think to say really helped because Miss Brindley still came with her motor car. *I'm going to have a nice ride in a car again. I'm going to look out the window and watch the fields and the cows, and not think about anything.*

Zilla and Rebecca said "Ta-ra," and walked off in the direction of school. I put my suitcase and gas mask case on the floor in the back, climbed in, and kneeled on the hard back seat. Through the tiny discolored rear window I saw that Zilla and Rebecca still hadn't turned the corner. Miss Brindley started the engine, the car began shaking and we turned around. We rode right past them as they walked along, and I knocked on the window, but they were busy talking.

We rode on, to a building near the station where we'd all arrived in Banbury less than a week earlier. She stopped the car, "Now you wait 'ere, there's a good lad," and disappeared into the building. I sat there, waiting; it began getting hot from the sun and I wound down the window and just sat, thinking: *I could escape, no one is watching!* Nobody came by, not even a cat or a dog. *But where would I go?* Gradually, the sound of a train welled up from a distance, louder and louder. Soon, trailing behind a big black puffing steam engine, a row of cargo transports rumbled and rattled slowly through the station — in the opposite direction from that of the train we'd all arrived on, which meant this one was going toward London! It was traveling slowly enough that I could maybe run and catch up with the back of it, try to hang on to something — but I'd have to leave my case and gas mask in the car, and Mum would tell Abie I deliberately left my case of clothes. Just at that moment the door to the building swung open and Miss Brindley came out holding a bunch of papers. She came over to the car, noticed the window was open and looked in, at my face. "What be up with you?"

The rearmost carriage was clattering through the station; it was hard to speak. "Nothing Miss Brindley, it got very hot so, so...."

"You be alright there, young 'un?"

"Yes, yes, I'm alright thank you. Thank you."

When she started the car's engine, its clattering subsumed all other thoughts, and a few minutes later we were riding in the country. After a while she spoke: "You behave yourself an' you'll be 'appy there in Whitney. It's a nice 'ome you'll be going to, and they'll 'elp you stop wetting the bed like that."

So they'd told Miss Brindley also — everybody knew! When we'd been riding for about twenty minutes I felt a bit better and I asked her where Whitney was, if it were near London.

"It's about the same distance from London as Banbury is, about thirty miles."

"Can I see my sisters on some days?"

She hesitated. "We'll 'ave to see."

"Would I see my Mum sometimes?"

"When the war's over, don't you worry about it."

Finally the road widened and we entered Whitney's main street, with shops on each side. We passed a church, then Miss Brindley pulled the car to the side of the road and stopped the engine. As the shaking ceased, in the brief numbed stillness my stomach felt like a separate animal with its own life.

She opened her door. "You're 'ome," she announced as she got out. "Bring your bags, now."

We were stopped in front of a shop that had heavy white curtains closing off the wide downstairs windows, and similar curtains on a row of windows upstairs. Miss Brindley rapped on the door. Through the glass panel I saw a thin woman wearing a green apron, her bony face severe as she came across the shop. The door opened; inside, by a far wall, a long table was surrounded by a row of chairs. Miss Brindley gave the woman papers to sign, handed her another bunch to keep, then with a simple, "Now, you be a good boy," was back in her car.

The bony-faced woman spoke: "Come on in then, *Grose*-man." They always mispronounced the first syllable.

I followed her across the shop and through another door into a kitchen with cabinets around the walls, a huge black stove, and a square cloth-covered table with two chairs. She said: "Put your bag and your gas mask down by the wall over there. What's your name, again?" She referred back to the papers in her hand: *"Grose*-man. Zachary *Grose*-man."

"It's *Gross*-man, like Gross, it rhymes with… with moss."

"Grossman — alright then." She wrote something on the paper, then looked back at me. "Says 'ere you're a Jew."

"Yes, well, in a way, I don't believe in god."

"Don't even know if you're a real Jew or not! Hmm, that's alright. We already got two Jew kids 'ere." She pulled out a chair and sat at the table. "Course, we're English, we goes to Church of the Reformation, Sunday morning ten o'clock sharp, that's Church of England. You oughtta go too, do you good, but if you're a Jew Oi s'pose as 'ow you 'as to stay 'ome, they's two other Jew kids they stay 'ome Sunday morning. Now Oi don't want the three of you getting in no trouble, no coming in the kitchen 'ere into them cupboards. Clear? Don't know why you can't be like the rest of us, C. of E. ain't good enough for some people. Alright, sit down. Oi'm Mrs. Drednaulton, you calls me Mrs. D. — clear? An' Mr. Drednaulton, when 'e comes 'ome from work, you calls 'im Mr. D. Clear? Talk back, you don't get no jam for breakfast. Wet your bed and you get's no butter either, just bread. Them's the rules 'ere. Clear? You writes one letter a week to your Mum an' Dad so's they know you're doing alright. Don't stick the envelope down — 'ear that?, *don't* stick it down, you gives it to me, Oi takes it to the Post for you. Follow the rules an' you won't get in no trouble 'ere. Yes, all me boys is 'appy in this 'ouse. You starts school tomorrow morning, nine o'clock sharp. Clear?"

"Yes, Mrs. Drednaulton."

"It's Mrs. D., Oi said, an' you don't 'ave to shake like that, no one ain't gonna bite your 'ead off."

"Yes, Mrs. D."

"Now get your bag and your gas mask there and come with me."

I followed her up a dark stairway that smelled of cleaning liquid. At the top on the landing were two doors. She opened the one to the left and we entered a long wide room, as big as the shop below, and with a set of four windows along the right side. There were two rows of about ten canvas bunks each, the kind with folding wooden frames, one row a bit back from the window side, the other against the opposite wall.

"Pick one as don't 'ave no bedclothes."

Three bunks were bare, but I couldn't think of which one to take.

"Pick one, Oi said! Cat got your tongue, 'as it? 'Ere, you'll 'ave this one."

She had taken a blanket and pillow from a cupboard in the back wall, and now threw them onto the only empty bunk in the back row. "It'll be warmer 'ere, away from the windows. The lads'll be home from school in a bit. Make your bed."

She left. I put my bag on the floor and started making up my bunk. Then I slid the gas mask box underneath, rearranged my clothes in the bag so I could find everything, took out *Modern Astronomy* and opened it to the part about shooting stars. If it were possible to ride on a shooting star, in just a few seconds I would be all the way to London! As I sat on the edge of my bunk thinking about the mystery of traveling so fast everything would be blurred together, I heard the downstairs door open. There was some talking, Mrs. D.'s voice, then a crowd of boys came thundering up the stairs and into the room. They horsed around and even tipped over a few bunks; they looked my way, but left mine alone.

Mrs. D. called up the stairs. "Now you stop that John and Alec, right away, or there'll be no supper. Oi knows who it is."

A fat kid with red hair called across to me: "You're the new one. Your name *Grose*-man?" They were all watching.

"It's *Gross*-man."

Every kid in the room started laughing at my pronunciation. I picked up my book again and pretended to read as they continued messing around. The bunk's canvas edge was stitched around the wooden rail, and sitting up on the side I found myself sliding backwards and down toward the middle. Soon, the rail was digging in behind my knees. It hurt, and I tried to stand up before my legs went numb, but now I couldn't easily pull myself far enough forward. The bunk tipped sideways, spilling the bedclothes and me with it to the floor. Everyone started roaring with laugher, so I laughed also.

Mrs. D. called up "Supper!" They jumped up and raced across the room, jamming through the doorway and down the stairs. I ran down after them into the shop.

"Not so much noise or no supper for anyone," shouted Mrs. D.

The same redheaded kid showed me my place at the long table, which was now arranged with plain white plates and cups and a spoon and fork in front of each chair. I'd never eaten with a fork; we just used big spoons in London, and at Mrs. Abbott's we also had only spoons. Standing behind our chairs, one by one we handed our plates along, and Mrs. D. ladled out boiled potatoes from an enormous black pot. I was starving, not having eaten since Mrs. Abbott's porridge that morning. Leaning forward over the back of my chair I picked up the fork and began to push the prongs into the potato. Although I knew boiled potatoes couldn't feel anything, still the thought of the points digging into it hurt in the pit of my stomach.

Someone hissed at me across the table, "Ay, Grossman, y' mustn't start 'til Mrs. D. sits down."

Mrs. D. came back in with a big steaming brown and white china jug, and went around pouring tea. When she finished she went to her seat at the end of the table and stood there watching us. Everyone waited at their places; suddenly she sat down, and in unison the kids crashed into their chairs and dived into the potatoes.

After supper we had to play outside in the back yard until it got dark. Then we were called into the shop again. The table had been cleared of dishes, and now a pencil and a sheet of blue-lined paper lay before each chair: we were to write a letter to our mums and dads. After a while, as we wrote, she began calling us out two by two to wash our faces and go on up to bed. In the little room with the sink there was also a lavatory — that is, actually inside the house — and I made sure I went as much as I could.

As the boys came upstairs they got undressed and into bed. Some of them were quiet, but others joked around and kept talking. Suddenly, something stung my cheek — with an elastic band, someone had fired a tiny rolled-up ball of paper at me. I managed not to make any sound. Mrs. D. came in and said, "Alright now, no more talking," and switched off the bare lightbulb that hung on a wire from the center of the ceiling. As she closed the door the room became dark, and I watched the windows slowly resolve into soft blue rectangles. There was a bit of talking and giggling, but gradually everyone quietened down. Then someone began snoring.

"Shut up, Nigel!" a voice said. The snoring spluttered and stopped.

I heard the street door open downstairs, then slam shut. There were voices; it was Mrs.

D., and also a man's voice, right away shouting. Of course I knew it wasn't Abie, but immediately the blood was thumping in the sides of my head and my wrists. Another door closed down there, and it became quiet. I must have dozed, but with a start I was suddenly awake again: the stairs were creaking. A nearby door squeaked open, then closed, and again it was quiet. It was too dark to make out anything in the room, but through the top window panes above the white curtains, beautiful stars glimmered against the black sky.

The next thing I knew, the door was opening. Immediately I was wide awake; I reached down and felt my sheets: soaked, even the bottom of the jacket of my sleeping suit as well as the trousers. The room was bright, it was morning. Mrs. D. stood in the doorway: "Alright, 'ands up dirty pigs."

The other boys were waking, and gradually several raised their hands.

"Thompson, Collyer, Griffin, Schreiber, Robb, Cook, Moline, no butter, no jam for breakfast," she barked, then went out, leaving the door open.

Under the blanket I struggled to remove my sodden sleeping suit, and reached around to my bag on the floor for dry underwear. I left the sleeping suit under the blanket so no one would find it. As I moved my legs my skin stung from the pee, the way it always did before I could wash it off. They were getting dressed, going downstairs, and I lined up to use the lavatory and wash my face. I wouldn't be able to wash off my legs because that would take too long and the next person would probably guess why I didn't come out right away.

Suddenly Mrs. D. came running downstairs and straight over to me. She grasped my ear, pulled me out of line and half way across the room. "Grossman, you're a *double* dirty pig. A pig pees where it sleeps and sleeps where it pees."

A couple of little voices from the line recited with her, "…where it sleeps, sleeps where it pees."

"…But even a dirty pig ain't no liar. Back of the line!" My ear was hot and swollen as though she were going to pull it right off; she twisted me around and back toward the end of the lavatory line. "That'll teach yer you better put yer 'and up next time."

The skinny dark-haired boy who'd been in front of me called back: "Mrs. D. always finds out. No use not putting your 'and up."

"That's right. Alec 'ere knows the rules, don't cha, Alec."

"Yes, Mrs. D."

Finally we all were seated for breakfast. At the head of the table a scruffy man in an old workman's shirt sat in front of an egg nestled in an egg cup. After cracking the shell and removing the top pieces, he tore strips off a slice of bread and poked them carefully down into the yolk, now and then sloshing everything down with gulps of tea. Mrs. D. handed along a piece of bread to each of the kids, then walked around the table pouring tea from the brown and white china jug. Some kids didn't take any butter; I guessed they were the ones who'd wet their beds. Nobody spoke; everyone seemed to know exactly what they were allowed to take. I didn't touch the butter, and Mrs. D. didn't pour me any tea either; instead she took my cup into the kitchen and brought it back with water. Some of the boys were helping themselves to jam from any of several jars set out along the table, but I remembered the other rule: if you wet the bed you mustn't take any jam.

"Why ain't Grossman 'aving no tea?" a small kid across the table asked above the clatter of knives and tea-spoons.

The man at the end looked up angrily. "Shut up. Keep your mouth *shut!* No talking while you're eating." Everyone ate silently, but some kids looked around a bit as though they might say something, and I was afraid of what Mr. D. might do.

Despite his harsh reproof, Mrs. D. did answer the question: "Grossman ain't getting no tea 'cause 'e's a liar, plain an' simple."

We walked to school in groups. The street was wide, with low buildings, a bit like a cowboy town in an American picture. I kept up with the edge of one group, though I couldn't think of anything to say to join their conversation.

In the school building we were split up and ushered into different classrooms. In mine I recognized only a couple of the kids from where I was now living. One of those pointed at me and said to the teacher, who wore a round white collar and black robe like a priest: "Sir, 'e's a Jew!"

The teacher looked over at me, and walked down the aisle toward my desk. He smiled. "Son, are you a Jew?" he asked gently.

"Yes, sir."

He smiled again. "Very good...."

"But I don't believe in god," I added.

He hesitated. "My son, God loves you even if you haven't found Him yet." He stood by my desk and addressed the whole class, telling them about someone called Moses who kept walking around in a desert for forty years. He said Jews suffered to save everybody in the world. He told us that Jews were not ordinary like the rest of the kids in the class — Jews were chosen, God chose them, and when you meet one you'd better be especially nice toward him because he's been chosen.

Every kid in the class had turned to look at me — it was terrible. Later, in the playground nobody came near me. Some of them watched from a distance, whispering among themselves.

At dinner time on the walk back to the shop, Moline, the one with red hair, asked me: "Does it feel different to be chosen?"

I tried to think what it felt like. "It makes you feel... a bit hot."

The evening was like the previous night: we washed our hands and sat at the table while Mrs. D. served us boiled potatoes and cabbage. Again we played outside in the yard until it began to get dark. I felt too awkward to join in, but John Collyer was nice; every time he caught the ball he threw it to me. There was one kid who stood alone on the edge of the yard by the fence, not playing, so I threw the ball to him to help him join in, but he didn't even try to catch it. Instead John Collyer picked it up, then came over and whispered to me: "Don't throw it to Schreiber, he doesn't play."

Shortly, Mrs. D. called the kids in two by two, not to write a letter this time, but to get ready for bed. She called me in along with Morris Schreiber, the one who didn't play. As we walked in I said to him, "I'm Zachary." He just looked at me, and didn't answer.

"'Urry now! Make sure you use that lavatory, Schreiber, an' you Grossman!"

Upstairs I pulled back the blanket to check: the sheets were dry and smelled clean, and my sleeping suit had been laundered and lay folded on the pillow. I undressed and got into bed. Some of the kids horsed around for a while, Mrs. D. called up to stop the noise, then a bit later she came in and switched off the light. I lay there and thought about Zilla and Rebecca; they probably were getting ready for bed at Mrs. Abbott's in Banbury. In London, Katherine was probably also going to bed now.

I must have started to doze when I was awoken by a loud bang that shook the bed. For an instant I thought it was Abie, but I was in Whitney, and it was the downstairs door slamming shut. A man's voice was shouting, and there came another crash.

Suddenly Mrs. D. was shouting back: "Boozing with your mates again, think you can just come 'ome pissed any time you like!"

"'E's 'ome," someone whispered, and subdued laughing circled the darkened room. A little later the two of them came thumping up the stairs, and their upstairs door slammed closed. Silence, then: "Sshh, listen!" — it was the same kid whispering.

And from the other room came a creaking of bedsprings.

"They're doin' it!"

"Sshh, Mrs. D.'ll come in and we'll all be punished 'cause of you," said a voice I recognized as John Collyer's.

"She ain't gonna come in if she's doin' it!"

                            •   •   •

The following week I wrote again to Mum, and every week after that, but I was afraid to write that I hated it there; you had to give your unsealed letter to Mrs. D. and she might read it and you'd be in trouble. I never received any replies, and I wondered if Mum might have been killed by a bomb in London. But someone would tell Mrs. D., and she probably would have told me by now. I wondered if Mrs. D. actually posted the letters we wrote or was just piling them up somewhere. I asked John Collyer; he said Yes, she did post them because he got letters from his mother.

The same routine continued for several months, and it began snowing. At the table, Mrs. D. served us tea and our boiled potatoes with cabbage, this time with carrots. She said: "Tomorrow's Christmas, so tonight we're 'aving our special treat, Christmas pudding." She cut slices off a dark raisin pudding, and gave us each a piece so thin it fell over on its side in the plate.

Alec spoke. "My Dad said Jews never 'ave no Christmas."

Mrs. D. looked across at Morris Schreiber: "Well, say something, cat still got your tongue?"

Morris just stared down at his plate.

"Schreiber, it's all of 'alf a year since your dad took sick. Moping like that ain't gonna bring 'im back now, is it?"

Morris didn't respond, but Philip spoke up. "Mrs. D., we have Hanukkah, that's better than Christmas."

"That when you killed Christ?" asked Alec.

Mrs. D. looked at Alec. "Who told you the Jews killed Christ?"

"My dad. My dad knows everything."

Philip responded angrily. "No he doesn't then, 'cause Jewish people didn't kill Christ."

"Well who did then? Bet Schreiber did!"

Most of the kids laughed, but Morris didn't answer, his eyes remaining locked onto his plate.

Philip spoke up again: "No Morris didn't. Christians say that to make people hate you if you're Jewish."

"I don't 'ate Jews," said Alec. "I got a friend back 'ome what's a Jew. 'E mustn't eat no bacon or 'e won't be a Jew no more. 'E comes in our 'ouse."

Mrs. D. brought the conversation to a close. "Leave Schreiber alone then, if 'e don' wanna talk to 'is friends that's 'is business. Now, eat your pudding, an' outside in the yard to play, all of you. Don't forget to muffle up."

•   •   •

February. One Sunday after everybody returned from church and we were going into the yard to play, John Robb came in from the front and said: "Grossman, your Dad's 'ere to see you."

I ran through to the shop, and there he was! "Dad! I can't believe it! Oh! Dad, I didn't know you'd come!"

"Well, uh come on the train, yeh, the train. Eee, what a long ride it was there, like going on an' on...."

I ran back into the kitchen to tell Mrs. D. my Dad was here. I saw Morris Schreiber looking through the glass pane in the back door.

"We knew 'e was coming," Mrs. D. said. "Thought we'd give you a little surprise. Maybe you wants to take your Dad for a walk an' show 'im 'round Whitney. We're pretty proud on Whitney, you know."

As I went back into the shop I heard Mrs. D. again: "No, Schreiber, you stay out in the yard with the rest of 'em."

I walked with Abie in the bitter cold. I asked, "Where's Katya, is she home in Morgan Street?"

"Nah! Not in London. Yeh, she's alright, Devon, it is. They took 'er away in Devon, they took 'er... Tiverton, near Devon."

"Why did she go to Devon?"

"Nah, she 'ad to be evacuated away, like evacuated from the bombs, the Germans, the bladdy Germans they 'ave bombs in London, all the time they 'ave bombs, terrible, eee, you should only see."

It was mid afternoon and an overcast sky threatened.

"Where is Devon? Is it a long way?"

"It's a long way. Eee, it's a very, very, long way, a long way away, like, hours 'n' hours...." He seemed to reel as he contemplated the distance.

We trudged empty snow-pocked streets. Abie needed to urinate. He found a deserted space between two buildings and opened his navy blue overcoat and double-breasted jacket, unbuttoned his fly and urinated through a snowdrift blown high against the wall. I stood away and watched the steaming vapor as the stream etched deep into the snow. He buttoned up his coat and we continued walking.

"Dad?"

"Wha's a marra?"

"Dad, I hardly ever pee in the bed anymore, like maybe once or twice a week only."

"Good, it's good, see, they did good, funny eee, they know what to do. Oo ever 'eard a fella your age *pishing* in the bed, it's... it's... disgusting." An early darkness was descending, and the chill February wind blew in short snapping gusts. "Yeh, it's good," he continued. "Uh'll tell Lily, Mum, uh'll tell 'er, she'll...."

"Dad...."

"Wha'?"

"Dad, could I ever... come home, I mean, like if I don't *pish* in the bed anymore?"

"Nah, you don' wanna come 'ome." He looked at his watch. "Eee, it's late, the train uh gotta catch, uh'll miss the train. Yeh, it's a nice 'ouse like where you are there, yeh, it looks like a nice… they did good, eee, yeh they're clever, they know what to do…."

He turned and walked away. Along the empty street a solitary dog trotted towards us on the opposite pavement, leaning into the wind-whipped dusk. As Abie approached, it stopped and barked; he turned to see where it stood, kicked in its direction, then continued on toward the station. As his black silhouette diminished, the dog's barking reverberated against the buildings' icy façades. The backs of my hands seemed mauve; I had to get back or Mrs. D. would be angry. In the vestiges of daylight I trudged through brittle ridges of frozen slush for several streets, then knocked on the door. The cold cut through my coat and circled around my shirt; a small whirlwind of loose snow lifted off the pavement and coiled lazily toward the curb.

The door opened; it was Morris Schreiber. He stood in the doorframe looking at me, blocking the entrance. "I'm freezing, let me come in." He barely moved aside. "Morris, it's very cold, I'm freezing, I want to come in." I edged him to one side and squeezed around him.

The next day after supper I wrote a letter and again asked Mum, could I come home. Perhaps Mrs. D. didn't take my letters to the Post; there was never any response. I wondered what it was like in Devon, if it were cold there also.

•   •   •

One sunny Saturday morning in June, Mrs. D. said: "Grossman, pack your bag, you're leaving."

"Where am I going?"

"You're going back. 'Urry, the motor car'll be 'ere in ten minutes."

"Back? To London?"

"London?" She laughed. "No, the war ain't over by a long shot. They're taking you to Banbury."

A little car arrived and the driver, not Miss Brindley but an even older lady, said: "Is he ready?"

"Get your bag! 'Urry now! Into the motor car with you!" I ran upstairs, grabbed my bags and hurried back into the shop. Morris Schreiber was by the door. He gripped my shirt sleeve.

"Ta-ra, Morris, I'm going." I tried to pull my arm free. "Someone'll come for you, I bet they will."

"Get in the motor car, 'urry now," Mrs. D. called from outside.

Morris was crying silently, and he seemed unable to let go my sleeve. I had to hold his wrist so I could release my arm without hurting him: "I've got to get in the motor car."

—o—O—o—

We bumped along past fields, barns, livestock and occasional cottages, with nary a word exchanged, the driver observing me distantly in the rear mirror, her squinty little eyes quickly reverting to the roadway when I caught her glance. In less than half an hour the view outside resolved into streets, then a row of attached houses — and we were back in Banbury. The car jerked to a stop, the cessation of noise leaving a sudden dull stillness. We had pulled up alongside a white garden fence, woven with green vines. The driver got out, and with my bag and gas mask box I followed her as she limped through the gate into a garden high with flowers, even a row of tall hollyhocks against the side fence just like in London.

She half turned. "Young man, you're going to be living here with, hem, Mrs. Stewart." Her first words since we'd left Whitney, and the surprise was her accent — not midlands, but like on the BBC news. "There's one daughter, Eileen, six, and... let's see, Mr. Stewart is away in North Africa fighting the Germans for you."

For me? I tried to feel grateful, but too many new things were happening. She reached up and twisted a brass knob in the door, and inside a bell rang. A young woman with shiny blonde hair and brown eyes opened the door. She smiled nervously to the driver and then at me, said "Hello Zachary!" and signed papers the driver held out. As the car rolled away she waved after it the way a little girl would.

She lifted my bag. "Oi'm Mrs. Stewart, welcome to your new home. Come on in." I followed my new foster mother through the spotless front room and into the kitchen. *People in Banbury have shiny front rooms.*

"You'll have a little sister while you lives here." A little girl peeped around the edge of the door. "Come on, come in Eileen, meet your new big brother."

The little girl, also blonde and wearing a pink bow in her hair, came in.

"Say: 'Welcome to your new home, Zachary,'" Mrs. Stewart said, and the girl repeated, "Welcome to your new home, Zachary." I noticed her eyes were blue, not brown. Katherine's hair had been brown, the same as Auntie Cissie's. I hadn't seen Katherine for a long, long time, and I wondered where she was now, if she were still in Tiverton in Devon. If she could live here in Mrs. Stewart's house everything would be perfect. Eileen stood next to her mother, and their blonde hair made them almost twins.

"Let's put your bag down here for now, then we'll get you something to eat."

"Thank you. Will I be able to see my real sisters soon?" I asked.

"Your real sisters? Where be they?"

"They live in Banbury. They live with Mrs. Abbott."

"Well, Oi don't know any Mrs. Abbott, but if you have sisters and they be still living in Banbury, we can find out," she said. "Here, sit down, and Eileen, you sit down with your big brother."

Eileen climbed up onto a chair, and we sat at a round kitchen table covered with a clean red and white embroidered table cloth. Mrs. Stewart served us both a cup of tea and a sandwich with Spam, and she sat down also.

"Did your sisters write to you while you was in Whitney? If you 'as an envelope, it might 'ave their address."

"No, they didn't write letters. Maybe they didn't know the address where I was, in Whitney…."

"Well, you must want to see your sisters soon as possible, so finish your tea then we can all walk over to Mrs. Carter's and find out Mrs. Abbott's address where they be living."

"Thank you."

We finished eating. Mrs. Stewart put the dishes in the sink, then picked up my bag.

"Come Eileen, let's show Zachary his room where he be going to sleep from now on."

I followed them upstairs to a landing, through one of the doors and into a small room with lacy curtains. A bed, its headboard against a diagonal wall, was covered with a multicolored quilt illuminated by the sun. On one side of the headboard on a doily-covered table stood an electric lamp and a big blue and white china jug, and on the other side, a chair.

"We'll hang your clothes up later, when you comes back from your sisters."

The three of us, Eileen in the middle, walked side by side along the crown of the road. The white fences seemed to glow in the sunlight. It was a much prettier street than the one in Whitney.

"You can hold your big brother's hand."

Eileen took one hand, and Mrs. Stewart came round to hold my other hand. Even though Mrs. Stewart was now walking on the crest of the road, I noticed I was taller than she was! I was actually taller than my foster mother, and it made my head swim! Everything was happening so fast; then I thought about if I wet the bed! That would be the most terrible, the most horrible thing that could happen! I would be absolutely ashamed, and they would have to drive me back to Whitney, to Mrs D.'s.

"So, you was living in Banbury before," Mrs. Stewart said.

"Yes, with my sisters at Mrs. Abbott's, before I had to go… to… that place, Whitney."

"Mum, can we go to Whitney also?"

"When your Dad comes home, when the war's over."

We continued walking.

"Was you 'appy in Whitney?"

In an instant my face was hot — I wondered if she knew why I was there! "…A bit…. It was alright, but I'd rather be in Banbury."

Three streets away she knocked on a brown door, and through one of its little windows I saw a girl come toward us along the hallway.

"Hello, Martha. This here be Zachary." Martha looked at me, then down at Eileen holding my hand. "Be your mother in?"

"Mum!" Martha called, and a lady in a long skinny dress appeared.

"Mrs. Carter," Mrs. Stewart introduced me. "This be Zachary, Zachary *Grose*-man. He be the new young man from London what's going to be living with us."

"*Gross*man," I corrected her.

"Oh, Zachary *Gross*man." And she smiled again.

"Ah yes, from Whitney. Zachary, we know it's difficult for the evacuees, but we do hope you'll be happy living here in Banbury again."

"Thank you, ma'am."

Mrs. Stewart continued. "Zachary says as how he has two sisters he thinks still be living in Banbury, at Mrs. Abbott's house, but he doesn't know as how where it be."

Mrs. Carter invited us in. I stood in the long hallway with Eileen, who wouldn't let go my hand. "Can Oi come to see your other sisters also?" she asked. She didn't seem at all shy.

"Yes, if my sisters don't mind."

"Are you going to live in our house all the time?"

"I don't know."

"Oi told my Mum Oi wanted a big brother, that's why she got you."

"Oh."

"Gwen has a big brother."

"I see."

"His name is Tommy."

"Is Gwen your cousin or something?"

"No, course not! She's my friend, along Bloxham Road."

"Oh." Her hair was so pretty, even in the dusky hallway.

"Do you go to school, or you too big?" she asked.

"No, I still go to school."

A tall dark brown grandfather clock ticked away gravely as a swinging brass pendulum glinted behind its glass panel.

The two women emerged, and Mrs. Carter spoke: "Zachary, we have good news for you. Your sisters are still in Banbury, but it was too much trouble for Mrs. Abbott, so now they're living at number sixteen George Street, with old Mrs. Stecker. I imagine they'll be very surprised and happy to see you." She handed me a piece of paper with the address.

"Thank you. When can I see them? I mean, are they…"

"You can go see if they be home right now," said Mrs. Stewart, as we made our way to the door. "Come on, Eileen and me'll walk you there."

We began retracing our steps, again hand in hand, then veered off at the corner. At the end of that street, Mrs. Stewart pointed.

"That's it, that's George Street, go to the end then turn right. When you're finished visiting, come right home, here's our address…"

"Can Oi go with?" asked Eileen.

"Not today, daughter, another time."

"But Zachary said Oi can go!"

"Zachary wants to see his sisters alone this time." And to me, "Don't you get lost, now! Here, let me write it down… we're number thirty five Bloxham Road, Margaret Stewart. You shouldn't have no trouble finding our house alright afterward."

"Yes, it's got big hollyhocks in the garden."

"You like hollyhocks?"

"Yes, we used to have hollyhocks in London. So alright, I suppose I'll be back soon then." Continuing alone along the street, I looked back and she and Eileen were still standing in the road, watching. They both waved, like twins; Mrs. Stewart hardly looked old enough to be a foster mother. I walked on, rounded the corner, and found number sixteen. It also had a little gate, and an unpainted fence, but the garden wasn't very neat. *One whole year — supposing Zilla and Rebecca don't remember who I am?*

The unfamiliar door was also brown wood, and in a small diamond-shaped window a red and gold stained-glass angel leaned forward, holding a wand. Under the brass numbers a letter-box was framed by a knocker, and I knocked one knock. Footsteps inside, then the door opened. A glamorous woman in a nightgown stood there; she had long black eyelashes and dark green stuff smudged around her eyes, like in American pictures.

"Oh! Hello! What are you doing here?"

"Excuse me..." I started, but then I realized it was Rebecca! She even had lipstick on, and she looked completely grown up!

"They brought me back to live in Banbury now."

"Oh! Er... when did you come back?"

"Now."

"Oh... we're going out, I can't talk now."

"Could I talk to Zilly then?"

"She's getting ready. We're going out. Come 'round tomorrow."

"Tomorrow?"

"Yes."

"Alright."

The door closed. I stood there a minute, then went out through the cluttered garden to the pavement, and closed the gate. I looked back at the house, at the windows; perhaps I would see someone, but there was nobody. They probably lived in a room at the back of the house.

There was no point in just standing there, so I began walking home. Maybe Mrs. Stewart would let Katherine live in her house. Maybe she could sleep in the same room as Eileen, I wouldn't mind. I was thinking about all that when I realized I was lost; I asked a man the way, and finally got home.

"That was a quick visit!" said Mrs. Stewart.

"Well, I couldn't visit today because my sisters had to go out. They said I should come 'round tomorrow."

"Tomorrow?"

"Yes."

"Then come next door and meet Dereck." She walked us out her gate, into the next garden and knocked on the door. "Madge, this is Zachary, he's our new evacuee. Is Dereck home?"

Madge, who seemed like a giant compared to Mrs. Stewart, looked me over. "Yes... Dereck!" she called.

"Mrs. Carter said they'll be in the same class in Saint Leonard's."

"Uhuh," she answered.

"Just 'til supper's ready, Oi'll call you in," said Mrs. Stewart.

"Alright."

"Dereck, this is the new evacuee, what was it, Zachary?"

"Yes, also my name's Zech for short."

"Zech."

"Yes."

"Uhuh, you lads play outside then."

Mrs. Stewart went back next door, and I followed Dereck out into the street. He had a ball and a bat.

"Do you play cricket?"

"No, but we used to play German Cricket in London."

"Oi never been to London. What's it like?"

"It's nice, lots of houses and stuff. They don't have gardens in the front, only in the back."

"We got a garden in the back also, it's next to the pit. You go to Saint Leonard's?"

"I don't know, I only came here today. I mean, I used to go there last year, just for a few days." I didn't want to say anything about Whitney in case he knew why kids were sent there. I felt my ears getting hot, but he didn't say anything.

Eileen came out of our house. "Zachary, what did your other sisters say?"

"Nothing really, they were busy today. Should we all play German Cricket?"

"She's a girl, she can't throw."

"Oi *can* throw, look!" She'd taken the ball from Dereck's hand, and thrown it along the street. The three of us played until we were all called in for supper.

The next morning Mrs. Stewart walked me to Saint Leonard's. After they wrote everything down, I ended up in Dereck's class. I walked both ways with him at dinner time, then home again after school.

Mrs. Stewart gave Eileen and me supper, a kind of meat I never had before, with potatoes and gravy — she said we were eating lamb. We finished, and it was time to go over to George Street. Again, Eileen wanted to come.

"She can come, I don't mind."

Eileen looked hopefully at her mother.

"Alright then, but don't be a bother now when Zachary be talking with his sisters."

"Alright, Mommy, Oi won't say anything."

Actually I *wanted* Eileen to come with, in case Zilla and Rebecca were busy again. This time Zilla opened the door, and she also looked different, much older, and she also had lipstick on.

She looked down at Eileen. "Who's that?"

"Oi'm Zachary's sister," replied Eileen.

"Oo-er!"

"She thinks she's my sister because I live in their house now."

"Oo-er!"

Zilla beckoned us into the front room, and Eileen and I sat on a settee covered with a clean white sheet. It was cold in the room, even though it was summer outside. Zilla said, "Just a minute…" and disappeared into the other room.

We sat for a while. It was all quiet in the house, except for footsteps going upstairs. After a few minutes, when nobody had come, I called out, "Zilly! Rivka?" There was no answer, so a bit later I called again. Still no one answered.

"Can Oi say something?" asked Eileen.

"What? Yes."

"Oi'm cold," she said.

Then suddenly Zilla came down. "Tsk! We're late…."

"Oh, are you going out?"

"We're going out, I dunno, come back tomorrow. Can you come tomorrow?"

"Rivka said I should come back today, now."

"But… well, I dunno, come back tomorrow."

"Yes, alright."

That evening, Mrs. Stewart played a record on their gramophone in the living room.

"Did you ever hear this music before?" she asked. The music sounded very simple, with little bells, as though it were for kids. "It's Tchaikovsky," she said, her head bent toward the gramophone.

"What does Tchaikovsky mean?"

"That's the name of the man who wrote it, he was Russian."

"Oh, my Dad is from Russia," I said.

"Is he really! Then you should like it very much. It's called…."

"Let me say the name!" interjected Eileen.

"Alright, you tell your big brother what it is."

"It's the *Dance of the Sugarplum Fairies.*"

To me it sounded all mushy and pretty, and that was why I *didn't* really like it, fairies dancing!

But from the way she was listening, Mrs. Stewart liked it very much. "It's part of something called a ballet, *Romeo and Juliet.* Young men and women dance, it's very beautiful." She looked wistful. "When Oi was a little girl my mother took me to dance lessons. A nice young man played it on the piano."

Altogether I spent most evenings and weekends playing with Dereck, and with Eileen, sometimes listening to records. I didn't get to spend that much time with Zilla and Rebecca because they always seemed to be going out. At school I saw my big sisters in the playground but mostly they were busy talking to boys.

After I'd been attending St. Leonard's for several weeks, one afternoon as Dereck and I were walking home we met coming toward us another pupil who was also an evacuee from London. He told me his mother had been evacuated to Banbury, she was at the railway station where he'd just come from, and he said there was someone named Mrs. Grossman. So, straight from school Dereck and I raced over to Zilla and Rebecca's and told them.

"Yes, we know," Rebecca said. "We're getting ready. The bombing got worse in London now and only the men can stay, so Mum's been evacuated. So's Maudy, he's here also."

Marius! I'd almost forgotten about my younger brother!

"Do you think I could come with you?"

Rebecca looked at Dereck. "I'll go back," said Dereck. "I'll tell Mrs. Stewart you'll be home a bit later."

"Alright, thank you, Dereck. So Rivka, can I come then?"

"Yes, alright then."

I was very happy to go somewhere with my sisters. At the station we encountered crowds of people, mostly grown-ups, with mothers and little kids sitting on duffle bags and standing around. Cars were gradually taking people away. It reminded me of when we were first evacuated, when I got to Banbury the first time. And then — there was Mum sitting on a bag, talking with a boy! We pushed through to her. She looked very tired. Rebecca said, "Hello, Maudy," to the boy. I realized it was Marius, so I said "Hello" but I wasn't really sure it was him; he didn't look like Marius from London. Mum had deep lines on her forehead — I'd forgotten the way she always looked so worried.

"Hello, Mum."

"Oh, hello, it's Zachary." Mum just sat on the bag. I stood there; it was hard to believe that this was really Mum, in Banbury! When I was in Whitney I'd wondered if I would ever see her again, if she might get killed in London by a bomb, but here she was right in front of me and all that waiting was now like a silly kind of nothing. I hadn't realized I might feel so awkward I wouldn't be able to think of anything to say.

They called out Lily and Marius Grossman, mispronouncing the surname. Mum went first, then Marius, then Rebecca and Zilla busy talking, and behind them I carried one of Mum's bags to the waiting car. Rebecca asked the driver where Mum was going to live, and wrote down the address. We weren't allowed to go with, but we all visited in their room the next day, Saturday. Marius still looked different, but I was getting used to it.

Rebecca and Zilla did most of the talking. "So who's going to feed Abie while you're here?" asked Rebecca.

"Him? He knows how to look after himself. He hardly comes home at night because of the bombs. He sleeps in the tailoring shop."

"I'd rather 'ave the bombs, it's so boring 'ere, there's nothing to do!" said Zilla.

"So what have you been doing here, then?"

"There's some American airmen from the base, they come to Oxford or here."

"Ee, is it alright to go out with them?"

"Yes, they're nice, they're very polite always," said Rebecca.

"Yeah, they 'ave a lot of money, they don't mind, not like the English ones."

I visited Mum and Marius again a few days later, when Zilla and Rebecca were going there, and this time I brought Eileen with. She said "Hello, Maudy," and although he answered, he didn't play with her; he seemed suspicious of everything. Mum hardly seemed to notice her. I felt better the few times that Eileen came with because it was someone to talk to, but then Rebecca said I shouldn't bring her over to Mum's anymore because the room was too small.

The next time my sisters and I were in Mum's room, the woman whose house it was, Mrs. Wiggerstaff, knocked on the door and told us not to talk so loud. The room was very small, with two narrow beds up against opposite walls, a little table and two chairs, and on the wall in a heavy dark frame a picture of horses done with thick blobs of paint. The bed seemed small, too short for Mum to sleep in, though I realized I was now taller than Mum also. When we visited, we had to sit on the beds because there weren't extra chairs. Marius never talked to me, and sometimes he looked at me as though he didn't know who I was. He was six but he still cried, and he never wanted to come back with me to play. Anyway, Mum told me he couldn't, in case something happened and he couldn't breathe. While Mum lived in Banbury, Mrs. Stewart always said I should ask her back with Marius and she would cook supper for everybody. Mum usually said, "Alright, next week," but she never did actually come; she always seemed too exhausted.

So after school I mostly stayed around Mrs. Stewart's house and played with Dereck and Eileen. There was a tremendously big pit that dropped way down from behind our back gardens, then back up again way over on Maple Street. A factory had dumped clumps of corroded and oozing batteries along our side, and Dereck and I would break off one battery at a time and throw it across, seeing how high up the other side of the pit we could get it to land, sometimes even reaching the opposite people's gardens.

One evening after supper Mrs. Stewart put on a record of beautiful violins.

"What's that, Mrs. Stewart?" I asked.

"That's Tchaikovsky," she said.

"Oh, it doesn't sound like the other record." This one was smooth and slow, with strange interesting notes.

"It's another part of *Romeo and Juliet.*"

"It sounds different."

"Well, the young man's ladyfriend has just died because of a misunderstanding. And it's very sad, so everyone dances slowly."

Weeks later, Rebecca told me Mrs. Wiggerstaff didn't like it when Mum used the kitchen, and also they couldn't make any noise in their room, and that was the reason Mum and Marius finally went back to London, despite the air raids. I counted up: they were in Banbury only seven weeks.

And then, suddenly, just a few weeks after they were gone, when the leaves were starting to change and you felt a first nip in the morning air on the way to school, Rebecca told me she and Zilla were going back to London also — the next day!

"You mean, tomorrow?"

"Yes," said Rebecca.

"You mean, you're just going for a holiday?"

"We're going to stay there."

"You mean, stay in London?"

"Yes."

"What about the bombing, Mum said the Germans are still bombing London all the time."

"Oo cares about the bombs, we 'ate it 'ere, everyone's so ignorant," said Zilla.

"Where did you get the tickets for the train?"

"At the station, we bought them, what do you mean?"

"Oh!'

"Yes, we bought them... y'know."

"I mean... did Mum or Dad give you the money?"

"No."

"Oh... how...."

"We saved up."

"Oh!"

"We saved up the money."

"Could I go home maybe, with you?"

"No, Mum said not yet."

"Do you think I could also go back sometime?"

"I don't know, Mum said soon."

And suddenly I was the only one left in Banbury.

•   •   •

On Sunday the air-raid siren sounded; we knew it wasn't a test because the time wasn't six o'clock. I told Mrs. Stewart how they'd taught us in school to sit under a table, and she, Eileen and I sat under the kitchen table. We heard an aeroplane in the distance, and as it came closer I could hear that the engine sounded different from the English and American planes: not smooth the way ordinary engines sounded, but sort of deeper, and ragged. Mrs. Stewart put her arm around Eileen, and held my hand, squeezing it. Outside, there came a little bang, followed by another boom, much louder, and the table shook. In the street a man's voice shouted: "It's the yards, it's the yards."

After a few minutes the siren sounded *All Clear,* two ear-piercing tones that rolled up to continuous high pitches, stayed constant for about a minute, then suddenly dropped down in harmony and fell to a silence so absolute that your ears hummed and the air felt cleansed. We climbed out from under the table, and Mrs. Stewart said it was the first time they ever had an air-raid in Banbury.

"Can I go see what happened?" I asked.

"Me too, me too!" said Eileen.

"No, no, you'd better stay home, both of you...."

"Could I go if Dereck's mum says he could go? We'd be very careful."

"Well, alright...."

"Oi want to go, Oi want to go!" Eileen jumped up and down.

"Well... alright, hold Eileen's hand, don't go close, don't get in the way of the men."

At the railway yards the three of us clambered up the embankment for a better view. A part of the railway station building's roof lay on the pavement, and nearby a fresh earthen crater, about four yards in diameter, had been dug out of the asphalt. Chunks of concrete lay on the ground, and all twelve panes in the station's only window were broken. An open lorry with no sides was driving slowly out from the tracks area, and on the back two shapes were aligned under a bedsheet. Two pairs of feet protruded from under the white edge — a black workman's boot on one of the feet, the other only a dirty-white sock, and then next to that a pair of smaller, women's feet, bare. As the lorry went over bumps and debris in the roadway, the things under the sheet rocked, together, from side to side.

"What's that?" asked Eileen.

It had to be two bodies under the sheet, two dead bodies; the first time I'd ever seen the feet of actual dead people. Maybe they'd just been killed by the bomb. I looked over Eileen's head at Dereck; he looked scared, but we nodded to each other, meaning we mustn't tell Eileen what it really was because she was too young. So I said it was just something that had been delivered on the train.

That evening after Eileen and I had gone to bed, the doorbell rang. Mrs. Carter, the one in charge of billeting the evacuees, had come over with her daughter Martha. Through my closed bedroom door I could hear them in the living room.

"Now, Martha," I heard Mrs. Carter say, "tell Mrs. Stewart what you saw."

"Well," Martha's voice began. "Oi were hiding under the bridge by the yards, and this aeroplane come down, and it had a German cross painted right on its wing. It leaned over and the pilot he looked right at me and he winked at me, Oi saw him wink. Then he kept on going over right by the station, and he dropped something, a bomb. I seen it fall out and tumble over, then come down straight, like a black thing it were. Then Oi heard a bang and seen the smoke. That's when the station got hit with that bomb. Oi seen the aeroplane just keep right on going lower, then it landed in Niles' Farm and then it was bumping around and then it rode right into old Niles' cow and went off like a big bomb."

"Well! Martha's lucky to be alive today!" It was Mrs. Carter talking. "Now those Londoners can't tell us how terrible those air-raids are down in London. We haven't run away from Hitler, from the bombing, we know how to take it and carry on doing our duty!"

It was quiet for a while, then I heard Mrs. Stewart's voice, subdued. "Oi fears for my John, he be living with bombs falling every day."

Again it was quiet. "Margaret, we find our comfort knowing the good Lord watches over good people." That had been Mrs. Carter.

Why do people always think god will make everything all right? I lay there, thinking about the air-raid, and the German plane crashing in Niles' Farm, and the lorry and the two people, how their bodies were rocking like jelly together. Although it was dark, I got out of bed and opened the window. It was cold, a soft still night with no moon, and brilliant stars prodding through the shadows of the tree branches. Were those two people on the lorry, and the dead pilot, gone forever from the solar system, or even the whole universe? Would the three of them reassemble somewhere, maybe on another planet; and, how would the man and woman regard the pilot, knowing what they knew, what he did to them? Would the pilot ever be able to look directly at their faces? Maybe he didn't want to be a pilot and have to kill people; maybe he was really a nice person and the Germans forced him to drop bombs because of the war.

I couldn't sleep. The company left, and a little later I heard Mrs. Stewart come up and go into her room. She puttered around, and after a few minutes I thought I heard an unusual sound in the hallway somewhere; it could have been crying. Maybe it was Eileen; I'd never heard her cry, but maybe she was having a dream about the two bodies, maybe she really knew what had lain there under the white sheet. The noise continued for several minutes, and I got out of bed and opened my door. The hallway was dark, and the crying seemed to be coming from Mrs. Stewart's bedroom. And now I could tell it wasn't Eileen; it sounded too much like a grown-up.

"Mrs. Stewart, are you alright?" I called softly; the shakiness in my voice surprised me.

"Oh, Zachary... it's alright." I heard the creaking of her getting up off the bed, and she opened her door.

"Hello, Zachary, it's alright."

"I didn't know...."

"Oi were just thinking about something," she said. She wasn't crying anymore. "Come, Oi'll tuck you in bed."

I got back into my bed, and in the darkness she tucked the covers in.

"Having trouble falling asleep?"

"I suppose so, I was thinking about the German plane and the bomb, and those people," I said.

"You mustn't think about that, the good Lord'll watch over them." She sat on the edge of my bed in the darkness, and put her hand on my hair. I wanted to ask her how she could be so convinced god would look after them, and where the planet was on which he or it would do this good deed, but I didn't have time because she continued talking. "You must miss your Mum and Dad and your sisters in London."

"No, I like living in Banbury." I didn't want her to feel rotten, because she was better than Mrs. Abbott, and much better than Mrs. D. in Whitney.

"You be a good lad — a kindly lad," she whispered.

"Thank you."

She sat quietly in the darkness. Then, "Oi were thinking about Eileen's dad," she said.

"Is he Mr. Stewart?" Immediately my ears went hot; what a stupid, obvious thing to say!

"Yes." She laughed and cried, both at the same time, and blew her nose. "Now he be Sergeant Stewart."

"Do you know where he is?"

"He be fighting somewhere in North Africa, we don't rightly know where. Maybe one day you'll see him, he'll say what a fine young lad you are." She patted my hair again, and again I didn't quite know what to say. A long pause and she continued: "He be kind, also." She just sat there on the side of my bed for a long time, in the dim reflected light from along the passage. Then: "John be the kindest man, sweetest man Oi ever did meet."

"Yes"; and I felt embarrassed again, because I didn't actually know him.

She was talking so quietly it was almost to herself: "Oi worries sometimes, Oi worries in case the good Lord don't let him come home."

"Yes, well, but I don't know if…."

"Like, if you lost your Dad in London from the war."

"Yes…." It wasn't so much that I wanted a debate, but it seemed the longer I didn't respond the more likely she would think I just believed in it all like she did. "Mrs. Stewart, I don't know what to say, I feel silly, but I don't really believe in, believe there's a…."

"You don't have to say nothing, Zachary… Oi just…. Oi shouldn't be going on like this."

In the small light that crept from her room I could make out she was wearing a white flannel nightgown, its little printed flowers barely distinguishable.

"Oi'll lie down here 'til you falls asleep." She lay down on my bed, on top of the blanket. "We don't have to talk. Let's be quiet now."

"Alright."

"We mustn't wake up Eileen."

"Alright."

She was quiet for several minutes, then: "You must miss not getting no hugs from your Mum and Dad."

"Well, they didn't really hug me and my sisters a lot."

"That's because you got such a big family, such a lot of children to hug."

"I suppose so, yes. Well, they did have enough time, really."

She turned toward me on top of the blanket and put her hand on the back of my neck. "Here's a little hug for being such a good lad." She gave me a sort of squeeze toward her, not actually a hug, and I ended up with my face near her neck, under her chin. I could feel warmth coming from her chest and neck.

"Don't make a noise, we mustn't wake Eileen."

"Alright," I whispered.

She stayed still like that for a long time. In the dark I could hear and feel her breathing. Every time she breathed in it made her chest expand and her skin touch the side of my cheek. Her lying on top of the blanket, pulled the covers down hard, and after about a minute my arm felt trapped.

"Can I take my arm out?" I whispered.

"Out?"

"From under the covers."

"Why?"

Immediately I felt terribly embarrassed! I didn't know what to say — something that wouldn't sound stupid and embarrassing. I was glad it was dark because my face suddenly felt hot and I knew it must look bright red! But before I could say anything, she pulled the covers down a couple of inches and released my arm. Now my arm was along my side and also touching her nightgown, and that made me so disconcerted I had to concentrate completely on not moving. But even staying absolutely still, in that position I could feel heat radiating from her waist, right through the nightgown fabric. She lay there a short minute without moving, then quietly got up off the bed and crept out into the hallway. I heard her bedroom door close, and it got completely dark. I supposed she thought I'd fallen asleep, and she wanted to go to sleep now. But suddenly she was back, closing my door very quietly. She came over and lay on my bed again, it seemed in exactly the same position on top of the blanket, into the same indentations.

In the new darkness, she whispered: "Oi closed the door, we don't want to wake Eileen now, she wants a good night's sleep."

"Yes." We lay there, and my cheek became inflamed where it was touching her skin, touching her neck above the top of her nightgown. Then, even though I felt very hot all over as though I had a fever, suddenly I started to shiver.

"You be shivering!" she said.

"I don't know...."

She'd unbuttoned the neck of her nightgown a bit so my face was more fully against her skin, which was moving alternately closer to my cheek, then further, with her breathing. The whole atmosphere was very warm, and made me dizzy. Everything was silent except for her breathing, with me trying to bend my mouth just a little bit away and upward so as to breathe cooler air to help get rid of the dizziness. Then something messed it all up: something momentarily stuck in my throat, like swallowing a bit of phlegm although that's not exactly what happened, but it made me choke, and I tried to keep quiet, not to wake Eileen, and then all of a sudden before I realized what it was, as though I wasn't even in charge, as though something else was in charge of what was happening, I started to cry, I was actually crying and I felt so silly because I hadn't realized beforehand I was going to cry — I didn't have any reason to cry! She didn't say anything, she just patted my hair, then my back. She must have thought I was really stupid, and that must have been the reason she pretended she didn't even notice I was crying. And then to make everything unbelievably worse, just as quickly as I'd started crying, suddenly it stopped, all by itself, also for no reason! It even made me feel angry; I knew I was even more stupid, stopping crying like that, than I'd felt even *starting* to cry.

Thinking about the whole thing made me very, very tired. I just lay there. I was so tired, I was too tired to think. I was too tired to even think about anything. I just lay there for a long, long time, still feeling a bit dizzy on the lorry. I was lying on the back of the lorry, on the flat bed on the back of the lorry, and we were riding slowly out of the station, over a big bump, and we rocked back and forth. Everything was blurred from my being under the white sheet, and as the lorry rode along the street we kept rocking on the back. I could tell there was another body next to me. We rode faster, and I got frightened because of the sheet, because I couldn't see, in case we rolled off the lorry. I wanted to pull the sheet off, but my arm was locked because I was dead. The lorry was rocking side to side and back and forth, side to side and back and forth, it wouldn't stop. I could hear the breathing. My eyes were open and it was moving. The white sheet was moving. The bed was moving. Her chest was moving the nightgown. I lay there a long time. Then I realized the bed was moving. It was still moving, it was definitely making the bed move. It wasn't her chest, it felt harder; she had moved away, she was lying on her back and my face was against the top of her arm, her shoulder, that's why it felt hard.

"Mrs. Stewart, are you alright?"

Her shoulder was moving, pushing right by my face.

"Mrs. Stewart, are you alright?"

She was crying again, gasping little noises, almost as though she were trying to control her crying, trying to stop herself crying.

"Mrs. Stewart, are you crying, are you crying again?"

"No..." She huffed the word; she couldn't answer because she *was* crying, she was crying again!

"Mrs. Stewart...."

She seemed to be jerking, making little crying sounds, not like ordinary crying, and I wondered if she were having a fit. When Abie used to shout, Rebecca always used to make a joke that he was having one of his apoplectic fits. Maybe Mrs. Stewart was having a fit, a real one.

"Mrs. Stewart, are you having an apoplectic fit?"

She already seemed better now. She had moved away and was lying still, on her side, her back toward me, just breathing; the jerking had stopped.

"No, it's alright, go to sleep." She sounded extremely tired, the way I'd felt before. In the darkness I felt her swing around and put her legs down, then her feet on the floor. She sat on the edge of the bed, facing away. "Yes, Oi did have a fit, just a little one, but everything be alright now."

"Should we go to a doctor? I'll come with you."

"No, sweetie, it's alright." She stood up, and tucked me in again. "Now, you go to sleep like a good lad. Don't tell anyone Oi had a little fit, now. Don't you tell anyone as how Oi come in here to your room and tucked you in. Don't tell your little sister, don't you tell Eileen."

"Alright."

"If Mrs. Carter knew as how Oi had a little fit, she'd have to send you back to Whitney."

"She would?"

"You don't want to go back to Whitney now, does you?"

"No, Mrs. Stewart."

"Then you be a good lad, Oi never come in your room, we'll tell them. We don't want you to have to go back to Whitney."

And she quickly opened the door, padded out, and quietly closed it behind her.

•   •   •

Most weeks I wrote letters asking Mum if I could also come home, the same as Zilla and Rebecca had done. One day I got a letter; in it Mum answered that I could come back to London sometime, maybe when the bombing stopped, when the house was all fixed up and painted.

I was now eleven years old, and at St. Leonard's everyone in my class had to take a special test to see what school they would go to next. I got the highest marks, which meant I had to go to Secondary School. Although I was sorry Dereck was no longer in my class, I really liked the new lessons, especially science and geometry. Also, they actually taught us to read music, quavers and semiquavers!

Then, a whole year after Zilla and Rebecca had gone back, a second letter arrived. This one was from Rebecca. I opened the envelope, and out fluttered a train ticket.

—o—O—o—

8

At Victoria Station I was met by two ladies in short fur jackets, high heels, and stockings with a dark seam up the backs of their legs. Their lips were perfectly outlined with rich red lipstick, and when they blinked it was to the sweep of heavy black eyelashes.

"Well, come on, Zachary," said the thinner one.

"Where're you taking me, miss?"

At which they both burst out laughing. "Don't you know who we are?" the thin one asked.

"Oo-er, wha's'a matter with 'im?" said the other. "We're going 'ome, wha'd'y' think!"

If it had been difficult to identify Marius in Banbury, this time it was impossible to recognize Zilla and Rebecca. "I... but you don't look like them, I mean, you're, you're...." They looked completely grown-up, like real ladies.

"It's been over a year!"

"Yes I know, but...."

"You'll get used to your new big sisters by the time we get home."

Then what might Katherine look like by now? "Is Katya home also?"

"No, she's in Devon," said the heavier one, who had to be Zilla.

"Will she be coming home?"

"No, not yet," said the other one, Rebecca.

We got on the bus to Aldgate East. I'd dreamed for so long of riding a bus again in London that now it was happening it didn't seem real. It wasn't just that the streets were hardly recognizable with all the damaged buildings, and pavements littered with mounds of bricks and debris. It had been more the hopelessness of ever coming home, and although I knew now I really was in London, it would take time to become believable.

The bus took us alongside a shell of burned-out flats with blackened window openings set in charred frames, like dead eyes watching as we made our way along the road. Some structures had been reduced completely to rubble — smashed masonry and wood, rusted pipes pointing out like admonishing fingers. Along Whitechapel Road I saw a solitary interior wall that rose out of a mountain of crumpled bricks, wood and plaster, with an intact set of stairs still attached, climbing to nowhere like a giant unfinished dolls' house. What must it have been like for the poor people the terrible instant the building was struck? One moment sitting quietly in an armchair, maybe polished furniture, books, pictures aligned on clean walls, the anticipation of a cup of tea — and the next, the floor falling away, a compression that bursts your eardrums, then dropping down, down into a choking furnace.

At Aldgate East we got off opposite Lyons Corner House and walked over the road into a new trollybus terminus. There at the far end stood a real trollybus, London Transport red, a streamlined double-decker with adverts pasted along its sides between the upper and lower rows of windows. It was big, bigger than a regular petrol-engined bus, and on the roof were two parallel side-by-side hinged poles mounted about a foot apart, coil springs pressing them up into contact with the set of overhead electric cables.

Looking at the arrangement of poles, cables and spaces, I realized they formed a parallelogram! I pictured the trollybus riding along parallel with the cables and, when the traffic dictated, at an angle. All angles would modify simultaneously and the space defined by the poles, the top of the bus and an imaginary line bridging the cables where they met the poles, that space would always remain a parallelogram whatever the bus's angle! The translation from geometry class to the real world was overwhelming and I must have stood there for several minutes enveloped in a flooding calm. Rebecca was looking at me: "Are you alright, Zech?" and I said, "Yes, it's… it's the excitement of coming home." I could hardly say I just realized something about trollybus poles and parallelograms.

The three of us boarded the number 663 to Mile End. We stepped up onto the broad flat open boarding deck at the back, walked along the clean airy aisle and sat down in the new thinly-upholstered seats. The rails and handles were the white of ivory, not cold metal as on ordinary buses. Other people were boarding and sitting down, and from their faces none of them appeared particularly excited at the thought of boarding a trollybus; they'd probably never heard of a parallelogram.

Outside, the driver grasped a handrail and pulled himself up to his cabin, settling into his seat. He flicked a few switches, and with absolutely no sound beyond the crunching of tires we rolled off, slowly circling the wide terminus to its exit. We pulled out into the main road, and though the bus was loaded with probably seventy people, its acceleration still pulled me back hard into the seat! How wonderful to be in London, to witness the miracle of new inventions, to be coming home!

We were humming briskly along the wide Whitechapel Road when the air-raid siren began a murderously loud upward glissando, two tones pitched a musical third apart, climbing way up into a howling undulation that lasted about half a minute, then fell downward lower and lower to disappear into a massive silence. The driver steered the huge bus to the side of the road, drawing to a graceful stop. On the boarding platform, the conductor addressed us from under the black peak of her cap: "Easy, now, let's not 'ave the ol' Jerry see us runnin'." The passengers alighted with what seemed a familiar camaraderie, everyone helping the others, and we hurried over to the side of the roadway to enter a ten-yards-long windowless brick shelter that stood squat under its massive concrete roof.

Inside, my eyes slowly adjusted to the light cast by low-wattage bulbs burning in small wire cages, and I could make out rows of benches and double-decker bunks lining the perimeter. I asked Zilla and Rebecca, "Where are we?"

"We're in Stepney, remember? You know, Stepney Green. Oo-er, 'e forgot!" Zilla giggled. In the crowded shadows the two of them looked absolutely grown-up.

"You don't need to worry," said Rebecca as we sat on a bench. "It's safe in here, they never get hit. The *All Clear* will probably sound in a few minutes."

The lights flickered, then returned. Conversation paused in deference to a distant row of muffled thuds I felt through the ground as much as heard, and when that sequence petered out, the talk resumed.

"Bet you're glad you're coming 'ome," said Zilla. I summoned the courage to look straight at her; it was hard to believe she was actually Zilly.

"Yes, I can't believe I'm really here! I wonder if any of my friends came home yet?" Rebecca answered. "What's-his-name, Jack, you remember, he knocks on the door sometimes to ask when you're coming back."

"Really, Jack Pristein!" Jack hated his real name, Yakub, so we called him Jack.

"Yeah, and Manny, Manny Yanklewitz, 'e keeps coming 'round all the time," added Zilla. Manny and Jack! I wondered how grown-up they might be, if I'd recognize them, either.

"What are the air-raids like? We had one in Banbury, they killed a cow."

"Oo-er! A cow?"

"Well, and two people by the station. We saw the bodies on a lorry."

"Well you have to be careful here but it's mostly a lot of noise. Don't worry," said Rebecca.

After several consecutive minutes of quiet the bus driver signaled to the conductor, who spoke: "Ladies and gents, we might as well be movin' along. Can't let the ol' Jerry tell us what to do, can we now?" And as our whole gang flooded into the street and back toward the trollybus, some of them were singing, *Hang out your washing on the Siegfried Line...*, in an atmosphere too exhilarating for the conductor to check anything as mundane as tickets.

The *All Clear* sounded as we sailed silently past the traffic light at Burdett Road, where of the old La Bohéme cinema only scarred and burned walls now remained — no roof, not even doors! I'd seen so many pictures there on Saturday mornings with Manny; neither of us had had money, so after the picture began we'd sneaked in through a back door so fast there was hardly time to notice daylight flicker across the screen. And if it were a John Wayne picture, when it was over and we came out my chest would be swelled, I'd walk a special way and nobody would dare talk to me.

The bus pulled up opposite the Mile End Underground station by the two red telephone kiosks, a familiar sight except that now all their little glass windows were missing. We continued on foot toward our house, past where a bomb had destroyed about four houses from the row of elegant homes that lined our side of Mile End Road. And as I followed behind I noticed that the black lines that ran all the way up the backs of my sisters' legs were not in fact stockings seams. They weren't wearing stockings — they'd drawn false seams on their bare legs!

Around the corner we came to Tredegar Square; the tall houses on three sides all seemed intact, if older and more grey, not quite dilapidated but after the freshness of the countryside, almost... seedy! Of course the lovely tall black iron railings that enclosed the park had been removed years earlier, before we'd even been evacuated, but their absence now was still a jolt. And not even a trace remained of the multicolored flower beds. I counted four small new sloping brick structures intersecting the scrubby remains, each with a wooden door in its taller end from which an angled concrete slab roof ran down at thirty degrees all the way into the earth. "There are steps inside, down to the shelter, it goes all around under the park," said Rebecca. She had briefly turned back as she spoke, and I wondered if the false stocking seams were drawn with the same makeup pencil they'd used on their eyelashes. I followed beyond the park, across the road — and there stood 27 Morgan Street on the corner! So small — like a miniature reproduction of the house I'd remembered! The wall on the Tredegar Terrace side that housed the street door really did bulge outward! Bricks had only compression strength and needed to be vertical, in line with gravity; maybe some day that wall would burst outward and the unsupported floors would sag where the rooms hung opened to the world, the upstairs furniture sliding along the sloped floor and crashing down out into the street.

As we came closer, the street door seemed too tiny even to pass through. Rebecca and Zilla entered first, then I climbed the two concrete steps, remembering how disproportionately high they were, and hunched into the dark passageway.

"Lily, he's home, we got him!"

Rebecca and Zilla ran upstairs, those steps sounding a familiar motif of squeaks and creakings. I opened the living room door and there was Mum, dusting the mantelpiece, her hair streaked with grey, the deep wrinkled lines now firmly etched around her mouth and forehead. She looked even more tired than when I'd seen her in Banbury less than two years ago.

"Alright, you're home, sit down, I'll get some dinner."

"Hello, Mum."

She walked around me and out the door; I stood my bag and gas mask against the wall and looked about. The living room was claustrophobic, hardly room to breathe, and everything so worn and decrepit! The lump-ridden linoleum confirmed the indelible map my mind had faithfully recorded — every undulation, tear, every little brown circle where a raised nail head in the floorboards had pushed through. The brown-painted window frames were peppered with raw-wood-colored holes where blackout blinds must have been tacked up every night. The door on the low cupboard at the left of the fireplace still hung partially open and off its hinges, still uncloseable because of multiple coats of paint, probably still brimming with the same pile of odd shoes nobody wore.

I sat at the table before its peeling oil-cloth covering. Mum came back in from the kitchen and placed in front of me a soup plate of small boiled new potatoes with green peas in hot milk. I'd forgotten that combination — it had been my old favorite, something I hadn't seen in four years.

"Eat, eat your dinner, quick before it gets cold." She handed me a dinner spoon of mottled tin, its bent handle partially straightened in not quite the original spot. I'd forgotten about eating everything with a spoon.

"Thank you." With a small cloth in her hand she scurried back to the fireplace, flicking dust motes along the mantelpiece.

"How are you, Mum?"

"What?" She stopped, her head turned momentarily toward me. "What do you mean, how should I be?" Her eyes squinted as she peered directly at me for a brief second. "Quick, your dinner, it'll get cold, eat."

In silence I finished the dish. "Thank you Mum, it was very nice. For years I've been looking forward to having that, peas, potatoes and milk." Again she paused, and for a flickering moment the terrible lines that clasped her face seemed to relinquish their grip. "Mum, did you mind me coming home?"

"Mind? You're home, a *glick for dere,* you would have been better off there."

"I really hated it there, I wanted to come home to be with everybody."

An autonomous hand resumed the nervous dusting, "Ugh."

"Mum, can I go out in the street for a little bit?"

"Go, go."

I went out — and there coming along the street was Manny, Manny Yanklewitz! Although he looked older we recognized each other right away despite an odd chubbiness to his face. I was on my way to growing tall, so although he still was shorter than me he now carried a sort of compensatory girth that caused me a flash of embarrassment, and about which I thought I had better not joke.

"Manny!"

He whipped out a plaid cap which he promptly donned: "Wha'cha, mate." It was that put-on Cockney accent, pretending he was a laborer in a pub. "When did you come 'ome, matey?"

"Today, just now."

The cap disappeared back into his pocket, and in his normal voice he said, "I've been back over a year."

"A whole year! Anyone else back?"

"Old Jack, still swirling around in his black cape. And fat Izzy Mendelssohn — he never even went away. And that rotten fuck Reuben Berger, I've seen him hanging around."

It was a shock to hear Manny say that word — I'd heard it in St. Leonard's playground, but Manny had never sworn before.

"How come Izzy didn't get evacuated? Didn't everybody have to go?"

"I dunno, his mother probably threatened to kill herself if they took him."

"Do they make you go to school when you come back?" I asked.

"Yeah, they catch up with you in the end. I had to go back to Malmsebury Road. Wish it got bombed. I'll be late for school, I can't stay. Wanna come to Johnny Isaacs later?"

"Fish and chips at Johnny Isaacs! Is it still open?"

"Open? Take more than the Germans to close up Johnny Isaacs." In the distance, the church bells in Bow chimed twice in ponderous succession. "Christ, it's two o'clock, school time, I gotta go. I'll come 'round and knock after tea."

I sat on a turret of our little crenelated brick wall and watched my absolute best friend bob off down the street. At the corner he turned to wave and in a delirium I waved back, glad he was too far away to see my tears.

At four o'clock, Marius came home from school. I expected him to look bigger than in Banbury, but still I wasn't prepared. "Blimey, look who it is, ol' Zech *drek.*"

He was still small, but his face had grown lean and hard-looking like a hooligan's. And, he was rhyming my name with shit.

"What do you mean?"

"Mean? Nothin'. Why, wha'd' *you* mean?"

Mum came in with his plate. "Maudy, where do you get that language, from the lousey *yocks* there in school."

I thought that whatever *yocks* do, they don't say the word *drek.* "Maudy, I'm home now from Banbury."

"I knew you was comin' 'ome, Mum said you was."

"So, how are you?"

"Wha'ja mean?"

"Did you come from school now?"

"Yup."

"Do you go to Malmsebury Road?"

"Yup."

"Oh."

That evening, Manny and I walked along Mile End Road, past the Empire cinema in Stepney to where the wide street becomes Whitechapel Road. He'd been evacuated to a place called Grange, he told me, further north than Banbury, and he'd hated it there, too. He'd been the only Jew in the whole town, and also there was never anything to do there.

His mother had sent him a ticket to come home almost a year ago, and now they slept down the shelter sometimes, but mostly the bombing wasn't that bad.

As we approached Johnny Isaacs a crowd of big kids mingled on the wide pavement, just the way it had been before I was evacuated. So many things had changed, I was too nervous and excited to try to recognize anyone as we shouldered our way through.

Inside the shop we joined the queue for chips. Now I was tall enough to easily see over the high counter. Old Mrs. Isaacs served us our tuppence-worth of chips briskly; no-one there knew I'd just come back this morning, and that secret made my head swim. We sat to eat at one of the tables lined up against the opposite wall. The tables and chairs, I noticed, were really old wood.

"Johnny Isaacs is getting fancy," Manny said. "Now they put a piece of clean white paper on top of the newspaper before they shovel in the chips." He continued to bring me up to date. "Remember Muriel? She's home now, just a few weeks."

"Muriel?"

"You didn't forget Muriel Roffberg? You know, that pretty one from the other corner house, you know, with brown hair. Well, now she wears tight fuchsia slacks so you can nearly see her bum, and we both oughtta do her."

This time my ears got hot at what he was saying. And I wasn't absolutely sure what that word *do* — my ears went red just mulling it in my head — what *do* meant when you used it about girls, but I knew it was to do with sex, enough to make you feel embarrassed. I'd forgotten all about Muriel. I wondered what she was like now, in fuchsia — what was that, fuchsia? — in tight fuchsia slacks.

"Then there's Joanie Ungar and her stupid brother Stanley, and stuck-up Shirley Hyams, and Judah Schreiber...."

Four girls sat giggling at a table diagonally opposite us in the next row. A particularly pretty one faced us. She seemed to be looking at me and I turned away quickly, but not before I noticed she was wearing a white lacey blouse to contrast with her brown eyes and long, thick, brown tresses of hair, also tie-up shoes with dark stockings that disappeared up into the recesses of a red plaid pleated skirt. Compelled to steal another glance, I thought I saw through the lace openings of her blouse what seemed like bare skin. One foot was hooked around the leg of her chair and she swung the other one back and forth.

I dreaded the possibility of Manny saying something — but sure enough he did. "See that girl, looking at you?" he whispered.

"I dunno."

"She wants to get done."

"What?" I used to always have a good time with Manny and never had to worry about anything he said. I wished he'd talk the way we used to, just joke around and stuff. Everyone seemed so grown up, I felt stupid.

He continued relentlessly: "She wants you to do her."

"Whadjamean?"

He leaned toward me. "See the way her leg is swinging?"

"Well, I s'pose so."

"That means she wants to get done, that's the first part, and the second part is because she's looking at you that means she wants you to do her."

It was amazing how he could figure all that out! I couldn't ask him exactly what *getting done* was, because the way he was talking I felt really embarrassed, as though everybody knew automatically what it meant. Probably everyone in Johnny Isaacs knew what it was, except me.

"There's something called psychology," Manny went on. "Everybody's got psychology. Sometimes people don't even know themselves they've got it, but their arms and their legs do things, and that means something. That means they want something, but their mind doesn't even realize it. That's what psychology is." I'd never heard him say so many new things! "When someone swings their legs, it means they want to get done. I bet she doesn't even realize she wants to get done."

"She's only swinging one leg," I whispered.

"That doesn't matter, it doesn't make any difference how many legs they swing."

"You wouldn't ask her, would you? Just to test it, to see if it's true. I mean, I'd wait outside, first."

"Oh no, you mustn't ask people about psychology because they always deny it. Sometimes if you ask them right to their face they punch you, that's another thing."

It was terrible not to know about all this stuff. I wished I could find out without having to ask anybody directly. Maybe I could get a book on it from the Lending Library — but they'd remember I'd kept those other two books when I got evacuated, and they might be waiting to catch me when I came back in. Anyway, no one would write a book about doing girls — they probably wouldn't allow it. And, if writing about girls was part of psychology and people always denied psychology, then they *couldn't* have written a book because that would be a contradiction. What shelf would a book about girls go on? Also, they certainly wouldn't put it in the index file.

Well, at least I was sure *doing* had something to do with sex, I mean, it was a relief to know even that. I would always be much too shy to do anything with girls, but you could feel a lot better if you knew things, stuff about them, especially if they didn't even know it themselves for sure. You wouldn't have to *say* anything about it, you could just quietly *know* everything and act sort of confident. It sure was terrific to be home.

"Hello, Manny." A short slim girl with a big nose and pimples was standing by our table, and her low voice sounded husky and rough.

Manny was surprised, but caught himself. "Oh, hello," he replied in a flat mumble.

She stood there, waiting.

"I suppose you want to sit at this table. Lucy, it's imperative you sit here, isn't it? Admit it."

She laughed awkwardly, and sat down. Her head was lowered, but she did smile across at me, a quick smile. I felt better with her because she didn't seem as confident and stuck up as the other girls there. But Manny locked his gaze straight into my face as we ate our chips, making it impossible for me to make eye contact with her as a way of saying "Hello." She sat looking down at her hands clasped on the tabletop. I actually felt sympathy for her because she would probably never be able to feel stuck-up. Manny's cheeks quivered; we both continued staring at each other, he trying not to laugh, and I feeling worse and worse about ignoring Lucy. But at the same time I thought: *Here I am, back home from being evacuated, eating chips with my best friend in Johnny Isaacs, and there's a girl sitting at our table who came over especially, and she's hoping we'll talk to her.*

Just when the tension was becoming unbearable, Lucy broke the silence: "Manny, aren't you going to introduce me?" she pleaded.

"Oh, alright then. Lucy, this is Zachary, Zachary Grossman. Zech, this is Lucy Greenspan. She's barmy." Lucy swallowed; he continued eating his chips and, therefore, so did I.

Again, nobody said a word for several minutes. He looked around; and so did I. He yawned. Then Lucy stood up, looked first at me then back at Manny. She still wore the same fixed smile.

"Manny, I'm going home now."

"Uhuh."

"Manny, which way are you walking?" She looked at me again. "Is anybody walking toward Aldgate?"

More than anything in the world I wanted to say *Yes,* but Manny knew her, he knew about girls, what to do.

"We're walking the other way," he said.

"Oh," and she gulped. Then she turned toward me: "It was nice to meet you." Now she was too nervous even to smile, but I smiled at her and tilted my head, to try to help.

We both watched as, with her head still lowered, she hurried to the door. Around the edge of the blind and through gaps in the tape that braced the big shop window against bomb blast I saw her outside; she turned left and jostled her way out of the crowd. After she'd disappeared, I asked Manny: "I thought she's nice. Do you think she's nice?"

"Oh, she's okay," he said. "She likes me so I have to be rotten to her. If a girl likes you, you have to be rotten to show who's in charge."

That was what I suspected, but it was useful to hear the rule clearly stated. "Does she want to be... *done?" I said it!*

"Er... I don't know. I didn't ask her yet."

"Well I mean, does she swing her leg when she looks at you?" I felt a bit silly. "I mean, if you mustn't ask them about psychology, how can you prove it, if they want to get done?"

"I... I dunno, it takes a long time to learn all the details."

A little before ten o'clock the fish-and-chip shop began emptying rapidly. We'd finished our chips, so we followed everyone out. The crowd outside on the pavement was also dispersing.

"Where's everyone going all of a sudden?" I asked.

"They'll be coming out of the Empire in a few minutes. Don't you remember?"

"The *yocks?"*

"Yes. The picture finishes at ten o'clock and they come to Johnny Isaacs to get fish and chips, so we have to bugger off before they get here. I don't want to get my block knocked off."

From just beyond the perimeter of visibility came scuffling sounds, then a shout, "Ow!"

"Quick, let's cross the road," said Manny.

In the darkness we stepped off the pavement and found ourselves in front of two boys, one of them dabbing at his nose. "Is it alright?" asked the other.

"It's bleeding."

"The barstards!" the other whispered. "Here's my hanky, take it."

Manny and I crossed to the other side. "What happened?" I asked.

"They're from Brady's, I suppose he didn't get out the way quick enough."

We walked back along Whitechapel Road toward Mile End. Brief flickers of light erupted from the swinging doors where people were coming out of the Empire. To avoid confrontation we turned down a side road and cut across Grove Road, then past Coopers College to my house.

"Well, matey, see you tomorrow. Maybe I'll even see you in school if they find out you're home right away!"

"I don't know, they may not send me to Malmsebury Road."

"Why not? Why would they make you go somewhere else?"

"When I was evacuated I got a scholarship and I had to go to a Secondary school. If they find out they may make me go to a Secondary school instead."

"You must have used all those long words and they didn't know what you were talking about, so they thought they'd better give you a scholarship in case."

"Well, everyone in Banbury was pretty stupid. I dunno, I'd rather be in Malmsebury Road."

Manny was backing away into the darkness, toward his house in Antill Road. He'd pulled out his laborer's cap and set it askew on his head. "Welp! See you tomorrow, matey! Cor blimey, 'e got a scholarship, lah-de-dah-de-dah!" His voice trailed off in the distance.

I reached into my pocket for the heavy street door key. Perhaps Abie had come home already; I took a deep breath, and climbing the first high concrete step, guided the key through the worn hole in the wood and felt for the massive iron lock screwed to the inside of the door. A scraping resistance allowed the key just a half-turn, but the door swung wide and I had to grab it before it banged the wall over the cellar stairs.

In the living room the settee had been opened, and Marius was already asleep on the far end; I realized his cot was gone. Mum sat at the table with a newspaper. The house was quiet, and again everything seemed small and remote as if viewed through the wrong end of a telescope.

"Hello, Mum, I went to Johnny Isaacs with Manny."

"You'd have been better off staying in Banbury."

"I dunno, I hated it there."

"Ugh, what's the good? The old barstard'll be home soon, I never know when he's coming home. You're hungry, sit down."

"No, we had chips. Mum, Manny said he came back a year ago."

"So what else does she have to drive her mad, her husband left her, she's just got him in the house to worry about."

"No, his father was dead, Manny said his dad died when the war started."

"Well.... I wish the old barstard would also drop dead or leave, no such luck."

"Will he be home soon?"

"He's got his tailoring shop there, they drive him mad, so fussy, every detail has to be exact." With intense little movements she brushed crumbs off the table into a cupped hand.

She seemed so worried — even anguished — I felt guilty that I'd had a nice time seeing Manny and going to Johnny Isaacs.

"Maybe he'll make a lot of money, he said he'll make a lot of money, we'll all be alright he said. When he opens the snack bar, he said all the people in the factories there, he'll give them big cups of tea, I don't know already, I wish he'd leave me alone with his big plans all the time."

"He's going to open a snack bar?"

"In Burnt Oak!" Her look of surprise made me feel remiss, as though I ought to have known. "He said when the war's over he'll sell ice-cream cornets as well."

"Mum, do you think Katya can come home soon?"

She pulled the newspaper back towards her. "Ugh, what for, she's better off where she is."

"She's the only one who's away now. Did you see her, where she is?"

"Where would the money come from to go to Devon? Your father hardly brings home enough for food, the landlord, that barstard may he *gae in dreard,* like clockwork he's here for the rent."

"I suppose so."

"That's what it is, day after day."

"Where are Zilly and Rivka?"

"They went out with American soldiers, don't tell your father, he'll kill them. God only knows what time he'll be back, the old barstard. I got his dinner ready, for hours it's on the gas-stove."

"Mum, I'm tired from everything today. I'm going to the lav, then I'm going upstairs."

"Alright. Your sleeping suit it's in the drawer still, I haven't been up there."

"Can I take the torch?"

"Alright, don't flash it outside, don't keep it on, just to light the candle, be careful the air-raid warden doesn't see the light."

I took matches from the mantelpiece, and by the light of the torch found my way along the dark passage, and, shielding the beam, down the stone steps to the lavatory. A stack of newspaper sheets, torn into quarters, lay on the near side of the wooden seat that reached from wall to wall. I lit the candle lying there on its side, dripped wax, and anchored it among the cluster of ancient browned burns pockmarking the far side of the seat. High up, the old cistern clung precariously to the wall; from its lever the rusting chain descended to shoulder level, and flickering light glistened off the lacquered brown wood handle that terminated in a rusty screw-head. The cistern leaned out above the seat on two corroded supporting brackets; I used to think one day it would crash down onto my head as I sat there, or certainly fall when the chain was pulled. As I watched, a drip of water formed slowly on a rust mote protruding under one of the brackets; it swelled, fell and sputtered with a *plink!* into a dark eroded indentation on the seat. When I used to sit there, in summer, I'd count to fourteen seconds, gauging exactly when the next drip would splash cold tingling droplets on my bare bum. I stood there and unbuttoned my fly. Everything was so quiet! The urine rattled against the old china bowl and echoed around the walls and pipes. As I pulled the chain a scatter of rust dusted down, and the sound of swirling fresh water shattered the night. I snapped the candle off the seat, collected the torch and walked back outside and up the wide stone steps, to stand on the top step in the silken silence. The big tree by the back window, a welcoming green during the day, was thick and ominous at night in the candle's puny dance.

"Put that light out!" The stentorian shout from the other side of the garden wall shook me from reverie, and I blew out the candle.

The stars were exactly the same as when I'd gone away four and a half crowded years ago. Everything seemed so at peace it was difficult to imagine that somewhere a war raged. I went inside and quietly latched the back door, into the kitchen to replace the torch and re-light the candle.

The stairs creaked their familiar ode as I climbed up to the landing. Before me was the paneled front bedroom door; *Bobbeh* lived, slept, cursed and died in that room. If *Bobbeh's* spirit were still hurtling through the universe toward some unimaginable rendezvous, it would by now be vastly remote, probably reformed beyond recognition, so that if I met it some day there would be no easy identification. The landing window on the right — a tiny rectangle; outside, the extinguished street-lamp a barely discernible outline. I pushed open the door on the left, the one with the coat-hanging nail inside sunk into the middle of its crossbeam permanently enshrouded in numberless coats of paint, the room I'd shared with Katherine a lifetime ago. The gas lamp hung out from the wall to the left of the black iron fireplace; I turned the flattened thumb-knob, and at the hiss of escaping gas lifted the circular glass enclosure and held the candle up close. *Pop!* A bluish flame crept around both sides of the white ash that formed the delicate mantle, reuniting on the far side, and a white light grew and flooded the room with remembered detail: Katherine's and my bed under the window, the tan hairy blanket and dingy grey cushions. It looked as if the bed hadn't been touched since I left — I would hardly fit in it now. The old veneered wardrobe with the broken mirror in its front panel still leaned out as if lunging toward the window. And Marius's old ramshackle little cot had been moved upstairs and now stood along by the door opposite the fireplace wall — against the wall that had been covered with bedbugs the night Katherine ran screaming down to the living room because, she thought, the wall itself was moving.

There I was, in the mirror. Tall: that was good, I'd hate to be short, even a bit shorter and fatter, like... Manny. Manny was my best friend, but still we were different; that was okay. I had dark brown hair, his was much lighter brown. I examined my face sideways. In Johnny Isaacs, that girl whose leg was swinging, she really had been looking at me! I wonder what she actually wanted? Was Manny right about psychology, that she didn't even realize herself what she wanted? I bet she was looking because she thought how could anyone be so stupid? But she wouldn't actually *know* I was stupid, because I didn't say anything loud enough. And Lucy, Lucy had said *Very nice to meet you,* that could have meant she thought I was... handsome. If Manny had let me tell her I'd walk her home, what would she have said? But, maybe she really liked Manny, Manny said she liked him, so maybe she was just being polite to me and she didn't really like me. If I went back to Johnny Isaacs by myself, or maybe with Jack and she were there, she probably wouldn't even remember I was the one with Manny. Maybe Jack and I could both walk her home one night; I'd much rather someone else came with. It would be useful to be tall, dark brown hair, and handsome. Girls would invent questions just to talk to you, and you wouldn't need to worry about plucking up courage to speak to them first — all you'd have to do is answer.

My old tan and white striped sleeping suit lay in the wardrobe drawer where I'd left it. It was ridiculously tight — I could hardly get my legs into the trousers part — but until Mum got me a bigger one I tied the tassel anyway. The front opened like a "V." I turned the gas knob and watched the mantle dim from white down through yellow, a dim orange, ocher, and, with a near-silent *pop!,* off. I leaned forward, pulled the thick curtains aside, then climbed onto the bed, over to my side. The springs creaked more than I remembered. I lay on my back and looked out the window. The oak tree branch was perceptibly closer to the pane now, and beyond the moving shapes of darkened leaves, soft blueish-white stars laced the peaceful black of night. If I rolled my head a bit to the left, The Seven Sisters would line up against the wood frame with the upper left hand corner of the glass. I moved slightly, and there they were, predictable, serene, beautiful.

I was tired out. From my bag I pulled out the book I'd stolen from the Banbury library, *Music In the Modern Age.* Moonlight flickered beyond the moving branches and leaves, trickled through the window to lie on the page; words were barely visible in its dim cast. Page ninety-six. Tchaikovsky wrote *Romeo and Juliet* in 1869, and Prokofiev composed his own *Romeo and Juliet* in 1935 — sixty-six years later. Of course, Prokofiev must have known about Tchaikovsky's version; I wondered what he thought of it? Did he secretly borrow any of Tchaikovsky's notes and interpolate them into his own piece, hoping no one would notice? Maybe he hated the Tchaikovsky, the mushy, sickly dancing sugarplum fairies part — maybe he deliberately composed something entirely different. Mrs. Stewart had liked it because it was pretty. I felt embarrassed because I was the only one who *didn't* like it — it was *too* pretty; you knew exactly where every note was going to go before it went there. One day I'd like to have a gramophone.

Downstairs, the street door jerked heavily closed. I'd fallen asleep and the book had slipped down onto the blanket.

Abie's voice: "Lily, where's the girls?" The short angry sentence stabbed through me. That voice hadn't been so frightening in Whitney, yet now in this house everything was different. A thumping, thumping, and I realized that quite separate from my thoughts, my heart banged away. But this time he would be after Zilla and Rebecca, not me.

"Ssshh, they're asleep."

"Asleep? They're out with the soldiers, the lousy Americans they're out with. You think uh don't know? Wha'd'y' take me for a bladdy fool?" His voice was rising. "Prostitutes, that's what they are, prostitutes."

"What's wrong if they want to go out? They're young girls. It's normal they want to go out, someone to buy them pretty things. What else do they have?"

There seemed to be no response. Perhaps he was tired. I lay there; through the window the stars still glimmered steadily, like reliable old friends.

I woke again with a start, this time to hear Zilla and Rebecca padding upstairs with their shoes off.

"Ee, the old fucker's asleep." That was Zilla's voice.

"Ssh, he'll wake up! What do you think of Wayne, it's so funny with the Americans!" They both giggled. "Wayne! It sounds like a place!"

"You really going to go out with 'im? 'E looked like a dried up turd to me."

"Oh, he was alright," said Rebecca. "It cost him a lot of money, in the club."

"'E wouldn't 'ave done it if 'e couldn't afford it. They get loads of money."

"What do you think of the commotion? His friend, the other one, Billy, he started it, what do you think of it?"

"'The queen sucks cock!' Ee, what an expression, the way they say it!" They were giggling again.

"They do it deliberately to aggravate the English soldiers."

"Ugh! I'd never go out with an English one. They got rotten teeth and no money."

Conversation faded as their door clicked closed.

—o—O—o—

9

Late the next morning I awoke to an empty house; Mum must have gone shopping after she took Marius to school. Downstairs in the kitchen I rinsed my face under a new tap on the wall above a white sink — we had indoor plumbing now! — then boiled a kettle for tea. The London County Council authorities would be after me to go to school, but maybe I had a few days.

A wireless, a brown Bakelite Philco, now stood on top of the shoe cupboard. I switched it on and turned the round dial: Vera Lynn was singing *There'll be bluebirds over,* (deep breath!) *The White Cliffs of Dover....* She'd interrupted the sentence right in the middle; of course she should have taken a deep breath at the beginning instead, enough to carry her through. As I drank tea and listened to the vibrato, so wide you could hardly tell which note she was trying for, I analysed how Vera Lynn, famous singer, hadn't even worked out the phrasing before she'd made the record!

A rat-tat-tat on the street door; could it be someone from the London County Council, so soon? I opened the door tentatively — and it was Jack, good old Jack Pristein!

"Manny told me they couldn't stand you anymore, so they made you come home."

"Jack!"

"Welcome back. I can't stay now, I'm going home for dinner, then I've got to get back to Malmsebury Road."

"Okay."

"You'll be here after supper? I'll come 'round."

"Jack, I can't believe it, it's terrific to see you!"

That night, I sat with Manny and Jack on the little wall in front of our house, like old times. Jack! He'd grown taller, about the same height as me, both of us taller than Manny, and I couldn't help notice he'd developed a curve to his back. Even more wiry and animated, with the same small penetrating brown eyes and — thinning hair! He jumped up each time he began to speak, intense, aquiline in his dark cape, dancing lightly on his perch, ready to swoop down and peck at any unreasoned statement.

Rotten old Reuben Berger came over from across the road and butted himself into the conversation. "You're back."

"Yes, I came back yesterday."

"Where did you go, where'd they send you?"

Just then fat little Isador Mendelson showed up in the half-darkness; he'd also heard I was back.

"Where'd you go?" repeated Reuben. "The bombs are nothing, they don't scare me."

"I stayed here the whole time also," volunteered Izzy.

"That's 'cause your mother wouldn't let you go in case they didn't keep kosher in the country." Prudence dictated that Izzy overlook Reuben's slight. Reuben turned my way again: "So come on, what was it like?"

Jack chimed in. "Go on, Zachary, regale us with stories of far away lands and your exotic encounters with dragons. How many princesses did you rescue, or did you lose count?"

The magic in everything Jack said, the effortlessness of his words — poetry!

Izzy: "Oh shut up! Come on, Zech, what was it like?"

"Well, I didn't really like it much — it was pretty horrible. I'd rather be back. I'm glad I came back."

But Reuben wanted specifics. "Did you do a lot of girls? In the country, do they do a lot of girls?" His tone was insistent.

My ears, I realized in the darkness, were burning hot as I turned to face him. "Well…" I wondered if they were actually glowing, "well… not a lot, I didn't, I mean, just a few, not many really, well maybe…" I fumbled for a pacifying number, "…maybe… maybe… six."

Christ, I bet all of them can tell I don't know what that word "do" means exactly. Tomorrow I'll go to the library and write everything down, clear it all up.

"What was it like?" Reuben wouldn't give up.

"Well… it was, alright…."

"Did they come?"

I paused. "Come?"

"Come! Did… they… come."

My face flooded with perspiration. What did he mean? Girls? How could girls come? At that instant the air-raid siren began its climbing dirge. Yet even then he was not to be deterred.

"Did… they… come?" he roared above the din.

"Well, some of them did," I shouted. "Oh, I don't know. I didn't ask them too many details."

People were scurrying in the dark toward the shelter beneath Tredegar Square. Mum came bustling down the front steps, half dragging, half carrying Marius, his outline huge and limp like a sack of potatoes.

"Quick! Is that Zachary? Quick, into the shelter, the siren went."

"Hi, Mrs. Grossman."

"Alright Mum, I'm coming…."

"Hey, wait a minute…."

"I'll be there soon, Mum, we're just finishing talking." Then, to Reuben, "I've got to go in a minute, my mother…."

But Reuben was not to be thwarted. With Mum out of earshot, he continued: "I don't believe you did six girls. I think you're a liar. I think you're either a virgin or a nancyboy."

As I reeled in embarrassment, Jack's magnificent voice measured back and forth in my head. "Are you calling my friend a liar?"

Virgin? I thought girls were virgins, I didn't think boys could be virgins also. Was it an insult, was he calling me a girl? Could nancyboys be virgins because they were like girls, in a way?

"No, I didn't call him a liar. I just want to get to the bottom of all this."

If I said now I had to go over to the shelter, Reuben would know I was trying to get out of it, he'd know I couldn't think of an answer, and that would prove I was a nancyboy. From the distance came the sound of exploding ack-ack shells.

"Maybe you'd better go home right now," said Jack, evenly. His gamble saved my life: confronted with such a phalanx of stalwarts, Reuben conducted a slow and dignified retreat across the road toward his house.

An arch of tracer bullets lit the sky. In the distance came the *thump, thump, thump* of a line of exploding bombs.

"Reuben is a crude fellow," said Jack.

"A twerp, don't worry about him," added Manny.

With Reuben now out of earshot, tubby little Isador sewed it up: "Fuck 'im."

Whang! A loud metal-on-metal impact, then a dull thump right behind us. It was too dark to see anything; I ran into the house and retrieved the torch from on the mantelpiece. But outside, the shielded light detected nothing in the area behind the little wall. Jack took the torch from me and shone it down through the iron grating into our cellar.

"Look," he cried. "There it is!"

The four of us, buddies, crowded around the grating. Among the scattering of concrete chips, rusty nails and pieces of broken wood, a shiny, scarred tubular piece of metal a few inches long glinted back at us.

"Let's go get it," said Jack. We rushed into the house and down the stairs, paddled through an inch of sopping water out to the front, then through the disintegrating French doors under the grating. Jack, who held the torch, picked up the prize. "It's still hot," he announced. He shone the light up at the grating.

"Don't shine the light up!" gasped Izzy.

"It's okay for a second. See where it hit? It's probably from a German plane. I'll take it home and examine it, and give you the results tomorrow."

We silently assented; in Jack's competent hands, we'd be assured of the definitive answer. "Let's go down the shelter for a while," he suggested.

"You think it's a bit risky, out?" I asked.

"It is getting a bit thick, and the statistics say there are more casualties from falling anti-aircraft shell fragments than from German bombs."

Upstairs and outside again, the four of us marched triumphantly across to Tredegar Square, and down the stairs of the closest brick entranceway. At the bottom, the stairway opened onto a system of six-foot-high tunnels with curved roofs, dimly illuminated by periodic wire-encased electric lights. Double-decker bunks lined the wall along one side.

"It's Zachary, I thought something happened. Why did you take so long?" Mum was seated on a lower bunk, Marius sitting up guardedly behind her.

"Crikey, you took so long," Marius said.

"I was with Manny and Jack and Izzy."

"It's dangerous, isn't it?" Mum directed the question to her neighbor from along Morgan Street, Sadie Benjamin, who sat with her pasty-faced, skinny husband on the adjoining bunk.

Sadie responded in that reedy wavering voice I recalled: "Yeh, hello Zachary, you're home now don't be silly, don't take a chance, stay here, yeh, stay down here." Sadie's husband, sitting in the shadows behind his spouse, nodded his chicken-like head in boney affirmation of his wife's wisdom, "Yeh." We always assumed that Sadie's husband never actually had his own name because everyone addressed him to his face as "Sadie Benjamin's husband": "Good evening, Sadie Benjamin's husband, sir." "Yeh, er, good eve... evening, er, yeh."

"What, what's that he's holding?" Sadie saw the piece of metal in Jack's hand.

"We found it, it landed down the cellar," I responded.

"Ugh! Take it away," she shrieked. "It's a bomb, it'll explode, we'll all get killed!"

As though feeding at a trough, her husband's head jerked rapidly up and down: "You're right, Sadie, you're right!" Then, his head suddenly to one side, while we watched he peered rooster-like at his wife, and smiled.

"It's too small to be a bomb," counseled Jack. "But we'll take it away if you prefer."

We took off along the tunnel. Most of the bunks for the first fifty or sixty feet were occupied, with men, women and kids of all shapes and sizes lying down, reading, talking. Bags, shoes and bundles lined the floor. Some of the faces were familiar; I recognized one man, although now he wasn't wearing the familiar coat: Lunch-Box Nose. Before we'd been evacuated, every weekday morning punctually at twenty-five-past-eight, Lunch-Box Nose had hurried past our window on his way to the bus; he had a big square nose, and Rebecca had speculated it had a little door on the far side where he stored his lunch.

He recognized me. "Hello," he said, "you're back." The voice resonated with grave command, and as his statement was in fact true, any response would have sounded inept.

We kept going. Beyond Lunch-Box's cluster the tunnel was deserted, though echoing voices drifted through from a greater distance ahead of us. We walked through the empty section and around a blind corner to where a group from the Mile End Road side of Tredegar Square had established residence near another exit.

"They sleep near an exit in case they have to get out quickly," said Jack, and the rest of us knew he was right once again. We climbed a new set of steps between massive brick and concrete walls, then out the door to what was left of the scraggly grass. The distant sky flared intermittently with gunfire.

There came a series of hollow-sounding booms; Izzy said he was going back down the shelter, but Jack, Manny and I stayed and watched, entranced, the bombardment's ragged flashes collaborating with the majestic starlit sky to imitate the peaceful beauty of summer lightning.

I sensed an approaching figure, and out of the blackness someone came racing up. We all heard the fast padding simultaneously; a shadowy silhouette crashed into Jack, winding him and knocking him away from us.

"What's... happening? Jack, you alright?" I called into the night. Jack regained himself; he'd managed to hang on to the torch, and he shone it on the fleeing shape.

"What... what's... christ, I think it's Reuben Berger!" said Manny.

"He got the shrapnel!" cried Jack.

"What?" I couldn't believe it!

"He did?" shouted Manny. "He took our shrapnel? Let's go get him!" And the three of us stumbled off in pursuit among evanescent outlines to the edge of the park, and then sped along Morgan Street. It *was* Reuben! As we sprinted after him he raced up to his house, rushed inside and slammed his street door closed. We pulled up, ten yards short.

At the crash, Mrs. Berger's voice rang out from the recesses of the house: "What's going on?"

"It's Zachary Grossman, he's back and he's outside with his gang!"

"What! Let me 'ave a go at 'im!"

A thundering along their passageway, and the street door reopened. A massive Mrs. Berger, hands on hips, filled the doorframe. "What you doing to my Rube?" she shouted at us.

We fell back to the middle of the road. The next moment a brilliant, silent white flash from inside the Berger house simultaneously illuminated the two downstairs windows and the passageway, emphasizing Mrs. Berger's gargantuan bulk. In alarm she stumbled forward as smoke began to surround her and pour out the open street door. "What 'appened to me 'ouse!"

A few moments later, coughing and choking, enveloped in smoke, Reuben staggered out the door.

"What 'appened, what did you do now?" Mrs. Berger screamed.

"The curtains, must 'ave been phosphorus, the curtains!" Reuben choked.

As Mrs. Berger ran past him to reenter her smoke-filled passage, she delivered a smashing slap to his head, causing him to reel forward and fall to the pavement. Inside the house, her screams and shouts were interspersed with choking and coughing. Then she stopped, and the house became eerily quiet. In the distance the sputtering drone of a solitary plane approached.

"Do you think she's alright?" said Manny. "Maybe we should... go in?"

"We probably..." Before Jack could complete his sentence, Mrs. Berger burst from the doorway engulfed in a cloud of white smoke, dragging behind her a long piece of fabric enveloped in flames. She pulled the smouldering material into the roadway and began jumping on it. Reuben had staggered up off the pavement and started jumping on it too, ostensibly to help extinguish it but, I thought, probably to pacify his mother. Not so seduced, again she slapped him heartily across the face. He backed off up the street.

"Me curtains, you lazy barstard, you moron, I told you not to bring things into the 'ouse. Wait 'til your father 'ears of this. If the Jerries don't kill you, 'e will!"

"Sorry Mum, it was an accident...."

"Accident my arse! You bladdy moron, get back in the 'ouse and open all the winders and see nothing's burning, you lazy barstard! Tomorrow you're getting a job!"

The engines of the approaching German bomber, more raucous- and jagged-sounding than the smoother drone of Lancasters or Flying Fortresses, welled to a garish rattle. Fastened inside a cluster of searchlights the ill-fated *Luftwaffe* plane appeared, snuggled within its white puffed cocoon of exploding ack-ack shells. It must have been damaged because it made no evasive maneuvers.

Manny, Jack and I drifted to the opposite pavement and walked the short distance to my house, to sit side by side on the battlements of our little wall. In a contented trance we watched as the plane floated on, passing over our heads and continuing its dream-like passage toward the easterly horizon, attended by its entourage of dancing lights and popping shells.

"It must have been a tracer bullet that didn't ignite when they fired it," said Manny.

"You're right, and somehow Reuben set it off inside his house," added Jack.

The three of us, lined up, sat quietly — me in the middle, Jack on my left, Manny to my right. Peace. We were at peace — at peace with the rent and thunderous night sky, at peace with friendship, at peace with war.

—o—O—o—

10

The raucous blare of a low-flying plane woke me. A low light barely illumined the bedroom. I'd fallen asleep with the gaslight on low — dangerous, the room would have filled with gas if it had gone out completely and someone downstairs had put in another penny. In the soft glow the room seemed to float, its dimensions distorted by the strident clamor of the aircraft's exhaust, louder, then louder still, erratic, a stream of backfires. Then suddenly — silence!

Quickly I sat up, straining to hear. A barely perceptible whistling pierced the stillness, low and breathy, a sustained wind — followed a few seconds later by a tremendous explosion which shook the entire room. The door banged against its catch, scatters of plaster whirled from the ceiling and spiraled to the bedclothes and onto my head. Puffs of white dust drifted out from cracks where the window's frame jostled the plaster wall. The room's brief and mysterious adagio merged into an eerie, still silence joined only by sporadic clinks and thumps as broken glass and other debris returned to earth outside, to be quickly succeeded by yelling, agitated voices.

Zilla's voice in the next room: "Ee, it was a bomb!"

"Quick, let's see if Mum's alright," said Rebecca.

I leaped out of bed, scurried into my trousers, turned out the light and barreled downstairs after them. In the living room, the light was on.

"Oy a broch, oy a broch!" Mum was muttering to herself as she and Abie frantically threw on their clothes. Marius was still asleep on the far side of the open settee.

Abie was talking. "Eee, that was a close one, eee, uh'm, uh'm… we're lucky it wasn't closer."

I'd been home just three days, had already panicked at his voice, but this was the first time I'd seen him. He stood up, shorter than I'd remembered him from Whitney, and slid quickly into his shoes. He moved fast, already donning his jacket and a hat.

"The blanket, the blanket," Mum shouted as she pulled the cover off the settee and attempted to wrap it around Marius.

"I'll do that, you get dressed." Rebecca pulled the blanket from Mum's agitated hands.

Marius pulled away in his sleep, "Tsk! Stop it, leave me alone!"

Mum reached for her shawl. "Stop it, quick, it's a bomb, we've got to go to the shelter, quick!"

Abie turned to leave the room. "Eee, it's Zachary! Zachary, that's right, you're 'ome, from Banbury where is it. A bomb! Did you 'ear it? Eee, the 'ole 'ouse, it was like, shaking."

"Help, quick, with the blanket help me…" Mum tried to assist Rebecca wrap up a reluctant Marius.

"Quick, quick, Zilly, 'elp Mum... uh'll, uh'll...." Abie brushed past my sisters and me to open the street door. He peered cautiously outside, then ran lightly down the high steps. Head down, at a half crouch and with an arm bent high across his forehead, he disappeared into the beleaguered night.

In the living room, Rebecca helped hoist Marius, now over three feet tall, onto Mum's shoulder, then grabbed the bag Mum kept packed for such emergencies. I held open the street door to see them all out, ran back upstairs to grab my shoes and shirt, then raced outside. Acrid dust laced the night; in the near distance I could hear Marius' again-familiar coughing. Congregating fire engines and ambulances were jockeying at the far end of Morgan Street amid a pool of leaping red- and yellow-hued reflections. I ran toward the disorder, but just beyond Coopers College an air-raid warden loomed from the darkness: "Ey, where you goin'?"

"I... I wanted to see what was happening...."

"You live up there, lad?"

"No...."

"Then better you don't bother them tonight, laddy. Run along to the shelter now."

I returned, ran down the shelter steps and waded into the tunnel's odor. Further along, Abie stood by a stacked bunk. "What 'appened, where were you, eee, everybody's wondering...."

My family had commandeered several bunks immediately beyond the initial dozen already appropriated by regular overnighters. Mum and Rebecca were preparing the beds. "Blankets, we need more blankets," said Mum.

"Alright then I'll get 'em, I'll go," said Zilla.

"I'll come with you," I added, and followed her back toward the shelter entrance.

"I suppose we ought to sleep down here every night, the stinking Germans, the barstards...." Mum's voice faded as we turned the corner to climb the steps.

"Ugh, I don't wanna sleep down 'ere, it stinks," Zilla said. "Funny, we didn't 'ave any bombs close like that 'til the week you come 'ome! I dunno, I'm not gonna sleep down there with the whole of Mile End snoring and *fotzing* all night." We stepped back outside into the pungent smell of burned explosive. "Ee, it must 'ave fallen up there, by Grove Road."

"Yes, something's on fire but they wouldn't let me go close to see."

Our house appeared to be still in one piece. We collected various blankets and pillows, I stuffed my ex-library book *Harmony* by Walter Piston into a pocket, and we returned to the shelter, Zilla conceding she would try it for one night. After we'd distributed the supplies I walked a little way through the tunnel to see if Manny and his mother might have come down — but no. Jack had already told me his mother wouldn't use this shelter; on the other side of Mile End Road they had access to a brick and concrete surface shelter right by their street door.

I read for a while about major and minor intervals, the distances between two notes played simultaneously. After an hour with no more bombs I must have dozed, waking intermittently to the dim yellow glow from the ceiling lamp cages, realizing where I was. Toward morning I fell into a deep sleep, then heard Rivka get up. Mum was already up, dressed and fussing with the bedclothes; Zilla whispered something to her, then left. Next it was Abie's turn: "Lily, come on, make me breakfast, make me...." and he too was gone.

"Zech, wake up, bring the covers back, watch Maudy."

I arose.

"'Allo!" Marius' eyes were open, and he watched me collect the rest of the bedclothes.
"Good morning, Maudy."

"That another book?"

"Yes." I stuck it in my pocket.

"Why you always got a book?"

"I don't know... I like books."

"You going to carry me?"

"Carry you?"

"Mum does."

"Why should I carry you? You're big enough, you go to school already. It's just over
the road, and I've got all the covers to carry."

"Mum carries me."

"Well, do you want me to carry you?"

"I dunno. Alright then, I'll go myself if you don't want to carry me."

"You're six, isn't that too old to be carried? Why does she carry you everywhere?"

"Case I can't breathe."

"Can you breathe?"

"I dunno. Yes."

We climbed the steps into the bright daylight. At the end of the street the flurry of
activity continued near Grove Road.

"I'm going up there to see what happened. Want to come?"

"No, Mum'll be wild, I gotta go 'ome."

I walked Marius and the blankets home to the clanging bell of another departing ambulance at the end of the street. Marius climbed the steps ahead of me and opened the door.

From inside came the rasp of Abie's voice: "Where are you already, uh'm late, for work
uh'm late...." I deposited the bedclothes and book upstairs, and managed to avoid seeing
him as I let myself quietly outside again.

Many of the upper-story windows of Coopers College had been broken, with glass
shards and other debris littering the grounds. Virtually every one of the succeeding houses'
windows were shattered, and the final six or seven homes on each side preceding Grove
Road had been reduced to brick piles and wooden stalks of door- and window-frames.
Workmen were carefully turning over debris, then shoveling it into a lorry. The ambulance
returned, parked nearby and the driver jumped down to join the search among the wreckage.
Around the corner on Grove Road, buckled girders and chunks of concrete from the demolished railway bridge lay strewn across the roadway, and twisted train tracks jutted out from
where the track bed abutted what had been supporting columns. Like the sinuous curves of
some half-submerged sea monster, downed trollybus cables arched their way out of the
debris. And in the middle of the devastation, I realized that the old Victoria Pub, which had
stood alongside the bridge, had completely disappeared!

Back around on Morgan Street, I discreetly asked a workman sorting through the wreckage what it was that had landed there.

"Don't know, sonny, the old Jerry's still got a trick or two up 'is sleeve!"

"I live along Morgan Street, I heard it, it sounded like an aeroplane nose-dived."

Another man called across at me: "Run along there, son." He seemed to be a foreman,
and he came over. "Keep moving, Bill, every second counts, you never know we might still
save some poor blighter under there."

I watched from the perimeter, fascinated, wanting to know if they'd found any remains of an aeroplane. When the foreman moved to another area, I asked the man again if it had been a plane that crashed.

"We don't know what it was."

"But did you find pieces of an aeroplane? There would be pieces…."

"Sonny, you ask too many questions for your own good. Run along 'ome now, your mother'll be wondering what 'appened to you."

I started home in a dream of contemplation that the energy unleashed in a fraction of a second might cause so much damage. And there, coming along the street toward me, was Jack.

"Hello, you saw it?" he asked. "I was here earlier. I just went to your house."

"Don't you have to be in school?"

"I'm supposed to be. Were you down the shelter?"

"Not when it landed, but afterwards we all slept down there. I was watching them dig just now. Wonder what it was, I thought a plane crashed, it sounded like it."

"Yes, but I was there already and there isn't any crater."

"Crater?" How could I have not thought of that myself?

"If a plane had nose-dived into the ground it would have made a big crater, and there isn't one."

"Yes you're right, of course!"

"And there'd have to be pieces of the plane lying around," he added.

"Yes, I asked them about that part of it."

"But what's most important is how far the blast spread. Did you notice all those broken windows everywhere, right up the street?"

"Yes…."

"Well, if it had exploded inside a crater the blast would have been funneled upwards and it wouldn't have broken windows far away." Jack was amazing! "It's too spread out for an ordinary bomb."

"So what do you think?"

"Well, I asked the man there if they'd found aeroplane wreckage, and he seemed to be covering up something, some secret."

"Really?" They hadn't told me anything either, but I hadn't thought of it as secret.

"Yes, so I think it was some kind of a secret weapon the Germans dropped there."

"You do?"

"Probably to test it out."

"A secret weapon!"

"Yes, and the British government is as mystified as we are. We probably have a duty to tell them exactly what it sounded like as it came down."

But on the wireless at six o'clock Richard Dimbleby, reading the news, confirmed that the Germans had developed a secret weapon but the British government already knew all the details. It was a pilotless flying bomb which carried one ton of high explosives, taking off from across the Channel, from Holland. Code-named *V-1*, short for *Vergeltungswaffe-1* which was German for vengeance, it glided down to the target, exploding on the surface of the ground and causing extensive blast damage. Dimbleby said the first one had landed in the East End during the night, killing several families. I was elated at the news of a pilotless plane, though I did feel guilty about the people who died. But apart from that, an aeroplane that flew itself! Things were getting to be like the twenty-first century and Buck Rogers, in the pictures!

The very next morning my wish to observe a V-1 actually in flight was granted. Mum had been frightened yesterday by the news reader's 'secret weapon', and she'd kept Marius home from school. When the *Alert* sounded she was cooking in the kitchen; I hadn't wanted to hang around indoors with Marius, so I was outside looking at the sky. *"Oy, again!"* I heard her mutter as the siren began its climbing dirge, *"I'll never get anything done."* She came running down the steps carrying Marius and her handbag, and hurried into the street toward the park. She saw me and called: "Come on, quick! Maybe it's a secret weapon, the German barstards."

"Alright, I'll be there." I was contemplating how a pilotless aeroplane's instructions might be fed to the controls, and Mum had just disappeared into the park, when from a distance came a penetrating, rapid staccato, similar to that of two nights earlier. It became louder and more sharply etched, and then I saw it: a tiny black aeroplane, stubby wings engraved onto the greyish fleecy clouds, racing through the sky like a toy. As it drew closer I could actually see fire spurting from a tube extending over the tail, and my heart thumped; a real jet engine!

The machine dropped lower, the pitch of its engine rising to a shrieking whine. This one wasn't gliding; it was diving! Maybe the controls had gone awry: how exciting if artificial brains could rebel, then do their own bidding! High above my head the tiny plane rolled over, and in a large arc began curving downward. It gathered more speed as it fell lower and lower, and I rushed through the house and out into the garden, scrambling up onto the top of the Anderson to get a better view. As I watched, it drove vertically into the ground a couple of miles away, to the accompaniment of a shattering explosion. Awestruck, I saw a column of black smoke begin climbing from behind the intervening houses.

An old bike leaned up against the wall by the tap. I slithered down from the Anderson, grabbed the bike, ran it outside and began pedaling furiously toward Victoria Park, the direction of the explosion. Beyond the park's entrance people were moving toward the big duck pond where there used to be boat rentals. Riding carefully through the running crowd I came to the pond. Two policemen were at the pond's edge by a fresh crater filled with oily water. One policeman had his arm around the shoulder of a woman wearing an apron, crying and clasping her hands together. The other policeman poked into the murky water with a tree branch.

I stood at a respectful distance, supporting the bike between my legs, and asked a man next to me what happened.

"They said it's her son. He was fishing in the pond. It was a direct hit."

The policeman and another man were trying to hold the woman up, but she kept falling slowly out of their hands. Limp, she twisted around and down, and I saw her face directly, just a few feet from mine. It was all red and wet, and her eyes were rolling.

On the ride back to Morgan Street, I thought about Katherine. I didn't even know where she was other than it was some place in Devon, near Tiverton. Suppose she were dead? That meant I would never see her again.

—o—O—o—

11

Less than two weeks after I'd come home from Banbury, the school authorities caught up with me. They discovered I was back from evacuation and sent a lady from the London County Council to our house with papers showing I'd gotten high marks for reading, geometry and science in both Banbury and Whitney. That meant, the lady said, I'd now have to go to a Secondary school. Malmsebury Road was an ordinary school but I asked her if I could go there instead because my friends went there; she got angry and said that wasn't the reason children went to school.

Mum thought the closest Secondary school was Raine's School for Boys, on Commercial Road. Raine's was five or six miles away.

"Whose is that bike in the yard by the wall, could I go on that?"

"The bike? Your father brought it home, there was a bomb or something, someone didn't need it, they gave it to him."

"Really?"

"Who knows what happened, the old barstard."

"Can I go to school on it then, do you think?"

"Go, go on it, I should worry."

Monday I got up early, grabbed a piece of bread and jam and sneaked the bike out over the garden wall so Abie shouldn't see I was using it. I got to school before nine, and found everyone in the playground wearing a blue blazer with a special *Raine's School for Boys* insignia on the pocket. A grownup showed me the classroom and my assigned desk. A few minutes later the teacher, a Mr. LaRoche, in a grey suit and black tie and wearing a homburg hat, entered. Everyone quieted down. He came around from the front and began maneuvering between the rows of desks, checking that we pupils had writing pads and appropriate implements. As he moved, his shiny black shoes flexed, their thick soles clicking with the precision of a machine-gun. He terminated his interrogation of the first pupil, who apparently had only an ordinary pen instead of a fountain pen, by delivering a sharp crack across the head with the edge of a ruler he carried under his arm like a captain's truncheon. Several other pupils received the same treatment for no writing pad or similar derelictions. I had no supplies at all, so naturally I got hit on the head also. He had the pupil in front give me a few pages from his pad, and LaRoche himself lent me a pencil.

That night I told Mum, "Everybody has to have a fountain pen, otherwise we get hit!"

"Fountain pen! So who's going to pay two-and-six for a fountain pen, the teacher? Your cousin Seymour has a fountain pen because he's an accountant, ordinary people don't have fountain pens. You tell him."

LaRoche's forays, culminating in a sharp blow to the heads of the remiss, continued until Wednesday, when I was the only pupil still without a fountain pen. That morning I'd tried platting my hair into a weave so it was thicker on top.

"What happened to your hair, Grossman?"

"Nothing, sir, sometimes it goes like that itself."

Again he crowned me with the ruler, so at twelve o'clock before going out to the playground to eat my sandwich I waited by his desk and told him my mother said we didn't have enough money for a fountain pen. He seemed suspicious, but replied that if that were really the case he would let me continue using a pencil — adding sarcastically, "Do you think your parents have enough money for a pencil?"

My daily recounting after school of these humiliations prompted Mum to investigate further, and she discovered that Coopers College, which was on Morgan Street just two streets along from our house, was also a Secondary school. The lady from the L.C.C. hadn't deigned to tell us this, and with its high fence and barbed wire along the top of the enclosing wall we'd thought the place was a prison. So I transferred, counting the minutes until Friday at four P.M.

Coopers College, which neither insisted on fountain pens nor boasted a school jacket insignia, had a wonderful science laboratory. I looked forward to classes there for two reasons, the second being Joan Ingersall. Joan Ingersall had long blonde hair, hazel eyes and white teeth, and she didn't know I even existed. Out in the playground she was invariably surrounded by a clutch of half a dozen cohorts who, I noticed from a safe distance, wore expensive-looking clothing. I hadn't thought about clothes before, so at home I studied my own in the mirror, reaching an inescapable conclusion: I wore cheap *shmutters*.

A week or two after my transfer, the science teacher, Mr. Moore, paired the pupils off for a frog-dissecting experiment. Incredibly, he assigned Joan Ingersall and me to the same bench. I loved stars, planets and jet engines but was dubious about frogs.

"You start," Joan Ingersall said. My stomach lurched that she'd said actual words to me.

But how could I cut up a real dead frog? "I don't like to, you do it first, then I will."

Her large hazel eyes hardened into a shriveling stare, she blinked slowly, and her brows knit together over that perfect nose as she spat out the words: "You're the man, you're supposed to start."

It took me a moment to realize that her *you're the man* referred to me. Maybe she was right about men starting first, but still I felt sick at the thought of cutting into flesh, even if it were dead. "I feel sick. I'll faint or something if I start."

The look of scorn rendered her even more beautiful; she gathered herself, and by default began cutting up the frog. Right away *she* fainted, collapsing gently into an exquisite array of arms, legs, blonde hair and flowered fabric. She looked breathtaking on the floor, her tanned face framed in a rim of silken tresses, a beam of sunlight slanting down from the window to illumine a light golden fuzz where her bare arm lay across her waist, the skirt fallen up to expose a tawny thigh. In the time it took to absorb these revelations, Mr. Moore came running over. He scowled at me as though it were my fault she fainted, and boldly picked her limp form off the floor, sat her on a chair and leaned her forward so her head was down. I was angry at myself for being slow — *I* should have picked her up and gallantly sat her on the chair before he got there.

When she regained her composure, Mr. Moore asked her if she felt well enough to return to our bench.

"I don't want to be at the same bench again with Gröseman. He's stupid, he even pronounces his own name wrong."

"No, I..." I stuttered, "that's... it's, it's Grossman, it's *supposed* to be Grossman."

Mr. Moore didn't seem at all surprised at her assessment. He just let her go home — implicitly, I suppose, agreeing with her.

Later in the same lesson I was dreaming about how luscious she'd looked lying help-lessly on the floor, when out of the blue Mr. Moore shouted: "Wake up, you!" and asked me a question about frogs. He caught me off guard and I gave the answer I should have given for the previous class, a history lesson where the other teacher had been talking about some war with the French, whom the English had nicknamed "frogs." In that instance I hadn't understood they were talking about French soldiers; now, though I realized Mr. Moore meant actual frogs, I briefly thought he was referring to frogs that lived in France. After listening impatiently to my flustered response, he sent me to the headmaster's office.

Mr. Edward Hutchinson, Headmaster, read the glass panel in the door. I knocked.

"Come in," said a woman's voice, and I entered. Behind a desk sat a frowning woman in a dark, frumpy but lace-topped dress. She had a tiny head and what seemed like a black frizzy wig perched on top of grey hairs escaping around the sides, with heavy horn-rimmed glasses embedded over her nose. "What is it?" she scowled. The huge eyes appeared disembodied behind their thick lenses.

"Mr. Moore sent me down to see the headmaster," I said.

"What did you do wrong?" They automatically assume you've come down because you did something wrong!

"I answered Mr. Moore's question, and the other pupils were laughing."

"I'll get the facts from Mr. Moore. Wait here." She began to rise out of her chair, and as progressively lower parts of her frame came into view above the desk she became wider and wider until she resembled an isosceles triangle. She came around the desk balancing on little black patent-leather shoes, wobbled precariously over to the door, and was gone. Several minutes passed before she returned, swaying menacingly toward me, each eye floating independently behind its lens. "You're the one who caused the trouble with Joan Ingersall, we had to send her home. And this time you were daydreaming. We have you down twice for daydreaming last week!" she snapped. "Wait here!" And she teetered through the inner door to Mr. Hutchinson's office.

"Come in here, Grossman!" ordered a stern male voice. I went in. "Return to your desk Emily, and close the door after you. There's no reason for you to witness this unpleasant-ness." She left. "Grossman, I don't know what's the matter with you. It's not that you're a complete idiot — if you would only wake up you could be Prime Minister one day." He carefully selected a cane from among several in his umbrella stand. "Hold out your right hand... more, palm up." And he caned me with the thin, flexible birch stick, three strokes right hand, three strokes left. And as he did, he lectured: "You'll remember this day and be thankful." The cane stung so much that tears welled up in my eyes, but I was determined not to show any response. "Believe me, this hurts me more than it hurts you," he added between swishes.

•   •   •

That evening Jack showed up. He said he had to talk to me about two things, urgently. "Where can we talk where we absolutely won't be interrupted?"

"Let's go in the Anderson, no one goes in there."

From the street we scaled the brick wall into the garden and climbed down inside the musty spider-ridden Anderson shelter.

His older sister Sarah, he began, married two months to Fred who has one crippled leg and with whom she now lived in Manchester, came home three days ago because his mother received a telegram from the War Office. "My father's in the paratroops. It's a military secret so I'm not supposed to divulge this stuff, but he said he might be going away in a few weeks to somewhere dangerous. Then we got a telegram from the War Office. He's missing."

"Your father's missing? What do you mean... where is he?"

"They don't know. Maybe it's the Second Front."

"Oh, I'm sorry, I hope he's alright...."

"It doesn't necessarily mean... they just have to let you know."

"Yes...."

"So I stayed home from school yesterday."

"Because... of your father?"

"My mother said the three of us should spend the whole day together."

"I see. Yes."

"So Sarah started telling me about being married. She always talks a lot."

"About being married?"

"She wanted to talk, she was going on and on."

"Yes, I see."

And Jack related what Sarah had told him about marriage; that you couldn't snore anymore, nor could you *fotz* unless it happened in your sleep because then it wasn't your fault. The worst part was you always had to watch what you said in case it started an argument. But the best part about being married, she had said, was — and Jack's face became stern — sex.

"She told... you... about... it?"

"Yes. I didn't want her to tell me *everything,* especially things that women shouldn't talk about." His eyes flashed. "Anyway this *is* what she said. She said she lies on her back on the bed, and Fred climbs on top of her, and he's not wearing any clothes. She's being crushed under this big body, and there's such a lot of hairy skin that to a woman it's overwhelming and she can't even breathe, but that's okay."

"It's okay? It is... okay?"

"That's what she said." His eyes were grim, and I tried to be sympathetic by shaping mine similarly. "She wouldn't stop. She said sex is different from anything else."

"I see." I struggled to match Jack's look of disgust with his sister.

He went on. "Of course, I can't respect her anymore after telling me this."

"I see. I mean, yes, I can't either."

"But it is useful to know."

"Yes, it is. Yes." I wanted to make some observation that might help, but I couldn't think of anything. So, since he didn't have anything more to say, I suggested we get out of the Anderson. We climbed back over the wall, and in silence walked along Morgan Street. Approaching Coopers College reminded me about having been caned earlier in the day, a subject that might allay my discomfiture. "I got caned today. I hate school." It took a while for his own preoccupations to moderate, and I had to repeat what I'd said.

"Caned?"

"Yes, I got caned in school today."

"Caned... hmm, those things are to test you, to prepare you for higher consciousness."

"Higher consciousness?"

"They're indicators of your inner balance between ordinary consciousness and higher consciousness."

"I'm... not sure... what you mean."

He seemed to have forgotten about his family. "That's right! Things like getting caned are called 'mundane.' They're a test; if you handle them satisfactorily then you're ready for higher consciousness." Jack never spoke carelessly, so I listened with scrupulous attention. He described how his consciousness had evolved to where he could cause an astral projection of himself to rise from his body and float above his bed.

"An astral projection?"

"A projection of your incorporeal self."

"Incorporeal... what?"

"The part of you that's sort of... intangible, like your consciousness, your ideas, everything that's not the material part."

"Really? You mean it feels like a piece is floating?"

"That whole incorporeal part materializes outside your normal body."

"What does it look like? Does it look like there are two... people?"

"No, it can't happen when anyone is watching; anyway it's sort of a bit misty."

"You mean you feel like a ghost or something is coming out of you? You imagine it."

"No, it's when I lay down and everything's quiet, it's really happening."

"But..."

"And I don't have to just stay above the bed. Astral bodies can travel to different places."

"Well... I mean... how do you know you... it... really went somewhere, you didn't just imagine it?"

"No, it's really going there. You can actually visit other planets."

"What?!" This was my friend Jack? "I... I...."

"Yes, I've seen people on other planets, girls, people."

"What? Where?"

"On planets in other galaxies."

"Oh come on, how do you know there are people on other planets?"

"I've seen them, that's why, I've actually been in their houses, their bedrooms. You understand, astral bodies are invisible."

"I... I...." Maybe it was the shock over his father, but the obvious question was whether astral bodies could be enlisted to find someone whom the War Office had declared missing — yet I couldn't be that direct in case it seemed harsh.

He continued. "Your astral body can actually be right there in their bed before they even get in."

"What... why... what do you mean?"

"For observational purposes. Usually you just sort of... sort of float by the ceiling."

"I mean... I mean.... What?" Perhaps *Bobbeh* or Auntie Cissie were now astral bodies.

"I realize it sounds preposterous," he said, "but that's because people are only used to things in terms of ordinary consciousness. The astral body is a sort of manifestation of higher consciousness, it's not hampered by mundane things like time or space...."

"I... I..."

"Or even relativity."

"I can't believe you're saying this, you always liked science...."

"I do, but that doesn't mean there's nothing else."

"Nothing else! But Jack, I mean...."

"We have to keep our minds open. The universe is a big place."

"Well, this sounds a bit ridiculous."

"You want evidence."

"Well yes! I mean, this contradicts everything... you know, all the stuff we talk about, like gravity."

"No no...."

"Then, the speed of light, how can you travel to another galaxy, it would take years and years."

"It doesn't contradict Einstein and other things, just don't forget that that stuff is all mundane...."

"*Mundane!* But it's the most important thing in the world!"

"I didn't mean mundane like that, listen, I mean that Einstein was talking about natural laws that apply to ordinary consciousness. I'm talking about *higher* consciousness."

"Well, I don't know, everything would still have to obey natural laws otherwise... it... it couldn't...."

"Alright, alright. Let's do an experiment to demonstrate it," he said.

"Alright, but, but, how, what sort...?"

"And you'll be in the experiment yourself, so you can see whether it's true or not, alright?"

"Alright."

That very night, his astral body would come to my house. We agreed on a time when everything would be quiet: two o'clock in the morning. He — it — was to materialize downstairs outside the kitchen door, float along the passageway, then drift up the stairs toward the bedrooms where I would be waiting in the back room. Before retiring, I was to place three secret objects on the landing floor at the top of the stairs. His astral body would come to the top of the stairs right outside my room, and it would note what these three objects were.

He also said that if I were awake I was to carefully note whatever sounds astral bodies might make. If I were not sure of the source of any noises, I was to get out of bed *absolutely quietly* and look out the door to see what was happening. But if my movements accidentally woke someone in my house, then because of awareness of an astral presence the whole experiment would be ruined and his astral body would rush back instantly into his physical corpus. Such emergency was fraught with danger and was to be avoided at all costs. But assuming a normal return, his mother or his sister observing him asleep in his bed would notice nothing beyond a little more-than-usual eye movement, his turning over in his sleep, perhaps some breathlessness, maybe even a little thump. And then — the following evening he would be able to name the objects I'd placed at the top of the stairs, and I would tell him if I'd heard anything.

So, we bade each other good night. Before going to bed, I placed on the landing right outside my bedroom door one tube of model-aeroplane balsa cement, one right shoe from the living room cupboard, and the copy of James W. Dunne's *An Experiment with Time* I'd borrowed from the library in Banbury. I moved them a bit to one side so no one should fall down the stairs, but not so far over that an astral body might glide right by.

It was after eleven. Zilla and Rebecca were still out on dates with American soldiers. I turned the gaslight down to the lowest level where it would stay on, and checked the bedroom door; the hinge would creak if it opened, and that was certain to wake me up. Zilla and Rebecca would come in about one A.M. and go straight up to their front bedroom. Abie had already come home while I was arranging my experimental items. The gaslight seemed even dimmer than before; I heard him drag a chair out to the downstairs landing and clunk two pennies into the meter, and the light glowed brighter again. I got out of bed, checked the door for the umpteenth time, pulled aside the thick curtain to let in a little outside light, noted where the opening was in the crumpled bedclothes, turned off the light and leaped carefully back into bed and pulled the covers over.

I couldn't sleep. I reached out and pulled the curtains further apart. A half-moon shining through the leaves gradually precipitated outlines in the room: the cot against the wall, the monstrous old wardrobe leaning outward, its broken door mirror catching reflections from the dark branches right outside the window. Downstairs, Mum and Abie were talking; occasionally his voice rose angrily but they hadn't begun really arguing.

The empty bed in Zilla and Rebecca's room creaked once, although no one was in it — no one was *supposed* to be in it. The big branch across the window stirred in a sudden breeze, and its shadow mingled disconcertingly on the wall with the myriad shapes of discolored and cracked paint. The breeze picked up again and I experienced some alarm, a foreboding at the impertinence of Jack's and my impending experiment. The fireplace produced a low-pitched double-toned whistle when the wind exceeded some minimum speed over the top of the chimney flue — a giant playing his panpipe — and with intermittent gusts the parallel melodies climbed and fell ominously. As the restless hour progressed and the wind speed increased, the rising pitches spread apart; the music book had said minor thirds sounded sad and major thirds happy, but this sounded apocalyptic — an omen to Jack's and my arrogance that cosmic secrets might be susceptible to our puny investigation.

The street door! It was Zilla and Rebecca. Abie clumped out of the living room. "Where you bin, where were you, you... runnin' out all hours. Eee, like... two prostitutes, both of y', you... you... prostitutes...."

"Oo-er, oo-er, what?"

"My goodness, how uncivilized!" That was Rebecca's voice; she was really taking a risk.

Then, louder: "You... you think uh don't know what's going on 'ere? Disgustin', disgustin' for the neighbors it's disgustin'...."

"Ssshhh, the neighbors, they'll hear...." Lily interjected.

Zilla spoke up now, her loudest talking voice yet: "We don't 'ave to listen to this fuckin' shit, c'mon, Rivka, let's go out, let's go, who wants to put up with this shit every time we come 'ome?" Scuffling sounds, then Zilla screamed. "Take your 'ands off me you old barstard — ow!"

I pulled the covers up. The street door slammed open all the way against the cellar steps wall, and footsteps indicated my sisters had run back out into the street. Through the little landing window opposite my door I heard Rebecca: "The old blue-nosed baboon, now he's gone completely mad!"

A tremor ran through the walls as Abie smashed into the kitchen. Through the blanket I heard his voice, shaking as he mumbled: "Eee, uh'll show 'em, this time uh'll really show 'em...." The pedal wheel of his sewing machine squealed as he yanked the leather belt off its pulley, and he thundered out into the street. I crept out of bed to the landing window.

The girls had paused on the other side of Tredegar Terrace toward Litchfield Road, but when they saw him coming they took off again. Perhaps they thought they could outrun him, but his adrenalin-laced strides quickly shortened their lead.

"You fuckin' old blue-nosed barstard," Zilla called back over her shoulder. Neither of them seemed afraid to say anything!

"Prostitutes, you don't come in the 'ouse no more, you... you *drae pisherchs mit der* fu–uckin', *fu–uckin'*" — his voice rose to a scream — "your stinkin' Americans, the soldiers, like... common... prostitutes, like...."

My sisters had removed their high-heeled shoes, and now Rebecca stubbed her foot on a raised slab of pavement, "Ow!" and fell to the ground. Zilla hesitated, and in that instant Abie lunged forward and seized her hair. With the leather thong he began lashing her across the back and shoulders, but Rebecca reached up from the ground and grabbed at his trousers leg, pulling him off balance.

"Eee, she'll tear mu trousers, mu good trousers she'll tear!"

As he cried out in disbelief Zilla escaped his grip, and so he turned and began lashing Rebecca with the strap as she lay under his feet. Zilla pounced back, pushed him forward from behind, pulled Rebecca up off the pavement, and the two of them ran off to disappear around the corner. Abie stumbled over one of their shoes, a barely-there high-heeled curve of leather, and picked it up.

"Eee, the barsteds," I heard him cry, close to tears. "Don't come back to this 'ouse," he shouted along the street. "Uh don't want no *prostitutes* in my 'ouse." He ripped the shoe in two and threw the pieces after them, then stood there gasping for breath. "That'll show 'em, that'll teach 'em a lesson."

Several street doors had opened. "'Ere, what's going on, all this shouting this time of night, waking people up!" a gruff voice called out.

"Oo asked you to chime in?" Abie shouted back. "Keep your nose outta other people's business, y'... you barsted you, and y'... y'... your wife, there, uh'll, so 'elp me uh'll.... Go back to... to *bed,* that's... that's all you *deserve."* The door clicked closed, and the street was silent.

Lily waited outside the street door directly below me as he returned. "Where are they, what did you do you old *broch,* you? What, should they do never enjoy themselves, stay home and get bitter and twisted like you, you ignorant old barstard you?" She went back into the house, and from the stairway I heard her muttering, "Ugh, what a life, what a rotten stinking life!"

I hurried back into bed, and heard Abie in the kitchen remounting the leather belt onto the squeaking pulley. The floorboards creaked, the living room door closed and it became strangely quiet. I lay there a long time, and intermittently jumped as shouted words drifted up from downstairs, but I was tired out and must have finally fallen asleep. When I awoke suddenly one more time all was silent, and I assumed Zilla and Rebecca were now home and in bed.

Next morning when Mum called me for school, I came down as soon as I heard Abie leave the house for work.

"The girls didn't come back last night, God knows where they are, they could be murdered for all I know. Eat your breakfast, quick, you'll be late for school."

All day at school I wondered where my two sisters were. We would read about it in *The News Of The World* on Sunday: *MILE END WOMEN MURDERED IN DARK ALLEY. Father drives his two daughters out of house in the middle of the night, then murderer kills them. Father arrested, put in prison for the rest of his life. Judge says he has to be lashed every day with sewing machine belt.*

That afternoon I walked home from Coopers College to find Jack waiting on the door-step. "I've written down the names of the things you left on the landing so there's no chance I can accidently cheat," he said.

The experiment! With all the commotion last night I'd totally forgotten about our plan!

"So, I could tell when I woke up this morning the experiment went very well," he continued. "Did you hear any sounds in the night, anything at all? Did you stay in bed the whole time or did you look outside the door?"

I was too ashamed to tell him about Abie. Really, I just wanted to know if Zilla and Rebecca had come home. "No," I said, "nothing, I didn't hear anything... it... it was all quiet." Then, compounding my own discomfort, I added: "I stayed in bed."

"I knew it! There are only noises and things when it isn't running smoothly. Here's the list, what my astral body saw," and he handed me the piece of paper. On it was written: *One comb; one empty bag from Bassett's Licorice Allsorts, one book, one triangular piece of dark cloth suitable for a cape.* He looked at me intently. "Well?"

"Well, I didn't have a comb, but the other three are right."

"They are? Really?" He was ecstatic. "Three out of four right! You see? I told you my astral body would actually be there. We'll have to tell Manny. This is important information."

"I meant to put a comb there also, but I couldn't find it." I was sweating. "My sisters keep using it."

"You see? I wrote down 'comb' first of all, but I got a funny feeling about it. Four out of four! It's pretty obvious my astral body theory is absolutely correct. I knew it was correct anyway, but it's always useful to have proof."

—o—O—o—

12

"We have to take care of Lucy Greenspan," said Manny. "It's time."

"What do you mean?"

"Well, every time I go to Johnny Isaacs she's bothering me."

"Bothering you?"

"Yes, she's a pain in the bum, coming over all the time."

"I don't know, I s'pose she likes you, I mean, I don't mind her coming over, she seems okay to me... isn't she?"

"Well, she's alright I s'pose, but when a girl likes you you can't just ignore it, you have to show 'em you don't even care."

"Really?"

"You have to make 'em suffer, otherwise they'll... well, they...."

"Why is that, I mean, what would happen if...?"

"Well, otherwise they'll start making up stuff, they'll be telling people you like *them,* and by that time it's too late because they've gone mad."

"You mean *really* mad, like in a lunatic asylum?"

"Some of 'em. The two of us will have to do this together. I've worked out a plan, and it'll be good practice. For Lucy this is the easiest way."

"You mean, it'll stop her from *really* going mad."

"I've got the stuff over my house." We walked toward Manny's house on Antill Road. "My mother won't be back for an hour, we have time to get everything ready without Mum finding out."

"What are we going to do?"

"We're going to tell Lucy we had a fight over her. We'll both be so bandaged up we'll barely be able to move."

"So how... I mean, what will that do, how will it...?"

"When she realizes we're taking the mickey she'll be too embarrassed to ever come near us again."

"I... see... well, actually I don't really *mind* her coming near us, near me, I mean, talking, well, oh! I don't know...."

"Wait in the living room, I'll bring the supplies in."

It was the first time I'd been let inside Manny's house, and he ushered me into the living room. The furniture looked tidy and highly polished — and in the corner stood a baby grand piano!

"Can I look at the piano?"

"Well don't open it, don't touch it, my mother gets wild if someone touches it."

"I wondered… if I could just play just one note, that's all."

"Well, be quick while I get the stuff, then close it before my Mum comes home."

Amid the odor of furniture polish I lifted the dark shining lid, and there sat the long row of beautiful yellowing ivory keys, the narrower, higher black ones sandwiched between. Slowly I depressed one key. About halfway through its descent it resisted; I pushed through the detent and it continued all the way to the bottom. It hadn't produced any sound, so I let it it pop back up then pressed it down again, faster. This time a sonorous tone floated out of the oak cabinet. Again I depressed the key, this time in concert with another white one two places to its left, which I knew from my book would produce the combination called a third. Sure enough, two clear tones soared from under the lid and resonated against each other as they voyaged across the room. Holding my thumb and third finger two white keys apart I played a climbing sequence of thirds, and mere words on a page were now become visceral. Because only *some* white notes had a black key between them, these chaste differences swirled around my head, bouncing off the walls in a voluptuous intermingling, and I felt as though I might faint.

"Uuuuugh!" A long scream — and in the doorway stood Manny's mother. "What's he doing to Ronnie's piano, ugh, you… you… animal you, out of my house!" She was shrieking, her eyes open wide like a ferocious animal's. Suddenly her voice changed, as if she would cry: "Emmanuel, where are you, how could you do this to me?" Now she was almost pleading, "To your own mother you do this, I turn my back and this is what I get!"

Manny came running in from the back of the house carrying a big paper bag. "Sorry Mum, I, we just came back, to get something, we're leaving, he just wanted to play one note…."

"One note?"

"I said no he shouldn't…."

"One note? One note! Hundreds of notes he was playing, *thousands* of notes! Out, out, both of you out, this instant," and to me directly, "you *animal,* you!"

We circled around her into the passageway.

"Emmanuel, I'll speak to you later about this!"

"Alright Mum, I'll be back, I'm sorry, I'll be back."

We escaped out the street door, and the lock clicked immediately behind us.

"You shouldn't have played it."

"I… just a few notes."

"I said don't play it, my mother gets wild."

"I didn't know she was coming home, you said an hour…."

"She came home early."

"Who plays it usually?"

"Nobody, my Dad used to play it, since he died my Mum doesn't want anyone to touch it."

"I hope you won't get in trouble now."

"I won't be able to bring you round anymore, she'll remember. C'mon, we better keep all this stuff in your Anderson shelter 'til this evening."

"Show me."

"I'm lucky she never looked inside." He opened the bag to show pieces of white linen, four or five rolls of bandages, a scissors, and at the bottom a cluster of safety pins.

"What would she have done if she'd seen you taking the stuff?"

"I dunno, she wouldn't talk to me for a few days, maybe. Anyway, we'll need some long pieces of wood, also."

"What for?"

"Crutches."

That evening we retrieved the stuff from the Anderson and took it to Tredegar Square, just inside one of the normally unused entrances to the shelter. First Manny made a sling to put around my neck for my right arm, which was to be broken. Then I helped him bandage his left leg over his trousers, all the way from the ankle to above his knee. He hooked the end of that bandage back around his ankle so his left leg was bent up behind him. Now the only way he could get along was to hop on his right foot. He leaned against the wall while I went outside and found a solid piece of branch he could use as a crutch. He also had me bandage his whole face and head so that only his eyes, mouth and nostrils showed. Finally, I placed my arm in my new sling, and we were ready.

Suspended within our surgical raiment the two of us hobbled through the park to Mile End Road. It was necessary to cross to the other side for the bus. Manny hopped around and waved his homemade crutch piteously at the oncoming traffic, which swerved and stopped in deference to our distress.

A trollybus appeared and we signaled it to stop. The conductor climbed down to help us board. "Give these men that seat!" he ordered a woman sitting in the closest cross-seat. She relinquished the seat, and after we'd eased ourselves down and the conductor had signaled the driver, the bus pulled very gently away.

I was extremely embarrassed by our display, but for Manny this was just the beginning. He began making up Russian-sounding words, speaking in a penetrating voice.

"Vrishky slomensk predilsky omfartabrochelsky."

"Yes," I agreed, quietly.

"Habronskikoff lucygreenspanovich popofelsky." Then, at a higher volume he added "Brochfaceyanklewitz and maudyoskograd rubyfotzberger," simultaneously smiling sweetly to counter any intention the conductor might have had to throw us off the bus as a couple of frauds.

"Not so loud, sshh!" I whispered. Other passengers looked our way, torn between solicitousness and disbelief.

"'Ow far y' goin', mateys?" asked the conductor.

"Two three-'a'pennies, please," I began.

"Offbroskivilevich hexahydrotrinitrotolueneglycolovich!" shouted Manny.

"Righto, mate," accommodated the conductor; he gave us our tickets and stepped away to begin climbing the stairs to the upper deck.

"Manny, I don't know...." I whispered.

"Oh — No!" Manny roared, and the conductor and the entire complement of passengers spun around to see what had happened. Nothing, of course — and now his face wore only a simple, cherubic smile.

"Manny, shut up or I'll have to get off!" I mumbled.

"We're nearly there, anyway. This was just a test."

"Well, don't do anymore then."

"You mustn't let other people's reactions affect you." If it were possible to further compound my embarrassment, he now spoke in a normal voice, in total disregard of being overheard. "Just do it as if you're acting in a picture and you're saying your lines, and the people watching are also just acting."

At Whitechapel, the conductor let us get off by ourselves, where, according to our respective afflictions, we staggered slowly across the broad pavement toward Johnny Isaacs. Near the doorway stood Lucy Greenspan and several other people who regarded us as they moved out of our way.

Lucy peered more intently, then her eyes widened. "Manny?" She hesitated. "Manny? Is that you, Manny?"

We had by now shuffled through the doorway to the brightness inside Johnny Isaacs, and the door had closed. Mrs. Isaacs and the several helpers behind the counter stopped serving, and everybody's eyes clamped on our misfortune as we joined the end of the queue. Lucy had followed us inside and now Manny looked her way, his bandaged mouth moving as though he were still trying to respond to her question.

"My God, what happened?" she asked. Then, stepping back, she repeated uncertainly, "*Is* it you, Manny?"

Several times the mouth behind the bandages opened and closed piteously, producing no sound.

She seemed appalled. "Manny, what happened?"

I could scarcely bear the pain of Lucy's torture, though I knew we had a responsibility to go through with the plan. People ahead of us had moved aside to allow us faster service, and Manny hung onto the high counter rail and signaled with his stick for Lucy to come closer. She held her ear by his mouth. "It was a matter of... of..." he wheezed, unable to complete the sentence.

"What, what was it, are you alright?"

"...matter of... of... honor," he coughed.

"Honor? What do you mean, honor? Are you alright?"

He moved his head my way, becoming suddenly articulate: "Zachary, you'd better tell her. Come on," he gasped, "you might as well tell her the whole truth."

"No, I can't do it, you're going to have to tell her. I mean, you told the police everything, including... including... you know...." Fabricating a story sufficient to justify our considerable injuries was an onus I preferred remain on Manny's imaginative shoulders.

He hesitated again, and some who had stepped aside began ordering their fish and chips anyway. Manny started to explain — nearly — then seemed to resolve not to speak of it; then immediately prepared again to begin, his mouth discernibly open behind the bandage — but apparently, No. With each seeming commencement Lucy leaned closer in anticipation, only to halt, suspended on his next choice. This charade of reciprocal feintings and bobbings continued for a preposterous number of minutes, the queue wending its way around us. Then his shoulders dropped and resolution visibly weakened: "Alright, I'll tell you then." He gathered himself. "First, get two orders of chips for us, and we'll wait at a table." He shoveled the pennies he held into her hand, and I did the same. Then he added: "We'll both share one piece of haddock." He nodded his head slightly in my direction. "Is half a piece of haddock enough for you?"

"I suppose so." My response was in as melancholy a tone as I could muster, but I was disconcerted by his request for fish; my fourpence, which I'd just handed her, would only pay for chips. I'd been certain he'd given her only fourpence, too.

Lucy took our place in the line. With me following, Manny retreated to a table by the wall, knocking over an empty chair *en route,* and in an agonized largo took his seat.

"I only had fourpence, that's not enough for haddock also," I said. "How much did you give her?"

"Fourpence also. She's got money."

"But… but that's like… almost like stealing, isn't it?"

"It's not stealing, she's in love with me." He placed his crutch across the table. With difficulty he maneuvered his bandaged head to look around the shop, the arc of his gaze prompting staring patrons to return to their private conversations.

Lucy came over with three orders. Careful not to exacerbate Manny's plight, she sat adjacent to his side of the table. "So what happened? Are you really alright?" She unrolled the three packages and slid the one with fried haddock in front of him. Then, looking across at me, "Both of you! What was it, it must have been terrible!"

Manny broke the fish in two and placed half on my newspaper. "Want any?" He leaned toward Lucy, but she shook her head. He began forcing chips through the bandaged hole exposing his mouth. In tandem, with my usable left arm I shoveled my chips in too. Manny ate furiously, attacking the fish with a gusto that seemed to me not wholly appropriate for a recuperating patient.

"So what happened? Did you go to hospital?"

Manny looked at her, at me, then back down to the remnants of his meal. "It isn't easy for a man to admit this," he said, a piece of batter swinging from a cotton thread by his mouth.

I wanted to help her, but lacking Manny's expertise in relationships I had no recourse but to follow his lead. "Manny's right, I have to agree with him, it isn't easy to admit it all." I continued eating; we never could afford fried fish, so this unexpected ancillary to his plan was most welcome.

"Alright, I'll tell you, I'll tell you everything, but first let's finish the food. I haven't been able to eat in three days, and Zachary hasn't eaten in two days." The head rotated toward me. "Is it one day or two days?"

"Two days."

We finished the haddock, and he began. "You ought to know this already — girls are supposed to sense these things without being told."

"What things?"

"You don't know?" He backed away reprovingly.

"Please, Manny, tell me what it is. I'd tell you if I knew what you mean. Please?"

It was hard to believe she was taking it all seriously, and I was beginning to wish she would smash him over the head with her handbag and just walk away. But maybe she was in love with him, and maybe there's nothing you can do to save yourself when you're in love.

"Alright, I'll have to tell you the obvious, then." A tongue circled, scooping up shreds of fish. "Zachary and I…" he hesitated "…are… in love… with you."

"What?"

"Both of us."

"What!?"

"Didn't you hear? We're in love with you, both of us."

"Wha'd'ya mean? Come on, really?" She looked at me. "With me? *Both* of you?"

"Both of us," he said. "We've argued about you for weeks now, ever since Zech came home from the country."

"For weeks? Why did you argue? I don't know what you mean. Both of you? What do you mean, argue?"

"Well, I told him about you, then last week you came over, and that did it."

"I...."

"How do you think we got these injuries?"

"I don't know!"

"Manny, just tell her!" The words blurted out of their own accord. Even if we needed to inflict all this on Lucy, it was more than I could bear.

Manny, however, was made of stronger stuff. "We were both in such agony over you," he continued.

I could hardly bring myself to look at her.

"In the end," he went on, "we decided there was no alternative, we had to have a fight to settle which one of us would get you."

"You kidding?"

Manny eyed her as gravely as his bandages allowed. "No, we're not kidding. Lucy, sometimes I think you don't realize the power you have."

"Who, me?"

"Over men's emotions."

"Who, me? Really? Do I? No one ever... said... that." Her expression alternated between alarm and a nervous smile.

"D'you think it's easy to admit these things, especially to the woman I love, well... both of us love?"

She peered into his mummified slits and her mouth hung open. We became aware of people vacating their tables, and she closed her mouth. I looked at the clock on the wall: ten to ten.

"We'd better go outside," said Manny. "You'll have to hold me up. I'm so overwhelmed I can't walk." He put his right arm around Lucy's shoulder and she her left arm around his waist, while in his left hand he held his stick.

I deferred gallantly to her offer. "No, I'm alright thank you very much, I think I can manage."

Manny continued the saga as we lurched toward the door. "We decided the only thing left was to have a duel, and you'd have to go with the winner. Y'know, Zech and I we've been best friends since before the war, it wasn't easy fighting each other. Anyhow, we agreed that afterwards we'd go back to being best friends again."

"Manny... and Zachary Grossman? I had no idea...."

"We fought for one hour, and in the end they had to call the police to pull us apart. When he broke my leg I fell over and hit my face. I'll be scarred for life, hospital said."

"C'mon you're kiddin' me. I don't know if I believe you."

"A scar can be a badge of honor."

"Honor?"

"I'm proud of how I got it."

Someone held the door open for us, and we were outside. The earlier crowd had filtered into the darker perimeters, and a noisy mob of *yocks* was already coming up the wide pavement from the Empire. They looked at us contemptuously as they went through Johnny Isaacs' door.

"'Ey! Jewboys, 'oo bashed you up?" As fast as we were able, we hobbled away toward the curb. "Why'n'cha bollocks orf back where y' comes from, ay?"

They held the door ajar briefly for their group as more entered, a herd large enough that their queue extended outside on the pavement, all of them lined up behind a young man of swarthy complexion with dark hair, wearing a brown sweater — obviously Jewish — who alone had remained at the counter.

"They wouldn't act so tough if we weren't injured," whispered Manny.

From our vantage point in relative darkness close to the roadway, as the door flickered open and shut we could see into the shop. It was against the air-raid rules to let light shine out but they didn't seem to care too much. A skinny character with a pimply beetroot-red face, mean-looking, about six feet two inches tall and wearing a too-tight jacket, stepped out of the line and sidled to the front; as everyone watched he deliberately shoved the fellow in the sweater. The queue laughed and from the safety of the street we looked on in dread fascination. The sweater fellow turned and said something, at which the *yock* pulled himself up to full height until his jacket seemed ready to burst. Lucy gasped at me as I realized I'd involuntarily ripped off my arm sling.

"What?" she stuttered. "Your arm!"

Despite my untimely revelation, the attention of all three of us was drawn back to the shop where the greater drama was beginning to unfold. There, the sweater and the *yock* were facing off at each other as the rest of the queue backed away. Manny, on one foot for the entire evening, dropped his stick clattering to the ground and wobbled uncertainly. Lucy and I grabbed at him, but quietly so, in compensation for the racket of the falling stick. Somehow we couldn't quite grasp his clothes as he spiraled on his left foot, the right ankle still hooked up behind his knee. He teetered and I made a last futile grab but he fell, hitting his bandaged head on the pavement. Several people from the section of the queue crowding outside the door looked back at our shadowy commotion. Stunned, Manny said "Bollocks!" and sitting on the pavement he started tearing the bandages off his leg. Lucy choked in disbelief. I tried to help him up, but as his weight bore on his other leg and foot, probably by now totally numb, he staggered and fell over again.

Four or five men from the outside queue started toward us. In terror I grabbed Manny's arm and began dragging him along the pavement as Lucy ran off into the night. But once again the larger commotion beyond Johnny Isaacs' door compelled everybody's attention. People were scurrying from the entrance, and through that vaulted archway we witnessed a miracle: inside, the youth in the sweater was now walking toward the doorway, his extended arms holding captive above his head the tall skinny bully. The young man carried his flailing trophy through the scattering crowd, banged him through the doorway, then outside to the street. There, he half-turned in each direction as if to acknowledge silent accolades, bent his knees and hurled the man a good four yards into the darkened perimeter toward where Manny and I quaked in awe.

His victim lay winded on the pavement as the mob stared transfixed. Samson then turned around and quite incredibly strolled back into Johnny Isaacs, past the chastened queue and right up to the counter. The door was jammed open; nobody uttered a sound.

"One piece of haddock, fourpenceworth of chips, two pickled cucumbers." In the astounded silence his voice rang clear and true.

"Coming right up, sir!" beamed Mrs. Isaacs. Despite the distance from which Manny and I observed these proceedings, we could still appreciate the studied excess with which she filled the order and rolled it up in generous sheets of newspaper. "I've given you some pickled onions, also."

Before the stupefied mob our exemplar ambled over to a table, unwrapped the newspaper, sprinkled on salt and vinegar, wrapped it up again and walked calmly out of the shop, the nimbus of backlight from inside framing him within its halo.

His direction would take him right by Manny and me, both of us quivering with admiration and resolve. As he came closer he walked around his vanquished foe, now kneeling, muttering and brushing off his clothes in the diminished light from the still-opened door. Then he strolled on in our direction, ever closer, and spotted us in the darkness.

"Excuse me…" I started.

"Shut up!" His voice was extraordinarily commanding.

"Excuse me, that was incredible…."

In a flash he turned, grabbed my jacket lapels and swung me around and down toward Manny, who was still sitting on the pavement. With the same fist he was also able to grab Manny's lapels. He lifted us both up to standing, and then practically off the pavement. He was holding us up, both of us, with just one hand; his fish and chip package he held in the other. And as that hand pulled both our faces abruptly close to his face, from somewhere beyond the periphery of blackness we heard Lucy scream. I could feel his heavy breath; he had bushy eyebrows and his nose was bent to one side, a wart on the outside curve.

"Fuck off or I'll kill the both of you," he said, and thrust us violently away. I staggered back and managed to retain my balance; Manny fell over a third time, and the young tough strutted off into the night.

Lucy materialized, and again we helped Manny up.

"Why did he do that?" I asked. "I only wanted to tell him it was marvelous, what he did."

"Those bullies, they're all stupid. He thought we were *yocks*." Manny was brushing himself off. "All the Jewish kids left already. I've seen him doing gym at the Brady Boys Club. We'd better get out of here."

"Boy, was he tough!"

"I could'a handled him if I didn't have pins and needles in my leg," said Manny.

Lucy's voice sounded broken. "Why did you do this, Manny? If you… wanted me, you didn't have to make up a whole story."

"You wouldn't understand, anyway. Women don't have any idea what it's like to be a man, the responsibility." He turned to me. "C'mon, we'd better go home."

"You gonna walk me home? Both of you can walk me home."

"Well, my mother said I have to be home by eleven. How about you, Zech?"

"My mother said I have to be home by eleven also."

"So, we're late already from all this."

Evening buses back to Mile End were infrequent, and the two of us began walking.

"Phew! What a night!" I said.

"Christ, it was a pretty close call."

"If the fellow from the Brady Boys Club hadn't done what he did, those *yocks* would have killed us, that bunch coming over to the curb," I conjectured.

"I would've taken care of that four, but then the others would have started. I s'pose we were outnumbered."

"There must have been forty of 'em there," I said.

"And what'll we do about Lucy Greenspan now?"

He was asking me? "I know, I don't know, really, I thought that would take care of it, your plan...."

"It got a bit mixed up, what with the *yocks.*"

"Maybe she'll forget...." I tried.

"No... aren't girls different? They never forget things like that... do they?"

He was asking *me* about girls! I tried to help. "If she says anything maybe we can make out we don't know what she's talking about."

"You think...?" he responded tentatively.

Warming to the position of sage, I suggested: "We can say we weren't even at Johnny Isaacs this evening, she must have imagined the whole thing."

"Yes?" He reflected. "You think that would work?"

I didn't want to appear presumptuously knowledgeable. "Girls are mysterious aren't they, you never can tell the way they think about stuff...."

"That's what I said, they'll make you barmy if you let 'em."

"So, we can just insist we weren't even there."

"Yeah...." Manny pondered my solution. "Yes, we'll do it. She is mad. Just like Lucy Greenspan to make up something like this."

–13–

The Germans had regularly dispatched their manned bombers in squadrons, for mutual protection. When the siren sounded the *Alert,* Nazi aeroplanes would quickly release their bombs and then zoom back over the English Channel to safety. Between these raids came brief periods of respite — sometimes a couple of hours, perhaps even a full day — affording the civilian populace some surcease. But with the introduction of the V-1 flying-bombs the Germans embarked on a new strategy, launching the pilotless vehicles over the English Channel one at a time in sustained succession, virtually round the clock. This mode of onslaught was calculated to engender unremitting anxiety, since it became difficult for us to remember at any particular moment whether the air-raid status was *Alert* or *All Clear.*

Coastal Command strove to develop countermeasures against this new weapon. As soon as radio-location detected a flying-bomb approaching the coastline, the RAF dispatched a Gloucester Meteor, a Hurricane or a Spitfire to intercept it. The pilot would fly his fighter alongside and carefully maneuver closer until the V-1's wingtip overlapped his. Flying thus in conjunction, the British pilot would ease his stick to the opposite side, whereupon his rising wing would actually nudge the flying-bomb's wingtip upward, disorienting the vehicle's gyroscopic control and causing it to roll over and plummet downward. Depending on where this critical maneuver was executed, the doodle-bug would plunge and explode either in the Channel waters, or in the relatively unpopulated approaches of Kent and Southern England. V-1s that survived this gauntlet to reach London were simply left to crash where they would, saving the populace from the additional trauma of spent anti-aircraft shells falling to earth.

• • •

In Mile End the sirens now sounded so frequently that Lily decided we should move our blankets and belongings down into the air-raid shelter tunnels under Tredegar Square park and sleep there regularly. Manny's mother, Mrs. Yanklewitz, had reached the same conclusion, and Manny took a bunk head-to-head with mine. For me the war was turning into one long holiday: I'd be spending entire nights with my best friend!

During the raids some electrical facility might be struck, and the lights would dim or go out completely, sometimes for hours. Manny and I brought our technical expertise to bear on this problem. From a public war-effort box we retrieved two discarded round food tins of slightly different diameters. With a tin-opener we cut off the metal tops and inverted the larger tin over the smaller. A hole punched in the top, then Abie's heavy beading cord threaded through, the bottom can filled with paraffin, a match, and lo! here was a lamp immune to the vicissitudes of fluctuating electric supply. We carried this prototype down the shelter, and the next time the electricity failed, Manny's and my location was the only illuminated area.

Our fame percolated through to other sections of the shelter's labyrinth, and orders for our technological brainchild quickly followed. The next day we scrounged several more tins and manufactured a full dozen units. At threepence each, they sold fast that evening. Late that night when the electric lights duly flickered and died, paraffin lamps peppered on along the twisting tunnels. In a rare moment of accord, Mum and Mrs. Yanklewitz basked in regal acknowledgement of their offsprings' genius.

A couple of hours later I was awakened by the sound of Marius's hawking cough. The shelter air hung heavy with black soot, making breathing difficult. Manny and I jumped up simultaneously: the paraffin lamps! More people woke up coughing, babies were crying, and soon the entire shelter population was forced to evacuate up the steps and out onto the damp grass. And there, clients now shivering in the night air who only two or three hours earlier had extolled our ingenuity, were quick with castigations.

"What should we do?" whispered Manny.

"We'd better give them their money back, maybe they won't be so wild."

He ran with me across to our house and down into the Anderson shelter where we'd stashed the receipts. We grabbed a big shopping bag, then zipped back to Tredegar Square. Perhaps as many as a hundred and twenty people stood shaking in the two A.M. September cold, some holding blanket-wrapped babies. By dim starlight the two of us wandered through the crowd making refunds. Periodically, while Manny held the bag, I descended the flight of steps into the shelter to check the air quality, which seemed to be taking an inordinate time to improve.

"I didn't think they would make so much smoke," I confided to Manny.

Holding the bag of returned lamps that now reeked of dripping paraffin, Manny tried to be consoling. "I suppose when you invent something new you run the risk of people wanting to kill you if it doesn't work right."

I tried rapidly opening and closing the entrance door to fan some kind of a breeze, as the minutes ticked on toward two-thirty. Eventually I was able to call up the steps, "It's starting to clear!" Preferring the risk of asphyxiation to freezing, the expatriates began winding back down the steps.

Finally, Manny and I stood alone on the grass in the silken silence of the night. No distant explosions, no popping of anti-aircraft shells, no tracer bullets arching across the sky. The starry peacefulness was almost enough to assuage the failure of our business venture.

"Emmanuel, downstairs, to bed!" Mrs. Yanklewitz called up from the shelter entrance below.

"Alright Mum, I'll be right down." Then to me, "It'll be light in a few hours."

The two of us started down the steps that descended between the brick and concrete slab side walls. Manny, ahead of me, had just reached the bottom and was groping for the door handle for entry into the shelter tunnel proper when a flash of white light seared the walls, the door, the back of his head and his extended arm in a brilliance so overwhelming that everything was washed out, colorless, fragmented. Simultaneously, around us there erupted a stupendously loud explosion; the steps and walls swayed and the door was wrenched away from Manny's hand and flung wide open. A blast of pressure compressed my ears, leaving only a muffled ringing. From the visible strip of sky above the stairwell came the flaring alternation of reds and yellows, blossoming into what had to be hazed reflections of huge, turbulent fires. Then, even before I had time to absorb these impressions, a blast of hot choking air rolled down the steps, enveloping us in smoke and dust that mingled with the powdered and chipped cement jarred from the shaking walls. Screams and shouts came from inside the shelter. Though my sight had barely returned I tried looking inside; the dim lights had remained on and people stood in odd arrested postures, steadying themselves against bunk frames from which they'd either just jumped or been thrown. Amid the tumult and yet apart from it, Manny and I stood in the door-frame; and I realized my hearing had returned when a deep, full-throated celestial roar like pealing thunder began rolling slowly across the sky, obliterating all the shouts and cries.

He and I raced up the steps to the grass above. The inevitable bitter taste of exploded powder quickly seared the tongue and eyes, and a pall of airborne grit hung between us and the brightness of fires raging diagonally across the street. As the last of the thunderous reverberations diminished up into the heavens, the impact of falling masonry and crunching glass began its inevitable accompaniment. And as quickly as the whole spectacle had begun, so the rain of returning debris diminished to sporadic clinks and thumps. Hushed billowing eddies of dust and smoke rolled over the devastated landscape. In the distance the bells of ambulances and fire engines already rose up to invade the now ghostly quiet.

Voices, men's voices from the distance of the fires proved Manny and I were not the sole survivors in the above-ground world. Neither had we been hurt, though covered from head to foot with whitish powdery dust, nor even stunned other than by the surprise of proximity. Massive fires — much too intense to be the conflagration of only a house or two — burned to our left along Morgan Street. As Manny and I adjusted to their iridescence, and as our fear of subsequent explosions abated, we each began to grasp the implications of the devastation's locale before us. For me at least, an improbable miracle had come to pass: where Coopers College stood — the *late* Coopers College — were now burning skeletons of walls, shattered glass, buckled floors and fallen roofs.

"A doodle-bug must have dived straight into Coopers College!"

"Your dream come true!" sang Manny.

"But I didn't hear the engine; and also, didn't the explosion sound funny? The reverberations, the other noise, it went on for such a long time! Like thunder!"

"I dunno, it sounded good to me, your school's gone, maybe you shouldn't be too fussy."

Clanging bells rose up and signaled the fire engines' arrival as we ran in the biting dust to the edge of the park and on into the street, clambering over the debris-strewn pavement. One structure, the science building where Joan Ingersall had lain so exquisitely on the floor the day she fainted, remained as a forlorn cadaver among the destruction, raging colors licking inside its sightless window frames. In the center of the playground, flames reflected the sawn rim of a deep crater.

Exhausted firemen climbed down from their perches, and Manny shouted: "Let it burn!"

"Can't do that, sonny, wish we could 'elp you," said one, spinning out a coil of hose.

We crowded closer, blundering over bricks, sliding on dust and freezing spray, the more intimately to savor the unexpected taste of my deliverance. The brunt of the blast must have been absorbed by the burning row-houses on the park side of Morgan Street, those fronting the school. Yet, adjacent houses lining the street to each side seemed to have borne the explosion in suspiciously resilient fashion, considering their proximity to the mayhem.

We made our way back along Morgan Street to my house, which not only still stood but looked as though nothing of note had occurred. Manny and I checked through the various rooms. The only damage seemed to be cracked glass in the upstairs landing window over the street door, though bits of plaster in the upstairs rooms had shaken down onto the beds. On to Manny's house in Antill Road and again no real damage, no surprise since his house was several streets removed. On our way through the living room I opened the freshly dust-sprinkled piano lid and in the dark room played one dramatic major chord. It still played! To celebrate its survival I held the keys down, and at the top of my voice, with an operatic gusto appropriate to the drama of the demise of Coopers College, I sang *Mis-sus Yank-le-witz* eight times, once on each pitch of an ascending C-scale, doh to doh.

Back down the shelter we were returned to relative normalcy, braving the gauntlet posed by the row of earlier paraffin-lamp returnees, all of whom except for Lunch-Box Nose seemed, in light of their deliverance, to have granted us absolution. We were able to announce that 27 Morgan Street and 14 Antill Road were still standing — and, incidently, that I wouldn't need to get up for school in the morning.

Actually, I did get up for Coopers College — and joyously so, even if not in quite the sense that Mr. Hutchinson would have approved. I was there at six A.M. with Manny to confirm in the burgeoning light of day our exultant expectations. The entire school except for the science building had been reduced to rubble. It seemed appropriate that if one building were to be preserved, monument-like, it should be the skeleton of Joan Ingersall's science building.

The sun rose triumphantly over the wreckage to disclose a massive crater, perhaps thirty feet across, freshly adorning the center of the 'til now clique-ridden playground. As the sun's rays encroached deeper into the hole, retreating shadows depicted almost perpendicular interior walls, as though something had plunged vertically through the asphalt at unimaginable speed to explode underground, its depth directing the blast upward in tight focus to sculpt a sharp rim. Of one thing I was sure: this was no doodle-bug gently gliding in, nor even diving.

That evening on the BBC six o'clock news, Richard Dimbleby announced that during the night an electric generating station had exploded. We'd been hearing such descriptions of isolated exploding generating stations more and more frequently, and now I knew them to be a fiction. Some secret weapon had lain Coopers College low, and for some reason the news readers weren't being permitted to divulge the truth.

I talked to Jack about it that evening as he, Manny and I reconnoitered the scene. Jack's explanation came quickly.

"It's probably some form of projection, maybe even astral projection, where the Germans can place the explosive anywhere they want without actually going there physically."

Staggering! I hadn't been particularly convinced by Jack's talk of astral projection, but this idea could pull the parts together — particularly when it produced such promising results. It did seem reasonable, considering we'd heard nothing, no bomb-delivering mechanism, prior to the explosion. We sat on our little wall to marvel at the implications of this reconciliation of higher consciousness with the mundane.

Some theories, however, are destined for brief tenure. Late next afternoon, sitting alone on the wall and reveling in the thrill of no more school, perhaps ever, a distant glint caught my eye. As I scoured the heavens for its location, from a great altitude there came a brilliant flash. Then, in the same area, a remote puff of smoke bloomed. Two and a half to three minutes later, still digesting these amazing phenomena, the sharp clap of a distant explosion ruptured the sky, followed immediately by a long muffled and billowing roar that seemed to roll over the houses and up into the heavens.

This incredible sequence called for some quick figuring. First, the speed at which light traveled: one hundred eighty-six thousand two hundred and eighty miles per second — fast enough that I could disregard that fraction of time and say that the explosion's flash occurred virtually the same instant its light reached my eye. Sound, however, was different; sound traveled at only seven hundred and twenty miles an *hour,* which reduced to twelve miles per *minute.* The *sound* of the explosion had arrived, say, three minutes after the flash. Three minutes at twelve miles per minute… was… thirty… six… miles! Goose-bumps rose on my skin at the numbers' implication. Using a stone on the pavement I scratched out mathematical confirmation: whatever had occurred up there, it had taken place thirty six miles distant, and at the apparent angle I'd seen it from the ground, it had happened at least *thirty miles high!* That was much higher than an ordinary aeroplane could ever fly — thirty miles high was nearly in space! Therefore — I'd probably witnessed the explosion of a space rocket!

I clasped the wall to regain my composure, then sprinted across Mile End Road to Jack's house. Jack had gone to the Brady Boys Club.

"Mrs. Pristein, tell Jack I saw a new secret space rocket! It's very important! He has to come round as soon as he comes home!"

Next I ran to Manny's house. Manny was out. "Mrs. Yanklewitz, tell Manny he has to come round as soon as he gets back, it's very important!"

"Get away you animal you, I don't want you near my house."

When Manny got back he did come round, so she probably told him anyway. While we waited for Jack, I put two and two together: it had been a rocket that demolished Coopers College the previous night. That explained the deep crater and the negligible blast damage, because the rocket had come straight down so fast it had buried itself deep into the ground before it even had time to explode, so the blast was buffered by the walls of its own crater and had been directed upward. Since the rocket's trajectory must have taken it at least a hundred miles high to be able to reach London from Europe, it must have actually been in space for a good part of its trip!

In space! Not only had my school been blown up, but blown up by something that had traveled through space! Manny had to help me sit down again. All the evidence was falling into place. That first glint I'd seen earlier this afternoon had been the sun reflecting off a rocket's casing while it was still in space. Then, as it fell back onto the top of the atmosphere maybe it didn't hit exactly nose first — perhaps askew like a diver's belly flop — and the impact wrenched it apart and it exploded up there. Oh, life was sweet!

Manny was impressed with my enthusiasm, but not so much with the reasoning. "Then what about the funny rolling thunder sound we heard last night after it'd gone off?"

That answer came viscerally; didn't he *know?* "If the rocket is getting here *faster* than the sound it's making gets here, the first thing… wait, give me a minute… the first thing you hear is the rocket's arrival, okay — you hear it explode. Then *after* that sound, you hear where it was a moment *earlier,* but you're *hearing* it *later.* Then after that bit of sound gets to your ear, you'd hear the sound of where it was a moment before that, etcetera, etcetera."

Manny was looking at me strangely and his head began to turn away, "What?" To him, I'd gone completely bonkers. That look, that instant was infinitely telling. Manny suddenly looked physically smaller, and I felt dizzy from an incredible sense of power, of… of —

station: Manny didn't understand how it all worked together! It wasn't spontaneously apparent to him, the explosion, the crater's vertical sides, the thunderous pealing across the skies! What had happened was a mystery because he didn't understand the parts; he couldn't come up with plausible explanations for each of the scenario's components, which he could then privately weigh and choose a most probable.

"So!" Under the circumstances, I granted myself permission to conclude my analysis using the more erudite terms I'd culled from *Relativity Made Easy*. "Since you don't hear these sounds in discrete pieces as I've described them, but rather as a continuum, you're really hearing the rocket's travel *backwards*. You're hearing it as though time is reversed."

Manny hesitated; he must have sensed in my confidence and language something hierarchical. "Let's go back to Coopers College and look. Maybe we can find a bit of shrapnel that's been in space. Would it be alright to touch something that's been in space?" he asked.

My new stature demanded magnanimity. "Yes, certainly it would be alright."

–14–

"Eee, Zachary, er, Zech, you'll come to The Lane with me, yeh?" Abie giggled sheepishly. "You'll 'ave a good time, we'll ride on a trollybus."

"You've got time now all the week for your own things, he wants you to help him carry home the cloth," said Lily. "Two private orders he got, for costumes, it's extra money."

"Yeh, eee good money, extra money we'll 'ave."

"Alright, Dad, yes, alright."

Abie and I took the trollybus to Aldgate East, and from there walked to Petticoat Lane, where on Sunday mornings the shopkeepers brought their merchandise — housewares, gramophone records, secondhand suits, tailoring supplies — outside to the pavement to sell from covered stalls.

The crowds thickened as we drew closer, and for several streets Abie pushed ahead through the jostling crush. The shops mostly ran continuous on both sides of the streets, interrupted periodically by desolated sections of perhaps three or four shop-widths where bombings had destroyed the old structures. These collapsed areas sometimes carried across to adjacent streets, and were largely heaped with old masonry, a twisted door incongruously locked in its frame, jagged slivers of white enamel with plumbing still attached.

We arrived at Abie's destination, a small doorway in the corner of a blank and pock-marked two-story wall around the side of a store. I followed him into a tight passageway, and single file we climbed dark stairs to the top. Light seeped below a door, which opened onto a dingy room illuminated by two bare bulbs hanging on wires from the ceiling. The panes in the sole window had been taped with large Xs as protection against shattering. The room was stacked high with bolts of cloth in several rows. Abie took out a packet of Woodbines and lit a cigarette.

A bent, bearded old man appeared from behind the stacks. He and Abie nodded to each other and began bargaining in Yiddish. Quickly, their voices were raised; from the little Yiddish I knew, the emphasis on *gelt* meant Abie didn't want to pay the man's price. Finally, Abie threw down his cigarette, stepped on it angrily, wiped the side of his nose with his thumb and grabbed my arm: "Alright, ugh!, it's no good 'ere," and pushed me out to the top of the stairway.

The old man limped to the door after us. "A minute, vait a minute."

The ritual that necessarily preceded a transaction might take a while. "Dad, can I wait in the street 'til you're ready?"

"Yeh, alright, wait downstairs, eee, be careful, uh won't be long, in a few minutes uh'll be there."

Downstairs and out, I was immediately caught up in the skirmish of merchants and shoppers. I wished I had money for the half-sour cucumbers nodding in open-ended hooped wooden barrels of pickling spices, or for the cheesecake, the smoked salmon, perhaps a sandwich of saltbeef steaming on its wooden board. I watched an array of rainbowed garments swinging on pipe-frame racks, and the fresh-baked rye bread drawing itself back up to shape as a newly-cut slice curled away.

A woman ahead of me looked up to the sky — and gasped. Other people's gaze turned reflexively skyward, then more, their expressions turning to horror as panic engulfed the sea of upturned faces. Parents grabbed children, flung them down to the pavement. The rye bread bounced to the ground as its proprietor ducked under his stall. Like a rapidly flooding wavefront, the entire market's hundreds of occupants dropped to the ground, huddled against walls, pressed into corners. I looked up and there, just at the end of the street at an altitude of no more than fifty yards, a huge black flying bomb coasted above the stalls toward us, its engine silent. It was moving slowly, so slowly it certainly had to stall and crash before the end of the street where I stood awestruck.

Suddenly aware that I was the only person standing, I crouched down under a corner of the stall where I could still study the incredible visitor. Oval bolt heads stood in precise relief where the wings and tail were joined to the fuselage. On the leading edge of the large pipe that housed the now-dormant jet engine was a rectangular grill; that had to be where air, forced in by the plane's momentum, was mixed with fuel, then heated by combustion, with the expanded air and fire forcing itself out the back. That meant the grill had to open and close at an incredibly rapid rate, acting like a one-way valve so the reactive pressure of the heated air was only directed backwards! Isaac Newton: action and reaction!

"Get your head under!" The man next to me crouching beneath the stall pulled me back down. He looked into my face: "What are you, some kind of a maniac? Keep down!"

"I just... I just... I never saw one so close...."

"Tsk, Tsk!" He shook his head.

A woman, further under and behind me, said, "Stay under, stay under, where's your mother? Quick, is she under somewhere?"

The doodle-bug's square-tipped wings now embraced the full width of the roadway, glinting black against a soft blue sky festooned with wispy white clouds. It whistled softly as it floated lower and lower, at once directly above our heads, then gently on toward the row of houses that crossed at a perpendicular the far end of the street. The apparition seemed to take forever to reach that line of roofs, and now seemed so low that it would inevitably strike them midway. But somehow it cleared the crest by inches, its left wingtip toppling a chimney pipe that clattered down the roof and smashed to the ground while the plane sailed on and beyond, lowering itself majestically out of sight. The people crouched with me under the flimsy stall were clenched down, girded. Three or four seconds more of absolute silence — then the roofs capping the far row of houses peeled off in a left-to-right sequence, curling gracefully up into the sky. Like a line of toy balloons, the scalped houses puffed themselves up, and burst. Window frames, doors and furniture were launched skyward and sailed their arcing trajectories. Debris began raining from the sky, a dull thump here, a skidding crash there, to rapidly mushroom into a veritable cataract. People screamed, covered their heads with their arms, pulled children deeper under them. The deluge of wreckage was falling into a vast white cloud of dust blossoming around us. I stood up into this exotic storm and watched it gradually diminish to an odd scattering of residual *bangs* and *clinks*. Billows of choking dust pushed eerily along the roadway, enveloping overturned stalls, muffling the moaning and screaming to a ghostly babble. Slowly, as the sound level multiplied from what had been a silent abstracted picture, shouts began falling into coherence. The man who'd pulled me down now stood dust-covered next to me; absentmindedly he tried to right an overturned stall askew in a sea of smashed bottles, and I helped him bounce it back onto its sprung wheels and legs. He choked in the sotted air, which like a smothering parchment now overlay the street. In the distance, the familiar ringing of fire-engine and ambulance bells began crowding up.

Maybe my eardrums had been broken, but this time I actually had not heard the explosion, and even now all the wailing seemed distant and unrelated. I helped out from under our stall the woman who had spoken to me earlier; her clothes were completely white, but she seemed uninjured. Another woman sat disbelieving on the curb, holding a blood-soaked handkerchief to the side of her head. I touched her shoulder and took out my handkerchief, kneeled, and held it to the bloodied face. Then I remembered: Abie! Was he all right, what had happened? What about the flimsy building I'd left him in? I began to push through the stunned crowds in the direction of the building, the wall, the stairs, the room, closer to where the bomb had actually exploded behind the row of houses. It was difficult to breathe; the air was thick with acrid fumes of burned explosive, pungent enough to immobilize my tongue. Lying in the roadway face down was a thickset shirtsleeved man, a white apron twisted up and around his neck; two men rolled him over, but his bloodied form seemed lifeless. By his head, a brilliant crimson pool clotted the thick ivory dust on the roadway. Dead — that was what a dead person looked like. That was what those two bodies on the back of that lorry in Banbury would have looked like were it not for the flapping white sheet. Supposing Abie were dead! It was entirely possible that at this moment Abie was already dead. What would 27 Morgan Street be like, what would our lives be like with Abie gone? Would Mum be secretly relieved? Or would she curse herself for the countless times, when he was safely alive, she'd wished him dead?

I stumbled on, and there ahead on the pavement he stood among the bricks and dust, dazed, embracing his big roll of cloth. Shards of broken glass lay around him, his dark blue coat now a light dirtyish grey. Closer, and he looked aged — it must have been the dust on his face and eyelashes, the whitened hair.

He didn't seem surprised that I was uninjured. "Eee, *oy a broch,* can you believe it? Eee, uh could 'ave been killed, you, you could 'ave been killed!"

I grasped the other end of the roll, and with him in front we hoisted it onto our shoulders. He steered through the debris, picking his way around huddled clusters of people kneeling, moaning. Glass crunched under our feet as we stepped through empty rectangles. A small dazed group partially obstructed our passage: "Eee, move, y' bladdy fool," he said, pushing someone with the roll of cloth. As the man fell away, I saw that a disfigured body lay in the roadway, hair matted with chalky dust, a vivid cartoon-like contrast of bright red blood over its face and shirtfront. Where the upper legs should have been was now a bloody mix of fabric and intestines; both the shoes had been ripped off and lay at odd angles in the littered landscape. A cloth cap lay nearby, a soft cloth cap, the type that *yockisher* laborers wore.

"Come on, already." Abie was lunging ahead, the bolt of cloth pulling me forward. Coming toward us, an ambulance gingerly picked its way around debris that cluttered the roadway.

"Just a minute, Dad, it's heavy."

"Tsk! What do we wanna stay 'ere for, what's the good, it's no good 'ere, you'll rest at 'ome, you'll be alright."

Two women in uniform jumped down from the ambulance's cab. The ring of men parted. "'E's a gonner, missus," said one.

The taller ambulance woman kneeled and lay her ear to the prone chest. "Someone get me a towel and water!" she called. A woman in a kerchief watching from over by the curb disappeared into a windowless shop and emerged with a towel and a dish of water.

"Quick, *oy a broch,* already, what's a matter with 'im already!" Abie yanked the roll of cloth, and it slipped forward off my shoulder. I tried to catch it but it fell to the ground, almost pulling me down with it. "'Old it, 'old it already, 'e'll ruin mu cloth, an idiot, a... a... *shvunce melumid!"*

I looked again at the cloth cap lying forlorn in the roadway, and against some inexplicable resistance forced myself to step off the pavement and pick it up. A grey cloud of dust drifted off as I smacked it sharply against my side: it looked something like the brownish plaid cap Manny sometimes doffed for a joke. Through a rising panic I walked the couple of steps toward the kneeling ambulance woman to hand her the cap. She had wiped the obscuring blood from the white face, though a fresh crimson stream continued to ooze from the parted lips; the brown eyes were open but unmoving, the alabaster cheeks round and a little pudgy. Suddenly the left arm jerked, the soft bent fingers scraping against a clump of cemented bricks that lay skewed alongside.

I bent closer to the unknowing face.

"Pick up the fu–uckin' cloth already, what does 'e want over there!"

"It looks like Manny! Is it Manny?"

"What's that?" asked the ambulance woman.

"I... I... I.... It... might be Manny!"

"Sonny, do you know who this is?"

"It's Manny, it's Manny, Dad, it's Manny!"

"Excuse me son, are you able to identify the body, this... person?"

"It's his hat, this is it, his cap...." I was holding Manny's cap! "It's Manny's cap! He only wore it for a joke."

"It's alright, sonny, calm down, everything'll be alright."

"But it's Manny, it looks exactly like Manny...."

"Sonny, you could help us if you could identify...."

"What about his mother, what should we do, someone'll have to tell his mother...."

"What, what, what, wha'cha saying there, Manny? 'Ow can it be Manny? Nah!, 'e don't know what 'e's sayin', we came 'ere to buy the cloth, the roll...."

"Young man, do you know who this... this person is?"

"Yes, yes...."

"It's alright now...." Someone was holding my arm. "Sonny, would you be able to positively identify the body?"

"The body? It's Manny, it's my friend, he was round my house last night, he's coming over tonight after supper, we...." Manny, Manny! "Manny, it's my friend Manny, we'll have to tell his mother...."

Another ambulance was slowly picking its way around us and on along the debris-strewn roadway toward the wreckage at the end of the street.

The kneeling ambulance woman was talking. "I suppose this piece of masonry was the cause of death. I'd say it hit him squarely on the head, what do you think, Maude?"

Her companion nodded. "Yes, the other one, there" — she pointed at a smashed block of cemented bricks — "hit his knees."

"I'm sorry, sonny, if he was your friend. What's his surname? We'll need his surname, and his address."

"Manny? Eee, nah, you really think it's 'im? Nah, come on, come 'ome, get the other end of the roll, we'll go 'ome, you'll see, uh promise 'e's alright, 'e'll be there, nah, this isn't Man... Man... Manny, your friend Manny, nah!"

"Sir, let the boy give us the name and address."

I couldn't believe it. "What about his mother?"

"We'll arrange for a policeman to visit his mother and notify her... don't worry, we'll take care of everything."

"Yeh, don't worry, Zachary, they'll take care of it, she said, she just said they'll take care of it, everything, you don't 'ave to worry. We'll just go 'ome, what can we do, what can anybody do, 'e's finished, gone. Shame."

"Yanklewitz, Manny Yanklewitz, his house is at 14 Antill Road."

"And where is that? I'm sorry, sonny, it's a terrible thing for you to have to see. Where is Antill Road?"

"Mile End, it's in Mile End, you know, near Bow."

"Yes, we know, we'll find the house, try not to cry, just go home with your Dad."

"Alright then."

"We'll take care of everything. Don't tell his mother, let us, we can do it gently."

"Alright, then, thank you."

"'Ere, guv, let's give you an 'and." One of the men lifted up my end of the bolt of cloth, and as Abie picked the front end, the man eased it onto my shoulder. He patted me on the head. "We all 'as to be brave, sonny. We'll beat the old Jerry in the end."

The huge roll began pulling forward. I looked back; a stretcher was on the ground and some of the men were rolling him onto it. I wanted to go back, I didn't want to leave him there with all the people, strangers, they didn't even know him, how he said funny things always and deliberately embarrassed people.

Abie was pulling ahead, the heavy roll on my shoulder dragging me away. "Come on, ee, we gorra go 'ome, Lily, she'll be worried."

I'd have to tell Jack, the police wouldn't tell Jack. Izzy wouldn't believe it at first if I told him. Maybe I should ask Jack to tell him, then he'd believe it. It must have been the doodle-bug, the one I saw in such detail. How could science do something so terrible? Just three nights ago we were both so glad about Coopers College, begging the firemen to leave it burn.

I realized we were standing at the bus stop now, with the wailing of the *All Clear* descending to closure. "Dad, can I put it down?"

"...Yeh, eee, terrible, terrible, the barsteds, the German barsteds they are." Abie was talking to someone also waiting. "A boy, a young boy... 'is friend, yeh...."

In contrast with others in the queue I saw how covered with dust we were, and the roll of cloth, too. I brushed myself off as well as I could.

More ambulances were upon us as we boarded the bus, their gongs chiming, blue uniformed women swinging from brass grab-bars. On board the bus cleaner passengers surveyed us, emphasizing just how dirty the two of us were still.

"What was it, matey?" the conductor asked.

"A, a... what'd'y' call it, a... doodle-bug, yeh, a doodle-bug, right there, right in the street it was, eee, terrible, you should 'ave seen," said Abie. "People there, like eee, covered with blood they were, mu boy, 'is friend, yeh, shame."

Mute passengers peered out from the recesses of their seats. In supplication the conductor brushed dust off Abie's shoulder, and Abie put his hand into his pocket for the fare-money.

"Nah, matey, it's on us." The conductor spoke for everyone aboard. As the bus swept along Whitechapel Road, Abie pushed the money back down into his pocket. "Eee, thanks, thank you, er, thanks." He looked at me. "Eee, you see, we don't 'ave to pay."

—o—O—o—

November, 1944. Each morning, flocks of high-flying American Liberators and Flying Fortresses dappled the skies on their way south to the now-beleaguered Third Reich, returning by evening in wounded clusters high above a sheet of deep-throated British Sterlings and the newer Lancasters that roared off at lower elevations to indulge their nocturnal depredations. In North Africa, Monty's army was pulverizing Rommel's crack panzer divisions, and down the shelter spirits seemed buoyed on a tide of optimism that at long last the fortunes of war had turned irrevocably to our favor.

After the demise of Coopers College, the school authorities never again caught up with me; I had already scored my own private victory. Mum said if I were not going to school anymore I had to get a job and earn money toward the rent, so I showed up at the Unemployment Exchange on Mansell Street. "You're next, lofty," said one of the clerks from behind his wooden grill.

Lofty? "You mean me?"

"You're the tallest chap in the queue, basically."

I glanced behind me; it was true, I had become tall, and though I was secretly glad, still it was an embarrassment to have someone point it out in public.

"So!" he began, "We ought to start at the beginning, shall we?"

"Er, yes."

"Generally, what sort of work do you want to do, if you know what I mean."

"I, er, don't really know."

"Basically you'd have to try out a particular job, generally speaking."

"Yes."

"Alright then. Now, I'll ask a few questions, put us on the right track so to speak."

"Alright."

"Question number one: what do you think you're generally good at?"

"Good at? Er…."

"Like, what can you do better than anyone else, basically?"

"You mean, in the whole world?"

He blinked. "For now let's say just in London."

I tried, but failed, to think of something I could do better than anyone else in London. "Er, I don't know."

"Hmm. Very good, then." He looked through his papers, then back again at me as he tapped his pencil. "Do you know how to make fuse boxes?"

"Fuse boxes?"

"For tanks, aeroplanes and stuff, help the war effort and all that."

"No, I don't know really, I never made any."

"They'd show you how to make them, then."

"They would?"

"Basically, yes."

"Would I get paid?"

"You'd get paid..." he perused his sheet... "thirty shillings."

"A week?"

"Yes, a week."

"You mean, every week."

"Generally speaking."

"Would I actually be working inside aeroplanes?"

"Probably not. Basically you'd work in their factory, Cable Electric Limited, it's in the East End, you wouldn't have far."

"I see."

"So?"

"You mean, I wouldn't even go inside a tank."

"Not in the East End, no."

"Do you have any jobs where I could do stuff inside real aeroplanes?"

"They don't have aeroplane factories in the East End."

"Oh."

Cable Electric Ltd. was in Cable Street, off Commercial Road, a factory housed in an old brick building behind a broken wooden fence. Singing to myself, I pedaled through the nonexistent gate into their yard, an expanse of buckled asphalt with grass forcing its way through the cracks. Off to the far right a stack of tarpaulin-covered boxes sat on a wooden frame.

"Wha'cha lookin' for?"

"The office."

"Over there, guv." The man pointed to a door.

The office was not clean like a school office with a desk. Instead a high and narrow homemade wooden counter, littered with papers and clipboards, blocked off the tiny area, leaving practically no standing room in front.

"Write down your name and address," said the burly man on the other side. I filled in the form; at the bottom there was a space: *Wages.*

"What should I fill in here?"

"Thirty bob, starting wages." He took the form and perused it. "Alright, be 'ere 'alf past eight tomorrow morning, matey."

Riding a bike, I confirmed on the ride home, was a good place to practice singing because you could sing the same line over and over, experimenting with the phrasing until it was just right, and there was no one to make you embarrassed.

So, at eight-thirty the next morning I rode jubilantly through the gateway of Cable Electric. The same man, who now introduced himself as Bill, came out of the office and ushered me into the factory proper, a very long darkish and noisy high-ceilinged room with two wooden bench-like arrangements that ran its full length. Men sat working on high stools at both benches.

I followed Bill over to the first bench. Running down its center was a moving belt. At the far end an electric motor rotated a cogged wheel on a roller, and this arrangement drove the belt along the bench top at a slow, constant rate. Four- by six-inch metal boxes in various stages of fabrication jogged along the belt.

Two locations down from where we stood someone held a paintbrush, and from an open paint pail he was busy slapping grey paint on the outside of one of these boxes that had newly arrived at his station. He tore off a piece of newspaper from a stack, placed it on the moving belt and stood the freshly-painted box on it. The belt transported it to the next location, to Bill's and my immediate right. Here a man lifted the box by putting his fingers through an opening, careful not to mark up the still-wet paint. He screwed a short piece of threaded pipe into a hole on one edge. Then, holding the combination up by the pipe he manipulated it without getting paint on his hands and shirt, and so he screwed another short pipe into an opposite hole. Next came locking nuts, tightened with a spanner. He then returned the finished item back onto the belt — just as the next box arrived. As he carefully put his fingers inside this new arrival to duplicate the pipe installations, beyond him I saw the first man, the painter, again rip off a sheet of newspaper to place on the belt yet another box wet with paint.

The painted, pipe-fitted box had almost arrived at our station, and Bill prepared to demonstrate what was to be my part in its assembly.

"'Ere's what you does, matey. See this bunch?" And he grabbed a cluster of wires from one of several partitions in a wooden shelf arrangement adjacent to what would be my work position. "Now this 'ere bunch 'as two black wires in it, see?" He held it up: as well as two black wires, the cluster also contained several green and red. "Now, you takes it this end, 'olding it with the green wires next to you, an' you shoves it through the 'ole at the top of the box — see the top end? This end, with this shape on it, see?, it ain't the same, the bottom end's all flat-like" — he turned the box over again — "this end it's got a thing 'ere on the right side, that's for the screws but you don't 'ave to worry your 'ead about that, that's Charlie's job...." and he pointed to a man three stations further up the bench, "...'ay, Charlie!" Charlie acknowledged us with a barely perceptible flick of his screwdriver. "Then," — back to the bench — "Then, you gets this 'ere other bunch..." and Bill reached to grab from another cubby a different set of wires, longer ones, "this 'ere bunch what's got three green wires, plenty of other ones, black, red, but that don't matter, make sure it's only got three green 'uns, then you 'olds it wiv the black wires facin' you, see?, 'ere's the black ones facin', you shoves 'em through the other 'ole, that's the bottom end, see, it ain't got no ridge, see that?...." As he turned the box over once again to show me, this time he accidently smudged the wet paint with his other hand, "Bollocks!" He wiped the offending paint onto his shirt. "...And you puts this wire 'ook what's on this short black wiv a grey stripe around this screw and you screws it tight." And he located and bent out one short black-and-grey-striped wire from each of the two bunches, curved its little hook appropriately around a small screw mounted inside one side of the box, then screwed it tight. "You gotta be quick so's the paint ain't dry yet, you can still turn the screw." He then splayed the wires at each end, "like that, see?" At which he returned the completed artifact to the belt, where in a series of jerks it departed for the next station.

"Jim 'ere, 'e puts in the fuse-'olders," said Bill, and the man to my left brandished a small white rectangular ceramic plate with brass retainers, which he deftly screwed inside the box.

"Why is Jim wearing gloves?" I asked Bill above the hammering and clanging coming from the very end of our bench where the belt's journey began.

Jim answered for himself. "Me missus don't want me comin' 'ome with me clothes covered wiv paint, says she won't let me in the 'ouse."

"Then why doesn't...." and I nodded toward the man on our right, the one inserting the threaded pipe pieces, "why doesn't...."

"Bill," said Bill.

"Bill," said the man to my right.

"....Then why doesn't... Bill... why doesn't he wear gloves? The paint is wetter when he gets the box than...."

"Jim," shouted Jim above the racket.

"'Cause our Jim 'ere's a nancyboy," said Bill number two, his eyes squinting at the piece he was screwing into his current box. "My missus knows better'n to tell me what's proper and what ain't. I'd cuff 'er ear I would, and she knows it!"

"Knock it orf Bill, I told you," said Bill number one. Then to me, "Alright then, let's see you get workin'. We already missed four boxes what went past, can't be perfect the first day, can we?"

It was a lot of wires to remember and I was afraid I'd make some stupid mistake. The next box was arriving and I grabbed at it, sliding it off the belt toward me by its unpainted pipe. Nevertheless I immediately had grey paint on my fingers, which I wiped off onto my shirt. I looked to grasp the opposite piece of pipe, which should have been free of paint.

"'Old it lad, can't be slowin' the line down over a bit of paint on your 'and."

Quickly I leaned out and pulled the first bundle of wires from its cubbyhole and onto the bench.

"'Old it, 'old it," said big Bill. "I told you two black in the top bunch, three green in the bottom bunch." Somehow I'd pulled out the wrong bunch, though apparently from the correct cubby. "Top bunch 'old the greens toward you, bottom bunch 'old the blacks toward you." He grabbed my hand and twisted the bunch around: "Not that, them's red — can't get 'em mixed up, Jim 'ere won't know what to do, throw the whole line out, it will!"

Another grey box had chugged up during his explanation.

"'Ay! These boxes ain't wired up, who's pissin' orf along there?" shouted a voice from far down the bench.

"Now you 'old yer 'orses, Bert, we got a new lad, 'e'll be all straightened out before you know it 'e will!"

I began working in earnest. After twenty minutes I'd fallen into some sort of a frenetic rhythm, and Bill left to return to the office. Fifteen minutes after that, I was able to keep pace with the new boxes, in fact get a few seconds ahead, sufficient to straighten my back and take a deep breath.

Quite some time later, a voice shouted: "'Old it fellers, I gotta piss I 'ave."

"Charlie, stop the belt, 'ang on everyone, John's gotta piss again," someone called. A few of the men laughed; some stood up and stretched.

The belt stopped and my ears rang from the stunning quiet; the belt wheels had been the source of much of the screeching. Although the hammering on metal at the far end still continued, the respite allowed me a moment to try to separate and locate the sources of all the different noises. And that's when I noticed the strong smell of chemicals, of burning — a man on the opposite bench was soldering electrical wires together and each time he withdrew the soldering iron from its gas flame and dipped the hot tip into a tin of paste, smoke burgeoned to the factory's high ceiling.

The belt resumed its flow, and so the rhythm of regulated mayhem pounded on.

At twelve o'clock a clamorous bell rent the air. The belt squealed to a halt; simultaneously the hammering at the bottom end of the bench ceased for the first time since I'd been there, and the sudden, intense silence clamped around my head. I hadn't realized how unremitting the noise had been all morning.

A filthy white enamel trough ran along the end wall below a row of taps set into a pipe clamped to the black-painted section of wall above it. The taps sloshed water into the trough and the men crowded around, washing their hands. I managed to borrow some soap from Jim, but it wouldn't lather in the cold water. There were three hand-towels, and everybody grabbed at them as they finished at the taps; by the time I managed to get hold of the end of one it was dirtier than my hands, so I just shook the water off.

"Excuse me, where's the lavatory?" I asked Jim.

"Shit or piss?"

"Piss."

"You goes outside round the back, up the wall. Watch out for them old birds in those flats there, they'll fall out the bloody window laughing at yer."

I went around the back; no one was at the windows of the flats opposite. I peed, came back around the front, found a corner where the grass was thick enough to offer some seating, drew my sandwich from my shirt pocket and sat down to eat. Twenty minutes later, twelve thirty, the bell rang and it was back to work.

At six o'clock, a clanging signified the close of day. The painter placed a lid, canvas and board over his paint pail and stood his brush into a tin; Bill put down the spanner, and Jim wiped his brow one more time with his cloth. Outside in the yard we disentangled our bikes. "See yer t'morrow." "G'night." "Don't do nothing I wouldn't do!"

Twenty minutes later I was home from my first day's work. Tired, I needed to lie down before I ate.

"How much will they pay you?"

"One pound ten."

Lily figured. "Alright. You're tired? Go on, I'll wake you up for your supper."

Next, I was lying on the bed, awake, fully dressed — and it was dark. Rebecca and Zilla were talking in the other bedroom! I went downstairs and Abie was home already, eating at the table; I must have slept for hours! Marius was there too with Lily, on the settee, talking.

"I'll get your supper, you slept!" Lily peered at my face, the way she did sometimes as though she were seeing me for the first time.

I didn't want to eat while Abie was at the table, but I couldn't make a fuss: "Okay."

"Eee, so you went to work, you're working there, where is it, Commercial Road, Mum said." Abie giggled. "Now you know what it's like to 'ave to work every day." Again a giggle. "Terrible it is, eee, every day."

"Yes, I suppose people get used to it."

"Ugh, the barstard!" Lily was getting up off the settee and responding to Marius in a separate conversation. "He's trying to make a fool out of you, a baby they start on!"

Marius jumped up, coughing. "'Who said I'm a baby? I'm not a baby!"

"Terrible, 'aving to work every day, eee, every day!" Abie continued across the table. "Y' see? You should'a realized when you was in school, lucky you were, now every day you'll 'ave to work."

"Leave him alone already, it's the first day."

"What did uh do, uh'm only talking."

She returned her attention to Marius: "The barstard, he's making you look like rubbish in front of everybody." And then back to Abie: "If you were a proper father you'd go there and tell them, the bladdy barstards."

"Oh, shurrup, I don't care," said Marius.

"You 'ear? 'E don't care! Wha'cha making such a commotion, for nothing."

"He doesn't care, what does he know? You're supposed to be the father, you should do something."

"Then what should uh do, set the school on fire?" Abie guffawed at his joke.

"Ugh! Will you ever do anything except for yourself!" She stood up, and nodded in my direction: "Alright, I'll get your dinner." Her voice trailed off as she went into the kitchen.

"What happened, Maudy?" I asked.

His eyes twitched. "Nothing, Mr. Taylor, 'e was making some jokes."

"What do you mean, what sort of jokes?"

Abie ate his dinner dutifully, reading the newspaper.

"Oh, I dunno. It was in English class. 'E said 'I s'pose your uncle 'as a barrow in Petticoat Lane on Sunday,' and all the kids laughed. And 'e said some other stuff, I forget."

"Why did he say that?"

"Crikey, 'ow do I know?" Again Marius jumped up, his eyes and eyebrows twitching furiously.

"The nerve! It's because you're Jewish, they make out all Jews have barrows in Petticoat Lane. I'll go and tell him off!"

"No, don't do anything," he said, taking a deep breath. "It'll only make it worse."

"Worse! What do you mean, worse! So it *is* something! They do that to get the rest of the kids on their side."

"I dunno, 'e's alright really."

"Well, I'm going to go and talk to him."

"Yeh, go, go, you talk to 'im," interjected Abie. "Why should 'e say, like, things, like that?"

"Oh, shurrup," whispered Marius to me. "I don't wan'cha to say anything to 'im."

"I won't make it worse. Why should he get away with it?"

"I don't wan'cha to go there," Marius gasped.

"Maudy, I wish someone had told them off for me when I was in school. Don't worry, I know how to do it, I positively won't get you in any trouble."

•   •   •

I completed the week at Cable Electric without any mishaps, and by Friday when work ceased for the day we lined up outside the office for our wages. One pound four shillings for four days — I'd never held so much money before! I felt bold enough to tell Bill I would have to be a bit late Monday morning; my young brother needed me to go to his school to see the teacher, my mother couldn't go, and anyway the situation needed a man.

"Mr. Barclay 'e won't like that, 'oldin' up the line."

"I have to go, it's important."

"Well, I'll work yer place for one hour, but don't be any later, 'e'll give you the sack for sure." I pedaled home and proudly displayed the money to Mum; she took it and put it in her bag.

"Don't forget I'm going to see Maudy's teacher on Monday morning, I have to have a hat and a coat to look alright."

"Alright, I'll get you some clothes with it then."

Next morning, Saturday, she came with me down the Roman Road. When I got back home, the proud owner of a second-hand donkey brown mackintosh and a new brown fedora hat, Jack and Izzy were sitting outside on our wall, talking.

"Jack, did your Mum get any more news from the War Office?"

"No, not yet. How's the working class bearing up?" said Jack.

"It's alright, it makes you tired, all the noise and everything."

"I told you," said Izzy, "you should be a tailor. In my Dad's place there's hardly any noise, just two machines. And you would have been able to make that coat yourself, save yourself fourteen bob."

"I hate tailoring, I don't want to end up like all the *yiddles* here in the East End, being a tailor all their lives. Anyway, already I brought home wages from my job the first week!"

From Izzy's tone of voice I realized I'd hurt his feelings. "Well, I'm a *yiddle* and I'm glad I'll be a tailor," he said. And for the first time I noticed that his jacket was a sort of silky quality. "And I'll also earn money, real money."

"So your parents can give it all to the *shul,*" said Jack.

The man at the Unemployment Office had just picked out the job at Cable Electric; I certainly didn't *like* the constant noise and dirt, and actually it was pretty boring, but I hated the way Jews automatically became tailors. "I didn't want to work with my father."

"When I'm finished school my father'll teach me everything, he says women'll always want hand-tailored costumes." Izzy's future sounded ordained.

The three of us walked through the park toward Mile End Road. "I'm not sure what I'll do," said Jack. "My mother and I thought maybe architectural school."

Architectural school! I felt a flush run up from my neck and encircle my whole head, and I let the two of them pull a bit ahead of me so they shouldn't notice my face. There was no way I could ever become anything important like an architect; I was as excluded as I'd been when Joan Ingersall used to float among her clique with their private jokes and perfect clothes, everybody unflustered as though they were all rich and never had anything to worry about. That was why Manny had been my absolute best friend: his father was gone, his mother didn't really listen to anything he said, so the two of us tried making paraffin lamps, he tortured Lucy, and he talked embarrassingly loud Russian on the bus.

To stay part of the conversation I caught up slightly and tried to interject a *yes* or a *no,* but thinking about the grey paint on my clothes, the deafening, relentless hammering, breathing oily fumes all day, of being so worthless, it brought me to the verge of angry tears. How could I ever get to do something nice, like singing? Already, on the bike ride home every evening my head was spinning from the ceaseless noise there, and I couldn't even think about practicing.

In Johnny Isaacs we each ordered chips.

"I still can't believe it about Manny." Izzy unfolded his newspaper-wrapped package onto one of the tables, and nibbled.

"I'd hardly be surprised if he just walked in," said Jack.

"'Watcha, mate!'" Izzy doffed an imaginary cap, but he was much too fat to pull it off.

I tried to be part of the conversation. "He probably would have worked in the docks so he could have worn his cap all day."

"Ah well. Manny was a good friend but we can't turn back the clock." As usual, Jack said the right thing. "It's like we're all on a train and Manny just got off early. Anyway, I'm sure we'll meet him again one day."

"You do, you think we will?" I asked.

"Yes, we don't just die, that would be a violation of Newton's conservation of energy. But just as important, it's no good to look backwards; we have to think of the future, what we'd like to be when the war is over."

What we'd like to be! I ate my chips silently, too embarrassed to ask him all sorts of important questions, like if Mrs. Pristein had been angry when she first found out he wanted to be an architect. What would his father say — if he even still had a father. How could they ever pay the rent for their house if Jack didn't go immediately to work from leaving school? His father used to make barrels before the war, and coopers never got laid off at the end of the season the way tailors did — *Beer has no season,* Jack had quoted him. Maybe, if the War Office ever found him, after the war he would go back to being a cooper and earn enough for Jack to go to architectural school and not have to worry about the rent. I couldn't ever mention to Mum anything like a special school. I'd have to keep working at Cable Electric and see how things turned out.

At least on Monday morning I'd wear my new coat and fedora to see Marius's teacher at Malmsebury Road. I'd look rich. At least I'd get some revenge.

•   •   •

My mackintosh was buttoned up to the collar to cover the paint-splattered work shirt, and the fedora was jammed tightly on my head. I didn't know who Marius's headmaster was but I was determined not to be intimidated, so I tried to imagine him as strict but pretty normal, maybe like Lunch-Box Nose. On the walk over to Malmsebury Road I practiced how I would stride into his office and say something like: *I'm here to speak to Mr. Taylor, immediately!* — anything that would make me sound more grown-up than thirteen. Nevertheless, inside the school building, just seeing the familiar thick paint on the walls — dark green with a light green strip above — was still so unsettling that I had to keep reminding myself I was finished with school, I went to work the way grown-ups did. An actual father wouldn't feel nervous, and I was just like a father coming to see the teacher about something with his kid.

In the hallway, a woman directed me to the headmaster's office. She said, "That way, *Sir,*" as she pointed — so at least the coat and hat were working. I strode along the corridor and there it was, a brown lacquered door with a translucent bubbled-glass window inset. In disbelief I read the name: *Mr. Edward Hutchinson, Headmaster!* My old headmaster, the one who caned me in Coopers College — now he was here, he was Marius's headmaster! They must have moved him over to Malmesbury Road after Coopers College was blown up. If that rocket had only landed during school hours he would have been killed and I wouldn't have had this extra problem now. The thought of having to confront him was nerve-wracking; I'd have to be even more firm. So I banged really hard on the door and walked straight in — and who should be sitting there but that same sniveling triangular clerk he'd had at the other school: Emily, she with the thick horn-rimmed glasses and the dark wig that sat too high on top of her head and didn't match the scraggly light grey hairs that crawled out under its fringe.

"Emily!" She jumped. "Emily, I've come here to speak to Mr. Hutchinson. Immediately!"

"You can't burst into this office like that!" She rose up behind the desk, glaring. "Now go back outside right this moment, knock, and wait until I say *'come in'!"*

Her thick lenses made her round eyeballs seem huge, floating around disconnected from the rest of her face. That, coupled with the wig and the way her black dress got wider as she stood up, made her more imposing than I'd remembered. Before I could regain my composure I was outside in the hallway with the door closed. I took a few deep breaths then knocked on the glass, this time nowhere near as loud, but certainly somewhat louder than she would have liked. Nothing happened. I tried to look through the glass but the bubbles distorted everything. At this point I couldn't really knock again so soon, because she'd know it would be me knocking, and she'd open the door and say, "Why did you knock twice," and I'd feel stupid.

The only solution was to wait one more minute, putting a clear interval between what had already happened in terms of knocking and what would happen from now on. So I waited. Just to be reasonable I waited even more than one minute, but the door never opened, neither did she call "Come in!" The best thing would probably be to knock one more time, moderately, as a sort of addendum to the earlier knock. But as I lifted my hand up to the glass, the door swung open away from me — and there was Mr. Hutchinson! He looked up at me, frowned for a moment as though maybe he remembered me from Coopers College, then bent his head down to one side to ease himself around under my forearm, which was still raised ready to knock. I felt foolish at his exiting directly under my arm, so I began to lower it, swinging it out to the side to avoid coming down directly onto his head — at which he backed off apprehensively as though I were going to hit him, which of course I wasn't. As a matter of fact I hadn't even wanted to see him at all in the doorway to his office, especially after all that unanticipated stuff with Emily. The door began swinging shut as he strode up the corridor, so with my shoe I caught it before it closed.

I needed to concentrate on the original reason I'd come to Malmsebury Road, which was to tell Mr. Taylor off about Marius. I pushed the door open, put my head in and said as pleasantly as I could: "Miss Emily, I'd like to talk to Mr. Hutchinson, please."

"Mr. Hutchinson isn't here."

"Yes I know, I was standing outside the door. He just left."

"You mean... you *know* he isn't in his office?"

"Well, he just walked out, wasn't it, I mean, he just left."

"Then... what in heaven's name is the point of asking to talk to him if you know he isn't here?"

"I know he isn't here *now.* I meant when he comes *back* I'd like to talk to him."

The eyeballs rolled upwards. "Alright, wait outside. When he returns, knock on the door, introduce yourself, tell me you'd like to talk to Mr. Hutchinson, and I'll see if he's not too busy. Now, close the door."

I eased my foot out and the door closed: I'd understood exactly what she meant, she didn't have to explain something obvious like I couldn't talk to him if he wasn't there — it was more as if *she* didn't understand what *I* meant. It was hot in the corridor, maybe because of the macintosh and fedora. It was hot, but I didn't want to unbutton the coat because of my old working clothes underneath with all the grey paint. But while no one was around I did take off the fedora, and wipe perspiration from my forehead. The leather headband inside was already wet, and I hadn't come close to seeing Mr. Taylor yet.

Just then Mr. Hutchinson came walking briskly back down the corridor. If I were going to be stern inside his office I didn't want to come face to face again outside and have to say *hello* or something, which would make it that much harder to be severe later. So I put my hat back on, swung around and at a good clip started walking in the other direction. In about fifteen yards I reached the end of the corridor, a blank wall. There was one door to my right and another to the left, so I turned purposefully right as though that was the room I'd intended to enter. The footsteps behind me had stopped, and I hadn't yet heard a door-lock click, which meant Mr. Hutchinson was probably standing outside his own door, watching. So I knocked loudly on the door in front of me, yanked it open and walked inside; it turned out to be a storage closet, with folders and things on shelves. The door swung to behind me, and with my foot I just managed to stop it just before it closed completely, meanwhile noticing there happened to be no knob on the inside; if I hadn't caught it I would have been locked in and have had to start banging on the door to be let out.

It must have been a full minute before I heard Mr. Hutchinson's door open, then click closed. Perspiration had by now soaked the neck of my shirt. I came out of the closet, brushed my coat off, removed the fedora and again mopped my scalp and the headband. Voices. Around the corner beyond Mr. Hutchinson's door a kid was talking, to a teacher apparently, the echo suggesting it was from the hallway I'd come through earlier. Both people laughed — I hadn't realized a pupil could laugh at the same time as a teacher — then the pupil said, "Thank you, Mr. Taylor."

So it was Mr. Taylor around the corner! I took a good breath and walked toward the voices. "Alright, run on back to class," I heard him say. "I'll be right there."

A kid's footsteps trotted off. Then the teacher came into view, grasping folders under his arm. He glanced at me as he approached, then at the last minute as he was about to pass he looked at me more directly, smiled and nodded: "Good morning!"

"Good morning, Mr. Taylor." Since I'd been forced by his politeness to respond, I at least made a point of barely moving my lips. And, I deliberately didn't turn my head toward him; I had to include a smile because he'd smiled at me, but I made mine stiff. He opened a door on the other side of the corridor, and disappeared.

All these preliminaries were consuming a lot of time and I hadn't even seen Mr. Hutchinson nor Mr. Taylor yet, officially. Also, my new job! They might give me the sack if I got there after nine-thirty.

To draw a definite demarcation line between what had already happened and how I would handle everything from now on, again I removed the hat and drew a deep breath. Replacing it confidently on my head, I strode back along the corridor and knocked cheerfully on Emily's door as though I'd just arrived at the school — an optimistic, normal-volume knock. I waited five seconds, opened the door and walked right in, giving her no chance to object.

"Good morning, I'd like to speak to Mr. Hutchinson please."

"Well!" She began to stand up, but I had the advantage of surprise. "Well, hmm... wait here and I'll see if Mr. Hutchinson is in his office."

"He is, a few minutes ago I saw him come back." Immediately, I realized I'd said the wrong thing. To compensate, before she could tighten up and her eyes become detached I leaned right over her desk and smiled directly into her face.

She backed over to Mr. Hutchinson's door, which I now noticed had been partially open the whole time. She knocked: "Mr. Hutchinson, do you have time to see someone?"

"Who is it, Emily?"

"What's your name?"

"Grossman. *Mr.* Grossman."

"It's a Mr. Grossman."

"Don't we have a Grossman in school here?"

I answered for Emily: "Yes, we do, you do. It's Marius Grossman."

"Aha! Come on in, Mr. Grossman." I entered his office. "And you're Marius's father, I presume?"

The hat was amazing! "No... well, no. I'm not his father really."

Behind the papers on the huge desk he'd started to rise from his chair to extend a hand. Now he paused: "I... see! And, er, what can I do for you this morning, Mr. er... Grossman?" He was short, and my fedora made the disparity greater still.

"What you should have done last time."

He seemed perplexed, withdrawing his hand and sitting down again. "I... beg your pardon?"

"What you should have done last week, I mean this morning, early."

"I... er... and what exactly was it I should have done last week, early, that is, this morning?"

My mind had gone blank; it took a minute before I remembered: "I... I want to speak to Mr. Taylor. Immediately!"

"Mr. Taylor? Why aren't you in class? Why are you wearing your coat? And that hat?"

"I... I... because I'm not, I'm not...."

"Don't I know you?"

"No. I'm not. Definitely not you don't."

"Who permits you to wear a hat like that to school? What is it, one of those... fedoras? Did Taylor send you down for misbehavior?"

Like a buzzard, Emily chimed in from behind; she must have been standing there all the time. "He just barged straight in without knocking. First he told me he wanted to speak to you, now he's saying he wants to speak to Mr. Taylor."

"Grossman for heaven's sake pull yourself together and try to tell us why you're here in my office."

"I'm, I'm, I'm finished, I don't go to school anymore, I'm finished at school, I used to go to Coopers College... in Morgan Street."

"Coopers College no longer exists."

"I'm, I'm, I'm finished, I go to work now, I work for Cable Electric Limited, Mr... Mr... Bill will prove it."

"So that's where I know you from, Coopers College!"

"I don't know, but you definitely don't know me from here, from Malmsebury Road, I used to go here before we were evacuated, now I go to work."

"Now calm down, Mr. Grossman, and try to remember why you wanted to see me this morning."

"Mr. Hutchinson, I'm here for my brother, Marius."

"Your brother can't leave the school premises until four P.M., Grossman, in common with every other pupil in the school. You know that!"

"No, I don't mean to take him away, I'm here about something that happened."

"Why didn't your mother come? You have parents, I presume?"

I couldn't let Mr. Hutchinson talk to me like that, in a snotty tone as if I were still a pupil.

"Yes, I do have parents, my father didn't come 'cause he's working, and my mother had to go shopping, so they said I should come."

"Ahem."

"Yes, they said I would be able to take care of this situation very well by myself."

"Grossman, what exactly *is* this 'situation' you're referring to?"

"It's Mr. Taylor. Mr. Taylor has been saying things about Jewish people in front of my brother."

"Indeed!" Mr. Hutchinson coughed. "And kindly tell us just what, ahem, Jewish things Mr. Taylor has been saying in front of your brother, Mr., er, Grossman."

"I don't know, it was something about Marius having an uncle with a barrow down Petticoat Lane." The fedora was so tight I felt liquid dammed up all around the headband.

"Grossman, are you implying that Mr. Taylor's observation — if indeed your attribution to him of such a remark were, in fact, correct — are you implying something improper on Mr. Taylor's part?"

"Well... yes, I am."

"And precisely what is the nature of his alleged impropriety?"

"Well, it's against Jewish people, it's...."

"Grossman, I'm quite sure there must be a misunderstanding. Mr. Taylor would never say anything that could possibly be construed as anti-Jewish. Why should he?"

"I... don't know."

"Then we can consider the matter closed?" He glanced across at Emily, stood up again, and started toward a cabinet on the wall. "A misunderstanding, perhaps..." he continued talking without looking at me. "...and should you have cause to enter my office again, if you're still wearing that hat may I ask that you kindly leave it outside?" He opened the cabinet door and shuffled several papers. Without turning his head, he added: "You may leave now, Grossman."

I backed away a little, under the door frame to the outer office, with Emily right behind me. I wasn't even in his school anymore and he was calling me 'Grossman' the way teachers address pupils! Emily had clasped the sleeve of my new coat and was starting to pull at me. I jerked my arm violently enough to make her gasp and let go.

"Mr. Hutchinson," I called from just beyond the doorway to his private office, "I don't know why Mr. Taylor did it, but...." Repulsive Emily was now alongside me, glaring. "I don't know *why* teachers do it, but I do know exactly *how,* so it's hard to pin them down afterward."

Hutchinson was back in his desk chair, now looking straight at me through the open doorway, his face entirely expressionless.

I was not about to be dismissed that easily. "They always do it so they can worm their way out and say you misunderstood. I know what I'm talking about, and I do want to see Mr. Taylor *immediately.*"

"Hmm! Well well... Mr. er, Grossman...."

"And my name is not Mr. *er* Grossman, it's Mr. Grossman, and let me inform you that I intend to see that something is done about this situation." The words may have come out of my mouth in the wrong order, so I compensated by trying to feel furiously angry, the way I'd tried to feel when Jack was telling me about his sister Sarah whose husband Fred lay on top of her. The next thing, Mr. Hutchinson flicked his finger to beckon Emily around me and into his office; she leaned down and he whispered something in her ear. She came out, her eyes swimming furiously in their separate glass bowls as she passed me. The outside door clicked closed as she exited into the corridor.

Now it was just the two of us, in silence. Maybe he'd sent Emily to get a policeman. If so, I would stay calm and explain in a reasonable tone exactly what Mr. Taylor had said to Maudy — even though the policeman would automatically be on Mr. Hutchinson's side.

"Wait outside in the corridor, Grossman. You can talk with Taylor there."

"Yessir." Oh damn, why did I say *sir?* But at least that meant Emily had gone to fetch Mr. Taylor, not the police. And he hadn't referred to him as *Mr.* Taylor, just Taylor! Headmasters must be so stuck up they think they don't have to say *Mr.* to anybody!

I waited outside, and Emily came back glowering down the hallway. "Wait right here," she snarled, entered her office and closed the door. Then a moment later, ambling along the corridor came Mr. Taylor, the one with whom I'd already exchanged reluctant greetings.

"Hello Mr. Grossman, yes, I remember you from earlier. And what can I do for you?" His cheerfulness was not a good sign.

"You can start by behaving yourself properly."

"Excuse me?"

Louder: "You can start by behaving yourself properly."

"Behaving myself *properly!* Hmmm! Perhaps you'd like to explain."

"You know what I mean."

"Well, well, really now, Mr. Grossman! I understand it's something with your brother Marius?"

My hat, which by now I was sure had a dark liquid ring around the crown, made me taller than him, though I still had to look up to meet his eyes. "Yes indeed, it is to do with my brother." (Only teachers were supposed to say *indeed!*) "Maudy... Marius tells me you made remarks about his having an uncle with a barrow in Petticoat Lane."

He took his hand out of his pocket and rubbed his mouth. "Oh, no, there must be a misunderstanding."

Sweat that had oozed beneath the headband now ran down through my right eyebrow into my eye, and I wiped it off with the sleeve of my new second-hand coat; lowering my arm I saw the water stain had blackened the cuff. "Did you deliberately make scurrilous remarks at the expense of my brother so you could curry favor with the rest of the class?" Wow! That came out really good!

"Scurrilous! And curry favor, indeed! Mr. Grossman, you mustn't believe everything you hear. Ha, ha, I wouldn't do anything like that — it would hardly be necessary."

My whole scalp was beading wet under the hat. "And further, are you in the practice of making anti-Jewish remarks at the expense of people unable to defend themselves?"

"Mr. Grossman, I'm really surprised — and, if I may say, offended as well."

"I didn't mean my brother can't defend himself...."

"I do resent being placed in a position where I'm called upon to repudiate something I never said. If all you have are unsubstantiated accusations, I'll return to my class."

"Mr. Taylor you have a responsibility, you can affect the future behavior of thirty children by your conduct."

"My goodness me!" His eyebrows were knit together. "I resent this. I really resent this. Perhaps I mentioned Petticoat Lane — I don't remember precisely in what context — but that doesn't necessarily impute anti-Semitism. Obviously your brother simply took it the wrong way."

"Mr. Taylor," — *it was wonderful to start sentences with his name* — "Mr. Taylor, long ago when I went to school, it took me years of being told I was taking things the wrong way before I realized I was actually taking them exactly as they were intended. In your case, you've picked on the only Jewish person in the class to ridicule him. Mr. Taylor, I give you fair warning: one more complaint from Maudy, Marius and I'll have you up before the London County Council. Have I made myself clear?" My head was so hot and wet I just had to take the hat off, even if it did make me shorter than him. Salty water immediately ran down into both my eyes and around my collar. With my handkerchief I tried wiping my eyes and hair and collar and ears, but it was too much liquid.

Mr. Taylor reached into a pocket and handed me his handkerchief: "There."

"Thank you."

"Made yourself clear?" — he continued my question. "Abundantly so, Mr. Grossman. I still insist it was a misunderstanding. And I'll have you know there are several children of the Jewish faith in my class."

I put my sopping handkerchief back in my pocket, wrang his out onto the floor and went to hand it back to him.

"No, you may keep it," he said.

"Thank you."

"I repeat, there are several children of the Jewish faith in my class. You can't teach in this area and not have several Jewish children in your classes."

"Then that proves it! Good day to you, sir!" I spun around and strode along the hallway, heart thumping, salt water stinging my eyes and sweat vibrating off my cheeks. The fucker, I did it! I told a teacher off! I got a bit mixed up at the end, but I really did it, nearly all the right words, as good as him even, and he's a teacher!

I realized I was approaching the blank wall and the closet — I'd walked off in the wrong direction — so I spun around in a fury. A *real* fury — that is, not just acting angry but actually *being* angry; and the feeling was so wonderful I began striding back along the corridor after him; maybe I'd... I'd... I'd even.... But the door to Emily's office was just clicking closed; apparently he'd gone in to see Mr. Hutchinson.

With manic disregard I put my ear to the keyhole.

"Taylor! How did it go old chap? Did our young friend dress you down?"

"Mr. Hutchinson, things are really reaching a point, nowadays."

"Yes, they are feeling their oats these days; they like to think they can usurp any authority. I don't think I'd worry unduly about this particular chap."

"It's a trifle unsettling though, ha, ha! He said he might go to the London County Council."

"I doubt whether his family would take it that far, and of course there's no proof. But I am afraid we'll be seeing more and more of this sort of thing among the fringe classes."

"Really!"

"Yes, this American democratic fiction that every Tom, Dick and Harry is entitled to an opinion is beginning to poison British society as surely as it's done their own."

"It's a joke, isn't it? This is what we're fighting Jerry for, losing British lives, so we can be insulted with impunity!"

"Aha, the greater enemy always lies within. Mark my words, Taylor, whatever the outcome of this war, we're witnessing the end of civilization as we know it."

—o—O—o—

16

I strode back to the hallway, down the stairs and out into the fresh air. It was already half past nine and no one was at the house; I threw off the coat and hat, grabbed the bike and pedaled furiously all the way to Cable Street. Bill was at my position threading wires through one of the boxes. "We was ready to give up on you."

"Sorry, it got complicated, I rushed as fast as I could."

"Alright, 'ere's this one…" he got up off the stool and handed me the small grey box…"'ere's the black ones, twist 'em round and screw 'em up. Tight now."

Lunch, peeing around behind the building; then at long last the clangorous six o'clock bell. As with every evening the previous week my head felt tight as the banging and hammering ceased, replaced by a ringing silence. Already, I wondered how I would be able to bear working every single week for the rest of my life. I cycled out of the gate with the men, trying to think of a song title, something to sing to myself. But I couldn't and a few minutes later, as I turned off Commercial Road into New Road, a man's voice called: "Zachary!" A scruffy fellow waved to me from by the high factory buildings. I stopped and he beckoned me over, "C'm'ere." I didn't know who he was but I didn't want to be rude, so I lay the bike down in the curb and crossed the wide pavement. He was unshaven, short, even slight, and the clothes — baggy brown trousers, a jacket pocket torn out at ninety degrees — hung on his frame.

"Did you call me?"

"Yes… yes!" His agitated dark eyes sparkled too brightly in the unkempt face. "It's me! Er, you don't know who I am?"

"No…."

"Your uncle!"

"My uncle?"

"Albert… yes, your uncle… Uncle Albert, Lily… she didn't say?"

"What? I don't know…."

"Lily, how is she… Lily?"

"You mean Mum?"

"Yes, your… Mum, how is she, your Mum?"

"Oh, very well thank you. I…."

His hands seemed to be shaking, and he drew back a little. "Don't be frightened, I'm your uncle, I'm your mother's… brother, younger brother, you know, Zelda."

"Oh…." What did he mean, Zelda?

"Er, I'm surprised she didn't say."

"I don't know…. I know about Uncle Harold, and Uncle Sid…."

"Uncle Sid? He's not your…. er, well, he's your… father's brother, that's it." His head was shaking slightly from side to side as he spoke. "Abie's brother, he's... he would be your uncle on... your *bobbeh's* side. My mother's dead... a long time, I was... seven."

"Seven?"

"Seven... years old... I was seven."

"Oh. *Bobbeh's* dead also, she's been dead a long time, before we were evacuated." Even in the open air he smelled a bit the way *bobbeh* had, like rotting excrement, the night before she died.

"So you're working... Harold told me... you're working."

"Harold? You mean, Uncle Harold, Mum's brother, I got mixed up."

"Harold, my... brother, your mother's... brother, it's... the same. Yes."

"Well yes, I am, I'm working at Cable Electric around the corner, I earn thirty shillings a week."

"It's good. So... come on... I'll show you where I... I live."

"I don't know...."

"It's alright, she'll... understand, her own brother."

"Well, maybe I ought to go home."

"No, come on, I'll... show you where I... live... it's downstairs...."

"I really ought to go home, the supper'll get cold and she'll be wild."

"Come on, just... five... minutes."

I didn't know who he was, though he did know Mum's name, and the others, but still I thought I shouldn't go. Also, I was afraid because he didn't seem to realize his hands and head were moving in a rhythm, almost a slow shaking, when he spoke. "Maybe another time when I see you."

He paused; his shoulders fell and the movements briefly ceased. "Alright, maybe... another... time."

I left him there and cycled home.

"Mum, I saw someone today, on New Road, he said he was your brother."

"My brother? Who was it?" She peered closely into my face. "Was it Albert?"

"He said he was Uncle Albert."

"Ugh! Don't talk to him! How is he?"

"He was shaking, he said he was your brother."

"He's filthy dirty, don't talk to him."

"Is he really our uncle?"

"Tsk!, the less said the better, shame for him, who needs more trouble."

She went to the kitchen, called "Maudy!" and brought in two plates and placed them on the table. Marius came in.

"Eat, eat, both of you." She put bread on the oilcloth and handed us each a spoon. Marius began slurping the bean soup.

"Maudy, was school alright today?"

He turned his head and twitched his eyes. "Yeah, why?"

"I mean, did everything... was it, like, normal?"

"Yeah, wha'd'ja mean, why?"

"I mean, was it the same as other days or was it different, a bit different?"

"Wha'cha saying?" The twitching became more pronounced.

"I just wondered if Mr. Taylor was okay today."

"'E came in, then right away Miss Emily called 'im to see the 'eadmaster."

"I mean, when he came back from the headmaster was he alright?"

"Wha'cha talking about, was 'e alright? 'E came back and did the lesson!"

"That's all?"

"Well, then 'e brought 'is chair over to my desk."

"Your's?"

"Yeah, 'e sat down an' started doing the writing on my paper!"

"Really?"

"Then 'e went back to the front. Why? What did you do? I bet you did something."

"Guess what?"

"What?"

"I went to Malmesbury Road to see him this morning."

"What! You did? I didn't wan'cha to!" He dropped his spoon and blinked rapidly.

"That's why Miss Emily called him out, I was talking to him!"

"You were? Crikey!"

"See, I told you nothing would happen if I spoke to him."

"Crikey!" His eyes darted for a moment, then he picked up the spoon and held it. "Well, after, 'e did tell me to shut up."

"He did?"

"When I asked 'im what I was supposed to do 'e covered 'is mouth and whispered 'Shut up.'"

"Hmm."

"Well…"

"You tell me if he starts on you again."

His eyes blinked furiously. "I told you I didn't wan'cha to go, now the other kids'll start." He put his hand to his mouth.

"They won't know I went."

Mum came back in from the kitchen, and overheard the last sentences. "What happened?"

As Marius listened intently I told her how before work this morning I'd gone to Malmesbury Road, and how I'd dispatched Mr. Taylor.

"Good for you," she said. "Your *broch* of a father should have done it, he leaves it to his son instead of him going to speak up."

Considering how adamant Marius had been, now he seemed to be taking it well; I momentarily had Mum's sympathies, so it seemed an opportune time to tell her I didn't really want to work at Cable Electric.

"Not work, what are you talking about? We need the money! You got a coat and a hat, what more do you want?"

"Just that place, I mean, it's loud banging all day long, I hate it there."

"Of course you hate it, what did you expect? Nobody likes to work."

"I have to keep doing the same thing over and over all day, screwing up the same five screws. Look!" And I showed her my hands.

"Blisters! There are worse things in life than blisters."

I took a chance. "Jack's mother might let him go to a special school to learn to be an architect.…"

"An archi… what?"

"An architect."

"An architect!"

"They draw buildings and things."

"Buildings? What do you mean, what buildings?"

"I don't know, things like the Taj Mahal, Jack said. Also, he wouldn't have to be drafted if he's registered in a school."

"What are you, mad or something?" A hard disgust transformed her face. "They don't have to struggle every week for the rent. How many mouths they got to feed, two?"

"Jack and his mother, they get a pension from insurance and from the government, he said."

"So what do they have to worry about, then!"

"Well, maybe I could do something else, any other kind of work. I don't mean not to work, I know everybody's got to work…."

"Thinks 'e's too good to work."

"Stay out of this, Maudy!" she said. "So what other kind of work is there? You mean you want to be a tailor, all the aggravation with the customers all the time?"

"Crikey, you wanna be a tailor like the old barstard?"

"Don't talk about your father like that! I don't know where he gets the language, from school, from the *yocks,* I don't know…."

"No, I don't want to be a tailor, isn't there anything else? I mean, maybe we could ask Jack, he wants to be an… architect, maybe I could learn something…."

"You? An architect! How could you be an architect?"

"Maybe I could ask him… how they… how his mother found out…."

"You leave your job, your father'll kill you. The end of the season, they've got no work there for him already, at least he tries to get extra work. Altman's, I haven't paid them for two weeks even, she should *gai in dreard* there she should, that woman." She retreated to the kitchen, calling over her shoulder: "Don't talk to Uncle Albert."

We ate our soup, then Lily returned. "Mum, why mustn't I talk to Uncle Albert?"

"'Oo's Uncle Albert?"

"Someone started talking to me when I was coming home today, in New Road, Mum said he's our uncle."

"Sshh, he was in the war, the other one, the first war, who knows?"

"Did he get injured or something? As he was talking his head was shaking."

"Shaking? Crikey!"

"From the guns they said, in Europe," said Lily. "He embarrasses the whole family."

"What 'appened to 'im?" asked Marius.

"Nothing, the less said the better, don't talk to him, Zelda should only know!"

•   •   •

The next evening, at the close of the work day, I hopped on the bike and rode out the Cable Electric gate.

"Zachary!" It was Uncle Albert. "Come on, I'll… show you my flat."

There was still sufficient daylight, so walking the bike I followed behind him into a narrow space between two tall buildings. Ten yards into the alley, where clumps of grass grew among the cracked flagstones, we were beyond the slanting diagonal of late sunlight and into shadow. The buildings' rough featureless walls soared on each side. At the far end of the building to our right was a small window, low down, almost at knee-level.

"Come on, er don't be frightened." He leaned down and his quavering hands jiggled the frame. He smacked it hard and the top half of the window banged down. Inside was dark. "Lemme... go first, I'll... put the light on." He lifted one torn trousers-leg through the opened window, his shoe searching for a footing inside. Then with an unexpectedly adroit twist he bent himself double and, clutching at the frame, eased his torso inside and stepped down to floor level. "A... a minute." In the blackness he struck a match, then lifted the trembling flame to a gaslight suspended from the low ceiling. A dim light crept across a small newspaper-covered table, gradually illuminating two chairs, a sideboard littered with clothes, books and papers, then over to a bunk against the far wall.

"Give me your... hand." His voice was muffled.

"What about my bike?"

"Leave it... it's alright... no... one comes 'round."

Cautiously I felt through the opening for something to grasp. "No, your... leg, first your... leg it's... easy."

I swung through, my head grazing the ceiling. He helped me off the sill and onto a nearby chair. At the other end of the small room I could make out a door; in front of that stood a half-cupboard with raw wood open shelves extending above to the ceiling. Next came a gas stove, and beyond that another cupboard, waist high. The room smelled of musty dampness.

"A cup of tea... you drink tea... course you drink tea." A small saucepan rattled as he took it off the stove, and I noticed the top of the half-cupboard held a recessed sink, with a tap mounted on the wall behind.

"Alright, thank you." I didn't know what to say to him. "Do you live here?"

"Yes, it's... where I live, it's my... flat for... years."

"I mean, I mean, this is it, you live in this room."

"Yes it's... enough what do I... want more for?"

"Yes, you're right."

"Nobody troubles me here... it's... quiet here."

"Do you have a lavatory?"

"You want to... go? Er it's outside, I'll... I'll...."

"No, I just wondered if there was one, that's all."

"Yes, well, outside... in the back."

"Why do you go in through the window?"

"The... window?"

"Yes, I mean, is that the door? There, behind the cupboard?"

"Well, it's... a door. What do I... need it... for?"

"I mean...."

"Other people... let them have a... door. I... just want to be... left alone... this way it's... no trouble." From a shelf he took two cups, and held one toward me. "It's alright? For tea it's... good."

"Yes. Thank you."

"I don't... trouble anybody here it's... like... quiet." A china lid clattered noisily into the sink as he drained a dark brown teapot which had been standing on the stove; without rinsing the pot he placed it back down. As he motioned to lift the saucepan, which was not yet near boiling, I stood up because of his trembling hand. Immediately he interrupted: "No... sit.. sit... what do you... what do... I manage alright, what do you think?"

I didn't want him to think I was implying anything, so I quickly sat down again. The edge of the saucepan tap-tap-tapped against the mouth of the teapot as he managed to pour most of the hot water into it. He put the saucepan down and covered the puddle of spilled water with a small towel. Next he brought empty cups over to the table, "Sit, sit"; I must have looked as if I were going to get up again. He placed a cup of sugar in the middle of the little table. "In Russia... they had a whole block of... sugar on a... string from the ceiling it hung on a piece of... string. You could... pull it over and... lick it... if you wanted... sweet."

I was grateful for something to say. "Really? Were you in Russia, then?"

He was returning the two cups to the stove. "In Russia no... my mother... she told us what it was like there... they... didn't have much sugar... expensive it was expensive. She... died... when I was seven... she died. I remember about... the sugar."

In one hand he held the shaking teapot, and in the other a small wire strainer. He managed to fill both cups without a spill, then brought them trembling to the table again. Back at the stove he retrieved a glass bottle of milk from a half-full pail of water which stood on the floor next to the sink-cupboard. "Milk, here's the milk." Water dripped onto the newspaper as he poured milk into each cup.

"So, do you go to work?"

"Work... no I can't work."

"You can't?"

"I tried to... work."

"Really? Are you a tailor also?"

"I... tried to work but it's no good... I get like... on edge... I have to... go home."

"Home?"

"Here."

"You mean, here?"

"Yes I live here. It's... my flat."

"I see."

"It's... quiet here."

"Yes, it is quiet."

"Harold."

"What?"

"Harold. Your Uncle Harold... every week he... comes."

"You mean Uncle Harold, he comes here to see you?"

"If Zelda only knew she'd have a... a fit she would."

"What does he do, I mean, Uncle Harold? I mean, I know Uncle Harold, he's very nice, but I mean why does he come?"

In the dim gaslight his thin yellow unshaven cheeks were stark. "Every week, he... brings... he brings me."

Mum would be wondering where I was; I didn't want to be rude so I tried to think of one more thing to say, then I would drink my tea, make an excuse and leave. "Were you really in the army? Mum said you were in the army."

The cup wobbled as he held it to his lips. "A long time ago I was... in the army. They made me go to France... in France I was... in the army... the B.E.F.... the British Expeditionary Force."

"Was it in the war?"

"This war? No!" His voice seemed muffled. "The other war... the Great War..." he laughed a thin laugh, "World War One they... call it now. I'll... show you." He went to the rack of half a dozen clothes hangers at the end of the bed. "Look... come here." He held a uniform, a khaki-colored uniform on a hanger. "This is... it... my uniform... I... wore it in the war... in France."

"I see." I stood up; in the shadow it was difficult to make out details, but under the jacket was a shirt. "Brown... they made it... brown, for camouflage. They used to be red, you remember? Bright red the jacket... right away the Germans they'd... see you. Then they made them... brown so you shouldn't get... killed. Khaki... khaki."

"Did you ever see anyone get shot, get killed?"

His lean face bent to the side. "Don't go... in the army Zachary... don't go... whatever they say. I... should have gone... to America I should have gone... Abie's brother Joe he went... to America... I should have gone before the war started. I would have been better off... we all would have been... better off."

"Was it terrible in the army?"

"What did we know... children we were... what did we know?"

"I suppose, yes."

"One year. One year I was there... in France. I couldn't stand it... on edge... all the time you're... on edge... you never know what's happening... the next... minute. I didn't want to fight... to fight with anybody... they... they... tied me... to the wheel they tied me."

"What do you mean?"

"The cannon... they were shooting... at the Germans they were shooting... firing... field artillery... a fancy name they... have for everything. Every time they... pulled the string it twisted... the wheel jerked... the whole thing the... ropes they cut my neck... my chest my wrists all bleeding... all over the jacket the shirt... blood. Twenty-four hours it was... twenty-four hours they... sentenced me... the court-martial... that's what it was... in... insubordination... twenty-four hours on the wheel... sometimes it'd... jerk back so far I was like up-side-down. The noise the smoke... everybody shouting... you can't even remember how long it is. You have nightmares all the time... your head every time it goes off. They sent me back to England... they said I was no good they said... yellow... they said." A wistful laugh, "my favorite color... yellow."

I tried to absorb what he was saying. "Are you alright now?"

"Alright?"

"I mean, are you better, did you get... better?"

"Better? Yes... I'm... better now."

"Mum will be wondering where I am, I don't know, I suppose I should be going home."

"You can... stay here for... a while if you like."

"Well, Mum makes supper for me, it'll get cold...."

"Want to see a... secret?"

"What do you mean?"

"A secret... I'll er show you a... secret."

"Well, Mum will...."

"One minute... I'll show you a secret." He went to the cabinet by the sink, opened the door, and brought a long thing to the table, iron and wood. It looked like a gun. "See? It's a rifle." He lay it lovingly across the table. "See? They don't know I took it... when... I came back... they don't know... I took the rifle. See here?" He raised a knob and slid it backward, exposing a black elongated opening. "Bolt action. In there... that's where... you put the bullet."

Mum had told me not even to talk to him; maybe she knew he had a real gun, maybe that was the reason.

"One... more thing."

"What? I really have to go, Mum will really wonder where I am by now...."

"One... more thing... one minute... one more minute won't make any... difference." And he went back to the cupboard, and returned with a metal tube with a shaped piece on one end and a small knob on the other. "Look!" With shaking hands he slid the shaped metal piece over the end of the rifle barrel and clicked it into place. "Look," he repeated, and slid the knobbed scabbard off to expose a spike about eight inches long, the end sharpened to a point. "A bayonet! That's what we had to do... they... showed us... we were supposed to... kill the Germans with it... on the end of... the gun!"

"Is it a real gun? Did you... I mean, did you... did it ever actually shoot anyone? Or... you know, like... with the bayonet?"

"No they told us over and over... but I couldn't I couldn't do it... that's why... in the end they had to tie me to... the wheel."

"Why do you still have it, I mean, why did you keep it?"

"Well... er... you never know."

"I mean, why did you keep the rifle... now?"

"In hospital there, terrible it was...."

"I mean...."

"Why? I s'pose if I... can't go on."

"Go on?" I really wanted to leave. "Listen, I really have to leave." I stood up.

"Look! A... bullet! See? This part's the... bullet...." he held a tapered brass cartridge; at the narrower end a half-inch-long plug of silver metal curved gracefully to a point.

"I've got to go, I've got to go." I climbed up on the chair by the window and placed a foot on the sill. He just remained on the other side of the small table.

"You pull back the... bolt... there... it goes in... here it goes in... the... breech they called it... all the names I remember...." He was standing, thin, wan, steadying his quavering frame with a hand on the rickety table, holding the cartridge and pointing it at the rifle glimmering in the dim yellow gaslight on the tabletop between the two cups of tea. As I put one leg outside the window, his shaking hand placed the cartridge down on the crumpled newspaper. I jockeyed through the opening while from inside there came a rustling, a rolling sound, then a *clack!* Looking back, I saw the brass cartridge had rolled off the edge of the table onto the ragged linoleum that barely covered the cold cement floor.

—o—O—o—

17

"Come on Zachary, I suppose we should go over, he was your friend." Mum was putting on her coat. "It's a pity for her, we'll bring her something."

"Alright, I hope she doesn't…."

"What?"

"Well, last time she really shouted at me."

"She *shouted* at you, what did you do?"

"Nothing, she came back and I was just playing about two notes on their piano."

"She got a piano as well? Humph! She did alright for herself!"

"I went with Manny back to his house for something, some bandages or something. I was waiting for him and I just played a couple of notes and she came running in screaming at me."

"Just for touching her piano?"

"I told her I only played two notes. She called me an animal."

"A fire in her *kishkas!*"

"Manny thought she was out shopping."

"Ugh!, we'll go anyway."

"She even shouted at Manny when he came down! He said she never shouted at him."

"Well, now she doesn't have anybody left, I suppose it's a shame for her." Mum locked the street door, and we headed over to Altman's on the corner.

"She said the piano was Manny's father's, no one was even allowed to touch it since he died."

"She told you he died?"

"He's been dead for…" I counted — "…four years."

"Hmm."

"Yes, she just keeps it standing there with the lid closed all the time, nobody can play it."

"So she told you he died!"

"Well, Manny told me, his Dad died when the war started."

"Alright, alright already."

At Altman's, Mum picked two apples for Mrs. Yanklewitz. Mrs. Altman started to say something, but immediately Mum put a threepenny bit down on the counter and Mrs. Altman's mouth closed again as she handed Mum a penny change.

Then, on to Antill Road. "Which one is it?"

"Over there, number fourteen."

We walked over, and Mum scoured the door's stained glass insets. "Tsk!, where's the knocker?" She twisted a little brass knob protruding from the frame between the glass panels, and inside a bell rang. "Humph! Look, she's got a fancy bell, a door knocker isn't good enough."

Nobody answered, so Mum turned the knob again. Upstairs a window opened.

"Who is it, what do you want from me already?" It was Mrs. Yanklewitz.

Mum backed away from the door to look up. "It's me, Mrs. Grossman."

"Mrs. who?"

"It's me, Mrs. Grossman, Zachary's mother."

"What do you want?"

"I came to see if there's anything I can do, to pay a visit, if you need anything."

"Need anything?"

"Some food or something…."

"Need anything! A family, that's what I need." She began to sob. "I need my family!"

"I'm sorry, it's terrible what happened to your boy."

"Terrible? It's worse than terrible! To you it's terrible, to me, I'm his mother, it's not terrible, it's *worse* than terrible."

"Alright, it's worse than terrible."

"My boy, *mein* only *kinderlech,* I lost my whole family, my life, they took my life away."

"I'm so sorry, what can anybody say? Look, I brought you some apples."

"Apples? So what's apples going to do for me? Will it bring me back *mein kinderlech, mein* boy?"

"What can I say, Mrs. Yanklewitz, we came over to pay our respects…."

"Respects!" She patted her eyes dry. "Mrs. Grossman, with all due respect, what do you know about dying, about losing your whole family?"

"Look, I'm sorry it happened to your son, what can anyone say that will change anything? Look, come downstairs, let me give you the apples."

"Four? What is it you got, four *kinder?*" She dabbed at her eyes again. "Alright, I'll come down." The window slammed, and a few moments later the street door opened. I barely recognized her in a bright shamrock-green robe, her face all puffed up, her eyes red. She held a white handkerchief the size of a pillowcase. "My boy, my *boubala,* my Manny, my life it's finished. First my husband, then one I've got, and now, nothing!"

"I'm sorry…."

"Sorry! Everybody's sorry, then they go, back to their family they go…."

"I…."

"They go home, they've got their family still, what've I got?"

"What can anybody do really?"

"What've I got? Nothing, that's what I got, nobody, an empty house I got!"

"If there was anything I could do that would make a difference…."

"How many you got?"

"Five *kinder,* you think it's easy?" Lily handed her the bag containing the two apples.

"Five! *Oy a broch!* I thought it was four!" She threw the bag to the pavement and the apples rolled out. "I'm sorry, I'm so upset, I'll die I will."

I picked them up and put them back in the bag to hand to her.

She looked straight at me. "You!" she said, sobbing. "Why did it have to be my Manny, why couldn't it be you?"

I felt guilty and didn't know what to say.

"What?" Mum said.

"Why did it have to be *mein kinderlech?*" She pointed. "Why couldn't it be somebody else's family?"

"What?" Mum drew back. "What are you saying already?"

"You got five, why couldn't it be him?" Now she was crying openly. "My only boy, my whole family, my life, I might as well be dead, I am dead, I'm as good as dead already…."

"What do you mean, why couldn't it be him? My boy?"

"You'll have four others left, I don't mean anything, why does God punish me like this, why me, why me?" She dabbed at her eyes with the huge handkerchief. "Why didn't it happen to someone else instead, you've got plenty…."

"Plenty? *I've got plenty?*"

"All I had, one wonderful boy…."

"Wash your mouth out, you…."

"One wonderful boy… and now, nothing."

"A terrible thing to say, *feh!* how could you even think such a thing?"

"I don't mean anything, you'll still have four left, why does God do this terrible thing to me, why to me? I'm a good person."

"*I'll have four left?*" Mum grabbed the bag of apples from my hand and flung it at Mrs. Yanklewitz; it struck her on the forehead and she staggered back into the open doorway. Again the two apples rolled along the ground. "A fire in your *kishkas,* may you take a *broch* already."

Mrs. Yanklewitz backed against the door. "What's she doing, I didn't mean anything…." The door inched open under her weight.

Mum's voice was getting louder: "A filthy thing to say! No wonder your husband ran off."

"What? What!?"

"No wonder your husband left you, *feh,* you're as ugly as a man, you are!"

"What? What's she saying…?"

"Wha'd'y' think, it's a secret? The whole street knows," and now Mum was shouting: "He left you for a *shiksa,* you think nobody knows? Everybody knows, I don't know how he stayed…."

"What, what, what's she saying, she's, she's…." Mrs. Yanklewitz made several futile grasps behind her back for the doorknob.

"Where he works, he ran off with the *shiksa* from the office there…."

"*Oy… oy….*" Mrs. Yanklewitz' other hand was to her chest and she was sliding down the door. "*Oy…* I can't breathe…."

"You think you're better than everyone else, like reading… books all the time down the shelter there. And you think people didn't see you tweezing your chin under the covers all night? It's a beard, a man's beard you got there on your chin."

"Ugh! Ugh!" she gasped. "Help me, somebody, help, help me, she's gone mad…." Now she was practically sitting on the doorstep, trying to scream, but the words were faint, "Help, help!" Several nearby doors opened part way, and heads peeped out.

"Take a *broch!*" Mum shouted. "I come here to… to… to give my… to say I'm sorry, to bring a little something, and the… the *pig,* she's telling me my boy should get killed instead! *Feh!* May you rot, may you join him there, under the earth may you join him!" Mum was pulling my arm: "Come on, we're going, who wanted to come here in the first place…."

I followed Mum away leaving Mrs. Yanklewitz screaming louder and louder, sitting on her doorstep, one hand hanging onto the doorknob. When we reached the corner I asked Mum: "Is it really true about Mr. Yanklewitz, he didn't die? Manny said he died."

"True? Sure it's true, everybody knew he didn't die, she's such a *broch* he couldn't stand her anymore."

"Christ!"

"He ran away, with the one from the office he went. She was so ashamed, for a week they sat *shiva* there, she had the rabbi say *Kaddish,* she even bought a plot in the cemetery."

"What's *Kaddish?*"

"A prayer when you die, she lit *yahrzeit* candles there in the house like he really died."

"I wonder why Manny didn't tell me? He always told me everything."

"You don't know the whole story, she didn't tell Manny, can you believe she didn't even tell her own son? Everybody in the neighborhood knew."

"Really? I didn't…. What a terrible thing for Manny, he would have been able to see his father sometimes."

"So, now, what's the use?"

Returning along Tredegar Terrace back toward the house, we could still hear Mrs. Yanklewitz shrieking in the distance. "Christ, listen to her!"

"Listen to her, with her nose stuck up in the air always! I knew I shouldn't try to do anything nice for that *broch,* ugh!, *feh!*"

18

Normally Zilla and Rebecca slept late on Saturday, but today they both were up before ten, bustling around, getting ready to go out.

"We're going to get Katya," announced Zilla.

"Katya! You are? Where is she?"

"We're going to the station to get 'er. They're supposed to put 'er on the train in Taunton this morning."

Katya, Katya! She'd been away so long it was almost as though she were no longer part of our family!

Through the window I saw that Jack and Izzy had just walked up. In the six weeks since Manny had died, a tacit understanding had arisen that Jack, Izzy and I would meet regularly in front of our house, whatever happened. Today Jack was to show us around the Brady Boys Club, but Katherine's return was much more important. I rushed outside. "My sister's coming home today! You remember Katya, Katherine?"

"She's the little one," said Izzy.

"She's twelve now, I can't believe it! She's really coming home, and today, she'll be here soon!"

Jack saw I was too excited for Brady's. "So I'll just take Izzy today, and you'll come another time, then?"

"Yes, definitely, I have to be here now."

"Why did she stay evacuated so long, until now?" asked Izzy.

The question was an embarrassment. "I don't know…."

Unaware, he continued: "There's hardly any air raids any more, the war's just about over."

I didn't want Lily to possibly overhear. "My parents said it's safer there." I couldn't say the real reasons — that we hadn't had the fare-money, that Mum had said it would cost extra to feed another mouth at home.

They left, and I went back in. Rather than going with my older sisters to the station to get her, I was secretly glad that costing an extra fare on the Underground gave me a reason to stay home by myself with the news.

For two hours I sat at the window in a reverie, singing silent songs the way I used to when Abie would be shouting and throwing plates. Bow Bells reverberated peacefully in the distance — quarter past, half past, quarter to — and I lost count. Then suddenly all three of my sisters were coming across Tredegar Square from Mile End Road, Zilla carrying a suitcase, Katherine a gasmask case strap across her shoulder. Just as I'd not recognized Marius in Banbury, nor Zilla and Rebecca years later at Victoria Station, so I could hardly believe this thin, much taller, shorthaired person could be Katherine. Katherine had had long hair; this one looked almost like a boy! I was nervous to go outside to greet her, afraid to interrupt the trio's approach in case it might cause the newcomer to be someone else. They crossed the road and slipped past the window's purview. Before anyone could unlock the street door I rushed to open it, and there they stood: Rebecca already on the step and wielding the key, then Zilla, and beyond them a fragile stranger and a big bag. Rebecca came in. Next, Zilla bumped the bag up the two steps. On the pavement below, alone, stood Katherine.

"Hello, Katya."

"Hello, Zech."

"Why is your hair short?" I heard my voice break.

"They cut it off."

"Do you want to come in?" It was as though someone else were saying the words.

"Yes." She came up the steps, and I was afraid to touch her. Zilla, behind me, turned toward the stairs; I didn't know which direction to go, so I picked up the suitcase and backed into the living room. Katherine followed me in just as Rebecca came out of the kitchen. From the bottom of the stairs Zilla called up to Mum: "We're back, she's here, we got 'er."

From upstairs came Mum's voice: "Alright, I'm cleaning, I'll be down."

"I want to get ready, we're going out," Rebecca said apologetically, and following Zilla she clattered up to their bedroom.

Awkwardly alone with Katherine in the living room, I stood her bag down. She unshouldered the gasmask case, stood it on the settee and started to take her coat off. I went to take it, to hang it on the door, "No, it's alright," and she lay it over the settee's arm. Her face was so different, with the thin pale cheeks of an anæmic boy. She just stood and looked around the room as if remembering, then walked over to see out the windows.

"Was it alright there, in Devon?"

"No, I didn't like it."

"Who cut your hair off?"

"Mrs. Bottom."

"They did?"

"She said it was easier to manage."

Again, neither of us spoke.

Then, "Katya, maybe I should tell Mum to come down, maybe she didn't hear."

"It's alright, she'll come down."

"Katya, would you like some tea? I can make some tea."

"Yes, alright."

"Katya, I wanted you to come home for a long time."

Still looking out the window, she shrugged her shoulders.

Suddenly, inexplicably, I burst into tears, "Tsk! I don't know why I'm crying!"

"It's not worth crying about."

And with just as little warning, of its own accord my crying stopped. We stood there. Then she giggled one time — the first time she'd looked even slightly happy — and that allowed me to do the same thing although my eyes still felt wet. We stood there, half a room apart, laughing at nothing.

"I'll put the kettle on." I went into the kitchen and filled the kettle. As I leaned over the gas stove on the kettle's handle, voluminous tears began streaming again from my eyes, confounding me; it would have been understandable to cry when she was away, not now she was home. Again I wiped my eyes and went to the bottom of the stairs to call up: "Mum, Katya's home."

"Alright, I'm nearly finished up here, a terrible mess it is up here always, I don't know why you make such a mess everywhere."

I went back to the kitchen to check the kettle, though it couldn't be boiling so soon. Mum's footsteps clumped down two or three stairs. The broom swished. She stopped every few steps to clear up some other bit of mess. Before I heard her reach the bottom I pushed the kitchen door almost closed so she should go straight through into the living room.

Instead, she brought the broom and shovel into the kitchen. "You put water on, alright. Is it enough, did you put enough on for tea?"

"Yes, there's enough, I put on enough."

"Alright." Her face seemed gaunt. "So I s'pose I'll go in." Outside the kitchen again, she first checked the street door, opened it and closed it. She swept up some crumbs on the floor by the doormat, opened the street door again and swept them outside, closed the door. Then she went into the living room. "So, you're home."

"Hello, Mum."

"Ee, you're so thin." I heard puttering movements. "You're hungry, I'll make you some potatoes."

"Zech is making tea."

"Alright, I'll make some tea."

"Why couldn't I come back?"

"What do you mean, you're back, a *glick,* what's the good?"

"The others came back."

"The others, don't start already! Zachary he's back, I don't know, a little while, the girls they got tickets somewhere, who knows, where's the money coming from for everything? I'll make you something, some potatoes."

She came back into the kitchen. "I'll make her some potatoes," then to me, "you want some potatoes?" She pulled the bag out of the cupboard over to the sink and began peeling them nervously. "Go in, go in, I'll make the tea, go on, talk to her."

I went back into the living room as the big girls came slithering down the stairs, all black-seamed shiny stockings and ocelot jackets. "Ta-ra, Mum!"

"You should eat something, you didn't eat, either of you."

"'S alright, I'm not hungry, we'll eat later, ta-ra Katya, Zech." They waved into the living room as they traipsed out.

"Where are you going?" Mum called after them.

"Up West, we'll eat there."

"Don't be late, your Father he'll start screaming." The street door banged shut. A moment's silence, then, from the kitchen, "Ow, my finger, *a broch,* no, my finger with the peeler, ugh!" Mum was talking to herself. She called me: "The tea, come get the tea already," then her voice went much quieter, "ugh, leave me alone everybody, leave me alone already...."

"You alright, Mum, what happened?" I asked.

"Nothing, nothing, my finger...." She had wrapped a serviette around her finger. "No, leave me alone, take the tea, take the tea."

I took the two mugs of tea that stood on the stove and carried them to the table in the living room. Katherine and I sat down.

"Mum cut her finger."

"Yes."

We drank our tea in silence. I could hardly look at her, she seemed so unfamiliar; I was almost frightened that she might suddenly announce she wasn't really Katherine. But I did look — the hair color, the nose and the mouth, the lines. Again I thought I might cry, as though I no longer had control over starting or stopping crying. I tried to say something, to have some conversation. "Katya, I wanted to leave my job, I go to work now, but Mum said I have to stay there, where I screw wires into boxes, one after the other. I hate it."

"If you hate it you should leave."

"She'll tell Dad, he'll kill me, she said." She didn't answer. "She'll tell Dad," I repeated. She shrugged. "You have to find a job you like and don't worry about what happens."

Katherine was right: it was that simple. I'd go to the Unemployment Exchange and not say anything to Mum. Maybe she'd tell Abie, but it would be too late to go back to Cable Electric with the constant hammering and the thick haze of smoke. We each drank our tea in silence across the table, and Mum found ways to busy herself in the other room.

Katherine stood up. "I'm going round the corner to see if Hazel's there."

"Can I come with?"

"If you want."

The kitchen door was pulled to as Katherine left to visit the friend she hadn't seen for four and a half years. I followed her down the outside steps. As we walked side by side along Tredegar Terrace, as I tried to have our different size steps fall into some graspable rhythm, I remembered Manny. "Manny's dead. He got killed by a flying bomb."

"Manny? Manny from Antill Road? Really?"

"Yes, down Petticoat Lane. I saw him when he was dead. I was there with Dad."

"How horrible! I remember him, he was a bit dumpy, his nose looked like a sausage."

"He was nice, he was very funny."

We reached Litchfield Road, Hazel's house, and I stood away as Katherine knocked.

The door opened to a dark rectangle. Whoever stood within its frame remained still for quite half a minute; then, quietly: "You came home." It must have been Hazel.

"Today." Katherine lifted an arm into the darkness. "Just now."

A hand emerged and touched Katherine's sleeve. "You want to come in?"

"Alright." Katherine looked back, "My brother...." Hazel noticed me standing back, by the curb.

"I'll go, my friends are coming, they'll be here soon."

I walked back along Tredegar Terrace to the house; I knew Hazel used to be her very best friend. In the direction of the City, the sky had turned a dusky ochre. On the far diagonal of Tredegar Square I noticed Jack and Izzy approaching. I didn't go forward to meet them, requiring more time, to recover, to think about Katherine being home at last. As they crossed the road from the park and I waited by the wall, so Katherine came back along Tredegar Terrace with someone, a girl.

I needed to introduce my sister. "Katya, do you remember Jack?"

She looked at Jack. "Yes, I remember. You know Hazel? This is my friend Hazel."

Hazel! I took a closer though circumspect look, and it certainly wasn't the little Hazel I remembered! This one was tall with a frilly white blouse, a bit skinny, with pale skin and what seemed in the declining light to be wavy auburn hair.

I didn't know what to say; "I'm Zachary, Katya's brother."

"I know who you are, you just came to our house."

"Oh, yes...." I felt foolish.

"Also I seen you in the shelter," she added.

"You did?"

"Yes."

"I didn't see you — oh, maybe I didn't realize it was you." My embarrassment compounded.

At that moment there sounded a distant but substantial explosion. It was followed by a thunderous pealing that reverberated and rolled echoing across the early evening sky. That could mean only one thing. "A V-2!" I said.

"What are we supposed to do?" Katherine asked the question quietly; she didn't seem the slightest bit alarmed.

"Katya just came back, today," I said to no-one in particular.

Jack addressed Katherine. "It's alright now," he said reassuringly. "Whatever's done is done. It was a rocket, a V-2 rocket." Above the housetops in the direction of Hackney a magenta glow flickered, lighting alternate patches of sky and augmenting the darkening clouds. "The Germans only send one at a time, so there's nothing you can do once it's landed. There wouldn't be any point in going down the shelter now."

Lily was at the opened door. "Ee, what was it, a rocket, the barstards, what do you think of that, I hope Zilly and Rivka are alright."

"They were going up West, that's a different direction," I said.

"It looks like Hackney or Stepney, Mrs. Grossman," said Izzy; nobody had mentioned him nor even introduced him, but he was used to being ignored.

"Hello, Mrs. Grossman." It was Hazel's soft voice in the dusk.

"Who is it, who's that?"

"Hazel," said Katherine.

"Tsk! Terrible, terrible, the barstard Germans. The potatoes, you didn't eat the potatoes, I'll eat them then." She went back in and the street door closed.

We walked. I stayed ahead with Jack and Izzy, but my attention was distracted by the two girls' footsteps behind us.

Jack danced around to walk backwards for several steps. "So this is your initiation, your first day back."

Katherine emitted an unlikely high giggle. "They probably knew I was coming back, that's why they did it."

At the end of Morgan Street, Jack pointed: "Katya, see that? That's all that's left of the railway bridge, and the Victoria pub and the houses."

"I don't even remember it!"

"It was the first doodle-bug to land in London," said Izzy.

"You have the honor — it landed on your street," continued Jack. "But now that the Allies have captured most of the launching sites there are hardly any more doodle-bugs. Also..." and he half-danced back to address me, "Zech, did you hear about the M-9 Predictor?"

"The what?"

"The M-9 Predictor. It's reduced the injuries from falling anti-aircraft shells."

"I... I never heard anything about it...."

"Some American mathematician, Norbert Wiener, worked it out, it uses radar readings to aim A.A. guns more accurately. Just two or three weeks ago the Germans launched over one hundred V–1s to hit London because the launching sites were about to be captured, but because of this M-9 Predictor equation, only four actually got through."

"Really? Wow!" Some other time I'd ask for details, but right now, continuing along Grove Road, I was intrigued by how different Hazel looked. "Hazel, how long have you been back?" Too shy to dance backwards like Jack, I settled for asking the question over my shoulder.

"About a year, I came back last March."

"Where did they send you?" asked Jack.

"St. Andrews."

"Scotland!" I exclaimed, sounding more surprised than I actually was. And, having again embarrassed myself, I couldn't abandon the startled tone too abruptly. "Wow! What a long way!" Anyway, St. Andrews *was* much further than I'd been — Banbury, and Whitney — further even than Devon.

"Was that the place where the Germans landed a sabotage crew from a U-boat?" asked Jack.

I didn't even know that!

"No, that was near Froon, it was stupid, they caught them right away."

"Christ!" said Izzy.

"But that was all, nothing ever happened there. I just lived with a family and went to school, it was boring, we went to church Sunday mornings, that was all we ever did."

"Didn't you tell them you were Jewish?" I asked. "They tried to make me go to church, also."

"I'm not Jewish, we're Christian."

"Oh!" This compounded my stupidity! I didn't even know she was Christian!

Either wittingly or through inadvertence, Jack rescued me as he swirled around to Katherine. "What about you, what was it like?"

"Oh, I don't know, nothing," Katherine said.

The flickering glow reflecting off the base of the low-lying clouds raged brighter as we approached, and we could hear the distant sounds of scrambling activity and shouting voices, of fire pumps and diesel engines. We rounded a corner, and several streets ahead of us bright lights had been set up behind a tall building of flats. Lately the authorities didn't seem to worry any more if lights showed at night since the only things reaching London now were flying bombs and rockets, where visible lights didn't matter.

From the distance it appeared the rocket had blown out the facing walls of two adjacent buildings of flats six or seven floors high; the still-smoking crater was right between them, with wreckage strewn everywhere. An air-raid warden wouldn't let us through, but you could plainly see the ripped-open rooms, the drooping unsupported edge of the floors. The thought of being inside one of those rooms as the explosion occurred made me feel nauseous. Firemen were directing hoses up at the fires, but the jets of water were unable to reach higher than about the fourth floor, so above that level flames and smoke poured unchecked from the shattered rooms. On the ground there were various movements among the rubble and smoke, and it was difficult to tell in the blinding floodlights and the confusion if these were people, or stirrings caused by the spraying water and swirling debris. As we looked, something, some massive piece of furniture slid from a top-floor flat out of the gaping opened side of the building. Enveloped in flames and a shower of sparks as it twisted down, a corner glanced against a ripped-open wall producing a cortege of debris and sparks that accompanied its plunge. It smashed to the concrete below in a dizzying fountain of black and golden projectiles. The sound! On the heels of its impact came a peculiar ring of notes like the arpeggio of a strummed harp.

In astonishment I realized what it was. "It must have been a piano!"

"'Ey, get back there, get back." A grizzled air-raid warden was ordering us and several other peripheral onlookers back.

"I think you're right!" said Jack. "It was a piano!"

Katherine's mouth was open. "How terrible, oh, those poor people!"

"I'm sorry you have to see this your first evening home," said Jack, and he actually put his arm around Katherine's shoulders. She didn't say anything, but stood there, frozen. I wondered if I should have done something like that to Hazel; as I glanced her way I quickly saw she had momentarily looked at me then averted her gaze. Why was I always slow, why hadn't I done that automatically, without thinking, the way Mr. Moore had picked up Joan Ingersoll when she fainted? A glance showed Izzy still looking at the fire scene ahead. Izzy never noticed what was going on between people, never seemed to even think about girls. Girls never looked at him anyway, because he was too short and fat.

At a distance, the diminutive figures of ambulance women threaded stretchers among the rubble, and every few moments an ambulance departed, its gong ringing mournfully as it negotiated its way. I was wet, then realized we all were wet; the wind had carried spray from the firemen's hoses the full length of two streets. For ten minutes the five of us stood silently in the chilled glare, and I was grateful when a voice suggested we return home.

Back at our house, Jack gave Katherine a little kiss on the cheek and called "Good night," as he walked off into the darkness, Izzy trailing behind.

I now had to pluck up courage to make up for being so slow, earlier. "Hazel, can I walk home with you?"

Katherine came with us also; after all she was her friend, and it probably hadn't even occurred to her not to come. At Hazel's door, although I wanted to kiss her on the cheek too it just seemed impossible. Katherine said they were going to talk some more, she'd be home soon. I left them and walked home alone, and let myself in. "Hello Mum, it's me."

"The potatoes, they're cold, eat some. The girls they didn't come back yet, I hope they're alright."

"Alright, I'll save one for Katya. She's at Hazel's house, she said she'll be back soon."

"Another one staying out all hours already, I don't want more trouble with his shouting."

I ate my potato. "Mum, I'm going up to bed."

Upstairs as I undressed and put on my too-tight pyjamas, I went over everything that had happened. I turned out the gaslight and climbed into bed, slid over to the window, and pulled apart the curtains. Dim starlight shone into the room.

It was impossible to sleep. Katherine would be back soon, then Zilla and Rebecca would return from up West, and maybe if Abie were home first there would be another round of his screaming.

A little later I heard the street door hinges creak. Under my door a crack of light from downstairs appeared, then quiet voices as Katherine spoke briefly with Mum. Shortly after that, soft padding feet up the stairs, the bedroom door opened, and Katherine came in.

"I'm awake," I announced.

"Oh, alright."

"Can you see?"

"Yes, it's alright, I'll leave the door open."

"Are you going to sleep here, I mean...."

"Mum said I should sleep in that bed — your bed — 'til she gets another one."

"Oh."

She began to undress among the dim shadows, and I turned away and looked out the window. I felt my face get hot and red, and I was glad it was as dark as it was, that the stars were such a welcoming anchor.

"Mum said this is where I sleep; is it alright?"

"Yes," I gulped.

She closed the door, lifted the covers, and there she was on the other side of the bed. I wondered if I would be able to sleep at all, and lay there uncomfortable and silent for several minutes.

"Zech, when did you come home?" she finally asked.

"Nearly a year ago."

"Why didn't she let me come home also?"

"Mum?" I felt guilty, as though I had conspired to keep her away so long. "I dunno, I asked her if you could come home. She said when we got the house fixed up."

"She'll never get the house fixed up."

Once again I was amazed at the simple directness of Katherine's answers. I had to say something. "What was it like in Devon?"

"Terrible."

"Really?"

"Yes."

I felt awful that Mum had let her be there all alone for such a long time; I could have really made a fight and forced them to have her come home sooner. And suddenly here she was, lying under the covers on the other side of my bed — grown-up, twelve, a stranger.

Starlight played on the motionless covers.

"Are you going to let your hair grow long?"

"Yes."

"Manny was just about my best friend, since I came back — well, him and Jack."

"Good people always die young."

"They do?"

"Always."

I lay there, looking at the dappled shadows cast on the window by the big branches and the leaves. If it were true that good people always die young then I wondered how it worked, what the actual sequence of events would be from the time you could tell they were a good person until when they died. The causes and effects would have to include some sort of relatedness that could be understood, theoretically.

I came out of my reverie; she was breathing a bit fitfully, but regularly. She'd fallen asleep; of course she'd had a long and momentous day. And for some reason I felt too embarrassed to look directly at her face in the faint light, even though she wouldn't even know.

The next evening, Sunday, at bedtime it was again embarrassing, and I had to make a point of going upstairs early, to be in bed by the time Katherine came in from Hazel's. I left the light on very low; when she came upstairs she didn't turn it off, and she didn't ask me to look the other way. Maybe she was too young to think about those things, but she did face away from the bed; she took her dress off, put on a nightgown first, then under that took her bloomers off. She couldn't reach the gas, so I went to stand up on the bed to turn it off, but as I began I realized I had an erection — a hard-on, that was what Manny had called it! I felt ashamed; it would be so visible when I stood up, especially in my too-tight pyjamas. *What are little boys made of? Snips and snails, and puppy-dogs' tails.* My face had turned a deep beetroot red, but I had to turn the light off or that would draw even more attention. *And that's what boys are made of, made of.* I must have hesitated for a critical moment.

"You alright, Zech?"

"Yes, yes, nothing." I faced away as much as I could as I stood up, then turned myself around toward the light with my back to her, reached across to the knob and doused the light. When I got back under the covers my ears were in a raging heat; the erection was completely gone, but I felt so mortified that everything was swimming around in my head.

"My friend Eileen Wiggington came back also," she said.

"Did she?" I tried to remember if *Did she?* were real words, a proper response to what she was saying. The words swirled around, echoing: *Did. She.*

"Yes. She hated it also."

"Did she?" Now those two words sounded definitely wrong, stuck together with shapes and corners that pushed against my teeth.

"You alright?"

"Yes. Where was she?"

"In Scotland. Her foster father where she was evacuated did the same thing to her."

"The same thing?" My ears caught fire again, in dread of some terrible revelation, that Katherine would give a flat factual description of some new unheard-of depravity. "What... what did they do?"

"In Tiverton, Mr. Bottom put his hand up my dress."

"What? Why did he do that?" It was unbearable; I wanted to just jump out the window and get it all over with, never have to feel anything again.

Her reply came simply. "That's what men do."

That's what men do! How dreadful! It was hard to breathe. *That's what men do!* Mum was right about men: they're all filthy, repulsive animals. Either they're doing terrifying things to girls or they're shouting and punching. I wished I were a girl; at least girls don't have to feel ashamed and guilty just existing, just being alive, guilty when they haven't even done anything.

—o—O—o—

When I got up on Monday morning and went downstairs, I acted as though I were preparing to leave for work at Cable Electric as usual. But, emboldened by Katherine's certitude, I hid the bike behind the hollyhocks at the far end of the garden, climbed over the wall and secretly took the bus to the Unemployment Exchange on Mansell Street.

"You again."

"Yes."

"Hmm. You're here for a job."

"Yes, I want a job, a different one this time."

"Different. Alright. What was wrong with the other job, basically speaking?"

"Everything was all dirty and noisy there."

"In that case what sort of work are you looking for this time? If you know what I mean."

"Yes, where there isn't a loud noise all day long, like hammering."

"Was the other job hammering?"

"Yes. Not me but somebody else. And paint and smells."

"Hmm. There are jobs that basically fall into what you might call the generally quiet category. Specifically I'd suggest an office job."

"I don't know anything about offices, would they show me?"

"You'd have to actually try out a specific job to see if it was quiet enough, if you know what I mean."

"Yes."

"Also they don't use paint in offices, as a rule of thumb."

"I see."

"So we'll start again at the beginning, shall we?"

"Alright."

"I want to get it really right this time."

"Yes."

"So I'll be asking you certain questions, put us on the right track, so to speak."

"I remember, yes."

"That's right. Okay, number one, what do you think you're particularly good at? Or let's put it like this, what would you say you could do better than anyone else, much better than anyone else?"

"In London?"

"Let's say all Britain."

"You mean, including Scotland and Wales."

"Yes, we want to get it right this time, try, at least."

I remembered Mr. Taylor. "I think I'm good at, well, people, telling people off some-times..." he looked up from his papers, "like teachers who say stuff and you think they're saying...."

"We wouldn't have any jobs specifically in that category...."

"I...."

"No, I wouldn't even need to look through the lists."

"Oh." Probably I shouldn't have mentioned that.

He returned to his sheaf. "How does a stock room job sound? Generally it's quiet in stock rooms, though basically you'd have to try out a particular job, generally speaking."

"What do you have to do in stock rooms?"

"Basically you move things around from one spot to another, although I'd have to say we don't know specifically about this particular job, basically speaking, if you know what I mean."

"Yes."

"It's definitely not a paint stock room though."

"Yes."

He sent me to the City, to Delhi Imports, Ltd., the premises of Mr. Bandi and Mr. Purushotham, who were importing cotton from India for military uniforms. In the back of their suite of two small offices and a clerk's desk in the hallway they had a big room stacked with loose-weave cotton swab bundles — not really rejects, said Mr. Bandi, "but still not quite, as they say in your country, up to snuff." And he laughed a high-pitched laugh.

My job was to be bundling the swabs into packages and taking them to the Post. The company would pay me one pound fifteen shillings a week — a five shilling increase! Mr. Bandi showed me around the stock room and started me off packing. It was completely quiet in there; in fact, too quiet. Periodically the clerk, Miss Eunice, came in with a list of addresses and the number of swabs I was to pack for each customer. I was grateful when she came in again later because she was the only person I'd seen all day since I began. During the morning she had left the stock room door open when she came in, but this time she closed it behind her.

"Why do you call me *Miss* Eunice?" she asked in a low voice, as though someone were listening. "Just call me Eunice."

I gulped. "Yes, Eunice." She was grown up, at least seventeen or eighteen, a real clerk, and I was only being respectful. Another thing, she didn't seem to realize she had long blond hair that swayed back and forth as she walked into the room. Particularly, when she was leaving, it was difficult because her hair reached almost down to her bum, which also swayed as she walked but in the opposite direction from her hair, making it a strain to try not to look. This time she was standing uncomfortably close, and I could smell powder on her face; she had big brown eyes and long eyelashes, and under the powder were three round pimples on her forehead and two irregularly shaped ones on the inset of her chin. She must have done up her eyelashes with the same stuff — mascara and a little brush — that Rebecca and Zilla did before they went up West, but hers weren't made up as thick as theirs.

She flipped back and forth through the address pages she was holding. "Do you like me?" she asked without even looking at me. For the moment I didn't realize she was talking to me, except there was no one else in the room.

"Well, yes, why not, wha'd'ya mean?"

"You'd like me more if you kissed me," she continued relentlessly, still looking down at the pages. Suddenly she lowered the notebook and pressed her mouth hard against mine, making me stagger backward against the wall. She leaned into me, pulled my head down, and again banged her mouth against mine. Her teeth dug into my bottom lip, and in surprise I hit the back of my head against the wall.

"Blimey!" she said, "look what 'appened!" A cotton swab lay at my feet, and on its bleached white surface a stark spot of bright crimson crept into a widening circle. "That you? You're bleeding." She looked alarmed. "Quick, any blood on me?"

I did a nervous survey of her face and blouse: "No, I can't see anything...." And she rushed out of the room.

My lip was swelling up, and I picked up another swab and dabbed the blood away, then another swab until the flow seemed to stop. Mr. Bandi might give me the sack if the very first day he found wasted swabs with blood on them in the dustbin, so the only thing to do was pack them up — which I did, adding one each to three different packages so that no single client would be unduly victimized.

On the way out to the Post I stopped at Miss Eunice's desk for postage money. "Eunice, not *Miss* Eunice," she hissed.

That night I told Katherine that I'd secretly gone to the Unemployment Exchange, that I had a new job.

She put down her book. "Good for you."

"It's better than the other one."

"I know."

"How do you know?"

"Because I can tell you're happier."

"You can? What are you reading?"

"Something about poetry."

"Poetry?"

"The Life of Byron, Baron of Rochdale."

"Oh, I don't know anything...."

"That wasn't his real name, it was George Gordon. He wrote beautiful poetry."

"I see. Anyway it's quiet in this place, and there's no paint smell all the time."

"See? You just have to make up your mind and then do it."

"There's a big girl there, also."

"Is she nice?"

"Well, she's older than me."

"That doesn't matter."

"There weren't any girls in the other place."

She lay her book on the floor and snuggled down to go to sleep. So many changes were happening: Katherine was home, I had a new job and Mum didn't even know yet, and when she did find out I'd be able to tell her I was now earning one pound fifteen. And Miss Eunice wanted to kiss me; that could mean she thought I was nice. I looked at Katherine lying next to me. I wondered if Katherine would ever be so fierce with a boy if she liked him. If girls didn't like you, which was nearly always, there was absolutely nothing you could do to change it, but if you found out they did like you, then all of a sudden they became really fierce. Manny had been right about girls, in a way. Girls were so mysterious; like wild animals they didn't seem to actually think, or worry about things, they just *did*.

•   •   •

The next morning, Miss Eunice again came in with the list. And when she again closed the door my stomach started to feel funny. So I thought, if she's going to start kissing I'm going to try not to be nervous — as she's doing it I'm going to try to stop thinking, totally stop thinking. But she was quicker than I imagined and I didn't get a chance to execute that plan; I just fell backward into the mound of swabs. She fell too, on top of me, and I could feel her breasts rolling like jelly against my chest. Just then the door opened and Mr. Purushotham stepped in.

"What's going on here?" he cried in that high-pitched clipped Indian vernacular. "We can't have these goings on here, you know! Eunice, come into my office."

An hour later I gingerly carried my crop of packages through the office hall on the way to the Post. In silhouette behind the frosted glass, Mr. Purushotham sat opposite Miss Eunice, leaning toward her, talking confidentially.

I knocked timidly on the glass. Mr. Purushotham looked up, but Miss Eunice kept her head facing away: "What do you want?"

"I need money for the Post."

He came out, opened the small metal box in Miss Eunice's desk drawer, and handed me five shillings.

I was sure he and Mr. Bandi were going to give us both the sack. I got into the lift, and the lift man smiled, "Good mornin'." It certainly wasn't a good morning for me. I'd never be able to go back to the clerk at the Unemployment Exchange because of getting the sack; Mum would tell Dad, and that would be the end of everything. But amazingly, after I returned neither Mr. Purushotham nor Mr. Bandi said another word about what had happened, though for the rest of the day Mr. Purushotham, not Miss Eunice, brought the address sheets in.

That evening when I got home, Mum was waiting by the door. "What happened, I saw the bike in the garden, they gave you the sack, *oy a broch!*"

"No, I...." It was time to tell her I had a new job, and just hope everything was all right despite Miss Eunice.

"Where were you all day? He'll kill you he will, when he finds out."

"But I got another job already."

"How much will they pay you?"

"One pound fifteen."

"That's more than the other one, with the wires."

"Yes."

"Alright, then don't tell him. The other one will have to get a job also, Katya, she doesn't want to go to school. She should go live with her *shiksa* friend already, she's there all the time except when she wants to eat."

The next day Mr. Bandi surprised me by walking into the stockroom with the address sheets, then mentioning in an almost casual tone that Eunice was now vice-president of Delhi Imports, Ltd. I couldn't believe it, how that could have happened instead of us both getting the sack. Later, going through the hallway with my packages, she sat at the same desk, and she still gave me the five shillings. Apart from her trying not to look directly at me, she didn't seem any different — a blue blouse today, but the same pimples on her forehead, and she still smelled of powder.

That evening I related to Mum about Mr. Purushotham and how he had reprimanded Miss Eunice because she came in the stockroom and closed the door; I could never, never tell her about the kissing part. "Then she became the vice-president."

"The vice-president?"

"Mr. Bandi came in and told me she became the vice-president. I thought she was going to get the sack."

Mum didn't answer, and her face went smooth. The ends of her mouth tried to curl, almost into a smile, but then juddered back into a straight line.

"How could she become the vice-president all of a sudden?"

Marius was obviously listening, but he didn't say anything either. He just sat there looking at me, waiting for something to happen. Even with Marius, four years younger than me, these situations were like a conspiracy of grown-ups, with me the only one left out. Without a word, Mum walked away into the kitchen.

"Maudy, do you know what I mean? Like, how...." I asked.

"'Ow do I know, I don't go to work yet. Crikey, 'ow should I know?"

"I don't know, you looked as though you knew what happened... sort of why she was the vice-president all of a sudden...." I felt foolish in front of Maudy, so I tried to change the subject. "I... I saw Uncle Albert last week again, I went to his room."

"So? So what's so special about goin' to someone's room?"

"He... he used to be a soldier in the First World War. He showed me his uniform."

"Well, alright. Crikey, is that all?"

I felt even more foolish. "He showed me his gun."

"Gun? 'E's got a gun?"

"It's a rifle. He took it home with him when he got out of the army."

"Took it 'ome? What's it like?"

"It's long, it's a rifle, with a thing you pull back to put the bullet in."

"Bullet! Does 'e 'ave bullets also?"

"He had a box of bullets, a small cardboard box."

"They're real bullets?"

"I don't know, I suppose so, he said they were."

"Does he keep 'em in the gun, is it loaded?"

"No, they were in a cardboard box, a little box. In a drawer."

"Crikey!"

That evening when I got into bed, Rebecca and Zilla were already in bed in their room. Katherine came back late again, from Hazel's. I turned away, and she undressed in the dark.

"Hazel likes you."

"She does?" This was surprising because Hazel never tried to be fierce. But first I wanted to settle what had happened at work, so I told her about Mr. Purushotham and Mr. Bandi. I had to mention Miss Eunice and me falling over in the cotton swabs, otherwise it wouldn't have made sense, but I didn't give any embarrassing details.

"Do you like her?"

"Who?"

"Eunice, Miss Eunice."

"What do you mean, she's seventeen."

"That doesn't mean you can't like her."

"I mean, like her? What do you mean...?"

"Well, don't tell Hazel."

"Hazel? Why Hazel?"

"She'll be jealous."

"Jealous?"

"Hazel said she likes you."

"She did? She actually said it?"

"Yes, she's too shy to tell you."

"Really! I wonder why?"

"What do you mean, you wonder why?"

"I mean, why would she like *me?*"

"Because you're handsome and you're my brother. She'd kill me if she knew I told you, so don't say anything."

I'd never have the courage to tell someone if I liked them. "Oh no, I wouldn't say anything."

"I'm only telling you because you're my brother."

"I won't say anything, I'd be too shy."

She climbed into bed. "I hate my job."

"What?"

"I hate my job."

"You started work?"

"Yes, this morning."

"You didn't tell me...."

"I'm selling shoes for a fat greasy *yenta,* in Burdett Road."

"I didn't know, Mum didn't say...."

"Six days a week, *Anya's Fashion Footwear.*"

"Don't you like it?"

"You can't stop for one minute or she starts nagging."

"Christ, I'm sorry, maybe you could do something else, go to the Unemployment Exchange...."

"Fifteen shillings for six days."

"Only fifteen shillings? They pay me one pound fifteen! And it's only five days."

"Girls, women only get half as much as men, and they have to work twice as hard."

"They do?"

"That's right."

"But... why, that's terrible, why doesn't somebody...?"

"Because that's the way it is."

·   ·   ·

At four o'clock the following Monday I was taking the last bundle of packages to the Post. The lift attendant wore a big grin as he slid open the door.

"Did you 'ear about it?" he asked as I entered.

"No, what?"

"The old Jerry surrendered!"

"They did?" The stockroom had no access to the outside world other than through the office and hall, and there Mr. Bandi and Mr. Purushotham talked only about cotton swabs. "They did? I can't believe it!"

"Signing it tomorrow, they are."

"I can't believe it!"

"Yup, May the eighth. Wait 'til you gets outside, they're dancing right there in the street they are!" As he pulled aside the lift door at the first floor, car hooters were honking outside. "Been like that for a bloody hour, it 'as."

I balanced the packages against the wall as the news' implications flooded through me: at last it was true, the war in Europe was over, finished, we'd won, we'd beaten the Germans! No more rockets and flying bombs, no more swarms of Lancasters and Flying Fortresses droning out every night and morning. But my reactions included numb pangs of confusion, even emptiness. No more sleeping in the shelter; in a way I'd miss the camaraderie down there, though since Manny was killed it hadn't ever been the same with just Izzy. After the regular air-raids had petered out, hardly anybody slept down there anymore. When Izzy wasn't around, all I did was stand outside on the dilapidated scrub of Tredegar Square and explain to the old Jewish men about *triangulation,* how the Germans controlled the flying bombs with radio signals from two separate locations on the Continent; how two signals homing in on the flying bomb comprised a triangle, how by measuring the signals' return time the Germans could locate the bomb's position, and then describing how they could transmit a signal for it to crash. Every night my audience doddered open-mouthed, touching one anothers' arms to acknowledge emphases, nodding, muttering; and the following night these same men would want me to explain the identical thing, only to be freshly amazed at the marvels of the modern world.

As I pushed open the swinging door to the street, the deluge of festivities catapulted me from reverie. The street was engulfed in an improbable parade of cavorting dancers, prancing women in neat office dresses, men in suits and ties swinging their briefcases, everything to a blasting accompaniment of bus hooters and bicycle bells. Through the tumult an irregular counterpoint of tugs' klaxons drifted up from the distant Thames.

I stood there, the packages again slipping from under my arms, the ruckus unfolding about me but separate from me. Above my head a strip of soft blue sky was unreeled between the tall buildings; up there all was silence and peace save the wheeling and plaintive cawing of gulls, indifferent to the news that their domain would no longer be invaded. I gathered the packages and inched a way forward. Opposite the Post Office, a more restrained chorus of revelers was singing: *There'll be blue-birds ov-er, The White Cliffs of Do-ver, To-mor-row just you wait and see.___ There'll be joy and laugh-ter, And peace ev-er af-ter, To-mor-row when the world is free.___*

–20–

Delhi Imports, Ltd. never gave me the sack, and within a week Miss Eunice was bringing in the address slips again. While inside the stockroom her big round eyes and their mascara'd lashes sometimes lingered a little longer than necessary, yet now she always left the door ajar. And when she walked out, the blonde hair still swished in the opposite direction from her bum as I tried to focus on the address slips. And thus my trips to the Post continued for the balance of the summer.

When I returned home from work one Tuesday evening, briefly alone in the living room I happened to turn the wireless on — and it was Beethoven as usual. They played Beethoven and Mozart so relentlessly you had to wonder if, besides a sprinkling of sea symphonies and larks ascending, those were the only records they owned. Then, while Lily was still in the kitchen, the announcer Stuart Hibberd cut in to say he would repeat an earlier news bulletin. For the BBC to interrupt Beethoven, the matter would have to be important. "Yesterday the Americans dropped on the city of Hiroshima an entirely new type of weapon, an atomic bomb that uses as its explosive force the power of atomic energy, the energy that powers the sun. One single bomb has completely destroyed the city, which is now burning."

Atomic energy! An atomic bomb! For a minute I thought I hadn't heard right! Wasn't atomic energy one of those things you just dream about, like perpetual motion? As the wireless voice droned unbelievably on, I felt I'd lost contact with reality! Lily brought out a bowl of soup with matzoh balls but who could think of eating? If what he'd said were true, this was more than just another incredible scientific invention — a jet plane, a rocket — this was… this was… atomic energy! As soon as they worked out the details and put it into engines it would mean an inexhaustible supply of power! My mind raced: manual labor would be redundant, no one would ever have to work anymore, the weekly struggle for the rent would be permanently resolved for everybody in the world, nobody would have to worry about anything. I'd be able to leave my job — though that would mean Miss Eunice wouldn't come into the stockroom anymore.

"So eat your supper then."

The ramifications were piling up so fast, my head ached. "Alright." Because manufacturing things used energy, the cost of everything would eventually come down to zero — except maybe having someone lubricate the machines once in a while. Still, they'd be able to practically give stuff away in the shops!

"So what do you think I'm standing over the stove all day for?"

"Alright, I'm sorry, I'm…." And it wouldn't even matter what something was made of, because they'd be able to transmute elements from whatever they had plenty of into whatever they needed, so you could never run out of raw materials! They'd be giving away gold and diamonds for nothing! "No, I'm, I'm, I just heard on the wireless about atomic energy, they dropped an atomic bomb in Japan."

"Atomic bomb! So will it pay the rent when the landlord comes round?"

"Well, actually…."

"When they do something for the working-class then I'll listen."

"Well, actually…."

"Your friend, what's-'is-name came round before, Jack, straight from school he came, he said he'll come round after supper."

So Jack must have heard about it in school! I tried to eat, but before I'd swallowed a single matzoh ball someone knocked on the door. I jumped up and shakily got the door open; Jack and I looked at each other, and it wasn't necessary to say a single word. Out of the corner of my eye I saw Izzy coming across the park. Izzy didn't understand these things, but even he must have realized he'd better be here.

"He should take a *broch* already!" I heard Lily's voice inside. "Finish your supper, by my life I'll give it all to the cat."

"Alright Mum, alright," I called back; and to Jack and Izzy, "I've got to go inside for one minute, wait here I'll be right out."

I ate three more matzoh balls in ten seconds, then rushed outside. Izzy held my arm and steadied me over the wall, then stood guard while Jack and I sat there, dazed.

Jack spoke first. "What an incredible reconciliation of energy and consciousness."

"Energy and consciousness? You mean…."

"This will be the demarcation point in mankind's casting off the old fetters."

Izzy looked at him, but kept prudently silent.

Lily opened the window. "Finish your supper, you *broch* you, what do you think I went shopping all day for?"

"Mum, this is the most important day in history. I'll be in soon."

The window closed. People walked by, their faces as bored as they were the day before atomic energy, ignorant people who didn't understand that soon the whole notion of work would be something you read about in history books!

Again the window opened. "Here's the rest of the dinner, eat it before it gets cold." I swiveled around for the plate that Lily handed through the window, embarrassed in front of my best friends to have to eat on the same day atomic energy was first used.

And so we sat there for hours, quietly reeling. Izzy left around ten to report in to his mother. "You'll be alright?" he called sympathetically as he headed into the dusk.

"We'll be alright," said Jack.

"If I ever recover from the shock," I added as Izzy faded away. "Remember that article in the paper where some scientist said he'd proved that atomic energy was impossible?"

"Whatever miracles transpire, there's never a shortage of naysayers."

At eleven o'clock, Abie came across the road from Tredegar Square.

"Dad, they invented atomic energy."

"Atomic energy? Nah!" And he went inside.

Finally, Jack stood up to go. "What a shame old Manny couldn't hang around long enough for the three of us to hear this together."

I knew how Manny would have felt. "This would have been a dream come true for him also," I said. "I keep expecting him to show up, I feel like he's actually here right now, sharing it with us."

"Well, he certainly is. We'll both see him again in another dimension, mark my words."
And Jack danced off into the charged and starry night.

•   •   •

The Japanese stuck it out for a few more days, hoping the Americans didn't have any
more atomic bombs, but three days later Nagasaki was demolished, already by a new and
improved model — trust the Yanks! And plutonium! They'd already created a new element,
beyond the ninety-two ordinary ones!

"We're living in momentous times," said Jack that evening. "With engines that run on
atomic energy, they can make rockets to go to other planets. I've written down exact descriptions of what my astral body saw on other planets, including the names of people I spoke to
there, so we can compare when someone goes there in a rocket and takes actual photos."

At the time we'd done Jack's experiment with astral projection I'd hardly been convinced by the outcome, but now at least I could be sure about atomic energy. "I'd love to
find that article I mentioned."

"Which one?"

"In the *Evening Standard,* where that twit specifically said he proved that getting
energy from inside atoms is forever impossible." I said. "I'd send him a letter really telling
him off."

"Why waste your time, he just had no imagination," responded Jack. "He's probably
only acquainted with Boolean logic. The Americans must have used quantum mechanics to
make the atomic bomb." I perhaps looked mystified at the words *quantum mechanics,*
because he added: "Quantum mechanics doesn't use Boolean logic."

"I mean I've heard the name quantum mechanics but I haven't read anything about it
yet. And the other thing, Boolean logic, what's that?"

"Boolean logic is what happens when you're looking at things, mostly."

"Looking? What do you mean?"

"A thing can happen one way if you're looking at it and another way if you're not."

"Well...." What was he talking about *this* time? "Okay, things can happen in different
ways, but what's that got to do with whether or not you're looking at it?"

"It's important whether you look or you don't look."

"To you, maybe, but of no significance to the thing that's happening. I mean, a thing,
what's happening, doesn't care... and *it* can't know if you're watching."

He regarded me gravely. "I see you don't know about quantum mechanics."

"I'm getting a bit mixed up." I certainly wanted to know about quantum mechanics and
Boolean logic, but in a straightforward way without loads of extra words.

"Let me put quantum mechanics clearly: if a thing happens, it happens one way if you're
looking at it, and maybe a different way if you're *not* looking at it! The thing is, you can't
tell."

"That's ridiculous! Isn't it? I mean, you can ask someone *else* to watch it, then they can
tell you what happened."

"Whether or not you look as it's happening," and he looked straight at me as he said it,
"affects the outcome."

"Well, wait a minute, how can *looking* at something make any difference — looking isn't
contacting it, like, poking something in, a stick, interfering!"

His face had changed into that same superior look that teachers have, that I'd seen in
pictures of insane people. "Boolean logic is what happens when... say, when you throw a

ball in the air, you know it'll come down again. But that doesn't always work for things you can't see, for instance when you're not looking at the moon."

"The moon? I...."

"For example, Boolean logic isn't what happens inside atoms, or, say, with Schrödinger's cat."

"*Whose* cat?"

"Erwin Schrödinger, he's a scientist with a cat, he got the Nobel prize."

"C-a-t, like an ordinary cat?"

"Yes, it sleeps inside a sealed box."

"Then how can it breathe?"

"That's the whole point, there's no way of knowing if it's dead or alive until the morning."

"I'm getting lost."

"Well, there's a difference, a big difference with non-Boolean logic, it's sort of mystical. Things don't happen the way you expect them to. It's sort of like magic, probably from other planets, normally you don't see much of it around."

"Magic? Are you serious?" This was Jack, who wanted to be an architect?

"Certainly!" He even laughed! "You only notice it when circumstances change, if it sweeps by from another planet, or I expect when you deliberately create it to make an atomic bomb."

"But what do you mean exactly, magic? You're not trying to tell me there's such a thing as magic, are you?" Jack could be so exasperating, but I had to be careful because sometimes he was right.

"It's hard to explain the theory," he said. "I'll draw an example." He picked up a stone, and on the pavement screeched out a rectangular oblong, which he divided into three sections — three rooms, with two doors, he said.

"See? Three rooms in a row, connected by doors *x* and *y*. If you want to get from room one to room three, you'd expect to have to go through door *x*, room two, and door *y*."

"Alright...." That I could follow.

"Imagine rooms two and three are empty, there are two dozen people in room one, and both doors are closed."

"You've drawn them open."

"That's only so you can see they're doors. Imagine they're closed."

"Okay."

"Twelve of the people are Jewish, and the other twelve are *yocks*."

"Alright...."

"Here's the non-Boolean part. Imagine the doors are special quantum mechanics doors — only Jews can go through the first door, door *x*, not *yocks*."

"Well..."

"In other words, these doors they're not Boolean logic doors, okay, anyone could go through those."

"Okay, then," I said cautiously; I was really going to follow his reasoning without judging beforehand. "They're not ordinary doors, like a door in my house."

"Right. Yours are Boolean logic doors. The ones I've drawn are quantum mechanics doors."

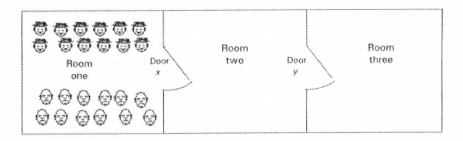

"They look the same in your drawing."

"They look the same but they're not — use your imagination."

"Alright."

"So, when you open door *x*, all the Jewish people run into the second room to get away from the *yocks.*"

"Alright…"

"So, the *yocks* are trapped in room one, they can't chase the Jews because they can't get through door *x.*"

"You mean because only Jews can go through door *x.*"

"That's right."

"Wow, is that it, is that all? I'm not sure…."

"Wait, that's nothing yet! Door *y* is special too — only *yocks* can go through door *y.* You open it, but nothing really should happen, should it?"

"I… don't know…."

"Nothing should happen, because the Jews can't go through it, and the *yocks* are still stuck in room one. Now, that's only if they're ordinary doors made out of Boolean logic like they have here on Earth. But with quantum mechanics doors, you open the second door and *boom!*, room three fills up with *yocks* from room one…."

"Wait a minute…."

"Wait, here's the important part! All the *yocks* from room one end up in room three, *without going through room two!*"

"But, but… yes, but, but… what? But…."

"I know, that's what used to be called magic in the Middle Ages, but when scientists do it these days they have to call it quantum mechanics, otherwise they'll get the sack."

"But Jack, you didn't really *explain* anything, you just stated…."

He didn't even hear me! "Luckily for us it hardly ever happens accidently otherwise engines and things wouldn't work properly."

"So then how do you know it actually can happen?"

"It happens all the time on other planets. I've seen people just materializing in rooms, which you couldn't do using Boolean logic, and nobody there gets surprised. They just have to be careful not to materialize inside something nearly solid, like a jet engine — especially while it's running."

An uncomfortable silence ensued as he remained deeply in thought. Most of what he'd said seemed too nebulous for me to be sure I'd followed it properly, and I didn't want to offend him. Perhaps I could write to the American government for information about their atomic bomb plans, see if they mentioned any of this.

"You notice the rooms didn't have any windows," he suddenly said.

"Er, yes."

"That's because if anybody looked in, the quantum mechanics logic could easily change to Boolean logic."

It was obvious I was going to have to spend a lot of time in the library clarifying all this. But for the time being, I changed my approach. "I'm also a bit worried about it all, apart from the bombs," I said. "If they can understand the actual shape of atoms and what's inside exactly, they can figure out how to make any molecules they like. That means they can design unstoppable atomic explosions, or one-hundred-percent-efficient poison to kill everybody in the world."

Jack's eyebrows rose. "That's a bit morbid, isn't it?"

"Well, it's dangerous in a way, what they've done...."

"But this is a wonderful development, in terms of evolution of the human spirit, of higher consciousness, everything...."

"Well, they could manufacture self-reproducing biological sort of animal things to take over. It could be like *1984.*"

"Come on Zech, I've never heard you so pessimistic! Isn't this our dream come true? The three of us talked about it enough. You assume they'll do the worst, but I'm sure they'll do the best."

"Maybe I am too pessimistic. Well, I hope you're right. When I was listening to Stuart Hibberd reporting on the wireless, I thought: *what hath man wrought?*"

"Then there's your trouble, Zachary. Stay with modern English, old fellow, you'll feel much better."

—o—O—o—

–21–

"Lift up the ol' joanna, together now."

"Easy there, mate!"

"Okay, lift, easy does it, together now lads, push, push, right straight in. We'll turn it round when it's up the steps an' all safe inside."

The street door was swung all the way back to the wall over the cellar stairs as the three men jacked the big black instrument up and eased it into the hallway.

"Alright lads, take a breather." They mopped their brows; it was not easy lifting an upright piano that weighed all of forty-eight stone up two high concrete steps. "Now let's turn it around, easy now, that's right, that door there."

In the living room the armchair with its torn cushion, the one that no one ever sat on, had been moved away from the wall to make room.

"Isn't it lovely? Ee, I can't believe I got it!" Zilla was jubilant. She reached out to play one note while the men were still nudging it into place.

"'Old orf, miss, five minutes and you can play it all day long."

The previous week, while riding home on the Underground from her job as a shorthand-typist in the City, she had seen the advert in a copy of the *Daily Telegraph* that chanced to lie on an empty seat next to hers: *Steinway upright piano, good condition, owner moving abroad, five pounds.* When she alighted at Mile End and came up the stairway into the evening dusk, she had gone straight over to one of the pair of red telephone kiosks outside the station to ring up the number. It was a lot of money, five pounds, and she was saving every penny to emigrate to America. But she knew it would take a while until she could afford to go, and in the meantime she could indulge herself and enjoy something she'd always wanted. When it came time to leave, she would sell the instrument and recoup the money: it was as good as straight into the savings.

And now, after paying the delivery men their four-and-six, plus threepence tip for un-loading the heavy instrument so carefully from their two-wheeled cart with which they'd delivered it without so much as a scratch, the movers' boss reached into his jacket pocket and handed Zilla the shiny silver locking key. The men left, and Rebecca, Lily and Zilla stood lined up before the keyboard.

"Try it, go on," said Zilla. Lily tentatively pressed down one key, but it produced no sound. Her daughter further encouraged her: "Go on, a bit harder."

When she tried again she inadvertently pressed down two abutting keys, and the old room swelled at the sonorous dissonance as the strings chorused their exotic opus. *"Oy a broch,"* Lily giggled. "The neighbors, what'll the neighbors say? We've got a piano, they'll think we're rich like Bella Yanklewitz!"

"Fuck the neighbors," said Zilla, and Lily blanched. "I always wanted a piano and now I got one." And to Rebecca, "Now we can have Wayne and Robert and Gil and the others come here, Dave, all of 'em, we'll have a party."

"If the old *broch* doesn't interfere!" Lily interjected.

With one finger Zilla played the beginning of *Underneath the Spreading Chestnut Tree*, and the rickety pock-marked window frame buzzed in sympathetic resonance. "We'll have a party on Saturday when the old barstard isn't here. If he comes home he won't have the nerve to say anything in case we tell the Yanks to smash him up!"

"It's funny, she's right," Rebecca giggled. "They're so tough, they'd kill him in one minute if we told them to."

Zilla kissed her fingers and touched the ebony case. "Come on Rivka, we're late, let's get ready to go." She carefully closed the fallboard over the keys, inserted the silver key into the lock and turned it until she felt the confirming click. She tried the lid to verify it was indeed locked, placed the key in the snappered money purse of her handbag, then followed Rebecca upstairs to begin their metamorphoses into potent evening garb.

•   •   •

Rebecca was speaking: "Mum, this is Gil, this is Wayne, this is Duane — Wayne and Duane, they're a set — Robert, John, etcetera, etcetera, oh, yes, sorry, Dave, David."

It was a week after the piano arrived, and Lily and I were at the table having a cup of tea. We backed away as the living room began to crowd with American servicemen. "Well, maybe I should go upstairs," said Lily. "I don't want to interfere...."

"Oh, no, Mrs. Grossman, please stay, sure, we'd like the pleasure of your company as well as your two fine daughters."

"You see, you see how polite Americans are?" said Zilla.

"Mum, the funny thing is they really mean it, they're not just saying it, they really mean it! Come on, stay down here!"

I had backed away to the far end of the living room. "Oh, yeah, this is our baby brother Zachary."

"Hi there, Zachary. Mrs. Grossman, ma'am, we took the liberty of picking up some snacks and a few bottles of... of... what's this stuff?"

"Tizer."

"A few bottles of Tizer."

"Oh, or the girls can make you some tea...."

"It's alright if we stand them on the table here, ma'am?"

Zilla made room on the table. "Yeah, stand 'em over 'ere, let's put all this rubbish in the other room."

Lily collected some plates. "Ee, I should have done it before you came, I'll help you."

Rebecca pulled my arm, "Zech, help with this stuff."

I carried the balance of newspapers and tabletop clutter into the kitchen.

In the kitchen, Zilla said: "What do you think, Mum, aren't they nice? They're so funny, they're always joking around, they always make you feel nice!"

"They're so tall, they fill up the whole room!"

"I know, funny, six of 'em, we been seeing 'em for a few months, we didn't bring just anyone, anybody we don't know! They're airmen, it's called the U.S.A.F., they're all in the same crew, they go in a Flying Fortress."

"Wow, a Flying Fortress?" I said. "It's the biggest bomber ever built!"

"Yeah, it's a shame now the war's over they'll all be going back to America...."

Lily pulled open the kitchen door to leave. "I don't want to be in the way, I'll go upstairs...."

"No, they really mean it, don't worry you don't have to do anything, just sit and listen, you'll see how nice and funny they are! And eat the noshes, you should worry!"

"Well...."

Rebecca's head poked out of the living room. "Yes, stay downstairs Mum. Do you like their uniforms? They're lovely, aren't they?"

"I don't know what to say, they look like strapping big boys, ee!"

"Now you know why we can't stand the English ones," whispered Zilla, as Rebecca disappeared back into the living room.

"They seem like nice young men." Then Lily dropped her voice: "I bet they're all married where they come from, in America."

"Oo-er, I don't think so, anyway, who cares?"

I'd plunked my stuff down in the kitchen, and I asked Zilla: "You mean, you'd go on a date with someone who's already married?"

"Wha'd'ja mean, oo-er, they're thousands of miles away, how can you worry?"

From the living room, someone ran an arpeggio up the piano keyboard.

"Oh Mum! You have to hear him, it's Wayne, he plays really nice, come on in the other room, come on!"

Zilla propelled Lily back into the living room, and I followed.

Rebecca was placing cups on the table. "I'm sorry we don't have glasses, uh, I can't worry about it all, the Tizer'll taste the same from a cup. Especially this one," she giggled. "The handle's missing, be careful."

"Cup's just fine, that's a step up for Gil, he's used to drinking straight from the bottle."

"Ha, ha, ha!"

"And here are a few plates, someone'll have to share."

"No problem."

"Can I pour, anyone?"

"Sure, gimme a swig of Tizerooney — *in* the cup, not down the outside, old buddy!"

"Can I sing something, oo-er, I dunno, really...." said Zilla.

"Sure, sure. Wha'd'ya know?"

"Oo-er, I dunno, I feel silly...."

"No, c'm'on, sing something!" chorused the Flying Fortress crew.

"I dunno, do you know *There'll Be Bluebirds Over,* maybe?"

"That's the one they were all singing, how does it go...." and Wayne searched for the opening melody. "I've heard that, it's pretty — is it, yeah, Vera Lynn sings it."

"Ugh, Vera Lynn!" said Zilla. "She's terrible, she's got terrible vibrato, all kvichering and shaky."

"Is this okay?" asked Wayne.

"I dunno, I think it's too high...."

"You start singing then, I'll find your key...."

Zilla began: *"There'll be Blue—birds O-ver,__"* Wayne scouted through a few notes, found the key, and began accompanying. *"The White Cliffs of Do-ver,__ To-mor—row, just you wait and see.__ "* Then, "Oo-er, I feel silly...."

"No it's great, you sound great, keep going!"

"'S great, sexy! More!"

Duane looked admonishingly at his crew-mate: "Dave, watch your language, huh?"

"Sure...." Dave swung around to Lily, "Sorry ma'am, no offense."

"It's the Tizer, Dave has trouble holding his soda."

"There'll be joy and laugh-ter,___ And peace ev-er af-ter,___ Oo-er, I forgot the words!"

"Tomorrow-when-the-world-is-free."

"To-mor—row,___ when the world is free.___"

"Rivka," I whispered, while Zilla sang, "would you go out with one if you knew he was married in America?"

"Sshh, I don't know. Why?"

"Well, isn't it terrible to go out with someone who's already married?"

"Sshh, let's listen to the music, I'll explain another time. When a war's on, things are different."

The living room door opened and it was Katherine: "Oh, what's...."

"Ladies and gentlemen, meet our baby sister, Katherine. Come on, come in!"

"My friend is here, can she come also — it's Hazel."

Lily interjected, "Ee, the floor will fall in, that'll be the end of it all."

"Mrs. Grossman ma'am, you have three beautiful daughters."

Framed in the doorway, Katherine blushed as she entered, Hazel behind her. Hazel looked so pretty! I'd never noticed before that her eyes were exactly the same color as her hair — auburn. She didn't even look so skinny this time. She was wearing a skirt with a very wide belt, and a white blouse with frills down the front under a thing, like a sort of open bolero jacket. It made her look at least sixteen, even though Katherine had told me she was actually fourteen.

"Hazel, you're all dressed up, where've you been?" asked Rebecca.

"We just came back from my aunt's, it's her birthday."

Someone knocked on the street door. John, who happened to be closest, leaned out into the passageway and opened the door.

"Ta-ra, Fred." Marius was bidding his friend good-night, and he appeared stunned as he looked into the crowded living room — American airmen, noise, the piano being played. "Crikey, what's goin' on?"

"Oh!, this is Marius, our babiest baby brother," said Rebecca.

"He's not a baby," said Katherine.

"Oh!" Rebecca giggled. "Sorry, I didn't mean he's a baby, no, he's a big boy, I meant...." Her face was turning red.

Zilla completed the sentence: "She meant Marius is a big boy, but he's our youngest brother."

"No," said Katherine. "We've only got two brothers, so he's our young-*er* brother, not our young-*est* brother."

"Crikey," said Marius.

Gil smiled. "I see these youngsters really keep you older daughters in line."

"Come here, Maudy." Lily beckoned across the crowded room. "Have some nosh, they brought nice things to eat."

Marius went over to the table and piled two slices of cake and several chunks of wurst on a plate.

"Maudy, don't *frass* up everything," I whispered, "take one piece."

"Oh you're always startin' on me, 'e's always startin' on me!"

Lily took Marius's arm. "Maudy, don't speak like that, so rough, it's *he,* with an 'H'."

Hazel said: "Mrs. Grossman, Fred speaks like that, I know his big brother."

"That's where you get it from, the *yocks,*" said Lily.

Rebecca, bending over the table, froze, her face aghast. Zilla, still standing by the piano, covered her mouth. Wayne noticed the girls' expressions and swung around on the piano chair to see what had caused it. At that moment John and Dave, both lifting cups of Tizer to their lips, noticed Rebecca's stunned countenance, and they too stopped in their tracks. A total silence had suddenly descended on the crowded room.

"Mum, don't say that!" Zilla tried to whisper, but in the stillness of the noise's aftermath her words were sharply audible.

"What... what did I say?" Lily asked.

"Yocks," Rebecca whispered even lower as she covered her reddening face. "Sshh, nobody's... Jewish."

"Who's not? Oh, you mean.... No, I meant he plays with... like... rough... children outside."

Wayne whispered to Zilla: "What's wrong?"

Zilla tried unsuccessfully to speak but instead giggled nervously, whereupon Wayne swung back to the keyboard and played a few generic opening chords: "Time for another song! Who's gonna sing next? Rivka, how about a song from you?"

"Oh, I don't know how to sing!" Rebecca responded, her face still stung red at her mother's provincial tactlessness.

"Who then? Come on somebody, we got a room full of people here!"

I realized that Lily had said *yock* in front of everybody, but even Hazel didn't seem to mind, and I wondered if she remembered what it meant. But anyway, the Americans wanted someone to sing, so here was my big chance. "Can I sing?"

"Zzzzachary! Sure, come here, come over here, sure!" I edged my way through. "What do you want to sing, mister?"

Now everybody was looking at me, including Katherine and Hazel. But I *would* sing; I'd done it in my head so many times that although I felt nervous and excited I wasn't at all shy! "Do you know *This Love of Mine?"*

"This Love of Mine! Hmm!"

"Frank Sinatra sings it."

"Frank Sinatra. Okay, you start."

"Well, I'd do it in B-flat."

"Wow, he even knows the key! Okay!"

He played a little introduction, and slowed it down a bit toward the end. Then he repeated the note *F* a couple of times, which was unnecessary because the chords easily showed me where I was supposed to come in.

I took a breath: *"This Love of Mine,__ Goes on and on.__ Though life is emp-ty,__ Since you are gone.___"*

"Hey, you're okay, kid!"

"You're al-ways on_ my mind,__ Though out_ of sight.___" And here I snatched a big breath the way Frank Sinatra did, because the following phrase was long and you had to sound as though you didn't need to breathe again in the middle: *"It's lone-some through_ the day,___ And oh_ the night.____"*

Wayne raised his eyebrows in seeming approval at my not needing an extra breath. And so I sang through to the end of the song. Everybody applauded, and I felt absolutely wonderful and silly at the same time and my ears got hot and red, but I didn't care.

"Hey, your kid brother's quite a singer! Sinatra better watch out!" said Wayne. Then again to me: "You're okay, kid."

"Thank you!" I felt so uncomfortable by now I had to go out of the room — through the passageway and out into the yard. I did it! I actually sang! And with a real pianist and he said I was okay, which I knew I was anyway! I needed to pee right away. I used the lavatory and pulled the chain, and as I came out Katherine and Hazel were out the back door standing in the dwindling daylight, waiting for me.

"We wondered where you went," said Hazel.

They both beamed at me, and Katherine said, "You should really be a singer."

"Really?"

"Yes."

"Yes, you should," added Hazel.

"Really?"

"Absolutely," said Katherine.

"Whew! I really liked it, I really like singing."

"Well, you should do it for a living."

"I wasn't shy at all!"

"We could see," said Hazel.

"Whew!"

"Really."

"Isn't it funny?" I said.

"Funny?"

"I mean, it's so easy, singing is so easy!"

"It's always easy to do what you're good at," said Katherine.

"Really? Well, I suppose so."

"How did you know what key?" asked Katherine.

I hesitated. "Well, don't tell Zilly or she'll start."

"You know I won't."

"Well, I found out if you put a knife blade in between the lid and the bottom part and push it sideways, then the lock opens so you can get to the keys."

"Boy! That sounds good!"

"So when no one's there, I open it and I play it."

"Congratulations!"

"Don't tell Zilly!"

"I already said I won't."

"So that's it! Whew! Hazel, when it's finished, I mean the party, when you're going home, I want to walk home with you, see you home."

Hazel flashed a glance at Katherine, then looked back at me. "Alright."

Two hours later, Hazel and I turned the corner into Litchfield Road.

"Thanks for walking me home."

"Oh that's alright, I wanted to. So… good night." I knew I should kiss her, especially because Katherine had said she liked me, but in just the short walk from our house I already felt too shy. If Katherine hadn't been with us earlier when we were out in the garden I certainly would have kissed her then. "So long then, maybe see you tomorrow."

"Alright, er... let me find my key." In the dusky shadows we stood by the street door. "Is anyone home? It seems dark inside."

"Mum and Dad were still at Vera's when I left, she's my aunt. I caught the bus home myself, it was a boring birthday party, just relatives."

"Will you be alright by yourself in the house?"

She held the key. "I don't know."

"Should I come in for a minute, just to see if everything's okay?"

"Yes please." She entered first. "You can hold my elbow, if you like," she added, and guided me along the dark passageway. Grasping her elbow made me sharply aware that although I'd known her since before the war, this was the first time I'd ever actually touched her. And it was also the first time I'd been inside her house. With her other hand she reached around a doorframe: click, and light flooded the room ahead. I released her arm. Beyond the door, two green armchairs and opposite a brown leather sofa under a dark-framed wall mirror, meant that this was their living room. I followed her in. Between the armchairs stood a low wooden table covered with pages of handwriting. Next to a window draped by a floor-length curtain, a dark wooden cabinet with the name *Philco* in curlicue script was balanced precariously on spindly curved legs, and its glass dial with knobs in the front panel suggested a wireless, but much more expensive than our little Bakelite one. Beneath a wooden rail near the ceiling hung two framed pictures of red-jacketed men on horseback.

"You can wait in here if you like," she said.

"Don't you want me to check anywhere else?"

"I'll do it, you stay here."

I waited, listening as she continued through the house. A light went on in the passageway. Then another, maybe a kitchen because of the slight extra echo from the electric switch. The rims of several flat thin black disks protruded from among the sheets of paper lying on the table. Perhaps they were records; maybe the cabinet contained a gramophone. A different switch clicked, closer; the light in the passageway brightened then dimmed again, and her footsteps returned.

"Everything's alright — downstairs," she said from just beyond the doorway.

"Okay. We only have gas lights in our house."

"I know, my father had electric put in."

"That's terrific."

"I'm a bit frightened to go upstairs."

"I can go if you like."

"No... thank you."

"Do you have electric lights upstairs also?"

"Yes."

"So... what should I do, shouldn't I go upstairs?"

"No, you mustn't go upstairs."

"I see." I felt awkward. "So I suppose I should leave... do you think... should I go, then?" I asked.

She came into the room. "My parents didn't come home yet."

"I know...."

"I could make you a cup of tea, if you want."

"No, well, I had such a lot of Tizer...."

"Me too."

"So!"

She beckoned toward the sofa. "You could sit down, if you like."

"Should I?"

"If you like, you can."

"Alright." I knew I wouldn't be able to sit down smoothly, without jerking.

"You can, if you like. That's where I always sit."

"Alright."

"It's the most comfortable."

"Okay." I turned, trying to smooth out my body's motions as my legs, arms and neck juddered down onto the sofa. She didn't seem to notice anything wrong.

"Can I sit here also?" she asked.

"Sure. Yes. Sure."

She sat by me, then immediately stood up. "I'm taking off this bolero, it's hot." And she took off the little sleeveless jacket and threw it over to one of the green armchairs, then sat down again. Now she just wore the blouse with the frills down the front, as well as her skirt and shoes and socks. "So!"

"So!" I responded; I couldn't think of anything else to say.

"I really liked it when you sang."

"Did you really?"

"Yes, you're a terrific singer. It made me feel like I was all... well, all melting or something."

"Melting?"

"I mean, my legs got sort of squishy, you know."

"Really?" I knew I should do something positive and masculine right that moment, but I couldn't think of anything. It was certainly interesting knowing she felt like that, like she was going to melt. I'd never felt as though I were going to melt.

She squinted her eyes. "It's so bright."

The light came from a single electric bulb in the middle of the ceiling behind a frosted glass shade. "Yes, it is bright."

"I saw you lots of times down the shelter."

"Did you? I don't remember, I mean, I was with my friends a lot." She was pretty enough that I felt sure I would have remembered if I'd seen her.

Suddenly she stood up again. "Just a minute, I'm going to take this upstairs." She picked up the discarded bolero, exited, and ran upstairs; she'd probably forgotten she was afraid. A couple of minutes later a door closed up there and she came running down. As she came into the room, she paused. "I'm going to turn off the light. I mean, do you mind if I turn off the light because it's so bright, there's a light on in the passage so it won't get dark much in here."

"Yes. I mean, no, it's okay, yes, it won't get dark much."

She switched off the light; it was pretty dark, with just an angled beam from the passageway shining on the wall around the corner to the left of the door. She came and sat down again on the sofa. "Do you want anything?"

"Anything? What? What do you mean?"

"Like, tea? I can make you some tea if you like."

"Oh, no thanks, I'm still not thirsty thanks."

"Whew!"

"Whew!"

"So! What do you want to talk about?" she asked.

"Oh I dunno. What's your second name, I don't even know your second name."

"Stapleton. Hazel Stapleton."

"Oh, it's a nice name." I realized I *had* already known her second name.

"Thanks."

"Are you Jewish?"

"No."

I felt foolish for asking. "Oh."

"Why?"

"I dunno."

"Remember, I said we weren't Jewish when we went for that walk to Hackney, that V-2, when Katya came home."

"Oh yes, I remember."

"Do you care if I'm Christian?"

"No, oh no, absolutely not at all, no, not at all. I suppose I just feel a bit silly or something, I don't know what to talk about."

"We don't have to talk."

"I know, we don't have to." That was a relief, but just then I thought of something to talk about. "Hazel?"

"What?"

"How old are you?"

"Fifteen."

"Are you? Katya told me you were fourteen."

"Last week was my birthday. My birthday's always one week before my Aunt Vera's."

"I'm sixteen."

"I know. Your birthday's November the ninth."

"How did you know?"

"Katya told me."

"I see."

"Zachary?"

"What?"

"Do you mind if I call you Zachary? It sounds nicer than Zech."

"Yes, sure, that's okay, I don't mind."

"Zachary?"

"What?"

"Zachary."

"What?"

"Zachary... why don't you kiss me ever?"

"I don't know, I feel a bit shy, I s'pose...."

"Do you want to, do you want to kiss me?"

"Well, yes, I do really, I suppose I'm a bit shy."

"I bet you wouldn't dare to kiss me."

"Wha'd'ya mean?"

"I bet you, you wouldn't dare to."

"I would!"

"I bet you wouldn't."

"I would, I bet I would."

"Let's see then."

"Alright." And I half turned and kissed her, right on the lips.

"Umm, that was nice," she said.

"Was it? I mean, yes, that was nice."

"You can put your arm around me if you like."

"Alright then." I put my arm around her shoulder. "S'posing your Mum comes home."

"They won't come home yet."

"How do you know?"

"They won't. Let's kiss one more time."

I kissed her again, and this time it was a longer one because when I went to take my head away she stopped me.

"They're supposed to be slow," she said.

"Are they? I mean, yes, it's better when they're slow, but, well, oh I don't know."

"Zachary, don't tell anyone, will you."

"What?"

"That I let you kiss me."

"Alright."

"Zachary?"

"What?" It was very hot in the room.

"I was going to ask you something, but maybe I'd better not."

"What?"

"Maybe I'd better not."

"You can, I don't care."

"You sure?"

"Yes. Absolutely, yes you can, I don't care, sure. Certainly."

"Alright. Did you ever... no, I can't say it."

"What?"

"Alright, I'll say it quick then." She took a deep breath: "Did you ever... put your hand inside someone's blouse?"

"No, no, I didn't, I never did."

She sank back. "Okay."

"Yes, I didn't, I never did."

She leaned forward again. "Did you ever... want to?"

"I feel too embarrassed, oh, I don't know, oh, I suppose so, but I didn't, I never did."

"Suppose I said if you wanted to put your hand inside my blouse for a minute it was alright, I wouldn't say anything?"

"What, well, what, then what?"

"Would you?"

"Would I, well er... what?"

"If I *said* that, would you put your hand inside my blouse?"

"I suppose I would."

"Alright, in one minute I'm going to say that, to see if you really would."

"Well, I really would, if you said that."

"Alright then, go on and do it."

"I don't know...."

"Alright, I'll close my eyes, then you can."

"Alright."

She closed her eyes. My left arm was around her shoulder, so with my right hand I felt for the front of the blouse, but it had lots of frilly things in the way. "All those frilly things...."

"Alright, don't look and I'll unbutton it. Then I'll close my eyes and you can do it."

"Alright." I closed my eyes.

She fumbled with the buttons. "Ready!"

"Alright." I put my hand through the opening and touched her skin, in the middle of her chest. It didn't feel hard and bony like mine where my ribs met, and the shape bulged out a bit, soft and smooth; but wouldn't that mean she didn't have a brassiere on? I lifted my hand away and very carefully moved my middle finger across, then quickly bent the tip; her other breast seemed to have fabric covering it! With the same fingertip I again touched the side nearest me — bare, definitely bare! Was she or wasn't she wearing a brassiere? Jack! Quantum mechanics! Maybe it depended on me, I was the observer; maybe whether she was or not depended on how I checked it out.

"What you doing?" she said.

"What?"

"I mean, you're like...."

"No, I was just... well...." I lifted my hand; the concept would be too complicated to explain.

"I took my brassiere off."

"Oh, you did?"

"I wear a brassiere, already. When I went upstairs, I did, I took it off. So go on, do it."

But I'd felt fabric against the other breast! "Alright then." Gingerly I lowered my hand onto the breast nearest me, the definitely-bare one. "What about the other one?" I asked.

"You can touch the other one also, if you like."

"I mean, did you take the other brassiere off also?"

"The other brassiere?"

"The one on the other side, I feel silly."

"What you talking about?" I probably hadn't phrased it right, and now I felt too foolish to move. Finally she said: "Go on, move your hand then."

I was baffled, not wanting to seem too analytical checking the other side out; perhaps it had been the blouse fabric.

"Well you're just staying still, come on then, you're supposed to move your hand."

So I slid my fingers slowly down the little curve, intending to unobtrusively walk them up the side of her other breast, and that way I'd know for sure if it were bare or covered. But at that moment we heard voices outside. She stiffened. Then the sound of a key in the lock.

"They're home! Quick, let me go!"

Let me go! I must have forced her the way men force girls to do things! I took my arm away, and as the street door hinges began to creak she was frantically buttoning herself up.

"Hazel?" A loud man's voice called along the passageway.

"Yes, Dad, I'm home, we're in the living room, I'm in the living room." And to me she whispered, "Quick, stand up, stand up!"

I stood up — and I had an erection, it was pressing against my trousers leg. In the darkness I could feel my face glowing hot and red.

"How long have you been home? Why's the light off?" Simultaneously two faces peered around the doorframe into the darkness of the living room, one head above the other. I was mortified in case they would notice my trousers, and I leaned forward to try to disguise it.

"The bulb's gone, it didn't go on, I tried to switch it on but it wouldn't go on, I tried a few times...."

"Then what are you doing, sitting in here in the dark?" His hand reached around for the switch. He pushed it down, and the ceiling light was suddenly brilliant and glaring. He stared at me, and I bent forward a bit more; then he looked at Hazel still sitting on the sofa. "Who's this, there's nothing wrong with the light. What's going on?"

"Nothing, it's Katherine's brother Zachary, we were just talking, I thought the light was broken, he walked me home because it's dark, it was dark inside, and...."

"Hello Mr. Stapleton sir, hello, Mrs. Stapleton."

"Hello," replied Mrs. Stapleton. "What's going on in here?"

"Nothing, Mrs. Stapleton, in case there was a burglar, or something...."

"A burglar?"

"No, we were just talking," Hazel said rapidly, "I went to their house, I was with Katya and then I just came home and Zech said he'd come inside for a minute to see everything's alright because I called out and nobody answered so I thought you weren't home yet so he said he'd just come inside for one minute and see everything's alright...."

Mr. Stapleton gently waved his hands. "Sshh, alright, alright. But why are you sitting here with the light off?"

Hazel and I answered simultaneously: "I, I, I...."

Mrs. Stapleton spoke. "Well Hazel, I think it's about your bedtime. Your father will see Zachary to the door."

In a flash Hazel was gone from the room. Mr. Stapleton followed me along the passageway.

"That was gentlemanly of you to escort Hazel home safely."

"Yessir yes, sir, alright sir, thank you sir, good night sir."

"Good night."

The door closed behind me, and I heard the loud click as he turned the latch inside.

I floated home on air. What a day, what a night! All was quiet in the house — the Americans had gone and the lights were off. I went upstairs to the bedroom and cautiously opened the door.

"Hello, I'm awake."

"Hello, I just came back from Hazel's."

"So what happened?"

"Well, they have electric lights in all the rooms."

"I mean, did you kiss her?"

"I'm not supposed to say anything."

"It doesn't matter, she'll tell me anyway."

"She will? She told me not to say anything to anybody."

"If *she* tells someone, it's different from *your* telling someone."

"Why is it different, I mean if… we both said the same thing?"

"It sounds the same, but it's different."

"It…. Her parents came home."

"Did they catch you?"

"Wha'd'ya mean? Kissing her? I only kissed her once, I mean twice."

"So was it alright?"

"What, well, kissing her, or her parents coming home? Oh, I wasn't supposed to say, don't tell her I said…."

"Was it alright when they came home."

"Yes, it was alright. Her father is nice, he didn't get wild with me being there."

"He's civilized."

"Civilized?"

"He's not like Abie."

I'd completely forgotten about being embarrassed getting undressed in front of my sister if she were still awake, but here we were talking and I was already in my sleeping suit! I climbed over her to my side and got under the covers.

"She said I was a terrific singer."

"She already liked you before that. I told you."

"But she said she *really* liked it when I sang. She said" — and I felt a bit silly — "she said it made her feel like she was… melting."

"Melting."

"Melting."

"Well. I'm sure it did make her feel like that."

"Yes, really?"

"Yes."

"Why would it make her feel like that?"

"It just would."

"Would it make… Marius feel like that?"

"No."

"How about Zilly and Rivka?"

"A little bit but not much."

"Or Mum."

"Nuh."

"Abie?"

"He'd punch you in the face."

"I suppose so."

"You know why?"

"Why?" I asked.

"He'd be jealous."

"Jealous? How could he be jealous of me, he's our Father."

"That's why he'd be jealous."

"But he's…. Sometimes you talk in… well, I… I don't know…."

She continued. "Izzy Mendelsohn came round yesterday." She giggled. "He's mad, he wants to kiss me all the time."

"Really?"

"Yes. Anyway, cousin Steve was here to fix the gas meter and they were both pushing in front of each other to stand next to me. Why are men so mad, it's funny! Izzy makes me sick with his pudgy fingers."

How humiliating to be a man! Wouldn't it be wonderful if girls pushed each other to be next to boys instead! Then you could sit back and wait until they did something, and then just enjoy it — you wouldn't have to always worry about things like wanting to kiss some-one, then feeling stupid because they might get indignant and say, And just what do you think *you're* doing? Girls are so strange. Girls must never feel stupid, or clumsy or anything — they're just *there.* I wonder if girls think — about *things,* like how things work, what makes things happen? Anyway, it was a relief to hear Katya giggle — she was mostly so serious.

"Steve said he likes me. We were sitting on the settee, then Mum came home. Did he jump! He told Mum the job's more complicated than he thought, he'd have to come back to finish the job."

I felt peculiar about this, about our cousin Steve, whether it was okay for him to sit on the settee with Katherine. Maybe they were kissing; I'd just kissed Hazel on her settee. But still, he was so old, twenty-eight, and anyway she was his cousin and she wouldn't even be fourteen until October. Listening to her now, she seemed so without doubt about every-thing, it was amazing! And Steve was another one who always was so confident, as though he *knew* it was all right. Maybe that's because he knew about science, he was an engineer, he knew all about gas meters and electric switches and things. With electricity things are not just a matter of opinion, you could *prove* everything objectively, so there was no need to ever be embarrassed about anything. Except for quantum mechanics, and you certainly couldn't count on that! Maybe you could fix up a camera with a string tied to the lever and take a photo while you're deliberately looking in the opposite direction — I wonder what quantum mechanics would do about that?

Katya snored; her presence beside me drawing me back from these imponderables. I looked at her — she was asleep. Although it was only my sister, it was so peculiar having a girl asleep right next to me, sort of tantalizing in a way, like I wanted to touch. I really needed to find out a lot more about girls so it wouldn't all be such a mishmash. Probably most sixteen-year-old boys knew hundreds of times more than I did about girls. I turned on my side to look at her; if she woke up I'd pretend I was asleep. I started thinking, *I wonder if I could just touch her,* only thinking it, but my heart started racing! I didn't do anything, I didn't even move, yet I could hear my heart and feel it, racing away! I tried not to think, not to think about that, but I couldn't make my mind think of anything else; it filled my whole head as though I wasn't in control. After a couple of minutes she hadn't moved, she snored one more time, so she was definitely asleep. My heart was thumping away and I was thinking, *I wonder if I just put my arm over her the way you can, accidently, when you're asleep and you turn over.* I didn't want to actually do it, I knew it was sneaky. But it wouldn't go out of my head, repeating and repeating even though I was trying hard not to think about it, trying to think about something else, electricity, science. But it kept getting stronger and stronger, pushing everything else out of my head, until in the end I took a deep breath, sighed to pretend I was having a dream, and moved my arm across under the covers to rest over her body, her hips. It was an amazing shock to realize her night gown was up and my hand was on her bare leg, bare skin, near the top of her leg. My heart was really racing, pumping away even in the side of my neck; I just lay there, snoring quietly and keeping my hand absolutely still, and wondering why I was doing it. *Because that's what men do* — the words came back like a nightmare.

My awareness that the palm of my hand and my fingers were on the bare skin of her thigh was flooding through me, more powerful than anything I'd ever known, something beyond ordinary thinking. It was as though my brain knew how to deal with science and singing and all that sort of stuff, but here was a different brain, one that made a sort of fluttery strangeness in my stomach and legs, almost pins and needles. If she woke up now and found out I wasn't really asleep, what I was doing, I would absolutely die of embarrassment — my life would be finished and it would be easier to just be dead. In school Miss Ratchet had made us sing: *What are little boys made of? Frogs and snails and puppy-dog tails.* Boys were disgusting, they had such uncontrollable thoughts about disgusting things with girls. Girls, *sugar and spice and all things nice,* girls never... never .... And, oh, no, supposing she told Mum! Mum would stand still, then look slowly at me and say, *What did he do!* Then she'd repeat it, slowly, slowly, *What did he do?* looking straight at me. I would have to kill myself right away.

Very carefully I lifted my hand up and away and rolled over onto my right side, so I could look out the window. What had I done! I must *never* do it again. Is that what men do? I would never, never be able to tell anybody, never. I wondered what Hazel would want, what would happen if I said something like that to her, could I touch her thigh? She'd think I was disgusting. I'd been too shy to put my hand inside her blouse, she had to tell me to. My heart was going in fast double beats, *ba-boom, ba-boom, ba-boom.* Maybe all this was sort of practice for boys until they weren't shy any more. I wonder what Steve did when he sat with Katya on the settee? She wouldn't let him do anything disgusting. But he wouldn't even want to, because he was a scientist — he knew all about electricity, which was a bit like being a scientist. And even if he wanted to do it, she certainly wouldn't allow it. Whew! The moon, the moon. There was the moon, think about the moon, two hundred and thirty-nine thousand miles away, no one had ever seen the back of the moon because now the moon's same face was locked to the earth by gravity. Science, science was cool and reasonable and predictable and your heart didn't need to thump and you didn't have to feel like a disgusting animal.

I don't know if I even fell asleep, but in the morning I was wide awake thinking about what I'd done. I climbed over Katya to the floor before she woke up. Quickly and quietly I started getting dressed.

"Good morning."

I'd probably woken her when I stepped over her; she'd probably pretended she was asleep, and watched me getting dressed! Getting undressed was easier because it was dark, but dressing in the morning was always in the light. She smiled! Why did she smile?

I mumbled something and went downstairs. Abie was still having his breakfast and Mum was making more tea. I was too ashamed to look at either of them, though after I'd passed by Abie's chair I glanced at the back of him, bent over the table, slurping his food without any self-awareness, any thought of how he looked to other people. I supposed I hated him, his ugliness; that must be the feeling when you hate someone, when a girl hates a boy who does something disgusting. I was afraid of Mum, how she always knew everything I did, how she threatened to tell him when I'd done something terrible.

Lily I was afraid of, but Abie I hated.

—o—O—o—

22

Zilla and Rebecca, through a series of delicately weighted letters, had coaxed Uncle Joe, the waiter, and his American wife Emily into sponsoring Zilla's immigration: the sisters' plan was for Zilla to go first. She had already borne the interview process at the American Embassy in Grosvenor Square, wearing long bloomers for the medical examination so the doctor wouldn't think she was a tart, and now she had secured her passport and visa. But when she returned home bearing in her handbag a transatlantic ticket on the *Queen Mary,* a further letter from Joe and Emily awaited: some conflict, they wrote from their New York apartment uptown on Claremont Avenue opposite the Juilliard School of Music, some conflict with their bank and the Immigration Department's legal requirement that they themselves pledge financial support if Zilla were unable to find work in America. These added burdens, they regretted, had forced them to renege on their promise to sponsor her.

The sisters were devastated.

"It's your father's sister Anya, the lousy *broch* she is," said Lily. "Who else? She must have written and told them about you both going out with the American soldiers."

"Why would she do that? What's the difference to her?" sobbed Zilla.

"She's like *Bobbeh* was, may they both *gai in dread!* Filthy stories behind our backs, who knows, she probably told Joe to be careful, maybe you're a prostitute or something. I never told you what went on before I married your father, Anya and her *becuckter* mother, the whole stinking family there they said he shouldn't marry me. They knew I was pregnant already, 'So get an abortion,' they both said. A fire on Anya, may she drop dead and be buried along with her stinking pig of a mother."

The American military had begun winding down its British bases of operations and, as part of its westward exodus, Flying Fortress crews, including Gil, Wayne, Duane, Robert, John and Dave, were returned to their various families in America. With these departures, Zilla's and Rebecca's lives lost an ebullience that, they realised, had become indispensable. They missed the romance and easygoing generosity that they knew indigenous males would be forever unable to provide. Reduced to dating British xenophobes with brown teeth, bad breath and meager finances conspired to harden their disgust into a resolve to emigrate to the United States. Over the course of a year of hard work where they saved every penny possible, this determination gradually came to embrace taking the entire family with them — excluding of course Abie.

So Zilla and Rebecca modified their plan. They would now write Joe and Emily afresh, the letters ostensibly from the younger sister Rebecca, each dispatch seeking to anticipate and carefully assuage any conceivable American apprehensions. Then, once Rebecca was ensconced in New York she would first find a job, then her own flat — and with it her freedom. No longer dependent upon Uncle Joe's precarious mercies, she would work round the clock to get Zilla a ticket to America. And subsequently, as the two sisters worked hard and saved up for more tickets, the rest of the family would follow.

After the Americans had left, Rebecca had begun dating — albeit reluctantly — a Michael Wolf, an amateur boxer from Stepney Green, the pride of the Brady Boys Club. Michael wore short-sleeved turtleneck sweaters that showed off his swelling biceps. Rebecca and Michael had little in common; they couldn't even agree on what picture to see on Saturday night, though following Mickey's obligatory objections he usually acquiesced in her choice. And after they came out of the Empire in Stepney Green, or the new Odeon that had been built in Mile End Road opposite the ruins of the bombed-out La Bohéme theatre, he never would discuss the picture with her. In fact, he never discussed anything — it was difficult to elicit from Michael any complete sentence beyond a peremptory demand. And on those rare occasions when Rebecca was able to ambush him in the murky waters of nuance, what with all his stumblings, qualifications and mid-course corrections she still was never sure quite what he really meant.

Because Rebecca was ashamed of the loud and senselessly belligerent atmosphere that prevailed at home, she rarely allowed Mickey in the house. And she felt equally disinclined to go to his flat, where he still lived with his parents. So they would meet at a bench in Tredegar Square, and at the close of evening conduct their good-byes at the same venue. Although Rebecca felt physically secure in Mickey's company, the relationship was unsatisfactory in every other way, bearable only because of her private knowledge of its temporary nature.

Concurrently, Zilla was dating a gentle, red-haired, prematurely-balding guitarist named Lew Green, who was happy to talk continuously about everything. Lew was anything but a fighter. He cultivated the callouses on his left fingertips for clean fretting; his livelihood and his passion depended on sensitive hands. He played his guitar with *Sid Milward And His Nitwits*, the comedy band that, dressed as tramps, toured the music hall circuit. Whenever the band came to be booked in at the nearby Hackney Music Hall, Lew loved to have Zilla come with him to see the show. She would sit in the center of the front row and beam with self-concious pride as he appeared on stage. When the band reached the middle of a number, Lew would suddenly stand up, and as the music raggedly petered out he would walk to the edge of the proscenium and there, dead pan, stare down at Zilla, then solemnly tear another rip in his tattered tuxedo as the audience roared with laughter.

Meanwhile, Katherine was still temporarily selling shoes at Anya's Fashion Footwear in Burdett Road. And I, between taking packages of cotton swabs to the Post, wondered afresh each morning whether today might be one of those rare occasions when Mr. Purushotham spent an hour or so away from the office — time for Miss Eunice to come in and safely close the stockroom door.

•   •   •

"I'm going with Jack to the Brady Boys Club Saturday morning," I said.

"You realize Jack said they start every activity there with prayers," Katherine responded.

"Well, I don't have to join in. They do stick up for Jews, though — I suppose that's good. One of them I saw in Johnny Isaacs one night while you were still in Devon, it was wonderful the way he stood up to the *yocks*. Maybe as they're mumbling their prayers I'll just read aloud from Bertrand Russell's *Why I Am Not A Christian* — that ought to partially satisfy them."

"Can I come with?"

"You?"

"Why not?"

"To Bradys...? It's a boys club."

"Well, I have no objection to boys. I'll watch from a safe distance where I can't contaminate them."

"I don't know what Jack will say if I ask...."

"It's not fair, why should there only be a boys club? What are girls supposed to do?"

"I... don't know...."

"Well, do you think it's fair?"

"I... I don't know, what about Hazel, and Eileen, don't they have... I mean, isn't there a girls' something or other?"

"Yes, they teach you to cook and clean lavatories."

"Well, you can come, I just hope you won't feel uncomfortable. Anyway, you work on Saturdays."

"I'll tell Anya the fumes from someone's bunions were infectious, I have to take the day off."

"Alright."

Saturday morning, Katherine, Hazel and I accompanied Jack on the bus to Whitechapel, to the Brady Boys Club. Katherine said she was bringing Hazel along for moral support.

Inside the building we followed Jack through the hallways to a large gymnasium. The cavernous room echoed to the strains of physical exertion, balls bouncing off the far wall, the rattling of metal connectors where young men slithered up and down ropes suspended from a grid frame hanging from the ceiling, and the grunting of tensed stomachs as muscled youth performed sit-ups and push-ups on a row of pads lined up on the floor against the wall.

Katherine's face bore a look of derision. "Is this what they do all the time?"

The room reeked of perspiration. I felt a bit embarrassed at Jack's having to defend what went on. "No, they have classes, Jewish history, things...." he said.

"Look, Katya, that one...." Hazel pointed discretely in the direction of the wall bars where a darkish, hairy young man in shorts was pulling himself up then lowering himself, repeatedly, using only one arm; after much huffing and blowing he changed to the other arm.

"Wow!" I'd been forced to do enough gym in school to know how hard that one was.

"It's impressive, isn't it?" said Jack to me; I avoided Katherine's look.

Another fellow closer by was doing push-ups on a pad. Every time he came to the top of a cycle he bounced, held still, and flexing his biceps, smiled across at us.

"Who's he smiling at?" asked Hazel.

"He's probably mentally defective," said Katherine. The girls giggled. "I think they all must be, if this is what they do all day."

"There are some pretty bright people here," countered Jack. "It doesn't automatically signify no brains if you keep yourself in good physical trim."

The young man had stood up from his pad and now started across the gym toward us, whereupon an older man seemingly in charge and bearing a whistle in his mouth blew a short blast at him, causing him to turn and revert to his mat.

The older man came over to us and spoke as well as he was able without removing the whistle: "No girls allowed in the gym."

"I'm sorry, we're leaving," said Jack, as he, I, and Hazel turned to leave.

Predictably, Katherine stood her ground: "No girls allowed in the gym?" she repeated.

"I don't know if you noticed but you have a whistle or something in your mouth. That might be why you're having trouble talking."

The man spluttered and the whistle fell to the length of a cord around his neck. "That's right, miss, we don't permit girls in the gym."

"Katya, we should leave now," said Jack. "I'm sorry, we're leaving."

"We're not girls," said Katherine, straight-faced.

The man looked momentarily nonplussed. "Miss, I don't make the rules...."

"We're boys, yes, Harry and I just like to dress like girls. They're lucky" — she pointed at Jack and me — "their voices sound normal."

I gulped. Hazel grasped Katherine's arm. "Katya...."

"We both have high voices." Katherine's face was rigid and brightly colored as she continued. "It's easier if we just dress like girls, we don't have to make so many explanations."

My face had flooded too. "Katya come on, we'd better go."

"Not until he signs us up. Sir, the four of us want to join."

"I'm already a member," mumbled Jack, "and I...."

"Miss, you'd better go to the office."

The young man on the mat, who had resumed his push-ups, stopped again and still sporting the same vacuous smile gazed at our group's disarray. Jack and I simultaneously grasped each of Katherine's arms, turned her around and began walking her out through the large swinging doors.

"I'm sorry, Katya," I began, "It made me embarrassed for Jack."

Katya brushed herself off. "The old fart with the whistle's the one who should have been embarrassed."

"They're the rules, it isn't his fault," said Jack.

Katherine's answer came quickly. "That's what they said at Nuremberg, they were just following the rules."

"Oh come on Katya, how can you compare...." I began.

"Sometimes the rules are wrong," said Katherine.

"She has a point," said Jack.

I felt caught in the middle. "Well, Jack said we can come with, but I mean, I didn't want to make him uncomfortable...."

"That's alright." Jack slapped me on the back. "Your sister's argument is logically consistent, and I'm with her in spirit."

Behind us the gymnasium doors swung open again, and the push-up fellow trotted toward us; his smile hadn't changed one iota. "Hello, I'm Ben, Benny." He focused on Katherine.

"Jack." Jack extended his hand. "Zachary, Katherine and Hazel."

"They don't allow girls in the gym."

"Yes," said Katherine, "your friend just explained it all to us."

"They don't mean anything against girls, it's just the rule."

"My sister thinks it's not fair," I said. "She's right, in theory."

Katherine began to walk along the passage. With the celerity of a coiled snake, Benny was at her side.

"I want to ask in the office why they don't let girls in the gym," Katherine said.

Still smiling, Benny responded: "They'll just tell you the same thing, it's the rule here."

"Then I can make them think about their rule."

Katherine left the door to the office open, and we waited outside, listening. "…Because as I've already said three times this isn't a mixed club, it's a boys only. If it was a mixed club, you can rest assured the girls would also have a gym."

"You're a girl, female, they let you in here."

"But I don't go to the gym, I don't *wish* to go in the gym."

"But that doesn't answer the question, why can't girls go in the one gym you already do have? There's enough room."

"Miss, we don't allow girls in the gym, that's the long and the short of it, and quite frankly I think your question is… indecent. If you're determined to use a gymnasium, try Jews' Free School in Bell Lane, they used to have a girls' gym. And now, I'm ordering the whole bunch of you to leave the premises."

Katherine came out, looking flushed.

"We can leave," said Jack. "Is that okay, Zech, you've seen enough?"

"Yes, yes…."

"Wait," said Benny. He seemed breathless. "Wait a minute, I'll get my stuff. Katya, Katherine, don't leave." He sprinted off down the passageway and fifteen seconds later he was back, fully dressed, carrying a bag.

Downstairs and in the street, Hazel said: "Well, that's why Katya's my best friend."

"But Jack invited us, I didn't want to…."

"I already told you not to worry, Zech, there's no harm done." We started walking.

"Zachary," asked Hazel, "don't you think she's right?"

"Yes, I just… well, she could have gone back some other time so as not to…."

"Zech, I repeat, your sister's quite right," said Jack. "As a matter of fact I'm glad she did it. I'll be famous now when I go back."

Benny had pulled Katherine ahead. "Is this the first time you've been to Brady's?"

"Yes, it is." She laughed. "The last time, also."

"It's pretty nice really."

"Well I don't like it."

"You go with anyone?"

"No."

"Very good. So will you come to the pictures with me? It's *Stairway to Heaven*, David Niven and Kim Hunter."

"Ugh!" said Katherine.

"It's supposed to be good. We could go tonight."

Katherine looked back to Hazel. "Will you come with to the pictures tonight?"

Benny looked perturbed by Katherine's invitation, but as Hazel hesitated he spoke up: "You can all come if you like."

"I'm busy tonight," said Jack.

Hazel looked at me, then away, and I plucked up courage: "Hazel, would you come to the pictures with me?"

"Tonight?"

"Yes, I mean with… those two."

"Well, yes, alright then."

Katherine actually giggled. "Well, in that case I'll go, too."

"So that's it, a foursome," said Benny as he pulled Katherine further ahead.

Jack, Hazel and I brought up the rear. "So Zech, think you'll join Brady's?"

"Er...." I was more concerned with the thought of the pictures tonight. I'd have to be careful when we filed into our seats so I would be next to Hazel. Benny seemed experienced with girls, so I'd let him stand in front of me in the queue and if he bought Katherine's ticket then I'd quickly borrow Katherine's ticket money so I could buy Hazel's. Maybe if I were careful I'd be able to put my arm around her shoulder in the dark. Though maybe she didn't like me any more; after that evening in her house she'd never asked me to see her home again. When I'd put my hand inside her blouse I probably did it wrong, and she most likely thought I was stupid.

"...There are some nice fellows there...." Jack was still going on about Brady Boys Club. "They have speakers come in, they talk about Jewish traditions. It's boring but it's good to know something."

"I don't know, I'd rather learn about science, or music."

"They teach you Hebrew songs."

"I mean more like Tchaikovsky, or Frank Sinatra."

"Hmm."

"Anyway, in school I hated gym."

"It is a sweaty bunch, you're right, I don't go to the gym much either."

"And the prayers, I don't want to put up with all that god stuff! Prayers mean they have a firm conviction in the existence of something for which there isn't a vestige of evidence. There are lunatic asylums for people like that."

Jack lowered his voice. "You're as terrible as Katya! Well, the way I see it, other people don't let us forget we're Jewish so it's good to be able to defend yourself. Oh yes, they have trips to the country, they hire a Green Line bus."

Katherine's and Benny's conversation fell within earshot. "...Tailoring, my dad was a tailor, he taught me," Benny was saying. "I've been working over two years."

"It sounds a bit like a nightmare to me, my father's a tailor."

"It's a decent trade, you try to make people look good, they pay you for it, what's better than that?"

"I suppose so."

"I'm pleased I chose tailoring."

"Pleased! Ugh!"

"What?"

"Nothing, I was just pleased you felt pleased. Anyway, what happens when finally everybody has a suit and they don't need any more suits?"

"They change the style so everyone wants a new one."

"Good god!"

"I know, it's wonderful, isn't it!"

My primary attention returned to Jack, who had still been talking, "...So I'm registering for architectural school this month. If I'm already registered when I finish Malmesbury Road then the military can't draft me...." He was right; I would also have to worry about getting drafted into the army if I were still working — at Delhi Imports or anywhere — when I turned eighteen. "...I'm really looking forward to learning architecture," he continued.

The Mile End bus pulled up to the stop. As Katherine, Hazel, Jack and I boarded, Benny waved. Still wearing the same smile, he said: "See you all at the Empire, six o'clock."

—o—O—o—

23

"So what'll we do if you don't make any money there, then?" Lily asked.

"Don't worry so much, the kids, four kids they're all working, so for a few weeks they'll pay the rent, it's not so terrible, we'll be alright."

"A few weeks! So then what, then what'll happen? Already we owe Altman's for nearly a month!"

"So will it be worse than Lipman's there, 'No more work, go 'ome, we'll come 'round when it picks up.' When it picks up! *In drerd* they should go with their work there!"

"Well, I don't know...."

"Uh tell you Lily as sure as uh'm, uh'm... uh'll drop dead there and we still won't 'ave the rent for the barstard every week."

"Well, I don't know... you, opening a shop!"

"Stop worrying so much, already uh got two orders, a costume and a skirt, first she'll try out a skirt that one said, don't worry, a few weeks and we'll be alright, may uh live so long we'll be alright."

"Who knows, maybe you're right this time. You really think you'll make a lot of money?"

"Uh'll make a lot of money, on my life uh'll make so much money you won't recognize it you'll be so surprised you will."

"Drink your tea...."

"Uh'm late, lemme go already...."

Abie bounded down the outside steps and trotted off through Tredegar Square toward the Mile End station. After riding the Underground for forty-five minutes to the other side of London — far, far from the East End — he alighted from the Tube train at Burnt Oak station. From there he strode purposefully through the clean, almost quaint suburban enclave, across Edgeware Road, then one block beyond to Quail Lane, the quiet side street in which he had rented a shop. He removed the key from his pocket and tenderly inserted it into the door lock. Inside, he switched on the electric light, closed the door, and rotated the *Open* sign to face the glass panel. He surveyed his newly-laid-out workshop: the broad wooden bench he'd constructed to be exactly the right height, the sewing machine carried two weeks earlier on the Underground from home in several thicknesses of paper bag, the array of cardboard boxes containing cottons, needles, basting hooks and other accoutrements neatly arranged on four shelves on the wall opposite the wide window that looked out onto the narrow street. He still needed to make a curtain for that window, but right now he had to get on with the orders; he'd promised them for this week and already he was behind.

But he didn't care if he worked late, all night even, this was his own place. Ee, marvelous to sit here and work, no foreman nag nagging him to rush, he could make a cup of tea, close his eyes for five minutes, listen to the wireless instead of that... that *barsted* Hirshberg all day with his boasting there. He turned the knob on the Bakelite case that sat over on the shelf, tuned it to The Third Program and they were playing... that was it, yeh, the *Warsaw Concerto,* real music, not like that other one what's-'is-name, the stinking American one, Crossly, Bing Crossly, fah! with 'is groanin' there, enough to make you sick!

He settled in to work at his new bench. The black and white sign in the corner of the big window, "High Class Ladies Tailor, from Saville Row," while not strictly accurate had already garnered two customers, both of whom freely advanced sufficient deposit for him to buy the necessary fabric down Petticoat Lane. Here in Burnt Oak he was free, here he could catch his breath. It was like a whole new beginning.

He worked all the day and evening until after midnight, stopping only for a cup of tea, then lay down on the other end of the bench for a few hours sleep on two rolls of cloth — one roll each trip he'd brought, so the shop would look busy, like he had plenty of work.

At sunrise he shaved, went out for breakfast at The Broadway Eatery around the corner on Edgeware Road, and on his return resumed sewing. At mid-morning the shop's doorbell rang. "It's a handsome costume, Mr. G." The buxom lady turned herself slowly in front of the tall mirror, examining her new suit from every angle.

"Uh'm sorry it took so long, ee, lots and lots of sewing, basting out the collar it took hours and hours, like extra."

"Well, I have to say it fits extremely well." She turned again, admiring her reflection. "So it was worth waiting an extra week, though to be honest I was becoming rather impatient."

"It fits perfect, perfect, the shoulders, it lays perfect, you'll be 'appy, believe me it'll wear, like iron it'll wear."

"Yes yes, I do like it. The ladies are sure to be asking who made it up! Maybe I should keep you a secret!"

As the door closed behind her, Abie pressed the lever on his new cash register and the drawer sprang open. He carefully added the fourteen one-pound notes to the small stack already tucked neatly in the bottom of the drawer. Outside, beyond the filmy white curtain that now softened the wide window, workmen passed by on their way to The Broadway Eatery; it was dinner time.

A motor rattled and spluttered to a stop, followed a moment later by the slamming of a vehicle door. There came a knock; just in time he'd gotten her out of the shop. He closed the cash register drawer, locked it and deposited the little key safely in the bottom of his trousers pocket, then opened the door.

"'Ello, Mr. G., 'ere she is, all ready for yuh." At the curb stood an old but shiny-black two-door Morris van. Abie went outside and walked around the small vehicle, scrutinizing it. "Bang-up paint job we got yuh, won't find a nicer job in the 'ole of London, you won't." In one or two areas, the gleaming black paint had encroached on the perimeter of the windscreen. The man saw Abie notice those excesses: "Oh, that ain't nothin', it comes orf easy wiv a razor blade, that's 'cause 'e used lots of paint 'e did, nice and thick I told 'im." Abie completed the circuit to his apparent satisfaction. Encouraged, the man added: "Even got a spare tire in the back in case yuh gets a puncture," and he jerked open a flimsy back door to display a tire lying on the wooden floor, its rubber tread worn smooth. "So! That'll be sixty-five pounds, then we'll be all squared away like."

"Alright, wait 'ere a minute, uh'll, uh'll, uh'll get the money." Abie let himself back into the shop and closed the door behind him, leaving the man outside. He fished for the little key, opened the cash register, lifted out the tray and from underneath removed an envelope. He counted out sixty-five one pound notes, returned the envelope and tray, closed the drawer and locked it, then took the money over to the workbench and counted it two more times. Satisfied, he stuffed the notes in his trousers pocket and went back outside. "'Ere, 'ere's the money."

The man took the money, counted it quickly, and pushed it inside his jacket. "'Ere's the door key, Mr. G. Want me to park 'er in the alley for yuh?"

"No, no, uh'll park it, uh want to look at it, later uh'll park it."

"Remember, push the clutch down before you puts it in gear, like I showed yuh."

"Alright, well uh got to practice so uh can 'ave the license, yeh, uh'll park it in the alley later, it'll be like good practice."

The man left. With a razor blade Abie carefully removed the offending black paint adhered to the glass. Again he strolled around the vehicle, seeking any other imperfections. He opened the driver's door, eased himself comfortably into the seat and perused the array of knobs and buttons. He turned the steering wheel to the right, then to the left, exercised the three pedals, jiggled the gear lever, and ratcheted the parking brake one extra notch higher. Then he climbed down, closed and locked the door, circumnavigated the van one more time, retrieved the blade from off the curb and returned inside his shop. There, he pulled aside the new white curtain, and pushed to the side of the workbench the jacket he had been felling, in order to better enjoy the view — which now included his own van.

That evening before dusk, jubilant but tired at the end of his long working day, Abie put on his jacket and went outside. He unlocked the van and climbed in. He remembered: first, the ignition switch, which he pushed up. Next, the starter button, which he duly pressed. The engine fired, barely caught, then with a clattering vibration continued running. He grasped the gear lever and slid it into the slot marked R. The van jerked violently backward several feet, and stopped. The motor too was stalled and its accompanying rattle silenced; for a moment he sat enveloped in an extraordinary quiet. Again he clenched the gear lever, which resisted his efforts to haul into neutral; he pulled harder and harder until it finally jumped free of its unseen restraint to float loosely in the gate. Once again he started the engine, and after six or seven grinding attempts he remembered the admonition to depress the clutch pedal before engaging the gears. This he now did, and slid the lever into first gear, removing his foot from the pedal. The vehicle leaped forward, to continue along the narrow roadway in a series of spastic jogs. It bucked its way to the end of the street, and, as Abie quickly turned the wheel, rounded the corner. It continued through a sequence of four smartly executed left turns which brought it back toward the shop, where in the nick of time a violent left turn directed it into the alley. Inexperience compounded anxiety: Abie had commenced the final left turn as he still struggled to release the parking brake, and the unyielding corner of the building ran several green grooves into the black paint. By the time he remembered which pedal was the foot brake he was deep into the alley, and the van ground to a jabbering halt.

Abie reapplied the parking brake, alighted and checked the damaged paint. Two minutes later, with a wet cloth from inside the shop he rubbed the green building cement from the black finish, buffed the damage lightly with his sleeve. He locked up the van for the night.

Back in the shop, he turned off the gas iron which he'd inadvertently left burning, donned his jacket, took one last look around, switched off the electric light, exited and locked the door. Halfway to the Burnt Oak Tube station he hesitated, turned around and ran all the way back to the alley. There, he unlocked the van, depressed the ignition switch to the *off* position, locked the van door, and as he exited the alley, noticed that the *Open* sign still hung in the shop door's glass panel. He opened up, reversed the sign, then trotted back to the station. One hour later, at eleven o'clock, he was home. When he entered, the gas mantle in the living room was turned down to a half-light and Marius lay snoring in the opened settee.

On hearing the key in the lock Lily jumped up from her chair, hurried into the kitchen, and returned with a huge soup-plate of potatoes, carrots and onions, which she placed on the table. Abie sat, picked up the spoon and began eating.

"So where's the money, did she come for the costume?"

"Nah, she came, just for a minute she came, tomorrow she said, she was in a hurry, tomorrow she'll bring the money."

"Tomorrow!" Lily's hands fell limp to her sides. "What do I tell Altman's there, may he drop dead, how can I tell him tomorrow again?"

"What can uh do? Tomorrow she'll come, so 'e'll wait, 'e won't die if 'e waits another day."

"*Oy!*" Lily fell into a chair.

"Where are the girls, they're out with the stinking American soldiers there this time of night?" Abie was tired, hungry and happy, and the agitation he manufactured was only perfunctory.

"What are you talking about, the Americans they've gone back already, what are you, mad? Rivka, she's out, she's out with what's his name, that one Mickey I told you, from Stepney."

"This time of night she's out? What girl is out this time of night, only a prostitute!"

"Ssh, keep your voice down, you'll wake up Maudy, he's sleeping. They're in bed, all of them, Rivka she'll be home soon, eat your dinner, don't start."

"Start! Alright, uh won't start."

Abie picked up the newspaper and ate, and after a minute or two found himself humming; he coughed, and continued eating. Lily undressed down to her slip, climbed into the settee under the covers and moved over to the middle, next to Marius. The settee's movement caused Marius to turn over; he coughed and began choking, then gasping. Lily patted him on the back several times, and slowly his loud breathing fell to a more regular rhythm.

"Turn the light out when you're finished."

"Alright, you don't 'ave to worry so much."

Abie continued his dinner, reading quietly. After five minutes or so the room's hush was regulated by Lily's quiet snoring, Marius's counterpoint, and an occasional click as Abie's spoon glanced against the soup plate.

Coincident with the tranquil scene that had now descended on the Morgan Street living room, Rebecca and her boyfriend Michael, the pride of the Brady Boys Club boxing circle, came walking together across Tredegar Square. They had just seen *The Best Years of Our Lives* at the Odeon. Rebecca had loved the picture; Michael hated it, not least because he insisted it painted a misleadingly sympathetic picture of the United States. "You think that's what America's like?"

"I don't know, I suppose it's something like the pictures. I know it's not the same but still it seems nice to me, a lot better than here."

"They're not real, they're just the pictures."

"I just like it better than here, that's all."

"You sound like you already lived there, like you know."

"Look, I liked the Americans when they were here, they're polite and they're funny. Mickey, I'm sorry if my liking it doesn't fit your ideas."

"You think they'll be any different back where they live?"

"What do you mean?"

"Different from the English?"

"I don't think they started brushing their teeth just because they were being sent to England. Look, let's talk about something else? I can't explain it, I just like it and that's where I want to go."

"I don't want you to go."

"I'm sorry, that's what I want to do, I told you about it and that's the end of it."

"I want you to stay."

"Please, lay off me! Look Mickey, I appreciate you want me to stay but what do you think, just because *you* want me to stay I'm supposed to be so overwhelmed I'll just... forget about all my plans for the rest of my life?"

"You'll be making a mistake if you go."

"*If* I go? I told you I *am* going, definitely, there's no *if* about it. Anyway you don't need to worry, you'll have your pick of all the girls in Stepney."

"I want you to stay."

"Oh, lay off me already!"

When Michael insisted on walking her all the way through Tredegar Square to her door, they forwent what had become their usual goodbye at the park bench; in a strained silence they exited the square and crossed Morgan Street. Meanwhile inside the hushed living room, Abie had finished his dinner and folded the newspaper. He carried the empty plate to the kitchen, and as he went to place it in the sink for Lily to wash in the morning he heard the scraping of a key and creaking hinges as the street door opened. Rebecca walked through into the kitchen where he stood at the sink.

"What... what... where you bin you barsted, this time of night, like a, a... prostitute, you...." and he raised the plate threateningly.

"Mickey!" said Rivka.

"What? Wha'cha... what?"

The kitchen door opened further. Michael Wolf stood in the doorway — only five feet nine inches tall, but stocky, his broad chest clearly spreading apart the jacket lapels above his slim leather-belted waist. His massive biceps seemed to tax the seams in the jacket's sleeves almost to bursting.

"Mickey, come in the room please," she said.

Michael took an easy step forward into the gaslit kitchen.

"What... what... eee, er...."

"This is Michael Wolf."

"I... er...."

"Mr. Grossman if you'll excuse me sir, it's not right to speak to your own daughter like that, that kind of language...."

"I... er... no, you're... uh didn't mean that, uh meant something else, uh was like just saying, you know, it's dangerous, a young girl out by 'erself in the dark, these days you never know...."

Michael placed a muscled arm around Rebecca's shoulder. "She wasn't out by herself,

Mr. Grossman, I was looking after her."

"Yeh, it's good, uh'm glad you're looking after 'er, thanks, it's good, yeh, you're right, uh mean uh'm glad you're looking after 'er.... Eeeyeh." A stifled wheeze came from Abie's throat; he turned back to the sink, opened the tap and began slowly and meticulously washing his dinner plate.

Rebecca and Michael retired to the passageway, pulling the kitchen door closed behind them. They whispered. "Will you be alright?" "Yes, he won't do anything, you better go home now" "I want to see you tomorrow after work...." "No, I've got packing to do, I've got lots of things to get ready." "You're serious about this, you think you're really going to go...." "I'm tired, I've been working all day, I can't go through this anymore, please." "Don't go. I don't want you to go." "I'll see you on Saturday, let me go to sleep, I've got to be up early." "What time on Saturday, then?" "Six o'clock, I'll meet you in the park at six...." "How about two, you can come to the gymnasium and watch me spar." "Michael, I've told you a thousand times I'm not interested in boxing, it's nice, I'm glad you're tough, I just can't keep talking about boxing all the time...."

"What's the matter, what's going on there?" Lily's sleepy voice called from the living room.

"Ssh, see, we're waking my mother up," whispered Rebecca. Then louder, "It's nothing, it's just me, I'm going upstairs now, see you in the morning." Again, a whisper: "Go on, you have to go now, I'll see you on Saturday, six o'clock, don't come early."

The house again fell silent save for the coursing of water down the drain in the kitchen sink, and in the passageway subdued rustlings, a barely audible, "See you Saturday," low creaking of door hinges, then the quiet padding of stockinged feet up the stairs.

–24–

When Abie came home from work I could hear Lily downstairs, angry at Dad's brother Joe having reneged on Zilla's sponsorship. "Speak to your sister Anya, ask her to do something to help."

"Anya, uh can't speak to Anya, she won't talk to me."

"Do anything already with your *becuckter* family, the rotten *brochs,* after all the girls' plans."

"Maybe uh'll talk to Harry, uh didn't ask 'im to lend me, a long time now uh didn't ask 'im."

"So what'll your brother-in-law do?"

"Uh'll explain to 'im someone must 'ave said something 'orrible, 'e'll tell Sarah 'e will."

"You think that'll help?"

"'E's like a decent fella, 'e'll tell Sarah she should write a letter. Maybe Joe'll listen to Sarah, she was always 'is favorite, oo knows?"

Abie's plan worked. Two weeks before Easter we received a letter from Joe and Emily in New York: their bank had made an error with the account, it was all cleared up now and if Rebecca wanted to immigrate they would sponsor her and put her up for a week or two in their apartment. But, they added, she'd have to find a job right away.

I saw the letter when I got home. "Rivka, are you really going?"

"I sure am! Mum rang me up at the restaurant to tell me, so this afternoon I checked it out at the Cunard office in the West End, and they exchanged the ticket already. Tomorrow I'm getting a passport, and it'll only take two or three days to get a visa."

Mum came in with my supper. "She'll be going in ten days, sit down and eat."

"Just ten days!"

Rebecca continued. "I have to work fast in case someone else in his lousy family makes up more lies."

"It'll be… strange when you're… not here."

"Don't worry Zech, everything is going to work out alright."

"Yes, I suppose so." Rebecca! We were losing the most level-headed person in the family.

"Eat your dinner," said Mum.

"The minute I get there I'll get a job so I can get a flat for myself. Joe sounds as repulsive as Abie, I don't want to stay in their place a minute longer than necessary."

"He's… ugh!," said Mum. "One of these days I'll tell you what he did to Aunt Muriel."

"Anyway don't worry both of you, once I'm there in a short time I'll get Zilla's ticket, then in no time we'll get tickets for everybody else."

"Yes." It was hard to look that far ahead.

"It'll take a while but not too long, don't worry."

"No it's alright, I'm not worrying."

"Then we'll get Mum next...."

"Yes."

"....with Maudy. Then we'll send for the rest."

"Yes."

"Except the old fucker of course."

"Eat your dinner."

On Wednesday of the following week, Delhi Imports gave me half a day off. I went early with Rebecca, Zilla, Mum and Marius to Waterloo Station; Anya's Fashion Footwear didn't allow Katherine time off. On the platform next to us stood the stacked steamer, two suitcases and the several small bags Rebecca had been packing and repacking for the past week. The boat train backed toward us as a porter, unaware of the import of our small drama, casually wheeled her luggage toward the baggage compartment. The engine engulfed us in its swirling steam and a panic rose up in my chest. All attention was focused on Rebecca, so I was able to keep secret my silent struggle.

"Lily, in the meantime try not to argue with him, whatever he says just agree."

"Be careful in America, Joe is a real barstard like the rest of his family."

"Everything will work out. Ta-ra, Maudy, look after Mum, I'll see you both there in two or three months even, ta-ra Zech. Zilla, I'll write as soon as I get there."

Doors slammed and the train inched forward under the girded iron and glass station roof. As it plunged into its black tunnel, a palpable emptiness hovered among us standing silent on the empty platform. Then Mum grasped Marius's hand, and I his other as in a trance we followed Zilla out of the smoke, up the stairs, across the vast echoing marble floor and out into the dazzling bustle of the street. Mum's and Maudy's bus to the Aldgate terminus arrived.

"Funny isn't it, like it's not real," said Zilla as their bus pulled away. For the first time I saw tears in my eldest sister's eyes. She and I stood at an awkward remove on the busy pavement.

"I know, I hope she'll be alright, I hope nothing happens."

"Nah, what do you mean, what should happen? Soon we'll all be there."

"I feel a bit ill."

"You alright? Where're you going now?"

"I've got to go back to work, to the stockroom."

"Go home if you don't feel well," she said. "Fuck 'em at work, you'll be in New York in a few months, you should worry!"

"Do you think she'll really be able to arrange for everyone else to go, all the money and everything? I feel a bit like everything isn't real."

"I hope so, who wants to stay here? Funny, I'll be the next one!" said Zilla. "So, I suppose I better go back to Buck & Hickman's."

"Yes." I had to get back too. Mr. Bandi only gave me off 'til ten A.M., and there in the stockroom I wouldn't have to think. "Yes, I'll go back to work, also."

• • •

"I want a pair of women's shoes, green, a leaf green, you know the kind with thin leather thongs bunched under a metal clasp over the toes." He was handsome, romantic-looking, though his long hair was a dusky blondish grey, and curly, not the sweeping rich brown that Katherine favored in her dreams. His carriage was sensitive, poetic; he'd even displayed a slight Byronic limp as he came up the steps into the shop. "You know, the heel bare, a thin strap?"

"A sling heel, what size?" Katherine asked, and hoped he wouldn't notice the high heat that had flashed to her cheeks. She found herself acutely aware of the shop's confines.

"Small, I don't know what size, exactly." He looked down at Katherine's feet. "About your size." A crimson brush painted her face. "Small. Petite."

He stood in the middle of the shop as Katherine went to the rear stock aisle to rummage, and catch her breath. She climbed atop the wooden step stool and looked at him over the top shelf: he was wearing a bottle-green cor-du-roi jacket with patches on the elbows; he must like green. His mass of dusty light curls, billowing enough to be those of a girl, fell over his ears and around his shoulders, forward onto the open-at-the-neck pink collar of his shirt.

She brought down a size six and opened the box. In the dim light between the aisles it seemed not a leaf green — too bright, flashy, too yellowish, almost a kelly green. He'd think she couldn't tell shades of green. But they were the only green in that style.

She stumbled down from the stool, brought out the box, and opened it.

"They're a bit... yellow, do you have...."

"I'm sorry, I know it's not the right green exactly, this is the closest we have in that style...."

"Would you try them on?"

"Me?"

"To see if they fit, I'm not sure of the size, they seem right...."

Katherine sat on the chair and removed her own shoe. With shaking hands she pulled one shoe from the box and slid it on; a leather thong caught clumsily on her big toe. She went to stand.

"Would you put on the other one also? That way I can see what they're like when you walk."

She put on the other shoe and tried to stand; one heel slid under, her ankle twisted to the side, and he briefly caught her arm.

"Would you... walk... just two or three steps?" He stood aside. She wanted to walk but her knees were giving way and her neck and chest had caught fire. The display window moved, swung to the right, then up to the ceiling.

Two faces were peering down at her. Anya: that hairy mole on the end of her lip; close up, she was even more repulsive. She'd been gone on a lunchtime errand, she must have just walked in.

The other face was nestled inside a halo of nutmeg curls that now fell forward. "Are you alright?" he asked. "You fainted. I think you hit the back of your head on the hard floor."

"I'm alright...." said Katherine, and moved to get up. Ow!, her head really did hurt. She fingered through her hair to the beginnings of a lump.

"Let me help you get up." He lifted her by the arm. "Excuse me, maybe if you got some water." He addressed Anya as he helped Katherine to the chair, "A glass of water?"

How embarrassing, to faint like that, just when she really wanted to seem unconcerned! Anya wrapped the shoe-box. "That'll be thirteen eleven-three altogether."

He took out a ten-shilling note and counted out four more shillings. The cash register rang, and she handed him back one farthing, then the shoe-box.

"Are you alright?" he asked Katherine. She had stood up, but still felt groggy. "You look white. Maybe you should go home, I'll take you home."

"Anya, I don't feel well, I'd like to go home."

"Alright, go, go, better you fainted here than on the train platform, all the strangers there. I can't pay you for the rest of the day, we don't make enough here, a little place, the rent I got to pay every week."

"Where do you live?" he asked. "Can I walk with you, see you get home alright?"

"Near Tredegar Square, the other side of Mile End Road." Katherine put on her coat, and together they walked toward the end of Burdett Road.

"My name's Artemis." The early afternoon sun shone faintly, and his jacket seemed barely sufficient against the April chill.

"Mine's Grossman. Katherine Grossman. What's your first name?"

"That's it, that's my first name, Artemis."

She felt like an idiot. "Oh." His hand clasped her arm as they crossed Mile End Road. Then: "What do you do, what do you work at?" she asked.

"I'm a poet."

"Oh! You mean... you write poetry?" Again she felt stupid.

"Yes."

What else could he have meant! "At a place? I mean, you go to a place and you write poetry?"

"No, my parents have a restaurant in Aldgate, I work there."

"Oh."

"I just like to write poetry, that's all." They were walking through Tredegar Square. "This is a pretty park. The branches, they're black, just about black."

"A little later in the spring it'll be all green. Is green your favorite color?"

"How did you know?"

"You're wearing a green jacket, and you bought green shoes."

"Yes."

Before she knew it, the words blurted themselves out: "Are they for your girlfriend?"

"Well, I wouldn't call her quite a girlfriend."

"Oh." Why would he buy shoes for someone other than his girlfriend? "So, I live over there, on the corner."

"I'll walk you to your door." They crossed Morgan Street. "Can I see you, another time?"

So he did ask! But it was silly: she was seeing Benny three, four times a week. "Well yes, but what about your girlfriend?"

"She's not my girlfriend. I'll prove it. Sit down here." He motioned for her to sit on the little wall in front of the house. He knelt down, opened the package and took out the shoes. From her feet he carefully removed the shoes she was wearing. She didn't want him to lean too close, she'd been standing on her feet all morning, thank goodness it was outdoors! Gently grasping her ankles he replaced her shoes with the green sling heels he'd just bought. "They're yours, I want you to have them. I hope the color is alright."

"I can't take them, they're a week's wages!" And she giggled.

"I want you to have them, they look better on you than they will on anyone else. I want to see you again, when can I see you?"

"Katya, is that you, so early?" Lily's voice came from the street door just around the corner.

"Oh, I wasn't well at work, I fainted, so I came home."

"You fainted? *Oy a broch!* Who's...."

Katherine and Artemis walked around to the street door to see Lily looking out.

"We just got back from the station. Who's...."

"My sister just went to America, this morning she caught the train to Southampton. Mum, this is Artemis, he was in the shop when I fainted so he walked me home."

"Nice to meet you, Mrs...."

"Grossman."

"Mrs. Grossman." Then, quietly, "I've got to run; Katherine, when can I see you?"

"Sunday? Early, like ten?"

Maudy had pushed forward from behind Lily. "What about Benny, 'e said 'e's coming round on Sunday."

"Who's Benny?" asked Artemis.

"Nobody, nothing, I can see you for a bit Sunday morning, then I have to... I'll be...."

"Where did you get those shoes?" interjected Lily.

"They look 'orrible," said Marius.

"They're... nothing, nothing." Katherine held the shoe-box containing her old shoes. "Sunday, then."

"It has to be just the morning...." Katherine called after him, but already he was halfway across Tredegar Square.

"So what's this?" Lily asked Katherine when they were inside the house. "A new one already? What'll you tell Benny?"

"Oh I don't know, he just walked me home that's all, what's it got to do with Benny? It doesn't mean I can't have any friends."

•   •   •

A knock on the street door, and Katherine opened it. "Hello, did you hear anything yet from Rivka?" It was Michael Wolf.

Rebecca had left strict instructions to say nothing; she would write to him herself when the time was right. "No, she didn't write, I suppose we'll get a letter soon."

"I'll come round tomorrow, then."

Actually, every day or so another letter arrived from Rebecca. Joe and Emily argued continuously, she wrote, and once she'd seen him hit Emily. Neighbors in the building avoided Rebecca simply because she lived in that apartment. Mum was right, he was as bad as Abie, it must run in the family. But Rebecca was busy working on Wall Street as a waitress and in only four weeks she'd earned enough to move out. She had taken her own apartment, on 175th Street just off Broadway in Washington Heights. All she had there was a bed and a dinette set, but it was all she needed for the time being. Working in London it had taken her well over a year to get enough money for her ticket, she wrote, but here in America it was wonderful — the customers were nice, she was making good tips and the way everything was going she expected to be sending a ticket for Zilla in just eight or ten weeks.

At home, Zilla was saving hard too, preparing to leave. She'd scheduled a repeat medical examination at the American Embassy, and had already placed an advert in the *Daily Telegraph* to sell the piano. A big new suitcase lay open on her bed.

—o—O—o—

25

Miss Eunice came into the stockroom and closed the door behind her. Her tasseled blonde ponytail swung like a semaphore. "I come in with this morning's list."

"Miss Eunice, are you really the vice-president?"

"Vice-president?"

"Mr. Bandi said you were the vice-president."

"I dunno. S'pose I am if 'e says so. 'E's alright, 'e always says I can bring in the list."

"I see."

"Purushotham said I'm not supposed to come in the stockroom."

"I know."

"'E said it'll be the end if I come in 'ere."

"The end?"

"The end."

"Won't you be the vice-president anymore?"

"Huh! More 'n that, likely."

"Oh."

"'E's out now."

"Who?"

"Purushotham, 'e's out 'til twelve. So do you want to kiss?"

"Well, yes I do, but supposing he...."

"'E's out."

She came close, and I put my face forward to kiss her. Our mouths touched. Then she started opening her mouth wide, pressing closer, practically pushing me backward. She pushed her tongue so far back into my mouth I began to gag. "Your arms, put your arms round me," she wheezed out the side of her mouth. I put my arms around her. "'Arder," she seemed to rasp, but her voice was hoarse and I wasn't sure I'd understood.

The only way I could breathe was by twisting my face sideways: "Do you mean, squeeze your body?"

She pulled her face away and tsk'd. "Don't you know 'ow to kiss a real woman?"

I wilted: here was something else I didn't know, something probably obvious to everyone else! "Do they kiss real grown-ups different from girls, I mean, younger ones?"

"They? Who's they?" She was smiling, leaning against me. "Boy, you're really something!" she said, and we toppled, spiraling down into the mountain of cotton swabs that were not only stacked up the wall but also covered a full quarter of the floor. We landed with me over her, my weight pushing her deep into the mound, in one moment both of us inundated with additional swabs falling on top. She was completely out of sight under me; I shoveled swabs away so she wouldn't be suffocated, but she just kept her arms tight around my neck, pulling me down, giggling.

"Just a minute, just a minute…." In my struggles I managed to throw a few swabs away, backwards; one of them hit something unexpected and fell to the floor right near me, and I turned my head. It was Mr. Purushotham, standing right there behind us! "Miss Eunice," I tried to whisper into the rumpus, "Stop, stop…." But either because she was buried and didn't hear, or she thought I was playing, she just kept bouncing around, giggling, and swabs kept falling down onto us faster than I could throw them out.

"C'mon, c'mon, fraidy-cat," her muffled voice came from beneath the turbulence. I looked back again and Mr. Purushotham still stood there, vertical, stern and silent. So that he shouldn't be any more angry than absolutely necessary I tried to support myself on my arms in a rigid stance over her, to disassociate myself in some degree from the commotion below, but it was difficult because she still hung on my neck.

Gradually she realized something was wrong and raised her head out of the morass. As she saw him, her mouth opened. I twisted my head back again and saw that his skin color had broken through the Indian brown into a sort of mauve. He glared past me at Miss Eunice below; I'd never noticed before that he had bloodshot eyes. Abruptly he spun around, walked out of the room and closed the door — quietly, which to my ears sounded more ominous than had it been slammed shut.

Miss Eunice pushed me off her as though it was all my fault, and clambered disheveled out of the mess. The loop that bound her ponytail was gone, and the blonde tresses fell in wonderful disarray around her shoulders. The blouse, dark skirt and little matching jacket were completely covered with flecks of white cotton — it would take an hour of brushing her to get it all off. She grabbed her handbag and started fixing her lips.

I knew I ought to do something masculine and decisive. "I… I…."

"Don't talk to me! It's all over!"

Probably I should have grabbed her firmly by the shoulders and assured her I was in charge of the situation. The two of us could have walked out through the hallway past her desk, her arm looped proudly into mine, our heads high. *"You can consider this latest intrusion into the privacy of my stockroom the final straw. We're both handing in our notice, and I hope you can find replacements as honest and hard-working as we've been. Good-bye and good luck!"* Edward R. Murrow always ended his news reports on the wireless with "Good-bye and good luck!"; it would have been a generous closing, free from malice and resentment.

"You alright?" She suddenly seemed concerned; maybe my contemplating the drama of our departure had made me look strange. "You don't 'ave to take it too 'ard. Whatever 'appens you can always get another stockroom job."

You can always get another stockroom job! I knew it, working in a stockroom was the lowest kind of job a person could have. I'd love to work at something that made me proud, something where I could earn loads of money so I could pay the rent for ten years in advance. Like an architect, or singing; or maybe being a scientist. But how does a person get to be a scientist, someone from Mile End?

Two hours later I was ready to go to the Post. Out in the hall, Purushotham gave me a fishy smile. Miss Eunice was still at her desk, but as she handed me the five shillings for postage she kept her head turned in the other direction.

•   •   •

"Eee, the customers they'll come, you won't believe it!"

"Really, you think they really will then?" Lily asked.

"Yeh, from the factories there, crowds and crowds, twelve o'clock every day they're going past outside to that place 'round the corner, you know on Edgeware Road there, 'e should *gai in dred* there. Eee, uh'd 'ave to be ready, they'll be banging on the door already, twelve o'clock to come in."

"So would you make any money then?"

"Money?"

"So what's the good if it wouldn't make any money?"

"Oo said it wouldn't make money, loads and loads of cups of tea uh'd be serving there, uh wouldn't even be able to keep up with it all."

"Mr. G's! So that's the name you'll call it!"

"Yeh, the painter, a big sign uh'll get painted, nice, on the window, *Mr. G's Snack Bar.*" Abie giggled.

"So then you won't earn any money with the tailoring."

"Tsk!, everything's no good, with you it's always no good, like a failure, before uh start even it's no good. Uh'll make time from the tailoring, in the morning on the way uh'll buy loaves and loaves of bread, uh'll make the sandwiches, like cheese, big sandwiches uh'll make, not the lousy little scraps they give you...."

"Big sandwiches? I don't know if it's good...."

"...like the one round the corner what is it, The Broadway Eatery, with 'is stinking little cups of tea, like one sip and already it's empty. 'Ere uh'll give 'em big cups, like a mug, eee, for tuppence they can drink all day if they want."

"So how will you make any money then?"

"Money, money! All I ever 'ear is money! Don't worry, they'll all, they'll come back, uh'll make loads of money, from the tailoring uh'm making already, you'll see 'ow much money uh'll make with the snack bar. You don't believe me uh'll make a load of money? Look, uh'll show you something, you'll be so surprised you will, you'll faint already." Abie stood up from the dinner table. "Come outside."

"Come outside? What for?"

He put down his cigarette. "Come outside, don't worry so much, uh'll show you." Lily followed Abie as he opened the street door. "Look."

She looked out the door into the evening darkness. The corner gaslight on Morgan Street illuminated only a short distance beyond their door. "What, what is it, it's dark, what should I see?"

"Look, look you idiot you, look, there." And he pointed along the street to the right, pushing Lily's head out the doorway. "Well?"

"So what is it already, some lights." She stretched the corner of her better eye to see further. "Some little lights, what is it, a car there or something."

"Come outside," and he took her arm and pulled her down the steps into the street.

"What's going on, what happened?"

"Happened, nothing happened, look, look." He walked her a few steps along the pavement. In the roadway opposite the gate in the wall that sided the garden a vehicle was parked, a barely visible light marking each front mudguard.

"So what is it, someone left their car there, so...."

"You bladdy idiot, can'cha tell the difference, it's not a car, it's a van."

"So, a van, who cares if it's a car or a van, what's the difference?"

"It's our van."

"What?"

"It's our van, uh said it's our van."

"Our van? How could it be our van, what are you, mad or something?"

"It's our van, you deaf? Uh'm telling you it's our van, it's ours."

"How could it be ours?"

"Because that's how much money uh'm making there, it's our van."

"You bought a van?"

"It's our van."

"So if you're making money enough to buy a van, where's the rent... and for Altman's?"

"If uh gave you for the rent, then we wouldn't 'ave enough for a van."

"A van? So who needs a van?"

"Oo needs a van! Uh'll 'ave two businesses there, uh need a van."

"You need a van? So that's where the money's going! You said you'll make a lot of money, we wouldn't have to worry."

"Well, we already got a van, we don't 'ave to worry about a van."

"*Oy,* a brilliant husband I got here, he gets some money, he throws it away on a van! Who needs a van?"

"Come, uh'll take you for a ride, you'll see."

"A ride? Who wants a ride, you can keep your ride."

Abie took a key out of his pocket, delicately edged it into the keyhole in the passenger's door handle, and opened the door. "Come on, we'll go for a ride we'll go."

"Now? In the dark?"

"Lights, there's lights in front, what do you think uh got a van without lights? Come on Lily, we'll go for a ride." He held her arm and helped her onto the running board and into the front passenger seat.

He went around and climbed into the driver's seat.

"The neighbors, we're making such a noise, they'll start."

"The neighbors, fu–uck 'em already the neighbors, they can *gai in dreard,* soon they'll all wish they 'ad a van like this." He pressed the starter button: *wow, wow, wow... wow....* The sounds from under the bonnet came slower and slower, until finally they stopped completely. Abie released the starter button, then pressed it again and again. All he could get now were clicking sounds. "Eee, wha's'a marra with it?"

"Me? You're asking me what's the matter with it? Ride then, go on, ride already."

"It won't go, uh dunno, it was alright, everything was alright, all of a sudden it won't go...." He pushed the button several times more, each press producing only a click. "The barsted, what did 'e sell me 'ere? Uh just come, from Burnt Oak all the way 'ome uh was riding, everything was alright. Now uh wanna go for a ride 'ere and it won't go."

"He probably took one look and saw he was dealing with a *schmuck* so he sold you one that's no good."

"Alright already, uh'll 'ave to 'ave it fixed, tomorrow uh'll 'ave it fixed."

"You don't have enough for the rent but you've got enough to get your new toy fixed?"

"Shurrup already let me think a minute, yeh, tomorrow uh'll 'ave it fixed, in the morning first thing."

"So what happened to the ride?"

"What do you mean what 'appened to the ride, you idiot, can't you see it's broke, uh'll 'ave it fixed."

"Tsk! Typical."

They alighted, and Abie carefully locked the two doors. As they began to walk back to the house, Abie noticed the little mudguard lights were off. "Eee, uh thought uh left the lights on, uh must 'ave the lights on, they'll take it away, the police, that's all uh need."

He reopened the van door. "The switch, it's on," he said to himself. He went around to the front, then to the back where he bent down and peered closely into the bulbs. "Eee, they're on, uh can 'ardly see 'em, like, there's no light nearly." He banged the dashboard switch on and off several times, came back outside and re-examined the lamps. "They're switched on, something's broke, there's only a tiny bit of light there," he mumbled. "Tomorrow uh'll tell 'im the lights, 'e'll 'ave to fix the lights, yeh that's why it won't go, the lights, there's something with the lights uh'll tell 'im."

· · ·

When I left work on the afternoon of my debacle with Miss Eunice and Mr. Purushotham, I didn't go straight home. I went instead to Jack's house to solicit his advice on rectifying the situation so I wouldn't get the sack. Together we went to Johnny Isaacs for chips, to sit down and talk it over. He thought there was probably nothing I could do, and what did I want that job for anyway, there was no future in it. That made me feel even worse, though I knew he was trying to help. We finished eating, I saw him home, and as I was walking across Morgan Street from the park Katherine was coming up Tredegar Terrace. "Hello, Katya."

"Hello, I hate my job," she responded.

"Yes, I hate mine also. They might give me the sack I think."

"I wish Anya would give me the sack. I just came back from Hazel's."

"I just came back from Johnny Isaacs, I went with Jack. Look at that van."

"Oh... yes."

We went into the house.

"Mum, someone parked a van outside."

"Someone! It's your father's."

"Your father's? You mean it's Dad's?" Dad was sitting at the table behind a newspaper.

"Who else? He bought himself a van with all the money."

I addressed Abie. "Dad?"

"What, what?"

"Did you really get a van, is that van outside yours?"

"Yeh, it won't go, uh dunno it's broke, tomorrow uh'll get the man, 'e'll come, uh dunno."

"You mean, it really is your van?"

"My van! It's our van, everybody's van. It's not only my van, it's everybody's, 'e'll fix it, we'll go for a ride we'll all go."

"Can I see it? Katya, you want to see, Dad's got a van."

Abie arose, and Katherine and I followed him out to the van.

I saw the lights were off. "You're supposed to leave the lights on after dark, aren't you? I think you could get a summons."

"The lights, they're broke, uh don't know."

"Broke?"

"Wha's'a marra with you, uh said it's broke, uh'll get it fixed tomorrow."

"Oh, *shoin,* don't start already, I'm going in." Katherine turned and went back inside.

"Start! Another one, like 'er mother!"

At that moment, Marius and one of his urchin friends came up out of the darkness. "Thought I 'eard 'is voice, grumbling as usual. Crikey, what's that?" In the low light Marius saw the van and Abie standing at the opened driver's door.

Abie's tone was mocking. "What's that, what's that? Piss orf with your lousy yockisher f... f... thief, there, that's oo 'e 'angs round with! When uh take 'em for a ride you'll stay 'ome you 'ump-backed barsted, you won't come near it."

"That your van? Well, you can stick yer van right up yer arse," said Marius as he and his buddy ran off into the darkness.

"Barsted," mumbled Abie. "With 'is coughing and choking there all night uh can't sleep, maybe 'e'll drop dead one night from choking so uh can fall asleep."

I turned to go back into the house.

"Listen Zachary, it's broke, the van, another time uh'll show you, when it's mended uh'll show you."

"Alright." And I went back in.

Abie came in ten minutes later. "Zachary, Zach, er, Zech."

"What?"

"Er... nothing, your name, that's all uh just said your name, can't uh say your name?" He giggled.

"Oh, I mean, did you want something?"

"Want something, no uh don't want something, uh'm, uh'm.... It's nice to see you, uh don't see you."

"Nice to see me?"

"Uh mean...."

"Well I come home every day...."

"Uh know you come 'ome. Uh... just, it's nice to see you, can't uh be friendly?"

"Er, yes."

"Listen, er, uh'll 'ave the snack bar there, it'll be real good, 'undreds an' 'undreds of customers, eee, it'll be so busy there like you don't know."

"Yes? That's good isn't it?"

"Well, if uh'm running both of 'em, like the tailoring also, it's too much, uh won't be able to manage all by myself."

"Maybe you should close the tai...."

"Uh'll need someone to 'elp out there, maybe uh thought...."

"You could hire someone to help, like someone to work for you."

"Uh thought maybe if you work there in the snack bar uh'll pay you money uh'll pay you, like wages, you'll see we'll make loads of money, you'll see."

"Me?"

"So what's so terrible if you 'elp out a bit, your own father...."

"Really? You mean, you really would want me to work for you?"

"So what's so terrible...?"

"No, I thought...."

"So work there, between both of us we'll make loads of money, you'll see."

—o—O—o—

26

Zilla was returning on the Underground from her day's secretarial duties at Buck & Hickman's. She had stopped to shop for some stockings and other items, and when she came up the stairway and out of Mile End station, night was falling. She crossed Mile End Road and headed toward Tredegar Square Park, wondering if there had been any replies to the advert she'd placed in the newspaper to sell her piano; it wouldn't be long before she left for America, and she wanted everything to be settled comfortably ahead of her departure. As she walked past the short driveway that ended with a large double door closing off a commercial garage, a furtive male voice called from the darkness.

"'Ey, miss, you wanna see something?"

Zilla turned round, but in the darkened recesses of the walled-in driveway could see nothing.

Again the voice called: "'Ey, miss, it's me, 'ere, look, you wanna see something?"

"What is it? What?"

"Look 'ere, miss, you wanna see, this 'ere, eight inches it is."

"What? Oo-er!" And as she looked, a seemingly youngish man who stood in the shadows, wearing a jacket and no coat, had dropped his trousers. "Oo-er, whasamarra with you?"

The man, still several yards away from Zilla, moved forward into the slant of light thrown by the street lamp several houses along by the perimeter of the park. His trousers sat hunched around his ankles, and in his right hand, it seemed to Zilla, he was holding his penis.

"Wanna touch it, miss, c'm'ere."

"Oo-er! You kiddin'?"

"Eight inches, miss, that's what it is, eight inches."

He seemed puny, not much more than a kid, and her initial alarm abated. "Oo-er, there's nothin' there!"

"Nothing 'ere? Eight inches it is!"

"You kiddin'? It's less than an inch."

"What! Look! It's not!"

"Why'n'cha stick it in the keyhole in the garage door?"

"Miss, you're cruel, that's what you are."

And Zilla ran home. Flushed, she told Lily what had just happened.

"Ugh!, the lousy stinker, so what did you do?"

"I told 'im to stick it in the keyhole."

•   •   •

I had just gotten home myself, and happened to be upstairs when Zilla arrived and related her story to Lily. For me the day had already been anxiety-ridden, Mr. Purushotham informing me as I left work that afternoon that Delhi Imports would no longer require my services. I'd stopped at Jack's house and spent an hour with him discussing my situation. And now, through the combination of the open door downstairs, Lily's questioning, and the agitation in Zilla's voice, I heard this story. And an unimaginable story it was; my skin flashed in a hot rash at yet another example of male depravity. How terrible, the affronts that women suffered at the hands of men! No wonder Mum said all men were dirty and disgusting.

By coincidence, Abie overheard Zilla's story, too. A motor mechanic who apparently had promised to appear at the house sometime after I'd left for work that morning had not shown up and Abie, still fearing a police summons for an unlighted parked vehicle during after-dark hours, had finally left for Burnt Oak, completed the costume he was working on, then forgone further construction of his proposed snack bar. He'd rushed home early, intending to take a closer look at why the lights weren't working and the engine wasn't starting — and perhaps even save himself the cost of a mechanic. Therefore, unbeknownst to Zilla as she related her tale to Lily, Abie, washing his hands in the kitchen, overheard every word of the turbid story. He charged into the living room. "What? What? Eee, disgusting the filthy barsted, where is 'e, uh'll kill 'im, by my life uh'll kill 'im."

"It's over now, I suppose 'e's gone."

"Keep your macintosh on, nah, quick, we'll catch 'im." He ran for his jacket. "Where's, where's Zech, Zach, Zachary?"

Lily called upstairs: "Quick, Zachary, quick, quick, your Father wants you."

I came downstairs, foundering in a bizarre sea of apprehension.

"Eee, Zech, Zachary, quick, come outside, we'll grab 'im, you'll 'elp."

"What's the matter…?" It was too difficult to acknowledge even having heard the story.

"The matter! Nothing's the matter, don't you worry what's the matter, get your jacket, Zilly, quick." And he herded Zilla and me outside and along the dark street. To Zilla: "Where is 'e? There? That garage, over there? Alright, you wait 'ere a minute, then you walk up there, like, like nothing you're just walking past. Zech, you wait there, yeh, by Tredegar, Tredegar, tsk!, uh can't think, the park 'ere, you wait on the pavement, don't let 'im go past, *grab* 'im if 'e runs, *grab* 'im and 'old 'im, in one minute uh'll be there. Uh'm going to go round, uh'll run quick round the other side, from Mile End Road uh'll run round. Eee, when uh catch 'im 'e'll be sorry!" And Abie flew off into the darkness.

"Zilly, what shall we do, what do you think?" I asked.

"I dunno, I suppose we ought to catch 'im, supposing 'e does it to someone else?"

"I, I, I, I suppose we have to."

"'E didn't seem tough or anything, like a skinny I dunno."

"Yes?"

"Yes, like a kid. You stay 'ere, 'e won't do anything."

Zilla began walking slowly and deliberately toward the garage. My fingers felt tingly, and I didn't know whether I'd even be able to intercept the creature, let alone hold on. Zilla walked further along the pavement, through the street-light's illuminated patch several houses before the garage. And there in the far distance came Abie, approaching the garage from the Mile End Road side, arms outstretched at the ready, bobbing from side to side in the close shadow of the wall as he loped toward us.

To synchronize the timing Zilla slowed her walk, and as she came abreast of the garage I heard clearly articulated the dreaded: "'Ey, miss."

She half turned: "What?"

"'Ey, miss, over 'ere," from near the garage door.

At which she cupped her mouth and shouted at full volume: "There 'e is, there 'e is!"

From the Byzantine recesses a man came hobbling out, his trousers down by his knees, held up with one hand. I knew I was supposed to run toward him, but I could muster little enthusiasm for getting punched by a crazed stranger holding his trousers up with one hand and perhaps his dick with the other. I couldn't make up my mind what to do, and in my indecision, lunging first toward him, then away, feinting sideways, the halflight must have set me forth as some ghostly warrior flailing an exotic multiplicity of weapons. Confounded, he spun around to take off in the opposite direction — only to crash directly into Abie, who had just bounded up from the other direction. The impact knocked them both to the pavement.

Abie, unencumbered as was his adversary by sartorial disarray, was able to jump up first, and he delivered a hefty kick to the small of the back.

"Ow, stop it, that 'urt," the youth cried, and stumbling, attempted to scramble to his feet.

"Zech, quick, punch 'im, kick 'im. You filthy barsted you!"

I ran forward. The fellow was up off the ground, but stooped, still trying to pull his trousers all the way up. Abie launched a huge fist toward his face, and the man raised his other arm to deflect the blow: "'Old orf, mister, I didn't mean no 'arm."

I grabbed at the arm still struggling with the trousers and managed to secure a hold, though not wanting to be complicit in the trousers' falling down again I didn't know which way to pull the arm.

"You twisted barsted you, you lousy stinking *perverse,* that's what you are!" Abie landed a punch squarely to the side of the man's head causing him to fall again, this time pulling me down to the ground with him. A thump, the arm jerked up, and I saw that Abie had delivered a kick to the man's face.

Zilla screamed, "Stop it, stop it, don't kick 'im like that!"

Again a kick, this time to his chest, then another to his face, then another. The arm was jerking, it seemed autonomously, and Zilla had grabbed at Abie's arm to haul him off. The man was groaning; his face seemed blackened, and I realized in the darkness it was covered with blood. Zilla managed to pull Abie, somewhat off-balance, a short distance along the pavement.

The man's face looked terrible. "Are you alright?" I whispered.

"'Elp me, 'elp me," he groaned.

I started to help him to his feet; Abie disentangled himself, lunged forward and went to land a crashing fist at the back of his head, but Zilla jumped between and prevented it from having much impact. I pulled the man away and we both staggered forward into the clear, while Zilla held onto Abie's arm.

Abie attempted to shake her hand away. "Wha'cha doing, what's going on?" he said in amazement.

"Leave 'im alone already," cried Zilla.

"What? Wha'cha talking, leave 'im alone?"

"Zech is, Zech'll take care of 'im, 'e can handle 'im."

"Zech, wha'cha talking about, Zech?"

We were afraid Abie would really kill him. I whispered to the man: "I'm not going to do anything."

"Wha'd'ya mean?" He didn't know which of us was his assailant.

We were face to face, his a reflection of what mine had been a few minutes earlier — terrified. "Sshh, it's okay," I whispered, "I'm not going to do anything."

"What should I do then, guv?" he moaned quietly.

"Pretend I've got you in a grip, put your hand behind your back, kneel down or something, make out I'm holding you down." He kneeled. "Dad, quick, run up to Mile End Road, get a policeman, I'm holding him, it's alright, go on, quick, quick!"

"A policeman? Er, er...."

"Quick, while I've got him, hurry...."

"Er... alright, eee, uh'll be quick, 'old 'im, 'old 'im." Miraculously, Abie ran off toward Mile End Road. "Don't let 'im go, 'old 'im," his voice echoed back along the street.

"'E's mad, 'e would 'ave killed 'im," said Zilla.

We stood up, and to prove I was not a belligerent I let go the man's arm. "Come on, sit down here."

As Zilla and I helped sit him on a low wall fronting the first of the houses, somebody opened the street door a crack.

"What's going on?" asked a woman's voice.

"Nothing, there was a mixup," I said. "Could we have a wet cloth please, this person's got blood on his face."

"Yes, some maniac started punching 'im...." added Zilly.

"Blood! Just a minute, I'll get a cloth...." and the woman disappeared.

"I don't wanna be bad, me Mum always said I'll end up a bad egg."

"It's alright, everything'll be alright," said Zilla.

"I don't wanna be bad, tell 'im I'm sorry, I don't wanna be a bad egg."

The door opened fully and the woman came down the front steps with a cloth. She looked at him. "You can't see to patch 'im up 'ere, bring 'im in the 'ouse."

Zilla and I helped him stand, and following the woman, walked him up the steps and through into the kitchen where I was able to get a proper look at this man who had done this incredible thing in front of my sister. He couldn't be much older than twenty five, about the same height as me, but thin and scraggly, with blondish hair, straight, falling forward. He wore a torn and threadbare grey jacket, double breasted like Abie's, and a white shirt open at the neck.

Suddenly from the very room in which we stood, a loud squawking tenor voice began to sing: *"Sur la pla - ce, Cha - cun pas se, Cha - cun vient, cha-cun va;"*

"What's that?" I asked in alarm; I'd seen no one else in the room, and the voice was too crisp to be from a wireless.

"Oh, that's nothing, that's just William."

"William?"

"William the Second. Me bird. 'E keeps me company. Named 'im after me dear old departed, I did."

"Drô - les de gens que ces gens là!"

"Shut up now, William."

There in the corner behind us, perched on a thick wooden rod strung from the ceiling by two pieces of wire, sat the largest parrot I'd ever seen, beautiful reds, blues and green, with a touch of yellow. His head bobbed up and down as he sang.

"Shut up now William, or they'll be no treat for supper. Do you 'ear me?" Then, more apologetically to us, "'E likes *Carmen*, you know, Bizet. It's 'is favorite opera. William the First — me dear departed, I calls 'im William the First — 'e liked Puccini, you know, *Madame Butterfly*, 'e loved *Madame Butterfly*, but old William the Second 'ere, 'e likes Bizet. There ain't no accounting for taste, you can't please 'em all, I always says. C'mon 'ere, luv, sit yourself down 'ere." She beckoned the man to sit. "What 'appened?" She started to bathe the blood from his face, affording me a chance to really see that face. In some perverse way it was guilt-provoking to steal a glance: hollow clean-shaven cheeks, almost emaciated, and small darting grey watery eyes under the dirtyish blonde sprigs of hair that hung forward over the forehead. No — I could heave a sigh of relief, it was not my face.

Zilla responded to the woman's question. "There's some maniac, he lives over there, that corner house" — she pointed through the curtains —"he started fighting with 'im, picking on 'im. We don't know 'im." She giggled uncomfortably. "Look, 'e tore 'is trousers...."

"I seen 'im, I seen that one before, I seen 'im chasing kids over the road. 'E's got a mouth on 'im...."

"Drô - les de gens que ces gens là!"

"Yes, 'e's always starting on people for nothing," said Zilla.

"Drô - les de gens!"

"Shut up now, William. What's your name, luv?" she asked the man.

"Bill. Bill Wiggins."

"Bill Wiggins." She savored the name. "You reminds me of me dear departed, 'e'd come 'ome all bashed up, blood all over 'im. Take me 'alf an hour to clean 'im up. What a man! 'E'd sit on this same stool, 'e would, and I'd clean 'im up, same as you. Same name, even — Bill." After a few moments she continued. "And what's 'is name, there, from the corner 'ouse what you said?"

"Abie. Abie Grossman," said Zilla.

"Well, 'e ought to be arrested then if you knows who 'e is...."

"The police..." *"Drô - les de gens!"* "...the police know about him already, they're planning to get him another time," I said.

"'Bout time, then! Shut up William. Ain't safe to walk the streets these days."

"...que ces gens là!"

As the parrot concluded this last refrain there came voices outside. "...And where is this suspect now, sir?" It was a policeman, with Abie.

"'Ere 'e was, they were, the three of 'em, 'ere, one minute uh left 'im 'ere, 'e was 'olding 'im, uh said don' let 'im go uh said...."

"There doesn't seem to be anybody 'ere now, sir."

From behind the curtains the four of us watched.

"That's 'im, right?" whispered the woman.

"Well, yes, 'e's the one who lives...." said Zilla.

"I'll go tell the copper, then. Maybe 'e don't know."

"Sur la pla - ce, Cha - cun pas se, Cha - cun vient, cha-cun va."

"No, no, it's alright," began Zilla, "the police are planning to get 'im another...."

"Shut up, William!" Perhaps the woman hadn't heard Zilla because of the parrot, but she rushed out of the kitchen, out the street door and down the steps.

"'Ey, 'scuse me copper, you oughta arrest that bloke, 'e's fighting with innocent people just walking along the street minding their own business! It ain't safe to go out your door 'ere these days!"

"What!? What!? Me? Fighting? Oo... wha'cha talking about?"

"You, you, you're the one, from that 'ouse there over on that corner." And she pointed in the direction Zilla had indicated.

"Wha'cha talking you bladdy idiot you're talking, she's...."

"Now now sir, let's watch our language, there's a lady present."

"Lady? She's telling me like uh don't know what 'appened? Piss orf inside yer 'ouse, you bladdy *broch,* she's telling me!"

"Now 'old it there sir, we won't 'ave that kind of language, we won't. Do you live in that 'ouse what this lady 'ere is pointing out?"

"'Ouse? What 'ouse? Where's a 'ouse?"

"*That* 'ouse, sir, where the lady pointed, that 'ouse right there on the corner."

"Uh... Uh can't see any 'ouse."

"Sir, then you'll kindly accompany me and we'll see for ourselves if you lives in that 'ouse. Madam, thank you for your assistance, you can count on us, we'll get to the bottom of this and see if 'e's our man."

As the policeman marched Abie away into the darkness toward the opposite corner of Tredegar Square the woman came back in, entering the kitchen and smacking her hands for a job well done. Through the window the remaining three of us had witnessed every detail.

"Well, ain't no use waiting. If they was going to get 'im, they might as well get 'im now before 'e does any more 'arm!"

"*Drô - les de gens que ces gens là!*"

"Welp! I betta be getting 'ome, me mother'll be wondering what 'appened," said Bill Wiggins.

"Shut up William, got far to go, dearie?" she asked.

"Nah, up Mile End Road a bit, nothing much."

"Alright, now you watch yerself, don't you go getting in no more fights."

"Nah, misses, I won't. Thanks a lot."

"We'd better be going also, I suppose," Zilla said. "Thank you, it was...."

"Always 'appy to 'elp out someone what's been caught unawares, like."

To the accompaniment of a parting French refrain, the three of us descended the steps to the pavement. The door behind us clicked closed.

"Thanks, sorry miss, didn't mean no offence."

"Oo-er, you kidding? Anyway, I wonder what the policeman's doing?"

"Mr. Wiggins, Bill, can I ask you something?" I asked.

"What?"

"I dunno, I feel a bit embarrassed.... Zilly, you wanna, er, I'll be back in a minute, just I want to talk to him, something...."

"You alright?" asked Zilla.

"Yes, sure, yes, absolutely, yes, I, I...."

"Alright, so I'll tell Mum you'll be home in a few minutes?"

"Alright, yes."

"You sure you're alright?"

"Yes, yes, absolutely, sure, oh yes, I'm alright, I just, yes, I'm alright."

Zilla walked off toward the house.

"Can I walk with you up to Mile End Road?"

"Well I suppose so, what is this, some kind of a trick...?"

"No, oh no! No! No, no, I just...."

We began walking, and I timidly broached a question: "I hope you don't mind me asking, but I wondered, I mean, I wondered, like...."

"What?"

"Well, I wondered, like...."

"Well then, spit it out, guv!"

"Well, I mean, I hope you don't mind, but I wondered why you, you, sort of, well, you know, kind of did... that, you know, I dunno, I, I just wondered that's all."

"Did what?"

"What? You know, what you, well, like what you... sort of... did."

"Wha'd'ya mean?"

"Well, like... tsk!, oh, I dunno...."

We had almost reached Mile End Road, and he turned to me: "Well, so long, guv."

"So long, good night, thank you very much."

"Yers, it's alright, guv."

He doffed an imaginary hat, and was gone.

Zilla would wonder why I'd taken so long; actually, I hadn't taken long, it was only about two minutes. I ran back along the side of the park. The street door to our house was open, with Lily talking in the doorway, and on the pavement the policeman held Abie's arm in his tight grasp. Lily saw me approaching. "Here he is, *oy a broch!*, he'll prove he lives here!"

"What 'appened, you bladdy fool you, you let 'im get away...."

"Now 'old it there sir, we said none of that there language!"

"Uh live 'ere, tell 'im uh live 'ere already!"

"He wants to wake Maudy up just to tell him he lives here, he's fast asleep," said Mum.

"Where's Katya, mu daughter, she'll prove it also, you'll see...."

"Benny came 'round for her, she's not home yet," said Lily.

I spoke up. "He lives here, he does, officer."

Zilla backed me up, "I already told him 'e lives 'ere."

"None of your cheek now, miss, I told you as 'ow we needs one additional confirmation, like, if said witness is available."

"Maudy just started his job," said Mum, "he's exhausted from working, he's sleeping, he needs the rest, how can you wake him up in the middle of the night, all this rigmarole?"

"Sleeping! 'E needs the rest! Uh'm also working, two places uh'll be running there at the same time, so what about me, what about what *I* need?"

"Just a moment there, sir, let's proceed with this identification." Then, to me: "Young fellow, do you know this man officially?"

"Yes sir, he does live here, he's my father."

"Then I'm placing you under arrest as a public nuisance," said the policeman, looking straight down at Abie from under his tall helmet. "Number one fighting with innocent passersby, and number two lewd behavior, exposing your private parts — excuse me madam and you, miss — exposing your private parts to ladies in the course of their using a public thoroughfare."

"What!? Me, you, you, no, tell 'im, Zilly, tell 'im what 'appened...."

"And I'd appreciate it you'd accompany me down to the station without any further trouble."

"It's not him...." began Lily.

"Tell 'im, Zech, Zachary, tell 'im what 'appened...."

"No, it's not him," repeated Lily.

"Madam, we've 'ad reports of someone — if you'll pardon the expression — someone what exposes 'imself to ladies, and now we've 'ad a positive identification by a lady what lives across the park, right by the spot where these indecent acts was perpetrated. 'E was even trying to blame it on someone else to divert attention from the perpetrator, namely, 'imself."

"No, 'e, 'e, you got, she got mixed up, uh, we *caught* the barsted oo was doing it, eee, uh would 'ave killed 'im, my boy, you *fu–ucking idiot,* you *coward* you, you let 'im go, uh said 'old 'im...."

"Enough of that there language sir, you're coming right down to the station with me, right now." And to Lily, "It's alright madam, I think I can safely say we 'ave our man."

"No it's not him, he's my husband...."

"It's alright madam, people usually don't know what a suspect's capable of, even if 'e lives right in the same 'ouse and acts all normal-like. Now come along, sir, no trouble now."

"Alright, uh'll go, Lily come with, officer, mu wife, mu wife she wants to come with, she'll explain everything, Lily quick, your coat, you'll be cold, you don't wanna get cold, eee officer, uh don't want 'er to catch cold, for nothing...."

While Lily was getting her wrap, the policeman noticed the black van standing without lights a short distance along Tredegar Terrace. "Sir, that vehicle, do you know who that vehicle belongs to?"

"The van, it's my van. Uh bought it, uh'll show you the receipt, it's...."

"Where are the parking lights, it's supposed to 'ave parking lights switched on at night."

"They're on, they're switched on, come uh'll show you, come, uh'll open it up and show you, by my life the switch is on."

"But the lights is s'posed to be on...."

"No, it's alright, the lights uh switched 'em on, it's broke, tomorrow the man 'e'll fix everything...."

"Sir, you're not allowed to park a vehicle on the street overnight without lights."

"Uh swear, tomorrow uh'll put it in the garage, you'll come 'ere tomorrow you'll see, tomorrow it'll be gone, uh'll 'ave it in a garage, the man, 'e'll fix it in the garage, everything 'e'll fix, uh'll tell 'im."

Lily came down the steps, a scarf flapping. "Zilly look after everything, there's potatoes on the stove, turn the light down, don't let it burn, you'll make tea?"

"Alright, Mum, don't worry."

Lily hurried along the street to catch up with the departing pair.

"Alright officer, uh'm going." Then, more quietly, "Lily you'll explain there, like the officer, 'e made a mistake, it's natural, anyone can make a mistake, like a mix-up with everything, heh, heh, you'll tell 'em...."

Lily's response was by now too faint to decipher as the distance increased. The policeman said something, then came Abie's stammer. Zilla and I stood on the pavement by the open street door as the trio's diminishing colloquium coalesced with the night.

—o—O—o—

27

Four hours of holding pieces of wood while Abie sawed and nailed them up was all I could take in one day. I was helping him build the new counter and the partition wall which would section off the snack bar from his tailoring shop. Maybe things wouldn't be too bad when it was completed and we opened up; at least he'd be tailoring on the other side of the wall while I handled the snack bar customers. I rode home by myself, leaving him working at the sewing machine on somebody's costume.

Mum gave me a bowl of delicious matzoh ball soup. "Thanks, Mum, that was nice." Still, I needed further respite from the family; maybe Jack would come with me to Johnny Isaacs. "Mum, I'm going over to Jack's for a while."

"Go, go."

As I jumped down the outside steps, Marius was approaching. "Hello, Maudy." He looked angry at someone or something, but apparently it wasn't me; I held the door for him as he climbed the steps, and then I was on my way.

Marius closed the street door behind him and ducked his head under the frame as he entered the living room. "I'm gonna kill that sodding barstard!" He took off his coat and hung it on the crowded hook behind the door.

"*Oy,* don't talk like that," said Lily. "What is it, Eric Lynch again?"

"Yeah, 'e thinks 'e's so tough! Trouble with 'im 'e's retarded or something."

"Ignorant *yockisher poyer,* he should take a *broch* in his *kishkas.* I'll get your dinner. How was work?" Lily peered at him. "Is it alright, they didn't give you the sack?"

"Alright, it's alright. Yeah, they been showing me 'ow to roll out the spring material on the cutting tables, it's 'ard work, makes me out of breath."

"Don't lift the rolls yourself, you've got to be careful, you'll get ill, you won't be able to work. You tell Fischbraun someone has to help you lift it."

"It's alright, Mum. Wha'cha got for supper? I'm 'ungry."

"I got matzoh balls with soup. Sit down, rest."

Marius sat down heavily on the old wooden chair. Hunched, he looked idly at the *News of the World* lying on the table.

Lily placed a big bowl of soup in front of him and handed him a spoon. "Eat, eat, you can rest, you don't have to do anything." He tasted the soup. "How is it? Is it good?" She spread the dishtowel she was holding across his lap. "Here, don't get your trousers messed up."

"Yeah, it's good." He looked more intently at the newspaper. "What's this?"

"What, don't let the soup get cold, what is it?"

Marius read haltingly: "Youth arrested for attempted burglary."

"So? There are always things happening…."

"Did you see the name! Crikey!"

"What? What is it, who is it, Eric Lynch? Burglary?"

"No, crikey, listen: *Reuben Berger of 18 Morgan Street, Mile End, was arrested in Aldgate on Friday night on suspicion of attempted burglary!*" Marius's soup spoon clattered down into his plate. "That's Reuben! Reuben from across the road!"

"Reuben?" Lily grabbed the newspaper. *"Oy a broch!* Reuben Berger! You think I'm surprised?"

"Crikey, Reuben!"

"Mrs. Berger, she'll be so ashamed she won't be able to show her face in the street!"

"Serve 'em both right!"

"A Jewish boy, a disgrace, I always knew he was no good."

"Ol' Reuben!"

"Stay away from there, don't go over the road."

"I don't even talk to 'im. I seen 'im in the morning sometimes running along Morgan Street to the Grove Road bus. Crikey!"

"Go on, your soup'll be cold already, eat, I'll get the rest of your supper." Lily retired to the kitchen and returned bearing a dinner plate with a small piece of boiled chicken and a mound of little round boiled new potatoes.

"Did the old barstard come 'ome yet? 'Is rusty old iron's still parked outside."

"Ssh, don't talk about your father like that, no, he's getting someone to fix it. He said he'll put it in a garage, I don't know, who needed more aggravation, with a van now."

"So did Zech go with 'im to 'is ol' dump today? Can't believe 'e's trying out with 'im there in Burnt Oak! 'Ow can 'e stand it?"

"They're fixing it up together there, maybe he doesn't have to talk to him so much, I don't know. Another one, he doesn't bring home any money now since they gave him the sack there in the parcel place. Your father said if he works there for him in the snack bar, when it makes enough money he'll pay him."

"Crikey, Zech believes that? If I worked for 'im and 'e didn't pay me I'd shoot 'is bollocks orf, I would."

"Ssh, Zech'll try it there with him in case they can't find him a job at the Unemployment, we'll see. Maybe both of them will make a lot of money, you never know."

"Fat chance!"

"Alright, eat your supper."

"Where's Katya?"

"Where? The usual I suppose, Benny met her at the shop, they'll eat somewhere then she'll go straight to her *shiksa* friend Hazel, she only comes home to change." There was a noise outside, and Lily looked quickly toward the door. "Is that him? I thought I heard something…."

"Nah, it's nothing."

"I hope he got the money, that woman there she should *gai in dreard,* everything's wrong, whatever he does she's not satisfied. She's supposed to pay him today, for the rent, we won't have the rent when he comes round."

"Every week I gotta listen to the same thing, 'We won't 'ave the rent, we won't 'ave the rent,' I'm fed up 'earing it already."

"Fed up hearing it! That's what it is when you're poor, it's terrible! Whatever you think about the old bastard, at least he tries to pay the rent every week. I hate his *kishkas* but it's a shame for him, what can he do?"

"Shame? So what did 'e buy a shitty old van for? It won't even go."

"Who knows with him, he said he needs it to get proper apple strudel in The Lane for the customers when he opens the snack bar."

"Pah! Like 'e got a fancy name for it, *Mr. G's Snack Bar!*"

"Maybe he'll make a lot of money there. If he wasn't so slow with the alterations, he takes an hour just to baste in a collar."

"The old *potz*, 'e'll never make a penny, don't even waste your time thinking about it. If 'e did, you think you'd see it? 'E'd go and buy another piece of rusty old iron or something. Once a *schmuck* always a *schmuck*, I say."

"Ssh, enough already, don't talk about him like that."

"The dinner's nice, Mum. Any post today?"

"From Rivka, there, it's on the table. She moved out of Joe's flat a week already she wrote there, she's going with a Polish one, from the camps." She looked at Marius. "What do you think, it's alright? Who knows what diseases they picked up there."

Marius read the letter. "Huh! She's like a real Yank, making loads of money. Crikey, she'll be alright."

"In a few weeks she'll send a ticket for Zilly, they'll both be gone!"

A knuckled *tah-t-t-tah-tah* sounded on the street door and a key slid into the lock. They both stiffened.

"Is he early tonight? He doesn't usually knock." Then Lily added confidentially: "He's in a good mood, that means she paid him."

The door opened and Katherine's voice came from the passageway. "Hello, everybody, I'm home, what's cooking, it smells good."

"Oh, it's Katya," said Lily. Katherine came in and started taking off her coat. "So what happened, Benny didn't come to the shop?"

"Oh hello, Maudy, how's the job?"

"'Ello, Katya matya, it's alright, I'm almost a cutter already. Where's Benny big dick?"

"I'll get you some soup. Here, sit down. Where's Benny?"

"I'm by myself, Benny's working late tonight. We had supper at his house last night, Bessie made it, the old warhorse. Nag! *Oy*, can she nag!" Katherine took a seat opposite Marius. "Thanks Mum," and she started on the bowl of soup. "I think she's grooming me to nurse her son. I tried to help put the dishes on the table, everything I do is wrong, it's not good enough. Her darling son just watches, he doesn't even say anything to her! I felt like punching her right in her big pimply Jew's nose, the old battle-axe. I had to leave both of them there in the end, I went to Hazel's to recover."

Lily was agitated. "You tell Benny to make her leave you alone!"

"Say something to Benny against his dear mummy? It'd take him a week to recover from the shock."

"So what you going with 'im for then if you can't stand 'im and 'is mother?" said Marius.

"I don't know exactly, both of you'll be in America soon, what am I going to do? I suppose there'd be some security with him."

"Us going to America?" asked Marius, surprised.

"After Zilly goes, you'll see, a few months and you'll be there also."

"We will? I didn't know we was really going also."

"Yes, you and Mum. Who knows what'll happen after that, I don't know if I'd ever get a ticket," she continued. "It'd take me years to save up the fare. I don't want to take a chance on being left here in the house with Abie."

"What about Zech, he'll be home," said Lily. "So you'll be here with Zech. Rivka said she'll send tickets."

"So how long will that be? Zech'll find a girl and he'll move out. Who knows, I wish he'd marry Hazel, that'd be perfect for me also, I could move in with them. Anyway I don't want to be stuck here by myself looking after the old barstard."

"Marry Hazel? Why should he marry a *shiksa?*"

"Why? Because Hazel's very, very nice, that's why."

"He doesn't have to marry a *shiksa.*"

"Oh come on! Anyway, it's a relief to talk about something other than Benny and his sweaty shitbag of a mother. And that's after I have to put up with that fucking Anya at work all day long, with the hordes of smelly bunions. I thought about committing double yentricide."

"What's that?" asked Marius.

"What do you think? Murdering two yentas, Bessie and Anya."

Marius was not inclined to sit through too much of the same dreary conversation. "I'm going out for a walk."

"Finish your dinner! Where're you going?"

"I dunno, I'll be back later. Maybe I'll see Reggie, 'stead of listening to this stuff."

"What do you want with Reggie, that's the only one?"

"Mum leave him alone, it's his friend, what's wrong?"

"A *gunif* he is, your father said he's a little thief."

"Crikey, Zech's got 'is friends, why can't I 'ave mine? Who cares what the old barstard says."

"Jack, he's a decent boy, at least he washes himself. That one there, a *yockisher* thief, he'll end up in prison he will."

"Oh, come on Lily, leave him alone! Have a nice time, Maudy."

"S'long, Katya. Talk of ending up in prison, look in the papers, Reuben got arrested!" Marius took his coat from the mound on the back of the door.

"Arrested?" Katherine asked. "Reuben, over the road? What do you mean?"

"Read it, you'll see."

"Don't go over the road, don't go near Mrs. Berger's house!"

"So long, Maudy, maybe I'll see you later. Mum, I was talking to Benny about Rivka and Zilly going to America, he said he might go also. Bessie hates me already, all she needs to hear is I'm talking her darling into going away to America...."

"Really? You both of you might go? Then... Zech would be the only one here."

"She probably wouldn't let him go, anyway. Believe me Mum I don't know what on earth I'm seeing him for."

"I've had more experience than you, don't let her interfere. You should only know the aggravation I had with *Bobbeh* interfering with everything, did I waste money here, why didn't I go to Isaacson instead, it's cheaper, did I cook enough chicken for her *buboula,* was it enough salt, right up 'til the day she died."

"They can be a prrrroblem, can't they, now."

"Every day I wished she'd drop dead, it took fifteen years. She hated the children, every one of you, in all the years she never said one good word."

"Anyway, you glad you'll be going? Leave the old barstard here?"

"Ssh, if he should come in, I don't want him to hear, I don't know what he'll do when he finds out. Anyway who said I'll go?"

"You'll go, and what can he do? It'll be the best chance you'll ever have of getting away from him."

"Let Zilly go, they're young both of them, they can make a life for themselves. What's an old *bobbeh* like me going to do there?"

"Rivka said she'll send tickets for you and Maudy. You know she always means it when she says something."

"So what'll I do when I get there anyway, live off the big girls? Ugh! It makes you shrivel up inside thinking about it. Maudy would have to get a job, I'd have to work there, they don't want to hire a middle-aged woman, what can I work at, they've got lots of young pretty girls there."

"Don't worry Lily, it'll work out."

And so the conversation between mother and daughter continued for another hour.

Outside the street door a footstep scraped and the knocker rapped out Marius's pattern. Katherine stood to open the door. "I'm going to go over to Hazel's for half an hour, they must have finished supper."

Marius entered the living room. "Still jawing, you two?"

"So did you do anything nice?"

"Nah, Reggie went to the pictures with 'is dad, I walked with Fred to Johnny Isaacs and back. I'm tired, I'm going up to bed."

"You're hungry? There's more soup," Lily called after him. "There's a clean sleeping suit on the mattress, it's the blue one. I'll wake you up in the morning in plenty of time."

"Okay Mum, goodnight. I got the matches."

As Marius started up the stairs, a key turned in the lock and Abie was home. He lumbered wearily into the living room, then brightened on seeing Katherine. "Eee Katya, Katya, you're 'ere, eee, you're never 'ome!"

"She's busy with her boyfriend, what's so terrible about that?"

"Hello, Dad."

"Terrible, oo said it's terrible? Where's Zech, did 'e come 'ome? 'E runs out the minute uh finish there, uh dunno like uh, uh, got... a disease or something."

"No, he went over to his friend Jack's. He'll be home later, I suppose."

Abie was removing his coat.

"Well, I'm going to go to Hazel's for a little while." Katherine stood up.

"You're always running, running, stay, stay already, it's late, it's time for bed already," said Abie.

Katherine put on her coat. "I'll be back in half an hour."

Lily returned from the kitchen with a big bowl of soup and placed it on the table as Abie sat down. "So did she pay you?"

"*Oy*, the aggravation with that woman you wouldn't believe, she should *gai in drerd*, she's giving me such aggravation like uh don't know. All day uh bin working on the collar and still it's not right for 'er, it doesn't lay right. Four times, she came *four times* to the shop she came, and still it's not good enough for — 'er... 'er... lady*shit*...already, it's not good enough for 'er."

"So she didn't pay you." Lily sucked air through pursed lips, then loudly exhaled. "And what about your stinking van out there, they'll take it away, all that money down the drain. A *broch* I married, I should have listened to Cissie and Rae! So what'll I do about the landlord now, what do you expect me to say to the old *fucker* when he comes for his rent tomorrow? He doesn't want to hear stories. He'll see the van there."

"What can uh do, the van I'll get someone, they'll fix it. When 'e comes you don't know 'oo's van it is, what's it got to do with the landlord? Someone left the van there, what's so terrible they leave a van there for a day, two days, it's not so terrible."

"So you want me to tell him when he comes we don't have the rent? Again we don't have the rent."

"She promised she'd 'ave the money tonight, the *fu–ucking* woman there she's *ricing* mu *kishkas* out with the *becuckter* jacket already, uh don't know what to do."

"Ugh! What a life, what a rotten stinking life. So *you* stay home and tell the landlord, I don't want to tell him."

"Tell 'im, tell 'im! Tell 'im you'll... you'll, 'ave the rent next week, tell 'im. What can uh do? Uh'm sick of it, working, morning 'til night working, all uh get is aggravation there from the customers, it's 'arder than uh realized, you don't know. Zech, 'e's s'posed to be 'elping there, a *schmuck* uh tell you, 'e's like a... a... an idiot. Sick, that's what uh am, sick of it all."

Lily returned from the kitchen with Abie's supper plate. "Katya said Benny told her he'll go to America, maybe."

"Benny? Believe me, Lily, uh wouldn't mind going, like a... a new start."

"You?"

"Maybe it'd be good. It couldn't be worse than all the aggravation 'ere, with the bills, more bills all the time, bills."

"You? You old *shmecktubbick,* you go to America? What would you do there, who'd pay for everything?"

"Uh'd work, what would uh do!"

"Work! You're so slow, someone can die before you finish their costume. People don't want to wait, there. How could you work?"

"Everybody else works, uh'd work. Uh'd try to go quick."

"And Maudy, what about Marius, do you ever think about him instead of shouting at him?"

"Shouting? Oo's shouting? Why should uh shout at Maudy?"

Marius called down from upstairs. "Will you shut up shouting down there, for christ's sake I gotta get up for work in the morning."

"Shouting? Oo's shouting? Wha'd'ya mean shouting?"

"You are, you're shouting."

"Shouting? You, you, you twisted-face *ponce* you, oo's asking your opinion?" Abie shouted.

"Oy a broch, he's off already," said Lily.

"Off? Off?" Abie jumped up from the table. "Wha'd'ya mean, off? From the minute uh get 'ome, nag, nag," and he grabbed the rim of his soup plate and flung it spinning across the table top. With the contents spiraling outward it skimmed above the table's surface, and on the far side smashed to the floor.

Lily grabbed the dishtowel and on her knees started mopping the soup and pushing pieces of broken china into a pile. "A misery my life is from one day to the other, every day a misery." And, shaking the flopping dishtowel at him from the floor, "You pimp you, you think I don't know why you're late, why you don't have any money? Mrs. what's-'er-name with her collar, very likely! Wha'd'ya take me for, a fool? I know why you don't have any money, you lousy pimp, you!"

"What? What's this? Uh work mu *kishkas* out from morning 'til night, for 'er uh work, and this?"

"You think I don't know why you got yourself a van? So you can take 'em for rides, show off like a *gunsa knucker,* a big man, my successful businessman, he can't even pay the rent, you pimp you!"

"This is what uh got to come 'ome to? Now she's calling me a... a pimp? You... you... you... turd, you, you stinking... turd, that's what you are! You don't deserve any... any...." And he ran out of the living room, smashing the door closed behind him with a force that shook the house.

Marius, hearing the commotion downstairs, leaped up from his mattress. He quickly slammed the bedroom door closed and leaned hard into it.

Abie, grabbing the bannister rail hand over hand, crashed up the stairs two at a time and began smashing, punching the door. "Open the *fu–ucking* door, you... you... twisted 'umpback barsted, uh'll... uh'll...." Pressing his back into the window frame for support, with the flat of his shoe he burst the door ajar, breaking the latch.

"Stop it, stop it Dad, stop it!" Marius, gasping, leaned ever harder into the buckling door to try to hold it closed as Abie heaved from the other side.

"Like your *fu–ucking* mother you are, with your... with your... your coughing and choking there, like a cripple, two barsteds, both of 'em." Hardly able to catch his own breath, Abie tried another, weaker, push on the broken wood.

Marius was trying to calm himself, leaning as heavily into the door as he was able while still trying to drop his shoulders and take slower longer breaths, as he'd been taught. "Don't Dad, please don't!"

Abie ceased forcing the door, and for quite several moments each stood still, gasping quietly. Between deep breaths Marius listened anxiously, and through the door he heard a muttered whisper: "Dead uh wish they were, every one of 'em dead. Uh'm desperate, desperate."

Several more minutes elapsed as they each stood on their respective sides of the broken bedroom door, in the darkness, the silence punctuated only by a duet of exhausted breathing. Finally, Marius dared to speak, quietly, shakily: "Now look wha'cha done. You broke the latch, you broke the door."

—o—O—o—

28

"What should I do? I really love your sister, if she goes to America I'll die."

I didn't know how to respond to Lew. Anyway he was probably exaggerating; I didn't believe he'd actually die. It was amazing that someone could like Zilla so much he would cry in front of you. She'd told me he cried sometimes, because he was a musician she'd said, and musicians are sensitive.

"Maybe if you're especially nice to her she'll stay here," I suggested.

"I don't know what more I can do, I've made it so plain I want her to stay."

"Do you think if you got married she'd stay?"

"Married? Zilla? Me, if I married your sister?"

"I mean... if she were your wife, well, then if she said she was going to America you could remind her...."

"Marry her!"

"Yes, well, I dunno...."

"I never thought of marrying her...."

A knock on the street door, and outside stood the three men who had delivered Zilla's piano almost two years earlier, their same two-wheeled barrow parked by the curb.

"We're 'ere for the old Joanna, lad."

"Who is it, what is it?" Lew called from the living room.

"It's the men for the piano."

"For the piano?"

"Yes, Zilly asked me to be here for them."

"Be here? What do you mean?" Lew ran to the passageway. "The piano, what do they want with the piano?"

"Well I'm home because...."

"Yes?"

"Zilly asked me, I've been helping my father partition off his tailor's place for something, I told him I couldn't work today, I had to stay home for the piano."

"What do you mean stay home for the piano?"

"Well, Zilly said she's...." I gestured at the men, then feebly at the piano. "They're s'posed to... the...."

"You can't let them take the piano!"

"I... I... Zilly asked me specially to be here, I was supposed to go to Burnt Oak."

"This is terrible, I'll die, if they take her piano I'll die."

"Didn't Zilly tell you? She sold it."

"She sold it, oh god!"

"I mean, Lew, would you actually die?" His round face was even redder than usual. "What would they write, you know, the doctor, write on that thing, the certificate thing they write?" His almost bald head and faint ginger-colored eyebrows were already beaded with sweat. "I mean, why would you die exactly, what would be the medical reason?"

The leader of the trio, still outside on the step, interrupted us: "Well, lad, we can't stand 'ere all day while you're arguing 'bout this 'n' that. We takes the piano or we don't?"

"My sister said you have to take it, she sold it."

He whispered to me, "Oo is this bloke?" and nodded surreptitiously in Lew's direction.

Since Lew was right behind me I could hardly whisper back, so I just lowered my voice a little: "It's her boyfriend, he's a musician."

"Well, we can't 'ave people butting in now, that piano weighs fifty stone if it weighs an ounce...."

Lew tried to interpose himself. "Don't take it, please don't take it, it'll be the end if you take it, my life will be ended."

"Welp," said the foreman, avoiding Lew's face by looking directly at me, "if your sister's already gone and sold it, someone paid for it and someone's gonna be waiting 'ome for it right now, so we better not disappoint 'em."

He really was right. "Yes...."

"So come on lads, let's load 'er up!" He grasped around the frame of the street door, pulled himself up and peered into the living room. "'Ere she is!" Brushing Lew and me aside, his two mates followed him in.

"I can't bear it, I can't even bear to watch!"

"Maybe we should go out in the garden while they load it up, then." I took the silver piano key from my pocket and handed it to the foreman: "Here, my sister said you have to take this also."

"Aren't you even on my side?" wailed Lew.

"No, no, I mean yes... I don't know, Zilly said...."

Lew and I sat on the stone steps outside the back door. I hardly ever came out to the garden anymore except to the lavatory, and it was strange to sit there and see what had changed. Where they'd removed the Anderson shelter after the war the ground was flat again, overgrown with uncut grass as though nothing had ever been there. The tall holly-hocks still made their way along the wall where Manny and I used to spray water on passersby, that time on Reuben, who'd threatened to get me in school but never did; I'd forgotten all about it until now. Reuben! Perhaps Reuben was in prison now, if he really did try to burglarize someone's place!

Lew, sitting next to me, was sobbing. His eyes reminded me of red cherries.

"I'm sorry Lew, I don't know what to say."

"What can anyone say? If she's determined to go, how can I stop her?"

"I don't know."

"That was a rhetorical question."

"A what?"

"Oh, nothing." We sat silently. "It's a terrible life to be a musician."

"Is it really? I would love to be a singer, like Frank Sinatra."

"Frank Sinatra? He's a good musician, a natural musician. Did you know, he phrases like an oboe."

"Does he? I love the way he sings."

"In this world, real natural musicians have so much pain."

"When you play the guitar it doesn't sound as if you're having pain."

"It doesn't sound like I'm in pain because real musicians have to cover up their pain."

"They do?"

"For a real musician — not *Sid Millward And His Nitwits* but when I play something serious, like, say an étude by Segovia — for a real musician, that's pain, every day is pain."

I looked at the red eyes, the huge, spotless white and dripping handkerchief he held. He usually did look in pain, even when he said he was happy.

"I have to stay here 'til she comes home, I can't go back to my flat, I'm too enervated. Can I stay here now?"

"Well yes, I mean if it's alright with Mum when she comes back from shopping, she went to the Roman Road."

"I must stay 'til your sister comes home from work, I have to see her, I have to plead with her."

"Alright."

●   ●   ●

"Uh'll wait outside in the van in case of the police, the barsteds, they're trying to drive me mad... 'e'll come round seven o'clock sharp 'e said, 'e'll be 'ere...." Abie had gotten home early, immediately after Zilla, and now even before he finished his sentence someone pounded on the street door. It was the mechanic.

"Abie Grossman?" the visitor demanded.

"Yeh, it's me, the van."

"Alright." The two of them walked toward the van which had remained standing on Tredegar Terrace for the last four days. "Switch on the ignition, I'll shove in the old crank 'andle and we'll give it a twist...."

"...The ignition?"

"The ignition, the ignition!" He came around and pointed. "That's right mate, that black knob there...." He rolled his eyes, "Jesus!"

Lew closed the street door behind them and turned again to Zilla. "How can you go, how can you just leave me?"

"Oh, fuck it already, you can buy yourself a ticket and go also, I'm not stopping you." Zilla lay her dinner spoon in the empty plate and swallowed the remaining tea from her cup.

Lily collected the plate to take it to the kitchen. "Ssh, it's not nice, such language, if he hears you...."

"If *he* hears me, you mean the old bastard?"

"Ssh, it's not nice."

"He's outside anyway, he's busy with his rusty old iron out there. Men, either they're punching you or telling you what to do."

"*Punch* you, when would I ever do that to someone I love?"

"Oh, not you, Lew. I dunno, I'm sorry I don't wanna make you feel rotten, you're very nice, but I *am* going, I *am* going, I *am going to America,* that's the beginning and the end of it. Sell your guitar and buy a boat ticket if you're that desperate."

"*Sell* my guitar! It's my life, could I ask you to stop breathing? Sometimes you're so cruel."

"Oh fuck, I'm going upstairs, I can't take any more." And Zilla left the room.

The street door opened again. "Eee, uh knew it would be alright, it's running, the engine, 'e made it run, quick, someone come to the garage with me, uh, uh...." Abie looked around, first at me, then past Lily, then toward Lew — who turned away further and lowered his head; apparently he didn't want to go either. Abie addressed Lew's back: "L, L, Lew, you'll come with me to park the van, yeh? It'll be... nice, like, you'll 'ave some company, we'll talk about the... music there... yeh, you'll tell me about your, er, g, g, g, guitar you got wha'cha play there, uh'm really interested, like *The Warsaw Concerto,* eee, lovely."

Lew's head dropped even lower, lost in anguish. But then he pulled himself up, and his face brightened as he swung around decisively to face Abie: "Mr. Grossman, I'll come, I'll come with you, I know how it feels when you're all alone, I'll be happy to help you out if you need someone...."

"Eee, good, good, uh'll be outside in the van, uh'll wait, don't be long, the engine it's like... 'urry, 'urry...."

"Alright, Mr. Grossman, one minute and I'll be right there to help."

Abie went outside, leaving the street door open. Among the multiplicity of backfirings, creakings and rattlings, the driver's door squealed open, and Abie climbed into the seat.

Along the passageway Lew called up from the bottom of the stairs: "Zilly, I'll be busy with your dad for a little while, I'm going to help your father at the garage, he needs someone, I'll be back soon, don't go out, I'll be back, I'll bring something nice with me, a surprise, something you'll really like."

No response consecrated his sensitive ear. He stepped out into the street, climbed into the van's passenger seat and slammed the door.

"Wha'cha, wha'cha doing there with the door, you'll smash, you'll break the... heh, heh!"

The vehicle lunged off into the evening, each occupant consumed in his own private imperative. They remained silent as the van juddered past Tredegar Square and on toward Mile End Road. There, Abie twisted the turn signal indicator to the right, then steered left into Mile End Road. As they rode along the main thoroughfare, Lew noticed Abie rocking rhythmically back and forth in his seat as he drove, on each forward motion giving the steering wheel a little push ahead.

"Why are you doing that, Mr. Grossman?"

"Doing? Doing what?"

"Rocking, pushing the steering wheel like that."

"Wha'd'ya mean, to make it ride along."

"Oh...."

"Uh'm driving it, uh'm 'elping it to go." The van continued along the crest of the wide roadway.

"I'm very happy to come with you, Mr. Grossman. Where is the garage?"

"Uh wanna go there, it's on that side where is it." Abie pointed vaguely across the street to the right side of the road. Suddenly, "There it is!" He squelched the brake pedal and pulled hard on the wheel. In front of the oncoming traffic the van crossed over the roadway and rolled into the dark confines of the garage. Abie switched on the headlights; ahead where the brownish-yellow dazzle illuminated the enclosed driveway, Lew could discern a fork. To the right the sign indicated ground-level parking where the lower drive curved around to run behind a line of parked cars. The left fork met a steep ramp climbing to the upper level. "We 'ave to drive up there on the roof, the last place uh got, they're full 'ere 'e said, they gave me the last place, uh didn't know they 'ad so many cars."

"Yes," said Lew, trying to ignore the hint of foreboding scratching at his stomach.

"Yeh, up there 'e said just drive up, it's straight ahead, you can't miss it."

Abie began backing the van out into Mile End Road to allow sufficient distance for a run up the ramp. He backed out in a series of alternating semi-circles, coming to rest in the middle of Mile End Road directly in front of an approaching police car, which sounded its warning gong and stopped. When the policeman climbed out and asked for his license, Abie said he'd forgotten it, it was at home. His heart was in his mouth, but luckily this policeman was not the same one who had walked him and Lily to the police station the previous week. From the tenor of *that* interrogation, Abie had realized he had to be very careful — the police were out to get him one way or another.

Lew sat in the passenger seat massaging his fingers, flinching as the traffic on both sides edged around the two stopped vehicles. He was unaware that Abie had to be careful not to concede explicitly to the policeman that he didn't *have* a license, that two weeks earlier when he'd taken the driver's test for the third time and been told again he'd failed, he'd leaned across to the passenger seat and threatened to wring the test-giver's neck. As Lew sat quietly flexing his hands, Abie was issued a triple summons: first, dangerous driving; second, driving a motor car while not carrying his license on his person, and third evasive, ambiguous and provocative responses to a police officer's legitimate questions at the scene of a suspected perpetration. The officer wrote on, handed him the three slips and added that the not-carrying-his-license-on-his-person charge would be dismissed if he produced the document at Bow police station within two weeks. Abie privately resolved to go again for the drivers' test, quick, before the two weeks; this time he'd have to be extra nice there and hope the man didn't recognize him.

The police car drove off. Lew took a deep breath as Abie started the van moving forward toward the ramp. The vehicle got only halfway up the slope before the engine stalled and began rolling down again. Under the best of circumstances Abie did not enjoy driving backwards; preoccupied now with searching for the brake pedal while seated at an angle of thirty degrees on the incline, he turned the steering wheel the wrong way, and about a foot from the bottom of the ramp the right rear wheel bumped down off the edge of the concrete, the van half rolling, half falling into the rear of a parked Vauxhall, one of the line of ground-level parked cars. Luckily there were no other observers of the incident; the attendant was gone for the day and the garage was deserted. It took Abie and Lew forty-five minutes to disengage the entangled bumpers, rock the rear of the van back up onto the ramp, apply the hand-brake, then push the broken glass over the edge and under another car. When they had cleared away the mess, from inside the back of the van Abie retrieved a brown paper bag of five-day-old apple strudel he'd bought in Petticoat Lane to sell in slices at Mr. G's and in a conciliatory gesture he left the package on the bonnet of the damaged Vauxhall.

Again the pair seated themselves. In a sequence of wavering oscillations they rolled backward out of the garage entrance, beyond the crest of the road and over to the far curb, coming to rest at right-angles to the direction of traffic; Abie hoped another police car wouldn't come by, but what could he do? He had to go back far enough to get up sufficient speed for the ramp. Lew, though terrified, was loathe to anger his prospective father-in-law by suggesting he get out and wait on the pavement; anyway with Mr. Grossman behind the wheel it was possibly safer inside the van than out.

The Mile End Road traffic paused briefly. Abie raced the motor in first gear, then with a bang released the clutch. The van leaped up and over the roadway crest toward the garage.

At high speed the pair rode up the ramp. This time the van did make it all the way to the upper level, but once there Abie kept going, aiming the speeding vehicle into the unoccupied slot approximately straight ahead. He sideswiped the car parked to the right, and their speed caused the van's front wheels to override the metal retaining lip mounted just before the edge of the rooftop.

Lew later told Zilla he thought Abie was going to drive right over the edge, and that was the reason he, Lew, vomited over his trousers and the car seat. As it turned out, his earlier restraint had been for nought: Abie still became furious because now that the driver's door was jammed shut against the sideswiped car, Abie had to slide over Lew's vomit-covered seat to get out.

The intrepid pair didn't get home until two A.M. On the walk back, Abie considered the best way to contain the incidents — the police traffic summonses, the damage to the two other parked cars. "L, L, Lew… don't say nothing if they ask what 'appened, you didn't come with, you don't know nothing."

"Mr. Grossman, I'm in love with your daughter."

"They don't 'ave to know; uh'll say oo knows, maybe someone stole mu van, 'ow do uh know what 'appens in the garage when uh'm working in Burnt Oak there?"

"I can't marry her right away, but as soon as I make some money I want to marry her."

"Like in the middle of the night uh should know oo's 'anging round in their garage!"

"She keeps saying she's going to America, she's tearing my heart out."

"What?"

"Your daughter, I'm in love with your daughter."

"Just don't say nothing, to nobody."

"What?"

"Uh was working in Burnt Oak, uh come to get the van, all of a sudden uh see it's all broke, somebody broke it."

29

Sunday morning there came a knock on the street door, and Katherine ran to open it. Although she knew beforehand it would be Artemis, still her knees went weak. Each time she saw him he seemed more handsome than the last.

They walked across Tredegar Square to Mile End Road.

"Let's get the bus to Victoria Park and go for a walk," said Artemis. In the park they strolled down to the lake. "Perhaps we could take out a rowboat." He rented a boat, helped Katherine in, and rowed out in the direction of the small island in the center of the lake. Carefully he helped her stand and navigate from her seat in the stern to come sit alongside him. He showed her how to grasp the single oar and pull using her whole body weight, holding it at an angle so the blade didn't skip above the water's surface. In tandem they rowed slowly toward the island, where he jumped out ahead and pulled the boat securely onto the grassy bank. Ignoring the nearby pagoda, they sat together higher up the slope, watching the tranquil waters lap peacefully at the boat's hull.

"Your name, Artemis, it's beautiful, I've never heard it before. Where did your parents get it from?"

"They didn't get it from anywhere; I found it."

"Oh, isn't it your real name?"

"No, it *is* my real name."

"I mean…."

"When I was first born, how well could my parents have known me?"

"I suppose…."

"The name they chose happened not to be suitable, it wasn't in any sense me, so I changed it."

"Oh! What was your name, the one they gave you?"

"Why do you want to know? It isn't my name; it never really was my name."

"Oh it doesn't matter…."

"In the sense of being appropriate, it never was my name."

"I… I suppose I was just curious…."

"The name they happened to choose for someone they didn't know isn't of any particular interest."

"Yes."

"I wanted my name to embody a certain cadence, you could almost say… a… quotient of feminine sensibility…."

"Feminine sensibility?"

"I didn't want a crude name, a coarse name."

"Yes."

And so Artemis talked and Katherine listened.

"I'm supposed to be back," Katherine said later. "A friend was coming round."

"Oh?"

"A girlfriend, someone…."

"Oh."

"But it doesn't matter, I can talk to her another time."

Two hours later they caught the bus back to Mile End, where at Katherine's suggestion they went to the little teashop recently opened a few doors before Anya's Fashion Footwear, to sit for a leisurely tea and sandwich. Next, they ambled along Mile End Road, past the Empire cinema in Stepney Green, and as dusk was falling, continued along Whitechapel Road until they found themselves outside the brightly illuminated London Hospital. There, they sat in the shaded seclusion of a recessed bench and talked for another hour, then continued their promenade all the way to Aldgate, to the restaurant of Artemis' parents. It was now after midnight; they let themselves in and, hungry again after their extended walk, in the echoing solitude of the kitchen Artemis cooked eggs, rashers of bacon, and chips. He showed Katherine a group of poems he said were by Shelley. She told him they were beautiful, whereupon he confessed he'd written them himself, to her.

He placed candles on the table and switched off most of the lights. The couple dallied over the romantic meal, then lingered in front of the gas stove as he prepared cups of tea. "I never said this before to anybody — I love you, Katya, and I want you to marry me." Katherine's eyes widened. "But before you answer, you must understand that I'll always need… space… to be myself, to have my own friends, to stay away when the need is strong." He poured loose tea into the teapot, then boiling water. "I've already made an irreversible commitment to myself, to remain free of negative exclusivity, you know, the pointless curtailing of… secondary relationships." She listened intently as he continued. "You know, it destroys spontaneity, it's what causes marriages to degenerate into hatred and loathing. You'll have to accept this. It's part of me and I can't change."

A considerable awkwardness descended as they stood in silence, in the low light, he leaning against the stove watching for her reactions, she privately unraveling the subtext of his speech. Suddenly they smelled burning. Artemis jumped away. "Sod it, the jacket!" The back of his jacket had caught fire. He ripped it off, and together they stomped out the flames on the floor.

The effect of this unexpected change of locus was to afford Katherine the opportunity to defer her answer. She was virtually committed to Benny, even though she had never explicitly promised him marriage, even though she had actually stood him up today. Benny was so… reliable and solid, even stolid, unromantic; but she supposed she would always be able to count on him. A Jewish tailor from the East End, but completely unembarrassed about it! Hazel might be right that Benny was another version of Abie, but at least he was down-to-earth, practical. She could count on his coming home after work; he wouldn't be trying to rationalize some "secondary relationship."

With Artemis she would always be unsure. He was ephemeral, like strawberries and ice-cream. She should just enjoy being with him as often as possible until the day she married Benny.

•   •   •

More than a week had passed since Mr. Bandi and Mr. Purushotham gave me the sack from India Imports for kissing Miss Eunice. The man behind the wooden grill at the Unemployment Exchange was only offering me jobs as dustman or men's-shoe salesman, and when he said that demobbed soldiers were basically snapping up the jobs, generally, that they knew what they wanted and were grateful just to be alive and home again, I gathered he'd finally gotten fed up with me. So after leaving the Unemployment and riding the Underground to Burnt Oak to continue helping Abie prepare his snack bar, I tried to size up whether working there would be bearable: at least, I'd be the owner's son. We'd completed the partition wall separating it from the tailor's shop, had put in a separate door and already installed stools alongside the counter. Mr. G's was virtually ready to open. So, since Abie had apparently assumed I would begin working behind the counter as my regular job, by default I let that happen.

The first day, I rode with him on the Underground in the eight A.M. rush-hour, because he wanted to show me Morton's, the grocery shop I'd be stopping at every morning. The train was crowded and we had to stand. As the doors hissed shut and we gathered momentum into the tunnel, the carriage's rocking motions caused one woman to fall against him; she was young and pretty, and Abie took her arm and helped her up again. But moments later when a man opened his newspaper close to Abie's face, he grabbed the whole thing from the man's hands, screwed it up into a ball and threw it away over people's heads where, despite the packed carriage, people managed to jump away. If I could survive this one trip with him, henceforth I'd be making the journey alone, after the rush hour, because Mr. G's wouldn't be opening until twelve o'clock every day.

We got to Burnt Oak without major catastrophe, and stopped at Morton's. Abie bought four loaves of bread, some butter, half a pound of cheese and two bottles of milk. At Mr. Morton's suggestion he sampled a slab of yellow pound cake left from the previous day, and bought that too. Thus loaded with provisions, we crossed Edgeware Road, turned onto Quail Lane and arrived at the shop. Taped inside the window was a sign: *Open Monday at twelve o'clock dinner time.*

Abie had designed the interior of Mr. G's to be long and narrow, about three yards wide. Standing customers were to crowd in behind the stools alongside the counter, which ran from the new glass-and-aluminium entrance door almost to the back wall. We placed the aliments on the counter, then sidled around the far end to get to the serving side with its cluster of mugs and stack of plates. Abie had acquired a collection of knives, forks and spoons that were uniformly old, mismatched, and bent; he'd largely straightened out the various handles and prongs, and the implements now lay on the shelf beneath the countertop where, he said, they couldn't be stolen. Behind us against the wall stood the gas stove he'd dragged home from some bombed-out building late one night near the end of the war, and which he'd subsequently retrieved from the two inches of stagnant water in our cellar at home to load into his van and bring here. Next to this stove he'd attached a similarly war-surplus sink to the wall, its front supported by a wedged-in box. Then came a long narrow worktable with four front legs, its rear edge also nailed to the wall. Several cardboard boxes were lined up on the floor under this table. The preparation area, a shelf under the counter, terminated by the window at a battered low refrigerator with two top-opening lids; this stood crosswise against the wall under a small sliding glass pane we'd installed for serving ice-cream directly through to the street.

"Quick, they'll be 'ere, first we'll make the sandwiches."

He cut a slice of bread, buttered it, covered it with a piece of cheese, cut and buttered a top slice. A dozen of these sandwiches he stacked in one of the cardboard boxes. From under the table he pulled out two jars of jam, and the next loaf became jam sandwiches.

"Eee, the water, they'll be 'ere." At the sink I filled the two kettles and lit the gas with the box of matches we were to keep on the shelf. "Quick, the cups." I lined up the cups. "The tea." From another box I retrieved a bag of loose tea and poured some into a round wooden-handled tea strainer. And from the furthest box under the table he took out two apple strudels. One of them had grey fur growing on one end, which he carefully scraped off into the sink. He cut both strudels into slices and returned them to the box.

Two workmen were already standing outside. "They're 'ere, they're 'ere! Quick open the door, yeh!" As I came around to the door, more men had assembled.

In rapid succession all the stools were occupied, and standees crowded behind.

"Tea."

"Gimme a cuppa."

"I'll 'ave a tea and a piece of cake, guv."

"Gimme a cheese sandwich."

"Milk. Where's the bloody milk? Can't drink tea without milk, guv."

"I'll have, er, tea and a jam sandwich, if you will."

It was a struggle to keep up with the orders. More and more workmen squeezed in and pressed up against the partition wall, which began to creak. Some men wanted the yellow cake bought at Morton's, others ordered strudel. Abie had planned huge mugs, in reaction to restaurants such as The Broadway Eatery that used such thick-walled cups there was hardly any space inside for tea, though now these mugs quickly emptied the kettle. Abie picked up an empty kettle. "You didn't do the kettle, *schvunce,*" he growled. I quickly filled the first kettle again and put it on the gas. A man who had sat near the door stood up and left. "Did you take the money?"

"No, I thought you did...."

The sandwich in Abie's hand slammed to the counter top as he rushed around the end to get to the door. Elbowing through the press of customers, he knocked over one man's cup of tea, "'Ey, 'old it guv!"

"Uh'm uh'm uh'm sorry, 'e just went out the barsted, 'e didn't pay, Z, Z, Zech make 'im more tea, uh'm sorry, 'ere give 'im a cloth there, on 'is trousers it went." He edged out of the door and ran along the street, but the man had already turned the corner.

"'Urry up wiv the tea there matey, we ain't got all day."

"This cake's stale!" Someone standing in the crush behind seated bodies shoved through onto the counter a plate with a half-eaten piece of strudel.

"Alright, just a minute, the kettle's nearly boiled, just a minute." It was impossible to keep pace with the orders, let alone track who paid, what was stale, what was a replacement for spilled tea. A man stood up, snapped a coin down on the counter, nodded and walked out just as Abie returned. I picked up the penny and handed it to Abie as he came around behind.

"What's this?"

"The man left it for his tea."

"Tea? Wha'ja mean tea, it's tuppence for tea."

"He just left a penny...."

"So why didn't you tell 'im, tuppence, tuppence!" His face darkened, but the customers seated immediately beyond the narrow counter top induced him to turn away and lower his voice. "Alright, from your wages you'll pay, maybe now you'll remember 'ow much!"

"I'm sorry I didn't know what he had...." The men were watching.

"What 'e 'ad! One penny! What's... what's... a *schmuck* already uh got 'ere...."

"'Ey, matey, we wants our tea. I paid you already, tuppence, I ain't got me tea yet." Another kettle was boiling.

"Alright." I poured his tea.

"And that ain't fresh tea there, I seen you, you bin pouring 'alf a dozen cups of tea wiv that there strainer...."

"I'm sorry...." I banged the tea leaves out into the rubbish box, put in fresh tea.

As I emptied the rejected cup into the sink, Abie came alongside. "Wha'cha doing? You're throwing it down the drain!" Then through tight lips, "Serve it to someone else oo's like, not looking...."

"Sugar!"

"Should we leave the sugar dish on the counter so they can take...."

"Nuh, take, take, they'll take, they'll grab everything, if they want sugar give 'em one spoon, uh won't be able to keep buying...."

I swung around for the sugar, and in the cramped space my arm knocked the kettle of boiling water off the gas stove. It fell into the opened cake box on the floor and the water gurgled out.

Abie jumped back. *"Oy a schvunce melumid* uh'v got 'ere, all the cake 'e's ruined!"

At five minutes to two, suddenly the snack bar was empty.

"Clean up, then you can go 'ome, you don't 'ave to stay, what for? Next week you'll stay 'ere 'til late, we'll sell the ice-cream, you'll stay open late."

Abie exited through the back curtain to work on his tailoring orders, taking with him the small cardboard box holding the money. Through the thin partitioning wall I heard the *ke-ching!* of his cash register. An hour and a half later I'd washed all the dishes and cutlery, dried them, wiped down the counter and the chairs, swept and mopped the floor on both sides.

"Shurrup in there already, uh'm trying to listen to the wireless, a commotion 'e's making in there all the time." I'd been singing without being aware of it, in my head listening to an imaginary chord progression dance by, practicing the melodic and lyric phrases so they meshed perfectly, beautifully, the way Frank Sinatra did them.

In the cloudy afternoon light I walked alone through immaculate Burnt Oak streets to the Tube station. I would give this job a definite time limit. Tomorrow I'd bring the other music book I'd kept from the library, *Orchestration,* to read on the Underground. I'd contemplate the differences in the sounds of instruments, how if you had, say, either a violin or a clarinet play middle-C in another room you could still tell which instrument was playing it, how the difference in sound was called *timbre,* actually the combinations of frequencies, overtones; Forsythe wrote his book in 1914 and they probably didn't understand the science exactly in those days.

An hour and fifteen minutes later I arrived home to find Zilla in a state of tremendous excitement: her boat ticket had arrived from America. Rebecca's accompanying letter said she was still seeing the same man, Berel; he was Polish and the American soldiers had freed him from Buchenwald. The Germans had tattooed a number on his arm, and killed his parents and brother. Americans were nice to go out with on dates and you could have a good time, she wrote, but with Berel you could talk about what life was really like, not all peaches and cream. When the *Queen Mary* reached New York, Berel would be driving her to the docks for

Zilla in the Buick he'd just bought, and from there to Rebecca's apartment in Washington Heights. Zilla would get a job, and with both of them working it would be only a few more months until they sent tickets for Lily and Marius. When the letter had arrived earlier that morning, Mum had gone immediately to the telephone kiosks outside Mile End Station and rung up Zilla at Buck & Hickman's to let her know, so she could ring Cunard right away and secure a berth: in fact she would be departing Wednesday of next week. Katherine, Marius and I already knew that when Zilla's ticket arrived we were not to say anything to Lew, so when he came around as usual Friday afternoon to wait for her to get home from work we were to keep quiet. She'd told us telling him would be difficult; she would have to break the news herself.

Jack, Izzy and I took a slow walk to Johnny Isaacs to get chips, and I told them about working in Burnt Oak, how one day I might perhaps take over the snack bar myself. Also, that my eldest sister was going to America next week. When we got back and they both went home, I couldn't bear seeing Abie or even hearing his voice yet again, so I went straight up to bed. I'd forgotten about the broken bedroom door; now if he started screaming when he came home, I couldn't even shut out the noise. I climbed into bed and a moment later the downstairs door opened and closed; Benny had brought Katherine back to the house, and left. Soon I heard her come upstairs.

"Hello, Katya," I called through the broken panel.

"Oh, you're awake, I'll come in, just let me get undressed." She went into the front bedroom, which she now shared with Zilla. Marius mostly slept on the old bed in my room, but tonight he was still out with his friend Fred. Maybe he'd even sleep at Fred's, to avoid Abie. I hoped he did, because we never had any kind of a real conversation, and also his snoring was always so loud.

After a few minutes Katherine came in and sat on my bed. "So, how's it working out with the old bastard?" she began.

"I don't know if I can stand it for long. He's swearing and cursing, even in front of the customers. Lucky they don't understand Yiddish."

"I couldn't work for him for one minute. Anya's like a pig, but compared to him she's charming! I bet when Friday comes round he'll find some reason not to pay you."

"Already he's deducting one penny because someone didn't pay enough for their tea, and sixpence because he said I didn't charge enough for the stale strudel."

"I'm not surprised."

"Then, it was so rushed I tipped over the boiling kettle into the cake box. I suppose that'll cost me a couple of shillings."

"I can tell you he'll find exactly one pound fifteen's worth of mistakes each week."

"One pound fifteen?"

"That's what he said he'll pay you, isn't it?"

"Yes, well…. I'll try it for a little while."

"Just, don't be disappointed."

"I s'pose. How's Benny?"

"Oh, he's alright, he was wild I wasn't home on Sunday, I told him a priest accidently locked Hazel and me inside her church. I met his mother last week, did I tell you? What a nudnik! We had supper there again tonight. She's constantly telling him what to do! He's so different when his mother tells him to do something, it's hard to believe it's the same person."

"Is he nice, I mean, do you like him, Benny?"

"He's bossy, he's always got to be in charge. Hazel said he's another Abie." Suddenly, though no one else was within earshot, her voice dropped to a whisper: "Guess what, I saw Artemis!"

"Saw him? What do you mean, you had a date?"

"Well, maybe it sort of… turned into an accidental date."

"What did Benny say?"

"You kidding? I never told Benny. Don't tell him, whatever happens!"

"Well sure, alright. Really?"

"Come on, tell Benny? He'd have an apoplectic fit! What he doesn't know won't hurt him. You've got to swear you won't say anything!"

"Alright I won't, but I mean, it's confusing isn't it, to see… is it right?"

"Oh, come on, right, what does right mean? Zech, one day you'll understand." Sitting on the edge of the bed, easily dismissing my apprehensions, she seemed so grown up. "Anyway, Artemis took me to his parents' restaurant."

"He did?"

"He's so romantic, not like Benny. He rented a boat, then we walked all the way to Aldgate and he took me to his parents' restaurant. It was closed, it was after midnight."

"Yes? After midnight!"

"He had keys for all the locks, and we went in the kitchen, huge, a great big kitchen and he fried eggs and chips in a pan, so big it must have been a yard wide!"

Downstairs the street door creaked then banged shut, and Abie was home.

"Don't let him hear, Katya, I don't want him to think I'm still up."

She dropped her voice further. "He lit candles and recited some poetry, it was lovely, from memory, he said it was Shelley, guess what?"

"What?"

"Then he said he wrote it himself, he wrote it for me!" She giggled.

Abie's voice was rising, and Lily shouted: "*Oy a broch* already, the minute he comes home."

"He asked me to marry him! He said he wrote the poetry especially for me!"

"Really? Can you get married when you're only fourteen? So what are you going to do? Do you… I mean, how can you marry him if you're going with Benny…."

"It's hard to believe it's real."

"So might you go with him then instead of Benny?"

Again she giggled. "I don't know what to do, I have to see, Benny's nice also, in a different sort of way, he's more down to earth…." The street door closed a second time, then came a crash, as though a piece of furniture had fallen. "Oh, christ, the old barstard! I suppose we should go down…."

"Leave 'er alone, you old fucker!" It was Marius, just come home, and shouting at him!

"We'd better go down," I said, jumping out of bed and grabbing my trousers. My heart was thumping, "Come with, yes?"

"Sure."

As we ran out onto the landing, the faint light was torn by a scream, then a thump that shook the house. "Ow!, Ow," It was Lily!

Katherine and I rushed, almost fell, down the stairs.

"Crikey, look what you done!" Marius' voice, "Look what you done, look what you done, look what you done…." He was crying, the words jumbled.

I burst open the living room door. Marius was kneeling on the edge of the opened settee; Abie was standing on the far side, the fireplace poker in his hand. There was no Lily.

"Where is she, what happened?" Katherine had run ahead of me, around the settee. "Mum, Mum!" she screamed, and fell to the floor. I rushed around; Lily was lying on the floor, her face white, and a trickle of crimson blood seeped through her hair and down the side of her face.

"What did you do this time!" screamed Katherine, and I was afraid he would hit her too. But he just stood there, the poker raised but his arm frozen.

"Nah, nah, what 'appened, what did she, uh'll... uh'll... eee, uh'll get a cloth...."

Katherine was crying also, "Get a cloth quick!" She lifted Lily's head onto her knee.

I bent down alongside; Lily's eyes were moving from side to side under closed lids, "Mum, Mum, are you alright?"

Abie was standing over us with a wet towel, "Eee, uh don't know what 'appened, she fell over...."

Katherine grabbed the wet cloth and started wiping Lily's face and hair. The eyes opened briefly, then for a longer moment. "Oh-oh-oh-oh-oh," came the faint quavering moan.

I took the cloth and tried to feel for where the blood was coming from. "Mum, Mum, it's alright, you'll be alright." We had her half sitting up on the floor against the edge of the settee.

"Oh, oh!" she cried weakly. On the side of her head above her left ear I found a raised raw welt, and held the cloth to it as carefully as I could without causing more pain.

Marius was screaming, crying: "You bullying barstard you, you could'a killed 'er, I'm gonna, I'm gonna...." He was still wearing his jacket, standing up on the opened settee in his shoes, clambering forward toward Abie, falling over the covers, up again on his knees. His face was pallored too, as he struggled to breathe.

Abie, his face a beetroot red, turned to face Marius. Slowly he bent and picked up the poker that had fallen to the floor. "Shurrup you twisted 'umpback barsted," he began.

"Stop it, stop it!" shrieked Katherine, "Both of you, stop it, isn't this enough already?" She shouted the words at the top of her voice; they both really did stop. Abie just stood there by the side of the settee, unmoving. Marius was now on his knees, all mixed up with the covers, and long gasping howls rasped from his throat as he struggled to open the neck of his shirt.

"Quick, help Maudy, he's choking," Katherine cried.

I patted him between the shoulderblades but it didn't help. "Maudy, let me, here, let me, it's alright, just, quiet, it's alright...." I knew I had to hit harder, hated hitting him so hard, but I had to, up and down his back. His lips were already blue; I pulled off his jacket, stroked his head, his hair. High strangled wheezes scraped out of his mouth. "It's alright, everything's okay, just, just be calm, it'll be alright." If I could quieten him he would catch his breath again; his whole face was getting that blueish tinge and his hands and fingers were jerking aimlessly. I grabbed his face, took a deep breath, locked my mouth over his and forced my breath into his lungs until mine were completely emptied, snatched another breath and repeated the process. I knew he might die, yet while I was doing it all I could think was how repulsive it felt to lock my mouth over his. Two more times, and his breathing began to regain a semblance of rhythm. The arms ceased flailing and gradually the dreadful sounds eased into a more regular pattern.

Lily was leaning up against Katherine on the floor. "Maudy," she said weakly, "is he alright, is he alright, *oy,* my head...."

"Yes Mum, he's alright, it's all over, he's breathing, everything'll be alright." Katherine held Lily's head. "Let me help you in the kitchen, I'll bathe it and put ointment on."

Marius had begun to shake. "It's okay, Maudy." I held his shoulders and stroked his head, stroked the foreign hair.

"Lemme 'elp 'er." Abie feebly raised his hands as Katherine edged Lily around the end of the settee.

"Leave her alone," ordered Katherine in so strong a voice it sounded like someone else. "I'll do it."

"No, it wasn't anything, it was an accident, uh didn't, she fell over...." Abie's arms fell to his sides. "'Er 'ead, 'er 'ead she banged...."

While I held Marius, Katherine eased Lily into the kitchen. A key scraped in the lock, and again the street door opened: Zilla was home. "What's going on?"

From the kitchen I heard Katherine's voice. "Mum, you'll sleep upstairs with us tonight."

"What's going on?" Zilla had followed Lily and Katherine into the kitchen. Suddenly she screamed: "What 'appened? Eee, what did the old barstard do this time?"

"No, it wasn't him, I don't know, I fell over, I banged my head against the corner of the settee or something," said Lily.

"You'll sleep upstairs with us tonight," repeated Katherine.

—o—O—o—

–30–

"'Ey, Zech, when you was at that other place, remember, that electric place."

"What place, Maudy?"

"Y' know, where you worked, yer trousers was all grey."

"Oh, Cable Electric, yes."

"Yup. That where Uncle Albert lives?"

"Near there, I saw him sometimes when I was riding home."

"What street's 'e live on?"

"Street? I don't think it had a name, it was an alleyway."

"I never seen 'im, 'e's our uncle, I was wondering where 'e lives."

"It's off of New Road, right near the Commercial Road end, it's like an alley, I didn't notice if it has a name."

"Is it 'ouses there then?"

"No, it's factories on both sides, he just has a room, it's half below ground, at the far end."

"On what side?"

"Why? What's…."

"Crikey, whassamarra with you? Just asking a question!"

"Alright."

"So, what is it then? What side's it on, when you go in the alleyway, what side's it on, I'm just wondering what side of the alley 'is room is on, that's all."

"On the right side, the furthest window along before the end of the alley."

"So, that where 'is door is, then?"

"He doesn't have a door, I don't think."

"Don't 'ave a door?"

"No, he goes in and out through the window, I don't think there is a door."

"You said 'e showed you stuff, stuff 'e 'ad from the other war?"

"When I saw him he did, yes, he showed it to me, I haven't seen him since."

"I'm going out. Tell Mum I'm going out, I'll be over at Fred's."

"Alright."

•   •   •

Amid a roar of steam, the boat train inched alongside the platform. "Ta-ra, I'll write right away, don't worry Lily, we'll send you a ticket, like in a few weeks, don't worry, just don't answer 'im when 'e starts."

"Maudy, Maudy has to go also, I can't leave him with the old barstard, no one'll look after him."

"We know, I'll tell Rivka, we'll get two tickets, we'll send two for sure, don't worry."

Lew picked up Zilla's carry-on bags. "Here, darling, I'll be coming soon, in less than a year I'll be there, you'll see, I've got nothing to stay here for now."

"Alright, Lew." Zilla kissed him so affectionately that I hoped no one was watching. "I'm glad you came," she said.

"It would have been too terrible if you just... disappeared," he whispered as he held her.

"I'd better go...." She was crying as she climbed through the carriage door, trying to change the sobs into a smile, even a laugh. "I'll see everybody soon," she choked, "we'll all meet in New York, you'll see, it won't be long."

Lew trotted alongside the train's open window, tears streaming down his face. To the receding window opening he offered up a big clean white handkerchief. Zilla's hand reached out and caught it.

•   •   •

With Zilla gone, I moved into the larger and brighter front bedroom, taking over her bed by the windows. Marius came into the front bedroom too, for the first time having his own real bed. Katherine now had the back bedroom, including the broken door panel, all to herself, and Lily remained downstairs with Abie on the opening settee.

Even though Zilla had spent very little time at home during the months since Rebecca had left, the house now seemed really empty. Lew came by frequently to compare our letters from her with those he received.

I had been working at Mr. G's three weeks, and Katherine's prediction had so far been accurate: no wages, just fare money, and money to pick up bread and groceries when I got off the Tube station at Burnt Oak around half past ten in the morning. The daily supplies had to be paid for first, Abie said, and the rest had to go toward the rent; there wasn't enough money yet for wages.

"Uh'll start with the ice-cream, it's warm out already, they'll buy, you'll see they'll all want. Then you should 'ave some wages, we'll make loads of money."

He was right about the customers: word did spread quickly, and that first Saturday I spent almost the entire day at the front window dispensing ice-cream cornets through the sliding glass panel. The queue was long, sometimes winding around the corner into the alley, and not only kids, but grown-ups. One reason for Mr. G's popularity was the size of the cornets; Abie showed me how to make the biggest cornets in London, two huge scoops of ice cream. On a couple of occasions the line at the window was so long that he had to drop the tailoring and come around to help. He lifted the stationary glass pane completely out of its frame so we could both make cornets and serve through the wider opening. All the money we took in went into his trousers pocket, and during a brief lapse he jangled the take: "Ere, you see? We're doing alright! You'll 'ave wages."

Later that afternoon, when he lifted his side of the refrigerator lid, his face dropped. "Eee, where's the ice-cream, there's no ice-cream, nothing, it's nearly all gone."

"I know, we sold all the chocolate ice-cream; there's a little bit of vanilla."

"So, what... what should we do?"

"I suppose we'll have to buy some more."

"Buy some more?" His face darkened. "What do you mean, oo'll pay for it, they'll want *gelt,* they'll want money."

"I... we'll have to, well, I mean if you want to keep selling cornets won't you have to...."

"Uh just took it in, uh just took in the money, and already 'e's, 'e's...." He stamped around angrily. I quietly washed the ice-cream scoop, not wanting to be perceived as a troublemaker. But a few minutes later when I had to turn a kid away because there was no chocolate, only vanilla, he began to appreciate the incontrovertible logic of my observation. "Alright, go, go, tell 'im we need more ice-cream, go already, what can uh do."

I went, and a little later the delivery van arrived. The driver brought in containers of vanilla and chocolate and dropped them inside the refrigerator. "That'll be eight and six, mate."

"Eight... eight and six?" Abie repeated in feeble disbelief.

"'Sright, mate."

"Eee... well, er... eight and six... er, right." And he proceeded to count out eight shillings and sixpence from his pocket.

"'Urry up, mate, I ain't got all day," said the delivery man as Abie counted and re-counted.

After he left, Abie was plunged into a perplexed despair: "A fire in 'is *kishkers,* a fire, you see that, eight and six 'e took from me like, ten o'clock this morning uh paid 'im already, now in one minute 'e took it again!"

But as the evening progressed and more customers lined up outside the window and his pocket began to jangle once again, so his spirits improved.

The following Saturday the manager from The Broadway Eatery on Edgeware Road came by. "Mr. G, you're cutting our throat what with your big sandwiches and your big mugs of tea, and them there double scoop cornets. You better knock it orf or you'll be putting us all in the poor 'ouse."

"What! What's this, you, you, you're *threatening* me you *barsted* you, *fu–uck* orf back to your stinking shit 'ole there with your polite cups of tea and your... your little finger stuck up in the air, there. Stick your finger up your arse, that's where you should stick it."

The manager left.

Around dusk a young fellow wearing a cap came in with his girl for two cups of tea and apple strudel. They sat at the counter and I put on the kettle. "One chocolate ice-cream cornet please," came a junior voice from the window. I put out plates for the strudel, then made the cornet and handed it to the little boy outside.

"Throopence, please."

"Alright." He took the cornet, and as he fished in his pocket, boiling water spluttered out the kettle's spout onto the hot grill. I quickly turned off the gas and poured the water into the teapot.

Abie came through the curtain at the end behind the counter. "What's going on with the kettle there!"

"No, it just boiled over a bit." I turned back to collect the throopence and the little boy was gone; out the opening I could see him running up the street. "Hey! You didn't pay!" I called after him.

"What! What did you do, you didn't take 'is money before you gave 'im the cornet?" Immediately his face was purple as he raced around the end of the counter. *"Oy, a schmuckisher* barsted uh got 'ere, 'e gives...."

On the other side of the counter the young man stood up from his stool as his girlfriend leaned away from the approaching whirlwind. He placed himself in the center of the aisle. "What's up, guv, there's a lady present."

Abie was forced to stop in his tracks. "Lady, lady, wha'cha...?"

"That's right guv, a lady, so you watch your language!"

"Ah, fu–uck orf with yer… yer… didn't you see, 'e didn't pay, the little barsted, quick…."

A click, and in the man's hand was an opened penknife.

"'Arry, don't!" the girl screamed. She jumped down off her stool and grabbed his arm, pulling him toward the door. "'Arry, we don't want no trouble, it ain't worth it for nothing, come on…." The young man's stance slowly softened, and he allowed her to pull him out of the shop.

Abie stood there, pale. "Eee, did you see, for nothing… like… and the other one, 'e got away."

"I… I…." I knew I should not have called after the boy.

Abie sat on a stool to catch his breath. "You *schmuck* you, *schvunce melumid!* Now you wasted the tea, also."

"Dad, it wasn't my fault, and I'm getting pretty much fed up…."

A woman was at the window: "Cornet, please."

I went over. "Vanilla or chocolate?"

"Vanilla please. Lovely evening ain't it dearie, nice and warm this time of year."

"Yes, yes."

From behind: "Take the money first, *first, before* you give it to 'er."

We stayed open until ten that evening, the drone of Abie's sewing machine buzzing through the thin partition, me selling half a dozen more cornets before closing. I tidied everything up, replaced and locked the windows, then the two of us raced to the station, barely making the last train home.

Upstairs, Katherine came in and sat on my bed. "Katya, it's absolutely horrible at Burnt Oak."

"Don't stay there then. Did he pay you yet?"

"No, I don't even want to get paid, I just don't want to go there anymore."

"Then go to the Unemployment, ask them for something you'd absolutely love."

"I don't know how to tell him I don't want to work there, who knows what he'll do?"

"If you have a proper job to look forward to it'll make it easier to tell him."

"Someone nearly started a fight there today, it was Dad's fault, the fellow had a knife."

"Christ!"

"Dad was saying 'fuck' or something in front of his girlfriend."

"Phew! If he'd killed him it would have solved everybody's problems."

"How can I take a day to go to the Unemployment? I think they're fed up with me there anyway."

"I'll tell you what, Thursday's only half a day at Anya's, I'll take the other half day off and go to Burnt Oak instead. Don't tell Abie you're not coming, I'll just show up there."

"Really?"

"Yes, what can he do?"

When Thursday morning arrived I gave Katherine Abie's money for the grocery supplies, and walked her to the Mile End station. "Thanks, Katya. I'm nervous, it's ridiculous."

"I'm not nervous, what have you got to be nervous about?"

"I dunno. I'll go to Anya's now and tell her you're ill today, you'll be back tomorrow."

"Fuck Anya, you don't have to."

"Well, I might as well."

"If you want to. Just try to get something good at the Unemployment, you could even ask them about singing with a band, you never know!"

"You're right! So I'll see you tonight."

"Be tough with them there, they *have* to find you a good job."

I got to the Unemployment Exchange on Mansell Street by ten-thirty. "Well it's you again, good morning then," said the same clerk who had gotten me the other jobs.

"Yes, good morning."

"What happened with the other job, basically?"

"Well, I'd told you already... I left." Of course, I hadn't mentioned Miss Eunice — and I could hardly tell him about Mr. G's.

He didn't seem as irritated this time as he looked through my file. "So are you basically looking for the same kind of work?"

"No, not really...."

"Alright, let's look and see what we have left." From the file he extracted a note. "You wanted it quiet, I see — and no paint."

"Yes, and especially nothing to do with food. Do you have anything to do with science? That's really what I wanted last time."

"Hmm. Science...."

"Yes. Or music. I like singing."

"Basically, you have to be trained for a job in science, you can't just, like, walk in. Also I presume for music, though I'm not certain about that; in fact I can't remember any time we had a job along that line — in a manner of... singing." He guffawed. "That is, speaking, of course I mean. Harrumph." He quickly straightened his face, and looked through the lists. "Now here's a position you might just be qualified for — a laboratory assistant, to learn." He pushed his glasses up to his forehead and picked up the sheet to peer at the smaller print. "They'll pay wages while they train you, hmm, jolly decent of them."

"How much would they pay me?"

"It's most likely quiet in laboratories, except when something's going wrong, har, har, har!" He coughed. "And generally you don't find much use for paint, unless it's basically a paint laboratory."

"I have to earn one pound fifteen, because...."

"After you'd worked there for a decent period you could ask, politely of course, if they'd let you play the wireless, like hum along while you're doing, say, nonessential work...."

"My mother's going away, I might be living just with my father, I need to earn one pound fifteen...."

"...work where the extra noise wouldn't actually interfere."

"Yes. I'll need to...."

"For instance, cleaning up equipment after use, things like that. You'd have to basically use your judgement."

"Yes."

"It's Wapping."

"Wapping?"

"It's not far, is that too far?"

"What is? Is what? Wapping?"

"The job. It's in Wapping. Bituminous Products, Ltd."

"Oh... I see."

"Alright then?"

"Well I always wanted to work in a laboratory."

"Jolly good then, this one should be right up your street."

"Yes. What does bituminous mean?"

"Doesn't say, probably a bit of this, a bit of that! Har, har, har! Wait a minute." He picked up the telephone and dialed. "Yes, Johnson, William Johnson from the Unemployment Exchange, yes that's right, Mansell Street." He put a handkerchief over his mouth and coughed. "Bituminous. Yes, what?" Silence. "That's what I thought it was. Yes. Alright then, yes. Tomorrow morning? Nine o'clock sharp, we'll have him there then." He replaced the receiver and turned back to me.

"Alright." He nodded. "Tar. Bituminous means tar."

"Oh."

"Tar, tar products."

"Yes. But I'd be working in the laboratory, not in the factory?"

"Tar distillates and residues," he said. "Pitch."

"I see, that's quite alright if it's in a laboratory."

"Sorry about the humor."

"That's alright. How much will I earn?"

"Good taste though, humor's always in good taste if it's not sarcastic, none of the low stuff. Gets a bit tedious here you know. At it all day, you realize." He wrote down the company address and handed me the slip of paper. "We buck ourselves up a bit. 'Ave to..."

"Yes. Thank you very much."

"I mean, basically we're people too, can't keep at it all day without letup, you know."

"Yes, it's quite alright, thank you very much."

"No harm done then?"

"No absolutely, certainly, yes I mean, thank you very much. Yes, definitely."

"Alright then. Nine o'clock tomorrow morning for the interview, clean shirt and tie. The wages are two pounds a week."

That evening I made sure I was in bed before eleven. I heard the street door open, followed shortly by Katherine's feet pattering up the stairs. "So what happened?" she asked.

"I told Anya you'd be back tomorrow."

"No, I mean at the Unemployment."

"Oh, it was very good, I've got an interview to work in a laboratory!"

"Really?"

"Yes, I couldn't believe it! I hope it goes alright, they make tar and pitch and things."

"Ugh! Is that alright?"

"I don't care, I mean I wouldn't be in the factory, just learning how to do things in the laboratory. Yes, I hope they take me, I'd love to work in a laboratory. I've got to be there at nine o'clock tomorrow morning."

"Do you want me to go to Burnt Oak again? I don't care, it's for a good cause."

"I didn't even ask, what happened there at his place?"

"I got all the stuff, he didn't get into any fights or anything. It was alright for one day. I ate loads of ice-cream."

"What did he say about my not coming?"

"He was surprised at first but then he didn't care. The workmen bought more stuff than usual, he said. 'Cause I'm a girl, I s'pose. Men are so dopey — if you don't mind my saying."

"I'm glad he didn't start shouting at you."

"No, it was alright. So, do you want me to go tomorrow also if you've got your interview? I don't care about Anya's, I'd love to get the sack."

"Oh, no thanks. It's early, the interview, nine o'clock, and I'll go straight on to Burnt Oak from there. It'll be alright."

"Alright then, if you're sure. I can hear plates rattling down there; I'm starving, I'm going to go down and have something. Woman cannot live by ice-cream alone."

She tripped out of the room and down the stairs, and a little later Abie's heavy boots began clanking slowly upstairs — not racing up, as in a rage. He came in. "You're in bed, what 'appened, why didn't you come?"

"I dunno, all of a sudden I had to do something, Katya said she would go instead. I mean, I made sure you wouldn't be stuck by yourself there."

"Eee, a surprise uh 'ad, uh didn't know what 'appened, all of a sudden uh sees Katya coming over the road with the bags, like through the window, schlepping."

"Yes, she's..."

"She's... eee, she's careful, like in no time she's serving everybody there, she's taking the money, not like... she's not like a... uh mean she's not like a *schmuck* there, she's... she's.... Yeh, eee, she's, she's... it was very good."

Early the next morning I quietly dressed and managed to slip out of the house without Abie noticing. Nervous and excited at the possibility of actually working in a laboratory, I caught the bus to Wapping. Bituminous Products Limited was on a narrow back street. Inside the building, stairs led to an upstairs office with two windows looking out over the Thames. A kindly man in a dark-green corduroy jacket, seated behind a desk, suggested I go down to see a Mr. Hitchcock, the chemist in charge of the laboratory.

Downstairs I knocked on the door, which was opened by a thin, tallish fellow around thirty-five, in a hairy brown and green plaid jacket. I couldn't help noticing white socks inside his brown shoes. "I'm Zachary Grossman, sir. The Unemployment sent me here."

Mr. Hitchcock regarded me affably. "So you're here to work at Bituminous!" He invited me into the laboratory, where we stood between two long black iron benches, a quarter-inch sheet metal top mounted on angle iron legs. On one bench stood what I remembered from Coopers College as a distillation flask; the thin glass tube extending from the side of its neck went through a bored cork into a Liebig condenser, and at the far end a pungent thin yellowish liquid dripped into a beaker.

He smiled. "I understand this will be your first experience in the lab?"

"Er yes sir, other than in school. I really want to learn."

"Excellent, then we'll say you're here in a sort of an apprentice-type capacity, shall we?"

"Er, yes sir."

"Call me Mr. Hitchcock, we don't have to be formal around here." A slight gurgle erupted from the equipment, and he turned to lower the already-low gas flame under the sand bath. "We have to watch out for the old distillate, you know. It's toluol, highly inflammable, burns like the devil if you let it come near the old Bunsen burner, haw, haw!"

"Ha, ha, yes sir, I see."

He pointed to the metal bowl in which the distillation flask sat in sand over the Bunsen burner. "That's why we use the sand bath."

"Yes."

"Safety precaution, you might say, haw, haw."

"Yes sir."

"But we don't want to pile the lot on you the first day, do we?"

"No sir, yes sir. Then can I work here then?"

"Oh... I thought you already were. Aren't you?"

"Well, if everything's alright and you said it's alright, so should I tell the office?"

"Jolly good idea! Run upstairs to the office, you're quite right, they probably should be told. You're going to work out well I can tell, good head on your shoulders."

"Thank you, sir."

"Just a minute — keep an eye on the old equipment while I run outside a moment, there's a good chap."

He hurried out a door to the side of the benches, grabbing a matching plaid cap on the way, and moments later the cap's peak bounced along the bottom of the laboratory's solitary window, a large bay housing a double-sink installation. I peeked out and saw him lean down into a red MG two-seater with its top down, parked just within the gate. A minute later he was back, holding a folded-up *Daily Express,* "Jolly good, thanks, er...."

"Zachary Grossman."

"Zachary."

I exited past the shelves of exotically labeled bottles and Pyrex beakers and wonderfully convoluted glass tubing. Back up in the office, an additional occupant was now at the second desk, and as I entered he stood up to shake my hand and introduce himself. He spoke quietly: "I'm Mr. Bitwood, I'm the clerk. Sit here, let's get all your particulars." We sat and he copied down my answers. "I'm here every day. If there's any questions, speak to Mr. Hitchcock"; he lowered his voice further, "or you can always come upstairs to see me." He looked at the calendar hanging on the wall behind his crowded desk. "Hmm... well, when would you like to start? I assume you want to give notice to your current employer."

"Yes, then am I... going to... work here?"

"Certainly, if Mr. Hitchcock said it's alright."

"Oh, yes, he did, he told me to come up here and tell you, just now."

"Very good. Well, you might as well be off for today; or," he almost whispered, "with Mr. Hitchcock's permission maybe you can observe in the laboratory for a while."

"Yes sir, thank you sir."

"How much notice will you need for your present employer?"

"Oh, nothing... er, I mean I already gave them notice, they...."

"Oh." He looked at me. "So then when would you be ready to start?"

"Now. Can I start now?"

"Well, how about we start you officially next week, Monday morning?"

"Yes, certainly, oh yes, that would be wonderful."

"Then let's say nine A.M. Monday."

The office's earlier occupant, now working quietly at the desk behind me, rose and extended his hand. "Welcome to Bituminous Products Limited, Mr. Grossman. I'm Mr. Margolin, I'm here frequently."

"Er, well..." Mr. Bitwood tittered deferentially. "Mr. Margolin, well, owns the company."

"Oh you do? Really? I see, then thank you sir, oh yes very much!" I shook Margolin's hand, then backed out of the office. "So I'll see you on Monday then."

Downstairs in the lab again, I told Mr. Hitchcock I was to start on Monday at nine A.M.

"Jolly good, jolly good show!"

"They said I can look around for a while if it's alright with you."

"Bang up idea, ask any questions you like. You might want to peek around outside in the yard; you'll be drawing samples from those tall tanks there...." And he pointed through the window. "The foreman, Mr. Smith, decent chap, he's floating around out there somewhere."

I looked at the bottles and read labels on the really big ones: hydrochloric acid, sulphuric acid, toluol, nitric acid, potassium nitrate. Mr. Hitchcock seemed engrossed in his work, and I didn't want to disturb him needlessly. In the yard outside, I saw that the downstairs laboratory and ante-room, with the offices upstairs, constituted the only building on the property. Across the yard, several slender metal tanks mounted on girdered bases soared forty or fifty yards into the sky, with steel-runged ladders running up their sides. At their highest extensions a maze of catwalks interlaced the sky between them.

A workman in grimy shirtsleeves and cap came over: "What's up, mate?"

"I'm going to start working here on Monday, in the laboratory. They said I can look around."

"Alright, I'm Mr. Smith the foreman round 'ere. Watch out where you're walking now, don't fall in that there evaporation tray." He nodded. "It's tar, it ain't deep but it won't do you no good, for sure."

I walked under the tanks, and on one steel ladder I tried a rung or two, then jumped back down to the sodden ground. A skinny fellow in a worn tar-stained jacket nodded his blackened face at me and straightened his cap. I looked out beyond the gate; directly across the narrow street and behind an opposite wall more than a dozen rows of 40-gallon drums were stacked up, eight or ten deep. A crane stood unattended, its boom leaning out above a dilapidated wooden quay that ran a short distance into the murky waters of the Thames. That was probably where the drums of unrefined tar arrived by barge, the tar we would be testing in the laboratory.

My watch said five to ten! I still needed to get to Burnt Oak in time for the workmen when they crowded in at twelve. The prospect of telling Abie that starting Monday I would no longer work at Mr. G's was, to put it mildly, daunting. But as usual Katherine had been right: now that I had an exciting job to look forward to, I wasn't — well — *terrified*. Whatever the consequences I would simply tell him, and get it over with.

Around the corner in Wapping High Street, I waited for the bus. A few other people were at the bus stop, chatting. Standing amongst them, my chest swelled. It was my private secret that starting next week I would be working in a real laboratory.

At Burnt Oak I got off the Tube and picked up the day's supplies at Morton's. Crossing Edgeware Road and turning the corner into Quail Lane, I was surprised to find Abie outside Mr. G's with a broom, sweeping the pavement.

"Eee, you see all this? Loads and loads of glass, all broke, somebody did it, like, deliberate."

In the gutter he'd swept into little piles the remains of dozens of broken Tizer bottles. Pieces of glass still littered the pavement.

"What happened?"

"Uh dunno, uh come 'ere and piles of broken bottles it was, all over. Someone, uh dunno."

"Christ!"

He handed me the broom and took the bags of food from my hands. "Uh'll take it, gimme. 'Ere, sweep it up, three times uh swept it already and every time there's more even. In the gutter, no one should 'urt themselves, when they come for the ice-cream they should be careful.'' I took the broom and pushed remaining shards to the edge. Although the mounds were spread beyond the tailoring section of his shop, most of the breakage seemed to have been concentrated in front of Mr. G's. "'Urry, they'll be 'ere soon the men, be quick, lemme start with the sandwiches. Eee, what barsted could'a done something like that, a terrible thing to do."

I swept away and shoveled most of the rest into the dustbin, then came inside and helped prepare the sandwiches. One thing at a time — I'd tell him about Bituminous later. Everything went as usual for the rest of the day, the men crowding in at lunchtime, the kids lining up for ice-cream after four o'clock. Maybe I'd tell him when we were on the Tube going home tonight; the presence of other people might force him to moderate his reaction. But when we did finally catch the train, it happened we were the only people in the whole carriage. I stood up to look through the window at the end; there were quite a few passengers in the next one.

"Dad, should we go through to the other carriage?"

"What?" He lowered his newspaper.

"I mean, there's nobody here, it's bouncing a lot isn't it?"

"Bouncing?"

"The carriage, isn't it… it feels funny, maybe it's smoother in the other carriage."

"What's 'e talking about already!"

"I mean the other carriage might be smoother, I can see people in it, like the extra weight of all the passengers. It stops it bouncing as much as this one."

"Alright, so you go in the other carriage then."

I wouldn't be able to tell him at home; I sat down again and considered. "Dad, can I have some wages?"

"Tsk! What does 'e want from me, wages!"

"You said I'd have wages."

"Wages, we don't 'ave enough, 'ow can you 'ave wages? Maybe tomorrow, when we get more money in, when we'll 'ave enough, you'll see, by my life, you'll 'ave wages, uh promise you'll 'ave, you'll see."

Perhaps it would be best to wait until tomorrow — Saturday, my final day. Then, when he still didn't pay me I'd have good reason to tell him.

Next morning we opened up, with one order of ice-cream delivered first thing. I didn't need to tell him right away — that would make the whole day unbearable. We arranged a second delivery around four o'clock, and by seven o'clock we were again very low on ice-cream. After I'd had to turn several kids away because we were out of chocolate flavor, Abie mumbled he was spending money from his tailoring just to keep the snack bar going, that as much as we took in he was paying out more just buying ice-cream and milk and apple strudel. I understood he was probably saying this to avoid paying me wages, so I kept my head down, cleaning the inside of the refrigerator. Mr. G's wasn't even earning its own rent, he continued, and maybe there'd never be enough for wages. The tailoring was different, he could make money there; maybe it would be best to close up Mr. G's for good. Miraculously he said all of this himself, and as he continued, it devolved that I never needed to interject one single word. I served three vanilla cornets to a man with a couple of little boys, then removed the last empty cardboard container, flattened it out and pushed it into the dustbin.

"Sometimes a business is no good, you'll find out, Zech. Uh dunno, uh never 'ad any luck. Come on, we'll clean up, we'll finish up 'ere, uh'll lock up, we'll go round the place there what is it, on Edgeware Road there, we'll tell the barsted we're closed up, 'e got what 'e wanted, we're finished, ruined."

It was only seven-thirty P.M., but he was right; there was no point in staying open just explaining to everyone who came to the window that there was no more ice-cream. "'Ere, take 'em, take 'em, what do uh want 'em for, so you'll 'ave a nosh you'll 'ave." He handed me the big cardboard box with the last of the cornets.

I could afford to be generous. "No, it's alright. You can eat them when you're working." Katherine had been right: in the three weeks I'd worked there this gift of a three-quarters-used box of empty ice-cream cornets was the closest I'd come to wages. For the first time it was still light out as he locked the door. I would never have to see this place again.

Together we walked around to Edgeware Road. All was dark at The Broadway Eatery, and a sign on the newly boarded-up window read: "Out Of Business."

—o—O—o—

31

Mr. Hitchcock sent me out to the yard with a shoulder bag containing three sample bottles, to climb a metal ladder attached to tank number three. "Let a pint or two run first to clear the pipe before you collect the sample," he'd said.

At a dizzying height above the miniscule workmen scurrying below, and hanging by one arm looped around the ladder's side rail beneath the catwalks that connected the high elevations of the tanks, I opened a valve. A bitumen-caked bucket strung from the pipe caught much of the initial tar as it oozed from the nozzle. But some missed as the bucket swung away, and my heart stopped as the turning strands plunged like twists of rope into the void beneath my feet, to be quickly caught on the breeze and carried diagonally along before slapping to the concrete pavement. I wondered how accustomed were the laborers down there to a black glutinous filament suddenly fallen across their hair and face — if there ever came a time when it no longer evoked shock. I unscrewed the bottle lid and collected a sample of the viscous dark brown fluid, capped the bottle and stuck it back in the bag. Down the tar-slicked rungs to the center valve I repeated the procedure. The bottom valve, which from above had seemed virtually at ground level, was actually far too high to leap directly to the safety of ground because of the height and breadth of the girders on which the tanks were mounted.

Scrambling over this delicate steel lattice was a requirement of my new job, the stuff that the real world of men was made of. Despite my fear of heights, what a difference from carrying puny packages to the Post — or pouring tea with knotted stomach as Abie glowered and cursed!

Back in the lab, Mr. Hitchcock weighed tar from one sample bottle into a 1,000 c.c. distillation flask, added several times its volume of toluol from a five-litre bottle off the shelf, then set the flask in the sand-filled iron dish, connected it to the Liebig condenser, double-checked the seals and, finally, lit the Bunsen burner. The purpose of the test, he explained, was to distill off and measure the volatile components of the tar, and incidently to reclaim the toluol. The sand-bath would contain the highly-inflammable toluol should the flask ever break.

The day went well, as did the next, and the following week after I'd collected that day's samples he had me set up the distillation myself. "Toluol is quite inflammable," he reminded me, "so make sure all the corks are a tight fit. We don't want to set fire to the place, haw, haw." He deliberately busied himself by his desk, facing away from me as I weighed the flask, first empty, then again with the tar sample in it, subtracted the flask's weight, added toluol, and was ready to light the Bunsen burner. He came over and checked the connections. "Jolly good show!"

The distillation went perfectly. Everything seemed so peaceful, so intriguing in a calm rational way. The toluol bubbled merrily away for forty-five minutes; I measured the distillate out of the condenser, disposed of the residue, cleaned the equipment and repeated the procedure with the second sample — then finally with the third.

"I knew you'd do a bang-up job," he said as he left for the day, leaving me to lock up.

"Thank you," I beamed.

•   •   •

When I opened the laboratory door as usual at nine A.M., Mr. Hitchcock hadn't arrived yet. I put three fresh bottles in the sample bag, and out in the yard I nodded to Mr. Smith, the foreman, as I climbed number four tank to collect the day's tar samples. Mr. Hitchcock had been late practically every day, though this time when I returned with the filled bottles half an hour later he was seated at his desk.

"Good chap, you got the samples already, I can always count on you. Let's set up the distillation." He proceeded to mount the sand bath over the Bunsen burner, and handed me the distillation flask to weigh in the sample. "Zachary, old chap, I'm going to be leaving for an early lunch, I have some important shopping to do for Mrs. Hitchcock and I won't be back. She's pregnant, you know."

"Oh, I didn't know. So you're going to be a father!"

"Yes, she's due the end of the year. It's not been an easy time, he'll be a huge fellow, already he keeps both of us up at night. Not just kicking, but actually punching." His thin chalky face waxed a proud, anemic smile.

"You said 'he.' Do you hope it'll be a boy?"

"Oh, he definitely will be."

"You mean you already know it'll be, or you want…? I thought you can't tell 'til it's born."

"As a matter of fact I've investigated the matter thoroughly, and by Jove it's quite amazing what I've discovered! The offspring's gender is determined by the degree of masculinity or femininity of the father."

"Really?" I stole a more analytical glance at him; he didn't seem unduly masculine to me, certainly not tough the way Mr. Smith and the other laborers were outside in the yard.

"I suppose an *extremely* feminine mother could influence the outcome, but that would be the exception, where the father's, well, shall we say… inclinations, haw, haw, were, well, shall we say, problematic? Haw, haw, haw! Mrs. Hitchcock does happen to be extremely feminine, haw, haw, but according to this list of criteria I've drawn up here" — he slid a sheet of paper he'd been working on to the center of his desk — "it's pretty obvious we'll have a boy. We plan to have just one child. I'm an only son, and that produced excellent results. Jill did want a girl, but secretly I'm glad he'll be a boy. You can relate to boys easier."

"Really?" I'd always found it much easier to relate to Katherine than to Marius.

"Oh yes, they're more, how can I put it… reasonable."

I looked at the paper on which he had compiled his list of paternal attributes militating in favor of siring a boy: father at least six feet tall, wiry frame, having been chosen for the college soccer team, high intelligence, a calm and reasoning disposition — and, red hair.

"Red hair?"

"I've checked it out among the people we know, and would you believe it, where the outcome is close, red hair seems to lock it into the… shall we say, male column? By the way, if Mr. Bitwood or Mr. Margolin come down, there's no need to mention I had to leave early; why stir up a bees' nest, I say, haw, haw, what?"

Around three, he left; I liked it when he left early because that meant I had the rest of the day to attend to my own private experiments. Neither Mr. Smith nor Mr. Bitwood, the only other people who might come in, were likely to notice what I was working on as long as the numbers were ready on time so that everything in the yard could go smoothly. I checked the distillation currently in progress. All was well, the flame under the sand bath was appropriately low, the toluol was bubbling gently, the corks were tight, and I could retire to the lavatory with *Stars and Planets,* my remarkable new book from the library. *Stars and Planets* even showed how the temperature of the sun could be inferred using a spectrograph to show the position of the spectral lines the sun emitted! Surface temperature, six thousand degrees centigrade, and at the center, fifteen million degrees! I was so exhilarated by the book's intricate reasoning that I sat on the lavatory too long.

Pulling myself back to more mundane affairs I trotted back across the passage to the laboratory. The toluene was low in the flask and I quickly turned off the Bunsen burner. A knock on the door and Mr. Smith looked in. "'Ow's it going, matey?"

"Okay, I'm a bit rushed, Mr. Hitchcock had to leave a little early, I'll have the first numbers in about thirty minutes."

•   •   •

As the weeks rolled by I became more and more familiar with the laboratory procedures, and came to enjoy being left to take charge of virtually the entire operation. Mr. Hitchcock regularly arrived late, around nine-thirty or ten o'clock, and quite often had to leave early. In fact, he seemed to spend so little time in the lab I thought I should bring up the possibility of my getting drafted when I turned eighteen in November. Although it was only March, my mentioning it now would give him time to prepare, perhaps think about getting someone to take my place — temporarily — in case the army did actually take me. "Mr. Hitchcock, you know I'm going to have to register in a few months."

"Register? Register for what?"

"National Service, for when I turn eighteen."

"Don't tell me you'll be leaving! Oh, goodness me, you've only been here — what is it — half a year! When are you leaving?"

"No, I may not be leaving, I don't know yet."

"Well actually, why would you *want* to register for the army? I thought you liked working here."

"I do, it's the best job I ever had. It's not my fault, the government makes everyone register when they turn eighteen. It wouldn't be 'til the end of the year, I just have to warn you ahead of time so you can make arrangements. You don't necessarily go into the army, I certainly don't want to, maybe I wouldn't have to, but sometimes they make you."

"Hmm, I see, I see. I must say I've gotten to jolly well depend on you opening up on time, sampling, everything, starting the distillations. That *would* be a jolly pest if they draft you." He waxed meditative. "How long would you be gone? Maybe we could get someone else... just 'til you come back, of course."

"If they take you they keep you for eighteen months unless there's a war, then they can keep you as long as they like."

"Haw, haw, haw, if there's a war with the Ruskies we'll all be vaporized so it won't make much difference will it, haw, haw. London must be top of their list." He stood up. "Alright, I'll think about it. I'll try to be here early in the morning."

"Yes."

"By the way, I'll be gone for the rest of today. Don't mention it if anyone asks."

"Certainly I won't."

And he left. That meant I had the entire afternoon to attend to a private experiment I'd been planning; the distillation was going well and didn't need my full attention. I mixed a little calcium sulphate and water into a paste, and put the mixture into a flat two-inch-square cardboard box I'd brought from home, that had contained — appropriately enough — an old Roman coin. To dislodge any trapped air bubbles in the mixture, I tapped the stuff down for a while until the surface was completely smooth and unblemished. A brand-new two-shilling piece I'd hoarded for this project was brought out and coated with a thin film of Vaseline. I laid the coin flat on top of the paste and gently pushed it down so that the surface of the paste was flush with the visible surface of the coin.

This all took time, because I needed to work carefully. Meanwhile the distillation had run its course, which meant I had to be extra fast preparing the remaining tar samples for analysis: clean and dry the equipment, weigh the tar sample plus flask, deduct the weight of the flask, pour the toluol (careful!), use the sand bath to catch the inflammable toluol should the flask ever crack, and finally, check the cold water flow through the Liebig condenser. Check all the connections for the last time, and then — re-light the Bunsen burner.

As soon as the new distillation was chugging merrily along, I returned to my little container of calcium sulphate. I checked that the coin and the paste surfaces were still perfectly flush, then carefully hid the whole thing away on the shelf behind the five-litre bottle of sulphuric acid. To give the paste ample time to set I would leave it undisturbed until the next day, then attend to it first thing in the morning, well before Mr. Hitchcock's little red two-seater drove up.

So! Everything was running smoothly, there still was a way to go on the distillation, and now it was lavatory-reading time. I grabbed my latest book and left the lab. Absorbed in the details of how anchoring a piano's very high tension strings in an iron plate — 160 pounds each, times 230 strings, equals a total of 20 tons tension! — differentiated the piano from all earlier keyboard instruments, again I overstayed my lavatory visit.

Back across the passage to the laboratory — and the flask had boiled completely dry! Luckily the beaker was large enough to hold all the distillate; if any had overflowed onto the bench it might have caused a catastrophe. Even then, the residue in the flask had baked to such a solid cake of pitch I couldn't soften it to clean it out. Hydrochloric acid wasn't strong enough for the job, so as a last resort I pulled down the sulphuric acid bottle, being careful not to jog the coin mold on the shelf behind, and carefully poured a little into the flask. In my haste some acid spilled onto the metal desk-top; I ran a cloth under the tap to wipe it up, but as the wet cloth came in contact with the small pool of acid it emitted a loud *pop!* and the cloth literally jumped right out of my hands. It was my fault: I should have remembered that when plain water touches full-strength sulphuric acid, the water immediately boils and expands to a much greater volume of steam; that's what had made the wet rag jump into the air. Still, the unexpected little explosion had made me anxious, because as I turned back to the bench, incredibly, I knocked the flask out of the sand-bath! It landed on its side on the bench top, and with the consistency of a thick syrup more acid globbed out the neck onto the iron surface. By some miracle the glass flask hadn't shattered, but still the situation was perilous; I grabbed the acid-slicked neck and ran the vessel over to the sink and turned on the water. I figured that a *lot* of cold running water on my hands would wash off the sulphuric acid before it had time to reach scalding temperatures.

I was right about that part, but some of the tap water got inside the flask and produced a loud, muffled *bang!* The overheated acid mixture immediately frothed up and spurted out the neck, peppering the window and discoloring the wall with fizzling splotches — luckily none hit my face, although hot slippery sulphuric acid ran between my fingers. Holding the foaming flask at arm's length and lowering it into the sink caused fresh globules of acid to splatter as high as the ceiling. I deflected the flask's neck to keep it pointed away from myself, and the spatterings flung themselves right across the lab, even beyond the far end of the metal bench-top. In the couple of seconds before I could tip it all the way down and into the sink, I watched in dismay as specks reached all the way over to Mr. Hitchcock's desk, where wisps of smoke and steam arose from each of the multitude of tiny impacts.

Rinsing the remaining acid off my hands I noticed that despite my precautions my shirt and trousers were also spotted, so with the rag thoroughly soaked in fresh water I dabbed the more conspicuous of the already-diluted markings.

What a fiasco! I'd endangered my job, the lab, the entire building and perhaps even Mr. Bitwood's and Mr. Margolin's lives! To salvage and try to contain the entire mess, the best thing would be to clean the flask quickly and start distilling the next sample. Then, while that progressed, I'd begin attending to what would be an extensive clean-up job. How I'd explain everything to Mr. Hitchcock tomorrow morning was a problem I couldn't cope with right now.

As I rinsed out the cloth, Mr. Smith knocked and came in. "'Ow's it going, matey, got those numbers for us?"

"Not yet, not yet, it won't be long." He didn't look around or seem to notice the acid spots.

"Welp, we gotta 'ave those numbers for the A.M., lad, so's we can start work proper like, early tomorrow."

"Yes, I'll have the distillations finished soon, I'll bring out the numbers as soon as I have them, it won't be long."

He left. I checked out the cleanup job more closely; there were spots all over the bench, the equipment and the floor, and even the storage bottle labels over on the shelves at the other end of the lab were dappled. As I expected, the spots turned out to be too small and diluted to actually pop or explode under the wet rag again, but nevertheless it took practically an hour to do just the bench. Each cleaned spot left behind a shiny silver dot on the sheet metal, and wiping off the red-outlined white bottle labels with their carefully printed names left them looking even worse than before I started.

I continued cleaning, progressing to the distinct little marks on Mr. Hitchcock's wood desk top, where I finally had to rub in a little floor dirt to camouflage the more egregious damage. While I did this, the second distillation finished. Mr. Smith would come in again any minute, so on the third sample I tried the flame a little higher to try to hurry it along, then resumed the clean-up job.

A swishing sound; I turned around, the brown toluol-tar mixture had frothed up inside the flask's neck and was running directly through the Liebig condenser and squirting out the end into the receiving beaker. As I rushed over to turn out the Bunsen burner and cool off the flask, the door opened again.

Mr. Smith: "Well matey it's six o'clock, should 'ave 'ad those numbers ready." He looked at the brown liquid in the beaker, then at me holding the flask high out of the hot sand with an asbestos glove. Thank goodness he didn't realize it all meant I'd messed up the third sample.

"Alright, I'm sorry, I'll be out with all the numbers in ten minutes; Mr. Hitchcock's not here, I had to do everything myself this afternoon."

"I knows, 'is motor car ain't 'ere."

"He had to go, it was urgent with his wife, she's pregnant."

"Hmm, well...."

"Maybe she was ill."

"Well, that don't 'elp us in the yard, do it, mate?"

"Ten minutes, just ten minutes I'll have the numbers."

The third sample was messed up, and I didn't have any time left to redo it. I would just have to fake those numbers based on the first and second samples. As he closed the door behind him I began figuring: the morning numbers had been 76 percent distillate, 13 pitch, 8 water and 3 percent ash. I'd keep the ash number constant, add and subtract a few points on the others, and keep my fingers crossed. Five minutes later he looked in the window. I'd written down the contrived numbers but to make them seem more legitimate I waited a few more minutes before presenting them. Mr. Hitchcock had faith in my handling the job, but if in addition to the smudged bottle labels and the silver spots on the bench tops he discovered any residual tar film on the beaker and other equipment he might get suspicious that the flask had boiled over, so I started meticulously cleaning out the beaker and the condenser; I still had no idea how I'd explain why the lab looked like it had the measles. Through the window I signaled to Mr. Smith, then went out and handed him the faked figures. Back inside, I poured the remaining contents of the flask down the sink; at least the residue wasn't baked hard this time, and with a little solvent I was able to get the flask completely clean.

Then — catastrophe: washing the flask, as I turned I accidently struck the bulb against the metal edge of the sink. That didn't break the flask directly, but it slipped out of my grasp, fell to the floor, spun around under the sink and hit the metal drain pipe. In dread I looked down and the entire neck, including the thin distillation arm, had snapped off. I'd actually broken a distillation flask! They were special Pyrex glass, expensive, one pound twelve and six each, almost one week's wages!

There was no way I could rationalize this culminating accident to Mr. Hitchcock. My first thought was: dispose of the broken distillation flask, say nothing, and tomorrow use the one spare we kept in the cupboard, hoping he wouldn't notice it gone. If he said anything, I'd have to plead ignorance about who could have taken it — unless there were some subtle difference between the two flasks that he'd recognize and know I was using the spare. In trepidation I removed the extra flask from the cupboard and compared it minutely with the broken one; they seemed to be identical. And, the only really safe way to dispose of the old one would be to take it home with me, so I retrieved my brown-paper lunch bag from the bin and placed the pieces inside.

I checked the coin mold. I'd better take that home too, even if the jostling would weaken the casting; if, when Mr. Hitchcock found the bottle labels spattered, he looked behind and found the mold, I'd be out of a job for sure. So I continued cleaning the acid stains off the bench top, the ceiling over the sink, the walls and window, Mr. Hitchcock's desk, his papers and the bottles and labels. The clock read eight P.M. when I finally left the lab, with the bag containing the broken flask pieces rolled up in one hand, the mold in its little box held horizontally in the other. Outside, the night was cold and raining, in darkness except for one light by the gate.

As I approached I was surprised by Mr. Smith stepping out of the shadows. "Oh! I didn't know anyone was here still!" Normally if I stayed late I'd unlatch the lock and swing the gate closed myself. I wondered how many of my string of misfortunes he might have observed through the lab window.

"Stuff to take care of in the yard. Now I'm 'ere, might as well see the whole place is all locked up, like." He looked at the items I carried. "What'cha got in your 'ands there?"

"Oh, nothing."

"Nothing?"

"It's not important, just a tiny box, a cardboard box."

"So long as you ain't knockin' orf the place."

The rain was spattering on the paper bag.

"Knocking off? No. It's nothing. It's just a tiny box." I held up that hand. "I'm bringing it back tomorrow, I'll show you when I bring it back."

"Then what'cha taking it 'ome for if you're bringin' it back in the mornin'?"

"I... I have to study it at home tonight. The bag..." I had to take a chance "...the bag, it's my lunch, I didn't eat it all."

The bag was already sodden and as I tightened my grip I felt the broken glass pieces inside move against each other.

"You scientist types, I dunno, you're all a bit bonkers if you ask me."

The gate clanged shut behind me. Belatedly I put the mold in my pocket; if I'd done that before getting to the gate I wouldn't have had two things to explain away. In the freezing rain I trotted to the bus stop and hoped I wouldn't have a long wait for a bus. The street lamp illuminated a mist rolling up from the Thames. In the darkness, a figure in a black coat with a turned-up collar and hat was also waiting for the bus. "Excuse me, there is another bus tonight, isn't there?" I asked.

He turned my way, and in the drizzly light he gulped: "Zachary Grossman?"

It was Reuben! "Reuben Berger!"

"What *you* doing here?" he asked.

"What are *you* doing here?" I thought he was in prison! But now, the way my response mimicked his but corrected the grammar, I realised he might think I was mocking him. He looked at the sodden paper bag in my hand. "It's broken glass, don't touch it."

"Why're you carrying a wet paper bag of broken glass in the freezing rain, miles from your house?" Reuben had a way of making everything a person said sound like a lie.

"I'm taking it home."

"Home? Why're you taking it home? The bag's gonna burst any minute."

"I had an accident."

"An accident?"

"Yes."

"What sort of an accident?"

"Well... it's a bit complicated, I work in a laboratory."

"A laboratory? I don't believe it is broken glass in that bag."

"I'm not asking whether you believe me or not. But if you grab this bag like you grabbed that tracer shell from Jack that night, it'll burst and you'll get your hand cut to ribbons."

The sound of an approaching vehicle rose up through the rattle of sleet on the roadway.

"I think you're bluffing."

"Christ, not again! Anyway, weren't you supposed to be in prison?"

He paused. "Prison? Here comes the bus."

"That's right."

"That was the *News Of The World*, they got it all wrong."

As the array of sparkling lights emerging from the waterlogged dark resolved into a bus, the bottom dropped out of the weakened bag and the flask remnants smashed to the pavement. Reuben jumped in surprise; one foot slipped down the curb and he fell backwards into a puddle of mixed slush and freezing rain, right in the path of the bus bearing down on us.

I hated his bullying nature: I had one second to decide whether he should live or die. But before I could seriously ponder the issue, I'd already grabbed his hand and pulled him up out of the puddle and back onto the pavement. The bus slid to a stop, squashing his hat. With such poor visibility the driver was probably unaware of the drama that had just unfolded below his windshield.

Reuben boarded first, whilst with my foot I pushed the broken glass pieces off the edge of the curb. I hoped Mr. Smith wouldn't be coming this way for the bus and maybe recognize the glass shapes, but with the bus ready to leave there was nothing I could do. The road sweepers would pick up the pieces early in the morning; Mr. Hitchcock would drive by much later in his little two-seater MG, but there was no reason for him to notice any pieces the sweepers might miss.

Stepping up onto the bus platform I saw rivulets streaming onto the floor from the back of Reuben's water-sodden coat. I didn't want to sit next to him, and he resolved that matter for me when without a word he clambered toward the front of the empty bus alone. He didn't seem to be inviting me, and so I took a seat mid-way. Neither of us spoke across that chasm for the entire twenty-five minute ride, and the bus finally rolled across Mile End Road to the next stop on Grove Road. We both alighted, and in the cold drizzle we walked side by side, though a good couple of feet apart, and silently turned the corner to begin the length of Morgan Street.

"That was the *News Of The World*, they got the name wrong." Then he added without looking my way: "And I don't believe you really work in a laboratory."

"Reuben, that is your prerogative."

He was shivering, he'd probably get pneumonia from sitting for nearly half an hour in ice-caked clothes, yet with all that he was still ready for an argument. "I'll believe it when I see it," he grumbled.

Reuben had always been such a preposterous boaster as well as a bully that it was difficult to squander an opportunity. "You really want to see it, where I work?"

"Well, at least then I'd know you're telling the truth."

"Alright, you can come and see it. It'd have to be late, after everyone has gone."

"Why?"

"Because... well, they wouldn't like me showing it."

"What, is it secret or something, now you're telling me you're doing secret research?"

"As a matter of fact it is secret and I'm really not supposed to divulge it to anyone, but you are an old acquaintance that I can trust."

He paused. "Okay."

"You can come one night late, I'll stay late and show you the place."

"So, when?"

"I'll let you know when it's convenient, I can't have you just show up casually in the middle of an experiment." He was quiet, so I added convivially: "And where do *you* work?"

"In the City."

"What do you do?"

He considered. "I'm delivering secret government packages, but I'm going to be actually writing the stuff soon."

Maybe he was working for India Imports, with Miss Eunice, taking cotton swabs to the Post, pretending it was important!

"I used to work in the City," I said. Would Miss Eunice want to kiss someone like him, ugly and tough, almost like a *yock?*

"You did? What did you do?"

I hadn't thought about it but maybe Miss Eunice wasn't Jewish; that would mean she was used to kissing *yocks.* "Well," I said, "it was the City, and also another place, my work was split between these two places. It was so important that when I left they made me sign a paper saying I'd never tell anyone what I did."

"They did? So what were you working on, then?"

"I can't tell anyone," I said.

"I'm not really interested, I just sort of wondered. I mean, you said you're gonna let me see the laboratory."

"Yes, certainly I can arrange that.... I would tell you about the other place but you'd have to promise you won't repeat it to anyone."

"Alright."

"You have to specifically promise, you have to say the actual words."

He finally looked directly at me. "I promise I won't say anything," he said.

This was wonderful! "Okay. Well, I was working for the government on the Copenhagen Interpretation."

"The what?"

"The Copenhagen Interpretation."

"What's that?"

"It's about quantum mechanics, scientific stuff, it's not easy to explain."

"Copenhagen, that's just the name of a place."

"Just! Neils Bohr made some pretty incredible discoveries there, we used his stuff when I was alternating between our office in the City — and Harwell."

"You were in Harwell? I read about that place in the *News Of The World,* they were doing atomic energy there."

"Well... alright, so now you've guessed, we were working on a British atomic bomb."

"The atomic bomb! I don't believe you."

"We were all quite surprised there to find out we did need the Copenhagen Interpretation to work out the formulas. It was complicated, it took me a while to learn even though I used to go to Coopers College." He didn't respond, so I continued. "It's related to why the moon isn't really there — unless you're actually in Harwell, looking at it."

"That sounds stupid."

"It's interesting you should say that, because for a while even I wondered. Listen, I can't give you a comprehensive run-down in three minutes. I told you it's complicated, it took me years." Icy rain continued to fall as we passed the desolate fenced-in remains of Coopers College, and I nodded deferentially toward the remaining rubble.

He mumbled: "Hmm. So when can I see the laboratory?"

"I'll try to schedule it within the next couple of weeks. I'll find out what's a good night and let you know."

"Alright, give me the address."

"I'll give you the location when I contact you."

"Hmm." He thought for a minute, "Alright then." As we approached my house I peeled off to cross over the road, and he mumbled a barely audible: "So long then."

I responded, even more quietly, "Good night, Reuben." And, like Humphrey Bogart, added: "I'll be in touch."

32

It was about nine when I opened the street door. In the passageway I shook the rain off my coat, draped it over the passage bannister and came in the living room. "It's horrible out."

Lily and Katherine were talking at the table. "Did you eat?"

"No, I've been at the lab 'til now — all sorts of things, I broke a flask."

"Ee, will you lose your job then?"

"No, I don't think so, it's not *that* serious."

"Alright, sit, sit, you didn't eat, I'll get you your dinner."

"Hello, Katya."

"Hello, we got a letter."

As I sat down the street door opened again and Abie walked in. Lily called from the kitchen, "I'll get his dinner, I'll get both your dinners, sit down."

"Hello, Dad."

"Eee, the weather, it's like terrible, were you outside?"

"Yes, I just got home from work also."

Lily came in with my plate as Abie hung up his coat.

"Here's the letter," said Katherine confidentially to me as she slid a handwritten page into my hand. It was from Rebecca: *Dear Mum, Everything is going according to plan here. I got an extra bed in my apartment for the time being, and Zilly loves it here. She's a secretary on Wall Street already, they love her English accent, she's earning thirty-five dollars a week, more than my wages, although I get tips. We're both saving as much as possible, we'll be getting the tickets for you and Maudy in just a few months, don't worry.*

Lily was already placing a heavily loaded plate in front of Abie's chair.

"Wow! So you really will be going!" As I uttered the words, Lily flashed a horrified glance at me.

"Ssh!" Katherine grabbed the letter, folded it up into her pocket and began reading a newspaper.

The massive silence that followed as Abie sat down told me I'd done a clumsy, stupid thing: Abie didn't know yet that Mum would also be going to America.

"Going? Going? Oo's going?"

"Nothing, nothing," said Lily, "nobody's going anywhere."

"What's going on, oo's going, where you going?"

"I'm going to go, to America, next year," said Katherine. I was shriveled at what I'd done.

"You're going, so go already," said Abie.

I ate a potato, then crept into the kitchen, ostensibly to make a cup of tea.

Katherine followed me in. "Christ, why did you say that?"

"I don't know, I forgot she was keeping it a secret."

"He'd kill her if he knew."

"What a stupid thing for me to say, I don't know, I just had a hectic day at the lab, things going wrong."

"Well, it's done already, let's hope he doesn't catch on. I'm going up."

"Alright, I'll be up soon as I finish eating. I hope everything'll be alright."

"There's no point in worrying, now. When you come up I'll come in with you for a few minutes."

I ate, sipped my tea and made small talk with Lily about the goings on at the lab. Abie just sat there behind the newspaper slowly eating his supper — not a word, and when the newspaper moved I couldn't detect anything in his expression.

Upstairs I undressed and got into bed, while in the other bed Marius snored. Katherine came in and sat on my covers. "You know," she said softly, "Benny keeps asking me to marry him."

"Really, you're only fifteen!"

"Girls get married at fifteen."

"Do they really, so young?"

"Anyway, I'll be sixteen in a couple of months."

"What about Artemis, though."

"Artemis's parents wouldn't have let him marry me, they want him to marry someone rich."

"I thought they had money, they own a restaurant."

"They don't have much, but anyway people with money only let their kids marry other people with money."

This was another of those conundrums that Katherine uttered with such certitude. "But if they have money already, then it wouldn't matter if the other person doesn't...."

Downstairs, I heard the settee being opened.

"Zech, take my word for it that's not the way it works. So, I have to think about it; marrying Benny wouldn't be the worst thing in the world, if I didn't have to see so much of his mother."

"But why do you have to get married now anyway?"

"If Mum's going to be going soon with Maudy, I don't know... it would just be the two of us here with Abie. Zech, you can always come and stay over, I'll insist, I'll tell Benny I won't marry him otherwise."

Downstairs there came a thud, then the smashing of crockery, and Abie's voice thundered: "Go, go to America with all your *becuckter* kids, go already, I'll be glad to get rid of you."

Marius was suddenly sitting bolt upright. From downstairs, Lily was crying. I dreaded going down there to the same old screaming and punching. But before I had time to move, Marius had jumped up off his bed and pulled out from underneath his mattress what looked in the darkness like a heavy stick. He rushed out the bedroom door with it and raced downstairs; I'd never seen him move so fast. Katherine followed directly behind, and I brought up a reluctant third place. We followed as Marius bounded along the darkened passage. And then, to my amazement, with a decisive flat of his bare foot to the door panel above the handle, Marius burst open the living room door. Light flooded toward us and I saw that the thing he held in his right hand was not a stick: it was a gun, a rifle. Standing in the frame of the doorway he lifted the weapon to his shoulder and took straight aim at Abie, who was standing beyond the bottom of the opened settee. Lily sat sobbing on the settee's far edge, the handkerchief she held to her face preventing her from realizing what was happening.

Abie had swung around at the violent intrusion, and it took a moment to dawn on him that Marius was pointing a gun directly at his head. He stopped, his face became chalk white, and his jaw moved up, then down: "What, what, wha'cha...."

The only movement in the room was Lily's handkerchief fluttering to her lap. *"Oy a broch!"*

Silence, and for several seconds the incredible tableau held. Abie suddenly giggled in disbelief, then his face became severe; then, awkwardly, he giggled again. Still nobody had moved a limb, not even he, and the scene once again fell to a fantastical stillness. After a bizzare interlude where the loud ticking of the clock on the mantelpiece resounded as the sole arbiter of reality, I realized Abie had slowly begun to move. Immeasurable at first, forward, sideways, even back, but overall he was inching incrementally closer to the doorway where Marius stood framed in the lighted rectangle, ahead of Katherine, ahead of me.

Marius recognized the feint. "Stop! Stop it, stay there, I'll, I'll...." He was already breathless, and in seeming trepidation he faltered, the tip of the barrel declining half an inch. An emboldened Abie continued perceptibly closer; Marius had caught himself, and the rifle was back up, pointing directly at Abie's face. It was difficult to absorb what I was seeing: Marius in his striped, wrinkled sleeping suit standing up ahead in the doorway, his back to Katherine and me, holding a rifle pointed directly at Abie's face now less than six feet away; Mum sitting beyond and to the left on the edge of the settee, aghast, unable to move; the clock's ticks marking off each protracted second. During any of these epochs, Marius's squeeze on the trigger might cause the gun to go off and, assuming it was loaded, Abie would fall dead. Abie would actually be dead and everything would be irrevocably changed — if Marius aimed right, and if a single bullet would have the power to kill him. He was so strong it might well take several, each of them requiring the bolt to be first pulled back then plunged forward again to reload a new cartridge, each shot carefully aimed, each of these separate acts enlisting a cumulation of loud ticks from the clock on the mantelpiece beyond our view. But Marius could never manage all that; he might fire once, and if a bullet hit Abie at all it would only graze him, maybe disturb the hair on the side of his head. Abie would swell to full size and come after us and kill the three of us, and after that, Mum as well. In the echoing ramble of time I found myself calmly reckoning: if Marius did shoot Abie, hit him even superficially, the police probably wouldn't allow him to go to America; he'd be in prison and the extra ticket would be wasted. Maybe Katherine would go instead, with Lily; then I'd be here in London alone in the house, with Abie in hospital. I didn't earn enough money for rent — assuming I still had a job. I'd have to move out. Maybe I could live with Jack; his mother was nice, maybe they'd let me move in with them.

Reality pulled together the meandering scatter of thoughts: Abie was significantly closer, and again the barrel wavered. Then, so unexpectedly that all of us jumped, Abie swerved violently to our left and down, ducking his head way under the barrel as he lunged forward, almost falling forward beneath the gun. A massive blue-veined hand reached up and grabbed the middle of the barrel from underneath, in one swoop pulling Marius forward into the room and wrenching the rifle from his grip. Continuing the same circular sweep, and without a word, Abie swung the rifle sideways, away, then brought the butt of the rifle back, back up toward the face, where he smashed its full force into the side of Marius's cheek just above the jaw. A dull, flat, sound. And Marius crumpled silently to the floor.

Lily's scream was blood-curdling: *"Oy a broch,* he killed him, he killed him, quick, quick, do something, get an ambulance, he killed him, he killed him...." Freed from paralysis she rushed across to where Marius's crumpled form lay in front of us. She toppled to her knees and picked up the lifeless shoulders. Abie had fallen back into the middle of the room, still holding the rifle at its center point. Mum screamed again, "Get an ambulance, quick, some-body get an ambulance!" Marius's face looked deep blue and red, with big pulsing blobs of blackish crimson blood pumping out of a gash in front of his ear.

"I'll run to the kiosk on Mile End Road," I gasped.

"You go, I'll stay and help Mum." Katherine's face was drained white.

I pulled open the street door; cold rain was still falling so I grabbed my wet coat off the bannister and leaped down the high steps into the street. As it dawned on me my feet were bare and I was in my sleeping suit, I pulled the coat over me. Running along the pavement and into the roadway to cut across Tredegar Square, the stones tore at my feet. I ran fast through the rain, as fast as I could, but with a strangely muted sense of urgency. I raced out of the far corner of the park and loped and splattered along the street toward Mile End Road where the two red telephone kiosks stood side by side across the road outside the station. While I ran I calmly assessed the implications should Marius die: the police would come, and Abie would be arrested for murder. Maybe Marius was already dead, right now; the possi-bility existed.

Two men walking along the pavement of Mile End Road under a wide umbrella backed off as I ran between them. Inside the kiosk a small placard read: *EMERGENCY: for police, fire and ambulance, dial 999.* I'd forgotten to bring money; luckily, for emergency calls the card said none was needed.

"Quick, we need an ambulance, my brother, I think he's dead."

"Alright, where is your brother?" From nowhere I suddenly started to cry, to sob so that I couldn't speak, a complete reversal from just a moment earlier. The kindly male voice came through the earpiece: "We'll be there right away, just tell us where he is so we can come right away."

I managed to stumble out the address, which the man repeated clearly; then, "Alright, you go right back, stay with your brother 'til we get there, that's a good lad. Don't let anyone move him, just stay there with him."

My hair soaked, rain running down my face, I loped at a steady pace back to the house, feeling yet again inexplicably quiet and composed. Marius, dead! He and I never had been close the way I was with Katherine, partly because it was so hard to talk to him; we were like different species. Trotting through the park I saw the soggy lights of the ambulance streak-ing along Morgan Street, heard the quiet *bong! bong!* of the bell — so quick! They would be there before me; this way I wouldn't have to be in charge, wouldn't have to know what needed to be done, I could delay knowing whether he were alive or dead.

As I exited the park and sprinted across Tredegar Terrace one man had already jumped out of the ambulance's cab and was knocking on the door. "Yes, that's the house," I shouted across.

Katherine opened the street door. "Oh god, quick, in here, in here."

The man entered and I pulled myself up the steps after him and cautiously looked into the room. Marius's frame seemed more straightened out now, less like a crumpled doll. The man kneeled over him, and as he dabbed his face and felt the jaw-bone I saw Marius's arm twitch; Lily and Abie stood stricken side by side at the foot of the settee.

"How is he, will he be alright?" Lily's voice quavered.

"He's moaning, that's a good sign."

"*Oy,* what can we do, what can I do....?"

"A bowl of clean warm water, missus, then leave it to us."

In a moment Mum was back in the room with a bowl. "It's nearly cold, I put other water on, it'll take a minute to get warm, will he be alright?"

I draped my macintosh back over the bannister, and wiped my head and feet with a towel from the kitchen. In the living room the kneeling ambulance man was bathing blood from Marius's face; every time he came near the jaw Marius moaned and pulled away slightly. "Looks like he broke his jaw." He tested areas, carefully touching around the head, neck and shoulders. "How did it happen?" The second man had a stretcher up the steps.

"He... he... there was a...." Lily looked at Abie, but before she could complete the sentence, Abie interrupted. "'E was, 'e was like, 'e... fell, 'e fell over."

As Abie was speaking I realized there was no sign of the rifle.

"Fell, did he? Must have landed real hard." The man stood. "Alright. We'll be taking him to London Hospital." And to his mate, "John, let's get him up and inside."

"Yeh, outside in the yard, the steps there, 'e fell, stone, like slabs they are, stone, 'e must 'a bin running up the steps, we found 'im."

"So, you found him out in the yard and he ended up in here," said the ambulance man quietly. They lay the stretcher down and gently eased Marius onto it. "We'll be taking him to London Hospital, Whitechapel Road."

"One of you can ride with us if you wants to stay with him," said the second man.

"Yeh, Lily, go...."

While Lily got her coat the two men hoisted the stretcher up and, keeping Marius level, toted him down the outside steps and up into the ambulance. The assistant stayed inside the rear with the stretcher, reaching out a hand to help Lily up the little iron step. The driver gently closed the back door and went around to his cab. "Emergency visiting any time, day or night," he called to us. The muffled pummeling of raindrops on the ambulance's roof was broken only by its subdued chime, then by the slapping of the windshield wipers as the vehicle turned around and accelerated smoothly away. Several street doors along Tredegar Terrace were open, people watching.

Abie closed the door. "Eee, uh don't know what got into 'im, did you see? 'Ow 'e could point a real gun at 'is own father!"

"Can you blame him?" The words were out of my mouth before I realized what they meant.

"Zech, don't start everything again," said Katherine.

"Start, start! Didn'cha see, 'e 'ad a gun, a real gun, a *meshuggener,* 'e was pointing it straight at me, uh would'a bin dead!"

"Where's the gun?" I asked.

"In the cupboard, uh 'id it for the ambulance men, disgusting it is, behind the shoes, eee, can you believe it?"

I felt behind the mound of orphaned shoes compressed into the cupboard. The gun lay along the back behind them, and I pulled it out. It was a bolt action rifle, identical to the one

Uncle Albert had shown me. I pulled the bolt up and back, and sure enough a bullet in its brass casing popped up. The bolt's knob slipped out of my still-wet fingers and the bullet of its own accord jumped out of the breech and landed atop the nearby folded-down sheet on the open settee. As I reached for it, it slid down the back of the soft pillow, through the springs, and the three of us stood watching as it bounced to the wooden floor beneath the settee and rolled noisily in a large arc, coming to rest against the open cupboard door.

•　　•　　•

Lily returned home by taxi around three A.M., and Katherine and I came downstairs to hear her report. Abie got the umbrella and went outside to explain to the taxi driver that Lily thought she was coming home on the bus; she was so nervous about her son in hospital she accidently got in the taxi by mistake. When the driver said everybody knows buses don't run at three o'clock in the morning, that's what they have taxis for, Abie rolled up the umbrella and started poking it through the opened driver's window. I gently eased the street door closed without locking it, then went into the living room.

The London Hospital had gotten Marius what they called *stabilized*, Lily reported. The bleeding had stopped, his jaw had definitely been broken, and he possibly had a skull fracture. If no further internal injuries became manifest, and if there was no uncontrollable problem with his breathing then he was not in critical danger of dying.

Lily said she would go back to hospital in the morning. Abie came in, slamming the street door; he wouldn't go to hospital, what for?, Maudy started it all, like a *meshuggeiner* 'e is, 'e must 'ave gotten the gun from 'is lousy *yockisher* friends. Katherine said she would take the day off and go with Lily to hospital, and if Anya didn't like it she could fuck herself. I said I absolutely *had* to get to the laboratory early to check everything before Mr. Hitchcock got there, otherwise I wouldn't have a job. We all retired to our respective beds.

I arose at seven, had a quick cup of tea, prepared my lunch, and remembered to include the coin mold in the lunch bag. It was about eight-thirty when I arrived at work, early enough to take care of anything I could have missed that Mr. Hitchcock might notice. A couple of workmen saw me as I entered the yard, and started toward me.

"Fuckin' Jewboy barstard, we'll get you," one of them called out.

I pretended I didn't hear, and continued walking toward the laboratory. One of the men ran around in front of me to stand in my way. Out of the corner of my eye I saw Mr. Smith over by tank number three, and I called out some fabricated question about the batch. He started to come over.

"Fuckin' Jews; they ain't one as ain't as bad as the other," said the vicious-looking tar-blackened member of the duo in front of me.

"You murderin' barstard Jewfucks," said the other, "you're all the same! Why'n'cha go back where you come from."

At that, Mr. Smith intervened. "Now let's 'ave none of that talk 'ere. I knows 'ow you feels, lads, but this 'ere bloke 'e ain't got nothin' to do with it."

"Old Schicklegrüber, 'e should 'ave finished the job, we'd all be better orf."

"Alright, back to work now, both of you." The two of them slouched off toward the wharf.

"What's going on? What happened?" I asked Mr. Smith.

"Don't you read the newspaper?" I must have seemed nonplussed. "Alright," he continued, "go to the lab, I'll bring you the paper."

Of course Mr. Hitchcock hadn't arrived yet, though there was always the possibility that he could show up early. I hung my coat on the hook and began immediately with a wet cloth. Some of the little whitish spots on the wooden desk seemed permanent, where the acid had eaten through the stain finish. A minute later Mr. Smith walked into the lab without knocking, and unrolled the *Daily Express* on the bench top, the paper covering half a dozen acid-silvered spots which he didn't notice.

The front page showed a photo of two British soldiers hanged by their necks from trees — members of the British Palestine Expeditionary Force, the caption read, the bodies discovered in a eucalyptus grove. And across the whole page the headline read: *Hanged Britons: picture that will shock the world.* The text elaborated: four British soldiers, two N.C.O.'s and two privates, kidnapped and murdered by the *Irgun Zvai Leumi.*

"It's a rotten business wiv them there Jews, Palestine, you know. You can't blame the lads outside, angry like. Four of our own, murdered, 'angin' there like they was criminals. 'Ow would you feel? Wish we'd finish the job there quick like, bring the boys back 'ome. Alright, Grossman, I'll talk to the lads, try to get 'em to lay orf you, I know it ain't directly your fault."

I went out to the yard to collect the first sample from the new delivery. Nobody came near me, but a couple of workmen stopped their shoveling in one of the big flat evaporation trays and leaned on their handles, their eyes following me as I walked over to the tank. After I'd collected the samples and climbed back down, they stopped work again to silently watch me return to the lab. Back inside, using the new flask I began the first distillation, at the same time continuing to clean up as well as I could the remaining evidence of yesterday's mishap. I found myself double checking that the door was clicked shut, so I'd hear if anybody opened it. By ten o'clock I'd done as much as I reasonably could. Mr. Hitchcock still hadn't arrived; he'd promised he would get there early, but he was even later than usual.

At ten-fifteen, Mr. Bitwood came down from the office. "Grossman, I got some news for you. Mr. Hitchcock won't be coming back to work anymore."

"What!"

"Mr. Margolin gave him the sack. Told him his heart wasn't in the job, taking all that time off and stuff. So now you're in charge 'til we get another chemist."

I couldn't believe my good fortune — there was no longer anyone to whom I'd need explain the acid spots, nor, as I thought about it, even the broken flask! And also I'd have much more latitude to mint coins and do my own experiments! But I did have to tell them about the possibility of my being drafted. "In a few months I might be leaving. Did Mr. Hitchcock tell you?"

"Leaving?" Bitwood's face clouded. "No, he didn't say anything to us! Why're you leaving? Mr. Margolin can probably pay you a bit more now, if you talk to him nice. I know he's very satisfied with your work."

"No...."

"But don't look like you're trying to take advantage. That won't go down well with him."

"No, I might have to go to National Service. I have to register in a few months, then if they draft me I'd have to leave."

"National Service!" He looked mortified.

"I definitely told Mr. Hitchcock."

"This is terrible, he didn't report it to the office. I'll have to tell Mr. Margolin right away." He glanced vacantly around the room, oblivious to the acid stains. "Alright then, for the time being you're in charge, and if anything's wrong you report directly to me. 'Specially if the samples test out too much water. Alright? You know how to do it all, don't you?"

"I can handle everything."

"Good lad, Zachary. That's why Mr. Margolin's been so pleased with you, we can always count on you."

I closed the door behind him. What fantastic luck! I grabbed the bottles and ran outside and up the ladder to collect the remaining tar samples. As I scaled the tank again and hung on the upper rungs of the ladder to unscrew the sample-bottle's lid, down on the ground the same two laborers who had accosted me stood watching.

Back in the lab I set the bottles down, checked the distillation and flame height, and got out my coin mold. Now that Mr. Hitchcock was out of the picture I didn't even have to wait for the afternoon! I spread a film of Vaseline over the top surface of the mold with the two-shilling-piece still embedded, added an inch of new calcium sulphate paste on top of the old, tapping it down to remove air bubbles, then put it away on the shelf again to set. Everything was hidden behind the bottles just in case anyone came poking around.

By the time I'd eaten lunch, gone to the lavatory and flipped quickly through *An Experiment With Time* by James W. Dunne, the mold had set sufficiently hard. The top and bottom came apart easily because of the Vaseline, and I eased the two-shilling piece out, careful not to damage the indented milled edges. Acetone cleaned off the Vaseline. The second distillation had just finished, and I placed the mold in the hot sand bath to dry it off quickly. In my anxiety I was a bit too hasty, and residual acetone that must have been trapped in the calcium sulphate vaporized and popped into flame. I blew it out with no problem, but accidently knocked over the sand bath and spilled sand onto the bench and floor. I stood still, and breathed deeply and slowly; maybe I was more disturbed by the laborers outside than I'd acknowledged. I swept up as much sand as I could, but it seemed too contaminated for the sand bath; the bits of dirt would smoulder and even catch fire when I lit the Bunsen burner. So I put the bath aside completely and replaced it with a wire gauze that had an embedded circle of asbestos. This setup certainly wasn't as safe, and would need careful monitoring. I began the new distillation, and where part of the flame flickered around the edge of the asbestos and played directly onto the glass the toluol mixture did boil fiercely, but by keeping the flame low the situation was controllable.

With a fine round file I incised a thin conical pour hole and a straight air-vent hole in the bottom half of the coin mold, painting both facing surfaces with sodium silicate to make them more durable. When that dried, I clamped the two halves together in a stand. Just the way the men in the hut at the end of our garden had made lead soldiers before the war, I melted lead pellets in a crucible over a Bunsen burner on the other bench, and poured.

I let it set, then eased the mold apart. The resultant coin was perfectly shaped even to its fine milled edge, but it was dull and discolored as though it had been in a fire. Dropping it on the bench produced only a flat-sounding thud. Maybe an alloy would produce a more authentic ring. Scouring the now-comfortably-spotted shelves for ingredients I ended up with a mixture of about sixty percent lead, forty percent tin, with just a touch of bismuth and antimony.

I retraced the melting and pouring procedure. After filing off the tiny pour- and blow-hole appendages the resulting coin was beautiful, with a newly-minted-florin shine and precisely milled edge! And, dropping it carefully on the bench, it rang out sweet and true. On a level with singing, scientific experiments were what I really loved most, though they consumed a lot of time! So I needed to quickly clean the flask and get on with the next tar sample. Because of using just the wire mesh with the asbestos circle instead of the sand bath, I had to be extremely careful setting up the distillation. I kept my eyes on it the whole time, while I experimented with producing a few more coins. Everything went very well, and by four-thirty I was able to give Mr. Smith the numbers.

When I got home, on the table was a note from Katherine: Lily stayed at hospital all day, and she, Katherine, was going back again to be with her. The doctors had moved Marius to a special ward where he was strapped in a bed so he couldn't move his head or jaw; he'd be there for a few weeks until the bones set. There would be nothing I could do, and anyway Marius couldn't speak yet, so there was no need for me to go to hospital. They'd both be back later.

After a bite to eat I went over to Jack's house to show him my freshly-minted cache. He wasn't as impressed as I'd hoped.

"My advice is don't make anymore."

"Why?"

"You can go to prison for it."

"Prison?"

"Of course, it's forgery. It's counterfeiting Her Majesty's coin of the realm."

I'd only meant it as an experiment; I hadn't thought about prison. "Then maybe I shouldn't tell Izzy in case he says something to his friends."

"Maybe we shouldn't tell anyone. They wouldn't understand you're doing it for scientific reasons." Jack was right: I'd put myself to the scientific test, the experiment had been a complete success, and now I had to destroy the mold. I felt a bit sad about it, after all the careful work. It would have been nice to show people a coin, then surprise them by saying I made it myself. I even could have looked like I had extra money if I bumped into Katherine and Hazel at Johnny Isaacs. But I would destroy the mold. He was right. I positively would destroy the mold.

—o—O—o—

–33–

After three weeks, Marius was discharged from hospital. His bandaged and taped face was still somewhat swollen and discolored when Lily took him to the American Embassy to initiate their applications for visas. He was scheduled to return to hospital in about a week for removal of the dressings that secured and protected his broken jaw until the bone was adequately healed. At the embassy, Lily admonished him to present his injury as the result of a fall.

They obtained their passports shortly after Marius's bandages were finally removed, though he was still not sufficiently recovered to attend the wedding of Katherine and Benny that took place in the clerk's office in the Aldgate Municipal Building. Lily had said of course she wanted to attend the wedding, but the day before it took place she told Katherine she couldn't manage because of the rush of preparations for their departure — getting Marius to the Embassy for his final examination, buying extra clothes for the two of them, another suitcase, etc.

In fact the only two witnesses to the wedding were Benny's mother Bessie, and me. Mr. Margolin gave me the morning off for the occasion — as many hours as necessary, he'd said, don't feel you have to rush back — provided I stayed a bit later at the lab the preceding evening to analyze one additional tank's samples so that Mr. Smith and the yard could continue production without a holdup that day.

At the clerk's office Katherine introduced me to Bessie, a fat short woman with blotchy red skin and thick lips drenched in orange lipstick. When I extended my hand and said, Pleased to meet you Mrs. Cohen, without looking in my direction she shook the tip of my finger and let go; not a word, nor did she look my way again. Katherine and Benny took their places in a short queue for the brief ceremony, which Bessie and I officially witnessed. Then we all followed Benny outside to the public telephone where he rang someone up and said he'd be back in half an hour.

Benny had arranged for Katherine to return to Anya's Fashion Footwear to complete the day's work. When she and I were riding back on the bus, I asked her if she minded going to work on her wedding day.

"I feel pretty shitty about it, he said we'll need the money. He went back to his place also."

"Who was he talking to on the phone?"

"Rosalind, the cheap tart in the office where he works."

"Oh, you know her?"

"I feel like I do. He has to show the foreman he's a hard worker, he says. I suppose he's practical."

"I see...."

"He said we'll put the extra toward a honeymoon. He promised we'd go to Scotland for two days as soon as we can afford it."

"Katya... I hope everything will be alright, you don't seem ever so happy."

"Ugh, I can't worry about it, I'll see how things work out. In case you get drafted I didn't want to be left alone with the old shitbag there."

"Yes, I hope I don't. Katya, what happened with Artemis Sunday night? I heard you come home."

She giggled. "I didn't know he was coming round, I had to tell him what was happening with Benny. Christ, I'm glad Benny didn't show up! Thank god Artemis came Sunday, I knew Benny was out with his Brady Boy's Club friends, it was one of those retarded men's-only parties, he still goes there."

"I heard when you came home, it was three A.M."

"Spying on me, huh?" She smiled. "We went for a walk. For god's sake, don't ever say a word to Benny!"

"Of course not. Christ, two nights before your wedding!"

"So what are *you* going to do when Mum leaves, she said, changing the subject! You'll be the one alone there in the house with the old fucker. You know I told Benny you can sleep on the settee in our flat whenever you want to. You'd have to run the gauntlet of passing Bessie's door downstairs, though."

"I'll see if I can bear it at home with Abie for a while, I'll see how it is."

"Thank goodness at least you like your job."

"I really do, I love it. I think the owner and the man in the office upstairs like me better than the one they used to have there, Mr. Hitchcock, the one they gave the sack."

"Good. Between a rotten job all day and Abie all night I don't think you'd last long."

We alighted at Burdett Road and I walked her to the shoe shop. As she climbed the steps and entered I heard Anya's voice: "Quick, quick, I got three customers at once, why do you think I pay you fifteen shillings?"

"You remember, I just got married? This morning?"

"Yes, yes already, congratulations, it's alright you'll be alright, he's a hard worker I can tell. You said you were coming straight in afterwards."

"No, you don't have it quite right. *I* didn't say I was coming straight in afterwards, it was my, ahem, husband who said I was."

"What's the difference..." she lowered her voice. "Shh, customers in the shop, I don't want any commotion...."

•   •   •

When I got home from work the evening before Lily's and Marius's departure, Katherine had just come round to help them with last-minute packing.

"Hello, Zech, how's the laboratory? Blown anybody up yet?"

"Not yet, everything's terrific. Haven't seen you in a few days, I'm glad you came now."

Mum brought in a final sandwich and cup of tea for me. "So how's everything with Benny?" she asked Katherine.

"Oh, alright, I suppose."

"What do you mean, is everything alright, is he treating you alright?"

"Well he's alright, he's very selfish."

"That's what it is with men, what did you expect?"

"He wants every single thing for his own convenience."

"Men, they're good for nothing, they expect you to wait on them hand and foot. That's what it is in this life."

"I don't know, it's Bessie as well, she's always sticking her greasy Jew's nose in and taking his side. This morning I told him to go fuck himself, I wasn't coming home tonight."

"Sshh, such language! Really, you told him? Zech, this one's too full, stand on it, Maudy, click it shut, quick, while he's pressing down, go on, careful with your face!"

"'Old it, 'old it," and Marius clicked closed the latches on the bulging suitcase.

"So you're not going back there tonight? *Oy a broch,* what'll he do, he'll... he'll lock you out or something."

"I should worry, so I'll stay here. He'll come round for me after a while, when he needs his dick rubbed."

"Sshh, in front of Maudy!"

"Sorry, Maudy."

"Ooer, I don't care. Crikey, so what did you get married for then?"

"I suppose it was a choice, Abie or Benny. Or Artemis."

"Katya, is Artemis like that," I asked. "I mean, is he selfish?"

Lily answered for her. "They're all the same, they pretend they're nice 'til you get married. The curse of the world, they are."

Around eleven P.M. the four of us paused for a cup of tea.

"It's nice to be able to eat proper food again, 'stead of all that soup," said Marius as he chewed gingerly on a slice of buttered challah.

"What do you mean," said Lily, "I brought chicken soup there every day, it's good for you."

After midnight Abie still was not home. "He's really late tonight," I said. "Did he say he'd be so late?"

"Who knows with him? He's usually home by twelve at least, I don't know."

"You should worry, Mum," said Katherine. "Come on, we'll finish the tea and pack some more."

"We can put a few more things in the steamer, that pullover, there's room," said Lily. "So you'll stay here tonight, it's too late anyway to go back, you missed the last bus."

"I told him I wouldn't be back tonight, oh that's definite, let him *plutz* for one night. Oh, I really mean it!"

"So, what'll you do, go straight to work from here in the morning then?"

"Oh, I forgot to tell you, I told Anya I wanted the morning off to see my mother and brother off to America, and she said, 'What again? More time you want off?' So I told her to shove her fashion footwear up her fat flabby arse and I walked out."

"*Oy a broch,* you mean you don't have a job now?"

"That's right! Benny will be charmed to hear that one!"

"Wow, I hope everything'll be alright," I said.

"Zech, you worry too much. What can happen at the worst, Benny'll tell me to leave for good? So I'll live here, you'll have your baby sister for company."

"Well I wish you did live here now, I don't mean anything about Benny.... I'm earning two pounds at the laboratory, and if Dad pays the rent, mine is enough for both of us for food."

"Thank you Zech, but Benny'll be here to get me as soon as he realizes I'm serious."

Lily put her hand to her face. *"Oy, such problems already!"*

"Lily, so I'll come with Zech to the station in the morning to see you both off. It's all settled, let's change the subject. Zech, I'm glad you like your job, that's very important."

"Yes, what a difference from my old job! Mr. Hitchcock, he was the chemist, he was in charge, he used to come in late and he hardly knew what was going on."

"Then 'ow could 'e 'ave bin in charge if 'e didn't even know what was going on?"

"Some people are like that, Maudy," said Katherine. "So long as nothing goes wrong, as long as Zech didn't set the laboratory on fire or something."

"Crikey!"

"Anyway they gave him the sack because he was always late."

"You should watch out for the *yocks* there," said Lily.

Katherine laughed. "Oh Mum, that's silly!"

"The *yockisher* workmen in those places, the lowest of the low, Zech you be careful, you think Anya's husband didn't have to be careful?"

"What do you mean?" I asked.

"He was making barrels in the factory, he was the only Jewish one there, one night they waited for him. He was lucky someone told him beforehand, he left early, he had to get another job."

"Really? I mean everything was alright at the Cable Electric place."

"Maybe this place is alright, maybe you'll be lucky, you just better be careful, that's all. You'll find out one day, I hope you don't."

"A couple of them started swearing about Jews after that business with the *Irgun* with those soldiers in Palestine."

"You see what I mean? You be careful!"

"But the foreman stopped them right away, I think it's alright there."

"Well you be careful."

As the clock ticked on into the small hours, it became increasingly apparent that Abie would not be coming home this last night. Marius was delighted, but Lily became more and more quiet, busying herself with last-minute details.

"Mum, do you mind that he didn't come home?" Katherine asked around three A.M.

"I don't know, he's probably got a woman there with him at the shop, one of his *becuckter* customers, no wonder he never brought home any money."

"You should care, now."

"You're right, I should care."

We all managed a couple of hours sleep and were up again, immediately it seemed, though the clock said six A.M. After a quick breakfast together — tea, bread and jam — I ran over to Mile End station to secure a taxi, and rode in it back to the house. The driver stood the steamer vertically in the open space beside his seat, and the other cases went in the boot. Lily and Marius bade a farewell to the old house, then while we sat in the back of the taxi Lily found it necessary to go back in alone, despite the running meter, to see if she'd forgotten anything. When she came out, her eyes were wet.

The four of us bore the ride to Waterloo Station in virtual silence. By the time we arrived my head felt thick, and I could barely discern the muffled words of the porter: "Where to, ma'am?" before he clattered the bigger cases away.

"Crikey, we're really going to America!"

As though through a veil, the crowds swirled across the vast marble-floored building in a muted haste. We traversed the hallway and descended the stairs to the number eleven platform. The boat train was already waiting.

"Bye, Maudy, look after Mum," said Katherine.

"And Zachary, you look after Katya, she's ill."

"Ill? Katya, you ill?" I asked.

"Nothing, it'll pass."

I tried unsuccessfully to put an arm around Marius but he seemed so nervous, twitching his eyes, fiddling with two small bags.

"Quick Mum, 'urry up, the train'll go in a minute." He dragged the bags up the steps into the carriage.

"Maudy be careful, your face, Zech help him with the bags."

I helped carry the bags up and lift them onto the overhead racks.

As I turned around, Mum was right behind me. "Look after her, the little stinker she is."

"What is it, what's the matter?"

"All aboard!"

"Quick, get off, quick, quick!"

I ran down the boarding steps. Through the darkened window the two of them were sorting out their seats, arranging things as the train pulled away; they never looked our way, and the last carriage was soon swallowed up into a turbulence of smoke and steam.

"Katya, what is it, Mum said you're ill."

"Oh, nothing, I'll be alright."

"They're gone."

"Yes."

"I wonder what it'll be like."

"We'll see."

"I've got to go back to work, to the laboratory. What are you going to do, you going back to Benny or to Morgan Street?"

"I'll go back to Morgan Street."

"You'll be alright? I'll come right home tonight, after work."

"Alright."

"Funny, the house'll seem deserted, especially if Abie doesn't come home tonight," I said.

"Yes."

"We'll have to make our own dinner."

"Yes."

•   •   •

"Zech, is that you?" the voice called. "I'm upstairs."

"Hello, Katya. You alright?"

"Yes, I'm coming down."

The four cups and plates from the morning breakfast with Lily and Marius, the dirty knives and spoons, still lay on the living room table. The cold tea had lined the cups with incrusted tan and grey circles. First, I'd wash the dishes.

Katherine came in. "I'm sorry, I didn't clean up."

"That's alright, it's not automatically your job just because you're a girl. You don't even live here."

"What do you want to do for dinner," she said. "You must be hungry."

"I suppose there isn't anything in the house. I don't know how to cook anyway."

"I'm not really hungry, do you want to go to Johnny Isaacs?"

"Oh, that's..." I thought... "that's a good idea."

"I was lying in bed upstairs. It's strange not to hear Lily grumbling."

The house was still and empty; I was secretly grateful Katherine was here. "So Benny didn't come round."

"He'd only just be getting home from work now. The first shock will be when he realizes I actually didn't come home again and make dinner; boy, I can see Bessie jump to make him something! I suppose as it gets later and later and he sees I meant what I said, his eyes'll start to bulge out of his skull."

"Are you going to sleep here then, tonight?"

"If he doesn't come for me, definitely."

"You mean, if he comes, you'll go back with him?" That would mean I'd be in the house either with Abie, or if *he* didn't come home again, alone.

"I don't know. Maybe I'll go back with him if he tries hard enough."

We walked over to Mile End Road to catch the trollybus to Johnny Isaacs. The fish and chips came to one-and-threepence a plate, and this time I paid for both using two of the two-shilling pieces I'd minted. I was nervous as Mrs. Isaacs took them, but she just put them in the cash register and gave me the change with no problem. But I couldn't do this again, and it would be a stretch paying double on a regular basis eating out. I looked around the shop, and apart from Mrs. Isaacs still serving behind the high counter, I didn't recognize a single person sitting there. Everyone seemed young, as though a whole world of familiar faces had evaporated.

After the meal and ride back, as we crossed the square, Abie's van came chugging along in the darkness, a working headlight on one side only. The vehicle turned into Tredegar Terrace, and Abie completed the elaborate ritual of locking it up as we got to the front door.

"Eee, 'allo, er, where's Lily, did she, did she...."

Katherine looked around in the darkness — I assumed in case Benny might be lurking somewhere. "Yes Dad, Zech and I saw both of them off this morning."

"You did? Yeh...." He paused for quite several seconds. "Let's go in then."

"Aren't you going to put it in the garage?" I asked. "I thought the lights would run the battery down again."

"Nuh, it's too much money, uh don't 'ave the *gelt,* it's one thing after another, uh 'ad to 'ave a new battery yesterday, they said if uh drive to Burnt Oak every day it'll be alright in the street standing one night, uh'll see, what can uh do? The headlight there it's broke from the street, someone broke it, uh was riding along and 'e stopped 'is car there, like all of a sudden for no reason in the middle of the road 'e stops dead, a *schmuck.* They should make 'im go in prison, uh told 'im."

I lit the gas mantle; the dirty crockery was still on the table. "I'll clean them up," said Katherine, "it was from this morning." She and I collected the dirty cups and silverware and started to take them to the kitchen.

"Eee, she really did go, both of 'em, uh thought maybe, like you never know...."

"Dad," Katherine asked, "why didn't you come home last night, just to say good-bye or something?"

"Uh was busy there, the battery, uh 'ad to make sure it was alright for the driver's test again."

"What happened with the test?" I asked.

"'Appened? By my life uh could'a strangled 'im the barsted, like writing in 'is book there like a teacher, to 'im it's nothing, 'Failed,' 'e writes, the fourth time the barsted, eee did uh tell 'im...."

"But you still could have come home," said Katherine.

"Come 'ome, come 'ome! Finishing with the costume, you should only know what it's like there, uh 'ave to rush rush, working all night practically uh was working." He followed us into the kitchen. "Where's Benny, is 'e 'ere, where is 'e?"

"I suppose he's home with his mother. He's in love," said Katherine.

"Is everything alright, uh mean, what's...."

"Everything's alright, I wanted to stay here the first couple of nights Mum was gone."

"So, did you... make, is there... like something did you make...?"

"No, I'm sorry I didn't make dinner, I don't know where anything is in this house."

"Wha'd'y' mean, three weeks, what is it, three weeks you're married and already you don't know where anything is 'ere?"

"Look Dad, I've got my own things to think about, my own problems, I didn't come here just to cook you dinner."

"Problems, problems! You just got married, 'e's got a regular job there, what problems you got, 'e's an 'ard worker, 'e'll be alright."

"Yes, I'm sure he *will* be alright, it's myself I'm more worried about."

"Worried! Don't worry, don't worry! You're always telling Zech don't worry, don't *you* worry also." He giggled foolishly. "If you made some dinner you'd eat, we'd all eat, and you wouldn't 'ave to worry!"

"Zech, I'm going up to bed."

"Yes, me also. Alright, Dad, see you in the morning, I suppose."

"Alright...." His diminished figure stood outlined in the living room doorway as I followed Katherine up the stairs. "Yeh, yeh, alright uh'll, uh'll see you in the morning."

"Yes, good night."

"And don't worry!"

"Alright," said Katherine. "I won't worry."

•   •   •

Jack was sitting on the little turreted wall when I got home from work a couple of days later.

"What-o old bean, what are you doing here? It's not the weekend."

"Izzy's mother told my mother that your mother's gone to America, so my mother said why not invite him to supper?"

I hadn't yet stopped at Altman's to pick up any food. "Convoluted invitation, but I accept. First I have to see if my sister is in the house."

"She's married, isn't she?"

"Yes, but sometimes they argue and she comes here." I let myself in; the house was empty, she had left no note that she was going to Hazel's, so Benny must have come for her. Jack and I started crossing toward Tredegar Square. "So, how's Malmsbury Road? I'm still at the laboratory, I love it."

"What are you making now, atomic bombs?"

"Next week they'll start plutonium deliveries, so in a few days I should have bomb number one ready to drop."

"Well, next month I'll be starting school if everything works out okay."

"Wow! That's wonderful!"

"I might as well aspire to something grand, it's what my Dad would have wanted also."

"Yes, absolutely!" I was so sorry about his dad, but at the same time grateful my own fabulous job permitted me to be happy for my friend without qualification. Jack would become one of those quietly important people whose name is forever associated with impressive buildings. One day he'd meet a woman who would fall in love with his accomplishments, just like in the pictures; they'd live in a pretty house and never need to worry about the rent. "My sister wrote from America, she said the skyscrapers in New York are marvelous when you see them up close or go inside."

"Americans are fascinated by buildings, but it's the Europeans who are interested in architecture."

"I don't know what you mean... I thought...."

"America goes more for the spectacular than the culturally appropriate."

"Well America is new, their buildings are new, what's wrong with that?"

"It's a big subject, I'm reading lots of stuff about it. Anyway, if everything goes alright I won't have to worry about being drafted," he continued.

"Yes, that's right. That's the one bad thing about my job, I'll still have to register in a couple of months."

Suddenly, a shout from the perimeter of the park, "Hey!" It was Reuben Berger. We slowed our pace and nodded acknowledgement. Reuben stood his ground for us to come over to him; we waited a moment and then, when he didn't move, we continued on our way.

"Hey, wait a minute!" he called again.

Again we paused and this time he crossed over the grass toward us.

"Hello Reuben." Jack's voice had an icy politeness.

"Hi, Reuben," I said, acutely aware that I'd never followed up on my several-months-old invitation for him to come to see the lab.

"So, you *don't* work in a laboratory, like I said that night."

"Yes, I do."

"What's the problem, Reuben?" said Jack.

"Problem? The problem is our friend here said he'd show me the laboratory he said he works in — which he obviously doesn't."

"I'm sorry Reuben, I've had a lot of things going on, I haven't had time."

"Why don't you admit you're just a tailor or something?"

Jack bristled. "Reuben, I don't like your tone of voice to my friend. Zech, you don't need to justify anything to this... this... character."

Tempers were rising, and all for nothing. "Jack, it's okay thanks, I did promise him he could come." My hand on Jack's forearm eased him away a short distance. "Reuben, I've been very busy, lots of stuff going on, I'll have you over in a couple of weeks, okay?"

"Couple of weeks! So when does that mean?"

"What is it now, August? Before the end of this month, is that alright?"

"Alright then, this month, August."

"Alright, I'll check out what day exactly and I'll let you know."

"We'll see."

Reuben left, and I went back over to Jack. "Sorry. Kind of stupid, I know."

"It's a waste of breath talking to that *schmuck.*"

"I know, I never see him really, the last time was… maybe six months ago, I bumped into him, he wanted to see where I work."

"Watch out he doesn't cause any trouble."

"Really? I dunno, he lives over the road from me so I just want… if it's that important to him I might as well show him where I work."

"He's a dishonorable fellow, be careful. You know, the court let him off that other time but it probably was him anyway." We continued on our way. "Anyway, I'm glad you like your job."

"Yes, I've got a lot of responsibility there. And if I do get drafted they have to take me back after my demob."

"I know, that's the new law."

"What with my mother going to America and everything, we couldn't really afford for me to go to a school… now…."

"Zech! Jack! Is that Jack? Yes, it is! Surprise!" Katherine was approaching from the direction of Mile End Road.

"What are you doing here, you coming over to our house?"

"Anya's just closed, I'm finished for the day. What a surprise to see you! What are you two doing?"

"Anya's? I thought you told her… I thought you left."

"Guess what?"

"What?"

"My dear husband did some calculations and decided to drag me back there." She looked at Jack. "I'm sorry to involve you in my domestic squabbles." Jack seemed perplexed as she continued: "So, in front of me he apologized to Anya for my lack of decorum, and here I am back squeezing sweaty bunions into fashion footwear."

"Christ! I nearly said crikey!"

"You're right, I feel the same way."

"I'm sorry, what's… going on?" As always, Jack was courteous.

"It's not worth explaining, just my new dear husband. Where're you both going? I'm inviting myself, I'll come with, you're my brother so you have to say alright."

"Jack's mother invited me to supper…."

She paused, "Oh."

Jack's unflagging gallantry saved me. "You can come if you want to, Katya, I'm certain it would be okay."

"I won't eat much."

"Were you going over to the house?" I asked. "I mean, is everything alright…."

"Well, I'd planned to stay at Hazel's for a bit, then go back to Benny's and see if he shopped on the way home and made supper by the time I got there."

"Katya, it sounds to me…" I began. As the three of us continued in the direction of Jack's house, sentences were out of my mouth before I'd weighed what was appropriate: "I wish that you… well, you two…." My ears flamed a beetroot red.

Even though I hadn't completed a sentence, Jack responded as though I had. "Katya's husband probably wouldn't be too happy if she committed bigamy. Anyway, I'll be in school now for four more years."

—o—O—o—

34

A school of miniscule hooting tugboats nudged the *Queen Mary* past a greenish-grey Statue of Liberty. In the harbor the water's surface was calm, yet the sense of unremitting motion still clutched at Lily's stomach as she struggled wearily to hold nausea at bay. Slowly, slowly the ship's bulk was nursed toward the jutting shoreline until it finally grazed, then compacted, a creaking wooden quay. It took a while for Lily to realize that for the first time in five endless days and nights, the relentless dipping and swaying had finally ceased.

Under intermittent sunshine, she joined the line that wended to a small table covered with weighted gust-blown papers. From beyond the lip of the deck came incomprehensible shouts of dock workers as they lashed hurled coils of rope, the vague noises marking the end of one ordeal and the beginning of another.

"Maudy, stay here with me, don't run, you'll get lost with all the people, careful for your face, *oy*, I don't know." Behind the table sat a dark-uniformed individual of serious mien, rubber stamp in hand, perusing documents at impossible speed; a nod upward, a disingenuous flash of smile, the stamp's imprimatur, then, "Next!" First-class passengers were already debarking from another, more insulated, venue. From the considerable altitude of the deck, Lily looked across the corrugated roofs of the hangar-like buildings immediately below, to the streets of the fabled New York. In the blinding sunlight, necklaces of parked cars sparkled along the edges of streets stretching all the way across toward a distant river. The zig-zagged array of skyscrapers was foreshortened against the blurring brightness of the sky, each outline hazily flattened into the next like superimposed pencilled sketchings. The bustle of car hooters drifted up in a remote and compacted anarchy.

Dismissed, they followed a middle-aged uniformed man rolling their bags and small trunk on a handcart down the unexpectedly-steep canopied ramp. Lily stumbled and grasped Marius's arm: "Crikey, Mum, why'n'cha be careful?"

At ground level they exited onto concrete. The baggage-handler beckoned them further along, into the yawning entrance of the first building. Inside and under the sweeping curved ceiling he discharged their smaller bags on the floor at the end of one of several short queues. "Stand on line there, Ma'am, watch your bags." He rolled their remaining steamer over to a railed enclosure and deposited it alongside.

"What did he say, 'watch your bags'?"

"So they don't get pinched, s'pose 'e means," said Marius. All around them was a sea of prominent American *r*'s, *can't* with the short *a* — not so much like those of the G.I.s Zilla and Rebecca brought home during the war — those accents had generally been softer, the speech less rushed; here was more the peculiarly harsh New York twang Lily had heard depicted in American pictures. Ahead of them a thickset black-coated man was protesting some indignity in heavy Hungarian inflections as a tall uniformed peaked-capped customs official rummaged through his suitcase. In a few minutes Lily and Marius were at the head of the line. The customs officer was kindly; when Lily asked what he meant, "declare?" and when he asked if she had brought with her any of several items he listed and she replied she had none, she and Marius were immediately dispatched not only without a search, but with the man's best wishes for their life in America.

"Mum!" And as Lily turned, there stood Rebecca, her face tanned, lines around her mouth, her eyes. Only nine months and she definitely looked older! And slightly behind her, it had to be, though Lily dreaded the possibility — Berel. This stranger standing there, watching; was that anger on his cadaverous face? A bit shorter than Rebecca; he looked like he weighed less than her — insufficient bulk for a man. The smaller ones, maybe they couldn't be such bullies; who knows, they might be more vicious even. An "Alright, let's get the bags," and he immediately turned away; with those few words she recognized the strong Polish accent.

"Lily, see, it's wonderful, we did it!" Rebecca embraced her joyfully.

Lily was embarrassed, people were looking. "So we're here! A *glick*, more trouble for you, now!"

Rebecca placed an arm around Marius's shoulder. "Maudy, we did it! How's your chin? I'd better be careful!"

"'S'alright. Take more 'an 'im to… to…."

The party followed the porter's trolley out to the wide dusty parking area. "Here, put them in the trunk." Berel unlocked the gaping boot of an immense black car that sported little chromed portholes along the front mudguards. The porter deposited the trunk and bags, Berel pressed the lid closed, then made a display of pushing paper money into the departing man's hand.

Rebecca directed. "Come in front with us Mum, in the middle, slide over, yes. Go on Maudy, in the back, see, you've got the whole seat to yourself."

"What a car! Crikey, it's big as a lorry!"

Lily sat between them on the high, wide front seat — wide enough that she didn't have to suffer contact with Berel's clothing — and the car floated silently through a bombardment of pedestrians, traffic signals, hissing bus doors, building façades and smartly-capped door-men. Berel pulled at the wheel and the car's prow swung around a corner.

"So how was the ship?" asked Rebecca.

"Stuffy, what can you expect, every day I was sick down there." Lily glanced at her daughter's profile: Rebecca — she had ventured all of this, the decisions, the upheavals; Rebecca was the important one now. All that was left now for her, Lily, was to go along with everything, try to adjust, to cope.

"She was sick on the floor, ugh, I cleaned it up," said Marius.

"He was a very good boy, he helped me."

"I told 'er come up on the deck, it was fresh air, she stayed in the room every day."

"Didn't you go outside, on deck?"

"She kept saying she was frightened, she wouldn't 'ave anything to 'old on to, crikey, I told 'er she could sit on a chair, they 'ad deck chairs up there."

"Well what's the use now, it's finished, we're here."

"Shame, Lily, it's a lovely ship, you could have had a nice holiday."

Berel listened, his passengers oblivious to his adroit adjustments of the Buick's controls as he maneuvered through the crowds; all three of them busy busy talking about the ship, the ship, already the ship was the past, they were *off* the ship now, they were in America, she'd have to make a life for herself and Marius — Marius!, what a name to give someone, like a British lord, Lord Marius, already he sounded to Berel like a *schmuck*, with his *crikey* — what was that, crikey? Rivka was always going on about Abie, how he cursed and beat everyone; now with Lily here he'd have to listen to both of them go at it! They should only know about beatings — the barbed-wire fences there, the filthy rags, exhausted sleeping on the freezing boards, the forty slashes he got when the *Capo* caught him with a shoe under his head as a pillow, grey ragged figures working 'til they collapsed; mother and father dead from starvation, his only brother Witjold pushed, tortured, then shot before his eyes; and always the chimneys, the smoke, the smell, four years and you never knew from one minute to the next — how could even Rivka, anyone who wasn't there, ever understand? He clutched the wheel, enough, enough, he'd take them back to the apartment, stuff their bellies then walk them right over to the room Rivka and he'd found for them, two blocks away on the other side of Broadway, not far enough for him.... Still the two women droned on, and he'd jump out of his skin if he didn't interrupt, change the subject.

He scrolled down the window: "Listen!" His beloved Buick slowed to a crawl and he shouted out one word to no one in particular: "Score?" Half a dozen hurrying pedestrians paused, glanced toward his car and responded in scattered arpeggio: "Seven to four." He ran the window back up. "See that? They're all *meshugeh* here. In America everybody's crazy."

"What is it?" asked Lily, *score?*, something, *ugh!*, the repulsive Polish accent, *feh!* her favorite daughter, a flower, she'd give someone the clothes off her back, this was the best she could do?

"Oh, they're mad here with their baseball, that's all they have to worry about in America," her daughter laughingly responded.

Berel berthed the car on 175th Street, by Broadway.

"Where is it, where are we?"

"Near Broadway." Rebecca pointed, "see, that's Broadway."

Lily looked: a mundane domestic Broadway with no flickering neon lights. Not the Broadway from the pictures at the Empire, of abutted theatres and imploring songwriters.

"We'll leave the bags in the trunk," said Berel. They crossed the wide pavement, and under an elaborately carved concrete arch entered a lobby furnished with mahogany tables and chairs that seemed to compound a funereal darkness. The lift door banged shut and they were jogged upward. Then, out into an echoing stone hallway, the pungency of bleach from the brutally slicked grey marbled floor drowning the *haymisha* aromas of dinner, of chicken. Berel's little brass key slid into the lock of a woodgrain-painted metal door: so, thought Lily, he'd already made himself a key to her flat! The door swung open to a large room, nearly empty — he didn't help her to buy anything, any furniture. To the left, isolated in an expanse of nondescript tan carpet, a sickly-blonde wood coffee table, three arms leaning up and out from its kidney-shaped base in perilous support of a too-large glass top. Behind, against the far wall a straw-like Kelly-green couch, a flimsy arm on one end and at the other a backless rounded curve. Off to the right of the barren room stood a cheap also-blonde wood cabinet harboring a curved glass screen — maybe he bought her a television, at least.

They went inside, and right away a buzzer sounded somewhere. Rebecca pushed a button on a wall-plate by the door; a few moments later there came another buzz and in stepped Zilla, come straight from work. "Ee, Lily, we did it, we did it, see, I knew we would, Maudy, so how are you, how was the *Queen Mary,* did you get sick, how's your jaw, the old barstard?"

They sat at the dinette in the bright kitchen, and Rebecca the waitress served. "We've found you a room. It's just two blocks from here on the other side of Broadway," she said as she ladled chicken and green peas into red ocher Melamine bowls on the glass-topped table with its curved aluminium rim embroidered in elaborately pressed floral relief. The matching metal chairs creaked and stiff plastic cushions hissed as her guests settled on the unforgiving buttons. Berel must have warned her, thought Lily, *after Zilla, no more relatives sleeping here,* that's why they got a room for us already. The opulent spread of fresh bagels, a fish-shaped plate piled with lox, a round plastic pot of cream cheese, the bright yellow enameled kettle beginning to whistle on the gas-stove, the chromed silverware and little serviettes of sculpted paper — so different from London, so pretty, how could she, Lily, have made a nice place there with no money in the house, not even the rent, Abie shouting all the time, smashing things. She looked out the window and leaned over to the dizzying distance below — the darting cars, the black top of a roaring single-decker bus belching twisted diesel fumes. Already she was afraid she'd feel panicked when they took her to the room, afraid when the door there would finally click closed; how could she tell anyone, what could she say after all the years of hating him? So he shouted; at least she knew where she was with him, it wasn't as terrible as it seemed to someone who didn't know him, there were worse husbands.

"So, how is Zech?"

"How should he be? He's working."

"Is this for afters?" asked Marius, reaching for a pastry.

"Yes. Maudy they don't call it *afters* here, it's called dessert," said Rebecca. "Lily, so what's happening with Katya and Benny?"

"Oh, the usual aggravation, what can you expect with the two of them."

A couple of hours later the quintet descended to the foyer. The wrought-iron glassed apartment-building door clanked closed as they exited to the outside street alive with fresh noise and burned petrol fumes. Dusk was beginning to fall as Berel lifted the bags from the Buick trunk, distributed two to Marius, one each to the girls. He reached in for the small steamer, checking that the strap was tightly buckled before pulling it over the lip.

"It's 'eavy; don'cha wanna drive it all where we're going?" asked Marius.

"We'd never find parking there," responded Rebecca. "It's funny, everybody owns a car here, it's hard to even find a place to park it. Go on, you hold one end."

The group labored across Broadway, then uptown a couple of blocks. They rested the steamer on the pavement a few moments, then turned left along 177th Street, crossed over and stopped at a building quite similar to Rebecca's.

"I'll get the elevator," said Zilla, and in the lobby she pushed the cracked black plastic button in its ornate brass plate. Just two months, and already Zilla was calling the lift an elevator! They dragged the bags off at the sixth floor, buzzed a little round doorbell incrusted with layers of paint, and Rebecca introduced Lily and Marius to a heavyset greying German landlady, Mrs. Henckel, who led them inside. The rented room, halfway along the passageway, measured ten feet by eight. Two small beds on opposite walls were made up with fresh-soap-smelling linen; a three-foot square plastic-topped table with two wooden chairs was lined up against the wall. At the room's far end a tiny white porcelain sink hung out under a small window oppressed by a neighboring brick wall. To the window's left, a locked door to the next room. Lavatory and a shower — no bath — outside, along the hallway. Rent, six dollars a week.

"So, Lily, both of you, you'll be alright here, we looked a long time, Mrs. Henckel is nice, at least you won't have any arguments, it's not like Morgan Street. Here, I've written down our phone number, the tenant's phone is outside in the hallway, I'll write Zilla's down also. Here's change, you put one of these in, it's a nickel, a silver one, you see, no serrations. Wait 'til you hear the dial tone, then you dial these numbers, it's easy, Mrs. Henckel will help you if you can't manage. Call me in the morning and walk over for breakfast, after Berel's gone to work, I'll expect you both for breakfast, I don't have to be in tomorrow."

"Er, Lily, I 'ave to be at work first thing," said Zilla. "I'll see you in the evening, I s'pose."

"Yes, Zilly's working tomorrow, you'll all come over for dinner tomorrow evening, we'll all be together. Don't worry Lily, everything's going to work out okay, it'll just take a few days to get used to everything."

As Rebecca, Berel and Zilla exited the room into the long passageway, Mrs. Henckel's door at the end clicked open. "Mrs. Henckel, the towels, they don't have towels...."

Marius closed the door, switched on the light, then moved over to the table, blocking the few remnants of daylight still creeping in the cramped window. "The light switch is up-side-down." Lily sat for a moment on the edge of the strange narrow bed. As she moved, the slow creaking of springs was startlingly loud in the tiny room. Floating up from the street came the ceaseless disembodied sounds of car hooters, of blurred voices. A muffled conversation — a man's and woman's voices, too loud, as though from the wireless or something — leaked from the next room through the brown adjoining locked door. She looked around — the picture rail on two crackled blue-painted walls, the plywood clothes cabinet, lightly-stained and still with protruding wood splinters, the little woven mat that should have softened the bare linoleum alongside her bed, a curved indentation like a mottled blotch in the ceiling above where her face would lie at night, the thick paint over the crack in the blue wall to the right of the sink. All this would be theirs for an unnumbered sentence of nights and days.

"I'll 'ang the clothes up then." Marius opened the steamer and began shaking out clothes and sliding them onto the hangers permanently attached to the wooden rod inside the narrow, flimsy, cheap clothes cabinet.

•   •   •

Day flowed into day. Lily had no income; the weekly fifteen dollars that Zilla and Rebecca each scraped to give her was barely adequate to get by. She felt humiliated, frustrated, trapped, even angry at the financial burden her and Marius's presence placed on the girls and Berel. Berel had found Marius a job delivering packages, but after two days the employer let him go because he took too long on his trips; one customer complained he'd spent half an hour in their bathroom.

In the bright Saturday afternoon sunlight the foursome walked along Broadway toward Washington Heights, to look in the 181st Street store windows. Berel walked in front beyond earshot to avoid the onerous conversation.

"That Berel, he's always looking at other women."

"That's nothing, he doesn't do it seriously."

"Look at him, always walking in front so he can look; see how he's looking at that woman there! Why should he look at other women? He'll leave you the first chance he gets."

"That's silly, come on."

"Mark my word I know what I'm talking about."

"Mum, you're making something out of nothing. Men like to look at women, it's harmless."

"Ugh! I hate him, feh!, even his name, it's a girl's name, he doesn't deserve a decent girl like you, I've had more experience than you, he's always walking in front, ready to run off."

"Crikey Mum, shurrup, stop nagging Rivka."

Later that afternoon Lily and Marius returned to 177th Street to go to their room. As they entered the hallway, Mrs. Henckel's door opened. "How are you, Mrs. Grossman, nice weather today."

"I s'pose so, we just came back, a walk with my younger daughter and her... her fiancé."

"That's nice, a nice change for you, I know you spend a lot of time in your room. If you want to watch television with my husband and me one evening... both of you...."

"Alright, thank you, maybe tomorrow?"

Lily was relieved to be able to tell Rebecca at dinner that she and Marius would be busy the next evening, they wouldn't be over for dinner.

The next day, walking home with Marius from breakfast at Rebecca's, the two of them stopped in the stationery shop for a writing pad, envelopes and a pen. The pen the lady showed her had a little ball on the end instead of a nib, but she'd try it, at least it didn't need an ink bottle. Back in the room she wrote a letter to Sadie Benjamin as she'd promised before she left: they were getting settled in, both her daughters had good jobs, lovely flats with big televisions, Rivka's fiancé had a beautiful American car, Maudy had already tried out one job, and a nice couple along the hall had invited them in to watch television. She stuck the envelope down and wrote the address, 13 Morgan Street, Mile End, London, E.3. The flimsy plastic pen actually snapped in her hand as she went to write the word *England;* she'd accidently been squeezing too hard. Tomorrow she'd buy a new pen, she'd be more careful, she had enough money. Then Rebecca would show her how to put the letter in the post with the proper stamp.

That evening, from the cold-water-filled tray she kept on the shelf over the sink, Lily removed the chilled quarter-pound stick of butter and the sliced cheese package and prepared two sandwiches on the little plastic table. She and Marius ate, and drank glasses of cold water. She carefully wiped up all the crumbs so as not to attract more cockroaches. At seven-fifteen the two of them knocked on Mrs. Henckel's door at the end of the passageway.

"Come in, come in," said Mr. Henckel. Despite the lipstick and the permed hair, Lily could tell — anybody could tell — Mrs. Henckel was a good twelve years older than her, but Mr. Henckel seemed considerably older still; his frame bent forward as he made his painful way across the room to his armchair. Two wooden kitchen chairs had been set close and to the side of the television screen for the guests.

"Would you like a cup of coffee, Mrs. Grossman?" called Mrs. Henckel from the kitchen.

"Tea, er, do you, well, alright alright, should I come in?"

"Please, make yourself at home, Mrs. Grossman."

Lily went into the kitchen.

"No, that's for Hellmuth, he likes it strong," began Mrs. Henckel as Lily reached for the filled cup on the counter top.

"I'll take it in for him, then."

"No, please, he likes me to bring it to him."

"What's the difference, it's the same tea... coffee." Lily picked up the cup in its saucer. "No Mrs. Grossman, I'll, I'll take that one, just a minute, here's...."

Lily was already walking the cup into the living room. Mrs. Henckel stood in the kitchen doorway and watched as Lily carefully lowered the cup and saucer onto the white lace doily covering the little Queen Anne table that stood alongside the armchair. "Here you are, Hellmuth."

Danke schön, thanks Mrs. Grossman." Mr. Henckel pulled out a handkerchief and coughed into it, then stirred the coffee and took a sip. Lily stood by; should she make her way back into the kitchen, with Mrs. Henckel in the doorway? If she returned to the chair next to Marius it would imply she thought Mrs. Henckel should serve her — both of them. She didn't want to impose, to be a burden. Mrs. Henckel turned back into the kitchen just as Lily decided to go over to the television and sit next to Marius.

Behind them, Mrs. Henckel pulled out a folding hand-painted metal tray from a rack of four. She opened it, latched the brown plastic snap catches onto the aluminum legs and placed it between Lily and Marius. Lily looked ahead at the blank screen.

"The program begins in a few minutes," said Mrs. Henckel. Her husband coughed. "Too hot for you the coffee, dear?" Again he coughed; china clinked against china.

Next Mrs. Henckel brought out two cups of black coffee, and without a word stood them on the tray. She turned a knob. "Do you take sugar and cream?" Crackling emanated from the television, and fluffy white streaks jumped across the screen.

"Can I do something, should I...?" began Lily.

"It's not as big as Rivka's," said Marius.

"Yes, the television, it is, it's the same, they're all big."

Mrs. Henckel rotated the large knob, and the streaks resolved into a singing commercial. Lily leaned toward the screen. "What is it? Is it..."

"The program will start in a minute."

"Oh, I thought this is, isn't?..."

"This is the commercial, after the commercial it begins." Mrs. Henckel turned off the wall switch, leaving the room lighted only by the low lamp on top of the television and by the dancing illuminations of the screen. "I'll bring you the cream and the sugar."

An hour later Mrs. Henckel stood up and switched on the ceiling light, then came over and turned off the set. "So, we'll be getting to sleep now."

Lily stood up. "Thank you, it was nice of you both to invite us, maybe another evening...."

Mr. Henckel coughed into his handkerchief. Mrs. Henckel opened the door to the passageway: "Goodnight, Mrs. Grossman, goodnight, Marius."

Lily and Marius walked toward their room, and behind them the door clicked shut. As Lily stopped in front of their door, at the end of the passage they heard the Henckel's bolt scraping home into its slot.

—o—O—o—

35

It was raining out, gloomy, too early in the evening for Abie's van to be parked outside if he were in fact coming home tonight. He often slept at his tailoring shop in Burnt Oak, and it was always a relief to have the house to myself, better still when I had Katherine to talk to. She and Benny were fighting so frequently that she stayed home in Morgan Street almost one night a week. The one time I'd accepted her invitation to sleep at their flat, in the middle of the night Benny's shouting in their bedroom had awakened me with a fright. When Katherine snapped back at him and Bessie had come lumbering upstairs wondering out loud why *I* was interfering when I hadn't said one word, to stay out of it I pretended I was asleep.

This evening on the table in the living room lay a scribbled note, which meant Katherine had been here earlier: *"I came over to lie down a while without being nagged by Bessie because I'm not cleaning or cooking. Between Bessie, Benny and Anya I'm beginning to understand what Mum meant when she used to say she's sick of her life. Sorry to grumble so much! There's a letter from Rivka on the table. Don't forget, anytime you want to sleep on our settee just show up at the door, I love it when you come over. I'm visiting Hazel for half an hour then I'd better get back. Ta-ra, Katya."*

I opened Rebecca's letter: *"Hope everybody's surviving without too many arguments. Maudy got laid off from another job, everybody has to be fast here and he's so slow you can get apoplexy waiting for him to move. We even got Mum a part-time job in a place that makes lace, just to keep her occupied, but the formaldehyde made her ill. We're working hard to try to save money for tickets for you Zech, and in case Katya still wants to come. It's not easy here altogether, but it'll all work out in the end. Love, Rivka. P.S., Zilly has a boyfriend with a strong German accent, Hellmuth, from Hamburg. Can you imagine, they were bombing us while we were bombing them!"*

If my sisters did get me a ticket I couldn't just go and leave Katherine here alone, fighting with Benny. The only one she'd have to talk to would be Hazel. Once I'd asked Katherine why she stayed at Anya's if she hated it so much there; after all, she'd advised *me* to change my horrible job at Cable Electric when she'd first come back from Devon. But she didn't really answer; maybe it's easier to see someone else's situation than your own. I'd gone with her over to Hazel's for half an hour the previous week; Hazel wasn't such a kid as I'd remembered her to be — and Katherine had warned me beforehand that she was going with someone at the moment, an older man who was their milkman, so I should be discreet.

I made myself a cup of tea and a sandwich for supper, and as I ate I examined the florins again; they really were perfect, Mrs. Isaacs hadn't given them a second look. Tomorrow was the day I planned to destroy the mold. I stayed up late, reading *An Experiment With Time*, ready to hurry upstairs if I heard Abie's van pull up outside, but again he didn't come home.

The next morning I walked through the lab door with a feeling of elation at being in charge of everything. With power came responsibility, and it was my responsibility to destroy the mold. Maybe just for today I'd make one quick coin while the tar was distilling, if only to confirm that the previous beauties hadn't been flukes. Then I could take the mold back with me in the evening and destroy it at home so there wouldn't be any incriminating fragments around the lab. The reasoning seemed... reasonable, so I made just one quick one. It was flawless. With this last one safely in my pocket I went out to the yard and scurried up the tank ladders to draw more samples. Back, and during the first distillation there was no compelling reason for not minting just one more really *final* florin, if I simultaneously kept an eye on the flask, the flame low and centered on the asbestos circle. By the end of the second distillation, since this was definitely to be the very last day, four more silver florins jangled in my pocket.

But, heating the metal amalgam, pouring carefully etc., did take time. The thumping of feet in the passageway outside made me rush to dismantle the mold, which was clamped in a stand in full view. As I hurried to hide it behind the bottles on the shelf I knocked the wire gauze with the asbestos circle off the tripod. Luckily I was between distillations and our only flask was soaking in the sink. Mr. Smith opened the door: "Well, what's it for today, matey?"

"Here are the numbers for tank one. I don't have number two and three quite ready yet."

"Two not ready! Two's cookin', 'ow am I s'posed to know when to pack it up?"

"Well, it's only three o'clock!"

"Don't get uppity just 'cause you're in charge. You knows we can't run the factory without the numbers."

"I'm sorry, I'll have two and three ready very, very soon. It's nearly ready. I'll come out as soon as it's finished."

"Okay matey, but 'urry it up. If we overcooks this batch, Mr. Margolin'll 'ave to know it ain't my fault."

A half hour later I had a total of twenty-four shiny florins. I resolved I wouldn't mention it to anyone, including Jack. Two pounds eight shillings' worth; in one day I'd made more money than I was earning in a whole week! My jacket was hanging on the rack, and I dropped the precious coins into the pocket then hid the mold back up on the shelf again, temporarily. Quickly, I cleaned out the flask, poured the final tar sample, set it up on the wire mesh and added the toluol.

I brought down the mold one more time. Fifteen minutes later, just as I was in the middle of pouring what was to be the absolutely definite last coin, an impatient Mr. Smith called in through the window: "'Ow's it goin'?"

Standing the hot vat down on the iron bench top I rushed through the door and outside to keep him out of the lab. "I'll have number three in ten minutes. I don't know what happened today, it's a lot of work with Mr. Hitchcock gone."

Behind me there came a *woomp!* sound from the other side of the window. As we both watched, to my horror a heavy yellow sheet of flame rolled lazily along the bench, and thick black smoke began billowing upward, pouring out the still-open lab door. Mr. Smith rushed immediately into the lab, and I followed him to see the whole bench top ablaze, oily yellow flames already licking along the ceiling.

"Jesus Christ!" Mr. Smith grabbed huge round work gloves from out in the passageway, put them on, rushed back in and started banging at the base of the flames. Both gloves caught fire; he ripped them off and threw them down, then grabbed the nearest thing that was visible through the now choking black haze — my jacket on the hanger behind the door — and threw that over the end of the bench where I could just make out the sooted remains of the flask. Dragging my jacket along the bench he smothered the bubbling rubber tubes, burning corks, notepad and other flaring items, in the process knocking over the small vat of still-molten metal. He then threw the jacket, sodden and flaming with toluol, down onto the floor. Beyond the sound of breaking glass and the frying of rubber tubing, I clearly heard the clattering, metallic ringing of florins hitting the floor and rolling in every direction. But Mr. Smith didn't notice; he dragged the flaming remnants of the jacket outside along the passage and into the yard, where we both stamped on it until the flames were extinguished. He turned to hurry back into the still-burning laboratory as I dropped down and scratched through the remains for florins. "Wha'cha lookin' for, matey?"

"There were some keys in the pocket."

"Blimey, look for 'em later!" He rushed back in. Among the charred and sodden remains of fabric I quickly retrieved eight florins, then followed him inside; again he'd grabbed the now-extinguished work gloves. The toluol seemed to have largely burned itself out and he was patting out remaining bursts of flames from burning corks and frothing rubber tubing.

"I found one of the keys." And on that pretext, while myself extinguishing small fires with our own asbestos glove used for holding hot flasks, I was able to peel the now-set puddle of shiny metal off the bench top, then search under work benches and in corners more diligently than might otherwise have seemed reasonable, surreptitiously pocketing six more florins. Fortunately, the far end of the lab with the desk and shelved bottles of chemicals was largely untouched, and in a quick moment while Mr. Smith faced the window clearing debris from the benches, I was able to rescue the unscathed coin mold and secrete it under a half-sandwich in my lunchbag, which I'd slid to the rear of the desktop.

At five o'clock, Mr. Margolin, Mr. Bitwood and Mr. Smith were lined up in the yard in front of me.

"Well, what happened?" It didn't really matter which one had said it.

"I don't know. It was hard getting everything done, with Mr. Hitchcock gone... it was late so I was rushing a bit."

"Well, fortunately for us all, Mr. Smith here saved the building," said Mr. Margolin. "We'll buy you a new jacket. Though with the several two-shilling pieces we found, you could perhaps afford a better one yourself."

My face flushed; I wasn't quite sure what he was saying. Maybe from the several coins I might have missed — I didn't know for certain how many, I'd been minting them in such a rush toward the end — he had inferred my avocation, and always courteous, this would be his gentlemanly way of telling me to stop.

•   •   •

It was almost eight when I got home, and to my surprise Katherine called out from upstairs, "Hello, Zech is that you?"

"Hello, you're here!" I went up.

She was in bed. "Yes, I came this morning."

"Oh, you've been here all day! Why are you in bed, are you ill? Mum said you were ill."

"I've been a bit run-down lately but I'll be alright. How are you?"

"We had a bit of excitement at work today."

"What happened?"

"I accidently set the lab on fire."

"What! You did? So did they give you the sack?"

"No, they were very nice. It wasn't exactly my fault, since they gave the chemist the sack I've had to do everything myself. They like me there, they'll fix the place up, clean off the soot and repaint it."

"Wow-ee!"

"I know, I was lucky the fire didn't go through the ceiling into the upstairs offices or anything. We'll have to order some new flasks and stuff, supplies — I won't bore you with the details, but actually it solves some problems as well."

"Boy, they must really like you if you didn't get the sack!"

"Yes, but anyway what's the matter, Katya, why are you in bed?"

"It'll pass."

"Is it because Mum went away?"

"No, nothing like that. I had a terrible argument with Benny over his fucking mother and the cooking. And something else."

"But why are you ill? I mean, is it because Mum's not here?"

"Well, in a roundabout sort of way. Oh, I might as well tell you the truth."

"What?"

"I had an abortion."

"A what! An abortion?" My sister had an abortion? "Katya, you did?" I was stunned. That meant she wasn't as shy as me about sex; she was much more grown-up than I was. I bet lots of people had sex, and I was the only stupid one. "Why didn't you tell me? Maybe I could've done something...."

"What could you have done? Stopped the bleeding?"

"I...I...."

"A few days before Mum went she came with me, a woman's house in Hackney."

"You did really, I mean, what?... christ!"

"It was Artemis. I didn't tell Benny when we got married, I suppose I should have...."

"Christ!"

"I don't know, I thought maybe I'd just have it...."

"Really? Christ! "

"He's so wrapped up in himself he probably wouldn't have even noticed."

"Really? I mean, really?"

"He's always complaining about my being tired, one thing and another, he was going on and on. He expects me to shop on my way home after a long day's work and then just start cooking. Then he wants to fuck, and I can't, I've been bleeding a lot, it should have stopped by now."

Boy, this was my little sister? "Christ, what can I do, will you be alright?"

"I'll be alright. He was shouting, just like Abie, sometimes I can't bear him to come near me. I couldn't stand it anymore so I told him, about the abortion, I thought that might dampen his enthusiasm a bit."

"Christ!"

"You've said 'christ!' about seventeen times, don't be so upset, Zech, everything will work out in the end. Anyway, christ is about the only name he didn't call me."

"What did he say?"

"The usual — slut, common, a few things. Apart from telling me never to come back there, he called me a whore, a prostitute, streetwalker. He's not very imaginative."

"Christ! Oh, I'm sorry, I can't stop."

"Funny how much energy I have when I really need it. When he called me a prostitute I explained a prostitute fucks for money; I did it for love. Yes, he liked that one."

"So what are you going to do? Did you tell Artemis, I don't know what he could do."

"No, what could he do, it's not him, I mean I can't blame him, I didn't exactly object at the time."

"I don't know what to say, what can I do?"

"There's nothing to do, nothing to say, I'll stay here with you and Daddy. Hazel will come over if I ask her."

"Well, I can buy food, I have money. You hungry? Can I take you to a doctor?"

"We don't have money for a doctor."

"I have enough money to take you to a doctor." I had two dozen slightly blackened two-shilling pieces.

Outside in the street, a car door closed. "I suppose that's Abie," she said.

"It didn't sound like his van. Anyway, I've got enough for food, and for a doctor." There came a resolute knock on the door. "I wonder who that would be, so late? Does Hazel know you're here?"

"Yes, she was over when she came home for dinner, but she wouldn't knock like that, so loud."

"I'll go down." I ran downstairs, opened the street door and there stood a policeman.

"Is this the Grossman household?"

"Yes, why, is anything the matter?" My first thought was that it was illegal to have an abortion. The second was that my pocket jingled with counterfeit coins.

"This is the residence of Abraham Grossman?"

"Yes, is something wrong?"

"Are you his son?"

"Yes, I'm Zachary Grossman, what's wrong?"

"Let me speak with Mrs. Grossman."

"She's not here, she lives in America."

"Lives in America? I was at this house this past summer. Mr. Grossman accompanied me down to the station, he did."

"Yes, I remember! Oh, so you were the one, I mean, the officer, the policeman." Now they must have arrested him for something!

"Yes, and a lady who claimed she was Mrs. Grossman accompanied us to the station."

"Yes, that's my mother, that's Mrs. Grossman."

"And now she lives in America?"

"Well yes, I mean she didn't then; *now* she lives in America."

"I see." He tapped a pencil on his fingernail. "Are there any remaining adults in the house?"

"Adults? No, well I'm an adult, I don't go to school anymore."

"Are you the closest relative then, here, in this country, that is?"

"To Mr. Grossman? Yes, I'm his son; I mean, he's my father."

"Yes, now I remember you." He straightened out a sheet of paper in his hand. "Well sir, I'm sorry to have to inform you your father has been involved in a motor car accident."

"An accident?"

Katherine was coming down the stairs. "What's the matter?"

I introduced her: "My sister Katherine."

"I'm sorry, miss, your father has been in an accident, a motor car accident, in Aldgate East it was."

"What happened, where is he?"

"He's presently in hospital, I'm sorry to report he's in serious condition."

"What does that mean?"

"Since your brother informs me that Mrs. Grossman is no longer in Britain, both of you are Mr. Grossman's closest next of kin, I take it."

"Yes."

The policeman looked at the sheet of paper he held. "According to the preliminary medical report, Mr. Grossman sustained several broken ribs, his lung appears to have been punctured, and he may have a cervical fracture."

"A cervical fracture?" I asked.

"Yes, I'm afraid so, sir."

"What is it, what's a cervical fracture?" asked Katherine.

"That's the medical name when your neck gets broken. His neck may be broken, I'm afraid, miss."

"Jesus christ!" I looked at Katherine. And to the policeman: "Do you want to come in?"

"If you wish, sir." The three of us sat at the table in the living room. "He was brought to The London Hospital. Do you know where that is?"

"Yes, I know it, it's on Mile End Road," I said.

"Actually it's Whitechapel Road, sir, Mile End Road becomes Whitechapel Road in Whitechapel."

"Yes, er, after Johnny Isaacs."

"Might he die?" asked Katya. "I suppose we'd better send a telegram to Mum."

"We want to offer any assistance we can, miss. I can take you to the hospital now if you want."

"Christ, Katya, I suppose we ought to go. You mean you could take us in your police car?"

"Yes, sir."

"Katya, do you feel well enough to go, I'm a bit nervous to go myself. My sister's ill...."

"Whatever you decide sir. Miss, I'd recommend against going to the hospital if what you have is infectious."

"No it's nothing like that, but I really don't feel well; I don't think I could get through this, tonight," said Katherine.

"Well I'll go, Katya, you stay here then. I'll come right back from the hospital."

"Just be careful, Zech, try not to worry, whatever happens, happens."

I sat in the back seat in the Wolseley as we sped quietly along Mile End Road. "According to the accident report your father was driving a van, reversing at high speed out of an alleyway into the main road. His vehicle was struck from the side by a bus."

"That must have been his van, he has a van. A bus?"

"London Transport, a trollybus. The collision spun his vehicle around, it was severely damaged. They had to enlist the local garage to extricate him from the wreckage."

"I see...."

"I didn't say all these details in front of the young lady, sir, in case you didn't want her to hear seeing as how she's ill herself, but the hospital doesn't know if he'll survive, I'm afraid."

"I see...."

Outside Johnny Isaacs, a crowd mingled in remote silence on the wide pavement. A little further along, the policeman pulled the Wolseley over to the curb. "Here we are, sir, I hope everything turns out for the best."

"Thank you officer for taking me."

"I hope your father pulls through, sir."

"Thank you."

As the car glided away I climbed the wide steps into the hospital lobby and addressed the fat lady sitting behind the desk. "I'm here to see my father, please."

"Your father's name?"

"It's Grossman, Abraham Grossman."

"What ward is he in?"

"I don't know; he was in a motor car accident."

"Oh, I'm sorry. When was he brought to the hospital?"

"This evening, the police just came round and told us, they just brought me here to see him."

"Brought in this evening, then he'll probably still be in Operating Theatre." She looked through a card file. "Yes, on the third floor."

"Is he... is he alright?"

"He is on the critical list." She smiled sympathetically. "I suppose they don't know yet; they may not allow any visitors. The ward nurse will explain everything up there."

"Thank you"

"Straight ahead along the hallway," she pointed, "then right-away you'll see the lifts on the right."

For the second time this year I crowded in among several passengers. The attendant slid the iron scissor-fold gate shut, and the large wood-paneled chamber jerked upward. Hushed voices spoke of private concerns as I stood among them, isolated. In one minute from now someone would tell me if my father would live or die. If he died, then all the punching, all the shouting would be finished, quiet, irrevocably sealed into a sudden past.

"First floor!" The words struggled to pierce the clogged air. Maybe he was already dead up there; maybe right this moment somewhere above my head they were wheeling a lifeless form away. I tried to cohere a dance of words into a sensible question but some jarring obstacle interfered, a lump, and I couldn't focus on what response I would be trying to elicit from the nurse by contriving my question this way or that way. A woman standing beside me inched away; I must have been muttering. Now my head flamed with thoughts of Jack, with his talk of quantum mechanics, of the Copenhagen Interpretation, how an outcome wasn't set until you observed it. Now the debris in my head was replaced with a sharp-etched clarity: this very instant, Abie was neither dead nor not-dead. In a few moments when I got out of this lift, some nurse would respond either that he was already dead or that he was alive, and in the phrasing of my question to her, I bore the responsibility for his living or dying.

The lift jerked again to a stop, "Second floor!" and the door clattered open.

If he were already dead, his body removed now to some macabre room, surrounded by quietly efficient strangers who didn't know him, didn't know about him — might he still sit up, shouting? Would he be shouting at them, or, unseeing, shout straight ahead toward whatever incidental wall they had directed his trolley while they first ministered to corpses that had preceded his? The attendants would soon recognize how strong he was, that dying couldn't easily stop him shouting, that it would take a while.

And while he sat up on the trolley, raging, if I were to be taken to that room, if I were slowly led in front of him, around and into his line of vision, and as I crossed into his line of vision he looked at me, might he see me, recognize me? And if he recognized me might he still shout, futile spit frothing between purple lips, yet gradually — increment upon increment — come to realize he was dead, that now it was too late? And could unfathomable time arrest its lonely plunge just once, just this once, and in the surcease have him look at me slowly, quietly — tenderly?

"I'm... my name is Zachary Grossman, I'm here about my father, Abraham Grossman, to see my father. He was in an accident, a motor accident...." The starched nurse peered up at me from a frame too diminutive to adjudicate life and death. "Is, is...?"

"Grossman, yes, the surgeon's going to operate, they're preparing him right now. I'll take you to the room, they won't let you in though, I don't think you'll be able to see him tonight." Before a wide swinging door she whispered with another nurse, then returned to me: "No, I'm sorry, they said no, it might be several hours. You can wait in the waiting room if you want, there's nothing you can do tonight. The best thing is go home and get a night's sleep, then ring up the hospital tomorrow morning."

Back at home, Katherine made me a cup of tea. The next morning I went to the phone kiosk outside Mile End Underground and rang up the hospital. He had survived, he was in intensive care still under anesthesia, I couldn't see him. I dialed Mr. Bitwood at work and told him what had happened. I didn't have to hurry, Bitwood said, the afternoon would be all right; until the laboratory was refurbished they'd have to send the samples out to another lab anyway. I went to the Post Office and sent a telegram to Lily in New York, stopped by Altman's and picked up eggs and milk and bread.

Katherine and I shared dinner at home. "It's Thursday, the landlord will be here this afternoon, what should I say?"

"Here's the rent." I handed her nine florins.

–36–

The next morning I followed the young nurse along the hallway. Ward doors were flung wide on both sides, and beyond them to my right, windows recessed into the massive white-painted walls with their tiers of light green ceramic tile directed streams of sunlight to flood along floors and over hospital beds. An old man's legs were hoisted on a coruscating torture rack; his trapped eyes glanced my way, and I, guilty in my well-being, smiled an obeisance. Hurrying my pace, but still not sufficient to escape his tacit entreaty, I nodded in helpless acknowledgement, pointed to the nurse disappearing before me, and mouthed silences as I glided to refuge beyond the door frame.

She had stopped. She turned my way, and beneath the white cap, large blue eyes waited under dark eyebrows for me to catch up. She beckoned toward the half-open door to my right bearing the legend "Surgical Ward." I followed her inside and kept my eyes timorously ahead, reluctant to precipitate out of the confusion of tiled walls, chromed tubes and starched white sheets a particular bed, a mutilated father. I counted peripherally: several beds to my right, eight to the left, and along the wall opposite a row of a dozen more lined up below the windows.

She saw my apprehension, "Don't worry now," and pointed. "He'll be in the end bed on the left, just before that curtain." I forced myself to look. "He's asleep," she added. "If he wakes up try not to let him move."

I stumbled toward the bed, around its foot to the chair on the far side close by a drawn curtain separating the end of the ward. Under the stiff white sheet, its top folded neatly down, a figure lay on its back. A barbaric metal head-dress framed the head, a padded rest bridging under the chin. A cable hooked to an anchor at the top of the contraption ran back and up over a pulley, then down behind the head of the bed. I looked underneath; metal weights drew the cable taut. The violently-opened mouth gasping for air, set in a gaunt, ashen, deeply lined face was barely recognizable. His thinning hair was laced with unfamiliar grey streaks, while heavy black hairs sprouted in profusion from the visible ear on the side where I stood above him. Yet the most startling was the stubble on his face, its preponderance of grey to black, the conflicting slants and whorls of beard. I had never been so close in a moment of quiet to the ragged topography of that face: the elongated lump that swelled under the right side of his chin, a discolored half-inch frayed splotch to the left of his forehead, the admixture of hairs protruding from cavernous nostrils, the coarse skin textured in bumps, crevices, and pimples.

Lower down in the narrow bed, below the shapes contorting the covering blanket, the remarkably foreshortened distance to the feet made his trunk and legs seem shrunken. I stood there enveloped in the tortured breathing, then leaned forward. The movement must have disturbed him and his eyes flickered and partially opened. They were puffed and watery eyes, and they blinked several times unseeing at the ceiling.

"Hello, Dad." No acknowledgement. I waited, then repeated: "Hello, Dad." They darted drunkenly and I eased away for the confusion to subside. Then, again, "Hello, Dad."

"Wha'?" The mouth moved the metal frame as it spoke.

Again I waited, then: "Hello, Dad, it's Zachary."

"Wha'... wha'... wha'...." The eyes spun uselessly. "Wha'? Oo... wha'rris... Oo?..."

I leaned closer, and by his face repeated, "Hello, Dad."

In silence the jaw tried to move.

"Hello, Dad, it's me."

"Wha'?"

"Ssh, hello Dad, don't try to talk."

The blinking ceased, and again the mouth struggled. "Wha'? Wha'? Is it, is it...?"

"Don't move, it's Zech."

"Wha'? Oo.... Zech, Zachary?"

"Yes, Dad, you don't have to talk, don't move, I'm going to stay here with you."

The mouth grappled for words. "Eee, uh'm, uh'm dreaming, Zech, 'ow, 'ow...." His barely audible utterances came slowly, incredulously. The head was unmovable in its mediæval dress.

"It's alright Dad, you're going to be alright, you don't have to talk." I reached over him and bent down, bringing my face close to the cheek sunken within its metal banded frame, into the fetid confusion of antiseptic lotions and venomous breath.

"Zech... Zech... Lily...."

"Ssh, Dad, just lie still, don't try to talk."

He lay there, gathering strength. "Wha'cha, wha'cha? Uh'm, uh'm...."

The same young nurse stood behind me: "Don't let him move, now." Then, gently: "That your father?"

"Yes, he is."

The prone figure sensed a feminine concern. "Lily, Lily, gimme... uh'm dying...."

"He thinks I'm somebody else, last night also he called me Lily. That your mother?"

"Yes."

"She coming to visit? Where is she, she alive, your Mum?"

"She's in America."

"Oh, America! I'd like to go there!"

"Yes."

"He keeps saying he's dying but he's not, he's coming along alright so far, we'll know in a few days. Careful you don't move him, now," she repeated. "Dr. Seymour will be making his rounds soon and you can speak with him."

"Thank you, miss." I leaned closer to Abie and whispered: "Dad, the nurse says you're going to be alright. The doctor will be along soon, I'll talk to him when he comes."

His parched and cracked lips tried again to shape a sound.

"Nurse, his mouth seems so dry."

"He mustn't have nothing to drink, make him vomit it will." At the sink she moistened a small towel which she carefully applied to Abie's lips. He touched them together and she applied the wet towel a second time, then turned to me. "Can't have him vomiting when his head's in traction."

"Yes, I see."

"He's been calling Sid, Sid!"

"That's my uncle, Sid."

She moved off to the opposite line of beds.

"Eee, gimme… gimme… ugh… a bladdy…."

In apprehension at his gathering faculties I pulled the chair to the side of the bed and sat. "Rest, Dad, don't get excited."

A scowl; his eyes flickered and closed, the mouth setting itself rigidly open. He began to snore. He was asleep.

I looked over his blanket to the line of beds beyond, and they swam into a fog. Suddenly, the doctor was above me and I stood up, groggy. "I'm sorry, I'm Zech, Zachary Grossman, Mr. Grossman's son."

"Yes, Mr. Grossman, I'm Dr. Seymour." He looked around. "Is Mrs. Grossman here?"

"Er, no, she's in America."

"In America! Very well, then. Let me say initially your father is a lucky man. We have him in traction as a precaution, considering he might have suffered a cervical fracture. But he has movement in all his extremities, which militates against that diagnosis, and which also speaks well of his rescuers. He's quite alert, even angry at the nurses; some may interpret that as a sign of vitality."

"I'm sorry…."

He looked at me quizzically. "He must remain here in bed for several weeks. Subsequently, depending on the outcome of the immobilization and assuming he survives, he may require some sort of sustained support for the neck, although right now it's too early to say."

"I see."

"And with luck, he might be ambulatory in four to six weeks."

"I see, that means he'll have to stay in the hospital maybe six weeks?"

"At least that." He frowned as though my question were a complaint. "You're lucky the people who extracted him moved him carefully, supporting his spine, not inflicting further injury."

"Yes, thank you very much."

"Hmm, yes."

"Do you think he'll be alright in the end?"

"It would be premature to say he would recover completely, we must wait and see, but he already exhibits a remarkable vigor."

"Thank you."

"Well then I must be on my way. Mr. Grossman isn't my sole patient, you know."

"Yes, I know, thank you."

Abie's mouth was still gaped open, his jaw askew in the contorted face pulled high by the frame.

The same nurse came back over. "He'll probably sleep for hours, now. You married?"

"Me? Oh no, I'm young, I mean, I'm not old enough."

"I got married when I was sixteen."

"Did you? My sister also got married, a few months ago, she only just turned sixteen."

"So you ain't too young for nothing."

"Yes I suppose so, I just meant…."

She looked at my mouth as I spoke. "He's lucky to have a son like you." I didn't know how to respond, but fortunately she continued: "You got a girl?"

"A girl?"

"Special, I mean."

"No, I haven't got a special one."

"Your dad won't wake up for a few hours, probably."

"I see. Then I wonder if I should wait?"

"There ain't nothing you can do, he won't even remember you been here."

"Maybe I should go to work then, I can come back tomorrow."

"If you comes back this evening he'll be more awake. Regular visiting's up at four, but they'll let you in for critical."

"This evening?"

She was straightening the already straight covers. "What time you get off work?"

"Five o'clock, I get off at five o'clock."

"I finish at six today, you could try to see your Dad after work." She smiled at me, and her large eyes reminded me of Aunt Cissie.

"Alright."

"My name's Melissa." She extended a soft little hand, which I took.

"And I'm Zachary, Zachary Grossman, Zech," I said.

"Zachary. Zech," she repeated. She looked up at me, which made me self-conscious of my nearly six foot height. "If he wakes up I'll tell him you was here."

•   •   •

Mr. Smith and two men from the yard were wielding paint brushes, putting the finishing touches to the ceiling. The benches were still covered with canvas sheets.

"'Ow's your Dad doin'?" Mr. Smith asked as I came in.

"They said he'll probably be alright, about six weeks or so. He's got his head in a thing to hold it straight."

"Well, we got this end finished, you can put your bottles and stuff back on the shelves now."

"Thank you."

"It'll all be done pretty quick. We got a delivery this mornin', we run it in number two and number three. Mr. Bitwood sent out for water content and ash but ain't no reason you can't double check. Right, the lab also, you got a box there, on the floor, stuff you ordered, arrived this morning, glass an' stuff. When you finished linin' up your bottles why'n'cha get samples, number two and three while we're finishin' up in 'ere? You'll 'ave 'em in 'ere ready, you can start settin' up y' testin' stuff on the bench over there and we'll be back in business."

From the small office ante-room where we'd temporarily lined up the large glass containers of sulphuric acid, toluol, nitric acid, and grouped the smaller ancillary bottles, I lugged everything back into the laboratory and up onto the shelves as the men continued painting the ceiling. Then, with the sample case and set of bottles across my shoulder, I went outside to scale the two tanks. By the time I'd returned with filled bottles, the brushes were soaking in naphtha and the men were tapping down the paint tins' lids and folding the canvas.

"Welp! It'll smell strong for a while, but it's all ready for yer, Grossman. All the winders is open, don't want you settin' orf them gas burners wiv the place filled wiv naphtha, does we now?"

"You're right. You were really quick fixing everything up. Thank you very much."

"Watch it now wiv them there chemicals, right?"

"Yes."

"Yep, we don't want another go 'round like this 'un."

"Right, I'll be very careful. First, I'll need some sand."

"There's a bin out there near number four, behind the 'vaporation tray." While his men finished packing up the painting gear I followed him out to a corner of the yard and scooped up sufficient sand for bedding the flask in the sand bath. "I'll let you know as soon as I have the numbers," I said, and returned to the lab.

"And you watch it," he called after me, "don't you go leavin' that room while them there chemicals is runnin'."

"I won't, don't worry."

I wanted to get back to The London Hospital before the nurse's shift ended at six. Although it was silly and I wasn't sure why I was hurrying — she'd clearly said she got married when she was sixteen — I applied myself to the series of distillations, and by quarter, to, five was able to give Mr. Smith a set of genuine figures for the next morning's run.

At five-thirty I ran up the wide steps, walked through the entrance hallway and got a visitor's pass. On the bus ride over I'd again considered that Abie might have died since the morning, but in a remarkable change of heart from yesterday that possibility seemed almost inconsequential. Melissa, at the other end of the ward, waved as she saw me enter. I waved back, and came to the foot of his bed. His head was still pulled up, the jaw jutting forward, his mouth pushed rigidly open, the same tormented breathing. Again I came around the side. "Hello, Dad."

Melissa had come to stand silently a good two feet behind me, yet her presence was palpable. "He's alright, we had to give him something to calm him down, he was swearing at Dr. Seymour."

"He was! I'm embarrassed…."

"It's not your fault, don't be embarrassed, he's him, you're you."

"Those noises, is it alright? He looks terrible, his face is so grey."

"Dreaming, something going through his mind. He's coming along right well considering, don't worry, he'll be out of the woods." She pulled a chair over for me. "He might wake up. I told him you was here this morning."

"Thank you."

She smiled. "I'll come by a bit later."

"Alright." She left, and I edged the chair closer to his face. "Hello." There was no interruption in the labored breathing's rhythm. It had been a long day and I settled back in the chair.

A hand was on my shoulder. "Zachary, sorry to disturb you." It was Melissa. "You was asleep."

"Oh! I…." Immediately I was embarrassed, but she didn't seem to mind.

"He hasn't woken up, I came by a few times. He'll probably sleep through the night."

"Really…."

"I'm knocking off in five minutes," she said. "I could stop for a cup of tea before I went home."

"Oh, er, you mean with me?" Stupid! I'd directly *said* the obvious! "Yes, alright."

"I'll take a cup before I catches the bus."

"Yes, we could go to Johnny Isaacs if you like, it's just a walk along Whitechapel Road."
At least, I'd thought of a place immediately the way men are supposed to, to be in command.

"Stay here then, I'll be back in two shakes of a duck's arse."

She returned, and this time she wore a blue blouse and plaid woolen skirt with a wide red belt. Her eyes looked even larger without the white hat, and her hair was black silk. She carried a bag and a red cloth jacket over her arm. "Ready!"

A last look at Abie, who somehow managed to appear even more repulsive than usual, and I followed her into the lift. As we exited down the outside steps into the chilly evening, she spoke. "You work near here?"

"Yes." I didn't want to say in Wapping, the area was so run-down. "I work in a laboratory."

"A laboratory! What do you do, research?"

"Well, sort of. We analyze things, chemicals and stuff."

"You like it?"

"Yes I do, it really is interesting."

"Bet you has to be sharp as a pin."

Thankfully she was making conversation. "I don't know, I do like it, it's the best job I ever had really but you have to be careful, we had an accident this week."

"Accident?"

I casually dismissed our serious laboratory fire. "Well, a little fire, nothing really." We walked along Whitechapel Road. "Do you like being a nurse?"

"It's something to do, to get out of the flat."

"What does your husband do? You said you were married."

"He's in the Merchant Marine, he won't be home for a week."

"I see."

"Do you mind?" she asked.

"Mind? What?"

"Having tea with a married woman."

"No, I just… didn't think about it, you seemed too young to sort of be, well, married already."

"You mean I haven't got that look yet?"

"I…. Here's Johnny Isaacs."

Most tables were empty this early in the evening, and she took a seat.

"I'll just have tea," she said.

I supposed I should pay; thank goodness I had three florins in my pocket.

"I'm sorry about your father."

"Oh yes, but the doctor said he could be alright in six weeks."

"My father took off when I was a kid."

"You mean he left you?"

"'Sright. He just didn't come home one night anymore and that was that."

"Wow! So what did your Mum do?"

"Cleaned people's houses. She wasn't sorry he left. He was one for the booze."

"My father doesn't drink but he's always arguing with people. He hits us, my brother and sisters, and my Mum."

"Thought your Mum was in America."

"She just went, a few weeks ago, with my young brother."

"I seen your Dad's got quite a temper on him, he lays in on the nurses. He still hits you?"

"He hasn't since I started working; he hit my brother a few months ago and broke his jaw."

"He did? I remember, the name, he had a funny name…."

"Marius, Maudy."

"Yes, that's right, Marius Grossman, like Marius Goring in the pictures. We set his jaw, he went home in a few days. His mum said he fell down the steps, she did."

"My mother was embarrassed."

"You seemed nice to your father now then, considering."

"Did I?"

"He's been going off at us in the ward, he's got a mouth on him."

"I'm sorry, I feel embarrassed."

"Why should *you* feel embarrassed?"

"Well, he's my father."

"It ain't your fault if he's like that."

"What's it like being married?"

"Well, he does drink a bit when he comes home."

"Drink? I thought that was your father, the one who left you, your mother…."

"Eric, my hubby, also. When he comes home he's been on the boats for weeks. He does a bit of drinking with his blokes so I just goes to sleep early."

"What happens when he comes home then?"

"Sometimes he gets into bed quiet like, don't wake up 'til next afternoon. Sometimes he's looking for trouble." She stretched a small scar over her left eye. "That's when this happened."

"Really! He did that?"

"Yup."

"Wow, I would have thought after your father…."

"You'd think I'd 'a' learned something, wouldn't you?"

"I…."

"You coming to see your Dad tomorrow, then?"

"Yes, I suppose. After work, I'll come in the evening."

"Maybe when you finished visiting, you can come home with me." She looked into my face. "I'll make dinner."

"You're inviting me to your house?"

"It'd be alright."

"Really?" I wondered if her husband would be angry. "Well, okay then, alright."

When I got home, on the living room table a yellow envelope was propped up against a cup, along with a penciled note from Katya: *Benny came round, I made him promise he'll behave and take me to a doctor. There's a return telegram from Lily in the envelope, it came this afternoon. Can you believe it, because of Dad she's coming back! She probably misses the arguments. If you don't want to stay by yourself tonight you can come over, don't worry Benny won't do anything. We're going to the hospital in the morning. The landlord came for the rent, I gave him the two-shilling pieces you gave me.*

—o—O—o—

37

Next day at the lab, all I could think of was Melissa's invitation to her place for supper. Supposing her husband came home while we were eating? I'd have to explain about Abie and the hospital. But she'd said he was a merchant seaman, away on his ship. Another thing, I couldn't go empty-handed — what did people bring? There was a sweet shop opposite the hospital; I could use another florin and buy two bars of Cadbury's, a Fruit-and-Nut and a Caramello, fourpence each. After work, when I bought the chocolate, the shop-keeper barely gave the coin a look, and I didn't count his one-and-fourpence change until I got outside. The very word *counterfeit* was ugly; I'd intended just a purely scientific experiment — but now someone had to pay the rent while Abie was in hospital.

Up in the lift and along the corridor I arrived at Abie's bed, and she came over. This evening, well-defined dark eyelashes that I didn't recall from yesterday draped her blue eyes. Further, her eyelids and the area under her eyebrows seemed tinged a bluish grey, forcing a disconcerting compulsion to look.

"I met your sister Kathy this morning. She came with her hubby."

I tried to sound unperturbed. "Katya, yes, she left a note that she was coming."

"They just stayed ten minutes, he seemed jittery, said his place was waiting for him. I told your sister I met you and we chatted a bit." She blinked.

"Did she say anything?"

"She just said, good." Now she looked at me more searchingly. "So, we're going to have supper at my flat?"

"Yes, are we, is it alright?"

"If you still wants to…." Again she blinked, this time more slowly.

"I was thinking about it at work, I wondered — will it be alright with your husband…?"

"Well," she almost snapped, "there ain't no need to send him a telegram," and in that moment her eyes became hard; Aunt Cissie's eyes never became hard. Then she smiled to soften the admonishment. "He won't be around, his boat ain't docking 'til the end of next week, eight more days like I said."

That must mean she planned not to tell him; maybe that's what people did. "Yes, alright." Not knowing what else to say, I turned to Abie. Beyond the padded steel hoop and his facial stubble, he was even more grey. "He still doesn't look very good."

"He ain't over the hump yet but he's coming along alright. He was awake for a few minutes when your sister was here, he was talking."

"That's good, isn't it?"

"Yes, your Dad's going to be alright. So," her face softened and she cocked her head to the side, "so you coming home for supper?"

"Well yes, thank you, I'd like to."

Momentarily, Abie's eyes opened to the ceiling and in his stupor he jerked. "Did you get the drink, uh'm, uh'm dying uh'm so thirsty, where's the *fu–ucking* drink already, uh'm, uh'm...."

"He's really got a mouth on him!" She moistened a towel at the sink behind us then put it to his lips. He licked a few times, then was back to oblivion.

"I'll stay here with him 'til you're ready," I said.

"Right-e-o, I'll be half an hour."

It was hot, so I hung up my pullover with the chocolate bars in the side pockets, and pulled the chair over. He moved. "Hello, Dad."

"Wha'...? Oo... oo...."

"It's me, Dad, Zech."

Again his eyes opened. "Eee, Zech is it?"

"Don't move, Dad, don't try to talk."

He sought to loosen his jaw. "Eee, they said uh 'ad an accident, uh don't know what 'appened." His eyes closed again. "They took me 'ere, eee mu van, all the things, material, eee, from The Lane uh 'ad material."

"Ssh, don't talk, Dad, you don't have to talk."

"Talk, talk! Wha'cha telling me don't talk? Uh'm thirsty, uh don't know why they took me 'ere." He began to struggle.

"Try to stay still, I'll see if the nurse can get something for you to drink." I attracted Melissa's attention; she signaled, then came over. "My father is still thirsty. Is he allowed to drink anything?"

"We can get him a little something." The silky almost black hair tried to escape from the trim white bonnet, and she pushed it back under.

I whispered to her: "He's moving, he's trying to...."

"Don't move now Mr. Grossman... how's about a spot of something?" I made room as she poured something from a glass into a spoon and held it to his lips.

"Anything, anything, uh'm dying, anything already."

"You're not dying, you'll be up and out of here in two shakes of a duck's arse." She fed him a spoonful, straightened the sheet, winked at me and left. I sat again, and Abie continued.

"Yeh, they took me 'ere, i's like terrible, uh can't move." Again his agitation was mounting.

"Ssh." I pulled his covers up higher.

The liquid had revived him and his eyes were more focused. "The nurses 'ere, well, uh don't know what to say, they won't bring me nothing to drink, you can die 'ere before anyone comes."

"Ssh..." He spoke so loud I was sure the other visitors were listening.

"...Uh can't call." He licked still-dry lips. "They're all deaf in this place, you can die 'ere."

"Rest, Dad, don't make yourself so... agitated."

"Agi...tated?" His throat rasped as the cracking voice struggled louder. "You call 'em and they're, like, uh dunno, they're deaf." The effort was too much, and his head lowered reluctantly into the pillow. The jaw continued to move as his eyes flickered closed; then the mouth set, hard, open, and he was gasping, snoring.

She was back, in a red cloth jacket and dark wool skirt with a wide belt, carrying a bag. The voluminous hair bounced as she moved. "Ready!"

Outside and across the road we caught the Bow bus. She slid in by the window, and I followed and settled next to her, enveloped in an unexpected cloud of perfume. She continued. "You got sisters and brothers at home then?"

Her arm and leg jiggled against me as the bus moved. "No, they're all in America except Katherine."

"So who was you gonna have supper with now your Dad's in hospital?"

"By myself, I suppose. I try not to eat with him."

"Would'a thought you'd have lots of girls after you to make supper."

"Oh…. I know one girl, Hazel, she's my sister's friend but she's too young. You said you're eighteen."

"Nope. Guess again."

"I don't know, I know you're older than me a bit. Nineteen?"

"Right. Nineteen, been married three years."

"I… I, er, I mean, I didn't know a married person could invite someone to supper."

"What do you mean?" She spun at me sharply and I knew I'd said a stupid thing. "You from Mars, something? There ain't no book of rules! You just does… whatever, whatever's alright."

"I'm sorry, I didn't mean…."

"Boy, bet you ain't never…."

"What do you mean…?" I dreaded an elaboration.

"Bet you ain't never done…. You ever had a steady?"

"Steady?"

"Girlfriend!"

"Well no, I mean I didn't have one yet."

"You ain't never, well," and fortunately she lowered her voice, "slept with someone?"

"You mean, like with a girl?"

"Hmm!" Her eyebrows went up. The bus was sweeping past the Mile End station, and though I'd have loved to change the subject I didn't want to mention I lived there. Bow, where I'd never been, was probably not so dilapidated.

"I s'pose you been sorta… protected?"

"Protected? I don't think so, no we weren't."

She changed the subject. "I eats by myself a lot."

"So do I now."

"It gets to you, it ain't good."

"I know, I don't like doing it every single day."

"Eric, me hubby, he's on the boats so you has to get used to doing everything by yourself."

"Yes…."

"Like fixing things round the flat, when he comes home he ain't about to fix things what got broke."

"Is he away a lot?"

"So much I went back to nursing. I was bored outta my mind, least at the hospital I've got people to talk to. How many times can you rearrange the furniture?"

"Did you know he was going to be away a lot when you got married?"

"Yes, but I had to get away from Mum, she was right mean. Eric's sweet the first couple of days home, then he gets fidgety. Sometimes I'm glad when he goes out for a drink with his blokes, 'cept he might be a bit boozed up when he gets home. That's when he did this one," and she turned her face to again show me the small vertical scar on the left side of her forehead.

"Yes, how did he do it?"

"Threw a vase at me."

"My goodness!"

"What must you think, me telling all this family stuff!" She looked out the window. "Sometimes I'd like to just go a long way away, start all over again."

"Do you have any children yet?" I asked.

"How could I go to work if I had kids?"

"I don't know…." Even my questions felt inept. "Maybe your mother, someone, could look after them…."

"My mother don't know how to look after nobody. Well, we're home." She stood up and pulled at the signal cord, the bus rolled to a stop, and I helped her down to the pavement. The street was a row of fairly shabby tenements on either side. She fished in her bag for a key, and opened a paint-peeled street door in the old brick building adjacent to the bus stop. "It ain't much but it's home, to coin a phrase."

As I followed her up two flights of stairs I was relieved at the peeling walls. At the top on the small landing she unlocked one of two adjacent brown corner doors, reached her hand inside and found the light switch. The living room had a sofa, a side chair and a low table with a vase of flowers. On the opposite wall a dark cabinet stood on shaped legs, a series of plates arranged vertically behind glass panels in the doors. A brightly colored raffia mat covered the floor in front of the sofa, picking up the hues of the flowered wallpaper. She took off her coat and hung it behind the door. "Hang your stuff up. S'cuse me a minute," and she disappeared into what I assumed was the toilet. I hung up my pullover and waited, determined not to be nervous. It was several minutes before she was out again. I followed her into a kitchen also wallpapered with a floral design. Another vase of what seemed like silk flowers stood in the middle of the dining table.

"You like flowers." That sounded alright.

"Yes, s'pose I do. I wallpapered the whole flat by meself. Eric said I done a real good job. You gotta be careful so's you don't get half a flower here and half a there."

She opened the door to what was probably a refrigerator, then stood by the sink cutting Xs in brussels sprouts. I didn't know what to do or say. In the awkward silence she glanced at me; I said "I'm sorry, I didn't mean to stare."

"That's okay," she responded. She continued paring, then suddenly stopped and wiped her eye with the back of her hand.

"Are you alright?"

"Yup." She wiped the corner of one eye with her apron, and smudged the mascara. "Nothing."

"Really? Would you… did I do anything, do you want me to leave?"

"Oh, no, no, it's not you. I don't know why that happened, it's silly." She laughed. "Sometimes I cry and I don't have no idea what it's all about."

"Where are the dishes, I want to do something to help."

"That cupboard there, yes, the middle one, there's plates." I took out two plates, hoping they were the ones she wanted. She put down the paring knife. "It's okay, I'll do it. Here, sit in the living room while I get things ready." She led me into the other room. "You like Vera Lynn?"

"She's, er... okay." At least I'd be able to say something about music, about singing.

She opened a lid in the corner, clicked something, and tinny violins began to swish. Vera Lynn began: *"Silver Wings In The Moonlight..."* She switched on a floor lamp and turned off the ceiling light. From the kitchen her puttering noises intermingled with the record. *I wonder if she'll want to have sex after we finished dinner, is that what the invitation was?* Sputtering sounds indicated something was frying. Vera Lynn's singing was horrible as usual; she didn't have the faintest idea about phrasing, and her vibrato made you feel seasick. "Should I do anything?" I called.

"Turn it over, you know how to do it?"

"I think so." I clicked the mechanism and my head swam, as much because of the tension as the horrible singing.

Then, "Ready, come on in!" She had covered the kitchen table with an off-white lace-patterned tablecloth. Different dinner plates from those I'd pulled down, with matching cups, and silverware on folded starched serviettes decorated opposite sides.

"Wow! It looks beautiful!"

She beamed, and brought back the flowers from the counter to place in the center. "Take a seat, sir!" From the stove she brought over a pot and ladled out onto the plates a dark thick mixture that looked like intestines covered with heavy gravy. "Hope you like bubble and squeak!"

"Bubble and what?"

"Bubble and squeak, do you good after working all day."

I had no idea what it was. "Oh yes, I love it."

She added brussels on top, chips along the side, stood a teapot on a wood trivet, then sat. She began eating. "So."

"So."

"Eat."

I ate.

"Your Dad, he must be a terror at home, that mouth on him."

"Yes, I don't really see him much now, especially since my mother went to America."

"Can't say as how I blames you. Why'd your mum go to America, get away from your Dad?"

"In a way. Two of my sisters are there."

"So, you ain't never had a steady."

"Well, not what you'd call a real steady girlfriend."

"You never been to bed with no one?"

I gulped. "Well, I dunno...."

"Want more bubble and squeak?"

"Yes please." It tasted horrible, but at least it would delay whatever hovered on the horizon — perhaps including her husband bursting through the door. But inevitably, even eating slowly as possible, Judgment Day arrived.

"I'm finished as well," she said. "Help me with the dishes then we can sit on the sofa."

Feeling a little sick, I helped her with the dishes.

"How old are you? You knows how old I am."

"Seventeen. I'm going to be eighteen next month."

"And you ain't never been with a girl."

"Well, I...."

"Don't mean no offence, but you ain't a homo are you?"

"Homo?"

"Nancyboy, queer, a faggot! You don't have to be ashamed of what you are."

"No I'm not! Wow! Why d...? Certainly not, whew, why did you think...?"

"Well, you're kinda, I don't know, you ain't never.... Don't you like girls?"

"Well yes definitely, of course I do, I s'pose I'm shy, that's all!"

"Let's sit on the sofa then." She finished with the dishes and I followed her into the living room. "You want to hear more Vera Lynn?"

"Well, not really. Do you have any Frank Sinatra?"

"We only got Vera Lynn."

"Alright, Vera Lynn then." She stood up and again clicked on the gramophone. I needed to take charge; that would help prove I wasn't a faggot. Questions might do it. "Tell me why you got married young. My sister said she didn't want to have to take care of my Dad when my mother went to America."

"My story ain't pretty."

"You can tell me."

"Want another cuppa?"

"Yes, alright."

"Come help me make some more, then." I followed her back into the kitchen.

"Well, my Mum used to work in the shop, just mornings, made sandwiches for the fellas at Smith and Rumstead, you know, the metalwork place? She'd be outta the house early, like six o'clock, we lived in a house." She filled the kettle and put it on the gas. "Dad 'd come across... 'e'd come across to get me." Her voice went quieter. "I'd have to get into bed with him and we'd... he'd make me have sex, do things."

"My god." I wasn't sure I'd heard right.

"Yeah. The first time he pulled me over his side of the bed... I felt this thing, I didn't know what it was, I was just a kid. His voice was different. I was real scared... I did it, I just did what he said, well, really I thought I did love him. Heard enough?"

Girls, women, were amazing! I really needed to realize that girls weren't shy like boys could be — things were actually the opposite way around from what I'd always thought.

"Heard enough?" she repeated.

"No, I just... it sounds... I don't know."

She rinsed the cups out and stood them on the table. "He was the only father I had, I s'posed he knew."

"My god, you read about it, how terrible."

"Well, you better believe it happens. He started around me eighth birthday, February, Mum had a miscarriage and stayed at the hospital a coupl'a days. It was winter, it was cold in the house, his bed was warm. He'd pick me up and... touch me up. I figured that's what dads do — I hated it but he was me Dad and I loved him too. Mum used to fight him about it, she knew what was going on, she'd hit me for it, I was scared she'd be looking." She glanced over. "You alright?"

"Of course, if you don't mind talking about it, of course I want to listen," I lied.

The kettle was steaming and she poured through the strainer into each cup. "That one morning she come back early and there I was right in her bed, s'pose it was bound to happen sooner or later. She hit me, me nose it was bleeding, blood all on the sheets, every place. She was trying to hit Dad and she was screaming bloody murder." She replaced the kettle on the stove and took milk out of the refrigerator. "Sit down, might as well have it here. You alright?"

"Er... yes. 'Course I am."

We sat, and she went on. "First he didn't do nothing, that got me real scared, then he started shouting" — her face was flushed — "I was real scared, he mostly didn't shout none. Well, he was hitting her, he knocked her on the floor. I took off for the kitchen; he called out after me, 'Look after your mother,' and out he went, I s'posed he went to work. Mum come right in after me and she swung that fist," she gulped, "she knocked me on the kitchen floor and I threw up right on the floor... she grabbed me hair and shoved me face right in it, she was shoveling puke right back in me mouth. Oh, God! I couldn't breathe."

She seemed so upset I reached across the table to touch her hand, but in her agitation she quickly pulled away. "Melissa," the name was a lump in my mouth. "Can I put milk in your tea?"

"I'm really going on, I gotta stop, I'll stop now. It's getting late, I s'pose you'll be wanting to get home."

"I don't mind if it's late, I better not miss the last bus, that's all."

"Tomorrow I got the eight 'til four. You seem like you never did wanna hit nobody."

"Me? Er, I usually talk my way out of fights, then I end up feeling like a coward."

"That ain't no coward, getting outta fighting."

"I hate fighting, that's all we had when I was growing up, nothing as bad as yours though, what you had. Christ, you must have felt terrible when you heard him coming to get you."

"Real scared."

"Were you afraid he might kill you?"

"Kill me? If I'd'a told on him he sure would'a'."

I wondered if girls actually liked some of it a tiny bit, not the threatening stuff, but when someone took over sort of decisively, like maybe a tough boyfriend telling them they had to have sex. "Melissa..."

She looked. "What?"

I felt foolish; how could I actually ask? "I... I...."

"Well, what then?"

She'd been so outspoken so far about everything; maybe it was alright to ask. "No, I just wondered, did...?" Consumed in her own story, it was almost as if I weren't there. "No, I don't know, I just wondered if you, if girls...."

"What you trying to say?"

"Well I dunno, I... was it terrible, I mean, all of it, did...?"

"Terrible? You mean me dad taking me in their bed like that?"

"Well I... I just wondered if women might... like it a little bit, only a *little* bit, oh I dunno...."

"Like it?"

"No, not exactly, not everything, oh I don't know, I don't know what to say...."

"Well out with it then."

"I just wondered... I just wondered about all of it, I know it must have been terrible, but sort of if women...."

She started to cry; my question had been so stupid it had made her cry! "That's what people don't understand, I wasn't a woman, I was a kid...."

I tried to touch her hand, but she pushed her chair away from the table.

"Melissa I'm sorry, I didn't mean to be so stupid, to make it worse."

She stood up. "Would ya believe it, I was gonna ask if you wanna stay tonight, now I don't know...."

"Stay with you? All night? I thought you'd hate me now."

She exhaled loudly, her face softened, and the mascara became completely splodged as she wiped both eyes. "Well, I don't hate you." She sat down again. "D'you want to stay with me tonight?"

"M... Melissa... sure, sometime, but maybe this time I'd better go home, my sister may be there, sometimes she waits for me to come home, I mean she's a bit ill, I'd definitely like to stay the next time...."

Now she laughed, although her face was still wet.

"You're laughing at me. Am I like a stupid kid?"

She wiped her eyes. "Yup. But, you're still kinda cute."

Whew! I needed to think about everything before I could actually stay — maybe all that stuff with her father had made her a bit insane and she might wake up in the middle of the night and I'd be trapped; also her husband could come home with his friends after they'd been drinking beer, and they wouldn't be in the mood to listen about Abie and the hospital. "Melissa, I definitely want to stay next time please, just, we don't have a telephone at my house and if Katya comes over and I don't come home she'll think something happened and I wouldn't be able to ring her up or anything...."

"Okay, okay, okay, okay, I'll walk you down the stairs then."

"Oh, thanks, thank you, thank you for the lovely dinner."

"Dinner, oh yes. C'mon, you'll miss the bus!"

I got my pullover and followed her down the two flights of stairs and out into the street. "So the next time, can I stay? I mean I really would like to stay, I'll tell Katya if I'm not home the next time she shouldn't worry, I'm, I'm...."

The bus was approaching. "You tell her you're staying with a married woman."

"Yes?" I didn't know if she was joking. "I mean, I really would...."

She put her arm around my neck and gave me a long juicy kiss right on the lips as the bus pulled up. "It's alright. Next time, when you're a little more... calm... you'll stay with me, okay?"

"Okay." I got on the bus and sat down, and looked to see what was pulling at the pockets of the pullover. It was two bars of Cadbury's — a Caramello and a Fruit-and-Nut.

•   •   •

Mr. Bitwood came into the lab. "So, everything's under control since the fire."

"Yes, I'm being very very careful with everything."

"Mr. Margolin knows you've had a lot on your shoulders since Hitchcock went."

"Yes, but I'm getting it all better organized bit by bit."

"Mr. Margolin didn't want to give him the sack, you know, especially since they just had a baby girl last week."

"A baby girl? Who?"

"Hitchcock, didn't he tell you?"

"A girl? I thought he was going to... they were supposed to have a boy."

"What do you mean, supposed to? They had a baby girl."

"Oh... I don't know."

"Pity, Mr. Margolin warned him nigh on a dozen times to pull his socks up."

"Yes. Mr. Bitwood, don't forget, my mother and brother'll be coming in tomorrow afternoon."

"Mr. Margolin said take the afternoon, he appreciates you ask ahead 'stead of just disappearing."

"Thank you, I'll come in a bit early so I have time to get the numbers on tanks one and two in the morning before I go. That'll keep the yard humming for the rest of the day."

"Good lad."

Next day, directly from work I went to meet the boat-train at Waterloo Station. At first I didn't recognize Aunt Zelda waiting on the platform, she looked so much older under her prim little hat.

"I'm also part of the welcoming committee," she said. "How have you been, it's years already."

"I know. How did you know Mum was coming back?"

"Lily wrote a letter, didn't you get a letter?"

"Yes, she sent a telegram."

"She told me about your father's accident."

"Yes, they said he's lucky he's not paralyzed, at first they thought his neck was broken."

"She never should have married him, we all told her but she wouldn't listen."

"Well...."

"And how's little Katya? Where is she, I heard she got married, I thought I'd see her here also."

"She's alright, she's been a bit ill, but she's alright."

"Did you know Auntie Rae is going for tests? Let's hope it's nothing."

"No, I didn't know."

"How you've grown! How many years is it? The big girls there in America, I bet they have American accents already."

The boat-train from Southampton squealed to a halt, engulfing us in a deluge of noise and steam. Zelda waved politely, and from among the swarm of debarking passengers Lily came toward us, and behind her Marius dragging three bags. Lily walked right by me — I couldn't tell whether she even noticed me — and put her arms around her sister. Zelda's hat fell off, exposing hair so thin you could easily see her white scalp. The two of them held an unmoving embrace for a full minute.

"So Lily, you're home from your world travels," said Zelda finally, picking up her hat and dusting it off.

Marius stood by the bags. "'Ello, good to be back, yup, I'd rather be in good old England than New York."

Lily partially turned my way: "Ee, how's your Father?"

"The doctor thinks he'll be alright Mum, maybe six more weeks."

"Huh, still rather be 'ere spite of 'im," grunted Marius.

"So how was the voyage, the ship?" continued Zelda. "Did you get seasick?"

"Not this time, Maudy made me sit outside on the deck. It was a wind but it was better than being sick."

"It's good you had Maudy with you to help with everything."

She smiled at Marius. "He's been a very good boy, the whole time he's been good."

"And the girls, how are the girls? I bet they're real Yanks already, I can imagine!"

"They're alright, Rivka got married, ugh!, you should only see him, she likes him, what can you do? They both have good jobs, the three of them, they've got plenty to eat." Finally, Lily turned to me and I was able to see her eyes were glistening. "So, we're back!"

"Mum, I'm glad you're back, I suppose it's a shame in a way...."

"How's Katya?"

"She's alright... I mean, she's been a bit ill for a long time. Benny's supposed to take her to a doctor."

"Still, after all this time, *oy a broch!*"

"I have to get back to the office," said Zelda. "Lily, I'll come round, maybe Saturday after I go with Rae to the doctor, we'll both come."

She left, and Lily, Marius and I gathered up the bags.

"What about the steamer?" asked Marius.

"We don't have to schlepp it right away. The two of you, you'll come back, you'll get it tomorrow maybe."

We caught the Underground in the direction of the East End.

"It's 'orrible in America."

"Really?" I was surprised. "Rivka and Zilla love it there, that's what Rivka always says in the letters."

"It's different for the girls," said Lily. "They've got their boyfriends, they're settled, they got good jobs, what more do they need?"

"Yup, they're girls, they're always busy. I didn't 'ave no friends, nothing to do 'cept go to work."

"He missed his friends, it's understandable. For both of us, it was hard there."

"Mum, when do you want to see Dad?" I asked. "We go right past Whitechapel station."

"Now, I'll get off at Whitechapel. Maudy, you'll come with."

"Who wants to see the old barstard the first day!"

"Sshh, you'll come with. Zech, you take the two big bags home, Maudy you bring that one with. We'll be home a bit later."

"Alright Mum." I'd seen Abie most days, and today I really didn't want to contend with Melissa; who knows, her husband's ship might have docked already. "I'll pick up something at Altman's to eat with a cup of tea when you get home. Maudy, you know the way in the hospital, it's the same floor where you were for your jaw."

"Least the ol' barstard won't be able to start punching if 'is bladdy neck's broke!"

"Don't talk about your father like that!"

"No, they're pretty sure it's not his neck, Maudy, it's his ribs and concussion and things."

"Crikey, we gotta see 'im again!"

Lily began: "Well, just try to be a bit nice, it's only for an hour maybe."

"Nice to 'im! I'll be nice to 'im even if 'e don't deserve it, but will 'e be nice to us?"

"Come on, you can't start with all the old stuff right away," said Lily. "He'll be different now after all this."

"Fat chance!"

I tried to engender a little sympathy. "Maudy, when I'm there he's still delirious mostly."

Then I went to give Mum some English money — almost English money, my one-from-the-last counterfeit florin.

"What do you mean," she said, "we changed back the money on the ship."

"I forgot, the *Queen Mary's* British."

The train jerked to a stop at Whitechapel, and the two of them alighted. "See you in a few hours," I called after them. "Leave him alone, Maudy."

Next, Stepney Green; then at Mile End, as I was exiting the station and dragging the two heavy bags across Mile End Road, a voice called from the Burdett Road bus stop: "Zech!" Again, it was Reuben Berger.

"Oh, hello Reuben."

"Walk down Burdett Road with me. Where're you going with those bags?"

"They're my mother's and Maudy's, they've just come back from America."

"They came back! What was it, too hard for 'em?"

"No, my father had an accident, different stuff. Here, carry one for me." He actually took one of the bags!

"So, it's nearly December already and the last time you said the end of that month you'd show me around where you work. That was August."

"Reuben, showing you my place isn't the only thing I've got going on."

"I knew it was a lie when you said it, I knew you didn't work in a laboratory."

"Christ, Reuben do you ever believe *anything* anyone says?"

"I do if they're telling the truth."

"Alright, this week I'm still too busy, with my mother coming back now. How about Monday?"

"Monday? Next Monday?"

"Be there Monday evening, let's say half-past-six, pretty much everyone should have left by then."

"I'll be there."

"Right. It's round the back from where I met you getting on the bus that time, when it was sleeting."

"I'll be there."

Back in the house I deposited the bags in the living room. From upstairs, Katherine called out, "Is that you, Zech?"

"Yes!" I ran upstairs. "Katya, you're here again, what happened?"

"Did they get here?"

"Yes, I met them at Waterloo Station but they went to see Dad on the way back, they'll be home soon. But what happened?"

"Oh, the usual, Benny was going to take me to the doctor this afternoon and he never showed up."

"He never showed up?"

"That's right, he just left me waiting there."

"Do you think he's alright?"

"Benny's *always* alright. I know what happened, something at his place, he didn't tell anyone he was supposed to be taking his wife to the doctor."

"What a rotten thing to do!"

"There's something even more rotten."

"What do you mean?"

"Well, I think he's still fucking that slutty Rosalind in the office there."

"What!"

"Excuse my language."

"What? You mean…."

"Sorry, don't mean to shock you. Zech, the world isn't quite as pretty as you'd like it to be."

"Christ, well, I mean, what should I do, I can go and tell him off…."

"I'm not sure if he is, but when I went there the way they both are, he doesn't look straight at me…."

"Well…."

"No, it's alright Zech, I'll handle it when I feel better."

"I'm sorry Katya, it sounds terrible… I could ask Reuben to come with me and maybe the two of us could like, scare…."

"No, no, no, I shouldn't have said anything."

"The barstard, christ! Don't worry, Katya, Mum'll be home in a little while. Tomorrow I'll bring some money from work and Mum can take you to a doctor."

"Where will you get money? I don't s'pose Mum has any."

"Katya, I absolutely promise that when I come home from work tomorrow evening I'll have enough money for you to go to the doctor. That's a promise, that's the end of it, no more discussion."

"Really?"

"That's it. I'd better run over to Altman's to get some butter and milk and stuff before they close. See you in ten minutes."

"Where're you getting the money from, what's going on?"

"Nothing."

"Nothing? What, did you rob a bank or something?"

"Nothing. Don't ask."

I ran downstairs and across to Altman's, and spent my last coins on milk and bread and butter, and some fruit. Back, I called up to Katherine, "You want tea? I'm putting the kettle on, I'll bring it up."

A few minutes later I brought both cups of tea upstairs. As I sat on the edge of the bed there came a knock on the street door: "'Ere we are, we're 'ome."

"They're here!"

I gave Katherine my cup, ran down and opened the door. Lily walked past me into the living room. "It's so dark."

"Oh, I forgot to put the light on." From the kitchen mantelpiece I brought in matches and lit the gas mantle. As the light crept across the room, she looked around. *"Oy,* it looks like it hasn't been cleaned once."

"I don't know, I cleaned it a bit."

"I'll have to start cleaning right away."

"So 'e's stuck in the 'ospital now, serve 'im right!"

"Ssh, leave him alone, it's a shame for him."

I took the bag from Marius and put it down. "Katya's upstairs," I said to Lily.

"She is? Benny's not here?"

"She had an argument with him, she stays here when they argue."

"How is she, is she alright?"

"She's in bed, go up and see."

"Ee, it's too long already." Lily lay her coat on the settee and went upstairs. Marius and I followed.

"Katya, you're still not well!"

"Hello Mum."

"Did you go to the doctor?"

"We don't have money for a doctor."

"A *broch* on Benny, he doesn't have enough for a doctor? You should have told Dad."

"You're right, I should have told Dad I had an abortion and it keeps starting bleeding again and I feel faint and I need money for a doctor."

"Crikey, what's an abortion, that what Aunt Cissie 'ad?"

"No, Maudy, hello, how was America?"

Lily sat on the very edge of Katherine's bed while I stood in the background. "Zech, maybe the butcher's still open, run quick and ask him for a nice fresh chicken, they're upstairs, their flat, knock loud on the door if he's closed. I'll pay him... tell him I'll pay him Friday. You get paid on Friday?"

"Don't worry Mum, I'll bring some money home tomorrow."

She looked at Katherine. "I'll make you some soup. You're thin as a bone."

On the way over to the butcher I burst into tears. Perhaps it was having Mum back in the house again, maybe it was that she'd look after Katherine, see that she ate. However shabby the house was, at least it would start to feel lived-in. Mum would clean everything. It would be a home again.

—o—O—o—

38

Uh'm lying 'ere. Uh'm in a bed. Uh thought it was dark, a minute ago it was dark, all of a sudden it's light out, it's like daytime already. Maybe uh fell asleep before, uh just woke up. Uh remember uh want to get up but uh can't get up. Maybe uh could 'ave a drink, they'll bring me a drink. They painted the ceiling.

Ugh, what's this on mu mouth, like a wet *shmatta*, uh want a proper drink uh'm so thirsty. A white jacket she's wearing there, linen, stiff linen uh mean starch, the loose shoulders, it's like a loose-fitting jacket she's wearing. 'Er name, 'er name, uh can't remember 'er name, uh!, uh can't even remember 'er name, with a spoon she gave me some water before. She said something, a long way away, oo knows oo she's talking to. The ceiling, *now* uh remember, at last they painted it.

We got 'ome with the oranges from the cart, what is it, a barrow. Uh looked out the window yeh, feet, loads of feet going past the window, women's feet, men's feet, it was low down, downstairs, a cellar, the rooms. If 'e came, if 'e chased us 'e'd 'ave to bend right down in the street to look in the window. 'E couldn't catch us, 'ow could 'e catch us, by the time 'e knocked we'd be out into the yard already. All 'is customers, *oy vey ist mir,* they'd be 'is customers alright if 'e came after us, they'd clean 'im out in one minute they'd clean 'im out. 'E'd come back to 'is cart, they'd take 'is 'orse even, everything they'd take.

The voice! It's Sid!

Sid! Mu voice won't come out, like mu mouth is funny, uh'm so dry. When 'e comes over uh'll tell 'im, in a minute, yeh, uh'll tell 'im Sid, mu mouth is funny, uh wanna drink. Then uh'll tell 'im about the ceiling. Sid, they painted the ceiling. Mu mouth, if uh 'ad a drink then uh could talk, yeh. Gimme a drink, Sid, gimme a drink.

All of a sudden she's back, "Be careful Mr. Grossman."

Uh remember when they painted the ceiling. The landlord sent someone, the barsted 'e never wanted to fix anything, paint, 'e just wanted the rent alright, but *at last* 'e sent someone to paint the ceiling, in the end 'e sent someone. Uh 'ad to look at the ceiling, the way we all slept in the attic, eee, all lined up on the floor! Sid, 'e was alright. The others, ugh! to sleep with any of 'em. Move! fidget! move! fidget! that's all they did all night, move, fidget 'til you could jump out of your skin already. Uh was lucky, in the end uh slept by myself. Afraid like uh was gonna do something, all of 'em they were afraid! What could uh do, what did they think uh'd do to 'em, uh was so terrible? Let 'em all take a *broch!*

Voices, what is it? Eee, it's daytime. My goodness, tsk, tsk, they're keeping me 'ere a long time, they think uh don't know, like uh don't realize, uh've been 'ere a long time already, you can crank your *kishkas* out before they'll get you something. Uh'll get up, true as uh stand 'ere uh'll get up an' uh'll go 'ome, uh'll get mu clothes, uh'll walk right out.

"Mr. Grossman?" someone's calling, "Mr. Grossman!" from outside, what is it? Abie, can you 'ear me? Joe, 'is idea of a joke! Joe, a real barsted 'e is. Eee, 'e pulled the covers right off me, 'undreds of times 'e pulled the covers off uh'm freezing, eee, and there 'e is *noch,* a little baby all bundled up like nice and warm, *nabuch,* uh'm freezing cold 'ere. Uh kicked 'im, eee!, uh kicked 'im, in 'is sleep uh kicked the barsted, with mu feet uh pushed 'im *right out,* 'e rolled on the floor, 'e didn't know what 'appened to 'im! They all said What's going on? What's going on, they should worry they're not sleeping with 'im, the barsted. 'E won't sleep with me again! *Uh'm* the *meshugener?* Uh should worry! Joe, Joe *'e's* the meshuggener, they should all *gai in drerd* they should go.

"Mr. Grossman, how are you feeling today?" a man, it was a man up there, like a doctor maybe, people standing there, others, white, white things they're wearing. More voices, talking like quiet whispering there, what is it already with the secrets? Gimme some fu–ucking water already. Uh'll tell 'em, uh'll show 'em they should give me water already. Uh can't talk. Eee, a terrible 'eadache, mu 'ead, uh can't even move mu 'ead, the way it's aching. What is it, a spoon, she's putting a spoon in mu mouth, yeh, at last, some water. Uh feel sick, ugh!, uh'm going to be sick, eee, Lily, quick.

"Don't move, Mr. Grossman don't move your head, just stay still."

What's this, in mu mouth, uh'm sick, it's all in mu mouth, uh can't breath, what's she doing to me already, uh can't move. Right in mu mouth! That's not Lily, where's Lily, where is she, that woman when you want 'er she's not there if you want something, ugh!, it's all in mu throat.

"Don't move, don't move your head. Now everything's going to be alright, we're cleaning your mouth out, you just rest there."

Mr. Grossman, the doctor said, you had an accident. Accident? 'Oo 'ad an accident? Uh didn't 'ave no accident.

It was red. Orange color. We 'ad to get fruit, some nice oranges, off the cart. First Sid and Sarah went, they talked nice to 'im, like to make out they were bargaining. The people by the cart, standing 'round the cart, their faces, like orange-colored, the sun, all the oranges were shining. Sarah, eee, she was good, she made out like she was bargaining on the other side, then all of a sudden Sid and me we grabbed the oranges and we ran!, eee, 'e didn't know what 'appened to 'is oranges all of a sudden. Like two *gunifs* we ran! Uh was starving 'ungry, eating and running all the way along The Waist back to Cephas Street, everybody was looking what's going on there?, we came in with oranges, eee did we 'ave oranges! They all grabbed one, Anya, Momma, Chona, Joe, even Morrie took one. Uh told Joe to go… go *fu–uck off,* no orange for 'im.

Someone's calling, what is it, Dad or something, like from the other room. You could *plutz,* every week 'e came for the rent alright, just one thing you 'ad to say, one word, all of a sudden 'e couldn't 'ear, deaf 'e went, 'e was stone deaf in case it would cost 'im a penny, to paint the ceiling.

Hello, Dad, someone's calling me. Someone's standing there. Mu neck, uh can't look. Oo is it, what is it, they're bending on top, over.

"Hello, Dad."

'Oo is it? What?

"Hello, Dad, it's me."

"Wha'?"

"Ssh, hello Dad, don't try to talk."

Zech? What? Uh can't believe it! "What? What? Is it Zech, Zachary?" Uh can't believe it! Eee, uh'm, uh'm dreaming, it's Zech, eee, uh sound all dry, crackly, eee, uh didn't think anybody would come. Uh can't 'ardly talk, uh can't believe it! 'E can't even 'ear me, uh can't 'ardly make any noise out mu mouth.

"Don't move, it's Zech."

"Wha'? Oo.... Zech, Zachary?"

"Yes, Dad, you don't have to talk, don't move, I'm going to stay here with you."

"Eee, uh'm, uh'm dreaming, Zech, 'ow, 'ow...."

"It's alright Dad, you're going to be alright, you don't have to talk."

Eee, 'is face, 'e's like leaning right over, eee, 'is face on mu cheek, silly, it's mu boy, 'e's 'olding my arm there, like a dream, it's like a miracle. There's another one, 'oo is she, they're talking there, ugh!, ugh!, uh just wanna talk to Zech, 'e'll get me a drink.

"Zech... Zech... Lily...."

"Ssh, Dad, just lie still, don't try to talk."

"Wha'cha, wha'cha? Uh'm, uh'm...."

"Don't let him move, now."

"Dad, the nurse says try not to move, you're going to be alright. The doctor will be along soon, I'll talk to him when he comes."

"Lily, Lily, gimme... uh'm dying...." Uh can't believe it, mu good luck. "Eee, they said uh 'ad an accident, uh don't know what 'appened." Mu mouth, to lick. "They took me 'ere, mu van, eee, from The Lane uh 'ad material." Uh knew Zech would come, what a boy uh got, a wonderful boy. "Yeh, they took me 'ere, uh been 'ere a long time, it's terrible, uh can't move, they're deaf 'ere," uh'm so aggravated, "the nurse she don't bring me, they don't listen" — Zech, a drink, mu throat — "if you call, you can die 'ere before anyone comes. Eee, uh didn't think anyone could come, eee, Zech uh thought you'd 'ave to go to work."

"Dad, don't talk. I'll see if I can get something for you to drink."

She's putting something, a wet *shmutta* on mu mouth. "Eee, gimme... gimme... ugh... a bladdy...." See?, she's worried, now she's worried, *at last* she'll get me a drink, now... yeh, ugh, yeh, like a spoon in mu mouth.

"Careful not to move your head, now," she's so good that Rivka.

Eee, wet, it's marvelous, oh, thanks, Rivka... thanks, thanks, like — uh don't know — she's good as gold. Uh told 'em, a 'undred times uh told 'em, a drink bring me. "The nurses in this place, well, uh don't know what to say, they're terrible, they never bring me anything to drink, they don't listen if uh call, uh can't call, it 'urts, they're all deaf in this place."

"Rest, Dad, don't get excited, don't tire yourself out, just rest. You don't have to talk."

"Excited?" Huh, excited — 'e's telling me uh shouldn't get excited! They're deaf, you call them and they're, like, uh don't know, they're deaf. Mu son the *schvunce-melumid,* like a coward 'e doesn't know 'ow to tell anybody, 'e can't punch, 'e's frightened of everybody. That little barsted what's 'is name Arnie punched 'im, yeh in the street there, 'e comes running in, 'is nose like pouring with blood, eee you should see. Uh said 'Oo did it, uh ran out, uh caught Arnie the little shitbag with one 'and, uh grabbed 'im by the throat uh grabbed 'im, uh gave 'im one punch in 'is face, they 'ad to take 'im in the 'ospital. With one 'and uh did it. My son, a *schmuck,* 'e's too *sensitive* to punch someone. You tell 'im Jump, and 'e jumps like 'e's frightened, *nebuch,* in case 'e might 'urt somebody's feelings. If they want to punch 'im 'e'll tell them 'oh that's quite all right, yes, certainly.'

Banging. Someone's banging on the door. Joe comes back in, it's someone for Obbah the Meshugginer, 'e says, Eva's 'ere for Obbah the Meshugginer. Obbah the Meshugginer, 'e's calling me! The barsted what does 'e know, always trying to make me like… like shit, Joe the *kitseler,* 'e *kitsels* in 'is trousers pocket, no woman wants 'im, no wonder fah!

Morrie said Why did you tear up your shirt, you mad or something? Uh told 'im, didn't 'e realize uh told Momma to press the shirt, it's wrinkled up the front is all wrinkled up, uh want to go out, uh got to 'ave the shirt.

'E tore up 'is own shirt. 'E's mad.

Abie, you ready? she's asking, Yeh uh'm ready. Laying on 'er bed in the corner, Whitechapel Road it is, that's right, near the Empire, the window with a curtain, lace, the springs a loud noise!, before 'er *becuckter* brother comes 'ome from work, eee, she's nice, Eva, a real nice girl, friendly, shame, shame for 'er parents, yeh, both of 'em got all burnt up there, eee the whole building it was terrible. When uh'm 'ungry she gives me a slice of bread and butter from the cupboard there, she makes me a big cup of tea, a real big cup. Uh shouldn't oil the springs, one minute it would take, it's embarrassing the noise, Jimmy would smell the oil! Jimmy told 'er off for going out with me! Jimmy, shmimmy, 'e should mind 'is own bladdy business the barsted uh'm going out with 'is sister not 'im. Eee she's shy to say something, she likes it really she'd run out if she didn't like it, it's nice and quiet in 'er flat, she's quiet, like… like… peaceful; the others they're always arguing, shouting at 'ome there. She gave me 'er violin, uh didn't take it 'ome, uh should'a taken it 'ome.

Eee, the violin, the other one, that's right, uh was skating in the street, all of a sudden the kid there 'e wanted the skate, all broke the wheels were, uh gave 'im the skate, what did 'e know, 'e gave me the violin, we like, what is it… exchanged, yeh. Uh took it 'ome, uh played the violin, uh played it. All of 'em, they were laughing, he!, he!, he!, uh 'ad to 'ide under the table, eee, uh was so… ashamed, it was embarrassing. Especially Joe, Obbah the violin player *noch*, Obbah will now play a concert, what does 'e want from me already. Lucky Chona came 'ome, she told me to come out, she told 'em all off, eee did she tell 'em off. They broke the violin already, already they broke it, the part where mu fingers go 'round they smashed. Uh glued it with strong glue, uh went in the cupboard to play, each time uh tightened the strings, again it broke.

Mu neck, oh, yeh, it's Zech… eee, uh'm lucky 'e came, what a stroke of luck, uh'll tell 'im, 'e'll take me 'ome, Lily'll look after me there, she'll make me a cup of tea. Uh'll give 'im some money, some real money. Listen, it's very important: "Listen, Zachary, uh want to tell you something, like, something… really important… come 'ere, uh'm… uh'm… uh'm going to give you, uh'm going to give you — ten… ten pounds." Ten pounds uh'll give 'im! There!

Uh'm too 'ot. Papa was a good presser, with a match 'e showed me 'ow to light the gas in the iron. The rabbi's jacket, uh made the iron too 'ot, it was an accident, brown it got burned there right on the flap. Papa saw the brown, 'e got ill but 'e didn't do nothing, uh was lucky. For 'ours 'e was working, extra material from the seam 'e made a new flap. For nothing the stinking rabbi wanted it, like a thief, with 'is god there, 'is miracles! Maybe 'is god'll make a miracle and sew a new flap on the pocket. In the morning Papa said, Come on Abie, come *mit mir* to the *shul* we'll go *dovan. Dovan!* Uh'm 'ungry, 'ere uh should go *dovan!*

Uh told 'im, uh can't go to the *schul,* uh 'ave to go to work.

Then uh went, it was the other time, we went to The London 'Ospital, uh said Papa don't wear the *yarmulka.* Papa said they don't 'ate the Yiddisher, they're doctors, they're educated men, they're from in college. All morning we waited on the bench in a big room, the doctors said Mr. Grossman, your diabetes 'as to be treated, eat one bacon sandwich every day and come back in one year. When we 'ad money Papa 'ad bacon on a piece of bread. Eee, when 'e gave me a bite uh loved the taste!

Morrie and Joe came in from selling the papers. Put a penny in the meter we'll 'ave tea, from the other room Papa called out. Morrie stood on a chair, 'e put a penny in and Momma put the kettle on and took one piece of bacon out the bag for Papa's diabetes. *Zaida* came round, Vat's dat smell, vat is you cooking?

"*Oy*, mu throat, *oy*, mu throat!" In the kitchen Papa was choking from the bacon, straight from the frying pan 'e tried to eat in a rush *Zaida* shouldn't see the bacon. What did *Zaida* know from diabetes? Quick, Sarah said, she brought Papa a cup of water for 'is throat. *Zaida* put 'is nose *right* in the pan, eee, to see what it was!

"Mr. Grossman, how are you feeling this afternoon?" It was a nurse. "I've got a little dinner for you. Think you can eat a little dinner?"

Mashed potatoes, like water ugh!, no taste, and a tiny bit of juice in a spoon.

"Mu 'ead, uh can't move mu 'ead."

"You hurt your neck when you had your accident; your head is held still so's your neck can heal alright. It's coming along, you're going to be up and out of bed in two shakes of a duck's arse."

"Where's Lily? Is Lily going to come?"

"You had a visitor today, your son."

"Yeh! Zech, it's mu Zachary, uh forgot. My son it is, mu eldest son, where is 'e, 'e's a good boy, yes, 'e'll take me 'ome."

"Sure he will. You're lucky to have such a fine family."

"Uh'm going to give 'im ten pounds, uh'll give 'im."

Uh went to their flat. 'Arry, y'know Anya's 'Arry, what a good fellow 'e is, eee, 'e earns a lot of money, 'e gave 'er the gramophone. They told me to wind it up and uh listened, Galli-Curci, eee, she was wonderful, dee, dee, de dee, deee, de de de de de dee, deee, for 'ours uh could listen to 'er sing, like a bird, a miracle, 'er voice. Sid came with me to listen. Caruso, eee, marvelous. In a minute the record's over, so quick, for 'ours it should 'ave played. 'Arry, what is it, barrels, a... a... cooper 'e is, eee, 'e's very quick, 'e makes good money, five pounds. They 'ave dinner there, every day they 'ave dinner in their flat. 'E told me to make Anya a suit, a brown 'erringbone worsted, it was strong, under the arms a good fit, like perfect. Uh bought the material down The Lane, yeh, a nice material, we carried it, uh told Zech come with. Eee, there was a bomb there, a doodle-bug, terrible it was, 'is friend, what was it, we carried it on the bus, they said don't pay the fare, she loved it she was 'appy, very very careful uh made it. Eight pounds 'Arry paid me, they 'ad loads of money, it was good. Yes, they went to the... the theatre even, Chona spent all the money, she should 'ave saved a lot of money.

Momma said, "Chona why don't you save a little bit of money? Every week you'll save a little bit, don't tell 'Arry, one day if you need it God forbid you'll be glad you did it, you saved it."

'Arry came round, uh was in the other room, uh couldn't 'elp it, 'e was so wild!, 'e told Momma, Fannie 'e said, 'e called 'er Fannie, Fannie, 'e said, please stay out of our affairs. They were rich, no it's good, they 'ad affairs like rich people. 'E said, Your daughter can spend as much as she likes, uh'm making good money.

Uh saw Johnny in The Waist, Johnny Hirshberg, the stinkweed. *Arbeitest du?* 'e said, uh said, Yeh, yeh. Yeh, 'e said, they came to tell me from Lipman's uh should come in tomorrow, they want me in the morning, like a liar, a... a stinkweed 'e is, with 'is twisted face there. Lily, every week uh take 'er to The Waist, she's walking so slow like a snail, uh should buy 'er this uh should buy 'er that, she should only know 'ow uh crank mu *kishkas* out to make a few bob. Hirschberg was there, do you think uh'd talk to 'im, right past 'im uh went, uh told Lily not to even... even... *nothing.* Uh took 'er to the pictures, what more does she want, she likes the pictures. *Chu Chin Chow,* mu favorite, after the picture on the stage in front they come, the clothes like all Chinese, from China. Especially what is it, *Maid Of The Mountains,* it's nice the music, dee dee deee, de dee dee de deee de.

"You must be feeling happy, Mr. Grossman. That's 'cause your son came to see you, I bet."

Where am uh? Where's Lily? It's Zachary. "Zech, did you get the drink, uh'm, uh'm dying uh'm so thirsty, where's the *fu–ucking* drink already, uh'm, uh'm, uh'm...." Ten pounds! Like a *broch* I'll give 'im ten pounds!

Uh know they 'ate me, Cissie, and Rae and Zelda, the three of 'em like three *brochs* there, always interfering. Taking their side she is, she's always on their side she thinks uh don't know Cissie put ten shillings, a ten shilling note on the mantelpiece, they want to make me feel like... like rubbish, like uh need their money. The barsteds, the three of 'em telling Zilly and Rivka to go out with American soldiers they told 'em, *drai pisherchs,* they think uh don't know. Like dried up prunes, ignorant, they're giving advice to mu daughters they're giving their advice, like they should be like prostitutes, like... common, uh don't know what, disgusting. Zilly and Rivka, did uh give 'em both, terrible, in the middle of the night they thought uh was asleep. The strap the leather one from the machine, in the street Tredegar Terrace there, eee, uh 'it 'em, eee, they won't forget that, disgraceful what they're doing, all the people in the 'ouses to wake up in the middle of the night. Prostitutes, both of 'em prostitutes going with the lousy Americans, disgraceful for all the neighbors.

"What, Dad?"

"Disgraceful, like... like... common prostitutes... coming 'ome, so late...."

"Alright, Dad, listen, Dad, I'm going home, you understand? I've been here two hours, I have to go home now. In the morning the nurse will look after you, her name's Melissa, she'll get you anything you need. She'll be here all day so just call her if you want anything, she'll get you a drink, anything. Tomorrow Mum and Maudy will be here after dinner, it'll take them a little time 'til they get off the train with their stuff and everything, but don't worry, they'll be here."

"Lily? And Maudy?"

"Yes."

"They're coming?"

"Yes."

"Lily's coming?"

"Yes Dad, Lily's coming."

"With Maudy."

"Yes, with Maudy."

"Zachary, eee, thanks for coming, uh don't know what to say."

"You don't have to say anything, Dad."

"Uh'll be 'ome in a few days, yes?"

"A few weeks, Dad, not long."

"Uh 'ave to go, to the lavatory uh 'ave to go."

"I'll tell the nurse, on the way out I'll tell the nurse, she'll bring the thing."

"When uh come 'ome, uh'm going to… to treat you… uh'm going to give you… two pounds, two pounds like all for yourself."

"That's alright, Dad, you don't have to give me anything. Just don't worry, everything's going to be alright."

It was 'ot, she turned the covers down.

It was so 'ot, uh couldn't bear the smell, uh was choking already. It was terrible, the conditions. Uh 'ad to go, we all 'ad to go, uh 'ad to take mu trousers down and like crawl along the wood to the middle and 'ang, like… far out over the pit. If uh didn't 'ang all the way out the shit got all on mu trousers, ugh! Eee, it was slippery, real careful you 'ad to be. Aaron 'is feet they slipped out, eee, 'e fell right down into the shit, eee, we got 'im out with a pole. They kept 'im in the 'ospital tent 'e got so ill, in one minute 'e got *seriously* ill. And the flies, mosquitoes, thousands of mosquitoes! The second you started from the end, the mosquitoes started. The others, they waved branches to keep off the mosquitoes, while you're straining to go, just when you 'ave to go, your 'ands, your arse, biting, biting. No wonder uh got malaria. The others got malaria, Albert, Hymie, Michael, all the others. Poor Hymie 'e died, it was so bad what 'e got. Uh was careful, uh didn't drink no water 'til it was really boiling, uh 'ad to *see* it boiling, first. *Still* uh caught it. The others 'ad diarrhea, uh never 'ad diarrhea the whole time, 'til the war ended. Eee, what a place there, filthy dirty. Maryse, uh took 'er some food to the Chartel Yahud, right near Cairo it was, Hymie gave me food from the mess, uh took it and we ate it in 'er room, Maryse, *oy!* did she eat, they were starving, 'er sister, what was 'er name Régine. They come from… Paris, yes she said, uh gave 'er sister a few pennies, Régine, what was it, nothing really, uh sent money every week for Lily.

That woman what was 'er name, may she drop dead wherever she is, she made Lily wait by the wall, for 'ours she stood there, she let the whole queue go first in front, for 'ours, eee, Lily told 'er off! Told 'er off? Uh would'a… *punched* 'er, in front of everybody right in the face uh would'a punched 'er. At last Lily reported 'er, she wrote a letter, uh told 'er to write a letter, uh told 'em just cause you're Jewish you 'ave to wait for 'ours to get your money, she 'ates the Yiddisher that woman! What did the Germans ask, they just shoot you especially yeh, like the Jewish Brigade, the uniform they made us wear that was it, eee, did they 'ave it in for us, you don't stand in a line! You don't go to the back of the line to wait for them to shoot you just 'cause you're Jewish! Ignorant, ignorant… *poyer* she was. The next week Lily went she was gone, they gave 'er the sack, right away uh told 'er to write.

"Ssh, quiet…."

Wha's going on?

"Crikey, 's that 'im?"

"Ssh, ee, ssh, quiet…."

What is it?

"'Ello, Dad."

What is it? Wha'… wha'? Is it Maudy? Eee, it's like Maudy, 'e's putting down the bag, yeh! Eee, yeh it's Lily, at last it's Lily, Lily! Eee, uh forgot, mu memory, ugh! A lucky stroke! She'll look after me, eee, I'll tell 'er, I'll tell 'er everything I'll tell 'er, she'll take me 'ome. Now everything'll be alright.

"Eee, Lily, what's a matter, ssh, all the commotion there, everybody's looking, ssh ssh, wha'cha… wha'cha…what y'… what are y'… like, crying?"

—o—O—o—

39

"So come with me to The London Hospital, then."

"To the 'ospital? Just to see the ol' barstard?"

"Ssh, don't call him that, he's still your father, it's a shame for him."

"Shame! So 'e got a taste of 'is own medicine at last, 'bout time."

"He could have been killed... what are you laughing about, it's a joke? Your own father?"

"Nah, I'm just thinking 'ow 'e said it, the policeman." Marius pulled his normally-stooped shoulders up straight, and puffed out his cheeks: "Ahem! Madam, Mr. Grossman's vehicle was observed driving out the alley at a 'igh rate of speed — in reverse.' Backward!" he chortled. "Can you picture 'im? The bus driver must 'ave wondered what 'it 'im. 'E probably thought the Germans started all over again!"

"He never should have bought it, throwing away good money for nothing, I knew it would only make more trouble. So he's not a good driver, what can you do, it's not his fault, he tries."

"Not 'is fault! Then 'oo's is it, if it ain't 'is?"

"Maudy what's the good, what's done is done, come with me to the hospital, be a good boy."

"Alright, I s'pose I'll go. But I'm telling you if 'e starts shouting I'll shut 'im up for good."

"Stop it already with the jokes."

"Anyway, Zech don't go anymore."

"Listen, he went every day when we were in America. What's the good, grumbling? You'll come with, you're starting with work on Monday, when else will you be able to go? Katya will be there, you'll see Katya." From a saucepan she poured hot chicken soup into an empty milk bottle, pressed a couple of matzo balls through its narrow neck, then topped up the bottle with more soup. She replaced the cardboard cap and wrapped the bottle in a small towel. "Here, you'll carry it, it's hot, be careful with the top, don't upset it."

Thirty minutes later the pair arrived at the hospital. Marius faced away from the lift's other occupants to hold the still-warm package away from his coat in case its contents should be spilled by the jolting. On the third floor they exited, Lily hurrying ahead to the ward. Marius entered moments later to see his mother straightening the bedclothes where Abie lay on his back, snoring.

"Ssh, put the soup down, on here." Lily made room on the bedside stand. "Ee, his face is white, quiet, don't wake him up."

"Wake 'im up! 'E can keep on snoring the 'ole time, far as I'm concerned."

The disturbance disrupted the rhythm of Abie's breathing. Blinking, and then amid coughs and splutterings, he slowly gathered his whereabouts until his eyes clamped on Lily. "Eee you're 'ere, eee, Lily, where you bin, all the time uh bin telling 'em where is she."

"Ssh, rest…."

"Eee, uh wanted…."

"Ssh, keep quiet, just rest."

"Already she's telling me quiet…."

"Crikey…."

"Maudy, it's Mm… Maudy, eee uh didn't know you're 'ere also, uh didn't see you."

"Mum said I should come with, so I came."

"Yeh, she's right, it's good you should come, course you should come to see your own father in the 'ospital 'ere, like uh can't believe it 'appened, oo knew?"

"Ssh, lie quiet, don't get yourself aggravated."

He inched himself up. "Like *you* wouldn't be aggravated if they smashed up your van in the street, broad daylight there it was."

"Ssh, ssh…."

"Maybe the middle of the night like uh could understand, but broad daylight? 'E comes rushing along the street like 'e don't care about anyone, nothing 'e don't care about, terrible."

"Soup, you'll have some soup."

"Uh dunno what 'appened, uh didn't even see 'im already, the next thing uh'm 'ere, they got me 'ere in the 'ospital."

"Ssh, don't get…."

"Zech it was, yeh, Zech 'e comes 'ere, uh'm in the bed 'ere with the doctor…"

"Ssh."

"Tsk, with the doctor 'e's talking, 'e says uh 'ad an accident, all mu things uh got there in the van, oo knows from an accident?"

"Soup, I got soup I brought, ssh, I'll ask the nurse, she'll sit you up for the soup, she'll make the bed." Lily signaled discreetly and the nurse came over.

"A dish?" The nurse cranked a handle at the foot of the bed. "We shouldn't raise him too straight." She fluffed the pillow behind his head. "You Mrs. Grossman then?"

"Yes, why, I got a thing downstairs at the desk to come up…."

"No, s'alright, I had a cup of tea with your son Zachary, he said you and your son was in America."

"We came home because my husband…. My son sent me a telegram his father had an accident so we came home right away."

"Mr. Grossman must be happy." The nurse was straightening his blanket. "He's been asking for you from the day he was brought in, ain't that right, Mr. Grossman?"

"Er, yeh, yeh."

The nurse perused the chart that hung from the foot of his bed. She looked over at Marius and smiled: "I know you, you was here for your jaw, fractured it was. Before you went to America."

"Yup, 'ello."

"How is it?"

"Me jaw, or America?" asked Marius.

"Here, help me sit your Dad up a little bit more." On opposite sides of the bed, as Marius reluctantly grasped Abie's arm, they both raised him a little higher. "Well, first how's your jaw, and second what's it like in America."

"Me jaw's okay, thanks. America's 'orrible, ain't nothing to do there 'cept look in the windows of the shops all the time."

She straightened the covers. "'How did that happen with your jaw, fight or something?'"

"Oh, that...." Marius considered. "I was walking down the yard steps in my 'ouse and all of a sudden this big 'eavy step jumped right up in the air... and...."

"Tsk! Oh Maudy stop it...." said Lily.

"I'll see if I can find a dish for him."

As the nurse left, Lily returned her attention to Abie. "Katya, she said she was going to come also maybe."

"Eee, Katya, yeh nice, uh'd like 'er to come, uh'd like everybody to come, eee, yeh."

The nurse returned with a small bowl and a spoon. Marius stood away while Lily poured soup into the bowl and eased a matzo ball out through the milk bottle's mouth. Sitting on the edge of the bed, Lily held the bowl before Abie's chest and raised a spoonful to his lips.

Abie spluttered, choked and spat out onto the bedclothes. *"Fah!* It's all freezing cold... ugh!" He wiped his mouth on his sleeping suit sleeve. "...What she's bringing me 'ere...."

"Crikey, well it come all the way on the bus, wha'cha...."

"Ssh, don't make a... they're watching, it's not nice for the other people."

Abie subdued his tone. "No, uh mean it's like cold there, it's not 'ot."

Marius pursed his lips. "Wha'cha think it's gonna keep 'ot all the way from Mile End?"

"Wha's 'e... wha'cha?... Wha'sa marra with 'im there...." Then to Lily, "Can'cha like... oo wants to drink freezing soup? Wha'cha think...."

Visitors at other patients' beds had discreetly turned their heads away from the commotion. Lily was embarrassed. "It's such a loud... ssh, I'll ask the nurse, maybe there's a gas-stove."

The nurse came back. "Having a bit of trouble, Mrs. Grossman?" She looked at the fresh chicken-soup stains on the folded-over sheet.

"It got cold," said Lily. "Do you have something, a gas-stove maybe, if I could warm it up a bit. I won't get in the way."

"He had his dinner twelve o'clock." She further straightened Abie's sheet. "Still hungry, Mr. Grossman?"

"Uh... uh... well, like, it's like, well it's different, it's not like the *fah!* what they give you 'ere...."

Just then, Marius noticed Katherine's head peep around the ward door. "'Ey, look who it is!" he said to Lily.

Katherine remained outside a few moments longer, evidently concluding an exchange with somebody beyond the door frame. She entered alone and came over to Abie's bed.

"'Allo, Katya matya!" Marius greeted his sister cheerily. "You've come at the right time."

"Eee, it's Katya! Eee you came, it's nice you came, eee."

The nurse backed away. "Well, seeing as how your whole family's here Mr. Grossman, I'll be getting right back to me duties."

"Can you warm up the soup a bit?" Lily called after her. "Just a bit so it's not freezing, I don't want to give him cold soup, it'll just take a minute. If you've got something, I'll do it."

The nurse returned for the bowl. "Well I'm not supposed to...."

Katherine was removing her coat. "What's going on?"

Marius was quick to respond. "We brought soup on the bus all the way from Mile End, and 'e's spitting it out over 'is covers 'cause it didn't stay 'ot."

"Ssh, don't start with your father...."

"Start, crikey what did I do? Katya asked what's 'appening so I'm telling 'er."

Abie's face had darkened. "Wha'sa marra with 'im, the way 'e talks!"

Holding the bowl and spoon, the nurse backed away.

"Stop it, stop it everybody, ssh," cried Lily, handing the bottle with the rest of the soup to the retreating nurse.

"Looks like I've arrived in time for the fireworks," said Katherine.

"Quiet everybody, we just came to visit, who needs any commotion?" Lily ruffled Abie's pillow afresh and smoothed the bedclothes. "Everything's alright now."

Marius turned to Katherine. "So, is Benny big-dick coming in? Why's 'e 'iding outside?"

"Well, I can't stay long this time...." Katherine smiled to Abie: "So, how's the patient today? How're you feeling, Dad?"

"Eee it's nice you came, 'ours an' 'ours uh'm 'ere all day, it's nice when you come, it's like a... a... relief."

"You look much better. I bet they'll be letting you out soon."

"Uh told 'em already uh wanna go 'ome uh told 'em."

"Well, good. Then, Benny and I'll come to visit you at home, and you'll wish you were back here again."

"Yeh... Benny, tell 'im to come in also, why's 'e outside, tell 'im 'e should come in also, yeh it'll be nice to see 'im, Benny."

"Well, er, he had to ring up the phone now, he had to telephone someone about something, with work, we can't stay long, I told him to go and ring them up now while I visit you, he'll come in the next time."

"'Is work? They laid 'im orf, 'e got the sack?"

"No, nothing like that, don't worry everything's alright. Hello Mum, I didn't even say hello yet."

"Hello, Katya!" Lily squinted at her daughter. "So what's wrong, what's going on?"

"Wrong?" Katherine laughed quickly. "What's the matter with everybody, who said anything's wrong?"

The nurse returned with a larger bowl, big enough to contain all the soup. "Careful now Mr. Grossman, we don't want you scalding yourself now, do we!" She handed the spoon to Abie. "Mrs. Grossman, you sit on the bed now, yes, right there and I'll hand you the bowl so's he don't spill none over himself. Righteo?" Lily sat. "Watch out, it's hot, don't you go spilling any now, either of y's!"

"Eee, it looks 'ot, at last! Oo wants to 'ave freezing soup?" Abie offered a wry laugh to Katherine. "Like before, uh'd come 'ome, working 'ard there in the shop all day, hours an' hours, so cold soup like *pischerchs* she used to give me, ugh!, uh was sick from 'er soup already!"

"Tsk!, nothing," Lily said. "I'm bringing him soup so he should have something nice to eat, who expected such a commotion."

"Blimey, try to be nice with 'im? When you gonna learn something Mum, you shouldn't even try!"

Katherine regarded Marius admonishingly. "Come on Maudy, leave them alone." She began picking up her coat.

"Wha', wha', where you going already?" asked Abie.

"I can't stay this time, I'll come back soon, tomorrow maybe. You just get better now."

Lily held the bowl close to Abie's chest. "Drink, take some, not the *knaedel,* it's hot, just a spoon of soup first, taste it."

He raised one spoonful to his lips. *"Eeee!"* He spat it out, flung the spoon down to the foot of the bed and grabbed at his mouth. "Eee, scalding 'ot it is, eee uh scalded mu mouth uh did!"

Quickly, Lily pulled the bowl away.

"Crikey, 'ere 'e goes!"

"'Ere 'e goes?" Abie mimicked Marius' tone. "Take a *broch, gai in dreard* you barstard you, oo wants you 'ere in the first place, with 'is *'ere 'e goes!* Fu–uck orf out of 'ere!"

Every head in the ward was turned toward the eruption.

"Quick, make space," said Lily as she held the hot bowl over the bedside stand.

Katherine had begun slipping an arm into a coat-sleeve; now she ran around the bed and with her free hand moved items on the stand to make space for Lily to place the bowl down. Then she clutched her coat and picked up her bag. "Well, cheerio, must run along now, you know." With the coat flapping behind her she trotted briskly through knots of other patients' visitors, out of the ward and into the passageway beyond.

"You're leaving really?" Marius called after her.

Lily was still holding the bowl. "Ssh, everybody's watching, let's all be quiet now. I thought she'd stay a bit. Quick, get the spoon. There it is, on the covers there."

"For 'im? Let 'im get the bladdy spoon 'imself!"

Forgetting the restraint of his bandages, Abie tried to lunge toward where Marius stood at the foot of the bed. The movement knocked the bowl's steaming contents splattering onto the bedclothes and the floor. Lily lost her grip on the bowl itself and it fell, glancing against the side of the bed then smashing to pieces on the floor.

"Ow! ow! mu belly, mu belly, she scalded, *oy!* all over she did it... you fu–ucking *idiot* you, wha'cha done, she's done me in for good this time."

The nurse called out the ward door: "Maud, get Bill in here quick!" As she ran over to the bed Marius moved away. She ripped the blanket and sheet down to the foot of the bed and quickly lifted Abie's jacket to examine his skin. "Move over, Mrs. Grossman." Lily backed away. "You got me in enough trouble for one day, I'd say!" She grabbed a flannel from Abie's drawer, hastily soaked it under the cold tap at the end of the ward, ran back and applied it to his belly. A heavy-set aide in blue cotton coveralls trotted into the ward, and she called him over. "Careful the broken china. He'll be wanting new bedclothes, his wife upset a bowl of hot stuff over him."

"I'm sorry I couldn't help it...." Lily began.

"No," said the nurse, still addressing Bill. "He's alright, wasn't hot enough to scald him, bit of ointment, I'll take care of it." She felt the mattress. "Dry. Just two sheets, blanket and a change of peejays should do it."

"Righteo Melissa, back in two shakes." Bill left.

"Try to sit up now Mr. Grossman, alright?" The nurse took Abie's arm. "Here, help your dad, get his other arm," she said to Marius, who still stood apart at the foot of the bed.

"Uh don't want 'im 'elping me...." Abie began, as Marius remained where he stood.

Lily leaned over and grasped Abie's other arm to help him up. "I'm sorry, who wanted all this trouble?"

"Well Mrs. Grossman, like I said he had his dinner twelve o'clock, I never should'a let you give him hot stuff right after he just finished eating." She pulled Abie into a more upright position. "Here we go, try to swing your legs round, I'm holding you, you can do it," and she helped him ease his legs over and down until he was sitting on the edge of the mattress.

Bill returned with fresh bedclothes.

"I'm gonna wait outside," said Marius.

"Outside, 'e can *gai in dreard* for all I care," said Abie. "And don't come back, uh don't want you coming 'ere no more!"

"Ssh…" began Lily. The nurse was pulling down the sodden bed clothes. She signaled Marius to remove his coat from the chair then helped Abie down and eased him into the seat.

"Don't do me no favors," shouted Marius as he backed away. "Mum, I'm going 'ome, I 'ope I never see 'im again, I 'ope 'e dies 'ere, be better for everybody if 'e never comes 'ome."

"Watch your tongue," said the nurse. "You can't talk like that in here, you're upsetting the other patients."

"Well, young man," interjected Bill. "I never did 'ear a bloke talking 'bout 'is own father like that!"

"You don't know 'im," cried Marius. "'E's a real barstard."

"Watch your language, young fella," said Bill.

"Go 'ome, you twisted 'umped-back *schvunce* you!" shouted Abie, pulling at the nurse's restraining grip on his arm.

"Mr. Grossman, don't you get all excited now," said the nurse, holding firm. And to Marius, "You better wait downstairs, getting your dad all riled up like that!"

Marius had tears in his eyes as he donned his coat. "I'm going 'ome, Mum, don't let the bladdy barstard wear you out. 'E knocked over the soup 'imself, it was 'is fault."

"That's enough!" snapped Bill.

Marius left.

"Bill," said the nurse. "After we've made up the bed, get the broom and shovel and clear up that broken china on the other side, there's a dear."

• • •

Outside, Marius began walking home along Whitechapel Road. He walked quickly and swung his arms, the exertion gradually purging him of anger and frustration until he could think more clearly about what he should do. He strode past Johnny Isaacs, deserted this early in the day. By the time he passed the Empire cinema in Stepney Green he was out of breath. A trollybus approached, and he flagged it down.

Back home, he put on the kettle and made himself a cup of tea. As he sat at the table and drank, a key scraped in the street door lock. Lily bustled into the house and hung up her coat.

"'Ello, Mum."

"What a commotion there, a disgrace for the other people to see."

"You shouldn't put up with it."

"What do you mean? I mean you, speaking to your father like that, in front of everybody."

"'E started it, 'e always starts it."

"If you just didn't… like… say anything to him, so he'd stop in a few minutes. I'm going to have some tea."

"The water's 'ot."

Lily called from the other room as she poured her tea. "When he comes home you'll just leave him alone, don't answer him, you should worry."

"I don't want 'im to come 'ome, we shouldn't 'ave to put up with 'im all the time."

Lily brought her cup to the table and sat down. "He's your father, what are you going to do, just try to be nice."

"Nice! 'E's not going to talk like that to me no more, I ain't putting up with it, that's not what I come back to London for."

"What can you do, he doesn't mean anything really."

"You shouldn't put up with it either."

"Ugh, it doesn't bother me so much, so he goes mad for a few minutes! There are worse fathers."

"Well, I'm telling you I'm not putting up with it anymore, so 'e'd better not come home, least while I'm 'ere."

"What do you mean, where will you go?"

There came a pounding on the street door. "Who's that, what is it?" Lily spilled tea onto the oil cloth.

Marius jumped up and went to the door. On the step stood Benny, his face flushed, his fist raised to pound once again.

"Crikey, what's going on, what 'appened?"

"Where is she, is she here, I'll kill her the little barstard."

"Who, what's going on?"

"Who? Who d'ya think? Katya, where is she, Maudy you'd better hold me back, I'm telling you, I'll kill her!"

"It's Benny!" Marius called out to Lily. "Come in, what's the matter?"

Benny poked his head into the living room. "Katya, where is she? Is she upstairs?"

"Upstairs?" Lily was alarmed. "No, what do you mean, what happened, what's the matter, did something happen?"

"Is she upstairs!" Benny demanded.

"Upstairs? No, she's not here, she was with you, this afternoon, at the hospital."

"Hospital? I never went to the hospital this afternoon. What's going on here, something fishy and I don't like it!"

"Fishy? What do you mean, what's going on? Where is she? Did something happen?"

Benny raced up the stairs two at a time, stomped into each bedroom, kneeled to search under the beds. Nobody was there. Lily and Marius stood in the passageway as he clumped back down again.

"The little fucker, I'll kill her when I catch her I will, so help me! Sorry Lily."

"Come in, come sit down, I'll make you a cup of tea."

"Yeah, I need a cup of tea to simmer down." He grimaced. "I just had a fight with Mr. Stapleton!"

"A fight? Crikey!"

"Sit down." Lily ushered them both into the living room. "I'll put the kettle on again. With Mr. Stapleton?"

The three sat at the table. "She didn't come home for two nights already, I'm going out of my mind."

"Where is she then?"

"I dunno, I guessed she was staying at Hazel's or something. I couldn't bear it at work, the boss said I could leave early. So!" He puffed air out between tight lips.

In the kitchen the kettle began to bubble; Lily got up, poured a cup of tea and brought it in.

"First I went to Anya's shoe place, she wasn't there. So I went to Hazel's. Mr. Stapleton opened the door," Benny continued. "I said I wanted to see Katya; he said she wasn't there. I told him I knew she'd been staying there, if he didn't tell her to come out I was going in after her."

"Christ!" said Marius.

"He said, 'You calling me a liar? Your wife is not in this house!' I lost my temper, I smacked him round the face." He sipped his tea.

"Round the face?" asked Lily.

"Yeah, he pushed me out and slammed the door. Just now. He said he's ringing up the police. I came here."

"Crikey!"

"I didn't know what to do. It's your daughter, she's so stubborn, I don't know what she wants already! All I'm asking her is to be satisfied like other wives, what does she want? I work hard, I bring home money." He took another sip of tea. "She was at the hospital, you said?"

"Yup, this afternoon, I thought you were... she said about you phoning up some-one...."

Lily kicked Marius' foot under the table. "No, for a little while she came, she had to leave to go back to work...."

"Work! I went to Burdett Road, Anya said she hasn't been in to work the whole week!" He banged his cup down on the table and the handle snapped off in his fingers. Hot tea spilled all over the table. He sobbed. "I'm sorry, Lily, she's driving me mad with worry, she is."

"I'll make you another cup, it's alright, it was an old cup anyway."

—o—O—o—

40

"If you'd rather be in the Royal Air Force, just keep on writing *RAF* wherever it asks if you have a preference. Just *RAF, RAF. RAF* everywhere." From under his ginger mustache, the RAF officer who interviewed me lowered his voice: "I must admit — confidentially, of course — it's true, we do get a finer class of chaps than the army. Not to derogate Her Majesty's Army, of course, they're a grand bunch, especially when it comes to enemy occupation duties, house-to-house, that sort of thing. You know, the basics, where the old grey matter isn't of such consequence."

After I'd completed the paper work, he directed me toward another large room where, with twenty other potential recruits, I lined up in the echoing December-cold hall. As instructed by a fierce red-faced sergeant, in unison we dropped our trousers. An army officer, presumably a doctor, a short baton tucked under his uniformed armpit, strutted in front of us, peering resolutely at our genitals. Occasionally he would pause, then with the tip of the baton lift a hapless penis for closer inspection, until finally he reached the end of the row. "Bend over!" shouted the sergeant, and the doctor continued his sojourn behind us. I wondered why this official preoccupation with arseholes and dicks, but mine must have passed scrutiny because I subsequently received another letter, this time from the Royal Air Force, instructing me to report to the induction center in two weeks.

• • •

Monday evening. *Tap, tap, tap.* I looked up to see who was knocking on the window, but the darkness outside had turned it into a mirror. Then a face leaned closer to the glass; it was Reuben Berger.

"Reuben, come around through the passage there, yes, on your right, I'll open the door." He came in. "For the minute I thought it might be the foreman come back again for something." I hung his coat on the rack. "How did you get in the yard? The gate is locked from the outside."

"I jumped the wall." He turned to look around. "So it really is a laboratory, then."

"I told you that's where I worked."

"Hmm!" He walked around the desk. "What do you do here all day?" I showed him various equipment, the shelves of chemicals, where I distilled the factory tar samples and measured the water content. I did not show him where I'd temporarily resumed manufacturing counterfeit two-shilling pieces for unanticipated family household expenses. "And you see the sooty corners on the ceiling? That's where I set fire to the lab."

"You really did?"

"Yes."

"What did the boss say?"

"I don't have a boss. Well, I had a boss here for the first few weeks, but now I'm in charge."

"What do you mean, how can you be in charge?"

"They used to have a chemist here, but they gave him the sack. Now, whatever I say, goes." Reuben pursed his lips as I continued to rub it in. "Presently that's just with the laboratory. Soon it'll be most of the factory as well." Maybe I was laying it on a bit thick; his eyes narrowed, relaxed, then opened to that cryptic impassivity.

"Well, you must answer to someone. What did they say when you set fire to this place?"

"It was an accident, you have to be careful with chemicals. I get along very well with the owner. He understands there are risks."

As we puttered around he mumbled something. I wasn't sure what he'd said. "What?"

"I said," he repeated, barely louder, "do they need another person here?"

"Oh no, I handle everything myself, easily." I'd made my point, and now I didn't care to stay later than necessary. "It's getting late."

"Late? I only just got here."

"Well, this is it really."

He was peering at the equipment shelf. "I'd like to look around a bit more."

I could collect the tar samples for the morning, that would impress him. Then I'd pack up and we'd leave. "I'll go out to the yard and take samples of today's final run, and some for tomorrow while I'm at it."

"Outside?"

"Yes. Come and watch, it's pretty impressive. But look out for the evaporation trays, they're dangerous."

"It's cold out, I walked from the bus stop."

"I have to climb a forty yard high tank. You can watch me fall off the ladder and kill myself. Then you can have my job."

He sucked in his cheeks and averted his eyes before answering. "I'll wait here."

"Alright, I'll be back in fifteen, twenty minutes. Don't touch anything, it's dangerous, like that toluol on the counter." And to drive the point home, I pointed to the ten-litre bottle of sulphuric acid standing on the shelf. "See that sulphuric acid? That's really dangerous stuff. Mess around with anything and you can easily kill yourself."

Again he mumbled, in that flat dead voice: "Do they know you used to sleep with your sister?"

For a moment I thought I hadn't heard right. "What?"

"Do the people here know you slept with your sister every night for years?" he muttered through a blank countenance.

"What are you talking about?" My face flamed with embarrassment! What did he mean, how did he know who I slept with at home? It was my fault; the very day Katherine came back from evacuation I should have taken the mattress off the bed and made two beds again, whatever Mum would have said. Maybe he *didn't* know, maybe he was just guessing.

"You look nervous," he went on.

"Nervous, no, what do you mean, why should I be nervous?" At the bus stop in the freezing rain that night in March, I could have just let the bus run over him. I wonder who he told? Maybe Jack also knew but was too polite to say anything; maybe Izzy, maybe everyone along the street knew!

"So!" he said.

"Look Reuben, I don't know what you're talking about. I'm going outside and get samples."

"So," he repeated even more quietly, his gaze still directed away from me.

"What the bloody hell's the matter, Reuben?"

"The matter? I just asked if they need another person here."

"I already told you they don't. Look, I don't decide whether they're going to hire someone or not!"

"Thought you said you were in charge of everything."

I was already putting on the heavy sampling jacket and gloves. "Reuben, I think you'd better leave now."

"Might as well wait 'til you come back if you're only gonna be fifteen minutes."

If he left now he might hang around outside, for whatever reason went through his furtive brain. My fault for inviting him, just to show off! Toting the bagged set of bottles I went out the passage to the factory yard, glad to get away for a few minutes to cool down and think what to do. If I tried to lock the fucker outside the gate he might even start a fight; anyway, he'd come right back over the wall. I'd sort it out while I was collecting the samples; when I came back I'd say as an aside that Katherine and I had always had separate beds. Maybe he didn't know really, maybe it was a bluff.

Yard lights, mounted high on the tall vertical holding tanks, cast a speckled light through the elevated metal walkways, connecting ramps and ladders, draping everything in a tangle of shadows. During daylight the yard was an impressive enough sight, but at night the metallic web took on an additional eerie contrast of glittering reflections. I shivered. The chilled air had again rolled a mist up off the Thames, cloaking the entire yard in a translucent envelope.

With the sampling kit strap wrapped around my wrist I climbed the vertical ladder attached to tank number four. The evening's moisture covered the metal rungs, making them slippery under my shoes' crêpe soles. It was a long way up; I kept an arm looped around the side rail, as Mr. Smith always insisted. Under the best of circumstances when I made this climb to the top my stomach roiled, and I envied the ease with which the workmen scaled these cobwebs. Tonight my nerves were jangled and I had to concentrate on every single step.

Two separate beds. Or, no details, just deny, deny. Instead of buying the coat, the Fedora and then the brown herringbone jacket I should have put the money toward a real bed. Mum said no more beds in that room. I could have argued her out of it and used that money.

Was I climbing the right tank? In the spangled light the top port showed tar: the tank was full. I descended a couple of slippery steps and with one arm between the rungs turned on the first sampling valve. A couple of pints discharged, the heavy brown liquid, shiny black tonight, slurping down into the tin. Despite the erie stillness the gurgle was muffled, choked by the heavy fog. Hanging on, I looked all the way down. Supposing Reuben came out into the yard? I extracted the first bottle, and with one hand between rungs and the other wrapped around the side rail I filled it from the valve, capped it, and returned it to the bag. Then the descent to the fifteen yard level. Christ, what was I going to do? Probably everyone in Morgan Street knew; I wouldn't be able to look at anybody in the street. At the lower valve I collected the next sample. Then at ten yards I placed the third bottle into the bag but my trembling hand knocked the run-off tin from its hook. Though I caught the wire handle just in time, a pint or more of tar slopped out. The oozing liquid flopped and squelched as it fell through the latticed rungs and buttresses beneath me. I kept my eyes up; it was frightening enough looking down even from ten yards, but to look down onto something that was falling was a hundred times worse.

"Ow!"

Reuben! I froze at the shout from below; perhaps he'd been watching me surreptitiously the whole time! I peered down but it was hard to see clearly, impossible to precipitate anything solid out of the fractured shadows. Across the open yard was the lighted laboratory window but from the angle of my perch I couldn't see inside, couldn't see if maybe he was actually still in there and I'd imagined it, imagined the shout.

"Reuben?" My voice rolled out into the damp silence and reverberated against the tank walls. "Reuben, is that you?"

He wouldn't come out in the dark by himself; I'd warned him about the dangers, the open evaporation trays. I steadied the run-off tin and continued down to the lowest valve, the three yards. Then just as I was removing the last bottle from the bag, there came a soft *clang,* the sound a metallic structure might make as it flexes under the stresses of a shifting weight. Someone *was* there! Maybe even above me, up on one of the ramps! How could he have climbed up above me without my hearing it? Goosebumps crawled over my skin. In my alarm the bottle slipped from my gloved hand. The loudness startled me as it struck a concrete footing and smashed, a deafening noise in the stillness, followed by a couple of *chink! chink!* sounds as shards of broken glass bounced against the tank wall and metallic legs.

"Reuben? Reuben!" Oh, but this was ridiculous, this was the sort of thing you paid one-and-ninepence to see at the Empire! Well, I knew I hadn't imagined *that* noise, the flexing of stressed metal, that was for sure! But, to be scientific about it, it could also have been that the falling night temperature had introduced some asymmetry to the contracting metal parts. Here I was, making myself nervous over perfectly ordinary noises. Hanging out from the ladder I scoured the adjoining walkways above me: "Reuben? Where are you? Are you out here in the yard? Be careful, you know what I said about the evaporation trays, they're dangerous." I dreaded the possibility that the disparate glints and shadows might resolve into some corporeal thing, maybe on the walkway right above me connecting the top of this ladder. Nothing. For several more minutes I stayed absolutely still. No breeze, no movement, no sound at all. I realized I was in a sweat, but shivering at the same time.

There was no point in just staying up there, and I needed one replacement bottle anyway. Reuben would be inside the laboratory waiting, and I'd tell him that collecting samples was an interesting part of the job, he should come out with me while I got the last one. At least I'd know where he was. What a stupid thing to leave the samples so late, so busy all day minting money for Lily that I didn't leave enough time to collect samples when the workmen were still here. And, my god, if Reuben found my cache in the back of the top left desk drawer!

I started down the remaining rungs and was almost to the bottom when there came a single loud reverberating clang, this time loud enough and clear enough as though someone had hit the side of an empty tank full force with a hammer. That settled it: he was definitely out here, trying to frighten me.

"Reuben? What's going on?" I tried to make my voice as angry as I could, but my mouth was dry and the words sounded shaky. Hanging on the ladder I swung around slowly and carefully, peering in all directions, but nobody was in sight, no movement, nothing. "What the hell's going on here?" I shouted, and the words jumbled around between my chattering teeth. "Who is it?"

That hammer blow had definitely come from below, from the base of one of the other tanks. Certainly I would have felt the reverberation through the ladder if it had been this one, and anyway the sound wouldn't have lasted so long on a filled tank. Maybe I should go back up, quickly. He wouldn't know the walkways up there as well as I did, so maybe I *should* run back up and come down at the back of the yard. Fuck it, who needed something like this with such a moron, especially when no one else was around?

As I started back up, another very loud clang of metal on metal rang out, but this time from way above me, over by one of the other walkways. Christ! He must have thrown up a piece of iron pipe to hit something that high.

But if it had been Reuben throwing something up, then I ought to have heard it again when it fell back down. Could he have caught it? Not in this light. Could he have climbed up somewhere, the back of the yard maybe, and come closer, but overhead? No, it always makes lots of different noises when someone moves along a walkway. That fucking thick-headed bully, he could have hit me with an iron pipe; this wasn't kid stuff anymore. And another thing: nobody knew he was coming here this evening, not even me for sure until he showed up.

Probably the best thing was to jump down to the ground, then run. I knew the yard, I could probably outwit him and get out the gate. Or maybe it would be better if I quickly scaled the wall. That way he'd be locked in and it would take him a minute or two to jiggle the latch or find a place in the wall to climb. Even then I'd have two streets in pitch-dark fog to run through to the bus stop, but maybe someone would be there, a policeman. I'd get a policeman, I really would — this was beyond a joke.

I took a last careful look around, then quickly ran down the last few rungs and jumped to the ground, landing haunched and ready in case he was right there. And as I peered carefully into the immediate darkness I saw something, something hovering in the shadow of the huge tank number three, about ten yards away, a shape that could be a figure, almost standing, but hunched over, like me — ape-like. Blood was banging in my ears. "Reuben you fucking moron, what's going on?" The thing stayed perfectly still; maybe it wasn't a person. Then, rocking slightly from side to side it seemed to move forward a few inches, and I saw that one of the arms was raised. "Reuben, is that you?"

The figure now glided closer a whole step, coming half out of the tank's shadow. It seemed too slight and wiry, not as solid as Reuben. Then, one more step closer, and it spoke: "'Ey, Jewboy, shit in yer trousers yet?"

It was one of the workmen from that other morning! He held a stick in his raised right hand, maybe a length of pipe. We each stood there, hunched like two cowboys ready for the draw. My mind had become suddenly focused, the anxiety gone, and I knew with conviction this character was going to get more of a fight out of me than he anticipated. I shouted as loud as I could, "Reuben! Reuben! Quick!" But you never could hear anything from the outside when the window and doors were closed. I'd try to trick this fellow into coming closer to the laboratory, then bang on the window and Reuben would come out and help.

"Pretendin' you got a mate 'ere what'll save yuh?"

Good, he thought I was kidding, he didn't know Reuben was here! But just as this sense of power girded my tingling arms and hands, there came a scurrying down number two tank ladder about ten yards further into the yard. Please, let it be Reuben! But no, it was the other *yock,* his buddy from the other day! All the strength I'd accrued so effortlessly now dissipated through my fingertips.

This second one paused on his bottom rung for a moment: "'Ey, Jewfuck, we ain't gonna kill yuh like we oughta, we just gonna 'ave a little game, like." As he sprang to the ground he reached up and with his hand slapped a horizontal buttress over his head. "We ain't gonna 'urt 'im, are we."

"'S'right, we ain't gonna 'urt 'im — much."

"Just 'ang 'im up a little bit. From this 'ere pipe," and he jumped up and again slapped the metal bar that crossed above his head. "Show 'im what it feels like."

The closer man, the one grasping the pipe, momentarily looked his buddy's way, and quite before I realized what I was doing I'd lunged forward and swung the loaded sample bag in a wide arc that took it behind his head. I pulled forward on the strap, and the bag — a soft case, but with three full bottles inside — made a loud crack as it encircled his head and smacked him sharply on the side of the face. He reeled, and dropped the pipe. The other one jumped forward at the upset, and I took off as fast as I could across the open yard toward the laboratory. Racing into the passageway, I found I still held the sample bag. As I slammed the passageway door shut behind me I caught a glimpse of them both trotting somewhat leisurely toward the laboratory, strategically separated by five or six yards, the one again holding his piece of pipe, rubbing his face with the other hand.

Reuben heard the commotion and opened the laboratory door: "What's…"

"No, quick…" I pushed him inside and slammed the door. "Reuben…" I was out of breath… "Reuben, two men, two *yocks,* they're trying to get me, they've got an iron pipe or something…."

"What?" He didn't realize the urgency.

"They work here, they're laborers, they hate Jews, they're trying to get me. Quick, put out the lights." I grabbed the light switch and pushed it off. "Because of the business in Palestine, y'know, with the *Irgun Zvai Leumi.* Sshh, don't let them hear us."

"So what'll they do?" whispered Reuben.

"I don't know, they said they're going to hang me from a pipe!"

"Hmm!"

The dim light from the window outlined the benches and the desk and chair. I went to go through the storage shelf area toward the outside office, but Reuben caught my arm, "No…" he said, and I looked at him, "don't go there."

"Why?"

"Let's hide here, they'll think you went somewhere else."

Maybe he was right. "Okay, let's get down by the sink."

On our haunches, heads down, we crept between the benches toward the big window. This window, with the sink installed in its bay, allowed a panoramic view of the yard. In the murky outside light the two of them approached, the one with the pipe coming straight toward the window where we crouched, the other veering farther off, presumably to go around the back of the building to the other side in case I came out there. They wouldn't be able to see into the darkened laboratory, but I kept down; no need to take unnecessary chances.

"That one'll probably go around to get in by that other door there," I whispered, motioning to the second door at the far end by the desk beyond the storage shelves.

"Uhuh."

The one with the pipe walked right up to the window while we crouched as low as we could. He tapped the pipe on the glass and in a sing-song voice called out: "'Ey, Jewboy, we're coming to get yuh!"

"He didn't break the glass!" I murmured. "He may be afraid of damaging anything. That's in our favor."

"Our favor? They're not after me!"

"Jesus christ, Reuben!"

The outside passage door, which I'd locked, rattled; the man leaned into it and pushed. It creaked under the strain, then *bang!,* it flew open and hit the wall. A moment's silence, then creeping footsteps along the passageway. From our concealment below the sink I reached up and over to the bench top to grasp a heavy glass measuring cylinder. It was more than a foot long and pretty hefty, its bottom stand a thick disk of molded glass. I could hardly imagine myself hitting him with it, but I'd done pretty well with the bag of sample bottles. I reached up for the second cylinder I knew to be there.

The passageway door began slowly opening into the laboratory. I could hear my breathing, and Reuben's. Silently, I handed the other measuring cylinder to Reuben but he pushed it away; maybe he was used to using his bare fists. The low light showed the door opening to midway, and the first thing to poke around was the end of the pipe, followed slowly by a hand, then the arm. From behind the door he swished the pipe around in figure eights. Belatedly, I thought one of us could have hidden there and grabbed the pipe from him before he even entered.

Now he was into the room. He was short, shorter than either of us, still crouching like an ape. With the pipe raised he swung slowly around. We were both huddled way down below the bench-top level, and with the illuminated window above and behind us he should not have been able to see us in the black cavity under the sink.

As he stood there holding the pipe we heard a noise in the outside office, and suddenly that interconnecting door banged wide open.

"Oo is it?" yelled the pipe man into the darkness. There was trepidation in his voice; I hadn't entertained the possibility that he might also be frightened of me.

"'Sme, Bill...."

"No names, stupid," the pipe man croaked. "Where is 'e?"

"I ain't seen 'im, this is where 'e works, ain't 'e in 'ere?"

No reply. Through the bench legs we watched the second man as he came through the door frame and into the far end of the room. He advanced slowly — but then suddenly lunged forward, his arms flailing ahead into the darkness as though he'd been knocked off balance. He stumbled past the desk into the relative light of the supply shelf area.

"What? What's... 'Ey!"

There came a brief scraping, sliding sound as on wood, followed by a moment of total silence. Then, a tremendous smashing of heavy glass as something, a huge bottle, crashed down onto the linoleum-covered concrete floor: "Ow! What's that, wharisit...." I was stunned at how loud the sudden noise was; then, "Oow! Me eyes, me face, ugh..." and the last syllable rose in a glissando to a piercing scream that penetrated and filled every crevice: "...uuugh!"

"Wharisit mate, what's up, what's 'appenin'?" shouted the pipe man.

"Me eyes, me face, 'elp me 'elp me quick...."

"Where's the bloody light, can't find the bloody light… what's goin' on 'ere…."

"Someone done at me wiv somethin', it's stingin' me bloody eyes out, it's burnin' me mouth, uuugh…."

"'Old on, 'old on…."

"Me jacket, I'm covered wiv it, 'elp, 'elp me quick, Bill, quick…."

Clang! — the pipe was thrown down. "Let's get you to the bloody sink…. Ugh! Easy there mate, don't wanna touch the stuff meself, that won't 'elp nothin', Fred…."

Both men were stumbling forward into the dark, their fumbling arms outstretched as they made their way to the sink where Reuben and I remained hidden. The one who had been holding the pipe came first, leading his stricken comrade. He seemed to have no inkling that anyone was there, and I thought that with the apparent urgency of the moment he'd temporarily forgotten about me. But we were still very much in jeopardy and I'd have to hit him somehow, as hard as I could. As they approached, my terror was evaporated, supplanted by cool reckoning, even exhilaration! It would be the first time I'd ever hit anyone seriously, really seriously.

In the darkness he was coming closer, his buddy behind him screaming, "'Elp me, gawd 'elp me, uughh…."

"Alright mate, 'old on, I'm doin' as best as I can…."

As the first one felt his way around our end of the bench, I carefully lifted the glass measuring cylinder, took aim, and with the solid edge of its base struck him a vicious blow across the shin. The force of the impact felt as though it could have broken the bone, although the glass remained intact.

"Ow! Ow! Ow!" He danced on the other foot, hopping and swaying; and as he folded over he lost his balance and toppled all the way forward. A dull *thump!* and to my amazement crumpled to the floor.

"'Elp me, gawd 'elp me…." his colleague moaned aimlessly, arms still outstretched, flailing.

"Christ, he must have hit his forehead on the corner of the bench!" He'd fallen forward into the sharp rough cut iron edge of the bench top. Reuben was already coughing, and I started choking as I realized acrid fumes were filling the room.

This whole sequence of events had been incredible: the unexplained shattering of a glass bottle, and now my single blow, the totality of our defense, and the two superhuman marauders seemed to be vanquished, sliced to ineptitude!

"Oo is it?" It was a pitiful cry. "That you, Grossman? 'Elp me, 'elp me, Gawd 'ave mercy, it's burnin' me eyes out, me mouth…."

"Alright, stay where you are, don't move." I stood up. "Reuben, can you believe it?" Then, "Okay, stay still while I get the light."

I ran between the two benches, and near the far end had to catch myself as I started to slide on the syrupy floor.

The light came on and the sight was incredible. Near the shelves the floor was covered with curved shards of glass where the ten-litre bottle had apparently been dragged from the shelf and smashed to the floor. The floor itself was covered with thick pools of liquid, and choking vapors rose from the frothing linoleum and billowed to the ceiling. By the sink stood the laborer, his arms outstretched toward the window, his hands and face already raw and blistering. Wisps of white vapor rose from his shoulders and head where whatever had doused him was disintegrating his hair and scalp. In front of him lay the other fellow hunched into a fetal position on the hard floor, his mouth hanging open. I looked along under the bench: yes, the face lay in a gathering pool of blackish crimson blood.

And standing by the sink, expressionless, was Reuben.

"Come outside, quick, follow me outside," I ordered the drenched man. "We'll wash you off with the hose from the outside valve, that's the quickest. Follow me, follow me." I touched his jacket sleeve to guide him but immediately a heavy clear syrup oozed onto my fingers. I squeezed the thick liquid between finger and thumb and smelled it. It burned my nose and throat: it was sulphuric acid, one hundred percent, undiluted! Already it was burning through his head and eyes and arms, and would start to burn through the skin of my own fingers in about fifteen seconds.

"Outside, outside!" I shouted at him, "get outside quick!"

He bumped along the wall.

"Watch out, the back of the door, right, come around it, okay, go to the right, that's right, quick, now come on along the passage, watch your step, down, one step down."

I was already out in the yard. I'd turned on the outside valve under the laboratory window to wash my hand off, and as the freezing water touched the acid-laden fingers of my left hand the mixture boiled, hissed and spat. I would have to hose him down with lots and lots of water, before the acid could make the water boil and scald him to death!

As I screwed on the hose I shouted at him: "Quick, pull your clothes off, fast."

"'Elp me, don't, don't 'urt me, I didn't mean no 'arm…."

"No, I'm trying to help you."

"'Elp me…."

"I'm *trying* to help you, you fucking idiot!" I found myself almost in tears as I shouted at him. "Get rid of 'em, your clothes, rip 'em off right now. When the water touches the acid it'll boil and scald you, so we have to wash it off as fast as possible. Your clothes they're soaked with acid, they'll get boiling hot, rip 'em off now, get away from them and I'll hose water over you, every second counts."

"'Elp me, I didn't mean no 'arm…."

"For fuck's sake, do it, do it, do it!" I sobbed. "If you don't you'll be blind! Stop fucking moaning and do it, quick, quick, quick, every second counts!"

He started tearing his clothes off. As he pulled at them, sodden disintegrating chunks of fabric fell away. The hose discharged icy water; this was a freezing night. The man stood there almost naked.

"Everything, your underwear, your socks, anything with acid on, it'll get scalding hot the moment water touches it!" I was crying, I don't know why — shouting at him, crying for him.

He ripped off his underwear and socks. From a distance of a couple of yards I played the icy water first onto his face and head.

"Ow! Me 'ead, ow!, ow!"

Steam rose from the top of his head where there had sat a frothing, unrecognizable mess. What skin was left would be raw, blistered and bloody, and I was sickened and grateful I couldn't see it clearly. Then the spray to his shoulders, arms and torso, legs and feet. In the stark light of the big laboratory window he stood there, naked, shaking with cold, his arms held out unnaturally before him like some stricken somnambulist.

"Hold up your arms, stay still, I know it hurts, we gotta do it, stay still!"

"Ow, ow, ow, ow, gawd 'ave mercy, I didn't mean nothin' I didn't, I didn't mean no 'arm."

The water ran off in puddles, some running under my shoes. Popping sounds like gunfire came from under the soles where they'd been contaminated with acid as I'd slid along the linoleum floor. The beads of water, vaporized in tiny confines under my shoes, kicked up miniature explosions that pushed up at my feet.

"Turn around, keep your arms up, let's get it all, the quicker we get it all, the better."

Reuben now stood in the passageway, a dim wordless shadow.

"Reuben, how's the other one?"

"I…" He turned to go back inside, then I realized he probably also had walked in acid.

"No, come outside first, let me wash your shoes off." He stepped down into the yard, and I sprayed his feet. "Underneath, as well." I sprayed the soles of his shoes. "I wonder how the other one is?"

He stood up on his toes by the window and tried to peer inside beyond the sink, then moved a few steps and looked again from a different angle. "Can't see anyone."

"What!"

"Can't see that far down."

"Oh!" I'd thought he'd meant there was no one there now! I went back to the window and looked myself; everything inside was hazy from the smoke, and the sink and draining board arrangement prevented a sufficiently steep view to the floor. "Christ! Then we'd better watch out for him, in case…. We'd better get an ambulance for this one." I couldn't fathom the expression on Reuben's face. "Are you alright?"

"Yeah I'm alright."

"Then while I do this, go around the other side, don't walk through the passageway because of the acid, go there where I'm pointing, round the back to the other side of the building, the door must be open where this one got in. Upstairs in the manager's office there's a phone, call a hospital or an ambulance or something. Watch out for the other one, in case!"

He walked lazily toward the rear of the building.

"Hurry Reuben, every second counts, it could be the difference between saving this one or not."

He broke into a little trot — but, it seemed, reluctantly. I didn't understand; since this whole turmoil had begun he'd barely said a word, had done nothing to help and even now refused to really move.

The devastated, moaning, naked man standing before me in the frigid night seemed to have descended into some sort of isolate shock, "Gawd 'elp me, gawd 'ave mercy…" the repetition reduced to a litany bereft of meaning.

"You'll be alright, an ambulance will be here soon."

He began to shake. He shook violently, from the cold or the effects of the acid burns, or perhaps it was shock; nevertheless, I had to get him out of the cold.

"Hold on, the floor in the passage is covered with acid, I have to wash it away first." I leaned into the doorway and directed the spray inside. As water touched the floor, sporadic bursts of steam flung the putrefying liquid at the walls. For want of a better idea I thought I should flood the entire passageway floor to dilute the acid so he could walk through to the outer office. At least he'd keep from freezing until an ambulance or the police or someone arrived.

I sprayed the walls, pulling the hose further and further into the passage. Pungent clouds billowed from the open door. I bent under them and peered inside the laboratory, but the fumes were too thick to see as far as the sink. I pulled the door closed. With the passage reasonably neutralized, I needed to get the soaked man into the relative warmth of the outside office — the office from whose door he had burst in upon us.

That's right: he had burst through that door intending me great harm, and here am I in grief at his agony, anguished that I'm unable to save him from a permanent disfigurement, or worse. Abie always said, "Punch 'em, right in the nose punch 'em, make 'em bleed," but I hadn't ever been adept at separating my tormentor's pain from my own. I was a coward, and it was from Abie's watching me when I was afraid to strike out that he also knew I was a coward. And now, was it compassion I felt for this man? Compassion, the coward's refuge? A timorous entreaty: *See how I've cared for you in your distress; when you are sufficiently recovered that you may again do me harm, I beg you, remember my kindness.* Why, why such a compulsion to save this man who twenty minutes ago was ready to string me up the same way those British soldiers were hanged? Should I go over to where he stood, naked, sightless, frozen, and rescue my own future by emptying another bottle of acid over his head? Nine months ago my near-belated resolve had saved Reuben's life, and in repayment he was now holding the threat of public humiliation over my head.

I went back outside. The man still stood in the same spot, in the same posture with arms outstretched, but diminished, the violent tremors now coming in bursts, the dirge subsumed between his chattering teeth. Bedraggled clusters of discarded clothing lying on the ground around him steamed angrily — the scene a Hades.

I realized I too was shaking — with exhaustion. "Come on, an ambulance'll be here soon. Turn around, okay, try to walk forward, can you walk?" He stumbled and slowly turned, and in the new light I saw a repulsive scraggly scrotum dangling between his legs — and, yes — no penis! At least, none visible. Maybe it had shrunk into his torso. Maybe we're so conceived that when someone empties a ten-litre bottle of one-hundred-percent sulphuric acid over your head, your dick retreats to await a more benign pH reading.

His outstretched arms were partially lowered and no longer feeling the way ahead, but I was afraid to touch his ravaged skin, to guide him by hand. "It's okay, I'll tell you if there's anything in the way. Come on, okay, now careful, slow, there's the step right in front of you, right, up one step, okay keep going, very good, we're nearly there."

And on, I walking backwards in front of him, past the laboratory door, the lavatory, and through the far door into the outer office. I switched on the light, and, to contain the still-burgeoning clouds, closed off the door that connected the laboratory. Perhaps he would be able to sit on the chair alongside the desk, if the red remains of his cracked and desiccated skin could bend.

"Come, this way." I directed him to the chair. "There's the arm, lower, lower down, okay keep hold of it, turn around, and sit, slowly, sit down."

"Ow, ow, gawd 'elp me, gawd...." The muttered words escaped through unmoving lips.

He lowered himself onto the seat. Giant blisters arched over the red and bloodied skin of his head and face, a few black atrophied hairs stuck into his caved chest, and his eyelids were glued shut. A corpse, a living corpse.

Exhausted, I didn't know what to do next. "Do you want some water?" I got the mug and went out of the room. "Reuben!" I called up the stairs, "What's happening, is someone coming?" What the fuck was he doing up there? And I mustn't forget: where was the other man? In the lavatory I filled the mug and brought it back in.

Through the window I heard the civilized *bong, bong, bong* of a police car, then tires on loose gravel, the clacking of a motor.

"Help!" I shouted to the outside darkness. I didn't have time to give the man water. "We're here!" I ran back through the passageway and out into the yard, over to the gate. "We're here!"

"What's going on there?"

"I'm here, we're here!" I struggled with the lock. "I can't get the damn gate open, it's stuck!"

Someone clambered up the outside, and a policeman's peaked cap appeared over the top. "What's going on here?"

"We need help, an ambulance! Didn't Reuben tell you?"

"Reuben?"

"Yes, I told him to telephone the police."

"We have a Reuben Berger in the car here."

"You do?" Maybe he went out instead, to get the police. "He was supposed to telephone you."

"We found him running along the street; we thought he looked suspicious so we followed him then apprehended him. Is this your firm, sir?"

"No, I mean, I work here, we've had a terrible accident. Look, wait a minute, I'll try to open the gate." But the policeman clambered over the gate and jumped down into the yard. "Oh, good, look," I went on, "there's a man in there, he's been terribly burned, with acid, we have to get an ambulance."

"Alright sir, let's be calm. Is there a telephone here?"

"It's upstairs," I sobbed; at last here was somebody who would really help.

"It's alright now, sir, I'll follow you, lead the way." We rushed along the passageway. "What's all the smoke? Is this building on fire?"

"No, it's acid... they wanted to do something to me...."

"Do something?"

"I... I don't know, something...." Now we were alongside the outer office, and I opened the door. "Here's the man, first..." A burst of choking fumes swept out of the room.

The policeman grabbed a deep breath, ducked, then entered; I hadn't realized, but the outer office air was by now quite thick also. He crossed over to the chair. "My God, oh, my God!" I heard him mutter.

"Should we phone for the ambulance first? Then I'll explain how it happened."

"We have to open a window immediately for this man to breathe."

"Yes, yes, I forgot..." We pushed open the stiff window, left the door all the way back and next we were up the stairs. "Oh! I forgot! The other one!"

"The other what?" The policeman was already dialing.

"The other one, the other man, he was on the floor in the laboratory...."

"Sir, how many injured men are there?"

"Two. Two, just two."

"You're sure?"

"Yes, two, only two, I'm sorry, it's been terrible."

"Yes, two ambulances, we don't know, some sort of laboratory accident, yes.... Thank you." He hung up.

"What's the name of the proprietor?"

"Margolin, Mr. Margolin. We have to go into the laboratory, the other one was lying on the floor by the window, he hit his head on the corner, I don't know what happened to him since then."

He dialed a second call, and I ran back downstairs into the outer office. The air was much clearer now, and the burned man sat rigidly upright on the chair. His moaning had ceased, and now as he breathed his chest moved in a shallow jerking rhythm as though he were barely alive.

The policeman came trotting in as I pulled open the door to the laboratory. A new burst of acrid fumes billowed into the office. "He's in there, he was on the floor by the window, the other end...."

"We'll have to try to save him. We'd better not go in there. I'll get my partner. Follow me." We slammed the door shut and ran back through the passageway to the yard. He climbed the gate to call to his partner: "John, we have one seriously burned, and another, probably asphyxiated unless we move quickly." As he jumped down I was able to open the latch, and we swung the gate wide. "The crow-bar, bring the crow-bar."

"What about him?" As the second policeman, stockier than the first, got out of the car, the opened car door illuminated the interior to show Reuben slumped in the back seat.

"He didn't do anything... I don't think..." I said. Then more directly, "Reuben, you alright?"

Reuben still said nothing.

"Stay here in the car, sir, don't leave, I don't want to have to handcuff you. We'll want you to answer a few questions after we've settled this emergency," the second policeman admonished as Reuben's hulk hunched a little deeper into the car's recesses.

The two policemen and I ran back to the laboratory window.

"He was in there, just beyond the sink on the floor."

"I'm afraid I have to break the window, sir, give him air."

"Yes, sure... I should have thought of that before...."

He lifted the crow-bar and smashed several panes; fumes rolled out into the night air. "He's a goner, must be in that stuff," he said as he smashed a few more. He broke away the framing, put a handkerchief over his mouth and clambered up to look inside. "Where was he?"

"On the floor, right there, beyond the sink."

"There's nobody here. Down there?"

"Yes." I leaned into the choking fumes to try to see. "There was blood, there on the floor."

"There's no one here." He jumped down, and the sound of an ambulance's chimes rang along the street. I went back into the passageway, opened the laboratory door, and crouching to floor level where the fumes had already started to thin, peered along the room: he was right, no one was there.

Suddenly, I remembered! Pulling open the shallow center desk drawer I reached into the left corner, all the way back, and my fingers closed around the paper-wrapped package of twelve florins I'd secreted; I shoveled them as quietly as possible into my trousers pocket. Quickly I groped around for the mold; I opened the drawer further, but it was gone! Reuben must have stolen it while I was outside, and he didn't notice the package of coins. Voices outside; there was no time for the luxury of a more thorough search. As I went back out to the yard, the ambulance was backing in through the gateway.

Ten minutes later I sat on a box by the wall, drained, and noticed my trouser legs were sodden, freezing in the cold night air. The two ambulance men, bearing a folded stretcher, passed by me and into the passageway.

"You alright, sir?" asked the first policeman, the taller one. His mate was off, searching the yard.

"Yes. It's been terrible." I sat, the first relative quiet since I'd climbed the tank ladder less than an hour ago.

A minute later the white-coated ambulance attendants were returning along the passageway. On their stretcher lay the burned man, his knees bent up in a sitting position. His head and legs rocked to the stretcher's motions, but beyond that he showed no autonomous movement.

"Is he alive?" I asked.

"Ninety percent burns. Ain't good, poor bugger!" They were loading the stretcher into the ambulance. "We'll do our level best for 'im. 'E your buddy?"

"He works here."

"We'll do our level best, mate."

Stones crackled under the tires as the ambulance pulled away through the gate. As it drove off, another car pulled up, a second Wolseley, and a man in civvies climbed out.

"Peter Harrington," he announced. "Detective, with the police department."

"Yes sir," acknowledged the first policeman. "Apparently, intent to cause bodily harm, then some sort of accident in the laboratory, sir. This man" — he signaled my way — "was witness to the events, sir."

"Your name, sir?"

"Zachary Grossman. I work here, in the laboratory." And I gathered myself, stood, and now in greater detail described the evening's happenings.

As the detective, the policemen and I entered the laboratory, the blackened linoleum crunched and crumbled under our feet. "Be careful, acid must have splashed all over." I led them to the end of the bench. "This is where he was, where that blood is. He fell into the corner of the bench and hit his head. He was there on the floor, that's from his head."

"He's not here now, sir, so we'll have this officer search the building, and if necessary the yard."

"Officer Clarke is already searching the yard, sir."

"Yes, good man."

"And I telephoned the proprietor, a Mr. Margolin. Twenty minutes, he said." He looked at his watch. "He should be here any minute now, sir."

"Good man."

I went outside for some fresh air, to gather myself. A second ambulance now stood outside the yard just beyond the gate, its headlights forming ghostly shadows in the fog. I walked over. "They haven't found the other injured one yet," I said, and the driver nodded. I remembered Reuben, and looked down into the back of the first police car. The seat was empty!

"Bloke buggared orf up the road, 'e did. Not two minutes ago, just as we got 'ere, we saw 'im," said the driver.

"Really, he ran off?"

"Like a bloody ghost was after 'im."

Reuben was gone, the last straw in an evening of unbelievable happenings. I ran back into the laboratory. The detective was puttering around, jotting down notes on a pad, measuring distances with a flexible tape, and the taller policeman had just finished searching the building.

"Reuben is gone!" I said. "The ambulance men said he ran off, I don't know why, I didn't think he did anything."

The policeman described to the detective how they'd earlier encountered Reuben running one street away, and picked him up.

The detective turned to me. "And who is Mr. Berger?"

"He's someone I know... he lives near me."

He pointed to a piece of the shattered ten-litre bottle, the neck stem, that lay on the floor by the old desk. "Do you recognize this?"

"It must be a piece of the bottle, the neck, the bottle that fell on the floor."

"Look closer, sir — I mean this." A length of thin cord was tied around the broken neck's narrowest part. "Could you tell us what this piece of cord is for?"

"I don't know, it wasn't on there before."

"I notice that none of your other bottles has a cord tied around its neck."

"That's right, we never did anything like that. I don't know what it is, I never saw it before."

"And there's a length of the same cord tied to that shelf bracket." He pointed to the small shelf on the wall opposite the storage shelves, the one we used for manuals. "It appears that that cord might have been stretched across the room and used as a trip-wire to pull the bottle off the shelf."

"But why? Why would anyone do that?" I asked.

"That is for us to find out. I assume you know where Mr. Berger lives?"

"Yes, Mile End, Morgan Street, he lives across the road from us."

"The street and number?"

"Eighteen, eighteen Morgan Street, why, do you think...."

"We try not to think, sir — we enquire, and we assemble jigsaw puzzles."

The second policeman came panting into the laboratory. "Found him sir, he's a goner."

We all followed outside and across the yard where he shone his torch on a shadowed area behind the huge steam-heated distillation still. There in one of the shallow rectangular evaporation trays lay a body, face down, one arm above the head, the other along his side.

"My god! When he heard the police car he must have run to hide, and fell into the tray!" I said.

Someone was walking toward us across the yard. "Good evening gentlemen, what's been going on here?" It was Mr. Margolin. "I see the laboratory window's broken."

Again, I tried to describe the dizzying sequence of the evening's events.

"I'm afraid this is our latest discovery, sir," said detective Harrington, beckoning the policeman to shine his torch.

Mr. Margolin shook his head in disbelief. "How dreadful! We'll have to get Mr. Smith here to identify this poor fellow."

"The other one called him Bill, and _he_ called the one who's in the hospital, Fred," I said.

"We'll want to be absolutely sure before we inform his family; Mr. Smith will be our man for that. I suppose I should see if there's anything left of the laboratory and offices."

"Yes," I said as the taller policeman, the detective and I followed him into the building. "The offices are all alright, Mr. Margolin, it's mostly the laboratory, it'll be a big clean-up job again, mainly new linoleum from the sulphuric acid, but it'll be alright."

Upstairs in his office Mr. Margolin pulled out a folder. "Here's the file on all our work-ers."

"Does Mr. Smith have a telephone at his residence, sir?" asked detective Harrington.

"I'm afraid not yet...."

"Then give me his address and we'll have officer Clarke here drive over and fetch him."

Later, as we stood downstairs in the shattered laboratory, crumbling linoleum under our feet and wisps of fumes still rising above the floor, Mr. Margolin addressed me with resigna-tion. "Grossman, I'm horrified at these two men's intentions to do you such harm, yet perhaps you'll allow me the hope that when you're safely in the military, the laboratory can look forward to a period of comparative calm."

41

Came Monday the tenth of December nineteen forty eight, the day of my induction into the Royal Air Force. Jack took an hour off from school in the morning to come with me to the station.

"So, here we are old fellow, the Fates once again scattering us to the winds."

"Maybe I can talk the RAF into letting me bomb London, so I can bail out over Mile End."

"You'll be too busy explaining why according to quantum mechanics their bombs wouldn't work anyway."

The face of an oncoming engine climbed the tracks of the foreshortened curve, rising up to platform height and screeching to a halt. We grasped hands. "Jack, you'd better stop wearing your cape to school, they'll think you're Zorro."

"So long, old buddy, try not to start World War III."

It was a short ride, forty minutes, and by the time the train had slowed to a crawl my stomach was queasy — another train ride into the ominous unknown of a small country station, Padgate. The setting, presumably chosen as suitable for square-bashing, seemed too idyllic to harbor germinal warriors.

A young red-faced airman wearing a beret, with two stripes on his arm, awaited us. "RAF recruits, over here!" he called in a discreetly shrouded whisper. From among the train's debarkees he collected an aggregate of twenty acned youth. An RAF bus, seemingly manufactured without springs, lurched us to the camp.

The induction process consisted first of a haircut — virtually a head shave. The exit door from this chamber led into a freezing corrugated Nissen hut where from behind a low wide counter an angry elderly corporal flung at each of our troop two sets of underwear and socks, one working uniform and one dress uniform, a pair of shoes and a pair of boots. Next, we were herded with our bundles out across an open parade square bordered by Nissen huts and crowned with a flapping Union Jack, into a dormitory barracks. There we were assigned our respective bunks and commanded to change into working uniform.

The new uniforms were stiff and hairy, itchy, and nothing fit. The boots seemed to weigh at least one ton each — so massive that every step required a considerable outlay of energy to initially get it moving and then accelerated up to foot-swinging speed. And once at that velocity, in accordance with Newton's Third Law, an equivalent energy expenditure was required to slow it down again to a stop. Following which, the process was to be repeated with the other foot, and on *ad infinitum*.

On each bunk lay a bag for our civvies, and two labels for our home address. "Write your 'ome address on 'em, y' bunch o' bloody pansies, tie one label outside the bag, t'other inside the bag so's we can send 'em 'ome to y' mums, you won't be needin' 'em for a long time," roared the jubilant sergeant. He marched us, each out of step and struggling against the boots' inertia despite his allegro "Hup tar, hup tar, hup tar," to the mess hall. There we joined an existing queue inching toward the counter, where we were served on metal plates a dinner of stewed rabbit and waterlogged potato, dished out of monstrous pots by a line of white-coated scraggly recruits seemingly as bewildered as we. During the leisurely cup of tea that followed, every one of our crew admitted to being scared. Finally we dragged our boots back to the barracks to recuperate from our first day of service to the queen.

After six weeks of push-ups, saluting exercises and tea, we were deemed airmen.

●   ●   ●

Marius hung over the edge of the boarding platform as the trollybus slowed. Just as it drew to a halt he gathered his coat tightly about himself and jumped down. He trotted across the wide pavement and up the broad steps before the entrance to The London Hospital. Inside, he asked at the desk for a visitor's pass.

The lady behind the desk turned to look at the clock, which read one-fifty — mid-day. "Ten minutes yet 'til visiting, you're early," she smiled.

"Oh...."

She pointed. "You can wait on them benches over there."

"Yeah, alright." Still clutching his coat closed, for several minutes Marius paced the busy hallway. He noticed a door marked *Gentlemen,* and entered the room. Inside, he locked himself in one of the stalls, released the grip on his coat, and into the corner of the wall behind the toilet-bowl he leaned the rifle he had been concealing.

He urinated, shook his penis, pulled the cistern chain, closed the wooden lid and sat down. He swung around to grasp the rifle, and as he lay it across his bare knees he noticed how hairy his legs were becoming. He eased back the spherical black iron bolt handle and a shiny brass-and-silver cartridge rose to the mouth of the chamber immediately behind the barrel. He ejected the cartridge silently from the rifle's breech, and as he caught it in his other hand he heard the gentlemen's-room door squeak open. Somebody coughed, the door banged, and he remained perfectly still at the sound of clothes rustling by the open urinal right outside his stall. More coughing, the rattle of unsecured plumbing as a flush of water hissed against the ceramic fixture. Again hinges squealed, and the door banged shut.

He remained motionless for a full minute until he was sure no one else was in the room. Holding the ejected cartridge, he observed how the narrow end of its brass case was serrated with compression marks where it gripped the gracefully curved dulled-silver bullet insert. He rubbed it against his coat to remove any dust, then painstakingly reloaded it into the rifle's breech. Grasping the bolt's handle, he traveled it forward until it reached its stop, then eased the knob down to its rest position. In his coat pocket he felt for the last remaining cartridge. This cartridge, plus the one now safely ensconced within the breech, were all that remained of the three he'd found when for the second time he'd surreptitiously clambered through the window of Uncle Albert's room in the cellar of the industrial building off of New Road. He was lucky to have found more bullets and to have again gotten out of there before Uncle Albert returned; if he'd been caught, Albert might have deduced it had been his own nephew who'd stolen the rifle months earlier, before they went to America. Back then, Marius had imagined it would have been sufficient just to frighten Abie by pointing the gun at him after he'd hit Mum. And for his gullibility, his underestimating his father's overwhelming strength and cunning, he'd ended up in this very hospital with a broken jaw. Never again!

He'd already spent one of the three bullets very late the previous night, practicing among the debris-strewn shadows at the back of the deserted Coopers College grounds — he needed to be certain everything would work properly. He'd loaded the rifle, aimed, and fired just one shot, into an old mound of detritus which had jumped like a living thing when it was struck.

Now he stood up, pulled up his grey cord-du-roi trousers and buttoned the fly. Next he confirmed once more the rifle was properly loaded, then engaged the safety catch. Again, he secreted the weapon beneath his coat, exited the gentlemen's, and crossed over to the desk.

"I'm back miss, wanna see Grossman."

"You a relative?"

"'E's me father."

"Do you know what ward 'e's in?"

"Yeah, Rothschild."

She searched two times through her compilation of little cards. "You sure that's where 'e is?"

"Rothschild, that's where 'e was Sunday." He hadn't anticipated that they might move him elsewhere. Supposing he wasn't even in the hospital any more! No, that was silly, he must remain calm.

"Oops! Found 'im! Yes, they moved 'im into the sub-ward."

Marius clutched the concealed weapon tighter. "Where's that?"

"'It'll be the same room but they'll 'ave partitioned off the end, like." She handed over the pass. "Visiting's 'til four. 'Ope your dad's coming along alright now."

"Yup, thanks."

The lift was crowded with visitors, and he held his arms firmly crossed in front of his coat as the scissors gate slammed shut. Everyone was jolted upward, the attendant finally calling the fourth floor. The brass knob on the operating wheel sprang to center and the man slid open the gate. Marius sidled carefully out, took a deep breath and strode along the hallway.

A nurse stood in the ward's doorway. "Who're you looking for?"

"Mr. Grossman, 'e's in the sub-ward."

"Oh yes, through that far curtain." She pointed into the ward beyond the ends of the two rows of beds.

Marius was grateful for the additional privacy a partition might afford, though he was curious as to why they'd put Abie there. "Why's 'e in there 'stead of 'ere, miss?"

"There were some... complaints."

"Complaints?"

She lowered her voice. "Sometimes his language is a bit much, we don't want to upset the other patients."

"Er... oh!" Marius walked past the rows of beds, then through the break in the curtain and around a further screen. In this semiprivate area two visitors had just arrived at the sole other bed, placed against the opposite wall, where an elderly patient was sitting up. Marius nodded a cursory acknowledgement.

Abie looked repulsive lying there, unshaven, brow knit as though angry even in his sleep. He breathed heavily, sputtering through bubbling lips as Marius came around the far side of the bed.

"Abie!" The visitors looked up at the sharpness of Marius's tone. Abie moved his head, his eyes flickered at the interruption and his mouth closed and set. He settled himself deeper into the bed and resumed his loud snoring.

"Abie!" Marius reached over the bedclothes and rocked Abie's shoulder.

"Wha… wha'sa marra, wha's going on…."

"Dad. It's me." Then, more sternly, "Abie!"

"Wha'? Oo is it there, wha's going on?"

"It's me."

"Me?"

"Me, Maudy. Who did you think it was?"

The other patient whispered to his guests.

Abie's eyes were now fully open. "Oh, eee, uh thought… where's Lily?"

"She's not 'ere."

"She's… Lily's not 'ere?"

"No. This time I come by meself."

"By yourself? Wha's the matter, what 'appened, is everything alright?"

"Yeah, everything's alright. Matter o' fact everything's pretty good if you ask me."

"Alright." Abie gathered himself and edged a little higher against the pillow. "Eee, like… Lily, she couldn' come?"

"Yup, she couldn't come."

"She's alright?"

"Yup, she's alright."

"Wha's the matter then, why couldn't she come?"

"Well, maybe she could come, I dunno."

Opposite, the other patient now sat over the edge of his bed as his visitors helped him into a dressing gown.

Abie continued. "Wha'd'y' mean, uh mean, is she 'ere? Wha's going on?"

"Going on?"

"Yeh… uh mean…."

"Abie, I already said, nothing's going on."

"Abie?" Abie giggled nervously. "Wha'cha calling me Abie for all of a sudden?"

"That's your name, ain't it?"

"Maudy, wha'sa marra, you look funny, wha's going on 'ere?"

"Crikey, I already told you nothing's going on. *I* look funny? *You* look funny. You look funnier 'an me."

Across the room, the other patient's visitors had eased him up off his bed, and the woman was tying the belt of his dressing gown.

"Wha'sa marra with 'im already, uh'm in the 'ospital with bandages 'ere, 'course I look funny, what did you expect uh'll look normal, like everybody else?"

"You don't 'ave to worry, you'll never look normal so you can stop worrying 'bout that, 'bout looking normal."

"Eee, you're wild with me, uh'm sorry, wha' did uh do?"

"What did you do?"

"Ssh, eee it's not nice, like such a noise. Such a commotion 'ere in the 'ospital, like, other people…." Abie nodded at the trio edging around the foot of the other bed. "Yuh see wha'cha doing with all the shouting?"

"Didn't seem to bother you couple o' nights ago."

"Wha'? Wha'd'y' mean, wha's going on 'ere with 'im already?"

"I mean…" and Marius' voice became even louder, "I mean, you were shouting loud enough the last time, shouting at Mum *and* shouting at me. Didn't seem to bother you then making a lot o' noise, did it?"

"Shouting? Oo was shouting? Me, uh was shouting?"

The departing patient had been hobbled away as expeditiously as his condition warranted, all three avoiding any glance in the direction of Abie's bed. They hurried around the partition and beyond, and the curtain swung back in place.

"Who was shouting?" continued Marius. "You, y' barstard, you were shouting."

"Me? A *barsted* you're callin' me, eee, such language!"

"You're always shouting and punching all the time, everybody in the 'ouse, don'cha know you're always shouting?" Marius's vehemence caused him to briefly pause and catch his breath; he gathered himself, inhaled deeply, swallowed, then: "What are you, stupid or something?"

"Stupid? Maybe uh'm stupid, uh didn't know uh'm *always* shouting, sometimes uh shout a bit, you shout also, uh 'eard you shout."

"Me? I don't shout all the time, every time I open my mouth like you, I got no reason to shout."

"Uh mean you're shouting, now, right now you're shouting, and for what? Nothing even 'appened and 'e's shouting! 'E's telling me!"

Marius was coughing and he clutched his coat. "No, I mean…."

"See?" continued Abie. "You're choking there 'cause you're shouting, 'e's telling me 'e's not shouting!" He giggled. "While you're telling me, you're shouting, you're like shouting while you're telling me!" The curtains moved and a nurse appeared around the partition. "'E's not shouting, 'e's telling me!"

"What's going on here, Mr. Grossman?"

Again Abie giggled. "Nothing, wha'd'y' mean, nothing's going on, 'e, uh don't know, mu boy 'ere 'e came to the 'ospital, we're talking, nobody's shouting, uh'm sorry don't worry, no one's gonna be shouting."

Marius stood silently on the other side of the bed.

"People said there was shouting here, patients could hear it in the main ward."

"Uh'm sorry, for a minute maybe someone was shouting, don't worry it's alright now, no one's gonna be shouting."

The nurse looked at Marius. "Don't you go upsetting your father now, he's got to get better so's he can go home."

"Alright, I'm not the one who shouts…."

The nurse straightened Abie's sheet where the top edge folded over the blanket. "You just call me if you wants something, some water or something, Mr. Grossman." She turned and left.

Abie looked at Marius admonishingly. "Eee, it's terrible a commotion like that, for nothing, they're all listening outside there in the other room, it's not nice."

A darkness clouded Marius's face. "Why did you throw the soup on Mum?"

"Throw the soup on Mum?"

Squeezing his left arm close to his coat, Marius walked over to the break between the two partitions and slid them closer together. He returned to the side of Abie's bed. "That's what I said: Why did you throw the soup on Mum, over Mum?"

"Maudy, take your coat off, sit down, uh don't wanna argue, oo wants to argue all the time, it's like, silly." Abie beckoned to the chair. "It's silly, arguing all for nothing, your face there, it's all funny from arguing."

"Abie, why did you throw the soup all over Mum, are you going to answer or not?"

"Wha'sa marra with 'im, oo threw the soup?" Abie replied angrily. "It was 'ot, scalding 'ot, uh dropped the soup, on the covers uh dropped it, uh didn't *throw* no soup uh didn't throw! Muself uh scalded with the soup even, not Mum."

Marius shouted, "You threw the soup!" He drew a hoarse breath. "You threw the soup...."

"Uh didn't throw no soup, take a *broch* already...."

"You shut up and listen to me! You threw the soup! I carried that bottle of soup from 'ome 'cause Mum told me, she was still trying to be nice 'cause she'll never learn...."

"Uh didn't throw no soup! The nurse there she took the soup, she made it 'ot, scalding 'ot, on the blanket uh dropped it, wha'cha want me to do, get all scalded...."

Now Marius was sobbing. "Well you scalded Mum, y' did...."

"Uh didn't scald Mum, you *barsted* you, 'e's crying there like uh, uh, deliberately, it was an accident, it went on the blanket it went, a bit, a tiny bit went on 'er maybe like a splash...."

"You fucking barstard you...." Marius opened his coat and the rifle fell out. With his right hand he caught it before the butt touched the floor. He lifted the weapon to his right shoulder and aimed it directly at Abie's face. His right index finger found the trigger inside its looped guard as, with his thumb, he released the safety catch. "Come on," he shouted, "why did y' thr... thr..." He tried to take a breath, "why... why... why did y'... y'... thr... she was trying t' be trying t' be... I'll...." He gasped for his next breath, "I'll kill y', y' fucking... y' fucking..." His finger tightened on the trigger. "I'll... I'll..."

Abie leaned violently away and now hung half out of the bed on the far side, pulling the bedclothes with him as he struggled not to crash completely onto the floor.

Marius attempted with mounting difficulty to take another breath. "I... I...." He tried to breathe, to continue; his mouth was opened wide as he fought to inhale. Even then he tried to speak, with only a rasping wheeze issuing from his lips. His right hand left the trigger and clawed at his throat as the rifle, now supported only by his left, began to drop. As he scratched at his own throat, tearing at the skin, the tip of the rifle barrel came all the way down to rest on the bed's iron side-rail. His face was now turning crimson; the rifle clattered to the floor and he began banging on his chest with both hands, slapping himself harder and harder, one side of the chest, then the other, all the while emitting hoarse, hollow strangled gasps. The resolution in his arms, his hands, slowly degenerated from desperately focused clawing and thumping into an aimless flailing. His mouth stretched wide and his eyes stared ahead unbelievingly, the strangled wheezing growing quieter, more halting, as he sank to the floor. He collapsed on top of the rifle, which with a sharp *crack* discharged horizontally across the floor in the direction of the other bed. The bullet passed through a leg of the wooden bedside chest opposite, which jumped, then leaned precariously forward, the curved metal bowl seated atop rocking to and fro in a series of decelerating *dut-dut—dut-dut—dut-dut—dut-dut* clicks.

All was now deadly silent throughout the entire ward. Abie managed to pull himself back up to the center of his bed. "M.. M... Maudy! Maudy, what 'appened?" He looked around, but failed to notice his son lying on the floor, so close as to be largely concealed under his own bed. "Maudy, wha'ch'a doing, come 'ere, don't be silly... with a... gun already, 'e's like a, uh dunno, mad 'e is already...." But Marius was nowhere to be seen.

The curtain swung and the partitions burst asunder as the nurse ran in, followed by a blue-jacketed male attendant. "Mr. Grossman, what happened? Are you alright? Where's your son? What happened?"

"Uh, uh, uh, uh, eee, uh, uh, uh, a gun 'e 'ad, ee-eee, like a gun 'e 'ad...."

The nurse tore Abie's sleeping suit jacket off to scour his chest. "Where is it, where did he hit you, where is it bleeding?"

"Uh, uh, uh dunno...."

She ripped the blanket and sheets down to the foot of the bed, searching Abie, his clothes and the covers for blood. "Where does it hurt then, Mr. Grossman?"

"Uh, uh dunno, uh don't think...."

"Then did he hit you, did a bullet hit you?"

"Nah, nah, 'e, 'e, nah, 'e missed me, maybe."

"'E missed?" asked the male attendant.

"Yeh, 'e, 'e...." Abie glimpsed something irregular on the floor by the far side of the bed, and pointed.

The attendant leaned over and looked down. "Gawd, 'e got 'imself 'e did, blimey!" He and the nurse both hurried around to where Marius lay face down on the floor, the rifle barrel protruding diagonally from under his shoulder. They pulled him from under the bed and rolled him over onto his back. His face was blue. "'E ain't breathing," shouted the attendant. The nurse dropped to her knees alongside Marius's prostrate form, and grasping his wrist felt for a pulse. Quickly she moved her fingers to the side of his neck under the chin.

"Doctor Albright, get doctor Albright in Casualty, ring the emergency bell quick, quick," she called to the small group that had gathered at the mouth of the partition.

Again she felt for a pulse, without success. She lowered her head, "He's a goner." She searched his clothes for a wound, but found nothing. "Looks like a heart attack from his color." The attendant nodded agreement. She climbed up to the bedside. "Mr. Grossman, you're sure you're alright?"

"Yeh, uh'm alright, what 'appened? Eee, uh'm lucky, 'e could'a killed me with the gun there, eee!"

"I'm sorry, Mr. Grossman, this young man is... was your son?"

"Yeh, M... M... Maudy, Marius, a name, you ever 'ear anything like it? 'Is mother she called 'im Marius, Marius Goring in the pictures, that's what she wanted so what'm uh s'posed to do, 'ave a fight with 'er? Uh should worry what name she wants to give 'im!"

"Mr. Grossman sir, I'm sorry, your son is dead."

"Dead? Wha'd'y' mean? 'Ow can 'e be dead?"

"I'm sorry sir, he's dead. Looks like a heart attack."

"'Eart attack? 'Ow can 'e 'ave an 'eart attack, 'e's... 'e's... 'e's four... 'e's fourteen, fourteen years old only, nah, 'e can't 'ave an attack... an... 'eart attack." The attendant was moving Marius's arms down to his sides. The nurse stood by the side of the bed, holding Abie's arm. "An 'eart attack?" continued Abie. "'Ow can 'e 'ave an 'eart attack?"

The attendant stood up and beckoned to another blue-jacketed man coming through the group crowding the partition. "'Ey, Fred, get a stretcher, mate, we'll 'ave to run this one down to Casualty."

"An 'eart attack? Eee, 'e could'a killed me with the gun there, like a meshugginer 'e is, always like a meshugginer. An 'eart attack? Eee, Lily, uh'll 'ave to tell Lily, someone'll 'ave to tell Lily. Shame, 'is mother, she'll... shame."

—o—O—o—

–42–

"Terrible, terrible." Katherine wiped her eyes. "Why is everything so hard?" She and I were riding home from West Ham, from the cemetery at Plashett.

"It's hard to believe," I said. "I never realized his coughing was so serious."

"Congestion of the lungs — phew!" Katherine exhaled.

We were seated together on the bus, and my new RAF uniform felt hairy and stiff. "They told me at the hospital what it was, ugh!, it means your lungs fill up with fluid and you sort of... drown. God!"

"Our little brother, what a horrible way to die!" she said. "A rotten life he had, also."

"Shame, he said he didn't have a single friend in America the whole three months."

"I'm hardly surprised he wanted to kill him, after everything. Mum said every time she took him to the hospital the old fucker found something to start shouting about."

I recalled the gun episode. "The other time with that rifle when he came running downstairs...."

"...Yes, I thought he really was going to shoot him! Where did he get guns from, I wonder?"

"Uncle Albert showed me a rifle when I went to his room in that factory by New Road. While I was telling Mum about it Maudy was listening to every detail, then he wanted to know exactly where Albert lived."

"I suppose the police will settle whose gun it was, who cares, really."

"The characters he hung around with," I said, "probably any of them could have gotten one for him, like Alex, he seems the type."

"You're right."

"You remember, when I went to get the ambulance, Abie hid the gun in the shoe cupboard?"

"I know, Daddy was ashamed, *nebuch,* for the ambulance men to see it."

"When they were in America I checked that whole cupboard out, it wasn't there. I thought maybe Abie took it to Burnt Oak or something."

"No." Katherine gathered her coat; we were nearly home. "Maudy told me he gave it to a friend before he went, to look after it, he wouldn't say who." She stood up to alight, and I picked up her handbag. "Not that it makes any difference now," she said.

The bus jerked to a stop. Through the window I noticed over by the corner of Burdett Road two men in RAF uniform with on-duty peak caps, both wearing M.P. armbands; I'd never seen military police in Mile End before. As we got off and crossed Mile End Road they started over the road as well, toward us; what had I done wrong? Katherine was buttoning her coat and I quickly handed her the handbag: "Take your bag, if I hold it they'll think I'm taking the mickey or something." I checked my uniform: the jacket was buttoned up properly, my shoes still looked polished, the beret was square on my head.

"'Ey private, you on special pass?"

That might have been because it was Thursday, not the weekend. But before I could respond, Katherine took over: "We're coming back from our brother's funeral."

"Alright miss. Let's 'ave a gander at your pass, private."

"Oh, why don't you piss off, both of you, leave him alone! Don't you hear straight? I said we're coming back from our brother's funeral."

Their backs stiffened and I was caught in the middle. I tried to mitigate the situation by standing smartly to attention while pulling the pass from my jacket pocket. The first one took it and read it.

"He's my brother." As usual, Katherine wasn't to be easily stopped. "We're just coming back from the cemetery, our young brother died, yesterday."

He handed the pass back, said "Sorry about your brother," to me, then turned to Katherine: "There's no need for that kind of language, miss."

"Oh, fuck off!" She grabbed at my arm and, though half my weight, pulled me along the pavement. I glanced back to where they stood, nonplussed; one made a halting attempt at pursuit but the other pulled him back.

After a short distance, when no truncheon had descended across my head, I whispered. "Christ, Katya, I can get in serious trouble!"

"What do you mean, *I* did it, not you."

As we turned the corner I stole another look, and the two had returned to their post outside the station. "You can't do things like that!"

"I can't? But I did!" Katherine was still furious. "Everywhere you go there's some *fart* ready to tell you what to do! Why don't people leave people alone?"

"In the RAF that's what they do," I said. "They have to, otherwise the whole air force would collapse."

"Sorry, I didn't mean to make you nervous."

The incident was over, and I had to smile. "Katya, the way you tell people off and get away with it! You love doing it!" A welcome little smile eased the severity of her face. "You're so quick," I continued. "Like with the rabbi this afternoon."

"Yes, what did you think of that one! That fucker is telling *me* I can't go on the cemetery grounds! It's *my* brother."

"That's their Jewish things, they don't let women go to burials, I suppose."

"Did you see his face when I said, 'You just try and stop me!' And then of course Benny took his side! Reliable Benny, I can always count on him taking the other person's side against me. Just like Daddy." As we crossed into Tredegar Square, flecks of snow were dotting the grass. "Well, at least they wanted him back at the factory this afternoon, I have to be thankful for that."

"Katya, I'm sorry it's so rotten being married to him, I...."

"Oh, it's not as terrible as I make it sound sometimes. He's alright — some of the time. I should stop grumbling so much."

"No, I don't mind, I just wish I could do something."

"I'll survive. I don't have to go back there tonight, I've got a breather."

"Oh, you're staying home, with Mum and me?"

"I told him I have to stay with Mum for a few days. He'll have the pleasure of Bessie's company. Maybe they'll both kill each other."

"Remember before Mum and Maudy went to America — christ, the way I'm talking... Maudy, I can't get used to it...."

"Don't cry Zech, it's nobody's fault, what can anyone do?"

"...anyway, you said you didn't want to be stuck with Abie so you married Benny, and...."

"Well, who in their right mind would want to be left cooking and cleaning for the old shitbag?"

"I know, but you got married and I thought it would be better... I mean like... different."

Katherine fell to silence as we slogged across the park through the thickening snow-flakes. Finally she spoke: "Is that how it sounds, like I just made an exchange, from one shitbag to another?"

"A bit... I dunno."

We were across the square and the snow was settling, the road covered with a white film that sparkled in the new electric street lights. She spoke, almost to herself: "Maybe you're right, someone's a bit nice, you think maybe it'll be alright. Then before you realize, instead of the old *broch* to contend with you've got a younger one with more energy...."

It was too much to dwell on right this moment, what with the funeral just finished and Lily waiting at home for us. We slogged in muffled unison across Morgan Street, our shoes leaving a trail of perfect prints on the smooth black asphalt that obliterated the old cobblestones I'd thought so pretty when we'd first moved there.

"My pass is 'til Sunday night. I'm glad you'll be staying home for a few days with Mum and me." I inserted the key into the lock, and we let ourselves in. The living room door opened and Sadie Benjamin, from along Morgan Street, stood in the doorway.

"Hello both of you, Lily said you'd be coming back, I'm making something to eat." I hadn't heard Sadie's reedy quavering speech since the air-raid-shelter days. "I told Lily to lay down upstairs but she didn't sleep a minute all day. I told her I'll take care of everything, rest."

"It's nice you came round," said Katherine, hanging her coat up behind the door.

"What's a friend for then, that's what I say."

"Who is it, they're back?" Lily called from upstairs.

"Yes, Mum, we'll come up."

"Uh!, what for, I'm alright...."

Katherine and I climbed the stairs. Lily sat on the edge of the bed, a heavy odor of sweated bedclothes permeating the room.

"Mum, hello." Katherine sat beside her and tried to put an arm around her shoulders. Lily, hunched forward, seemed oblivious to the hesitant embrace.

Lily's back begin heaving. No words were exchanged, and after a few moments the restrained convulsions lessened. She half-turned: "There's a... there's a..."

Katherine reached back for a handkerchief that lay on the covers.

"Mum, let me put the light on?" I asked.

"I don't know, do whatever you want, put the light on then...."

"Not bright," said Katherine.

The match's flickering momentarily illuminated Lily's face — pale skin overlaid now with bright red blotches, her eyes rimmed and raw. Raising the gaslight's globe I lit the mantle, and when the yellow flame had crept to both sides and completed its encirclement I turned the knob to low. Katherine was sobbing now too, and her hand had slipped from Lily's shoulder. In the semi-darkness I stood helplessly by, as separate from Lily as the two women were from each other, Katherine's hand fallen to the bedclothes behind Lily's back, Lily bent forward on the edge of the bed, hands clasped on her lap, immobile but for the sporadic heaving of her shoulders. I waited, wanting Lily to move, closer to Katherine — but no — and a grieving beyond even Maudy's death caused me to burst into helpless tears.

Immediately at my crying, Lily pulled herself straight. "So, what's the good already." Katherine had again placed her hand against Lily's back, but again it fell away. "Come on already, we'll go downstairs, you must be hungry, both of you." Lily stood up.

"Let me go in front," I said, afraid either of them might slip or fall down the stairs. I extinguished the light and went down ahead of them. Downstairs, Lily turned abruptly into the kitchen where Sadie stood over a pot on the stove, stirring what smelled like chicken.

"Lily, I found this saucepan, it's alright to use, it's *flayshedik?* I didn't want to trouble you."

Lily barely looked. "Yes, I should worry, yes, it's alright." She sniffed. "Chicken, you made?"

"I made you some soup, half a chicken I got, it'll do you good, you didn't eat all day."

"Eat! Who can think of eating...." The sentence snagged in Lily's throat.

"Mum she's right, have some soup," said Katherine. "You'll feel better if you have something warm." She and I helped Lily into the living room, to a chair at the table.

"I'm alright, what do you think I'm an invalid?"

"Mum, sit." She sat, and I lit the gas mantle on the living room ceiling.

"Your mother's plate is ready," trilled Sadie. "There's a bit of meat in it, do you think you can eat a little piece of chicken Lily, it'll do you good." Katherine carried the plate through and placed it in front of Lily. "You, both of you," Sadie called again, "I'll bring in your plates, sit down also."

Lily's weariness was briefly eclipsed by Sadie's attentions: "Sadie, rest a bit, I don't know what to say, you're doing so much...."

"Don't say anything, just have the soup." Sadie came in and the four of us sat quietly, the pervasive silence broken only by the clink of spoons against china. As we supped, there came a knock on the street door.

"I'll get it, all of you sit, eat." Sadie got up and went to the door. Hushed tones floated from the doorway.

"Who is it, I don't know already, what's the good...."

I took Lily's hand and eased her spoon back to the soup. "Mum, sit and have the soup, Sadie knows how to answer the door."

Footsteps, and Mrs. Stapleton entered the room, Sadie standing behind her.

"Oh, er... Mrs. er...." Lily stumbled to get out of her chair.

"Emma Stapleton, sit, please Mrs. Grossman. We heard the awful news about Maudy, Hazel told us."

"Yes... I... it was yesterday, they were... at the hospital it was, he went to see my husband...."

"Don't tire yourself, no, no, don't stand up Mrs. Grossman, have your supper. I just wanted you to know my husband and I are terribly sorry for all you've suffered recently, your husband in the hospital, and now this terrible loss."

"Thank you, thanks Mrs. Staple..."

"Emma, please call me Emma."

"Emma, what can anyone do...."

"We wanted you to know how sorry we are and if there's anything, anything you need, anything at all," she repeated, "don't hesitate, send someone round."

"Thank you...."

"Hazel wanted to come with me. Katya, she wanted to come now but I told her you don't want to be disturbed at a time like this."

"I saw her this morning for a few minutes, maybe I'll come round for a short while this evening, I'm staying here tonight."

"Oh! Would... your... husband be coming also? I... maybe now's not the time to mention it...."

"No, he won't be here tonight. Why?"

"Well, he came around again last week, one evening, Friday I think it was, banging on the street door, he was looking for you."

"I'm sorry, he is a bit of an impetuous child."

"We really wouldn't mind but he actually went to strike Mr. Stapleton, you know Jim had a heart attack two years ago, we have to be careful."

"I'm terribly sorry, I can't control him, his temper. I'm sorry, anyway he won't be here tonight, he knows I'm staying with my mother, he knows I'm not at your house."

"Alright then, I'll tell Hazel." Mrs. Stapleton turned to leave. "Don't forget, Mrs. Grossman, anything you need, just send someone round." And the street door closed.

Sadie finished her soup and cleared away the dishes. I added more coal to the fire, and as the previous cinders collapsed and the flames burgeoned anew we pulled our chairs around in a semi-circle. I turned the ceiling light down.

"No, Lily, you sit on the sofa."

"The settee? What for?" Lily half stood, and Sadie went to move her chair over so that Lily would see the fire from the settee without obstruction.

"It's too high, the chair's too high, you have to *sit shiva,* it's low on the sofa."

"Ugh, what's the difference?" Lily was crying again. "Will it bring him back if I sit high or low?"

Sadie slumped into her chair. "Lily, it's just... respect...."

"Sadie, if she wants to sit on the chair, let her." At Katherine's tone, Lily sat again on the chair.

"It's just... just a matter of respect...." Sadie twittered.

"Leave her alone," Katherine continued. "Look, it's nice you came round and did everything, we're very grateful, but please don't start telling people what they can and can't do. And..." Katherine suddenly jumped up, and with two hands pulled away a piece of black fabric that had been draped over the mirror on the wall above the fireplace. "Who put this filthy *shmutta* over the glass, it's giving me the creeps."

"Ugh!" Sadie jumped. "Katya, put it back... Katya you're supposed to... it's not right, you mustn't have mirrors...."

"Oh, fuck the rules Sadie, we all feel rotten enough without making us feel even worse."

"Katya, your language!" Lily interjected feebly.

"Don't worry," Katherine continued at Sadie. "If god complains tell him it was all my fault. He won't deduct marks."

"She's... Sadie means well, it's nice of her to do everything, don't make a commotion anybody, I couldn't bear it."

"I'm sorry Mum, everything's alright."

Sadie remained standing. "Well..." she glanced at the clock on the mantelpiece, "it's getting late, Benjamin will be home from work, I've got to cook something for supper."

"I'm sorry Sadie, I didn't mean anything," said Katherine. "It was very nice of you to look after my mother all day, it's just we're all...."

"Course, you're all under a lot of strain. I'd better go anyway, it's late, he's nearly home, it's time."

"Sadie, thank you for...." Again Lily went to stand.

"Lily, sit down, I'll come round tomorrow, in the morning, after Benjamin goes to work."

"Alright."

"Try to get a night's sleep, that's the best thing." As she opened the street door to let herself out, again we heard subdued voices. "Lily, someone's here to see you, I'll let her in."

The street door creaked closed, the living room door swung wide, and there stood Mrs. Yanklewitz.

Lily jumped up, almost knocking over her chair. "Mrs. Yanklewitz!"

"Mrs. Grossman, can I call you Lily?"

"Yes, sit down, there, Zech give her the chair."

"Mrs. Grossman, I mean Lily, they told me about your boy."

"Mum, sit down." I eased Lily back into her chair.

"Lily, I came to... to tell you, to say... condolences about your boy."

"Thank you, Mrs...."

"Bella. You can call me Bella."

"Bella, thank you... it's terrible...."

"It's terrible." Mrs. Yanklewitz sat down. "It's worse than terrible."

Lily dabbed at her eyes, "Terrible, terrible."

We all sat silently.

Suddenly Mrs. Yanklewitz spoke. "You think I don't know how terrible it is?"

Lily looked cautiously at her. "You had the same thing, I...."

"You're right I had the same thing." She too raised a handkerchief to her eyes. "With me it was my only boy, *mine* only *kinder.*"

"Mrs. Yanklewitz," I began, "please don't...."

"Soup, get her some soup," said Lily.

"Thank you, no I don't want to intrude, you want to be left alone at a time like this, your family you want to be with, you don't want strangers at your table."

"You're not a stranger, stay, I'll... some soup, my daughter will... Katya, get Bella a plate of soup."

"Alright, thank you Lily, I'll have a plate of soup, I'll stay a short while, I don't want to intrude."

"No, it's alright, your coat, Zech, hang up her coat...."

I hung Mrs. Yanklewitz' coat on the door. Katherine placed a bowl of soup in front of her, and she began supping. "You've got your other children to help you, it's good. Zachary, you're home from the army, they let you come home?"

"Yes, its the RAF, they gave me a special pass, 'til Sunday night."

"It's good they let you come home to be with your family. The soup, it's good soup. Lily, it's cold out, snow, the soup, it's nice and warm."

"Yes, Sadie she did it, Sadie Benjamin, from the shelter, I don't know if you remember... oh yes, she let you in now, just now."

"Yes, your friends it's nice to have, but your family you need at a time like this, your family."

I lowered the gaslight a little more, and we three sat gazing into the shifting red glow of the fireplace while at the table behind us Mrs. Yanklewitz' spoon clanked. She finished the soup then came over, standing behind Lily's chair. When Lily half turned, she said: "No, no, stay." After several minutes in which none of us moved nor spoke, Lily's gentle sobbing again sundered the room's quietness. At that, Mrs. Yanklewitz, still standing behind Lily's chair, began sobbing too — muted, restrained. Neither Katherine nor I knew what to do, so we did nothing; a little later I saw that Mrs. Yanklewitz had placed a hand on Lily's shoulder.

Along that arc — Katherine, me, then Lily, all seated, and Mrs. Yanklewitz standing behind with one hand on Lily's shoulder — all was still and silent for the longest time, save inside the fireplace where coals glowed and small tongues of flame licked and ebbed. A hiss of white gases abruptly drew our attention, spurting from a hidden rift in the coal's polished black surface. With a *pop* the jet transformed into a thin pencil of fire that curled upward to a yellow dance then wavered, diminished, and died. For an eternity we watched the shifting embers unravel their miniature drama, glowing, settling, sifting through the metal gratings to join the bed of ashes that lined the hearth.

The silence was finally broken by Mrs. Yanklewitz: "My legs ache, I'm not as young as I used to be." She removed her hand. "When I lost *mein boitshick,* it was like a door, all of a sudden a door slams shut and that's where it stops, nothing ever moves any more. Mrs. Gro... Lily, it'll take a long time, a year, two, three maybe, but in the end you'll be able to... one day you'll realize you can bear it, it's terrible, but at least you can bear it." She turned. "I'll go now, before Altman's closes. You'll come to the cemetery with me, where is it, Plashett, the next time I go to see my boy *olov hasholem,* may he rest in peace there, you and me, we'll go together, we both understand." I started up to retrieve her coat. "No, don't get up." Then, again to Lily: "I'll come round in a few days." From the street door she repeated, "I'll come round in a few days." The door scraped shut.

Silence.

"Mum, do you mind if I go over to Hazel's for half an hour?"

"Whatever you want, I'll be alright, don't get cold, button up your coat."

"Zech, did you want to come? Lily, would you mind if Zech came? Just for a short while, Hazel's always asking about him."

"Go, go, both of you, I'm not an invalid, go."

"Hazel asks about *me?"*

"She's seen you about twice in the past year, she'll love the uniform."

"Really, the RAF uniform?"

"If you're wearing it."

"What? What do you mean?"

"Hazel misses you."

"Hazel misses *me?"*

"Why shouldn't she miss you, you are my brother. Didn't you know girls always like their friend's big brother?"

"Really, now I'm going to be too shy to go over there."

"Just button your lip and put your handsome RAF jacket and overcoat on. Do you mind, Lily, we won't be long?"

"Go, go already."

"In fact..." Katherine thought for a moment. "Mum, you can come also, if you want to. Maybe it would be a good idea for you to get out for half an hour or so."

"No, I'm alright now, I just want to sit, all the commotion with the visitors, I'm worn out, you go, both of you, I'll sit."

I put on my blue-grey military jacket, overcoat and beret, and followed Katherine out. Lily called after us: "Don't rush, I'll be alright, a bit of peace and quiet here."

It was still snowing lightly and we both raised our collars.

"I'm going to be too shy to go in...."

"Oh, knock it orf."

The street was quiet, and the softly falling snow lent an atmosphere of utter peace. I thought of snow falling on Maudy's grave. We were already down to the corner, by Hazel's street door, and Katherine had rung the bell. "Just follow me."

Mr. Stapleton opened the door; in the darkness I saw him look warily at me standing behind Katherine.

"Oh no, it's my brother, it's Zachary."

He immediately relaxed and held out his hand. "Zachary, come on in out of the snow, we don't see you now you're busy defending Her Majesty's emerald isles." Inside, he closed the door.

"Thank you Mr. Stapleton, I know, they don't let us out 'til we finish square-bashing."

"We were devastated to hear the sad news about your brother — dreadful, so young. Marius — was that his name, Marius?"

"Yes."

Hazel came down a few stairs. "Katya!" She looked beyond Katherine at me. "Hello, Zech, I heard your voice."

"I twisted his arm."

"Oh, Katya, stop it, tsk...."

"I'm glad you felt alright to come. Come on, we can go upstairs," said Hazel, and started back up the stairs; Mr. Stapleton turned into the living room, the room where he'd almost caught Hazel and me sitting on the couch in the dark that time — when was it? — four, five years earlier!

Katherine began following Hazel up the stairs, but somehow I felt too awkward. I couldn't change so quickly, and poor Mum was home by herself; supposing other people came round, like Mrs. Berger, or even Mrs. Harney from next door, she might have heard too. "Hazel, thanks, maybe I should go home, I'll come next time, I just...."

"Oh," said Hazel. "You can stay, if you like...."

"Thank you, I feel...."

"Zech, I'm so sorry about Maudy."

"Thanks." I turned around and in one moment I had the street door open and was outside. I heard them both coming back down the stairs, so I pulled the door closed and began walking quickly. It opened again; I began trotting along the slippery pavement toward our house.

"Are you alright, Zech?" It was Katherine, calling from the corner.

"Yes, I... I'll see you at home later."

At home, Lily was at the gas-stove boiling water. "You're back? I thought you were...."

"Katya's going to stay, I came home. I'll be quiet."

"I'm making tea, do you want a cup of tea?"

"Yes please."

Lily and I sat before the dwindling fire holding our teacups.

"So he'll be home Monday or Tuesday, they said."

"Dad? Oh, they're letting him out? Monday or Tuesday? I'm supposed to be back at camp Sunday night, how will you…?"

"It's alright, they told me to telephone them Monday, then we'll go on the bus for him."

So, I wouldn't have to plot to avoid Melissa any longer. It had been silly anyway; she was married, her husband might come home, and I didn't know what I hated more: Vera Lynn's singing or bubble and squeak. "Will it be alright for Dad to come home on the bus?"

"Katya'll come with me, she's staying, we'll bring him home in a taxi. I'm sorry they're giving him the van back already, more aggravation."

"They're giving it back to him? Who is? I thought it got smashed up."

"A letter we got from the garage. They fixed it up, London Transport paid to get it repaired, a *broch* on them. Who needed it in the first place? Maybe now he'll sell it. Him and his big ideas, a *gunsa knucker.*"

I added more coal to the grate and we sat silently for half an hour.

Katherine's key turned in the street door lock. "Why didn't you stay?"

"I… I don't know, I'm a bit tired maybe from everything."

"Should I make more tea?" asked Lily

"It's alright Mum, I'll make it." And Katherine went into the kitchen. "Everybody?"

"Yes."

Again, silence, as we sat around the ebbing fire and sipped our tea. I had opened the curtains and turned the gaslight off completely. Outside, a calm virgin whiteness reflected off the crenellations that punctuated our brick wall, off the pavement, the curbs, the gentle curve of the road surface.

Finally, Katherine spoke: "Did you notice what Sadie called her husband? Benjamin!"

"Yes." I had wondered about that. "Maybe people get in the habit of calling someone by their last name if the Christian name isn't so nice, whatever it is."

"No, that's his name," said Lily.

"I mean his first name," I said. "She called him Benjamin as though that were his Christian name."

"That's his name," repeated Lily, "Benjamin."

"His first name?" asked Katherine.

"Yes, that's his name. Benjamin Benjamin."

"Really?" Katherine burst out laughing.

"Christ!" I said. "I thought he actually didn't have a name, a Christian name."

"Benjamin Benjamin," Katherine mused. "I think that's even worse than no name at all."

Lily started to get up. "Well, that's his name."

"His mother must have hated him," laughed Katherine.

Lily giggled also. "He's so limp, could you blame her?"

—o—O—o—

43

My square-bashing RAF basic-training stint was followed by a two-month radar opera-tor training course. After completion, they assigned me to a radar station in Kent, just outside the small seaside town of Sandwich on the English Channel coast. On my first day there, wandering alone through the labyrinthine Operations Rooms of the radar complex, I happened upon a darkened cubicle containing a console replete with flashing indicator lights lined up below an inviting array of throw-switches. Calamity! Luckily, no aeroplanes crashed and there were no injuries, but the following morning when the commanding officer, Flying Officer Golightley, sentenced me to three days at hard labor I learned that the switches I'd experimented with had at first confounded, then aborted, joint British-American fighter interception maneuvers over the English Channel.

Hard labor consisted of reporting every six hours to the military police gatehouse at the entrance to the camp spiffily attired in dress uniform, brass buttons burnished to a blinding sheen, beret set at a precise thirty degrees, immaculately polished shoes. There I had to pick up off the grass all and every discarded cigarette butt and bring them in a tin to the duty police sergeant. He counted them, checked they were not contaminated with foreign matter, dutifully recorded the count in his official log, then took the tin outside and flung the butts back across the grass. "Alright, A.C.1 Grossman, pick'mup, on the *double.*" Overlooking the mispronounced surname, I commenced my next trove cycle.

Since one or another of the recruits had inevitably to be the first to go down, my new buddies, the twenty-seven other Air-Craftsmen-Ones occupying my barracks, were fasci-nated that I'd blazed the path. For this they helped me polish my gear, prompted me for the recurring gatehouse rendezvous between my regular duties, and generally sought to bask in the peripheral glow of my notoriety. Even the fellow in the next bunk, Brewster, a young tough of the type who had terrified me in school, offered to clean my boots.

But the most attentive recruit, one Garrick Sharansky, was barracked across the square, not even in my hut. Garrick had arrived at Sandwich just a couple of weeks previous to me, and he seemed convinced I'd committed my sabotage deliberately upon arrival to establish standing. As a consequence he regarded me with unabashed admiration. "You're famous! Everybody wants to know what you'll do next."

"Well, it was kind of an accident…" I protested in a carefully weighed demurral.

"Come on, don't try to look modest," he chided. "So, what are you going to do about Golightley?"

"Golightley?"

"The C.O. You realize he made sure you did your three days over the holidays."

"Holidays?"

"With a capital 'H.'"

"I... don't follow...."

"Pesach, Passover."

I hadn't noticed that coincidence, nor had it crossed my mind that Garrick was Jewish and might be aware of religious holidays. "Why, what makes you think...."

"Because he's a schnapps-swigging anti-Semitic fuckface, that's why."

"You think...?"

"There isn't a single Jewish officer in this camp. These things always look like chance 'til you think about it."

I hadn't thought to look. "Anyway, I'm not religious at all, god and I don't see eye to eye on a number of issues, and my being Jewish doesn't particularly interest me."

"But it interests other people."

"You're not religious, are you?"

"Mmm..." Garrick thought about it, "no, but...."

"Well, I'll stick with Occam's razor."

"Alright," he smiled, "since you want me to ask, what's Occam's razor?"

"Occam's razor dictates you opt for the more economic explanation. So I'll go with the universe appearing first, rather than this god character showing up in a puff of smoke and then creating everything; that would be an additional step."

"I... see...."

"Not to mention I just find superstition boring, the opiate of the masses, to quote my buddy Groucho."

He took a deep breath. "When they break your door down at two A.M., I wonder if you'll find it boring then?"

"I can hardly imagine that happening... though, now you mention it, I did nearly get bumped off at the place I was working because of being Jewish — you know, when the *Irgun Zvai Leumi* hung those British soldiers last year?"

"Really?"

"Yes, laborers, actually two of *them* died in the ruckus, and another fellow sort of tangentially involved, he's in prison. The whole thing was pretty gory, they reported it in the *News Of The World."*

"Wowee! You did all that?"

"Well, it was mostly accidental. But, you're not religious though, Garrick?"

"No, but I am Jewish."

"Hmm. You see yourself as embattled because of that?"

"Look, I've noticed... you have to be careful."

"To me, to believe in a god is to have a conviction about the existence of something for which there isn't a vestige of evidence. They have a clinical name for that — insanity."

"I admire your reasoning, but...."

"Want to hear more?"

He laughed. "Do I have any choice?"

"Actually, no! Well, first, the character who announces he *is* god, that type is usually pretty harmless because the sandwich board prevents him doing too much damage."

"Ahah! I'm taking notes."

"The greater danger comes from the more cunning members of the phylum."

"And how do we identify these — pray?"

"Generally they claim they've been directed to pass along strictures of great moral import to us lesser beings. Maybe they *met* god, chatted over a cup of tea or something."

"And?"

"They don black Zorro-type garb to frighten defenseless children, prey on the guilt-ridden and, you know, generally alarm the intellectually frail. And they contrive to even get paid for it all."

"I suspect you have rather strong feelings on the subject."

"I wouldn't go *that* far."

"Hmm, I've enjoyed your sermon, Zech, except I wasn't talking about any of that stuff."

"Oh, what were you talking about then? You should have interrupted me."

"Is it *possible* to interrupt you?"

"I'm not saying it's easy, but it is possible."

"I was talking about that ignorant barstard Golightley making you report over *Pesach* in such a way he couldn't be nailed down as an anti-Semite."

"Alright then. Hmm. You think he timed my three days deliberately?"

"Sure! Those smooth types are the most insidious."

"Maybe I'm naïve...."

"I just hope you've got something in mind to take care of him, you know, set him up so he can't weasel his way out."

"Well...." Despite the jokes, my celebrity status clearly incurred responsibilities. "I am working on it...."

"Good. Enough about all that stuff. Want to come back to my place some weekend?"

"Yes? Where do you live?"

"Forest Gate. You know it?"

I'd heard of it — it was in the suburbs, you had to be pretty rich to live there. "Past Bow and Stratford?"

"Yup."

"That's beyond where I live, I've heard of it, it's a bit further out." Our old house in Mile End was falling to pieces; I'd shrivel up if I had to invite him back.

"Come on, just say yes, this weekend, okay? Your three days'll be finished by Friday."

"Well alright then, Saturday morning."

"I'll be off at twelve. What time are you off, the same?"

"Twelve, after the morning parade."

"Then it's a deal."

"How do you get home?" I wondered if his father had a car, if they came for him.

"Hitch a ride."

That was a relief! "I imagine everybody'll be trying to hitch a ride at twelve o'clock — it'll be impossible." If Garrick were — if not loaded, then still pretty well-off — I'd have to compensate for my deficiencies with extra daring. "How about skipping the parade?"

He regarded me with renewed awe. "Really?"

"Someone said they come around checking the huts to see if anyone's AWOL from parade, so if we bug out across the field before nine, who's going to miss us?"

"I don't know, it's dangerous...."

"Come on, we'll do it. We'll be the only ones, we can get a ride with no competition. We'll be in London before the parade even finishes." While he was recovering I grabbed his hand, shook it, and left. Walking back across the square to my barracks I realized I was euphoric, breathless, as though some forceful persona had taken me over.

The three-day sentence was completed Friday evening, and in relief I took a quiet walk around camp looking for the Navy, Army, Air Force Institute — the NAAFI — a hut set aside for airmen's off-duty relaxation. The NAAFI, I'd heard, boasted a gramophone and some records. But, too preoccupied to find the place, I returned to my hut to pack for tomorrow's pre-parade departure.

The next morning, up bright and early, I was presented with an unanticipated dilemma: the entire barracks, twenty-eight men, had their bags packed and ready to go also.

"What the hell are you all doing?" The euphoria of fame had even changed my mode of speech!

They'd gotten wind of Garrick's and my plan, and tough Charlie Brewster spoke for them: "You're buggin' out, why shouldn't we?"

"'Cause it was my idea. Anyway, they won't miss one man, but twenty-eight! Are you all nuts?"

At the far end of the hut, D'Arcy Lewis, tall, pasty, with wispy blonde hair, volunteered an interesting point. "Grossman, at least half a dozen of us are definitely bugging out. If they see an incomplete squadron on the square they'll want to know where the rest of us are."

"'E's right," said Brewster.

Lewis continued. "But if the entire squadron is gone, the other units will just close up the gap. It's actually safer for *you* if we all go."

"'E's right," repeated Brewster.

I pondered this turn of events. "Well, er… yes, but… everybody! Wow!"

"That's right," said Brewster. "We're all cuttin' across the field."

"Alright, we'll do it!" I conceded. "We'll all have to be very quiet, sort of fade into the undergrowth." Jesus, twenty-eight men, twenty-nine with Garrick, all in uniform, racing across an open field — it would look like an invasion! A knock on the door and Garrick entered with his duffel bag. When I explained what was happening, he assumed I had orchestrated the change. "So instead of taking a little chance," I said, "now we're taking a bigger one."

"You mean if they catch all of us, then we'll see if you and I are the only ones up on charges."

I had to be quick; he and I *were* probably the only Jews in the bunch. "Yup," I responded confidentially, "you might call this a preliminary test prior to nailing Golightley." Then to the group, by now crowding around, duffels in hand, ready to go: "Alright fellas, one at a time, quiet!" I opened the back door, scanned the horizon, then sneaked down the wooden steps with Garrick close behind. One by one the rest of the recruits followed. A quick run across open grass and we were under the fence, which I saw had already been pulled apart; apparently we weren't pioneering the route. With a military precision that would have made the sergeant proud, the entire platoon mustered behind a clump of trees. Brewster climbed up on a branch, and with his assurance the way was clear, in a loud whisper I said, "Alright, spread out across the field." Duffel-bags bouncing, our intrepid phalanx fanned out toward the road that lay beyond the distant hedgerow. Garrick and I veered to the right, hoping to intercept a ride before it met the others.

As we finally broke through onto the road, an open lorry approached. The driver slowed down and called out, "London, mateys?"

"Yes," we shouted.

"'Op on then, lads." We threw our bags up and clambered on the open back, and within the next couple of hundred yards twenty other airmen were aboard. Forty-five minutes later we were in the outskirts of London, and individual airmen began alighting. Garrick and I stumbled down onto legs numbed by the lorry's jostling, and boarded the Underground.

In the City we changed trains, and on the ride east one of the train's stops was Mile End Station; though bright as usual with florescent lights, white tiled walls and colorful adverts, never could I volunteer that it was my stop. We rattled on further east to the end of the line, Bow Road. The connecting Forest Gate bus arrived — and it wasn't even a trollybus! At least we had trollybuses in Mile End.

On the journey I learned his mother was dead and he lived with his father; Mr. Sharansky was a wholesale chocolatier who ran his business from their house, one room of which was stacked with cartons of Cadbury's. Even though the war had ended four years earlier, it was still not easy to find chocolate in many shops, and of course sugar was still rationed — though not so in Germany, I'd read. We won the war; the Germans got the sweets.

The bus rode through streets lined with attractive row-houses in fine trim, many fronted by mowed lawns and neat fences. Closer to Forest Gate, the houses becoming more affluent, we alighted and began walking. Garrick lived on a quiet street of fully-detached residences, the lots ornate with softening hedgerows and mature trees. He unlatched a white-painted wooden gate, and under a trellis we followed a short curved path that even boasted a shaded bench.

With a key he swung the dark-stained street door open to an entrance hall, with a closet off to one side specially for coats. "Pop, I'm home!" he called. Mr. Sharansky, a little man barely half the bulk of his son, stepped into the entrance hall from the side room he used as his office. "Zachary Grossman, the *meshuggener* I told you about on the telephone."

"Welcome, welcome." He gave Garrick a cheerful embrace, and shook my hand. "Garrick, try to leave a few cartons to sell. Zachary, if he eats too much chocolate do me a favor and hit him, he's too big for me these days." And he disappeared back into his office.

We dropped our duffels to the floor and Garrick immediately took me into a side room stacked with cardboard boxes. He pulled back a top flap, and — chocolate, chocolate, and more chocolate. "Take some. What would you like?"

"Will it be alright with your Dad?"

"If I didn't take half-a-dozen bars he'd think I was ill or something."

"Alright, Cadbury's Fruit-and-Nut, please. Boy, how can you resist with so much here?"

"I can't. That's why I got pimples and my hair is falling out." The doorbell rang; it was a friend of Garrick's. "Uri, this is Zachary Grossman from the RAF; Zachary, this is Uriah Bliss from around the corner. We call him 'Urine' for short."

"Hello Uriah, nice to meet you."

"Hello, call me Uri. You just get back from camp now, both of you?"

"Yup, we hitched a ride on a lorry — my legs are still numb."

"So you been another week defending Her Majesty's empire. Not for me, that stuff!"

"We can't all plead insanity as convincingly as you."

"For that, I'll invite you to come and have supper this evening," said Uri.

I stood apart, assessing the banter for indications of how to speak and act in this unfamiliar milieu, what degree of wit or knowledge might warrant my participation. Garrick looked to me to see if supper at Uri's was alright. Everything was happening so fast. "It's okay with me," I said. "Thank you."

"Six o'clock, then."

Uriah's was the sixth house along the street, not as grandiose as Garrick's. In the dining room, under a glinting cut-glass chandelier stood a large dark wood table with curved polished legs, a blue lacey tablecloth, silver cutlery settings and neatly folded white fabric serviettes. Dark wood chairs, whose upholstery matched the blue curtains, completed the ensemble. In two corners of the room, table lamps shed additional low light on dark polished cabinets.

"You can sit down everybody," called a woman's voice from the kitchen.

We sat, Garrick next to me, Uri opposite. In the chair next to Uri's, facing us, his sister Sophy kept her eyes lowered. Uri introduced us: "Zachary meet Sophy, Sophy meet Zachary." Under a sweep of ginger hair her china-blue almond-shaped eyes raised momentarily, their color almost matching the chairs and curtains. Her brief glance included a smile; she said nothing, and my Adam's apple precluded anything beyond a mumbled "Hello," at which her attention returned modestly to her plate.

Mrs. Bliss, heavy-set, well-scrubbed, wearing a tidy nonfunctional apron and — yes! — a blue ribbon in her also-reddish hair, entered bearing two bowls of soup. "Pleased to meet you," she smiled, placing the bowls before Uri and the empty chair at the head of the table. "Sophy, help me with the dishes."

Sophy stood up: she was about five feet two, slim of waist, and as she retired to the kitchen her bum swayed gently. She returned, carrying two soup bowls and stood between Garrick and me to plant one in front of Garrick. Her torso never touched my shoulder, but it might as well as she leaned over to place the other bowl before me. I managed something like "Thank you," and felt myself breaking into a heat as she walked around the table to her seat. Though her white blouse had a modest neckline, its lace plunged disconcertingly down below the bust. To see her I had to look across Uri, which was discomforting. I noted her mother, now sitting at the end of the table from what seemed a greater elevation, commanding a view of everything. I wondered if that had been a brassiere visible through the holes in Sophy's lace, and struggled to resist the compulsion to check it out. How could she wear such a blouse without realizing how compellingly it distracted attention? Yet her demeanor was so innocent that maybe she hadn't given it any thought.

Mr. Bliss, small-framed, gaunt and balding, came and sat at the other end of the table, nodded at me, and started on the soup. The chicken soup was wonderful, and the *knaedels* were heavy and rich, better even than Mum's — compacted dumplings that slithered directly through the gullet to the bottom of your stomach.

Mrs. Bliss opened the conversation. "Where did you say you live?" she enquired of her new guest.

"Well... near Bow."

"And what do you do, what line are you in?"

Mr. Bliss picked up a newspaper and continued with his soup. Sophy leaned forward over her plate and her blouse swung away, revealing cleavage down to a bra, not white like the blouse but skin-colored — even more unsettling. At least that question was answered.

"You were telling us what line of business you're in."

"Oh yes, I'm in the RAF now of course, with Garrick; I used to work in a laboratory."

"A laboratory! Hmm!" She seemed pleased. "What did you do there?"

"Analysed tar, set the laboratory on fire and inadvertently contributed to the general mayhem."

Mr. Bliss looked up from his newspaper, and the interrogation lapsed. Then: "Zachary!" Her lips smacked at the name. "That's not a... well, a... Jewish name, is it?"

"Oh yes, Zechariah, my father was born in the U.S.S.R., in Podolsk, and my mother's family came from Russia also, a long time ago. I suppose it's Russian or something."

"Russian? It doesn't sound Russian."

"Well I don't know exactly; my mother liked Zachary Scott in the pictures."

"That American one with the shiny black hair...?" asked Uri.

"Yes, so she called me Zachary, that's all I know."

"Well, I'm glad you're Jewish," said Mrs. Bliss, "not that we would make... make the... others... any less welcome."

"I think," I said to Uri, "Zachary Scott puts motor oil on his hair to make it look like that."

Sophy nibbled demurely at her *knaedels;* her mother chewed on a small piece of chicken, then continued. "And what line is your father in?"

"He's a tailor." I felt ashamed; everyone's father in the East End was a tailor. "He specializes in ladies costumes, he has his own shop."

"His own shop!"

"Yes, in Burnt Oak."

"Burnt Oak! Isn't that somewhere near Edgeware?"

"Yes, he goes on the Edgeware line."

"Hmm, that's a rich section, isn't it?"

"I suppose so. He usually drives there in his van." I couldn't believe what I was saying. "He has a snack bar, also."

"A snack bar!" Her thick lips smacked together.

"It's like a little restaurant, it's next door his tailoring shop."

"Well then, my goodness me, your father sounds like a wonderful man, you must be very proud of him."

"Er... well...."

She stood up. "Sophy, help me with the next course."

Sophy followed her mother silently into the kitchen, from where I detected a brief spate of whispering. They reappeared, Sophy bearing fresh dinner plates which she proceeded to place before each of us, Mrs. Bliss depositing a large elongated covered dish in the center of the table. As the two of them retreated once more, my attention was riveted to the undulations of Sophy's elegant rear behind the swishings of her coral linen skirt. They returned with two more covered dishes.

Again Sophy came around between Garrick and me; she leaned forward to serve us each roast chicken, brussels and potatoes from the covered dishes, and the hair on my arms rose at her proximity. She reached out, and I saw the brassiere was also lace! What if the holes in the blouse lace happened to align with those in the brassiere? The realization that I was probably the only one in the room with those thoughts turned my face a deep red; I needed to concentrate on the chicken.

I'd never seen chicken roasted before; Mum always boiled everything in a saucepan. This tasted as wonderful as the soup — the best chicken I could imagine.

With everybody again seated, Mrs. Bliss resumed her interrogation. "Why does your family live in Bow, then?" Mr. Bliss looked up from his newspaper, perhaps for my explanation.

But I couldn't think of one. "What, well...." Compared to Forest Gate, Bow was still pretty shabby, but Mile End was decrepit. I didn't know any other mentionable areas — Whitechapel or Stepney or Aldgate were just as bad — and anyway she would probably question me further and I'd be trapped. Also I hoped none of them had been to Burnt Oak recently because Abie's snack bar with its moldy cake had been closed for two years. "Er, my two older sisters live in America."

"In America!"

"Yes, in New York."

"My goodness me, you have a very enterprising family."

"I suppose the rest of us will move sometime; we just didn't think about it." My ears were flaming, I knew, but Sophy was looking at me across the table and she seemed happy, so maybe my sweating wasn't apparent.

Mrs. Bliss found time to eat a piece of chicken. Then: "Are you in National Service? I mean, you didn't volunteer for the army — the Air Force, did you?"

"No! Oh, no!"

"And how did you meet Garrick?"

"Oh, Mum, please...." Sophy interjected; it was the first time she'd spoken, and the timbre of her voice was rich and soft. I was so taken aback I found myself looking directly across at her; she glanced up, lowered her eyes momentarily, and then, as though driven to establish herself by contravening some convention of decorum, looked up again right past Uri and straight at me. Her expression was quite serious as she bravely gazed directly at me for several seconds, then slowly the faintest brush of a smile caused her eyes to crinkle at the corners.

Mrs. Bliss had been talking the whole time: "You were going to tell us where you met Garrick?"

Everyone was looking at me now, including Mr. Bliss. "Er, well, we're both at the same camp. That's where we met... where I met Garrick."

"Well!" Mrs. Bliss pondered briefly, smacked her lips once more, then rendered her verdict: "We're glad to have you to dinner."

Fortunately for me, Garrick tried to lighten the atmosphere. "Before you get too glad, I should warn you that Zech's a bit of a dangerous *meshugginer.* He messed up the radar the day he arrived, he got put on a charge for it, and this morning he forced me to go AWOL."

"What's AWOL?" asked Sophy, her words obliterating every distraction.

"A-W-O-L — Absent With Out Leave." Garrick pulled me back. "He twisted my arm and we both bugged out of camp early, before the parade."

Uri added his tuppence-worth: "I bet it wasn't easy to find someone more *meshugeh* than you."

"That's not all!"

"Oh, Garrick, come on!"

"Listen to him, he's too modest! Listen, he also talked his entire barracks into going AWOL with us, to trick the C.O., the Commanding Officer."

Sophy asked me directly: "Why, why did you do that?" Those dulcet tones!

"The others seemed as if they needed a little extra time off also." I actually said it!

"He's kidding." Garrick swallowed a brussel. "See, I think the C.O. hates Jews."

"An anti-Semite?" asked Mrs. Bliss. "Really, what did he do?"

"Oh, it's a bit complicated," I said. "We'll explain when it's all over and we've trapped him."

"When Zachary here messed up the Channel maneuvers, the C.O. made sure his sentence ran over *Pesach.*"

"He did that?" asked Mrs. Bliss.

"Well, we don't have any evidence it was deliberate," I said.

"So Zachary set a little trap for him," continued Garrick. "We'll find out when we get back to camp tomorrow night whether he fell into it." What an ally Garrick was! He was determined to attribute not only intention, but even adroit skill to my bumbling! *Sophy must think I'm a real daredevil!*

The meal concluded, we stood up. Garrick grasped me across the shoulders in a big bear hug. In debonaire fashion I slapped him on the back, which move I calculated would appear suitably robust to the assemblage. We drifted outside to the street. Sophy hesitated at the door behind us, wanting to come with, it seemed to me. Garrick suggested a ride.

"A ride?" He caught me by surprise. "Oh, you have a car?" What a stupid fool I was! Fortunately it was dusk, because again my face flushed; how else would we go for a ride?

"An Austin. My father's."

We, a rank of three males, strolled toward Garrick's house. But as the two men talked I dropped back, ostensibly to allow older friends some privacy, but really as a signal to Sophy to come along too. Quickly she closed her street door; I held back and she trotted up, she and I finally walking side by side at a slightly awkward remove. A quick glance showed that from this view too she was extremely pretty, and that confirmation made me self-concious of my towering gawkiness to the point where it became difficult to amble my limbs spontaneously.

The car stood in his driveway, and under the outdoor light it looked like a new Austin A4, a beige four-door. Not wishing to usurp Uri's friendship I opened a rear door to climb in the back, and to my amazement Sophy scooted around to open the other back door. *That meant she wanted to sit next to me!* And suddenly she and I were together in the rear of the car, Garrick driving, Uri the front passenger.

They chatted in front, miles removed, Garrick relating the tribulations of Royal Air Force life, periodically addressing me for confirmation. Sophy smiled submissively from the darkness of her corner. With every glance she seemed prettier and prettier, making me even more shy — not that I could have done anything anyway having just met her, especially with her brother sitting in front. Because there wasn't much width across the back seat from door to door we were already squeezed together, but a bit later I thought she seemed to be pressed even closer. The jiggling of the car kept her thigh moving against my leg, which made me get an erection; I tried to force my mind to think of something else, but that just made it worse.

She spoke quietly. "Do you go out much in the Air Force?"

The timbre of her voice was so exciting I found myself thinking of that corny expression: like music! A richness of sound, so captivating — and I realized I hadn't noted what she actually said. "I'm sorry, what?"

"Do you and Garrick go out much in the Air Force?"

"Er, no, we don't go out."

"Do you go out yourself?" It was soft and husky, but also tinkly.

"No, not much."

"Do you go to the rink?"

"The rink?" It was already April, but Garrick seemed to have the car heater on high.

"Ice skating."

"Er, no, not really. I've never been."

"We go skating sometimes, Sunday afternoons."

"Yes?" She was pressed so close! "I see."

"Yes, we do."

"What?"

"Yes, we do. Go."

The lurching and the temperature were making it quite hard to remember what we were talking about. "Em…"

"Go skating."

"Oh, I see. Well…."

"Do you?"

"What?!"

"Do you skate?"

"I don't know how to skate; well, I used to roller skate on the pavement when I was little."

"I bet you're a terrific skater," she whispered. So that was part of the difficulty: her voice was getting softer by the mile, making it increasingly hard to hear what she was saying above the car noise, and I had to keep leaning down closer.

"I dunno," I whispered back. I didn't know why we were whispering.

"Tell me the truth, I bet you're a terrific skater as well."

"Oh, I dunno, I never bothered."

"You could come with us."

"Skating, alright. It'd have to be on the weekend, when we get a pass."

"You must know lots of girls."

"No, I dunno, well, not really. Well, I'm a bit shy, I s'pose." *Why did I have to say that? Now I made a fool of myself!*

"So 'm I."

"What? You're what, I didn't hear."

"Shy," she whispered. "I'm shy also."

"Shy? You?" She didn't seem shy. "You don't seem shy. I mean, you seem like you're not shy." The heat in the car was terrible.

She continued remorselessly. "Do you… go… with anybody?"

"Where?"

"Anybody special, I mean."

"Wha'd'ya mean?"

"D'y' have a steady?"

We'd slowed down and were turning into what seemed to be Garrick's driveway again.

"Well, um, well… no, I mean, not actually a steady." Oh, fuck, I'd really messed it up! "Well, one of 'em was a bit steady, I mean, sometimes we… we *were* steady… my friend said we were, steady." This ride had been a good opportunity, she was sitting next to me, and I'd done everything wrong. Now she probably thought I was stupid.

Garrick broke in. "We could take a trip tomorrow if you're not doing anything. Liz'll be back, so we'll all go, the five of us — how about Southend?"

"Southend? It'll still be freezing by the seaside," said Uri.

I supposed Garrick's girl, Elizabeth, would sit next to him, in front. That meant there'd be three of us, squeezed into the back. Suppose Urine sat in the middle! Well, I'd just have to say, let Sophy sit in the middle, then she'd be next to me.

"Zech, how about you sleep at our house tonight, okay?" Uri had turned in his seat toward me. I looked at Garrick — I didn't know what he expected.

"Sure. You sleep with that red-eyed monster, but watch out he doesn't rape you. I'll come around in the morning, about ten, for breakfast. I'll bring Liz."

Settled. Maybe Uri had a special bed for guests. Though I certainly didn't want to sleep with him, it did mean I'd sleep under the same roof as Sophy. I got my duffel, we said goodnight to Garrick, and I walked back with the two of them. Uri was trying to be nice, but I didn't feel as at ease with him as I did with Garrick. Upstairs in his bedroom I started getting undressed, realizing it was to be the two of us in his bed. It would be uncomfortable lying next to him and I hoped we didn't accidently touch in the night.

"You can use the toilet first," he said. "On the left and first door. Here's a towel." They had a separate toilet room, inside the house; I supposed all rich people did, like in the pictures. Even Melissa had had one, though her's was just a flat.

In my sleeping suit I took the towel and opened the toilet door. There was a white enamel bathtub standing on little legs, with two taps inside it at one end. Next to it was a sink, also with two taps. And to my left was the water closet, a tall pipe leading up to a white enamel cistern with a brass chain. There were four towels hanging over horizontal bars on the walls. Four towels! That must be one each, and the one Uri gave me must be just for me!

I turned on one tap. Wondering what the other tap was for, I turned it on, too: the same cold water ran out. Suddenly there came a *pop!* from a white enamel cylinder about two feet high by eight inches diameter fixed to the wall above the bath: a gas burner inside had popped on of its own accord. A moment later, the water coming out of the second tap became warm, then, scalding hot. Running cold *and hot* water! The gas burner was a water heater that turned itself on and off as the water flow dictated! I had to be careful not to make myself look dumb by marveling at all these sorts of inventions; probably people who weren't poor like us used them without a thought.

I peed, washed, and brought the towel back to Uri's bedroom. "Finished!" I said cheerily.

"Okay, er, you need the towel out here?"

"Well, no... I forgot, I was just carrying it."

"Give me, I'll take it back. You take that side." and he pointed to the side furthest from the door.

He left and I climbed into bed. The mattress was soft and massively thick, at least a foot high, covered with a brilliant white sheet that billowed up around me. Everything smelled of soap and furniture polish. A few minutes later Uri returned and got under the covers, staying well over to his side.

To forestall awkwardness, I initiated conversation. "How long have you known Garrick?"

"Since I was seven. We used to live in Aldgate, off Commercial Road..."

"Oh, I know Aldgate." *Everybody was poor in Commercial Road!*

"...we moved here in thirty-nine, just before the war, that's when I met him. Then Dad went in the army; Garrick's dad was too old. Dad came home in the middle of the war — I was twelve. They said he had a weak heart."

"You stayed home during the war?"

"Yes."

"What about Sophy?"

"We both stayed home."

"Wow!"

"Mum wanted to keep us home. She took us to Scotland for a year when the doodle bugs started."

"Scotland, I see."

"Yes, then again for a few months after the V–2s. Dad stayed home to work and look after the house."

"Did Garrick get evacuated?"

"No. He stayed home the whole war."

That's what it must be like when you have enough money not to feel inferior: if you don't want to go you just tell the London County Council, and they don't interfere. Izzy hadn't been evacuated either, but that was because he was terribly Jewish; his mother had probably insisted he could only eat kosher food. That meant Mum could have said No also.

"Dad had one heart attack, two years ago. His van went up the pavement and banged into a lamp-post, that's when he had the heart attack. He's worked part-time since."

I heard a floorboard creak outside the closed door. "Someone's outside, I think?"

"What? Who is it? Mum?" In an instant Uri had jumped out of bed and pulled the door open. Sophy, in a short-sleeved white nightgown, was turning around to go back to her room but Uri lunged for her. "What... I told you... you were listening!" He began twisting her arm.

"Ow!"

I was surprised; if they were joking, he seemed a bit rough. He whispered something to her, she cried "Ow!' again, and he came back in and closed the door.

"She's too nosey, my little *schvester.*"

During the night I woke several times. Light filtered in through filmy white curtains and around a plant-pot that hung from the window-frame, and I could make out the furniture spaced around the room: a swivel-mirrored chest with a chair in front, an armchair in the corner, a regular chair in the other corner with clothes on it, everything neat and clean. None of the furniture was broken — it all looked just-bought. It was hard to imagine that only this morning Garrick and I and the rest of the barracks had sneaked across the field such a long way away, as far south as the English Channel, and here I was in Forest Gate, with a very pretty girl I hadn't even met this morning, after a lovely car ride, sleeping in the next room.

I was awakened by the sound of the door quietly opening. Sophy's face peeked around; it was morning. She saw I was awake, *sssh'd* me quiet, and tiptoed into the room. I must have looked concerned, fully expecting Urine to kill her, but he just snored away in oblivion.

She padded carefully around to my side of the bed. "Good morning," she mouthed. "Don't wake Uri, he'd kill me if he knew I came in."

"I...."

"He doesn't hear well, since he had the mumps," she whispered. "He won't wake up if we're quiet; he never wakes up in the morning."

"I thought he broke your arm off last night."

"He looks after me." Silently she sank to her knees on the rug. "Did you sleep okay?"

"Yes." This was a dream. "Did you?"

"I lay awake for a while..." she hesitated, "I thought about you being in the next room."

She seemed anything but shy to me. The street doorbell rang, and in an instant she'd slid silently out of the room. Voices, footsteps on the stairs, then Garrick strode noisily in, dressed in civvies, a tweed jacket, open-necked white shirt.

He trumpeted reveille: *"Du doo d' d' doo, du do d' d' doo, du doo d' d' doo du doo doo."*
Uri opened glazed eyes, and though I assumed he was now awake, he continued snoring.

"Doo doo." Garrick repeated just the closing cadence.

Uri blinked, emitted a couple of snorts and with difficulty roused himself. "Yes, *Sir!* Good morning, *Sir!"*

"Come on, airmen," Garrick said, "let's see both you men hop out of that sack!"

Downstairs, Mrs. Bliss had set a full table for breakfast. The elegant surfeit didn't faze Garrick. "I'll just have tea, thanks. I had breakfast already. Liz came over early and started bouncing up and down on the bed, rotten bugger! She had an errand; she'll be here in a few minutes." He sat down. "Anyway, they serve us like this every morning in the RAF."

"Har, har, har!" That was Mrs. Bliss.

Fried eggs, bacon, toast, tea, and a tall glass of orange juice! With the creamy linen tablecloth and linen serviettes, glasses sparkling in the morning light where the soft April sun shone through white lace curtains onto the table, it was as in a dream.

"D'you people mind if I don't come with today?" asked Uri. "This is the only time I got to get some stuff ready, I need it for tomorrow. Did you want to go?" He directed the last question at his sister. "What a question!"

"I wanna go," said Sophy.

"Just the four of you can get by, I mean you won't be bored?" he asked.

I couldn't tell if he were serious. "We'll just have to suffer." My remark didn't sound as funny as I'd intended so I added a quick smile, though I felt my cheeks jerk their way into position.

Ten-thirty, and the doorbell rang again. Elizabeth breezed into the house. *"Good morning, good morn-ing,"* she sang, *"I've danced the whole night through, good morn-ing, good morn-ing, to you."* Garrick introduced me. "Hello, Zachary, nice to meet you. Garrick told me about your exploits." She was slim in her blue lace blouse and darker blue skirt, thinner than Sophy, with straight blonde hair and a whiter skin — more Christian looking, more intellectual, more æsthetic.

In the car, she sat in the middle of the front bench seat, squeezed unnecessarily close to Garrick. I wanted to put my arm around Sophy's shoulder but didn't want to be too obvious and crude. So I spent several agonized minutes inching my fingers along the top of the seat back behind her, contending with the daunting realization that she offered no discernible resistance. As my hand finally arrived at her far shoulder, to my alarm she leaned even closer to me. This rearrangement left my hand bereft of support, hanging outward in front of her shoulder. Although I could easily bend the elbow to swing my hand around toward the front of her neck, I could hardly hold her neck, so for a moment my hand bounced loosely up and down with the car's motions. This looked completely silly, so I contracted the muscles to make my forearm rigid, which quickly made it too heavy to maintain casually in that position; and also — more important — it didn't look at all natural sticking out like that. So I let it swing gradually closer around toward her neck until a propitious bump in the road brought my fingers into contact with the fabric of her blouse in front, in the center, at the top of the line of small white buttons. This was a bit lower than where my hand would have naturally fallen. I pretended I hadn't even noticed any of the foregoing, though to maintain the established beachhead I did grasp one blouse button, something to hang on to. She sort of settled in side to side, perhaps to straighten out the blouse; luckily this maneuver located the anchoring button more squarely under my fingers.

Then, for a second *her* fingers brushed lightly against those of my other hand, which rested on my thigh — and her left forearm and hand came to lie squarely on my right leg and knee! I was astonished at the ease with which this occurred: I'd been maneuvering in incremental distances, reassessing, all the while looking nonchalantly out the side window for a dreadful infinity of minutes, whereas she, in one bold and decisive stroke, simply placed her forearm along my leg and her hand on my knee. And, smiled up at me, to boot: "Enjoying the ride?"

"Yes," I gasped.

Simultaneously, I noticed that up front Elizabeth and Garrick had become particularly quiet. She sat ever closer to him, gazing up into the side of his face as he drove, her chin resting on his upper arm. Her far shoulder swung forward, and he, slightly hunched, peered at the highway with a focus somewhat in excess of what I imagined might be the normal burden of driving.

I must have needed those few moments gauging the situation in front as a respite from the intensity of my own straits. I wasn't at all clear how far I should take my own pursuit, or even clear about Sophy's assessment — even awareness — of it. But such concerns were quickly rendered irrelevant: she moved again, and in so doing jiggled her shoulders back and forth, dislodging my hand from the security of the button, my fingers this time falling against bare skin! I glanced down to note that quite a few of her blouse buttons had somehow become undone. Another bump in the road, and because of her contorted angle, of its own accord my hand seemed to slip completely inside her blouse. But my elbow and wrist were twisted downward; I tried to adjust to a more natural position, which move necessitated a partial withdrawal — at which she grabbed my hand and held it inside the blouse! Another bump in the road and she caved forward, loosening the constriction of her brassiere, and before I could stop I realized my hand was actually inside her brassiere! I must have jumped: through the fabric of the blouse she immediately increased the pressure of her hand over mine, and there I was, holding her breast — and I hardly knew her! She relinquished her grip; in case it had all been a curious sequence of accidents I went to remove my hand, but no! She grabbed my hand again and squeezed it into an even firmer grip. And between my middle and third fingers I could feel what would have to be the nipple, but it felt hard; I'd imagined nipples to be soft.

Here I'd been taking an inordinate amount of time pursuing painfully analyzed guilt-ridden advances, when it seemed she simply and directly wanted me to hold her breast. That caused me to wonder if, out of consideration for me, she had for the whole ride been accommodating my own juvenile awkwardnesses. At that humiliating thought I found myself perspiring. Nevertheless part of me remained cool, even — suave. This is what men of the world did. I shook my head to throw off a dizzying weakness, and looked at her face lying somewhat below mine. Very gently squeezing her breast, I held my breath and kissed her suddenly upturned lips, then looked out the window again to exhale — I hardly wanted to breathe right into her face. Her lips were all soft! That must be what they call *pliant lips.*

I wondered if they'd heard anything in front. Garrick wasn't looking in the rear-view mirror. Elizabeth had disappeared downward; she seemed to be almost lying down. Obviously, I couldn't look; Garrick did seem to be driving straight. I contorted my head downward to kiss Sophy again, and as I went to straighten out my spine she executed a deft exchange of hands on my knee, placing her newly freed right hand around and behind my head, with the ends of her fingers through my hair just the way Deborah Kerr did to Clark

Gable in *The Hucksters,* and pulled on my head to keep it down. The arched-over position was soon breaking my back and I tried to right myself, but she pulled down harder, and — moaned!

I hadn't realized she might also be twisted into a painful contortion. "I'm sorry!"

"No, sssh!"

I stayed bent until the agony was unbearable, said "Excuse me a minute," and forced myself up. I leaned back on my side of the seat and, so that she shouldn't misunderstand, pulled her toward me. She seemed welcoming of being flung into any position I put her. The back of her shoulder lay against my chest, her head and hair on my neck, and her hand on my knee.

Several minutes passed during which I tried to think of what words I should think about. Then she spoke: "I'm going on holiday in Bournemouth for a week, in May, the last week in May," she whispered. "We'll be staying at the Cumberland."

"I see." Could it be an invitation? *I see* was noncommittal, though perceptive and still quite masculine.

"I'm going with two of my friends, they're gonna be away on Saturday afternoon...."

"That sounds interesting." My ears were flaming because I wasn't sure if she were inviting me to visit her there; I ought to say something more positive, sort of powerful and decisive — worldly — yet sensitive enough to still be considerate.

She waited, and I couldn't think of anything. Then, after a minute, close to my ear, in a hoarse whisper: "Well, do you want to see me, do you want to come to Bournemouth?"

"Yes... I mean, yes... I mean, er, yes."

"Will they let you out of the Air Force that Saturday?" Maybe she only sounded hoarse because her mouth was virtually inside my ear.

"Well, sometimes we can have Saturday off — I don't know yet." My mind was reeling, but this got me off the immediate hook. Was she asking me to go to her room with her? Would she expect us to have sex? Her seeming worldliness was nerve-wracking. I had to respond, and quickly, but I realized in fact I could afford to *sound* resolute, because if necessary I could always say we weren't allowed out that day. "We never know beforehand if we're going to get leave, but, sure, I do want to come."

The ride had been so taxing that it was a relief when the car finally rolled into Garrick's driveway. I still had to walk her home. Outside her street door as I kissed her goodbye, something interposed itself — her tongue, which quickly pushed open my mouth, ran behind my lips and across my teeth. Again her action was so unexpected that I'd pulled my face away before I deduced this must be how that class of people kissed, people who already had everything, and pursued bizarre sensual experiences to compensate for their satiety.

•   •   •

Garrick changed back into his uniform, and that evening he and I caught the train to Sandwich. To be prepared for any eventuality, I needed to know where to procure a *Durex* for two weeks hence, but of course I couldn't ask him. So when I got back to my barracks I asked Charlie Brewster — he was the rough type who would probably know.

"You get 'em at the barbershop in Sandwich, but you won't be needin' any for a while."

"What do you mean?"

"They want you down at the gate'ouse."

"The gatehouse? What do you mean?" I started to feel panicky.

"Ol' Thompson was 'round earlier lookin' for you. Said you gotta report to the gate'ouse."

"But I finished my reporting there. I didn't have to go anymore."

"Look, Grossman, it ain't nothin' to do with me — I'm just tellin' you what I 'eard. Thompson said somethin' about you buggin' out before parade."

"What! But the whole barracks bugged out! Why do they just want me?"

"'Ow should I know? Go to the gate'ouse and ask 'em."

Maybe Garrick was right about Golightley! But what about Garrick himself? I grabbed my jacket and hat and ran down to the gatehouse.

"Sir, someone told me you wanted me to report here?"

"Aircraftsman First Class Grossman, you're to report to company HQ on the double."

"What for? Is anything wrong?"

"On the double! D'y' know what *on the double* means?"

"Yessir."

At headquarters, the corporal on duty told me they'd put me on a charge again, that it would be formalized in the morning. "AWOL."

"AWOL? For what?"

"Skipping out yesterday before parade."

"What? But that's not fair! Everybody else missed it too!"

"Fair?!" He burst out laughing.

"Well, lots of people skipped out — I mean, why should they just pick on me?"

"I'm just duty corporal tonight." He shuffled his papers, "it's nothing to do with me. Who knows? You already have a record."

I ran over to Garrick's barrack. He was lying relaxed on his bunk, reading. "Did they put you on a charge?" I asked.

"No, what do you mean?"

"The duty corporal said I'm on a charge for being AWOL!"

"Interesting, so they caught you! You're really famous around here!"

"Well, what I mean is, if you were on a charge also, then… you know…."

"What? You alright?"

"No, don't you remember we said, if you and I are the only ones put on a charge for being AWOL then we'd have proof Golightley is anti-Semitic…."

"I bet he deliberately didn't put me on a charge! He's shrewd."

"So then, how can we tell if he's… how can we do anything if he didn't get you, I mean… he can always say he's not anti-Semitic because he didn't put you on a charge also!"

"You're right. That plan didn't work."

"Yes."

"He really tricked you."

"Me?"

"Well, us…. See, I warned you, those slippery types. Now you'll have to come up with a whole new plan to trick him."

"Er, yes."

"You'll give it some thought, I'm not worried, you'll do it."

"Er, yes."

Once again the sentence was three days at hard labor. I wanted to say something about being the only one brought up on a charge, but Flying Officer Golightley looked as if he were waiting for me to rat on Garrick and all the rest of my barracks, so he could call me a coward.

"It's right over the end of *Pesach,*" said Garrick later. "See, the barstard knew exactly what he was doing. Let's polish your buttons."

At the conclusion of my third and last day of counting cigarette butts, there were two weeks left to Durex day. At least, now I was free to go into town. I went to the barbershop. The barber was giving someone a haircut, and a couple of men sat along the wall reading newspapers. How could I go in and ask, when they'd all hear me? I walked away to think about it. Well, it would be uncomfortable, but it had to be done.

I fixed a casual smile and strode in the door, straight up to the barber. He stopped cutting and looked at me. "Do you have any..." my voice dropped of its own accord, "Durex?"

"What?" he asked, in an unnecessarily loud voice.

I leaned toward him. "Any... Durex." The customer in the barber chair twisted around to look at me, and the two men waiting their turn had lowered their newspapers.

"Durex?" the barber articulated clearly. He coughed. "No, we don't have any contraceptives at the moment. Come back tomorrow." I started to leave, myriad eyes clinging to my back as I struggled across the shop. By the exit door I accidently knocked over an empty chair. Slowly and with dignity I bent over and picked up the chair, but in the process I must have hooked the heel of my dress shoe on a tear in the carpet, and I fell backward to the floor. Though the fall surprised me I did manage to restrain the chair, which I now held in the air a few inches above my tunic. I drew a slow breath, and from that prone position gracefully jockied myself up, the chair legs never touching the carpet until I chose to return it squarely to its proper place. I left.

The next day, Friday, when I returned, the barber spotted me before I had time to walk in, and in a peremptory move came over to the door. The entire clientele leaned forward to listen. "They're," cough, "not in yet. Try on Monday." What did other people do? In two weeks Sophy would be in Bournemouth. He'd better have them in before then.

My Monday afternoon shift on radar watch ended at four and I donned my dress uniform to go back to town. Garrick was at the door.

"I'll keep you company," he said.

"Oh, I was just going to buy something. You needn't come — I'll be right back."

"That's okay. I'll still keep you company."

I couldn't possibly tell him. After all, his best friend was Sophy's brother. In town, I bought a pencil and rubber eraser in Smith's.

"What's that for?" he asked.

"I have to write a letter."

"I've got plenty of pencils, and rubbers, and sheets of paper — even a stamp. Why didn't you ask me?"

"I didn't want to impose." We walked back to camp.

It was not until shortly after dark that evening that I was able to get out of camp again. Luckily the shop was still open. The barber looked up from trimming someone's hair and signaled me to wait outside. He disappeared behind a door, then came out and handed me a small package. His face was stern; maybe he'd found it best to look stern when selling Durex. "That's three and ninepence."

I paid him there on the street and walked off as fast as I could, clutching the hot package securely in my trousers pocket. When I glanced back he was still standing outside looking along the street after me — probably smirking with contempt. What did men usually do? I didn't have the faintest idea what men did; I just knew that as usual it had to be something different from what I was doing. Brewster had seemed alright polishing my boots when I had to report to the guardhouse, but maybe Garrick was more right than I cared to realize about anti-Semitism being everywhere: maybe Brewster had told me to go to the barber's shop so I'd look stupid, maybe there were easier venues. Of course, I couldn't ask Brewster, or anyone else for that matter about other places you buy them, because they'd know how inexperienced I was.

Anyway, the package was safely in my pocket, and I was ready for action.

44

The street door opened and Katherine came into the living room. "Oh Zech, you're home!"

I put down a letter addressed to Abie from Haine's garage. "Yes, I'm just here for a few hours today, I've got to go back soon." The letter was dated the sixth of May; Haine's garage had repaired Abie's vehicle two months ago but, it said, no one had come to collect it and it was taking up valuable space, so in one week they'd have to start charging storage fees. That incentive had speeded Abie's recovery sufficiently for him to take the bus there the previous week to pick it up. Now the vehicle was parked under the lamppost on Tredegar Terrace; a recent change in the law rendered it no longer necessary to leave the little lights on all night and risk draining the battery.

"Sunday, today, you came? I thought they let you loose on Saturdays."

"Sometimes they do, this week it was only for one day, I didn't feel like just hanging around there."

"I thought you'd be in Forest Gate."

"Oh, Mum told you?"

"Yes, where is she?"

"The two of them just went out, he's started taking her to the pictures again."

"Where did they go?"

"He's celebrating getting his van back, he's taking her to the Odeon to see Abbott and Costello."

"She hates Abbott and Costello! I love 'em."

"Well, first he said they'd go in the van if she wanted to go to the Empire. Then she said she doesn't want to go in the van, then he didn't want to catch a bus, so after the usual commotion they settled on walking to the Odeon."

"What a business with him and that piece of rusty old iron! The garage painted it, but that didn't last too long."

"Did he pass the test, do you know?" I asked. "Mum said last week he was going for his driver's test again soon as he got it back. When I mentioned it just now she shushed me up."

"Did he pass, are you kidding? I didn't get all the details, something about him scraping the van along the side of their office building there, and the man failing him and the old shitbag threatening he'd strangle him because he insisted he didn't scrape against the building."

"Did he scrape it? I didn't look at it."

"What do you think? It's all scratched and dented on the other side, and the door handle's snapped off. Ugh, I s'pose it's a comedy. Anyway, what's with this rich floozie from Forest Gate?"

"Oh, Sophy, yes. Well she's someone from — did Mum tell you about someone called Garrick?"

"She told me everything, but I want it straight from the horse's mouth."

"Well it's nothing really…."

"Oh come on, knock it orf, mate."

"Well I dunno, she's like, she's the sister of what's his name, Garrick's friend in…."

"So, are you fucking her?"

"Christ, Katya… I… I only… I only just met her."

"Well, Hazel wants to know."

"Hazel?"

"She always asks how you are, if you're coming home for the weekend instead of going to Sophy's."

"How does she know about Sophy?"

"I told her."

"You did?"

"Well, she is my best friend, what do you think?"

"What did you tell her?"

"I said you go to Garrick's house just long enough to be polite, then rush straight over to Sophy's and wait for everyone in the house to go to sleep so you and Sophy can fuck."

"Christ, you said that? We don't… do anything, we only sort of… are you kidding?"

"Well, no, I don't say it exactly like that, she'd get jealous."

"Really, Hazel gets jealous?"

"Zachary get with it, man!"

"Now I'm going to really feel foolish if I see her."

"You'll be alright. Anyway, I came round to give Mum something."

"Some money, you mean?"

"Yes, 'til the old shitbag's back in his shop, I take some from Benny's trousers while he's asleep and bring it round. She used up all those two-shilling-pieces you gave her."

"Yes, I know. I made an allotment from the RAF pay, a bit every week, help with the rent."

"Yes, Mum told me. I s'pose you hardly have anything left for yourself."

"Well, they give us meals and stuff, so I don't need much really. Mum said the girls send something also."

"Anyway, if Mum and the old shitbag aren't coming back for a few hours I'll go over to see Hazel for half an hour before I have to get dinner ready for fartface."

"Yes, how *is* Benny?"

"The same, I don't believe in miracles. So come on with to Hazel's for a while."

"No, I've got to go back to Sandwich."

"Oh come on you liar, you can manage half an hour. She wants to hear the truth, the whole truth, and nothing but the truth about Sophy."

"There's nothing, really. I mean I might be going to Bournemouth next weekend to see her at a hotel, maybe."

"Wow, so that's nothing? What's the occasion?"

"She's going to be on holiday there she said, so if they let me out I might go and see her. I can't tell Garrick in case Sophy's brother finds out."

"So, come on, come and say 'Hello' for a few minutes."

"I feel silly. Anyway I really have to get the train back."

"Coward."

•   •   •

"So, you're coming to Forest Gate after parade tomorrow?" asked Garrick.

"No, not this weekend, I have to visit my aunt... Aunt Zelda... she's... she's elderly, her hair's falling out, stuff."

Sophy's and my secret arrangements for our tryst were that she would wait at the Cumberland Hotel, or if she had to be out for any reason she'd keep coming back to the desk to see if I'd arrived. I'd told her that if they did let me out of camp I'd leave right after parade and should be at the hotel no later than one.

Despite a light drizzle, everybody seemed to be present at this Saturday morning's parade, no doubt chastened by what had happened to me. They marched, wheeled, saluted, then with dismissal bolted back to their barracks to grab their stuff and get out of camp. I needed to figure out how to proceed — if in fact I would even go to Bournemouth — and for that, I preferred to have all the other recruits leave before me. I sat nonchalantly on my bunk reading Forsythe's *Orchestration,* about the ranges of orchestral instruments and how composers balanced their relative weights.

"Not going 'ome?" asked Brewster as he raced to throw garments into his duffel bag.

"Not right away. I've got to visit some boring relative in Bournemouth, I'm not in a hurry."

Finally the last airman left, and in the empty barracks it was time to address my options. If Sophy were expecting us to have sex, first of all I never would have the nerve to put on a Durex while she was in the same room. Supposing there wasn't a lavatory, some place for me to go to do it? I'd never even seen a rubber, let alone tried to put one on. Probably there would never be a better time than right now.

I opened the little package I'd gotten from the barber and counted three flat sealed pouches inside. A perfumish aroma immediately filled the barracks! Why did they always have to do things with perfume, couldn't they bladdy well leave things alone? Any recruit coming back unexpectedly would recognize that smell, and I'd never live it down. I took the pouches into the lavatory, locked the door, then peeled one open. Inside, bedded among dry powder, was a circle of rolled-up transparent rubber. I undid my fly buttons, and with one hand propping myself up against the wall by the rain-streaked window, held the rolled-up thing against my dick. Right away I saw it would be impossible to put one on without having a hard-on. I tried thinking about Sophy and what was going to happen, but the only change was it got even smaller, which proved I was really scared. I began to roll it on anyhow; it went on a little way, but started pulling at hairs. Trying to roll it off again caught the hairs in the tight rolled-up part, yanking at my skin; I wouldn't be able to remove it without cutting the hairs.

I unlocked the lavatory door, and holding the trousers up around my knees hobbled out to the locker at the foot of my bunk, for a scissors in there somewhere. It wasn't in the shaving kit so I emptied out underwear and books. As I was rummaging I heard someone outside sprint up the wooden steps to the door. I dropped the locker lid and tried to pull up my trousers, but my underpants were still around my ankles. I yanked the trousers up anyway, and in a rush to do up the fly, the tip of the Durex wrapped itself over a fly button and became partially threaded through a buttonhole; now stretched tight as a rubber band, it was close to ripping out every hair still rooted in my groin. At that moment the door flung wide and Flying Officer Golightley strode in. To salute him with my right hand I had to change hands and hold my trousers up with the left.

"Grossman! What are you doing here? Everyone else has gone off for the weekend."

"Sir, I'm, I'm… I'm getting ready, sir."

He peered at my face, at the disarray of my shirt, then down at my trousers. Trying to inch them higher, I discovered you can't maneuver trousers all the way up by pulling only from the front with one hand. My arse was bare in the back, and the hairs ensnared in the Durex made me gasp with pain.

"You alright, Grossman?"

"Yessir!"

His eyes swept me in a suspicious glare, the bottoms of the trousers' legs bunched over my boots, the sharply sloped angle of the belt line at least implying a bare arse. "You sure you're alright, airman?"

"Yessir!"

"What's that smell?"

"Smell, sir?"

"Yes… something… in the air."

"I don't know sir, I don't smell anything."

"Grossman, are you using perfume?"

"Certainly not sir! Why… maybe it was one of the other recruits, sir."

His eyes squinted. "The truth, Grossman! You're not preparing some new stunt, some kind of fabricated medical emergency or something?"

"No sir, absolutely not sir, no sir!"

"Well, I must tell you quite frankly I've had about as much of your East End shenanigans as I'm inclined to take."

"Yessir! Certainly sir!"

"Look, I don't know what's going on in here, but if you are going, I want you out of here in five minutes. Is that clear, airman?"

"Yessir! I'll be packed and out of here in five minutes sir."

"Now you understand, I'm not ordering you to leave. You have the option of going out on pass or staying at camp, as you wish."

"Yessir. I understand, sir."

"You say you *do* want to leave the post. Correct?"

"Correct sir! Yessir!"

"Alright. Five minutes. I'll be watching for you." He turned around, scanned the whole barracks, sniffed at the air again, and as he took a final look at my drooping trousers I rotated a few degrees to keep my rear out of his line of sight. He marched out and closed the door. In agony I sank forward to relieve the tension, and hobbled back into the lavatory to unbutton the fly. Through the window I saw Golightley had stationed himself halfway along the side of the next barracks where he could simultaneously observe the front and the back doors of my hut.

I had to get the Durex off right away and there was no time to search for scissors, so I closed my eyes and tugged. The area wasn't completely numb, and the pain caused me to cry out; Golightley jumped at my shout. As I pulled the lavatory chain to flush the thing away he was looking rapidly in each direction to see what would happen next.

Despite these difficulties, I couldn't afford a subsequent fiasco in Sophy's hotel room. That meant I had to get it over with now and put a Durex on properly before I left. If ever there were a time an erection shouldn't have happened, this was it. Nevertheless — in fact, *supporting* my contention that penises have minds of their own, something in the bizarre situation contributed an inexplicably elevating element. But this was hardly time for philosophical ruminating; from my pocket I ripped open the second pouch, removed the content and rolled it on.

Immediately, I realized I'd never tried pulling up my trousers while I had an erection. I did manage that part — gingerly — but trying to button up the fly was akin to unanæsthetized surgery. I staggered out of the lavatory, threw a change of underwear, socks, shirt, the toilet kit and a couple of books into my duffel bag and hobbled to the front of the barracks. By the time I yanked the door open the hairs were again ripping my skin off at the groin. A heel caught on the back edge of the top step making me trip forward, and just in time I yanked the duffel bag around in front of me before I stumbled down the steps and ended up kneeling in the puddle of mud at the bottom. And there stood Golightley, legs set apart, hands on hips, his face a snarl of contempt. He said nothing.

I began to drag myself up, but the Durex pulling on the skin hairs forced me down again. Golightley just stood there, his hair dripping from the drizzle; he would certainly intervene if I went back into the barracks on the pretense of washing off the mud, so bent forward at the hip and without looking back I set off for the gate post. *En route* I experimented with various angles of posture, compromising at about forty-five degrees, where the pain was bearable and I could still be described as reasonably vertical. My béret, which had fallen off and missed the worst of the puddle, was still streaked with mud, as were the jacket sleeves and trousers' legs. And of course the duffel bag was more brown than blue-grey. If my nemesis Military Police Sergeant Murphy was on duty at the gate post he'd never let me through looking like this. In fact he might well arrest me on the spot if I approached with the posture and gait of a chimpanzee. There was nowhere I could go now to get the Durex off, since Golightley was sure to have posted someone near the barracks to report if I returned.

Anyway, I needed the thing on, so as I loped toward the gatehouse all I could do was try to focus my mind on something far removed: how scientists ascertain the temperature at the center of the sun. Obviously they arrived at the sun's surface temperature using a spectroscope. I sat down on a rock near a clear puddle of rain water, which offered a respite from the tension on my groin. From knowledge of the surface temperature, knowing the diameter of the sun and assuming uniform production of solar heat, you deduced the temperature at the center. I took out my toothbrush, dipped it in the puddle and started brushing the mud off. How do you find the diameter of the sun? You figure by triangulation, by the fact that the earth is in two extreme opposite positions every six months. Quite a bit brushed off, but the water left dark grey patches on the blue fabric which might disappear when it dried, but wouldn't much help in the short term — getting past the gate post. At any given time, the earth's position would be directly opposite its orbital location six months earlier. Shit! Or six months later. Lines drawn from the sun to those two orbital positions gave you a triangle with the sun at the apex. Fuck it, that was the best I could do. I put the toothbrush back in the duffel bag and slowly stood up. That's why they call it triangulation.

The rain had stopped, and springing around in small circles helped air-dry the water blotches a little. Five minutes later I gamboled up to the gate post. Sergeant Murphy was on the telephone.

"Yessir, he's just arrived now sir. Yessir!" He hung up. "Grossman, Flying Officer Golightley wants to confirm you've left the post. You look like a scarecrow, airman, but you'd better get your rear end out of 'ere right now."

"Yessir."

"And a word to the wise: when you come back tomorrow you'd better be cleaned up or we'll 'ave you up on another charge before you can say mercy mother o' god 'elp me."

Out of the camp, I lurched toward Sandwich. At the terminus the Green Line bus to Bournemouth was just pulling away. Already late, I threw the duffel ahead onto the bus's open boarding platform and lunged after the receding handrail. The driver hadn't noticed me and continued accelerating as I hung on, pulled into ever longer strides, to finally find myself twisted around and seated on the platform's edge facing backwards, heels skating along the roadway. At the commotion, the conductor came running down the steps to investigate just as I managed to pull myself fully aboard. Longing for an escape to anonymity I began dragging the duffel bag up the stairs, but he intervened, "No room upstairs, mate," and pointed to a single empty seat on the aisle: "There's one." I inched forward and came alongside, but the woman in the adjoining window seat took one look at my disheveled appearance and placed her bag on the empty seat. The conductor chided her to relinquish the seat, especially for our brave young men in uniform; she removed the bag and I sat down.

Striving for a disinterested nonchalance amid the passengers' stares I gazed noncommittally out the side window, which required looking past my new seat-companion's face. Soon she squirmed uncomfortably as though I were trying to steal surreptitious glances at her. Her agitation mounted, and when she half-stood to twist around for the conductor's attention, I realized it was safest to read. But a few minutes into Bertrand Russell's *Why I Am Not A Christian,* I felt her scowling at the page as she gathered her clothes and pulled herself as far away as the seats' confinement permitted.

After half an hour or so the conductor announced "Bournemouth," and I gratefully closed the book to alight. We were stopped opposite the Cumberland Hotel. My groin was so numb I found I was able to walk across the street virtually without pain. In the lobby, in the wall mirror behind the desk I saw myself: filthy, and still plenty of mud on my jacket and trousers. I hadn't been aware of it, but there was even dried blood under my nose where I'd fallen down the barracks steps. Luckily there hadn't been any MPs around when I got off the bus. I asked for Sophy Bliss.

"You Zachary?"

"Yes."

He signaled a young uniformed boy: "Run up to room 204, tell Miss Bliss Zachary's arrived." He turned back to observe me more closely. "Just back from the front?"

"Huh! Very funny."

Sophy came down the stairs. Her red hair and turquoise eyes, a diaphanous flowered skirt and white lace blouse that barely disguised her shape, once again pushed all other thoughts out of my mind. She gasped as she came closer: "What happened to you?"

"What do you mean?"

"Well," — she laughed a bit — "You look like you've been in a war."

I glared at the fellow still smirking behind the counter. "I had a little accident, with the bus. It hurts to stand up."

She became concerned. "Are you alright? Look at your face! Come on upstairs, I'll bathe it."

I started up the wide curved and carpeted stairway, grimaced in anticipation of the pain, then smilingly signaled her to go ahead. I really did need to be careful — the area was so numb I could easily rip the skin off and not realize it. Partially shielded behind her, alternately stepping sideways then hopping up a step I arrived at the top.

Hers was a large airy room. A double bed stood to the right of the large window, a line of big white fluffy pillows propped against the headboard. Alongside the opposite wall a smaller bed was strewn with magazines. Billowing filmy white curtains covered the window, in whose bay a table and four chairs looked out over the striped awnings of the beach to the ocean beyond. Armchairs stood to the sides of the window. "Give me your bag, sit here where the light is. I'll get a flannel."

She swept through a door that led off the room. So they *did* have a lavatory! The whole business with the Durex — unnecessary! She told me to lean back and began dabbing my face with a wet flannel. My expression must have seemed pained: "Sorry, I didn't know I was doing it so hard." She came round the other side of the chair and continued dabbing. It was nice to have her lean over me so attentively but I couldn't enjoy it too much; I wanted to get into the lav and check my groin. "I'll see if they've got any ointment here for your nose." She went back in and returned with a jar of Boracic ointment. "Maybe you'd like to have a bath?"

I'd never been in a bath. At home we washed with a flannel, and nobody had baths when I was evacuated. I'd seen a bath at Aunt Cissie's, but they kept coal in it, in a bucket, for the fireplaces, and although Sophy's and Garrick's houses each had a bath in the lavatory, I'd never gotten into one. "Might your friends come back?"

"Not 'til tonight. Anyway it'd be alright, they know you're coming."

She helped me toward the bathroom, and it was all so domestic as she turned on the taps to fill the tub, showed me a stack of sparkling white towels, stole a glance at herself in the mirror, then left and called through the door: "Tell me if you need anything."

I removed my trousers and — the Durex was gone! I checked the underpants, both trousers' legs, but it was nowhere to be seen. Perhaps it was lying out there on the carpet in front of the armchair, in full view! If I told Sophy I was coming out because I'd lost something she'd ask what it was, and look herself before I could get halfway across the room. So I put my trousers back on and just walked out.

"Oh!" She jumped up from a small mirror where she'd been adjusting her make-up by the window. "You need something?"

"No," I gulped.

"I mean, is there — do you have everything?"

I'd reached the armchair. "No, em, yes, thank you, I...." I circled it. "I think I... dropped something."

She sprang to help. "What was it, I'll look."

"Oh no, it's nothing." Dropping to my knees I jerked reflexively, then remembered the Durex was gone anyway, and sank back down. Behind the armchair and momentarily out of her view, I stole quick but thorough glances along the carpet in every direction — but nothing!

"Tell me what it was so I know what to look for." She leaned over me, "And I'll find it before you finish your bath."

"Er... well... I must have left it at the camp." She sat on the carpet alongside. "Well, it was nothing really, just a thing, you know...."

She placed a hand on my bare shoulder. "You have just the right amount of hair on your chest."

I gulped. "It was a, just a, y'know, one of those, wha'd' they call it, tsk!, boy!, funny, can't think, y'know on your uniform, I remember now it was in my foot locker when I, when

I... yes." We helped each other up. "Definitely, it was in my locker definitely."

Her eyes crinkled and she gave me a soft kiss on my forearm. "Are you nervous?"

"Nervous? Absolutely not! Why should I be nervous, I'm in the RAF, I've been around to all sorts of places."

"It's just... well, I'm a bit nervous."

Sophy nervous? "You are?"

"A bit."

"I see."

"It's the first time a man's been in my hotel room."

Man? She must mean me. "Is it really?"

"When no one else is here."

"Is it really?"

"Sort of."

"Really!"

"Oh! The water!" A slurping sound came from the lavatory; water had slopped over the rim of the bath and onto the tiled floor. Sliding on the wet tiles I reached into the clean hot water and pulled out the rubber plug while she turned off the taps. "Want to have your bath now?" She spread a couple of perfectly clean towels on the floor to absorb the water.

"Alright. Will they mind about the towels?"

"Who's gonna tell 'em?"

"Yes. Er... yes."

She said she was nervous, but she seemed so calm it made it extra difficult to be in charge. How would I handle everything when I was bathed, dressed and back out there in the room facing the big bed?

She closed the door. Lowering myself into a vessel full of clean warm water was amazing. The gentle heat soaked slowly through me and calmed me down. It was silly to worry about the Durex; probably it had fallen out of a trousers' leg while I was sitting on the Green Line bus. The woman in the window seat would have seen it on the floor after I'd gotten off, and that would have confirmed she'd been sitting next to a depraved rapist. I tried letting the wafting humidity seep in and loosen up the tightness in my teeth and jaw, my forehead. *There's nothing to worry about.*

A knock on the outside door and I jumped, slopping a tidal wave of water over the edge and onto the floor. Her friends must have come back early! I pulled the plug, grabbed some towels and quickly begin drying myself. A man's voice said something. A moment later, she called through the door: "That was our lunch arriving."

"Wow!" People who stayed in hotels probably knew how to have lunch actually sent to their room. I used up one towel after another then threw them onto the floor to try to sop up more water. "Sophy," — that was the first time I'd called her name, I could tell from the shape of it in my mouth — "I need some clean things, could I have my duffel, please?"

I stood on a sodden towel, opened the door a crack and she pushed the bag through. I'd brought clean socks and underwear, but I'd have to put the muddy trousers back on; we'd been issued only one pair of dress trousers. Using a hair brush lying on a glass shelf I brushed as much mud as I could from the clothes into the bath. A few minutes later, after running more water to scrub the mud down the bath drain with the hairbrush, I was dried, dressed, and combed. I sauntered out as rakishly as I could. She had set up a little feast on the table in front of the window.

"You sit here." She directed me to a chair.

"It looks so lovely," I said. We sat side by side at the table, looking out beyond the traffic to the brightly striped flapping beach canopies beyond. She had ordered one saltbeef sandwich that she'd cut into two, some pickled gherkins, and a pot of tea. The saltbeef looked hot, moist and delicious on its seeded rye bread — just like the sandwiches I'd never been able to afford down Petticoat Lane. We ate slowly; I ate extremely slowly, every extra minute warding off the moment of truth. And the truth loomed large in the form of the big jeering bed's implacable presence imposing itself into every sentence.

"It's a nice place. Do you come here every year?" My mind was going blank as I heard my voice — was it my voice? — chatting, unruffled, worldly.

"No. Joan, Joan Cohen — that's my friend — she's been here before."

"Uhuh."

"But this is the first year the three of us have gone away without our parents."

"Three?"

"Shirley, she's here also."

"I see."

"Where do *you* go, usually?"

"I... I don't go on holidays, often."

"Why not?"

"Well, we're a bit... we do other things, we move in different circles, we do other things... like discussions about things."

"Oh. What sort of things?"

"Oh I don't know, politics, science, classical music, stuff like that."

"I like Nat King Cole, we've got two records, do you like him?"

"He's okay, I meant more like Beethoven, Tchaikovsky and Mozart. Do you like Beethoven?"

"Hmm..." She giggled. "I don't know."

We stood by the window where dust motes sparkled on the afternoon sunlight as it slanted through the room and played across the unnaturally white pillows. My shirt sleeve came around her shoulder and my hand was close to the bare tanned arm; the tension of ionized surfaces was palpable. The unrelenting fact that hammered through the façade of my chatter was that it ought to be now, it had to be now, or cowardly disgrace, a confirmation of my ineptitude. I had to evade the conspiracy of terrors that danced through my head, and try to recall the softness of her first whispered invitation to Bournemouth, to forfeit reason to this large anonymous hotel room with its flowing curtains and ineluctably locked door, the welter of voices, car hooters, laughter and discordant street sounds floating in the phantom world beyond the window.

It was a short kiss; then again, more slowly. I was already out of breath, out of mind, but I found my hands gently easing her blouse from inside the belted skirt. When she didn't object, I paused in confusion and looked toward the window. God, this unbearable male burden of first moves, she needing only to restrain at her whim! I tried to feel passion but that didn't work; I kissed her again, acutely aware this kiss was identical, stagnant. Somehow she had maneuvered us to the edge of the big bed and she laughed as side by side we toppled, sundering the smooth covers into blasphemous disarray.

A knock on the door: "Finished with the tray, miss?"

Effortlessly she rolled off the bed, tucked in her blouse, "Just a minute." Hidden, her arm easily handed the tray around the door.

As she returned to the quilted surface, I faced her: suddenly it was easier, as though her own ease were infectious, as though it could all have been spontaneous, almost as if I *wanted* this, though the newness of it all was still too fraught for pleasure to intervene.

And so I kissed her neck as I fumbled with the buttons of her blouse, and still the logistics hammered: how would I make the trip over to my bag down there on the floor to find the next little pouch, the third and final pouch, to open it in her lavatory, to come out again and over to the bed, and all with nonchalance and *savoir faire?* She was unbuttoning my shirt; her hands were around me, under the shirt, on my bare back. She kissed my chest, somehow her bra and skirt were off. I went to the garter belt holding up her stockings. My brain was engulfed and I realized my hand was running the silk of her waist, fingers on her hip inside the angled elastic rim of her lace satin panties.

As abruptly as she had restrained me from removing my hand from inside her bra when we were in the back of the Austin, now her hand alighted firmly on the red satin, on top of my hand, to prevent me from progressing further. "N... no," she stammered. "No... I...."

"No?" I was swept back to reality.

"No... I mustn't...."

I paused. "Why not?"

"I... mustn't."

"But why not? I just...."

"Please, I can't. I mustn't. I promised...." I went to kiss her again, but she was stiff. "I... I promised, I had to promise...."

I didn't want to get up, I didn't want her to get dressed, I was amazed we'd gotten as far as we had. "Then let's just lie here."

"I...." She was still rigid.

After a minute I repeated: "Then let's just lie here. I understand, it's okay. It really is. It's quite alright."

"I...."

"It's alright, just stay here, we don't have to do anything, let's just lie here." Her anonymous promise had rescued me. "Everything is alright. Really." Now I could be gentle, demonstrate a protective appreciation of her girlish vulnerability. The remaining pouch would rest safe in my bag.

After a few minutes: "Why are you being so nice about it?"

"I... I...."

"I'm sorry, I shouldn't have let it go so far, I didn't mean to lead you on."

"No, no...."

"I'm not a... a... prick teaser." She blushed at her own choice of words. Then, her face turned away from me: "I ought to get dressed."

I spoke very gently. "You didn't make us go too far, there's nothing to apologize about. Everything has been perfect."

"Really?"

"It's wonderful just to feel you close to me. It really is."

"Is it? Is it really?" The lustrous reddish sheen of her hair, the eyes touched with a hint of darkness around the lids, her carved lips, were too perfect. I looked closer: the curves of her cheeks were not quite symmetrical, a small brown dot desecrated the rim of her lower lip; she was human after all. My hand lay on her chest, the silken crux of her breast nestled in the scallop of my fingers and thumb.

"I... I'd better get dressed, someone may come...."

"Sophy, you're unbelievably pretty!"

"Am I?" She looked at my mouth.

"It's like a dream, to lie here and hold you close like this."

"Really?" She smiled, her long slow deep smile.

"Really. Look at the light, the windows, the curtains, the sky, the white bed. It's all perfect."

The resistance, the anxiety seemed to wash away as she sank back toward me. "It is, isn't it? It is perfect."

"Yes, it is perfect."

I thought, what would Urine say? I thought, who cares?

45

"Can I try the piano?" I addressed the heavyset Salvation Army lady who sat typing on an ancient Remington behind the desk in the dimly-lighted NAAFI recreational quonset hut.

"It's there for you. We've been fortunate here at Sandwich, the family donating that piano appreciates the sacrifices you young men are making to protect Great Britain." As I pulled the bench forward, she added: "You're welcome to join our wholesome activities whenever you're off duty."

I opened the squeaking lid and tried a few notes, which rang hideously out of tune, replete with mechanical clunks, scratchings and twangs. Complimentary clicking sounds behind me came from colliding billiards balls where two airmen carefully angled their cue sticks to avoid the rips in their table's green baize. By one of the two windows another airman sat in a decaying armchair, riffling through a magazine. At the sound of the piano he swung my way. *"Knees Up Mother Brown. Let's 'ave a go at Knees Up Mother Brown."*

"I don't know that one, I don't really play."

"Oh. Sounded like you were playing."

"Just a bit, by ear." Another single key produced three different tones, almost a diminished triad give or take a few cycles per second.

The door to the NAAFI creaked open, and Garrick's head poked around. He saw me and came over. "Zech, I've been looking for you."

"They just got this old piano from someone in town."

"This is more important. I don't know what's up, but you're wanted in the C.O.'s office." My stomach twisted. "Oh christ, not again!"

"I was just there, Collins sent me to find you and tell you."

"What do they want me for now?"

"He didn't say, but Golightley wants to see you, as usual on the double."

I closed the lid but Garrick opened it again. "I might as well learn to play now you'll be busy with your cigarette butts."

"Keep your fingers crossed for me." I thanked the woman at the desk, and sprinted over to the headquarters building. Two barely audible male voices seeped through the door that closed off Golightley's office — Golightley and someone else, speaking in that quiet reserve employed for the gravest of offences.

"A.C.1 Grossman," I announced to corporal Collins, the clerk.

"Yes, Grossman, we already know who you are."

As he got up and walked over to the door, Golightley's voice on the other side fell briefly into focus: "You know of course he's a Jew."

"No, as a matter of fact I didn't know," came the moderate response. "All the more remarkable, don't you think?"

Collins knocked politely.

"What is it?" barked Golightley.

"He's here, sir."

"Send him in."

"Yessir."

Golightley was seated behind his desk, and on a chair to the left of the desk sat a stocky middle-aged man in a brown tweedish suit, white shirt and dark tie. As I entered, the civilian half-turned his chair to include me in his view.

I marched smartly up, my boots executing a loud, perfect one-two-halt: "Aircraftsman First Class Grossman reporting as instructed, sir!" I rendered an impeccable salute and stood at attention.

"Yes." Golightley acknowledged my presence with a curt nod. "Grossman, we have a report of your, well... I suppose the word is *association* with a crime — a most serious crime."

"Yessir!"

"Tell me, do you recognize this man?"

I regarded the man seated in the chair, but drew a blank. "No sir!"

Golightley addressed him: "Would you mind standing?" The man stood and faced me. "Now do you recognize him?"

The face was mildly familiar, but I couldn't recall from where. "I'm... not sure sir!" He sat down again but turned his chair a little more toward me.

"You're not sure."

"Yessir, I'm not sure sir!"

"Then does the name 'Harrington' mean anything to you? It should."

"Er — no, sir!"

Golightley turned again to the man: "Were you in civvies at the time or do you wear a police uniform?"

"Civvies *are* my police uniform."

"Well Grossman, I see no reason to prolong this further. This gentleman is Detective Sergeant Peter Harrington."

Harrington stood up and reached for my hand. "Yes, Grossman, you'll recall we met December last year at John Margolin's..." Suddenly I remembered! "...at John Margolin's factory in Wapping, ahem, a curiously interesting evening."

"Yes sir, now I remember!"

"As I'm sure you've learned, Mr. Berger was sentenced to six years incarceration at hard labor — a sentence, if I may say, most heartily deserved."

"Yes sir, I know, it was in the papers."

Still standing, he opened a leather briefcase that had leaned against Golightley's desk, and withdrew several typed pages. "However, I'm here not to speak of Mr. Berger, but primarily to address your participation in the events of that unfortunate evening."

"Sir, I answered questions in a deposition at the police station...."

"...participation in which this summary report and commendation describes your actions as little short of..." his eyes crunched into a friendly smile "...heroic."

"Short of... heroic?"

"Indeed 'heroic' is the expression used, and the Chief of Detectives has requested that I personally deliver one copy of the report to you and a second to your commanding officer.

And, Mr. Grossman, may I add personally, splendid show sir, splendid." At which he grasped my hand again and shook it vigorously. Behind the desk, Golightley rose to his feet.

Harrington swung around to address Golightley. "This young man matched wits with, as it developed, no less than three quite deadly adversaries, one of them admittedly wanting — perhaps even dull-witted would better describe one of the culprits, a Mr. Berger. Yes, Berger certainly is one of those bitter angry young fellows who seeks to find fault with everyone but himself. Be that as it may, Grossman single-handedly dispatched two of his assailants, and he was of inestimable assistance in the apprehension of the third, whom, as we have noted, is now safely ensconced in Her Majesty's prison at Wormwood Scrubs..." he laughed, and added "...where he has been afforded ample time to contemplate the foolhardiness of his ways."

Golightley leaned forward to interrupt: "Excuse me, Harrington old fellow, are we certain we have the right man here?"

"Indeed, sir, it is my privilege to confirm that we most certainly do have the right man. I'd recognize him anywhere."

Golightley fell back into his chair. I stole a glance; Golightley's mouth was taut, his eyes peering at me in squinted concentration.

Harrington turned back to me, and continued. "Margolin's foreman, a Mr. Smith, confirmed that the two deceased had in fact earlier threatened you. We apprehended Mr. Berger at his residence at two A.M. the following morning, and with the full cooperation of his mother brought him to the station. Shortly thereafter he supplied us with a signed statement confirming that he was indeed the culprit who, in effect, booby-trapped a large glass bottle of sulphuric acid with intent to cause grievous bodily injury. As you know he lay claim that earlier that evening you had deliberately humiliated him, implying, he hoped, ameliorating circumstances that would mitigate his sentence."

"Yessir! Wow, that was part of the statement I had to make out, that that wasn't true."

"Yes, we don't call military personnel on active duty to testify in person unless a defendant's claim is rationally defensible. This one was clearly rendered null and void by the premeditation required in the fabrication of his dastardly plan."

"Yessir! Wow, yessir!"

"Now sir, I must add that this verbal report to you is not without some criticism of your actions." At that, Golightley stood up again. "Your life was clearly threatened prior to the incident, yet you neglected to report this punishable offence to the authorities."

Golightley leaned forward. "And this neglect on the part of private Grossman is, I assume, a... punishable offence?"

"Golightley, old fellow, the only explanation we've come up with at the Yard is that Mr. Grossman's confidence in his ability to resolve this most vexing matter single-handedly was unusually strong. Luckily for all concerned, that confidence was well-founded."

"Th... thank you," I spluttered.

"Yes, well-founded indeed," Harrington concluded. He nodded his head and sat down.

Golightley's face wore a sneer. "Grossman, you never told us here at Sandwich of these exploits!"

"If I may," Harrington interjected, "men of this caliber rarely are boastful. It would be unseemly, quite out of character." Again he stood, and turned to me. "Mr. Grossman, it is my pleasure to present you with a copy of this Summary Report and Commendation, which one day you'll be proud to show your children and grandchildren."

"Thank you." I took the report.

Harrington swung back: "And, Golightley, the Yard has recommended you display copies of the report on the various notice boards inside the men's barracks. As of course you're well aware, knowledge of valorous actions by one airman cannot help but inspire other officers and men to seek to emulate him."

Seated behind his desk, Golightley stared coldly across at me as Harrington continued addressing him. "You have good reason to be proud to have under your command an airman who exemplifies those qualities that keep the word 'great' in the name Great Britain" — he slowly shook his head — "qualities so sadly lacking in modern-day youth."

Golightley's mouth had resolved to its usual thin-lipped straight line, and his eyes, now fully opened and bearing no recognizable expression, were riveted to my face. His indecipherable glare forced my eyes to meet his, and for what must have been well over a minute we each, unmoving, regarded the other with inordinate unblinking intensity. From the periphery of my vision I saw Harrington, who must by now have been at least confused, if not concerned, begin to lean over the desk toward Golightley.

Suddenly, with no discernible preparation, Golightley shouted: "Collins!"

Harrington and I both jumped. The door opened and Corporal Collins appeared: "Sir!"

"Take this report," Golightley extended an arm and handed the report across the desk, "and type up seven copies…"

"Sir!"

"…for distribution and display on barracks' notice boards…"

"Sir!"

"Dammit man, wait 'til I'm finished! …on barracks' notice boards, with a cover note indicating my authorization, then bring them in for signature."

Collins waited quite several seconds, then shouted "Sir!", spun on his heel, and exited.

"Well, this concludes my business here," said Harrington, "so I'll be getting along. Wish I could say I had this pleasant a day more often, but quite honestly they're not turning 'em out the way they used to." He picked up his briefcase. "Sometimes it seems the whole country's going up the creek, wouldn't you say, Golightley?"

"Em… in some areas, perhaps. Though I must say we have a superior, well-disciplined force of men here." The typewriter clacked away beyond the open door.

As he left, Harrington directed his final remark to me: "Grossman, if you should ever decide against the RAF as your career, remember, we can use good men like you on the force — staunch, decisive, at your best under pressure."

•   •   •

The following evening, Garrick once again put his head around the door of my barracks. "Zech, you're here! I saw your posting on the notice board! And did you hear the commotion in headquarters building? Golightley's been bawling out Collins all day long!"

"No, I didn't hear it."

He sat on my bunk. "So come on, how did you get Golightley to post a notice like that about you?"

"Well, it's a bit of a long story…."

"But, is it all true, what it says?"

"Well… mostly, those things did happen I s'pose, but…."

"But how did you force him to do it, to post a notice all over the camp that you're a hero?"

"It wasn't easy…."

"I knew you'd get the barstard sooner or later. And you set it all up without even a hint to anybody of what you were planning! Wait 'til Sophy hears about this!"

46

"Lily, you wanna go to the pictures? C'mon, you like going to the pictures. You're workin' so 'ard already, worrying all the time, like a change, it'll do you good."

"Alright," said Lily. "They've got Bing Crosby at the Odeon."

"Fah! Oo wants to 'ear 'im groaning? We'll go to the Empire."

"We can walk to the Odeon, I thought you didn't want to start taking a bus."

"So we'll ride in the van."

"The van? I thought you don't like to drive the van anymore."

"Uh'm trying to sell it, no one wants to buy it, uh dunno it's a good van."

"Ugh!"

"Uh gotta drive it a bit, 'ow long can uh leave it standing there, like months and months, people'll wonder like what's 'appening with 'is van already."

"I don't want to ride with you in the van. Wasn't last time enough?"

"A short ride we'll take. Your favorite one, what's 'er name er, er, 'Epburn, she's there in the Empire, she is."

"Oy a broch, who wants to ride with him in the van?"

And so Abie and Lily rode together to the Empire on Whitechapel Road in Stepney Green. Abie parked the van directly outside the front of the cinema, leaned across to open Lily's door to let her out, locked her door from the inside because of the missing door handle, exited and carefully locked the driver's door.

"Abie, for christ's sake don't start any business with the tickets. They'll catch us, for the neighbors it's not nice, don't start."

"Start? What should uh start, with the tickets? Uh'll buy the tickets, like normal people uh'll pay for two tickets, start! Don' worry, nobody's gonna start with you with the tickets." And, true to his word, Abie joined the queue at the cashier's window and paid for two tickets.

After the program they emerged from the theatre into the Sunday late-afternoon light, and walked through the waiting crowds across the wide pavement to where they had left the van. The van was gone.

"Oy a broch! It's gone," cried Lily. "Where is it, what happened?"

"Eee, uh bet they took it, someone took it, the barsteds," rejoined Abie.

Lily held a hand weakly to her heart. "What'll we do, that's all we need, more aggravation, what'll we do now?"

"We better report it to the police station. We'll go to the police station."

Lily peered into her husband's face. "You look funny. What's the matter with you, you look funny."

"Funny? Why should uh look funny? Wha'cha talking about? C'mon, we'll report it to the… the… look, there's a policeman, we'll, we'll tell 'im, we'll tell the policeman." He led Lily over to the policeman. "Er, officer, excuse me, officer, uh want to er, er, uh want to report something, something *very important.* Like we, er, we just came out, five minutes ago we came out, and it's gone, a thief maybe, uh don't know, what else, uh ask you. A thief, a thief they stole it."

"What is this, sir, somebody stole something?"

"Officer, as true as uh stand 'ere, we stand ere, like mu wife, mu wife," he waved an introductory gesture at Lily, "yeh, we came out, from the Empire we came out, like first we saw the picture then we came outside and it's gone! Can you believe it? The van. Someone stole it, it must' a bin a thief, oo else would do a terrible thing like that? It's gone, clean, clean away, they took mu van. It's terrible, nowadays."

The policeman had taken out his notebook. "Sir, if someone stole your van I'll write it down, but you'd be well advised to go over to the station and fill in a complete report, sir. We'll need all of the details before we can apprehend the person or persons as what perpetrated this crime."

"Yes officer, you're absolutely right officer, Lily, 'e's *right,* we'll go to the station, they'll fill in a report, we'll tell 'em everything, Lily you'll write it all down, every detail, like right now we'll go to the station, straight away. Thank you officer, it's wonderful the police these days, my goodness, you've bin wonderful, *oy,* Lily we'll go straight away."

And they caught a bus to the Bow Road police station where they officially reported the theft.

•   •   •

Late the following morning there came a knock. Lily, just returned from the Roman Road market, answered the door. A man in a dark business suit stood there, holding a leather briefcase.

"My name is John, Norman John. I'm the insurance investigator. Can I come in, Madam?"

"Why, what do you want?"

"The insurance company would like some more details, Madam, and quite frankly it'd be easier writing them details down inside your 'ouse 'stead of standing outside 'ere in the street."

"Well then, come on in, everything's a mess, I just got back from shopping, I didn't have time to clear up yet. *What's* your name? Mr. John? It sounds like a first name."

"That's right Madam, it does, thank you Madam."

Mr. John took off his hat and followed her inside. He sat down at the table, placed the hat carefully on a vacant chair, opened his briefcase and took out a sheath of papers. "And now, Mrs. Grossman, if you'd be so kind as to relate from the beginning exactly what 'appened with this 'ere van."

"What happened?"

"The events leading up to and including the disappearance of your 'usband's said vehicle."

"Well, we went to the police station and reported everything there."

"We 'ave that report, Madam, but the office 'as a policy of sending an investigator — that's me — what's trained in listening to stories related such as yours and taking down our own report. An extra copy, we likes to say, it 'elps us." He cleared his throat. "Sometimes, Madam, it 'elps us get at the real *truth* about what 'appened."

"The real truth? What do you mean, the real truth? We wrote it all down." Then, more angrily: "What are you trying to say?"

"Well, Madam, strictly between you and I and the wallpaper, it 'as been known to 'appen that sometimes the aggrieved party forgets some detail — some *important* detail — at the police station."

"What are you getting at, come on, out with it!"

"Well, Madam, since you're insisting we tells all our…" he coughed, "trade secrets you might call 'em, it 'as been known that sometimes the aggrieved party *arranged* — I says *arranged* — to 'ave 'is vehicle disappear from said location."

"Arranged? Who do you think you're talking to, *arranged!* You calling us liars, they didn't take our van? We're hard-working people, we work hard for our money; what do *you* do, sit in people's houses and ask questions and write things down with a pen? Work? That's not work! My husband works hard for his wages, he doesn't just sit there scribbling with a pen, calling people liars!"

"Now then Madam, I wasn't calling anyone liars, I was only saying what *some* people does. I'm sure you'd never do such a thing, you're obviously decent 'ard-working people. No offence intended, Madam."

"Right, then, but you watch your tongue."

"Certainly, Madam. Now then, there's these questions on this 'ere form." Mr. John slid a sheet of paper in front of Lily. "I knows some of 'em you already said at the station, but if we can go over 'em again, carefully like…."

That evening when Abie came home, Lily told him what had happened.

"Eee, so what did you say?"

"I told him what happened."

"Did 'e ask you questions, like more questions?"

"What's going on? Something fishy's going on."

"Fishy? Wha'd'y' mean, fishy? What's going on?" Abie giggled nervously.

"You *ponce* you, what did you do?"

"Do? What did uh do! What did uh do? They took the van! Is it my fault somebody took the van?"

"You old barstard you, you did something, I know you did something, and you let me get caught in the middle. They'll catch us, we'll both go to prison because of you, your tricks, you old barstard, you."

"Look, uh'm 'ungry. Uh bin working all day, riding on the Underground there, uh'm 'ungry."

"Alright, I'll get your dinner." She stood up. "His wife! He lets his wife answer all the questions for him, the brave, fearless protector. I'd be better off dead, I would."

•   •   •

Two weeks later, Abie told Lily he'd found someone to pay three hundred pounds to buy all their furniture and take over renting the house.

"So when do they want to come and see the furniture?"

"Don't worry. If they knock on the door say you're going out, anything, tell 'em anything."

"What? So will they pay you three hundred pounds without seeing the furniture? And the inside of the house, it's falling to pieces, nobody in their right mind would want to rent a shithole like this."

"Don't worry, you're always worrying!" He giggled. "Next month we're going, all we 'ave to do is be careful for five weeks, then when we're on the ship they can *gai in drerd,* uh should worry! In America we won't 'ave to worry! What'll they do, chase us on the ship to America?"

"Oy a broch, the aggravation with this man!"

"Look, if they knock on the door just don't let 'em in, you're busy, they should come back, later tell 'em to come back, tomorrow."

A couple of days later there came a new knock on the street door. Lily called out: "Who is it?"

"It's Joe."

"Joe?"

"Right, Joe. I wanna speak to your 'usband."

"He isn't home right now. Come back tomorrow."

"I can't come back t'morruh. I wanna speak wiv 'im nah."

"He isn't home now. He's at work. Come back tomorrow."

"What time's 'e 'ome from work?"

"Late. He comes home late. He won't be home 'til very late."

"Is this Mrs. G?"

"Yes."

"Then you tell your 'usband Joe wants to see 'im. You tell 'im it's *very important,* it is. 'E'll understand. Okay, missus?"

"Alright, I'll tell him, I'll tell him when he comes home."

Again that evening when Abie came home, Lily related her conversation.

Abie's face went white. "Joe?" he responded hoarsely. "What did 'e say, what did 'e want?"

"I told you what he said. What do you mean, what did he want?"

"Uh gave 'im the money, uh paid 'im already — what does 'e want, the barsted."

"Money? For what? What are you talking about you slimy old fart, what did you do this time?"

"Nothing…. Just… when 'e comes you tell 'im uh'm out, uh'm not 'ome. Tell 'im uh'm out."

"What's going on here, another one of your shifty deals you barstard, leaving it all on me to take care of?"

The next day, Joe returned.

"He's out. He won't be back from work 'til late tonight."

"Mrs. G, it's important, mark my word. I 'as to see 'im right away I 'as to."

"What's the matter? What is it? What happened?"

"Mrs. G, I can't rightly explain what's bin going on, like me standing out 'ere. I 'as to come inside so's I can tell you confidential like."

Lily opened the street door. Joe was a stocky five-feet-eight, roughly dressed and wearing a cap, but clean-shaven. Lily decided to let him in. Joe stuffed his cap respectfully into his jacket pocket, came in and sat down at the table.

"Nuh, Mrs. G, I dunno as 'ow if your 'ubby told you what's bin going on, but 'e owes me some money, 'e does."

"What do you mean? I don't know anything about it."

"Mrs. G, you seems like a decent lady what don't mean no 'arm, you does. Well, your 'ubby, 'e paid me ten pounds 'e did, to take that van of yours from Whitechapel Road, you know, outside the Empire."

"He did? To *take* it...? The old.... He never told me! I thought someone stole it, a thief. We went to the police station."

"Well, Mrs. G, not meaning no 'arm like, but you 'as to go to the police station when you gets a job like this done so's nobody gets suspicious, like. If you knows what I mean."

"Well... yes, I s'pose so. Eee, what should we do?"

"Well missus, I told your 'ubby as 'ow I'd be passing 'is van along to someone what does that, buys vans an' stuff like that. That's why I could do the job for ten pounds. Cost a lot more 'n ten pounds to do a big job like that, I gets paid a lot more 'n that, but I did 'im a favor 'cause I was s'posed to sell 'is van for twenty-five pounds, I was. Well! The bloke what buys vans says this van ain't worth nothing, so 'e takes it orf me 'ands, but I gotta 'ave more 'n ten pounds to finish the deal proper like."

"Alright then, I'll tell him when he comes home. I don't know what to say."

"Sorry missus, it ain't your fault, it ain't nobody's fault but that van it ain't worth nothing, not one penny it ain't worth. I can't keep coming 'ere knocking on your door, it's dangerous if I gets spotted. I'll come 'rand tomorrow, eight o'clock in the morning I'll be 'ere, an' you tell your ol' man to 'ave it ready."

"He doesn't have any money, he won't have any money tomorrow. He doesn't get paid 'til she comes to pick up... she picks up the costume...."

"Not meaning no 'arm, missus, but I 'ears them stories all the time in my line of business, I 'ears 'em. You tell 'im 'e'd better pay up what's due, otherwise I'll just 'ave to... to see what we can do about it."

"What do you mean?"

"Missus, when a man don't pay 'is debts, you 'as to... you 'as to do what's... *necessary* so's you gets what's coming to yuh."

"What'll you do, what do you mean?" Then, angrily but still nervous, "Who d'you think you're talking to?"

"It's alright missus, don't you get all excited nah. All 'e 'as to do is pay up what's rightfully due, that's all, an' nobody ain't gonna get 'urt."

When Lily related the conversation to Abie that evening, again the color drained from his face. "You tell 'im... you tell 'im...."

"Me tell him? Why, you coward you, you leave your wife to stick up for you, to fight your battles for you? *You* tell him when he comes. I won't be home."

"So... I'll get Benny to wait 'ere in the morning. 'E'll come over early, 'e'll be a bit late for work, you should worry!"

"So who's going to start going to Aldgate now to tell Benny to be here in the morning?"

"Tsk! I'll tell 'im, you'll tell 'im, oo cares. Eee, 'e won't try anything if 'e sees Benny, 'e'll be frightened, 'e won' come 'round 'ere again!"

"So now you want Benny to fight your battles for you? You'll have to tell him yourself, not me, I'm not going to tell him. Anyway, I don't want him here when he comes, I don't want Benny mixed up in your lousy stinking deals, a terrible embarrassment it is. He wants his son-in-law to fight his battles for him."

"'E's a big 'ulking man, what does 'e care, it's like nothing for 'im."

The next morning Abie left for work at seven. At seven thirty, Joe knocked on the door.

"I can't let you in," Lily called out. "He had to go to work early today, they told him to come in early."

"Alright missus, you just tell me where 'e works."

"I don't know where it is, he doesn't tell me where he works, ever."

"Missus, you just tell me the name of the place. That way we don't 'ave to trouble you no more."

"I don't know it. Really, he doesn't tell me anything, I don't know where he is."

"Is that your last word?" Joe called through the door.

"Yes. Honestly, I don't know where he is. What'll I do if you do anything? I don't know what I'll do!"

Again, that evening Lily related what had happened.

"You didn't tell 'im we're going to America in three weeks."

"No."

"Alright, if 'e comes don't say anything. Just say... just say uh'll bring the money 'round. Tell 'im, yeh, tell 'im uh'll bring the money 'round 'is 'ouse, next week, tell 'im uh'll bring it."

"I'm not telling him anything anymore, from now on you tell him yourself."

"So, oo needs you to tell 'im, then! You think uh'm frightened of, of... a stinking *turd* like that, a... a... weasel? Uh'll go to the police uh will, uh'll tell 'em to 'ide behind the door and when 'e comes 'round, they'll... they'll... uh'll tell 'em to... jump out and grab 'im, like, they'll... they'll 'old 'is arms down, they'll... eee they'll do 'im in!"

With two more weeks left before their scheduled departure, there came another knock on the door.

"Who is it?" a weary Lily called out.

"It's the Archers," replied a man's voice.

"Who?"

"Archer. Mr. & Mrs. Archer."

"Archer? I never heard of you. What do you want?"

"Mr. Grossman told us to come 'round this morning. He said 'Ten o'clock.' He's going to show us the house, and the furniture."

"He didn't tell me anything about it."

"He didn't? You ask him. He told us to come 'round now."

"Well, he's not here. He's at work."

"At work? He told us to come 'round at ten o'clock today, Tuesday. We paid him for the furniture and he told us to come 'round."

"Well, he's not home. You better come back tomorrow."

"Tomorrow?" There was a moment's silence. "Will he be home tomorrow?"

"I don't know. I don't know anything about it. All I know is, I'll tell him tonight when he comes home, I'll tell him you were here and you'll be back tomorrow." Lily heard a confidential exchange on the other side of the door.

"Mrs. Grossman, I'll write this number down on a piece of paper. It's a telephone number, we have a telephone. Please give it to him, tell him to ring us up on the telephone at that number." A piece of paper slid under the door. "Does your husband know how to dial the telephone?"

"Course we know how to dial the telephone, wha'd'y' think? Alright, I'll give it to him."

"Thank you."

•   •   •

Abie and Lily now had secured their passports, visas and Cunard tickets. They were scheduled to catch the boat train from Waterloo Station at eight A.M. on the 19th of April, a

Wednesday. On Sunday the 16th at around nine in the morning, three days preceding their anticipated departure, there came a loud knocking on the street door. Lily and Abie, sleeping late on the opening settee in the living room after packing until the small hours, awoke with a start. They hurried out of bed, and Abie pulled on a pair of trousers.

"Sssh, Lily, quiet, don't make a noise." Abie crept out along the passageway and up the stairs. Katherine happened to be sleeping upstairs; she'd had another row with Benny the previous evening and he'd threatened to hit her. She'd walked out on him, planning to stay in Morgan Street for the remaining days until her parents left. She was asleep as Abie silently eased the still-broken bedroom door closed; she usually chose the back bedroom because although the door was broken, still she wasn't directly above the living room when the arguing down there became too vociferous.

Downstairs the knocking began again, louder this time. Abie tried to peer out through the small landing window, but because it was closed he couldn't see down at a sufficiently steep angle. Very quietly he eased the window open and gingerly put his head out. He recognized the cap: it was Joe at the door. Abie crept downstairs, and in the kitchen filled up the kettle with water and stood it on the stove. He struck a match and turned the gas up high. The pounding resumed, even louder than before.

Katherine called down: "What is it, someone's banging on the street door, is it Benny? Don't let him in, I don't want to talk to him."

"Nah Katya, don't worry it's not Benny, call out the window, tell 'im just a minute, we're getting dressed."

Katherine got up and put her head out the window. "Hello!" The man with a cap looked up. "My father said he's getting dressed. Just a minute, he'll open the door." And she retired again to her bed.

The kettle was getting hot. Abie crept into the living room. Lily was quaking: "What shall we do, should we call the police?"

"You bladdy fool you, 'ow can we call the police?" Abie whispered. "What should uh do, call 'Police!' and a policeman'll come, like magic 'e'll show up?" From the kitchen the kettle began its preliminary song. He crept out into the passageway and passed the street door again; there were several voices outside. He padded into the kitchen and picked up the kettle, now boiling, tiptoed out and started up the stairs. On the landing, Katherine's door was closed. He carefully eased the steaming kettle out the small open window, then tilted it over. From below there came a scream. As he quickly pulled the kettle back in he accidently bumped it against the restriction of the small frame; it fell from his hands onto the landing floor, the lid came off and the remaining scalding water splashed over the linoleum and onto his right foot. He screamed in pain, jumping up and down on the other foot.

Katherine had fallen back to sleep but the commotion woke her again. "Oh Jesus, what the hell's going on out there?" The kettle and its lid were clattering, bouncing down the stairs.

Abie shouted with pain, and as he hopped around, his left foot slipped off the edge of the small landing and onto the top step. He lost his balance, crashed into a sitting position then went bumping down each step, grabbing at the banister railings to try to halt his descent.

Katherine pulled the bedroom door open just in time to see her father disappearing below the horizon. "What on earth is happening?"

Lily had crept out of the living room at the noise. She heard the continuing commotion outside the street door, and now saw her husband thumping to the bottom of the stairs on his back, moaning and clutching his foot. *"Oy gevult,* what's going on, what happened?"

"Lily, Lily, 'elp, 'elp, mu foot, mu foot, eee, mu foot"; then his voice rose to a scream, "can'cha see, you, you, bladdy idiot, you... mu foot, uh scalded mu...." Abruptly, he remembered the small crowd milling outside, and his voice dropped to a hoarse whisper. "Mu foot, uh scalded mu foot, 'elp, the fu–ucking kettle...."

"Hey, Abie, what are you shouting at Mum like that for?" cried Katherine. "What is this here, I've come from one madhouse to another?"

Lily began helping Abie up onto his other foot. He tried to straighten up, right foot still in hand, but before he could stand erect he winced: *"Oy,* mu spine, mu spine uh broke!"

Katherine wondered if perhaps he'd fractured a recently-mended rib, and called, "You alright, Dad?"

Lily was more direct. "What happened, *brochface,* now you fell down the stairs!"

"Mu foot, mu foot, uh scalded mu foot, the kettle it fell, *oy!* mu foot, quick, mu foot." Forgetting, again he went to straighten up: *"Oy, vey ist mir,* mu back!"

Katherine ran down the stairs, and the two women half carried Abie as he hobbled along the passageway and into the kitchen. Passing the street door they were made freshly aware of the hubbub outside, and as they sat Abie down on the chair next to the stove there came a single stentorian knock.

"Sssh, eee, don't answer it, ssh, ssh, keep quiet," groaned Abie in a strangled whisper. Nobody moved. There came another equally loud knock on the door. The three of them stayed perfectly still. After a moment Abie whispered: "Katya don't worry, go upstairs, very quiet, don't let 'em 'ear you, go up and look out the window, see what it is. We'll, we'll make out we're not 'ome, we're out. Lily, some ointment, gimme some ointment, eee mu foot, uh scalded mu foot, ssh."

"What's going on?" whispered Katherine to Lily.

"Who knows, his... his...."

"Business associates?"

"Ssh, stop with the questions already. Katya quick, go upstairs."

Katherine crept up the stairs. Out the window she saw several people: a man holding a white cloth to the head of a woman sitting on the brick wall at the corner, and another man wearing a cap. There came another sharp knock; she carefully eased her head farther out, looked straight down and saw yet another man, standing on the front step. When there was no response, this latter person stepped back down and reported to the others. "There doesn't seem to be anyone home."

"There's someone 'ome there alright," said the man with the cap. "Someone shouted out before, when I knocked. 'E don't wanna open the door that's all, thinks 'e can get away wiv something. Anyway, I gotta be getting along, me missus sent me out to get the newspiper." And he hurried off up the street.

Katherine came downstairs, picked up the kettle and lid and brought them into the kitchen where Lily was binding up Abie's foot with a towel. She reported her findings. Abie stood up slowly on his good foot. "'Ere, Katya, 'elp me, gimme your arm." The women helped him hobble into the living room where the three of them peered surreptitiously through the curtain. *"Oy a broch,* Mrs. Archer!" said Abie.

They heard Mr. Archer talking. "...And we'll come back with an officer, of course. We *thought* there was something peculiar about him."

"Eee, the 'ot water fell on Mrs. Archer's 'ead, just my luck it should go right on 'er!"

"Well," Katherine whispered, "perhaps this wouldn't be a bad time to visit Hazel. Mum, you want to come with, Mrs. Stapleton always says I should bring you if you want to get out for a bit."

"Eee, don't open the door, they'll... they'll... you mustn't open the door, wait, wait, maybe they'll go 'ome, yeh, they'll go 'ome, you'll see."

Katherine trotted back up the stairs. "I suppose I might as well get dressed."

"So how're you going to get us out of this one now?" asked Lily. "They'll come back with a policeman."

"Come in the kitchen, they'll 'ear us," whispered Abie, and Lily helped him hobble back and sit on the chair. Abie had a solution. "Listen. We'll all go out. We'll all 'ave to go out. We'll 'ave to stay out 'til Wednesday, 'til what is it, the boat-train there. Katya, let 'er go, 'er friend she'll go with, let 'er go. We'll all get ready now, then the minute they're gone, we'll go out."

"What do you mean, 'til Wednesday we'll go out? So where will we sleep? In the street?"

"'Ow do I know where we'll sleep! Sleep! You're always fidgeting, you never wanna sleep anyway."

"Oy, this man....."

"Then sleep in the street, sleep already! Oo cares where you sleep. Then Wednesday, eee, yeh, we'll go straight to Waterloo Station and get on the train."

"Him and his plans, I'll die I will...."

But the more Abie considered his stratagem, the better he liked it. "Te-he-he," he chortled, "wha'd'y' think of that? They'll come back 'ere the barsteds, all of 'em, and nobody'll be 'ome! They won't know we're going to America, they can *gai in drerd* for all uh care."

"And you? You can't even stand up inside the house, let alone walk around outside for three days. And what about the bags?"

"The bags?"

"The bags, all the clothes, all the things, *schvunce* — the luggage."

"So... we'll... we'll take it with us."

"You mean, the two of us walk around the streets 'til Wednesday, dragging suitcases and boxes? Typical!"

Katherine came down, dressed. "They seem to be walking up the street toward Mile End Road."

"Your father has a wonderful idea. You'll go to Hazel and both of us are going to walk around the streets dragging all the luggage, 'til Wednesday."

"Sounds like a wonderful plan."

"Jokes, jokes! So laugh! Everybody's laughing, har, har, har. So what else should we do, then? Tell me, tell me something better we should do!" Neither answered, and as Abie's plan cohered it came to embrace ever more nuanced elements. "Yeh, the bags, we'll 'ide the bags there, in the 'ut, we'll 'ide all of 'em."

"The hut?" asked Katherine.

"Yeh, where they, where the *yocks* they used to make the... the... the lead soldiers there, the end of the yard, it's all dark, Lily and me we'll sleep there, for three nights."

"Ugh! Me sleep there in all that filth, with the spiders? Nobody's even opened the door there for years. I can just imagine!"

"You won't die from three nights sleeping there."

"Sleep in there? He's serious!"

"So we'll take the blankets in, we're leaving 'em anyway, a spider won't come under the blanket, don't worry."

"I'm not sleeping in that filth, not one minute!"

"So you rather go to prison? Alright, you go to prison, uh should worry! Stay 'ere, so they'll come 'round and put you in the prison."

"Oh come on, leave Mum alone."

"Believe me she'll 'ave more spiders in prison, she will. Katya, you'll go and see 'er when she's in the prison there, you'll bring 'er the spray, she can 'ave a good time with the spiders."

47

"So, in just four weeks I'll be packing my bags and facing the rigors of Cadbury's Fruit-and-Nut, full time. Went fast, didn't it?" Garrick sat on my bunk at the close of our day's duty in the radar op rooms. His arrival at Sandwich about eighteen months ago had preceded mine by a couple of weeks, and now he was about to complete his stint and be demobbed.

But whereas for Garrick a return to civilian life meant the secure comforts of Forest Gate as the scion of his Dad's chocolate distribution business, my circumstances were fraught with uncertainty. Now that Abie and Lily were in America I'd go back to the laboratory at Bituminous; government law required employers to give demobilized recruits their job back. I'd see if on two pounds a week it was possible to rent a room, eat, and also afford a music school at night. Katherine had said I could stay with her and Benny in Aldgate as long as necessary, but Benny didn't like me any more than I liked him; I'd have to sleep on the settee in their kitchen, and what would happen when they argued and Katherine stayed at Hazel's? At least, seeing Sophy on weekends would be a constant.

The barracks door banged open and in barged corporal Collins: "Grossman, Flight Lieutenant Golightley wants you to report to headquarters this evening."

My heart sank. One problem at a time — I was still in the RAF. "What did I do?"

"He wants you to report after supper, seven P.M."

"Why, what's it about this time?"

"He wants to talk to you."

"Isn't seven after hours?"

He turned to leave. "After, during…. Grossman, when Golightley says report, you report," and the door closed.

"Don't worry," said Garrick. "At this point he's probably looking for your advice and approval."

Garrick and I walked across the square to the mess quonset and took our places in the queue.

"I'm so sick of the RAF, I'll be really relieved when I get my demob also."

"You'll only have to hang on for a couple of weeks more after I'm gone."

"That's when I'll probably get court-martialed for something, five years hard labor. I can't imagine ever getting out of here alive."

"So, another five years, it'll fly by. Seriously, when you get your demob you're welcome to come stay with Pop and me 'til you get settled."

"Really? I hadn't decided whether to stay with my sister for a little while or rent a room right away."

"Whatever you want, the offer's open, we've got the spare bed. Any kind of breather to help you avoid moving into Sophy's place."

"Sophy's?"

"That's right!"

"I mean...."

"You can be sure Mrs. Bliss will do everything up to and including enlisting La Sûreté and the M-5 to get you to move in there."

"You think so?"

"Think so? Pop and I've gotten enough hints from Uri about the various plots hatching. The matriarchal plans include setting you and Sophy up in a hairdressing shop, salon, whatever they call it — after you've married her daughter, that is."

"Hairdressing? Ugh!"

"Sophy's determined to marry you, you realize."

The dinner queue inched along. "Is she, you think...?"

"Her old man isn't happy about it, but the battle-axe herself is determined, so a word to the wise...."

"You mean the Mrs.?"

"That's the one. According to Uri she thinks you're confused, but you've got potential if you're guided right. And Sophy's driving them nuts talking about you day and night, so that's enough to put her mother in gear."

"Getting married, christ, I'm not ready for that! It's true, I didn't anticipate the complications. My sister also said I should be careful...."

"Tell me, did you ever say anything about being interested in music or something?"

"I told Sophy I'd thought about going to a music school after I get my demob."

"Old buddy, you can believe they'll be determined to wean you off anything like that! A women's body may feel nice and soft, but their heads are solid concrete. It's nothing personal, just a natural inclination to nudge you into something that'll pay the rent and feed the kids. Uri thinks within a year they'll have you as a research chemist in the lofty field of cosmetology..."

"Cosmology?"

"Cos-*met*-ology, cosmetics, and if that doesn't pan out they'll twist your arm into being a hairdresser."

We'd reached the serving counter. "A hairdresser! That's even worse than a tailor!"

"The old weasel wouldn't tolerate anything like music. He thinks it's about time you *wake up!*, as he likes to say." We leaned over to look in the pots. Dinner was rabbit stew again, with potatoes separately mashed to a pale greenish-yellow slime. "Old chap, all this is nothing against Sophy, you know I like her and so does Liz, it's just that they're all the same underneath the nylons and lace, whatever they tell you. You ask Liz, she's recklessly honest."

"The thing about Sophy is, I haven't really gone with anybody else before."

"My rule is, if you're not sure, don't make a move." Garrick looked around confidentially. "Golightley was your preliminary test. When you realized what was going on there you certainly settled his hash. When the time comes to decide about Sophy, you'll handle it."

"I don't have trouble knowing who I hate."

"Take your time and if she's really the one for you, you'll know."

"I just didn't want pressure from her family right away."

"Exactly. So if you do decide to move into their house, don't do it 'til after you've got your own things set up, you know, the direction you want to go. That's why you can stay with us a week, a month, as long as you need."

"Thanks, Garrick, for being such a good buddy."

"I'll leave my bill on your bunk."

"You're right, I have to be careful."

"Unless you secretly dream of being the world's greatest hairdresser, with a row of screaming baby hairdressers lined up when you get home at night covered with other people's dandruff."

"Whew! Maybe Mr. Bliss is right, I really need to wake up!"

"I wouldn't take *that* too hard either; according to him, everybody in Forest Gate should *wake up!*"

We downed the slop. "I'll stop by later and let you know what happens with Golightley this evening."

At seven, I knocked on the headquarters door. To my surprise Collins was still there. "Airman First Class Grossman reporting."

"Come in, Grossman." It was Golightley's voice, from the inside office. "Dismissed, Collins."

"Thank you sir, good night sir!"

Golightley opened his office door and I snapped to attention. "Airman First Class Gross..."

He interrupted me. "Yes, yes, let's forget about all that for this evening, shall we." And with a surprisingly non-military gesture his opened palm swept across the front of his unbuttoned field jacket. He was inviting me in.

"Yessir!" I saluted smartly.

He actually smiled. "As I say, let's agree to forgo military requirements this evening."

"Er, yessir, er, yes, okay, I mean, yes." I followed him through to his inner sanctum, and noticed that he wore no tie; even his shirt was unbuttoned at the neck, though the sleeves of his jacket were pressed with the usual razor-sharp edge, as were his trousers. I'd never seen him other than all correctly buttoned up, and a thought flashed through my mind: he was a *yock,* maybe he was drunk.

"Take a seat, Grossman." The speech was not slurred.

"Yessir! Yes."

He flagged me to a chair alongside a small table by the window wall of his office. From behind the desk he dragged his own chair around to the other side of the table, and seated himself at right angles to my left.

"You're probably wondering why I sent for you this evening."

"Yes-ss.... Yes."

"The truth is I don't know you that well, Grossman, apart from your... exploits."

"I'm sorry, sir! I mean, I'm...."

"No, that's alright Grossman, we're not here to talk about that." He took out a pack of cigarettes and offered me one.

"No thank you, sir, I don't smoke."

"You see, I didn't know you don't smoke. I try to get to know all my men in due course. Takes time, you know."

"Yes, I suppose it does."

He took out a lighter. "Yes." He lit up. "It does. We've been inordinately busy introducing the new radar equipment, and here you are only a month away from the end of your stint."

"Yessir, yes."

A cloud of smoke drifted my way. "There are only so many hours in a day."

"That's true. Twenty-four hours each day, exactly twenty-four every single day."

"I was speaking more… metaphorically."

As I averted my head to avoid the smoke I noticed two glasses stood on the table. "It's interesting how it works, it's related to how much the earth weighs, its mass. It would have to accelerate and decelerate to change, like a different number of hours some days."

"Yes, I…."

"The earth weighs a certain amount and the equation must stay equal, I mean everything would go flying…."

"Grossman!"

"Yessir!"

"How about… a beer?"

"A beer, sir?"

"A beer."

"To drink? I mean, you want to drink beer? Sir?"

"I'm asking you, would you like a beer? I'll have a beer too."

"Thank you sir, yessir, you mean, to drink."

"That's what people usually do with a glass of beer. You don't smoke you say, so maybe a glass of beer." He reached under the table and brought out a bottle labeled Watneys Pimlico Ale.

"Oh, yes I know, mostly…." In the nick of time I stopped myself saying that that was what Christians mostly did when they got together. "I'm sorry, I feel a bit awkward, sir. Jewish people don't usually drink beer."

"Don't drink beer?"

"No sir."

"Then what do they drink?" He coughed on his own smoke. "Chicken soup?"

Was he being sarcastic? "No sir, they do like chicken soup, but in a plate. A bowl. Not in a glass."

"According to records you're a Jew, am I right?"

"I am Jewish. I mean, I'm not religious, but according to the records, that's right, I am Jewish."

He placed the unopened bottle on the table. "So you are in fact a Jew?"

"Well, I am Jewish, I'm just not religious."

"Then, you're differentiating between Jew and Jewish. Let's see if I understand: are you suggesting a Jew adheres to religious doctrines whereas a Jewish is not so strictly inclined?"

"Er, no sir. There isn't such a thing as *a* Jewish. The word Jewish just sounds better than Jew. Jew sounds hard. Jewish is softer, it's nicer, Jews prefer it, I mean Jewish people prefer that word."

"Ahem. And is there a… difference between being a Jew and being… Jewish."

"Well, I'm of the Jewish faith. That is, I would be if I were religious. But I'm not."

He tapped the ash into the ashtray. "I'm trying to understand, Grossman. Are Jews Jewish?"

"Yessir! They are sir, definitely."

"You don't have to keep calling me 'sir,' we're just chatting informally this evening."

"Yessir. I mean, yes."

"Grossman."

"Yes-ss...."

"Try to make it simple for me; as I'm sure you've been told, we Christians are not as... *quick?*... as you Jews. Are you a Jew or are you a Jewish?"

"I was trying to explain, there's no such thing as *a* Jewish. It's a Jewish *person,* Jewish isn't... a noun, I think it is, I didn't go to school much, I don't know about the parts of speech. You can't be 'a Jewish,' you can only be a Jewish person."

"But aren't we only talking about persons? We're not talking about, say, dogs or cats, are we?"

His insistent manner was beginning to make me sweat. "Dogs or cats can't be Jewish... at least, I think so, I think they can't. I don't know all the rules, I'm not really interested in the whole subject to tell you the truth, a person would have to ask a rabbi."

"And what, then, is a rabbi?"

"Yes, a rabbi is a person who prays in a Jewish place, place of worship."

"You're referring to a church."

"Yes, well, it's not a church, they don't have rabbis in churches. They have priests in churches, you're Christian, aren't you, sir?" I laughed good-naturedly. "Probably you know a lot more about it than I do."

"You mean, in churches, in Jews' places of worship, they don't have priests."

"No, I'm sorry, in Jewish places of worship they have rabbis *instead* of priests, it's the same sort of thing I s'pose, just they use a different name. Yocks have priests."

"Who?"

"Well... I didn't... I mean, Christians, I'm getting a bit mixed up, I don't really know much about all this kind of stuff, you'd have to ask a rabbi, they know all about it."

He crossed his legs and settled in. "Then explain again, what is a rabbi?"

"It's a Jewish priest, a person who knows all about this stuff. I suppose like a priest, who's Jewish."

"Grossman, surely you must know that a priest can't be a Jewish. That would defeat his whole purpose, wouldn't it?"

"Sir, I really don't know anything about the whole subject. Can we talk about something else?"

He slowly lit up another cigarette. "If you insist, certainly." A long draw, and he exhaled a fresh cloud of smoke as for several moments he considered. "Then what is a yock? You used the word 'yock.'"

"A yock... is... a certain type of... Christian, I suppose."

"Grossman, you understand that a Briton such as myself doesn't know these things. I'm... simply trying to learn. Your reputation... suggests you might be able to clarify these things for me."

"Yessir."

"Someone once told me that *yock* is a derogatory term for Christian."

"Oh no sir, I mean, not every Christian."

"Then... just certain Christians?"

"Well, yes." The cloud of smoke was making it hard to breathe.

"And what type of Christian would that be?"

I could feel my face flushed. "I... I don't know, sir."

Golightley reached across the table for the bottle. "Grossman, are Jews permitted to drink beer?"

"Yessir."

"Then imbibing alcohol is not contrary to their religious beliefs, is that correct?"

"I think it's right, anyway, as I mentioned I'm not religious so I can't be certain, you'd have to ask a rabbi."

"Yes, alright. But more to the point, will you join me now in a beer?"

My throat was parched. "Yessir, I'll have a beer."

"Although you are... Jewish, as you say."

"Sir, I'm very thirsty."

"So am I to understand that because you're thirsty, although you're a Jew you'll drink a glass of beer."

"I'm Jewish, sir. Yessir."

"You don't have to keep calling me 'sir.'"

"No sir, I'm sorry sir I keep forgetting, it's hot in here."

"But nevertheless you are Jewish, and Jews don't drink beer."

"I *think* they don't."

"As far as you're concerned, Jews... don't... drink... beer."

"Well, alright."

"But, because you're thirsty you're prepared to abandon the Jew's practices, and in fact, drink beer."

"Jewish practices, well, if you want to put it like that."

"Grossman, I'm not trying to put it any way other than the way you've told me."

"Yessir. I'm really thirsty sir, can I have some beer?"

He eyed me evenly as he filled the glasses. It tasted funny, but I was thankful to swig it down.

"Grossman, you downed that as though you've been drinking beer all your life, ha, ha, ha."

"Ha, ha, ha."

"Right. Now, let's change the subject."

"Yessir, certainly, that would be good."

"Tell me Grossman.... Now..." he refilled both glasses, "how would you describe a Jew's sense of allegiance to country?"

"Country?"

"To the flag, to the Queen, say. To Britain."

"Well, I don't know really. I'm English, so I suppose...."

"You're English but you're still not British if you follow me, you come of foreign stock."

"I suppose so, my father comes from Russia, from Podol'sk."

"Uhuh, soviet! Communist, is your father a communist, are your parents communists?" He had finished his second glass already, and refilled it once again, emptying the bottle.

"Communists? I don't know, I never asked them."

"Well then, what did your father have to say about the Queen, for instance?"

"He's a tailor, er, once he said she's... well she's sort of, well... I don't want to be rude...."

"Come on Grossman, speak up!"

"Well... heavy, on top, he said it would need extra material."

"No, no, no, I'm talking politically. For instance, could you see your father laying down his life for the Queen?"

"Well I suppose not, no, he wouldn't. He said she should go out and get a job."

He looked directly at me. "In other words, he was unhappy with the job Her Majesty is presently doing to maintain Britain's standing in the world."

"Er, he was then, when he mentioned it, but I don't think he thinks about it a lot. Frankly he didn't really discuss things much, it was always a bit difficult to have a conversation with him."

"I see, he did not discuss things openly with you!" Another big gulp of beer, and he wiped his mouth. "Did you get the feeling he wanted to keep his real views on the monarchy private, under his belt, so to speak?"

"I don't know, maybe." It was getting harder to think coherently, and I wondered if it was the heat, the questions, or the beer.

"But more to the point, tell me about *your* allegiance to God, Queen and country."

"Well as I said, I'm not religious. I know some people are but I'm not, I don't believe in god."

"Go on, Grossman. I realize I'm asking you to divulge personal attitudes, but this is all strictly off the record, you have my word as an Englishman, as an officer in Her Majesty's Air Force." He finished his glass. "This isn't the Soviet Union you know." Again he wiped his mouth. "Nor, nor is it America, McCarthy and all those goings on. Though I must say he's clearing out a lot of spies and other people, disreputables. At least here in Britain one can speak one's mind fearlessly." He reached under the table, brought out a second bottle, opened it and poured himself another glass.

"Alright. I don't know what to say about *my* allegiance to the queen. I mean, I don't mind if they want to have a queen, it doesn't bother me."

"They! You said, 'if *they* want to have a Queen.' Who are *they?* Are they *yocks?"*

"Oh no sir, I mean *us,* the English."

"So! Off guard, you differentiate between you, as a Jew, and the normal British citizen."

I was all perspired. "What I mean is, I don't *care* if we have a queen, it's alright by me, but I don't feel a sense of allegiance the way I would for instance toward, say, Einstein."

"Einstein? Hmm." He tapped his glass. "He's a Jew, you know."

"Yes I know, but that's not anything to do with it. I mean, Einstein doesn't believe in a god, he believes in understanding things, how things work, like stars and relativity, the sort of things I'm interested in, *that's* why I feel an allegiance. I know he shouts at his wife, and he plays the violin out of tune. He has a tin ear."

"What has playing the violin got to do with anything?"

"No, it's just that he's a person like anybody else, but he certainly doesn't believe in god."

"Aha! I can correct you there, he does believe in God even though he's a Jew, he believes in the Lord..."

"Well, not really...."

"...whatever that means for Jews, he is reputed to have said, 'God doesn't play dice with the universe,' something like that."

"Oh, he didn't mean like a god, really, the one you're talking about."

"Then why would he say God doesn't play dice if he doesn't believe in Him?"

"No, Einstein was talking about the Copenhagen Interpretation."

"The what?"

"Yes, he was angry about quantum mechanics, he didn't like the idea of atoms and things being only statistically true instead of each individual particle... the way it used to be in classical physics, sort of, well, they call it deterministic...."

"I'll confess I'm not sure what all that chatter adds up to, but are you telling me he was taking the Lord's name in vain?"

"Who?"

"We're talking about Einstein, Grossman, although I confess I have no idea why. But then, I realize you Jews don't believe in God or country either, not to mention basic allegiance to our monarch."

"I don't know, I think they do."

"*They* do? We're back to *they* again?" His speech was slurring as his voice rose to a higher and louder pitch.

"Jewish people, I think they believe in a god and the other stuff."

"*A god?*" He slammed the glass down, and beer slopped over his hand. "I'm talking about God, the God who created this good earth! Of course, you even repudiate Jesus, the greatest Jew of all! Grossman, I don't know whether you're deliberately trying to anger me, whether you're too... well...."

"I'm sorry, you asked a lot of questions, I'm trying to answer sir, but I'm getting a headache."

"Indeed, clearly there's no point in going any further since it's obvious you have little inclination to... to... see any point of view besides your own. Tell you the truth, Grossman, I'm sorry for you that you were born a Jew."

"Sorry!"

He took another swig of ale, and a trickle ran along his wrist and inside his shirtsleeve. "Struggling... all that confusion, don't even know how to have a glass of beer and look natural about it. There's no doubt you'll always suffer from the burden of being a Jew. You'd think parents would think twice about the consequences."

Garrick was right — the barstard really hated Jews! "Well, I'm not...."

"Yes, I am sorry for you, you'll have a more difficult time here in Britain."

"Sir, most of my family has gone to America. When I come out of the RAF I might well go also."

"Aha, lots of Jews there, I'm told. They keep them out on an island, Long Island I believe it is. You'd probably be more at home with the Americans, they're coarse, garrulous, no sense of history, no dignity, no reverence. Can't even speak decent English!" Another drink. "Not to denigrate them you understand, they certainly were a jolly big help in the war, but looking at the facts that's probably where you'd fit in best."

"But Jewish people do have a reverence for their own history, sir. And it's a longer history than the British."

He swung toward me. "Yes, yes but don't you see, theirs is a history of complaint, not of accomplishment."

"Then what about Einstein?"

"Einstein again? The atomic bomb? I wouldn't say that's anything to boast about."

"No, that wasn't him, the atomic bomb was quantum mechanics, that's Oppenheimer and Niels Bohr and... what's his name, Archibald Wheeler, I think they're all Christian. Einstein discovered relativity, that's totally different. He got the Nobel prize, E=mc2."

"What?"

"That's right, what about all the Nobel prizes Jews have won?"

"They've persuaded the Nobel committee, they're very clever at that sort of influence...."

"Well, Einstein must have persuaded them two times...."

"...And don't forget about Palestine, we were trying to help them establish some sort of order there and look at the... beastly things they did, armed gangs murdering innocent Tommies just doing their duty, doing their best to help. Grossman, sooner or later you'll have to face up to it, you're tarred with the same brush. It's a simple fact you'll have to work that much harder to... to overcome the taint of your inheritance, develop a sense of fair play and all that."

"Well sir...."

"To be, to be more... more British, everything we British hold dear."

"Well...."

"But then, I wouldn't be surprised to hear you say you were actually *proud* to be a Jew; I've had Jamaican negroes under my command say precisely that, some sort of buffer I suppose against the obvious futility of their predicament."

"Well, no sir, I'm not *proud* to be a Jew, I mean in the sense that I didn't control it, I didn't arrange it; anyway, if I recall, pride is one of the seven deadly sins. But, sir, I can tell you I'm *grateful* to be Jewish — I'm grateful for the string of historical coincidences that finds me the beneficiary of a heritage that makes me, if you will sir, the kin of all those Nobel prize winners."

"Very poetic, Grossman, but I have to wonder whether detective Harrington would be so eager to have you on the force if he were aware that you don't even recognize allegiance to Queen and country, not to mention your obtuse refusal to admit the simple fact that if it weren't for the good Lord you wouldn't even exist!" He picked up his glass and realized it was empty again. "Why God gave us Jews, I'll never understand. Not to condone what the Nazis did, obviously, but one has to wonder." He reached down to drag out a fresh bottle, which he stood on the table. "I have to tell you frankly yours is a beastly attitude to the country that... that... took you in, gave you.... Perhaps in His wisdom, you represent our trial by fire." Drawing a deep breath, he concluded: "You may leave now, Grossman."

I stood up, and spoke evenly: "Good night sir."

He waved his empty glass at me.

—o—O—o—

48

Leaving Golightley's office, I went directly over to Garrick's quonset.

"So, what did the old boy want?"

"Christ, I don't know what the fuck he wanted. He was drinking beer, going on and on, loads of questions, mostly about Jews, Jewish people. I've got a headache from it. I tell you, I can't wait 'til the day I get that train ticket to London and I never have to come back. I hate the fucking RAF."

"Did you see the message on your bed?"

"Message? No, I came straight here."

He looked at his watch. "You mean, he kept you 'til now?"

"Yes, the fucking twerp!"

"Well, I spoke to Pop tonight and he said your sister Katya had rung him up."

"My sister telephoned your father? She doesn't even know who he is!"

"Apparently she'd rung up headquarters office, and they told her they don't relay messages. So she asked for our telephone at home, and then she rang my Dad."

"How strange! Is something the matter?"

"I've got no idea, she just left this telephone number." He handed me a piece of paper. "Pop told me she said you have to ring her up tonight. He said she sounded pretty cheerful about it."

"She wants me to ring up this number? It's not her number. Her's and Benny's, it's not their number."

"So, ring it up and find out."

I looked at my watch — nine-thirty! "That yockisher barstard grilled me for two hours! Alright, I'll go over to the gatehouse."

Sergeant Murphy was on duty. "Grossman! Wha'cha up to this time, airman?"

"Nothing, I want to ring someone up."

He stood up from his desk. "Well, there she is up on the wall then, airman, no one ain't stopping you." He nodded toward the pay-phone, then stepped outside.

The operator took the number, I deposited the money and a phone rang. A man's voice responded: "Hello, who's this?"

"It's Zachary Grossman, I...."

"Zachary, hello there old chap! It's Artemis at this end."

"Artemis! Wow! What's...? You mean the Artemis who...."

"Hold on old fellow, I'll fetch your sister for you, she'll explain."

"Hello, Zech."

"Katya! What's going on, is everything alright?"

"Yes, a bit of a mix-up, I'll explain when I see you. You have to come to London tomorrow, very early."

"Tomorrow? Tomorrow's Wednesday, they don't let us out of camp 'til Saturday morning, maybe Friday night sometimes."

"Well, you have to come, I have to see you tomorrow, extremely early, it's an emergency."

"Emergency? What is it Katya, are you alright? Why is Artemis there? Where's Benny, is anybody hurt or anything?"

"No, nobody's hurt, I'm just staying at Artemis's restaurant tonight. I'll explain everything when I see you, but I have to see you in the morning, really early."

"They won't let me...."

"Can't you tell them I broke a leg or something?"

"You broke a leg?"

"Tell them I was hit by a car, both my legs are broken, I'm in hospital, it's an emergency, they have to let you out."

"Were you really hit by a car? Katya are you alright really, what's going on?"

"Zech, first, don't worry, everything's alright, nobody was hit by a car. Second, tell them your baby sister's in hospital with two broken legs and they absolutely *must* give you an emergency pass because you're my only brother and everyone else in the family is out of the country. So far, can you do that?"

"Yes, alright, I'll do that. I'm sorry," I cupped the phone so that Murphy shouldn't overhear, "I got a headache from the fucking C.O. here, he's been grilling me for no reason."

"I'm sorry, are *you* alright, Zech?"

"Yes, I'm alright. What time in the morning? How early?"

"Around six A.M.?"

"Six A.M.! You mean in the morning, there, in London?"

"Yes, well maybe a bit later depending on where we meet. Where could we meet?"

"At your place? I can just come directly to your place if you like."

She coughed. "Ahem, I wouldn't advise that. You know Lyons Corner House, the one in Whitechapel Road, in Aldgate?"

"Yes, the one near Petticoat Lane, that's easy."

"Alright, meet me at Lyons Corner House, they're open all night, we'll have breakfast if you get there in time."

"Alright."

"So I'll be there waiting very early in the morning, I'll be there a bit after five, I'll just wait 'til you get there. Alright?"

"I'll have to go back to the office now and find out about the train schedule. Maybe I'll have to catch one late tonight if they don't have any that early tomorrow. What happened, you're staying with Artemis tonight? Did you murder Benny or something?"

"We had a little... tiff, you might say. No, I'm not staying *with* Artemis, his wife wouldn't care for that."

"His wife! So he's married also!"

"Yes, he married that hussy he originally bought my green sling-heels for, remember those shoes? I thought after he smelled my feet he'd be so hypnotized he wouldn't want her anymore. What do you think of the stinker!"

"I...I...."

"Anyway, this was an emergency so I rang him up. He owed me a favor, don't you think?" She giggled, and I heard Artemis's voice in the background; they both sounded pretty cheerful, which made me feel better.

"So you're definitely alright?"

"Actually, I'm better than alright. Okay I'll go now, Zech, see you in the morning. Be as early as you can, I'll be waiting, I've got to be out of this place by five A.M., before his parents show up, otherwise his wife'll leave him. No need to cause more trouble, even if I do hate her."

It was now five to ten, and the light was still on in Golightley's office. I took a chance and knocked on the door. "Who is it, who's there... knocking... there...."

"Private Grossman, sir!"

Movement inside, then: "Yes, Grossman, just a minute...." Shuffling, furniture sliding, and finally the door opened. "So it *is* you Grossman, yes yes, good, come...." Again an elegant sweep of the arm bade me enter, but this time he almost fell over. "Grossman, Grossman, Grossman. Can I call you Grossman?" And now his speech *was* slurred.

"Yessir, that's my name, sir."

"Grossman, I'm glad, ex...extremely glad you decided to come back. May I say... it's jolly decent of you to come back."

"Yessir, thank you sir."

"No, don't thank me. I've been going over our conversation, several times if I may say." He stumbled back to his chair behind the desk, and sat. "Sit, sit." He waved toward the other chair, which had been dragged closer to the front of his desk; on the desk stood the two glasses, the ale bottles, and another, smaller, somewhat flattened bottle.

"Yessir."

"Grossman, I'm going over your records." A folder lay opened. "Well, how can I say this... we *are* fellow Britons, I know you'll understand, I do apologize, yes, I do."

"Apologize?" The power of beer! "For what, sir?"

"Most sincerely so, for, for, for, can we just say... for going at you?"

"Yessir."

"Good. Sit down."

I sat.

"I went at you," he continued, "on the basis of, of... common hearsay. There's no point in my denying it."

"Yessir."

"It's clear from these records you've done nothing wrong." His voice was rising. "Your conduct has been ex...exemplary!" The bottles clinked as his fist to the desk emphasized the point. "Do you hear me, Grossman?"

"Yessir!"

"Don't call me sir! I've been unforgivably rude to you, Grossman. Don't ever call me sir again," he shouted. "That's an order, you understand?"

"Alright, yessir, alright sir, you didn't do...."

"Don't argue with me! When I go over Harrington's report here..." he was riffling through the papers, "well, I may say, I must say you put the other recruits to... to... virtual shame!"

"Thank you sir."

"Yes, indeed." He tried to pull his opened jacket together. "Your country called you to active duty in the armed forces of Her Majesty's government."

"Yessir."

"And... you answered that call, Grossman."

"Yessir. Thank you, sir."

"Don't thank me, Grossman. Despite the communist... how shall we call it... brainwashing from your parents, you answered your country's call with the patriotism of... of British stock."

"Thank you, sir."

"We all thank you. Your country thanks you. Britain, *Great* Britain thanks you." He lifted his glass. "Here, have a beer." With his other hand he tried to grasp the neck of one of the bottles.

"No thank you. It was nothing, sir."

"I salute you." He stood up and saluted, grabbed at the desk, then eased himself back into his chair. Remaining quiet for what seemed like several minutes he looked directly at me, his hand around the glass.

"Sir, I have a serious problem," I ventured.

"A serious problem? Tell me, tell me everything and we'll see what can be done."

"Yessir."

"Tell me and if it's humanly possible I'll take care of it."

"Thank you, sir."

"For every problem there is a solution."

"Yessir."

"I am the commanding officer, Grossman."

"Yessir."

"I can, if necessary, move mountains you know."

"I know, sir. Sir, earlier today my sister was run over by a motor car. I got a telephone call this evening from London, she's in hospital."

"In hospital!"

"Yessir. She... they think both her legs might be broken."

"My goodness me, in hospital! What hospital, where?"

For a moment I was thrown. "London Hospital, sir. London Hospital, Whitechapel Road, in London."

"Is that near what they call the East End?"

"Yessir, it's *in* the East End. I wondered if you could give me an emergency pass so I could go and see her. I'm the only family member she has in this country."

"Yes, yes, of course. The East End is where, well, mostly Jews, it's primarily a section for the Jews, is it not?"

"Er, yessir, mostly."

"Would corporal Collins be safe there?"

"Collins?"

"If I have Collins drive you directly to the hospital, would he be safe? He's not a Jew, you realize."

"Oh I know sir, oh yes he'd be perfectly safe. There are lots of Christians there, and Indians, he'd be perfectly safe." I did some quick anticipating. "Maybe it wouldn't be so safe for him to actually come into hospital, but it would be absolutely safe for him to let me off onto the pavement there, then he could drive straight back to Sandwich."

"Indians. You don't mean American Indians?"

"No sir, people from India, British Indians. Yessir, he and the vehicle would be quite safe, I guarantee it. I know the area well, I lived there for many years."

"Good. Grossman, you've told me everything I need to know. I'll go over to Collins' barracks myself right now and give him his instructions. When would you be ready to leave?"

"Well, if I could get there by five in the morning, that would be good."

"Five hundred hours! You're not leaving immediately?"

"I just spoke to the hospital and they said it would be better if I arrived at five tomorrow morning."

"Well then, they know best, certainly yes, understandably you prefer to follow their briefing."

"Yes, sir."

"Does an O-four-hundred-hour departure seem appropriate? No, make that O-three-thirty, give you leeway for variables, one never knows."

"Yessir. I'll be here at headquarters three-thirty A.M., sir. Thank you, sir."

"Private Grossman, frankly this circumstance eases my conscience somewhat, though of course I'm terribly upset at the news. Please inform your sister all the officers and men, the entire Sandwich complement of military personnel wishes her good luck. And a speedy recovery, of course."

"Of course, thank you, sir."

"Help me up, Grossman."

"Yessir."

"How do I look?"

"Perfectly okay, sir."

"Right."

"You look very good, sir."

"You look very good too, Grossman. And when you arrive in London, in… where is the hospital?"

"Whitechapel, sir."

"Whitechapel. You'll remind Collins not to get out of the vehicle under any circumstances, you'll do that?"

"Yessir, I will."

The lights were already out in Garrick's hut as I climbed the wooden steps. He was reading by the light of a torch.

"Hello! Everything alright with Katya?"

"Yes, I mean she's not hurt or anything, that's what I was worried about."

"Uhuh, good."

"Something's going on though, I don't know what it is. I'm going to London tomorrow, early, to see her. I have a feeling she's left her bullying fart of a husband, Benny. I'm glad about that."

"Tomorrow, Wednesday? So you imagine Golightley's going to let you out tomorrow because your sister left her husband?"

"Garrick," I whispered, "this is confidential. She's supposed to be in hospital, both legs broken!"

"That's a neat trick! Do you think Golightley will buy it?"

"He's already bought it. He's having Collins drive me there in the morning."

"What? Collins drive you all the way to London?"

"To The London Hospital in Whitechapel Road."

"Tomorrow morning?"

"Three-thirty A.M."

"I'll believe it when I see it."

"He just told me okay. When I left he was going over to Collins' barracks to tell him."

"Jesus! Zech how do you do it?"

"It just worked out that way."

"Oh come on, you and your 'it wasn't me, it just happened,' bullshit! Everyone else is terrified of the barstard, you wrap him around your little finger."

"No really, I… it really did work out that way accidentally, I'm telling you the truth, I didn't do anything."

"Bullshit!"

"I'm really knocked out and I've got to get up early. What an evening!"

"So will I be seeing you this weekend? Sophy'll be disappointed."

"As soon as I know what's happening. I'll ring you up Saturday at your house."

"I just realized! What happens when Collins decides to go into hospital with you to wish your sister *bien recouvrer la santé?*"

"Golightley is giving him strict instructions not to get out of the jeep in the East End in case he's attacked by the natives. He just ordered me to remind him myself he should just drop me off on the pavement, turn around and drive directly back to Sandwich."

"Get the hell out of here, Zech! I can't stand it anymore."

—o—O—o—

49

At five-thirty in the morning, out of breath from running and carrying my duffel bag, I pushed through the revolving door of Lyons Corner House in Aldgate. At a table at the back of the restaurant Katherine sat alone. "Katya!"

"Oh, Zech, am I glad to see you! You're really early!"

"Yes, what are the bags for?" A large soft dress-and-coat bag was draped over a chair's back, and on the seat her handbag lay on a magazine folded on top of a small suitcase.

"You're out of breath, sit down." She slid the remaining chair out. "You don't know how glad I am you could come. Was it difficult getting away?"

"Believe it or not, the C.O. had his corporal drive me all the way from Sandwich to London Hospital! It's amazing how things work out sometimes! I could hardly ask him to drive me to Aldgate, and no bus was coming, so I ran here."

"You alright now? We'll get tea."

"Yes, I'm fine."

"I didn't want to start going into details on the phone last night. And I hope this isn't too sudden Zech," she reached for my hand, "but I'm going to America, to New York."

"What? You are?"

"Yes I am, it's a long story!"

"You mean both of you are going?" That meant I'd have no immediate family at all left here when I got demobbed.

"Thank god, no, I've left shitbag junior for good! If I never see him again it'll be too soon."

"Really? Wow, so you've left Benny! Wow! Then when do you think you'll be going to America?"

Tears had welled up in her eyes. "Now. This morning."

"What? I'm stunned!"

"Eight o'clock, the boat-train. The ticket clerk in Waterloo Station should recognize us by now, we're both old hands." She sniffled and wiped her eyes. "That's why I needed you to come early, it's the last chance I have to see you."

"Jesus christ, give me a minute to absorb everything."

"Zech, I know it's a shock. You must have realized I couldn't bear living with shitface indefinitely."

"I… I… yes, you're right."

"So you'll have to make do with Uncle Albert and Auntie Zelda for a while when you're demobbed, but between all of us in America we can get you a boat ticket within a few months." On the table before her sat an empty cup. "I suppose you didn't have any breakfast yet?" she asked.

"No, did you?"

"A few cups of tea, but I didn't eat. I was going to wait 'til six or so then have breakfast if you still hadn't shown up, then get a taxi or catch the bus to Waterloo Station."

I looked around; Lyons Corner House was almost empty this time of morning, just one man in a mackintosh sitting at another table. "What do you want?" I stood up.

"I don't care, eggs and chips, and my fifth cup of tea."

"Alright, you stay here, I can manage it on one tray," I said.

"Let me just go and pee first, I couldn't leave everything 'til you got here."

"You go, I'll watch the bags at the same time."

As I approached the brass-railed counter entrance she called out, "With a roll, and the eggs basted."

I got the breakfast tray to the table as she returned, and we sat. "Boy, it's a shock! I mean I'm glad you're getting away from him, it's just a surprise." With a chip I punctured a yolk. "What time did you get here?"

"Five-fifteen or so." She looked at her watch. "Half an hour, it's been pretty empty except for him over there." She indicated the lone unshaven man at the other table. As I watched, his eyes drifted closed and his head nodded downward toward the table-top; just before striking the rim of his cup he pulled himself upright. "He's been just missing that cup about once every minute. Thank goodness there's a place open all night."

"You look a bit tired. Did you sleep last night, anywhere?"

"I couldn't ask Hazel, if Benny came smashing at the door again her father would have another heart attack. Artemis was very nice...."

"Yes, what's with Artemis all of a sudden — assuming it *is* all of a sudden."

"He let me stay overnight at his parents' restaurant. He had to leave at eleven otherwise his wife...."

"Yes, you said he's married."

"Yes, he couldn't stay later, she'd start wondering."

I must have looked overwhelmed.

"No," she continued. "I haven't been seeing him, don't look so... whatever-it-is you're looking."

"No, I'm not... I'm just surprised at everything moving so fast. You've always got so many exciting things going on."

"Zech, you're better off without my kind of excitement. Anyway, Artemis was nice, he gave me money for a taxi for this morning. Yesterday he helped me buy a steamer trunk, then we took it and another suitcase to the station. We'll get them when you come with me after we're through here."

"So what did you do, sit up all night after he went home?"

"No, I slept on a counter, it wasn't bad. He gave me tablecloths and things to sleep on. It had a thing along one edge and we lined up the backs of chairs on both sides. I just had to be sure I left before five when his father gets there. I got a better night's sleep than I ever did with fuckface."

"Well, you look tired but determined. How long?..."

"Oh, I suppose I knew from the first day I couldn't stand it forever, I'd end up like Lily, shame for her. Hazel and I planned this together, boy did Hazel have a good time! I think she hates him more than I do! She always got the post from New York for me at her address..."

"So that's how you kept it secret."

"… and for weeks she was holding whatever I could scrimp from the housekeeping money toward my big day! She's wonderful!"

"Why didn't you tell me what was going on?"

"You've been so busy with Sophy every weekend I never get to see you. I hinted broadly enough, the last few times." She laughed. "I just didn't tell anyone, all I needed was for him to get the faintest whiff and he probably would have murdered me. Really! That's what women have to put up with from their devoted husbands. I meant to tell you soon, but then this Saturday the boat ticket from Rivka came in the post, much quicker than we expected. Hazel rang me up at Anya's to tell me. Anyway, when I got home, Saturday evening it was, he was shouting about my nerve seeing Hazel without his lordship's express permission. 'Insubordination!' That's actually the word he used! Plus, shit-cunt and a few other terms of endearment. So Monday morning I rang up Cunard, they had a cancellation for this week, and suddenly here I am! I already had the passport and visa a few weeks, Hazel was holding them. I was going to tell you a couple of weeks before I actually booked a passage, but anyway, here it is. Sorry. It's a shock for me also, it happened so quickly."

"Well I'm glad it worked out alright. How did you get your stuff out, the bags and things?"

"I couldn't stay overnight at Hazel's any more; he already threatened to punch her father in the face if I stayed there again. So I thought, Artemis owes me a favor." She paused for a draught of tea, "Wouldn't you agree?"

"Well, I… I… yes, he does."

"So, I rang his parents' restaurant. He was there, and I told him I needed help in getting my stuff out of the flat without getting killed, also a place to sleep for one night."

"Christ!"

"He told me he was married, his wife might notice somebody extra in the bed."

"Uhuh, astute."

"So I met him in the street, he came with me to buy a steamer and some bags, then while fat-arse Bessie was out shopping at her regular time we both went in the house and ran upstairs and packed everything in about five minutes, like lightning. Naturally just as we got the steamer down and the taxi driver was tying it on, Bessie come wobbling along the street."

"Christ, what did you do?"

"Boy, did I jump in the back fast! She didn't know who Artemis was, standing out there with the driver tying the steamer on, so she just went on into the house. After a minute or two Artemis peeped through the glass thing in the street door. He said the kitchen door was ajar but he couldn't see her."

"Oy! to quote Sadie Benjamin."

"So," and she giggled, "can you believe this? The two of us crept back in and up the stairs, grabbed the rest of the bags and sneaked out downstairs and along the passage. I s'pose I should thank god for creating carpets! We rushed everything into the taxi — and then the street door opened and there was fat-arse. She must have heard the commotion and it took her 'til then to get to the door."

"What did you do?"

"Well, she looked up and down the street a bit, then went back in. She couldn't imagine something as fancy as a taxi having any connection with me."

"So, you left?"

"Guess what?" She looked at me sheepishly. "I couldn't resist! I told Artemis to wait a minute with the taxi. He didn't mind, he was having a good time."

"Don't tell me you went back!"

"I did," she giggled, and wiped her eyes again. "Let's get some more tea, you want some more tea? We've got half an hour yet."

"Whew! Yes, alright." I got refills and sat down again.

She continued. "I unlocked the street door again and crept back upstairs, by myself."

"Boy, you're brave!"

"Well, if she'd seen me, as far as she's concerned that's where I live."

"Yes I forgot, you're right."

"So I wrote Benny a note: 'Dear Benny, Bessie mentioned you've been fucking Rosalind again for the past six months.'"

"Who's Rosalind?"

"She's the cheap tart in the office there, at work, the boss's secretary. I'm sure he was already fucking her the time we met him at that Brady Boys' shithole, and he just kept on."

"Really?"

"Well, maybe he stopped for a week when we got married."

"Christ, I can't believe it!"

"Actually, I doubt he did stop, now I'm thinking about it. But anyway, let me finish telling you about the note. I wrote, "Darling, I deserved that punch in the belly. I realize you're too good a catch for me to throw away an opportunity of a lifetime over something like one little punch.'" She shrieked with laughter, the dozing man awoke with a start, and a woman and little girl newly ensconced at another table looked around at the commotion. "'So,'" still reciting her letter, "'I'm going out to buy black lace lingerie, you know, the kind that always makes you come before we even do anything.'"

The two newcomers must have overheard the last part, and I gulped.

"Sorry, your baby sister, I'm supposed to be sweet and innocent." She peered into my face the way Lily used to. "I'm embarrassing you."

"No, I don't know, I just, er...."

"Anyway, I signed it, 'Your loving wife,' stuck it in an envelope and wrote 'To My Darling,' on it." She giggled again. "I know, I'm terrible."

"Katya, when you get to America you have to become a playwright!"

"You're right; I spelled that w-r-i-g-h-t."

"You won't need to make up anything, it all happened already."

"Anyway to finish my long story, I went downstairs, and outside the kitchen door I whispered, 'Hello, Bessie.' She had a fit when she saw me. I told her I'd really learned my lesson this time, I realized now how much aggravation I'd caused. That seemed to slow her down a bit. I said I was the luckiest woman in the world that her son had married me, and from now on I was going to be a perfect wife."

"To quote Garrick, I can't stand it anymore!"

"I said I was going out for half an hour to buy something, it was all there in my note for her to give to Benny. And, finally, my magnum opus." Her face radiated gleeful malice: "I told her she shouldn't cook this evening, I was taking them both out to supper at the Carleton when he got home, some money Rivka sent me from America."

"Whew! What's the Carleton?"

"That's Artemis's restaurant."

"Artemis's? Why did you do that, why did you mention his place... in case... in case they went there or something?"

"I don't know…. I doubt whether she'd remember the specific name, I said it quickly."
She paused. "I don't really know what made me pick that name. Maybe unfinished business
or something, before I left?"

"Hmm. So, you had a busy day."

"I can't believe it was all only yesterday!"

"They must have gotten pretty hungry drumming their fingers waiting for you to get
back with the black lingerie. Maybe Benny finally went over to Hazel's and killed Mr.
Stapleton."

"I couldn't risk going to her house, but I rang her up late last night, no, he didn't go
there. I'll write to her as soon as I get to America." She finished her cup of tea. "Anyway, it
cost Artemis an extra ten shillings to hold the taxi, but it was the best ten shillings I've ever
forced someone to spend on me."

"What do you think Benny will do now?"

"As far as I'm concerned he and his mummy can have parallel apoplectic fits. Fat-arse
was always worried I'd take her baby away from her; maybe when it dawns on them I went to
America she'll convince him it's best I'm gone."

We'd finished the rest of our breakfast. "Do you want to get the bus now to the
station?" I asked.

"Alright." She checked her watch. "We're in plenty of time, you can have the taxi
money if you like."

"No, thanks, keep it for the boat, I'm alright."

"What will you do for the rest of the day? When do you have to go back to Sandwich?"

"They gave me a three-day pass, 'til Friday night, so I suppose I'm off 'til Sunday night
really. I've got an idea, Katya, should we use the taxi money for another train ticket so I can
come with you to Southampton? Sort of a practice run for me."

"Oh, that'd be wonderful!"

At Waterloo we bought two tickets, retrieved the suitcase and steamer, labeled them,
and followed the porter down to platform eleven where the boat train was waiting. Soon, we
were sitting together as the train gathered momentum out of the station.

"Funny, these train rides feel so something-or-other," she said. "You remember the last
time we sat in a carriage like this looking out the window?"

"You mean when the war started, when we went to Banbury?"

"Rivka and Zilla were opposite, busy talking, remember? Two boys came in."

"Like a different lifetime."

"September thirty-nine, I'll never forget that date."

I calculated: "Eleven years ago, christ! We didn't know where we were going, if we'd
ever see Mum and Dad again."

"In five days I'll be seeing both of them in New York, it'll be so strange!"

"I wonder if they have American accents yet."

"Him? He couldn't speak proper English after forty years in London."

"Katya, I'll miss everybody."

"I'm sorry Zech, don't forget you can come as soon as you want to. That's what Zilla
and Rivka say, something with the rate of exchange, it's easier there. Between everybody
we'll get a ticket for you in no time."

"Yes, maybe I'll go, I have to see about a few things, I suppose."

"You mean Sophy?"

"Well, I didn't expect her to be so serious about everything, really."

"Remember your baby sister warned you, before you realize it, it can get serious."

"I...I...."

"You haven't said you'll marry her or anything definite like that, have you?"

"No, oh no, no I haven't...."

"Even if you did you're entitled to change your mind, take it from one who knows. But anyway right now you're free, nothing's decided."

"You're right, nothing's decided."

"Zech, if you really like her, she could come also."

"My god, what would her parents say? Mr. Bliss, he hates me already the way he's always watching with tight lips and never saying anything."

"Just remember no one's forcing you to do anything you don't want to do. You can go without her or with her, it's up to you."

"I doubt she'd want to go, she wants to open her own hairdressing place or something."

"Hairdressing?"

"Yes, I'm a bit embarrassed to even say the word! Her parents would pay for everything."

"Hmm, that's a surprise, you've never mentioned hairdressing. I suppose it's not the worst thing in the world to have some help starting out, if that's what you'd really like."

"She said her parents would open a place for us in Stratford. I suppose it's a bit of a nightmare to think of fiddling with people's hair all day long."

"I hate leaving you here Zech, with everything unsettled."

"Do things ever get settled?"

"If I'm an example, no! You know, I feel creepy about leaving Maudy here, like I'm deserting him."

"I'd be the last one of us to go, so I'll *really* be deserting him."

"I didn't even have time to go out to the cemetery." She paused. "I suppose that's a bit silly. Ugh, I can't bear to think about it."

The houses had dwindled and the train now rode through a pattern of green fields, past scattered farmhouses and barns. *Déjà vu,* cows interrupted their chewing and lifted their heads to watch as we sailed by.

"So you'll go back to London tonight?"

"Er, I suppose so. I... I'll see...."

"When you're demobbed, where would you stay, Auntie Zelda's?"

"God, no!"

"Sophy's? Or Garrick's?"

"I don't know... I wouldn't want to stay too long at Garrick's with just his father there, I don't know what to say to him. Maybe Jack Pristien, I've bumped into him since I've been in the RAF. He's going to be an architect, he's going to a special school, he loves it. He has an extra settee in his room, in fact."

"Pity you couldn't stay at Hazel's. She'd love that!"

"They don't have an extra bedroom, I thought."

"I meant *with* her; no, you couldn't because of her parents. They're nice, but not *that* nice."

"If Benny showed up there we could all smash him up together," I said. "That would make for a pleasant evening's entertainment."

"If you do, give him an extra one for me, please."

"How is Hazel, haven't seen her in a while, maybe a year, I think."

"She's alright, still secretarying at the same office, Stratford."

"Is she going with anyone?"

"No, she went with the milkman for six weeks, then she found out he was married."

"Really, was she…?"

"No, she felt sorry for his wife, she told him he should stick with fiddling with cows."

"She's a nice gal."

"She really is wonderful, so easygoing and funny. I'm going to really miss her a lot. Maybe you'll bring her to America with you instead of Sophy."

"I.…"

"Didn't mean to embarrass you just because she's so wonderful and you're my brother and she'd be a wonderful wife."

"I was so stupid and shy in those days. Sophy's kind of determined, I suppose, she says she's shy but she sure doesn't seem it to me. You know, I've only had two or three weekends a month off, like, for one and a half years, so I suppose I've seen Sophy because she's up the street from Garrick's."

"That's as good an excuse as any."

"Well, I mean.…"

"I didn't mean excuse, I meant reason. Don't forget, Hazel's got your two suitcases as well as Maudy's things, so you *have* to be nice to her if you want to get them back. Maybe when you get demobbed you can have a cup of tea with her."

"I will. I've really thought about what you said about getting too involved with Sophy by default, the consequences."

"Yes?"

"Yes, you know the way Mum always used to say she was so tired, I'm beginning to understand what she meant, how you can put up with things just by habit."

"Once you get demobbed maybe things will be clearer."

"Yes. I'll go back to Bituminous, I'll get a room first, near there. If nothing else it'd be more peaceful than the commotion with Sophy's family, the mother, her brother. I'll ask her about going to America; if she said okay then I'd definitely go."

Finally the train slowed. It clattered over sidings between clusters of industrial buildings, then rolled into the station at Southampton Docks and screeched to a halt. Carriage doors swung wide and disgorged a host of passengers. We joined the melée of people hunting among the mounting stacks of luggage that piled onto the platform from the baggage compartment. Katherine's steamer was visible; we found her other big suitcase as well, and amid the general disorder found space in the flow of porters' carts for her belongings to be ridden over to the passengers' departure area, a huge shed adjacent to the station.

We followed behind the cart. With every distraction of the porter's attention Katherine reflexively shepherded the total of her worldly goods toward the departure area. In the brief surcease from conversation I noticed I could hear my own heart as it thumped. Above and beyond the building's walls loomed the masts and stacks of several vessels moored at quayside, but there was no mistaking the three huge chimney stacks of the *Queen Mary*. Inside the echoing building we joined a queue; Katherine retrieved from her handbag the blue stiff-backed passport and opened it to show me her picture glued to the first page — a slight but mature woman, big beautiful eyes and dark eyebrows, wearing a roll-collar blouse under the open jacket. No longer my baby sister, but a sophisticated woman of the world. I was happy for her even while I struggled with the sickly impact of my own stunning loss, even desertion. This was silly, irrational, certainly no cause for tears; in a month I would get my demob and be free to emigrate to America soon after to join my sister, all my sisters, and Lily and Abie, everybody.

"Katya, where will you stay? With Mum and Dad?"

"No, I wouldn't go back to that! Rivka said I should stay with her and Berel for a while 'til I find a job and get settled."

"Rivka's wonderful...." My throat was closing itself off though I wanted to talk normally.

"Thank goodness for Rivka, she's like a reliable aunt. They don't even know yet I'm coming this week, Hazel's sending them an air-mail." Her eyes were fastened to the man in the peaked cap and blue jacket as he questioned her. "No. No, one-way, permanent. New York. Queens. My family. Yes, two elder sisters and both parents." She even smiled though her face was white. "No, nothing...." The haughty temper, her usual immoderate responses to bureaucratic questioning — gone, the slate wiped clean.

I accompanied her through the wide doors and outside, over the concrete quayside. I couldn't bring myself to look directly at her as we walked together through the disarray toward the entrance of the long canopied ramp, didn't look at the side of her face, nor even down to the confusion of her silky brown hair as it bobbed along beside me toward the beginning of the ramp that led up to the black opening in the ship's side, the massive iron door that constituted its grand entrance. She moved aside to let others pass. "I suppose this is it, Zech."

I embraced her, both of us trying not to cry. "Be careful, Katya, don't get seasick."

"I won't, don't forget we'll all be expecting you to come also, as soon as you get out of the RAF."

Strangers bustled by and I stepped further back. "Yes, I...."

"I won't post anything to Sandwich because you'll be demobbed, I'll send everything to Hazel's 'til you send us your civilian address."

"Yes, I'll get in touch with her...."

"Zech, I know Sophy's nice, but don't let her talk you into anything you don't absolutely want to do...."

"No, no, I... I won't, I'll...."

"I mean..." she gulped, "I mean, I know she's affectionate and she likes to cuddle and everything, but so is Hazel, I mean, lots of girls are... girls love to be affectionate when they're lucky enough to find someone really nice."

"Yes."

"So that isn't a good enough reason...."

"Yes... I know you're right."

"I mean, that isn't enough reason just by itself, oh, I don't know what I'm saying."

"I know what you mean, it's alright...."

She turned. "I'd better go."

"Alright."

"Zech, if you have a chance to go to the cemetery, put a flower or something there for Maudy. I'll lie, I'll tell Mum I did go before I left."

"Yes, alright."

She began the climb into the darkness of the ramp. "I'll write as soon as I get there, I'll send it to Hazel's so I know you get it."

"Alright."

"Look after yourself, Zech."

"Alright."

Two minutes later, outside in the street on the unfamiliar pavement, I couldn't see clearly. I tried to focus, to see if there were any grey-blue RAF Military Police peaked caps around, ready to pounce. I must have looked ridiculous — six feet tall, in uniform, standing in the middle of the pavement spluttering and blowing my nose. I faced into a wall and wiped my eyes. There was a teashop ahead; I went in and sat down.

"Just a cup of tea, please."

She brought the tea. "Seen someone off on the *Mary?*"

"The *Queen Mary,* yes."

"Where're you stationed?"

"Oh, me? Yes, Sandwich, you know, on the coast, em...."

"I knows Sandwich. Bus goes to Sandwich this afternoon, it does."

"There's a bus to Sandwich from here?"

"Pretty much direct. Leaves..." she looked up at the wall clock, "leaves in three quarters of an hour, it does."

"Oh!" Perhaps I should go back to camp, forget about all the turmoil at Sophy's house with the parents, Uri, the questions; even seeing Jack, wondering where to sleep. "Where's the bus stop?"

"Over the road." She pointed through the big window. "Right opposite the station."

—o—O—o—

50

Reaching through the slats of the white-painted gate I lifted the latch, ducked beneath the ivy-festooned trellis, passed the bench and headed around the walkway. I dropped my duffel bag to the step and knocked.

The door opened. "Zech, you escaped!"

"Hello, old bean!"

"Come on in, *Mr.* Grossman." Garrick swung the door wide and grasped my duffel bag. "Don't tell me, Golightley tried to manacle you to the radar panel but you got him confused and *he* ended up wearing the handcuffs.."

I followed him in. "That's close enough."

"He must have been relieved to see you go."

"I don't know about him, but it'll take me a while to get over the shock of finally getting out of there alive."

"I still have nightmares about missing the last bus back Sunday nights." He held the duffel at arm's length in mock distaste. "It's scary to even touch one of these things."

Mr. Sharansky stepped out of his office. "Heard the door. Hello Zachary, Garrick tells me you'll stay with us for a while."

"Yes, if it's alright."

"Certainly, he said 'til you get settled, or… marry Sophy or whatever it was."

"What?"

"Pop, what's the matter with you!" Garrick's face colored, the first time I'd ever seen him disconcerted. "Listen, Dad, the telephone's about to ring, don't wait 'til the last minute."

"Zachary, you eat less chocolate than my boy here so you're welcome to stay as long as you like. Anyway Garrick knows all my jokes, I need a new victim."

"Just 'til I get my job back and get settled."

"Sure, sure, as long as you need." Mr. Sharansky turned back to his office. "Just finish one complete carton before you open a new one."

I followed Garrick to the kitchen where he put on a kettle.

"Sorry about my father, the Sophy thing, he knows Fannie."

"Fannie Bliss."

"Yes, the old battle-axe. A nice cup of tea, okay?"

"Yes please. Anyway, what's it like to be an old-time civilian?"

"A bit better than Sandwich, I can tell you. We're so busy with the orders, people still haven't recovered from the war. We don't even use adverts, still it's hard to keep up."

"Really!"

"Yes, Liz helps out at night. Pop and I've been talking about renting a warehouse maybe to keep up with everything, maybe get a van and a driver. There's only so much you can put in the boot." He gestured to a kitchen chair and poured tea. "My theory is it wasn't Roosevelt and Lend-Lease, or even stiff upper lips, it was the prospect of unlimited chocolate that won the war." He sat down opposite, opened a package of chocolate-covered biscuits. "So, Zech, it's good to see you in civilian-land at last! Where are your civvies?"

"They're at my sister's friend's house, Hazel, near Bow. Maybe I could get them this weekend, would that be alright?"

"Sure, I'll take you. Meanwhile you'll have supper with us tonight, of course."

"Thanks. Are you sure it's alright my staying a few days?"

"Course it's alright! Liz'll be here for supper, she can't wait to see what you're like as a civilian! I'm a bit suspicious, what's going on between you two?"

"Elizabeth's nice, Garrick, she's a really nice lady."

"Talking of ladies, I suppose you didn't stop by Sophy's yet?"

"No, she doesn't get home from work 'til after six and I didn't want to face the rest of them until I've regained my composure. I thought I'd go round this evening for a while, is that alright?"

"You can stay even longer than a while, we don't do bed check in this house."

"Alright, after supper then."

"Talking about the Bliss menagerie, did you know Urine's thinking of going to Israel?"

"Israel? You mean, for a holiday?"

"No, he told me he has an obligation to help out there."

"With what?"

"Fighting."

"But the English left, he's a year too late."

"He's sure something'll flare up there with the Egyptians, or those Syrian barstards."

"That's funny, he didn't get drafted because he got Conscientious Objector status."

"He did."

"But he wants to go there to fight the Arabs?"

"He's sure there'll be a war and the English will come in on the Arabs' side, so he wants to be there to do his bit. Another cup?"

"Yes please. So you'd be losing your best friend."

"Hardly."

"What do you mean?"

"He just happened to live along the street, he's a friend, I wouldn't call him my *best* friend. There's Maurice, Liz's cousin, I went to school with him...."

"Oh, I kind of thought.... To tell you the truth, I never feel very comfortable with Uri, especially the way he pushes Sophy around."

"It's the Sephardic blood."

"She just accepts it as though it's normal, it bothers me more than it does her. I'd never even think of bullying Katya like that."

"That's their way, the men looking tough, I don't have patience for it myself. The old battle-axe is actually proud he wants to go to fight."

I started my third chocolate-covered biscuit. "I hope nothing happens there, but I'm sick of wars, fighting. If he wants to go and it makes them all happy, who's to complain?"

"I wouldn't worry about it," Garrick said. "What I *would* worry about is if he goes, they'll have a spare bedroom in the house."

I hadn't thought about that. "You mean ready for me to move in."

"If I may coin a phrase, forewarned is forearmed."

"I suppose it would be easy...."

"Watch out for anything easy."

The doorbell rang and Garrick jumped up. From the street door he called back, "Guess who?" Elizabeth ambled in, slacks and a pale tan and gold silky blouse, and her slow smile and ease of gait filled the room. So composed, trim and unencumbered, the way high class *shiksas* comport themselves — not freighted with East-European angst. Like Garrick, she rarely seemed upset about anything.

"Liz the whiz!" Garrick swirled her around, pivoted her backwards like Ginger Rogers, then clamped his teeth around the tip of her nose.

She disentangled herself. "Hello, Zachary, so are you a free man?" I stood up as she came toward me. She put her hand on my arm and lightly kissed my cheek. I gave her a peck, and felt my ears redden.

Supper was quick and delicious: a saltbeef sandwich, cabbage and tea, then rhubarb with cream, and I stood up to wash the dishes. Garrick said no, I mumbled I wanted to help, Elizabeth said definitely not, she needed the practice, Mr. Sharansky disappeared into his office, and I found myself outside, closing the garden gate. On the short walk over to Sophy's, I tried to use the cool evening breeze to help me sort out my confusion. Elizabeth's calm refinement and intelligence were disconcertingly attractive, in a manner Sophy could never claim. And Elizabeth well suited Garrick's quiet confidence; Mr. Sharansky's business probably made enough money for a comfortable life for all of them, a lovely house, a car. Garrick could sleep well at night because in good time he would inherit that security, bringing a tangible *worth* to the relationship that balanced Elizabeth's grace. The mystery was why they both seemed to like me; maybe I was their exotic primitive. Did they really like Sophy too, or were they just accommodating me? Sophy was beautiful, but not elegant or sophisticated. Already, I was opening the gate to her front garden. Sophy was essentially physical, without much curiosity or quick wit; I realized I'd fallen into the habit of carefully phrasing my responses to soften our dissimilarities, because my enjoyment of sharp discussion seemed to bring her mostly pain. And what about Mr. Bliss? And Uri! In any future, they would invariably take Sophy's side. I took a deep breath and rang the doorbell.

The street door opened and there she stood — wide blue eyes crinkled into amazement, perfect white teeth and depth of lipstick reminiscent of Aunt Cissie. The silky red hair flowed over a pale blue lacy blouse tucked into a flowered skirt under a wide black belt. The wind gusted briefly behind me and the skirt billowed. Her mouth seemed agape in astonishment despite her knowing full well that I was coming. Backlighting from within the house briefly outlined her legs as with both hands she collapsed the pellucid skirt's hemisphere. The unblemished lips spoke: "You're home!"

My apprehensions of a moment earlier had been annihilated. "Yup, I'm home."

"For good?" Her arms were flung around my neck, breasts crushed against the polished brass buttons of my air-force tunic.

"Yes." What other girl from such a background could ever want me this much?

"They can't make you go back anymore, then."

"Right, I'm all finished with the RAF, except the reserves."

"It's wonderful! Let's go in." Mrs. Bliss was seated on the living room settee, knitting. In the armchair opposite, Mr. Bliss's head was buried behind the usual newspaper. "Mum and Dad, he doesn't have to go back to the air-force anymore!"

Mr. Bliss stood up. He turned to his wife, "Fannie, I'll be in the cellar." He tried unsuccessfully to fold up the newspaper, offering me a peremptory nod as he bundled the pages together to avoid brushing against either me or his daughter as he squeezed by and out of the room.

Mrs. Bliss called after him. "Sol, we'll have tea, you'll come up?"

"Tea? What do I want tea for? We just had supper, I don't need any tea."

Mrs. Bliss's tone was more kindly: "Take your coat off." As I removed the tunic jacket, Sophy fumbled to loosen my black RAF tie. "Sit, sit," Mrs. Bliss continued, a wave of her hand directing me to the vacated armchair. She corralled her several balls of knitting wool closer so that Sophy could join her alongside. "Did you have supper?" Sophy listened attentively as Mrs. Bliss launched her welcoming inquisition.

"Yes thank you, I ate at Garrick's. I'm going to stay with him next week 'til I get set up with my job and everything."

Having them seated side by side across from me, I couldn't help but compare: beyond the impact of Mrs. Bliss's considerable bulk, both of them had eyes the same color and degree of slant, but the mother's more pyretic, more baggy, and under nonexistent or — was it skin-toned? — eyebrows. Reddish hair, but of different shades; Sophy's head engulfed, silky and rich, Mrs. Bliss's laced with grey, and — clearly, white scalp in several places. "You can stay here with us if you want." For the moment I wasn't even sure which one had said it.

"Thank you, er, I'd like to stay on the weekend thanks, but tomorrow and next week I'll be busy checking out my job…" Sophy looked to her mother's reaction as I continued "… getting settled and stuff."

Mrs. Bliss wound the knitting thread more securely around the little finger of her left hand. "Uri's always pleased to share his room with you."

"Thanks, thanks, I…."

"So, will you be going back to your research job at the same laboratory, then?"

"Yes, I expect to. I only just got back this afternoon, I haven't had time to work anything out yet." I was tired of repeating that the job wasn't research, it was analysis.

"But you'll be living with a relative? Sophy mentioned you have an uncle near Commercial Road."

Sophy was looking at me intently.

"Uncle? Oh, you mean Uncle Albert… no, I couldn't live with him, he only has a…. I mean, I'll find a room to rent near the laboratory… for the weekdays, to stay on the weekdays, it'd be too far every day."

"Well then!" Mrs. Bliss gathered up her accouterments. "Good, you're getting started on your plans, then." She stood up. "I'll be in the kitchen. Sophy, make him some tea, there's a tray of… you baked those nice muffins."

"Alright, Mum." As Mrs. Bliss exited, Sophy jumped up and pushed the door to, then plopped herself down on my lap and planted a long and pliable kiss on my mouth. "At last you're really home for good."

"Yes." Her warm breath enveloped me, and as she snuggled in I momentarily turned my face to inhale a quick breath. Where my forearm came to rest along her thigh, my hand on her hip, the flowered tissue-thin fabric pulled and I felt the elastic of her underwear, and through the weave above that the bareness of her waist.

"I missed you every weekday, and the weekends when they kept you there," she said.

"Yes, so have I, it was pretty horrible in the camp, altogether."

"Might you be coming back to Forest Gate some weekdays also?"

"Yes, sometimes maybe."

"After work?"

"Yes, well, I'll be in Wapping, the laboratory is in Wapping, I mean I have to find a place near where I'm working otherwise it'd be too far every day."

"But you'll stay here every weekend."

"Yes, oh, definitely."

"Maybe I can… sort of… tempt you into staying…" her tongue was in my ear "…some week nights also."

"Yes, alright, well…."

"And…"

I waited. "What?"

"We'll have to see about getting you a nice suit and trousers, some ties."

"Alright. My stuff is at Hazel's, Katya's friend Hazel, remember I told you? Garrick is taking me there Saturday so I can finally change into civvies for good. When Katya went to America they took the suitcases over there 'til I got my demob."

"No not those, I mean nicer things, not that jacket in the snaps you showed me."

"Well, alright, yes."

"Those trousers were so baggy."

"Yes."

"The turn-ups were too heavy round your ankles, that's how you could tell they were out of date, like an old man."

"Yes."

•   •   •

Next morning Garrick and I had eggs and tea, and he drove me the short distance to the bus stop. Over an hour's ride, including the change, and the second bus dropped me off opposite the stop where Reuben had nearly slid under the wheels that snowy evening aeons ago. I crossed the road and walked around the old back street facing the wharf. The surroundings weren't totally as I'd remembered them; more crumbled, dirtier maybe. The stacked barrels on the left were the same, though the rusty green-painted crane leaned further out over the water. But surely Bituminous Products' wall to the right had been higher, and certainly not topped with this row of spikes. Maybe they'd done that to prevent anyone jumping over. I skirted a tar puddle on the pavement and passed through the gateway under its figured wrought-iron arch, now itself desecrated by welded spikes. It was reassuring to see Mr. Smith, burly as ever in his familiar tar-spattered work shirt and blackened headgear, step out through the still-new-looking passage door alongside the laboratory.

"'Ey, Grossman, wha'cha matey!" he called, the rough Cockney slang familiar and welcoming.

"Hello, Mr. Smith."

"Coming back to the lab, are you?"

"Yes, I'd like to."

He smiled. "'Ope you ain't gettin' ready to set the place on fire again."

"No, no, don't worry, no more of that stuff."

As I approached the laboratory window he dropped an arm in my direction and turned his hand away, his fingers gesturing to join him beyond the window's purview. His voice was low: "New man in there, be respectful like."

"Yes, alright."

"'E's alright, 'e just ain't easy goin' like old 'Itchcock." He scurried away to the yard and I knocked on the laboratory door.

"Come in!"

"Yessir!" The voice had been so peremptory I'd responded with a reflexive 'sir.' I entered, and the room was different: they'd removed the two long iron-topped benches and replaced them with a set of three shorter ones that ran from side to side. On the bench closest to the sink the distillation flask was bubbling merrily away inside a sandbath. The Liebig condenser was no longer dripping distillate into the open beaker Mr. Hitchcock and I had used; they'd modified it so now it ran down a curved tube, through a drilled cork stopper and directly into a narrow-necked receiving vessel, with a second vertical tube to relieve back-pressure. Presumably they deduced this new arrangement would help to seal off vapors from accidental ignition. And the new alignment of the benches, at right angles to the set-up we had previously used, brought the whole apparatus adjacent to the sink — though, I thought, water wouldn't extinguish burning toluol.

"What can I do for you?"

"Oh!" I'd been so absorbed I hadn't noticed a short stocky man standing by the far desk, in his hands a heavy open book. He wore a green linen hospital-type robe tied at the waist. "My name is Grossman, Zachary Grossman."

"And what can I do for you?" I couldn't place his accent.

"I used to work here, I was the assistant, then I had to go into the RAF."

"Grossman…. Then you're the one who set fire to the building."

"Er, well, that was an accident."

"Yes, accidents will happen. Especially if you give them an opportunity." He adjusted his glasses. "And what are you here for, Grossman?"

"Well, I'd like to work here again."

"Work here again." He removed the glasses, breathed on the lenses and polished them with his apron. "I… see."

"Yes, I've been demobbed from the RAF."

"By the way, my name is Nicolas. And what work would you do here exactly, Grossman?"

For a moment I was flummoxed. "I assume the same thing I used to do. I used to collect the samples from the tanks and distill them, you know, for water and ash content, like that." I pointed to the bubbling flask and Bunsen burner. "I mean, do you still, do they still do… tar and stuff, bituminous… the name, it still said Bituminous Products outside…."

The glasses went back on. "Yes, yes, we're still refining the same materials, raw materials."

"Then…."

"By the way, what were your qualifications?"

"Qualifications?" His tone was snotty. "Mr. Nicolas, I used to run the whole laboratory by myself after Mr. Hitchcock left, got the sack."

"*Doctor* Nicolas, if you will."

"Sorry, Dr. Nicolas. I mean I ran everything. Mr. Margolin, Mr. Bitwood will tell you."

"No, I'm asking about your academic qualifications. And Mr. Margolin is no longer here." He closed the book and put it down. "I understand you had no academic qualifications; is that still the case?"

"Er, well, yes…."

"Then, are you planning, would you be planning to enroll in any program... academic program?"

"Er, em, well not right away, I haven't...."

"Yes, yes, you're just... are you out of the service? The uniform...."

"Yessir, I just got my demob yesterday, I haven't got my civvies... my civilian clothes back yet."

"I see. Then I suppose you should run upstairs and speak to Mr. Bitwood first."

"Yessir."

"You don't have to call me 'sir.'"

"Yessir, I mean, doctor."

"Grossman, Dr. Nicolas will do very well, thank you, I do respond to my own name. Now run along upstairs, Mr. Bitwood will know the law regarding these things."

"The law?"

"Whether we're required to hire you again."

"Required? Yes, you *are* required, that is the law."

"Hmm. Well, run along upstairs then."

To exit the door that led into the outer office I had to walk right by him. As I passed, he rotated himself in increments to keep facing me. I closed the door behind me, and by the time I began ascending the stairs I realized I was shaking, angry. The way he'd told me to run along! I was probably a foot taller than him!

Upstairs, Mr. Bitwood grasped my hand warmly, "Grossman!" He eased me into the chair beside his desk. "Good to see a friendly face! So, when are you coming out?"

"I'm out. I got my demob yesterday."

"You did! Oh, it's the uniform. Yesterday — you're not wasting any time! So, you'd like to come back to Bituminous?"

"Yes, I'd like to have my old job back, the new law, they have to give it back when you get demobbed...."

"Well, yes." He hesitated. "Things have changed a bit since you left. Wait." He stood up. "I'll go speak to Mr. Richardson."

"Who's that?"

"That's right, you don't know. Mr. Richardson, he's the new owner."

"New owner?"

"Yes I'm sorry, I should have told you, of course." He sat down again. "Mr. Margolin sold the company, eighteen months now, must have been soon after you left. Mrs. Margolin..." he lowered his voice, "well, you know she'd come down with..." and he spoke more softly still "...she was very ill, capital C, that's why he couldn't come in every day, wanted to spend time with her. Decent man, Mr. Margolin, paid his bills on the dot like, you'd have to go a long way to find another one as decent." He put his fingers to his lips, then disappeared through the door to the inside office. After ten long minutes he came back out and quietly closed the door behind him. "Yes, Mr. Richardson said it's alright with him so long as Nick needs someone."

"Nick?"

"Dr. Nicolas, he's the new chemist."

"Oh, that one, I met him downstairs already. I don't think he liked me."

"He comes off a bit fussy, so long as you're careful I wouldn't worry too much. But don't call him Nick, either, only Mr. Richardson can do that! I'll put in a good word for you."

"Thanks, Mr. Bitwood."

"So much has changed around here. Like to get as many of the old crew back as we can. When were you thinking of starting?"

"Next week, could I?"

"Don't you want a little holiday first, take care of things?"

"I've got to find a room to rent, that's all really."

"You're not at the same address, where was it, Mile End?"

"I'm not, my family have all gone to America."

"To America, really!"

"I'm the only one left here, my immediate family, that is."

"There's a lady has a house on my street as rents a cellar room. That way you could walk to work, just four streets. She has a *For Let* sign up."

"Really?"

"Yes, here in Wapping, that's why I come to work by bike, it's only five minutes, you could get yourself a bike."

"Well, yes I'd like to see the room, do you think I could?"

He looked at his watch. "It's dinner time in ten minutes, I'll take you there if you want. I'll show you the area, it's not all factories and docks like they say."

I trotted after him as he rode the first street on his bike. We turned left onto High Street; there were tram-lines, and he jumped down and we both walked together, him pushing the bike. "Watch out for those tram-lines, if you ride parallel your wheel can get caught, then you can't steer," he said.

"They don't have trams here still, do they?" I'd imagined the whole of London had given up trams for trollybuses before the war even ended.

"No, there's regular buses here, you know, petrol, they're covering up the lines with tar. Look, people think Wapping is all factories." He gestured to the shops with first- and second-story flats above them. "There's even houses round the corner. Come on."

We crossed the tram-lines, he climbed on his bike again and began pedaling slowly. I followed; we rounded the corner onto King David Lane and he got off. Both sides of the street had houses joined in a row, like Morgan Street. "I live up the end there. Here," he pointed to the small sign in a window, *Room To Let.* "You want me to talk to the landlady? Mrs. Stokes it is, she's always ready for a chat — too much, if you ask me, idle hands and all that."

Mr. Bitwood waited while I followed Mrs. Stokes inside and down the stairs to a little cellar room with two small high horizontal windows that were barely above outside ground level. A tiny table and one chair, a chest of drawers and a single bed, a sink in an off-room the size of a cupboard. I could use the kitchen upstairs for light cooking, breakfast, then bring the food downstairs to eat. No overnight company, she didn't want to be surprised by strangers in her own house; but that was all right, I'd be at Sophy's every weekend.

Four shillings a week — and I told her I'd take it. "I'll mostly be here week nights." It was a relief settling this problem. Even if I didn't stay here every single week night, at least my things would be here — a token asylum.

•   •   •

The resolution of employment and living concerns had occurred with such ease — and it was still only Friday, my first full day demobbed! Which probably explained my exhilaration that evening when Garrick, Elizabeth, Sophy and I went for a drive toward the West End.

We rode through Ilford, then along Romford Road to Bow, and I realized we were approaching Mile End. With difficulty I restrained an announcement that we were right near where I used to live. Suddenly we were in Stepney, opposite the Empire.

"Want to go to the pictures, anyone?" The question was out of my mouth before I knew it, and Garrick promptly pulled the car over. Elizabeth read from the marquee: *The Red Shoes.*

"Oh, I missed it, I wanted to see it, let's go," said Sophy. Four car doors burst open and shut in unison, we crossed over the road, and moments later it was dizzying to stand in a queue at the Empire on Whitechapel Road with three aliens from the insular luxuries of Forest Gate. At the cashier's box Elizabeth fumbled with her bag, whereupon Garrick immediately snapped it closed and took a ten-shilling note from his wallet. Sophy made no such move; one-and-ninepence each, three-shillings-and-sixpence for both Sophy and me — almost one week's rent. The remaining demobilization money burning in my wallet would stand me in temporary stead, but it was clear my situation would rapidly become untenable if I paid double for everything on only two pounds a week.

Garrick and I sat on the outside, the girls in the middle. And there ahead of us in brilliant technicolor danced Moira Shearer, larger than life. Garrick's arm crept unabashedly around Elizabeth's shoulder, and as I started to do the same with Sophy, suddenly the persona of Marius Goring filled the screen. I'd forgotten he was in this picture. His white-powdered and brightly rouged — almost corpse-like — image jarred me into recalling why I hadn't wanted to see it eighteen months earlier when it had come out. Marius — the week after I was drafted; and now Marius — the day after my demob. In the darkness Sophy had turned toward me and begun kissing the side of my neck but, feigning some interest in the story, I drew a deep breath and was able to ease her face back toward the screen.

By the time the picture was over at ten-thirty I'd regained my equilibrium — even my earlier buoyancy. My world had not collapsed when I'd abruptly lured them from the seclusion of the Austin onto the grubby East End pavements. They'd all enjoyed the picture, this was my first day of freedom, and I had fourteen crisp pound notes plus a ten-shilling note in my wallet. "There's a fish and chip shop along here on Whitechapel Road."

"Perfect," said Elizabeth.

"We'll do it," confirmed Garrick, and we piled back into the car.

"I understand it's nice and busy, tables, a big friendly crowd."

In the back seat, Sophy threw her arms around my neck and pulled me down. "I'm having such a wonderful, wonderful time. You're really... terrific."

The car screeched to a stop outside Johnny Isaacs. The three of them hung on behind me as I confidently pushed through the noisy gathering and up to the counter: "Fish and chips for four people, please," I said to Mrs. Isaacs, and splurged by making the fish fried haddock, with pickled cucumbers, pickled onions, Tizer — anything they wanted. It came to twelve-and-ninepence, and in a rare delirium I took out a pound note and lay it on the counter.

"Oh no," Garrick protested. "You're not paying."

I pushed him away. "Oh yes I am, thank you very much!" Pocketing the seven-and-six change, ashamed of the quick private calculation that I had just spent more than three weeks' rent, I enlisted Garrick to help carry the food over to where the girls had commandeered a table.

Across the crowded shop, three girls sat at another table. One — thin, brown-eyed and sallow-faced, perhaps nineteen or twenty — looked our way. She said something to her friends, and they each glanced our way. After a couple of minutes she stood up and walked over. She surveyed my companions, then addressed me: "Hello."

"Hello, I, er…." I must have looked nonplused.

"Come on, don't you recognize me?"

I found myself sharply conscious of Sophy's flagrant scrutiny. "Er, I forget, were you… a friend of Katya's?"

"Who?"

"Katherine, my sister, she just went to America."

"Try again."

"I'm sorry, I…"

"Lucy, Lucy Greenspan, how could you forget?"

"Oh hello, I'm sorry, you used to go with Manny."

"No, I never went with Manny once."

"Well, I mean…. This is Sophy, Liz, and Garrick, I met him in the RAF."

"So you joined the RAF! I wondered where you disappeared to." Her two friends were examining us avidly.

"No I didn't join, they drafted me, I just got my demob yesterday." There was an awkwardness. "Well, we…."

"Okay, so long then." Sensing my discomfiture she returned to her friends, and pulled her chair around so that her back was toward us.

"When did you go with her?" asked Sophy.

"Go with her? Never, I didn't go with her. My friend Manny, the one who got killed by a doodle bug…."

"She said she never went with Manny."

"Come on, let's have our fish and chips," countered Garrick.

I hadn't even recognized Lucy, yet she'd remembered me! And, Sophy seemed — jealous! This was what it was like to be independent and adult!

A bit before twelve midnight, Garrick dropped us off outside Sophy's house. "Let's go for a ride in the morning, after breakfast," he suggested.

"Would you mind, could we go to my sister's friend Hazel's? It's near where we were tonight, I can get my stuff, my civvies."

"As good as done, sir."

Sophy and I entered the darkened house. "You want to lie down on the sofa?" she asked, quietly clicking the living room door closed. "Take your shoes off."

I removed my shoes. Sitting, lying on the sofa, answering questions about Lucy Greenspan when there was nothing to answer for, while on the wavering disk Nat King Cole nagged the background with piano fragments I already knew too well, it was difficult to constrain my vague anxiety and upset. "Do you mind if I change the record?" I sat up before she could object.

"Don't you like this one? Last time you said you liked this one."

"Well yes, but I thought maybe… you know, we had this one on all the time."

"There's *Mona Lisa* on the other side, turn it over then."

"Let's put the Frank Sinatra one on."

"I don't like him so much, I thought you liked Nat King Cole."

"Well I do, but Sinatra does some… some certain things, he breathes in certain places, he's very particular and it's nice to listen how he does it."

"But it's only supposed to be in the background. How can you listen like that, I mean you're just supposed to enjoy it, not listen like...."

"I don't know.... It is in the background but part of my mind still listens to how he does everything. He's very careful how he sings, about technical things." I stood up.

"Can't you just enjoy it instead of being so... like, fussy, listening to every single bit?"

I found the Sinatra among the pile, and by the window's outside light confirmed its label, opened the gramophone lid and clicked off Nat King Cole. "It was just playing so many times it was making me feel a bit..." I couldn't say *nauseous,* "I don't know."

"You shouldn't think about it so much, it's just... nice."

I lowered the arm onto the Sinatra record and stood, deciphering the street lights beyond the flimsy curtains. The needle crackled, and as Axel Stordahl's strings began their sweeping introduction the consonance wrought surcease to some torturous pressure in my head. I stood, transfixed by the curtains' lights, by the anticipation of the piano. And it came: Graham Forbes' delicately sensitive choices of notes, runs, implicate harmonies. "I love this piano introduction, it's so perfect."

"Alright, come and lay down then."

But some imperative required I remain by the window a moment longer, just until Sinatra's voice began.

"You don't like me any more, do you." The accusation from the couch came as a sharp blow.

"What do you mean, of course I do, why, no, it was just the other record, it was going on and on...."

"Do you want to lay down with me then?"

"Well of course I do, that's ridiculous, of course I do."

Quickly I sat, swiveled around, brought my feet up and put my arm around her back. Her uppermost forearm was behind my neck, and I kissed her; she opened her mouth hard against mine, making it difficult to breathe. I couldn't survive more than two or three seconds, yet she would interpret any small withdrawal as further evidence. Suddenly the door clicked open and in an instant the room was flooded with the painful glare of electric light.

"So, what's going on in here?"

As I pulled myself up, Sophy virtually jumped over me to sit on the far cushion. "Nothing, nothing." She scrambled with buttons, realized none had been undone. "Nothing. We were talking."

Uri stood just inside the door. "Talking! Huh! I can imagine."

The light's vehemence hurt my eyes. "We... we were just talking about some things," I said.

"Well, alright then."

Sophy had gathered herself. "I didn't hear you come in, I didn't hear the street door."

"I was already in when you got back, I was in the kitchen but that's none of your business."

"Oh, I didn't see the light."

"I heard Garrick's car pull up so I switched the kitchen light off."

"Oh alright."

"So come on Soph, it's time you went up to bed."

She stood up and brushed off her skirt. "Alright."

"What's the time?" I tried to focus on the hands of my watch. "Nearly twelve-thirty."

"Zech, you can talk to her in the morning."

He left, leaving the door open. As she collected her handbag from the chair, I got up and closed the door.

"Why did you do that? I have to go up."

"Sit on the couch again, please."

"But I have to go up, what's the matter?"

"Sophy, sit on the couch. I know it's Uri's house, your parents' house, not mine, but I just escaped from eighteen months of RAF people telling me when to go to bed and when to get up."

She sank back onto the couch and began to sob. "I don't know what's the matter, I thought we were having a terrific time at the pictures and everything."

"I did, we were, I'm sorry I... I... I don't mean anything's the matter."

"Something's the matter, I can tell."

"Nothing's the matter."

"What did I do?"

"Do? What do you mean, you've been, everything's been...."

"Why don't you tell me the truth?" she sobbed.

"The truth?" I was perplexed myself. "The truth about what?"

"I thought when you got your demob everything was going to be, like, perfect."

The truth was that I didn't know what the truth was.

Fifteen minutes later we crept upstairs. My mind wouldn't stop racing, and I was tired, immensely tired, thankful for a cessation of the need to think, grateful for a chance to get to sleep.

Uri was already asleep, and I managed to ease the door closed without his waking. By the soft white light of the moon filtering through lace curtains and around the obscuring plant that hung in the window's bay, his presence in the bed struck me this night as repulsive. He lay on his back, mouth ajar, not snoring so much as snorting in bunched outbursts. His frame was extended under the blanket, one leg way beyond the center line and into my exclusive territory. If he went to Israel at least I'd have the bed to myself when I stayed over. I undressed, donned the sleeping suit left out for me and crept into his bed, the flat of my foot gingerly easing away the intrusive leg.

I lay on my side, enveloped in a stampede of exhausted thoughts. The moon's visage grew a harder cast; its light flickered and modulated behind sheer skeins of racing backlit clouds — a terrible brilliance as waves of photons drenched the chaste, rubbled crater where I knelt. The searing incandescence expunged all detail, then gradually subsided, dimmed, dimmed, still, a stillness.

•   •   •

"You gotta get up, you gotta get up, you gotta get up this morning!" Uri stood in the doorway, spiffy in a white shirt and wide grey tie, his wavy black hair slicked back along the sides.

"Oh!" A pale summer sun had flooded the room.

"You were so fast asleep, no one had the heart to wake you."

"Really, wow! I...."

"I suppose this has been a pretty hectic few days for you."

"Yes.... Where's Sophy?"

"She's downstairs helping Mum get breakfast. They sent me up to get you."

"Alright." The clock said ten A.M. "I'll be down in a few minutes."

Crystal glasses winked and shimmered beside glistening plates, with cutlery nested alongside in scrupulously white cloth serviettes.

"No, you sit, I'll serve you." Sophy stood behind my chair, her hands resting briefly on my shoulders. She swung forward to glance into my face, then picked up my plate. "You want them basted, I know." Her manner bore no trace of the previous night's tensions.

"Yes please."

"They went into the frying pan as soon as I heard you coming down, and I already covered it." She placed the silver strainer on my cup, and poured from the brown china teapot. "There, I left enough room for plenty of milk. I already put two lumps in, I know that's what you like."

"Thank you, thanks, Sophy."

Uri was seated opposite. "Where else would you get that kind of service?"

"I know," I said.

"Where else *would* you get this kind of service?" It was Mrs. Bliss bringing Uri's plate of eggs and toasted bagel from the kitchen; she addressed me as she placed his plate before him.

"Oh I know," I said. "Everything is so... beautiful here, it's very very nice of you to make everything so...."

"Sophy did it all herself, I'm just the kitchen assistant this morning."

"It's much nicer than anything I ever had before...."

"So long as you appreciate it I'm sure she loves to do it."

"Mum, where's Dad?"

"He's seeing Moishe this morning."

"Where, in *shul?*"

"Yes."

In less than a minute Uri had wolfed down his breakfast and jumped up. "I'll see him in *shul*, then." He grabbed his jacket, "So long Mum, so long Zech," and hurried toward the door, pushing half a bagel between his teeth. "See you later, Soph," he managed.

"I don't know how anyone can eat that quickly," said Mrs. Bliss. Then to me: "Does your, did your family go to *shul* — synagogue?"

The kitchen door swung open and in came Sophy, balancing two plates.

"No, my family wasn't that religious."

I rested an arm around Sophy's hip as she put my plate down — perfectly basted eggs and a big poppy-seed bagel already sliced apart and buttered. "Oh Sophy it looks so lovely, the table, everything!"

"You like it?" The red lips parted in an immaculate smile.

"It's beautiful, you've taken care of every detail!"

She took her place in the chair beside me, her mother opposite.

A brief exchange by the street door, then Uri's voice: "He's here, hold on to your wallets!" The door closed, and Garrick walked in.

"Greetings ladies and other species."

I was grateful to see him. "Hello old bean, where's Liz?"

"She's busy this morning. I pleaded, but she wouldn't see reason."

Mrs. Bliss nodded: "Sophy, get him a cup." As Sophy hurried to rise, Mrs. Bliss reconsidered her dictate: "No, stay, I'll get it." Then to Garrick, "Have a cup of tea while they have their breakfast."

Garrick sat. "Thanks. We'll see Liz the whiz later. And where are we off to this morning, your lowness?"

"I wanted to get my suitcases, is that alright? At my sister's friend's house, near where we were last night."

"There's a remote possibility that might be arranged."

"Then if we could just take them to Wapping, that's where I'll be working, that's all."

Mrs. Bliss had returned with a cup for Garrick.

"It's Hazel what's-'er-name, the one you told me about?" Garrick asked.

"Yes."

"You're sure she'll be in this morning?" he continued.

"Er, I don't know, I suppose someone will be there...."

"Why not give her a ring, in case?"

"Yes, er, you're right, I...."

"Show him the telephone, Sophy." Sophy was already rising before her mother completed the sentence, and I followed her into the living room.

"I don't know the number," I began.

"What's their last name?"

"Stapleton."

"Hazel Stapleton; would it be in her name?" She lifted the receiver and proceeded to secure the number with an easy competence.

"Er, no, I suppose it's the parents'."

She was already dialing. "What's her father's first name, then?"

"I...."

She spoke into the telephone: "Yes please, Stapleton, Hazel Stapleton, it's in Bow."

"It's not actually Bow, it's..." and I was compelled to interject the humiliating words "...it's Mile End."

"Mile End," she repeated into the mouthpiece. Then to me, "Oh, you used to live in... Mile End?" Then, "There's a James Stapleton, that's the only Stapleton they have in Mile End."

"That must be it then."

She dialed and handed me the receiver. A click, then: "Hello, this is the Stapleton house." It was female, but fuller than Hazel's voice.

"Hello."

"Yes, who's speaking?"

"It's Zachary, Katya's brother, is this... Hazel?"

"Zachary! Oh, Zachary, where are you phoning from?"

"I'm, well, I'm in Forest Gate, I'm..." Standing inside Sophy's house, yet speaking to Hazel, made me feel disoriented.

"Are you still in the air-force, Katya told me...."

I sat down. "No, I was demobbed this week."

"Oh, so where are you then? We've got your suitcases, did Katya tell you...?"

"Thank you Hazel, I'm staying in Forest Gate for a while...."

"You're not staying with... what's her name, Katya told me, er, Sophy's family, are you?"

I was sitting in the armchair, with Sophy standing over me. "Well, er, I'll explain when I see you."

"Oh, are you going to...?"

"Hazel, I'm phoning from Sophy's parents' telephone, I wanted to ask if it would be alright to come and pick up my suitcases."

"You mean today? Yes, I'll stay here, I'll be home all day, what time do you think... it doesn't matter, I'll stay home all day."

Sophy sat on the arm.

"Thank you, we'll be leaving in, say, fifteen minutes so we'll be there about dinner time."

"We? Who are you coming with?"

"My friend Garrick from the air-force, his dad has an Austin so I'll be coming in a car, and also my... my friend, Sophy, yes, she's coming also."

"Oh."

"Is that alright?"

"I was hoping you could stay a little while, I've got three letters from Katya. Maybe you can read them another time, then."

"Alright, well...." Sophy had slid down off the arm and squeezed herself into the armchair beside me, and now she leaned her head sideways so it lay against my face. "Hazel, I've got to hang up the telephone now, so... let's see when we get there, if we have enough time."

"Alright."

"Alright, so I'll see you in about an hour or so."

"Alright then."

"Alright."

Sophy took the receiver from my hand, reached across and hung it up. "What was that all about?"

"What do you mean?"

"Is that how you describe me, your friend?"

"No, I... I didn't know what to say."

"I thought we're going together, you could have told her you're going with me."

"You are, we are, I'm sorry I was a bit nervous, I don't talk on the telephone such a lot."

Ten minutes later Sophy and I were following Garrick back to his driveway. She climbed in the back of the car and held the door open for me.

"Where shall I..." I began; I didn't want to offend her, but I also didn't want Garrick feeling as though I were just using him as a chauffeur. Luckily he resolved the dilemma by reaching across and opening the front passenger door for me.

"Can you spare him to sit in front this time? Can't afford too many distractions or I won't know which way to go."

As we drew closer to the East End, and High Street in Stratford became Bow Road, then Mile End Road, the houses and other buildings appeared increasingly dilapidated. We'd driven this same route the previous evening but it had already been dusk and I hadn't worried about the surroundings. But now as the car threaded deeper into the East End I found myself acutely aware of the proliferation of bombed sites, abandoned piles of rubble untouched since V.E. Day. Forest Gate showed no such decay, but here I was being dragged back to the mortification of poverty and neglect.

To get to Hazel's house on Litchfield Road we would need to make a right turn into Tredegar Square, then cross over Morgan Street and ride directly past our old house on the corner — unless, I thought quickly, we turned right one street earlier, on Coburn Road. "Here, yes here, I'm sorry, turn right, I... I should have given you more warning...."

"What happened?" exclaimed Sophy from behind, as Garrick pulled the wheel sharply and the car veered right, toward the center of Mile End Road, barely managing the turn ahead of oncoming traffic.

"I'm sorry, it's my fault...."

We were safely into Coburn Road; this way we'd be able to approach her street from the end, circumventing Morgan Street entirely. We rode slowly along the litter-strewn roadway, Garrick glancing my way for directions.

"A bit further... I'll tell you when we have to turn, it'll be to the left."

I'd thought of Coburn Road as more well-tended than the decrepitude that greeted us. Rusty iron railings enclosing a mound of rubbish next to a lidless dustbin, a garden gate hanging obliquely by one hinge, upstairs windowpanes missing and replaced with patches of taped cardboard — these fortunately too high up for Garrick, behind the wheel to my right, to notice. I glanced back, but Sophy's attention was taken by a swarthy young woman in a torn black overcoat, her hair shrouded in a *schmatta,* pushing a pram with three rubber wheels and the fourth a buckled metal rim that snapped against the frame at each revolution. As we passed rubbish-strewn gardens we approached a street corner to the left where a large shop window, cracked and taped, a display of vegetables behind its dirty façade, slid into view. Suddenly I realized that that window had to be the Coburn Road side of Altman's grocery shop on the corner at the end of Morgan Street; and there it was, the brown splintered double door that never would swing properly, the boxes of old vegetation stacked outside on the street. We were moving very slowly, and Garrick had begun to turn the wheel.

"No, no, no!" Too late, I clutched his arm. "I'm sorry...." I lunged at the wheel's rim and pushed it clockwise, away from me. Startled, he lifted off both hands; the car, already turned, steered itself in a semicircle across the width of Morgan Street toward the old pub on the opposite side. Garrick grabbed the wheel again and looked at me in surprise. "I'm sorry!" I took my head in my hands, "I don't know what I'm doing."

"It's alright Zech, take it easy old bean, we don't want the three of us to end up a bunch of has-beens, b-e-a-n, like in that shop window." He laughed. "You're a bit hepped up, that's all."

"I know, I know...."

"I thought you'd said turn left at the next street...." The car had completed a half-circle in Morgan Street's mouth, and was now back facing Coburn Road.

"I'm sorry, what's the matter with me today, I could have caused...."

"What're you doing, Zech?" Sophy was leaned forward between the front seat backs. "Don't make us have an accident, especially in this neighborhood."

"It's alright, Zech." Again, Garrick spoke with a gentle humor. "We've got time, we'll go slow, you just tell me where to turn."

"Garrick I'm sorry, go left here again the way we were going along Coburn Road, then it's the... *then* it'll be the next left turn into Litchfield Road." Sophy was again sitting back, and I turned to her: "Sophy, I must be a bit...." And as Morgan Street slid away through the rear window I couldn't avoid a glance that absorbed everything: Reuben Berger's house on the left with its defaced wall, Judah Schreiber's and his *stumah* mother's place on the right, Mrs. Harney's door alongside our little crenelated wall around what had been our cellar grating. In the time — was it nine months already? — since Lily and Abie had left, everything seemed to have fallen into unrecognizably squalid and humiliating disrepair. As the car pulled us around the corner and the scene was eclipsed by the corner pub, my relief barely masked a bizzare melancholy.

I looked up; we were continuing down toward where Coburn Road would dip under the railway bridge. "Left, left at the next corner, just before where the street goes under the bridge."

The car slowed further. "You're sure this is where we turn."

"You're sure?" echoed Sophy.

"Yes, yes," And we swung around onto Litchfield Road. "Along there on the left, yes, this side, there it is, the last door there before that first street."

The car rolled to a halt before the corner. "Is this correct, Lord Grossman?"

"Yes, yes." In a jumble of thoughts I realized belatedly that I could have had us avoid Coburn Road altogether by simply turning off of Mile End Road directly onto Tredegar Terrace; the houses there were better kept, we would have ridden alongside Tredegar Square Park, which despite its meager-looking chain link fencing was still clean and pretty with flowers and trees. Then as we crossed Morgan Street I could have simply avoided mentioning number twenty seven. "Okay, I'll check she's here and everything's okay." In a turmoil I jumped out of the car, hopped over the familiar pavement and rang the doorbell, noticing that the Austin's rear side window was aligned with Hazel's street door.

The door opened into darkness. Inside, beyond the mat on the slightly raised concrete step, I didn't immediately recognize Hazel as she stepped partially forward: slightly buck teeth, her gingery-brown hair a hoop of tight curls, tortoise-shell glasses resting on a pallid white nose. She certainly looked more grown-up than a year and a half ago; or maybe it was the dress, a blue halter-top with a matching belt, and yes, matching blue sling heels.

"Hello, Zech, it's nice to see you."

"Hello."

"Seems like such a long time." The voice was still diffident, yet fuller than when Katya and I had stopped by the evening of Marius's funeral.

"Yes, it's nice to see you too." It really was. "I hope it's not an inconvenience…."

"Oh no, do you want to come in or do you just want the… there're two cases of yours, and also one with Marius's things… also I've got three letters from Katya."

"Well, my friends…."

"They could come in… if you like."

"Just a minute." I looked around, and noticed the back window was now rolled down a couple of inches, though inside the car was too dark to resolve shapes.

She continued in a lowered voice, "Maybe don't read them this time though, if your friends come in."

"Why, what's…?"

Garrick opened his door on the far side and his head rose above the car's roof: "Need help schlepping the stuff?"

"No, thanks…."

"Well, she wrote a bit about, well, your girlfriend, maybe it's better you come round by yourself and you can read 'em then."

"We've still got to go to the other place, what is it, Wapping?" Garrick cautioned. "I told Liz we'd be back by two or so."

"Alright!" Then to Hazel, "So I'll just take the cases this time." I turned back toward the car. "Sophy, you want to say hello, I can't see you."

Sophy's forehead appeared as the window lowered itself barely another inch. "Nice to meet you."

"Nice to meet you," responded Hazel to the dark reflective glass, then turned back into the house. "They're in the passage, I carried them up."

"Oh you shouldn't have, I would've...." I followed her into the darkness.

"When do you want to come round then?"

"Em, well I'm starting work on Monday...."

"You mean in Wapping, in that laboratory?"

"Yes, how did you know, I...."

"Here's the bags, these are your two..." In the darkness I grasped a handle. "...Katya used to tell me everything, sorry, a bulb went out, Dad likes to change them himself, you're not going to marry her are you?"

"Marry her, I... I mean I only just... I mean I didn't even start work yet... I didn't think about anything yet."

"Katya said you shouldn't marry her," she whispered, "she says it in the letter, in the three letters, each letter."

"Really?"

A car door slammed and Sophy approached the street door. "Is there a light, it's dark." Her backlit figure peered into the blackness of the passage, the length of her legs fully visible through what seemed like a transparent skirt.

"Sophy I'm coming, the bulb went, I just... Hazel, I'll take this one out first, I'll come back."

I walked toward the light, and Sophy backed to the side as I lugged the suitcase out the doorway. Garrick, standing by the opened lid of the boot, helped me hoist up the case and lay it flat.

"There are two more, three altogether."

Sophy stepped aside again to let me back inside. "I'll help," she said.

"No, it's okay, I can do it."

Inside the passage, Hazel whispered: "So when do you want to read the letters?"

"I... er... soon... I don't know yet."

"You want to come this week?

"I... don't know...."

She helped me find the handle. "Also you can see our new Knight."

"Night? What do you...."

"Piano."

"Piano! You got a piano?"

"Yes, an Alfred Knight, it's new."

"Really, wow! Oh, I'd love to see it, let me think, I'll be staying in a room I rented in Wapping, I've just got to sort out a few things."

Sophy's head was leaned into the passage: "What you both whispering about?"

"Oh, nothing...."

Hazel was barely audible: "Then come over one evening."

"I'm staying in the room Monday night...."

"Then come over Monday evening, don't eat first, come straight from work."

"Yes? Should I...?" I mumbled under my breath.

"I'll be waiting for you, Monday evening."

Sophy had begun groping her way into the passage. "Zech, I'll help with the suitcases. How many are there now?"

"Sophy, it's alright, I'll be a couple of minutes, I'm just talking to Hazel for one minute, they got a new piano, I haven't seen her for a year."

"You can talk to her outside in the light."

"Jes-*us!* I'm coming." I started back toward the outside; Hazel remained within the dark recess of the far end of the passage. Outside, I carried the suitcase across the pavement, Sophy steadying it as I lugged it toward the boot.

"Here's Marius's things next," called Hazel from the darkness. I returned, and as I grasped the third case she whispered: "Monday. Don't eat."

The three bags barely fit. Garrick pushed the lid closed and began climbing into the car: "So long, Zachary's sister Katya's friend Hazel," he called. A disembodied hand waved back from within the doorway.

As I went ahead of Sophy to open the door on the pavement side for her to get back in the car, she whispered: "I want a kiss."

"What?"

She used my upper chest to block her face from the street door's view, and with barely moving lips she squeezed out, "I want you to kiss me."

Hazel wasn't visible in the passageway, but the street door was still open. "What for? Later, when we...." I opened the rear car door for her to get in

"Now, I want you to kiss me," she hissed, and took my arm. "Put your arm round me and kiss me."

"I feel embarrassed."

Garrick, over in the driver's seat, had turned at the delay.

I gave her a quick kiss but she wouldn't relinquish my arm, and through taut lips said: "Zachary, kiss me properly, slowly... now."

Imagining the hot stare of Hazel behind me, coupled with the embarrassment of Garrick discreetly looking away again, I put one arm around her and kissed her. Her other arm locked around my neck. "I want you to sit in the back with me," she said, pulling her lips away just enough to release the words.

Garrick started the engine. "Come on, meshuggeners."

I sat in the back.

"Which way?"

"Turn left." We turned onto Tredegar Terrace, and I realized I was covered with perspiration. As we rode directly past our old street door I couldn't resist looking. They had painted it a shiny dark brown, the gloss serving only to accentuate the familiar cracks in the wood. To the side, a chalked wicket had been drawn on the wall; the local kids must be annoying the new occupants with their games, just as they always had us. "Straight, keep going straight."

We crossed Morgan Street and I again looked back, at the big living room windows downstairs, and the upstairs ones where *Bobbeh* died, the frames now also painted the same brown. The only fresh-looking thing was the turreted wall in front where we used to sit and talk about aeroplanes and trajectories, quantum mechanics and relativity.

"What are you looking at?" Sophy pulled at me.

"I used to live there."

"Where?"

I didn't care! "There."

Garrick slowed. "That's where you lived? Why didn't you say, we can take a few minutes for that, you want to ring the bell, see if anyone's home?"

Bell! We never could afford a bell! "No, it's alright, it's not important…. Go straight, up to the main road there, Mile End Road, then turn right."

Sophy was still looking back. "That's where you used to live, the end one with the wall?"

"The little turreted wall? Yes, that's the one."

"Turreted? What's turreted? No, I mean that side wall, it's sort of curved outward, it looks like it's going to give way."

"That's exactly where I used to live. Sometimes when the bombs were close I thought the wall might crumble outward and the whole house collapse, but it never did."

"Everything's so… run down."

"Yes, it is. I had some wonderful friends here."

"This park looks nice, look at the flowers!" said Garrick.

"Yes, that's called Tredegar Square, we used to sleep down a shelter there during the flying bombs and things. It used to have high iron gates, it was all very pretty at one time."

A silence descended as we followed the bus route to Wapping, to park outside the house where I'd rented the room. Garrick jumped out to open the boot. "I'll help you in with them."

Sophy was standing next to us. "Which one is your brother's things?"

"The top one."

"Leave it in the boot, we can store it in my house, it'll be safe there."

Garrick looked at me as I thought for a moment; she was probably right, my room would be tight on space. "Alright."

Garrick hesitated. "Should I help you with the other ones?"

"Sure, thank you." He slid Marius's case to the side, handed me the top bag then lifted the other out to carry himself. Sophy watched as he centered Marius's case in the boot and closed the lid. She remained standing by the car as I rang the doorbell.

Mrs. Stokes opened the door. "Oh 'ello, got your stuff, 'ave you!"

"Yes, can my friend help me carry it down?"

"Don't see why not, dearie."

Sophy spoke up from the roadway: "I'll come in also," and started towards us.

"The car's unlocked. You stay with the car, Sophy," said Garrick. His voice carried authority; she hesitated, then turned and climbed in the back seat. Mrs. Stokes stepped aside as Garrick followed me through and down the stairs carrying the second case.

It was dark, despite the little windows at the top of the wall. I switched on the light, and a small-wattage bulb in the center of the low ceiling glowed reluctantly. "It's pretty gloomy-looking, I'll get a brighter bulb."

"It's a walk to your work from here?"

"Yes."

"Then if it's close to work and you're earning the rent, it'll do the job while you decide things."

"Yes…." I slid the case I carried under the bed. "Garrick, I'm feeling a bit overwhelmed with everything."

"You mean with Sophy, like how did I guess!"

"Suffocated, almost. She watches everything I do."

"Well, old bean, you're champion at handling the Golightleys of this world, and I'm good at other things like seeing the future. Take my word, renting this room may turn out to be, if you'll pardon the religious connotation, turn out to be a godsend."

—o—O—o—

51

Monday morning, Garrick threw together a quick breakfast. At Sophy's insistence the night before, I stopped by her house for a moment before catching the bus to Wapping.

"Don't forget to ring me up tonight, I'll be home after six," she said.

Rush-hour traffic made the two-bus trip slower than I'd anticipated, and it was ten-after-nine when I opened the laboratory door.

Dr. Nicolas was already setting up the distillation. "You're late."

"I'm sorry, the bus...."

"Run outside and collect the samples from top and middle valves number one tank right away, so we can get this distillation moving. You can explain later."

I went out into the yard with the bottles.

"Watcha, matey." It was Mr. Smith.

"Hello, my first morning back and I get here late."

"Did they tell you what 'appened, did Nicolas tell you?"

"Tell me? What?"

"Mr. Bitwood, Friday evening it was, same day you was 'ere, riding 'is bike 'ome from work."

"What, what happened?"

"Bus, knocked 'im right orf it did. Wheel got caught in the tram lines they said, 'e couldn't get out the way."

"So what happened, is he alright?"

"'Fraid not, matey, back wheel went right over 'im."

"Ugh, how terrible!"

"Killed 'im right out, didn't 'ave no chance, poor bugger. They got a new feller up there already, showing 'im the ropes. Don't waste no time, this Richardson."

"The new owner."

"That's 'im. Bitwood worked up there nigh on thirty years, Margolin would'a taken a day at least, show some respect."

"Yes. Oh, I can't believe it!"

"Everything's 'urry up, quick quick quick, these days."

"Mr. Bitwood! I can't believe it."

•   •   •

After the day's work I rang Mrs. Stokes's doorbell. As I followed her inside she handed me a key. "'Ere's your key dearie, so's you can come as you please." At the top of the stairs, she added: "You 'eard about that poor Mr. Bitwood, I s'pose."

"Yes, they told me where I work."

"Friday, killed 'im right out, the whole street was talking. Good sort 'e was, never 'urt a fly 'e wouldn't, always 'ad time for a 'good morning'."

"I know, he was always nice to me at work...."

"It's always the good uns as 'as to go. Don't pay to question, do it dearie?"

"No...."

I ran downstairs, rinsed my face and changed my shirt.

Thirty minutes later I was at Hazel's street door. It opened, and there stood a nice baggy cardigan, the same frizzy hair and tortoiseshell glasses framing a bucktoothed and welcoming grin. "I was wondering if you'd come."

The passage light had been fixed. "You said Monday evening...." I followed her along the passageway. "Didn't you, didn't we?"

She smiled back at me. "Yes, but because of your friends, I just wondered if...."

We passed the living room doorway, and Mrs. Stapleton put her head out. "Hello, Zachary, welcome back from your adventures!"

"Thank you!"

As she eased the door closed I caught a glimpse of a tall polished mahogany piano against the wall, its gleaming ivory keys a tantalizing smile against the resplendent red-hued wood. I followed Hazel into the kitchen, and noticed that her tush undulated as she walked. She really was a woman now; hers had been the first boob I'd touched, the only one beside Sophy's.

"You want me to take your jacket?"

"Okay." She averted her eyes as she took my coat, and I wondered if she was also thinking about that evening. I shook my thoughts clear and looked around their kitchen. A tidy row of wooden cabinets ran above a countertop inset with a sparkling white enamel sink. In the center of the room a crisp red and white checkered tablecloth, its corners almost draping to the floor, covered a medium round table. Surrounding chairs, four of them, had flowered cushions on the seats and backs, more homey than either Sophy's or Garrick's formal straight-backed monsters. A single window looked out through frilly bunched white curtains, presumably to their garden.

"You can sit if you like."

I was still stiff from working. "I've been sitting on the bus, let me stretch a bit."

"Was this your first day back at work?" She filled a kettle and put it on the stove; when she turned the knob, with a *pop* the gas ignited itself without a match.

"Wow! That was neat!"

"We got a new stove."

"Wow, even Sophy's and Garrick's don't do that, I don't think."

"Your blue-blooded friends," she joked in Katherine's fake haughty tone. I'd never seen her so outgoing.

"Well they kind of have nice things, I s'pose. Yes, today was my first day."

"How was it, going back to an old job?"

"To tell the truth it was difficult. I used to work there before I was drafted..."

"I know."

"I was sort of in charge and they left me alone."

"Katya used to tell me how much you liked it."

"Yes, well most of the people I used to know there are gone, and now this one man I knew from the office upstairs, he helped me rent the room I got, he got knocked off his bike when he was going home, just this Friday, that same evening, he got killed."

"How horrible!"

"I knew him for a long time, he was very nice always."

"I'm sorry."

"Also, the person I'm working under all day now, he's new, a chemist, he's kind of snotty. He makes remarks about my never having gone to a college. Phew!"

"Why don't you sit down and rest while I get everything ready."

"Are we all going to have supper, your parents?"

"No, they ate, they won't bother us."

"Then can I go out and get something for us, fish and chips or something?"

"I already picked up fish and chips on the way home. It's in the oven right now, to keep warm."

"Wow, let me pay for it...."

"Oh come on, you don't have to pay!"

"I got demobilization money."

"No, sit, do you want to see Katya's letters?"

"Oh yes." She handed me a group of envelopes from a cabinet by the window. It was almost perverse to see Katherine's handwriting juxtaposed alongside foreign airmail stamps. I sat down and opened the first one. *Dear Hazel, I did it, we did it! You have to come here! I was sick on the boat, all over somebody's lap at the table, but he said he didn't mind. It's wonderful here; in just two weeks of work Zilla made enough money to buy an old car that runs, if you don't mind breathing in thick black smoke. Can you imagine that in England! Hazel, you must come here even if you have to bring the milkman and his favourite cow....*

Hazel was setting out plates and cups. I opened the next bulging package; the multiple pages had barely allowed the envelope to close. A photograph fell out onto the table.

"Wow, a picture!" My family was lined up in a grassy area by a bench — Lily and Abie, Katherine, a man, Zilla, Rebecca and another man. On the back was written: "Bear Mountain."

"Yes." Hazel came over. "That one," she pointed to the man between Zilla and Katherine, "he's Hellmuth, the one at the end is Berel. Sounds like the U.N.O."

I read on: *...And make sure Zech reads this part, I went with Zilla and her sort-of boyfriend Hellmuth, he's the one between her and me (everybody's foreign here) we went to a place called Leonetti's in Manhattan where they have a talent contest every week, people get up on the stage and sing. Zech sings better than all of them. When they've finished, the manager holds his hand up behind their head one at a time and the audience claps, and the one who gets the most applause wins a prize. Zech would absolutely love it here, so tell him he has to come here right away, we've nearly got enough for his ticket already. If he says No, punch him in his nose, tell him you have my permission....* Then the third envelope: *...VERY IMPORTANT, show this to Zech, I found a music school, it's called Hartnett National Music Studios on 8th Avenue (the streets really have numbers, also the ones they call avenues don't have trees). Anyway, they teach popular music there, and you have to tell him to read this next part <u>at least three times:</u> the one who plays piano with Axel Stordahl on Frank Sinatra records, his name is Graham Forbes, Zech knows about him, well, he comes to Hartnett and accompanies the vocal pupils when they sing! So I waited after the class ended and I actually ended up having coffee with him! He knows Frank Sinatra, and I told him about Zech and he said, quote: 'tell him to get his rear end over to America right away!' That's considered polite conversation over here....*

The kettle was steaming, and Hazel brought it over from the stove to fill the teapot. "So did you get to the part about your idol?"

"Frank Sinatra's pianist, I know, I love the way he plays, and he actually said I should come to America!"

"Hot!" She whistled, as with a dishcloth she lowered the hot pan onto a pad on the table. "Help yourself." Next came brussels sprouts. "I know you love brussels." Before sitting down she topped off the center of the table with a small dish of half-sour pickles.

"Hazel, this is really nice." Her face reddened. "I really appreciate it, the last few days have been such a mixup for me."

She picked up a chip and deliberately stuck it in the gap between her teeth so it wagged as she spoke. "Any friend of Katya's...."

"That thing about the milkman in Katya's letter...."

She swallowed the chip. "That was months ago, it was nothing really, it's all finished."

"Oh."

She ate some fish. "I'd go to America also, I think."

"You would?"

"Maybe I caught it from Katya, helping her to get ready, it sounds terrific."

"Would your parents let you go, I mean, do you have any relatives or anyone there?"

"Katya's there, your whole family's there, I wouldn't be by myself."

"Yes, you're right."

"I don't think my parents would really want me to go, though."

"It's understandable."

"Katya would love me to come."

"Oh, I know she would, you've always been her best friend, that's what she's always said."

"Do you want to finish the fish and chips? I'll make some more tea."

"Thank you."

She spoke with her back to me, from the stove. "That milkman, I just went with him for a few weeks, that was last year."

"Was he nice?"

"I dunno, I found out he was married."

"You mean, he didn't tell you?"

"No, I found out from where he works."

"They told you?"

"Well I went there, the dairy, on my way to work, he usually got through by the time I was going to work, he worked very early. They told me in the office his wife comes around sometimes to check up."

"Really? Wow!"

"You can't always tell with people, I suppose. The first time he took me to the pictures my parents said they thought he was married."

"Did you ask him?"

"The next time I did, he just laughed. It was hard to tell, I felt silly."

"My Mum said if he says he doesn't have a telephone, that means he's married."

Around half past ten, her mother called through the door, "Hazel, don't stay up too late, you've got work in the morning."

"Alright, Mum."

"I don't want to miss the last bus." I stood up and took my jacket off the chair.

"You want to come another night?"

"Yes, okay, I can't wait to try the piano."

"How about tomorrow?"

"Tomorrow? I don't know, I'd better not come too much."

"Wednesday, then."

"Christ, I forgot to ring up Sophy tonight, she asked me and I totally forgot."

"You want to ring her from here, now? I won't listen."

"I don't care, no it's too late now."

"You want to come on Wednesday then? My parents will be out, you can play the piano." She scribbled on a piece of paper. "Here's our telephone number."

I walked to Burdett Road and caught the bus. Forty-five minutes later I was creeping down the stairs to my basement room. All was silent in the Stokes's household, my first night sleeping here. I reached around the door for the switch, and a feeble glow crept out to the corners of the dark walls. On the little bed lay a penciled note: *A woman rung up on our telephone at eight o'clock tonight. I said you wasn't home. Using our telephone is not in the rent, so please ask your friends not to ring you up on our telephone.*

52

Wednesday after work on my way to Hazel's, I picked up fish and chips at Johnny Isaacs, then hopped off the trollybus across the road from Mile End station. An Underground train must have just departed and a young man, the first of a swarm of passengers, came bounding up the steps; a second look — and it was my favorite scientist-philosopher. "Jack!"

He turned and jumped in the air: "Zech!" Although Mile End Road was crowded with vehicles at rush hour, we each ran out into the roadway, dodging cars and leaping over cyclists to the accompaniment of hooters, bicycle bells and less benign exclamations. In the center of the busy road we embraced.

"Jack, old bean, wonderful to see you, how are you?"

"I thought by now you'd be wearing an Air Marshal's uniform, at least."

"They offered me the job but I declined — gracefully, of course."

"Of course, previous commitments and all that."

Arms raised to deflect traffic, we threaded our way through to the safety of the pavement.

"So, what are you doing in Mile End," he asked.

"I'm going to have supper with — maybe you remember her — Hazel? She was Katya's friend."

"Certainly I remember her. What do you mean, *was* Katya's friend?"

"Katya's in America now, about a month."

"America!"

"Yes, let me ring up Hazel a minute." I slipped into one of the telephone kiosks outside the station and dialed. "Hazel, I just bumped into Jack, you remember him? I'll be a bit late, but I'll be there."

"You can bring him with if you like."

"Oh, thanks, I'll ask him. Jack, you want to come to Hazel's for supper?"

I held out the phone to his mouth: "Hello Hazel, it's nice of you to invite me, I can't, I've got studying to do."

I got back on. "He can't, so I'll be right there after I've said hello for ten minutes."

"Alright, I'll put the brussels on, don't be long."

"See you soon." I hung up the receiver and exited the kiosk. We began walking. "So you're still in school."

"Second year, two and a bit to go."

"Do you like it?"

"Architecture, I love it! I think you'd like it, the way it all evolves, the way the engineering changes when they discover new materials, I love it all!"

"It's wonderful you're doing something you like so much."

"It's sculpture, it'll be like getting paid to be in the arts."

"Sounds great...."

"Not to mention a very intelligent young lady in... well, she's in two of my classes."

"Oh, a girl in architectural... well, why not, that makes it even nicer!"

"We mustn't be dinosaurs, there are half a dozen female pupils. Binnie, Binnie Rudman, she's from the City, she's brilliant. Which is probably why she finds me so attractive."

"Naturally!"

"So, what's happening with you, old fellow, I assume they let you out. And Katya, they went to America! That's all your family there now, isn't it?"

"She went alone, the one she married used to hit her and stuff. You remember him, we met him at Brady Boys Club that time. She left him here and went, a month ago."

"Really! Your sister always was independent minded."

"That's Katya, alright."

"So you, you're demobbed I assume."

"Yes, just last week, I'm back in the laboratory already. I'm not sure what I'll do, whether I'll stay there."

"Is something cooking with Hazel, besides dinner?"

"Oh no, nothing, I kind of met a girl, another one, Sophy, through a friend in the RAF. From Forest Gate."

"Are you going with her?"

"Er..." I thought about it. "Well... I suppose so. Yes. I'm not sure."

"Hmm...."

"It's a bit complicated."

"Everything to do with women is complicated." We paused; here, our paths diverged. "So, do you have a telephone where I can reach you?"

"No, I just... not yet." Everyone had telephones!

"Then you'll have to spend the tuppence." He wrote down his number. "I'll introduce you to Binnie — after you're safely married to your Forest Gate lady."

"I'll ring you as soon as I'm settled in."

At Hazel's I pressed the bell and brought the fish and chips into the kitchen. She poured tea and we apportioned the goodies. "You're looking more like a real civilian," she said.

"I'm out of one war but there's no shortage of others."

She ate. "What do you mean?"

"Oh, things, Sophy, the job. Where are your parents tonight?"

"Up West, they went to a concert."

"You mean a music concert? Oh, they like concerts? What is it?"

"My Dad does, it's an all-Stravinsky."

"Stravinsky? I don't know much about classical music, I've just heard a bit of Tchaikovsky and loads of Beethoven and Mozart."

"Stravinsky's still living so he's not really classical."

"Oh, I don't know about those sort of classifications...."

"Have some more tea, the fish is delicious. What you mean is...."

"I mean I heard Stan Kenton records in the air force, they seemed so wild and imaginative, I really liked it. Also I like Mel Tormé, Dick Haymes, people like that."

"I don't... know those two."

"They sing but they're like natural musicians, a kind of complete understanding between them and the instrumentalists, they all seem to know exactly what the other ones mean."

"My Dad likes the high-brow stuff, Schubert, things like that."

"I heard a man on the wireless singing Schubert. That stuff's completely foreign to me, sort of trying to control the vibrato, straining for the notes, so cultured the words could hardly get out of his throat. I felt like reporting it to the Royal Society for the Prevention of Cruelty to Music."

"Maybe don't mention that when my Dad's here. By the way, he said Stan Kenton borrows from Stravinsky."

"Borrows? What do you mean?"

"When we're finished we can listen to a Stravinsky record if you like."

"Alright, I'll chance a little bit. How come your father knows about Stan Kenton?"

"Didn't Katya tell you, he writes music reviews."

"Really, he does?"

"Yes, for *The Evening Standard.*"

"No, I didn't know!"

"Yes, also for some classical music record magazine."

"So that's what he does, how interesting!"

"But they only pay him with free tickets and a few shillings, so he has to work in an office as well."

"Now I'll feel intimidated if he knows so many official-type things about music."

"Intimidated, why?"

"I don't know very much."

"He doesn't know that much about popular music, so you'd be even."

"One time someone was playing an opera record in the NAAFI, and a woman was singing, they said it was Puccini. I don't know if singing is the right word, she was shrieking like a lunatic."

"Dad does love Puccini operas."

"This one's vibrato was so wide you couldn't tell what note she was trying to sing. I thought if those noises hadn't been sanctioned by the upper-crust cultural elite, she'd be in an insane asylum."

"Opera's different from popular music, they train differently."

"This one was singing about killing herself. Personally I'd have recommended she did it before the opera started."

"Maybe don't discuss opera with my Dad either."

"I'll be discreet. Anyway, she could have gotten her vibrato copyrighted."

"I'm not... sure...."

"Just my corny sense of humor."

"Come on, eat up, don't forget we've got the piano to try out."

"Records, fish and chips with brussels, a new piano, and bumping into Jack! It's too many things for just one evening."

"Let's eat fast."

"Okay. Any more letters from Katya?"

"Since Monday? No. I forgot, was everything alright when you rang Sophy up?"

"Christ, well, I rang her up last night, yes, she didn't like my coming here for dinner, she was going on a bit."

"Did you tell her Katya's been my best friend since even before the war?"

"Yes, but she's a bit... I don't know. She doesn't want me to come here."

"She's jealous."

"On Monday night while I was here she rang my landlady up, she found out the number from the operator."

"She did really?"

"The landlady left me a note I should tell people not to ring up their number anymore."

"More tea? You ready to try out the piano?"

"Piano. Anyway, I just didn't mention I was coming here tonight."

"Leave everything, I'll clear up."

In the living room I lifted the fallboard and tried out a few notes, then sat on the bench and doodled, picking out a few lines until Hazel came in. "It's lovely, it's out of tune a bit."

She was kneeling on the floor by the bottom shelf of records. "They told us that's because it's new, the wires have to stretch or something."

I started to pick out a bit of *Laura,* along with the chords which came logically by ear, ones the harmony book had described as II-, V- and I-chord sequences. "I hope I can get a piano one day."

"You can always come round and play ours if you like."

"Oh, I'd love to."

"Sing," she said. "I love it when you sing."

"Really?" I wanted to sing but felt too shy, alone with one person — only Gordon MacRae did things like that.

"Yes, when you sang at your house that time, that's what you should do when you get to America."

"Maybe... maybe next time I come round...."

"Aha, here it is." She pulled out a record. "So, are you girded for Stravinsky?"

"Alright."

She opened the gramophone lid. "It's called *Firebird,* it's a suite."

"I don't know what all that stuff means."

The loudspeaker crackled as the needle touched down, and moments later the basses began a low bowing and scratching. The sheen of deep brass — trombones? — entered, strange clusters of tones, and it was clear this was not classical music metered in the sense of predictable chords plodding by — certainly not Schubert! Hazel hovered over the instrument, poised to interrupt the record if I asked her. But then a scattering of agitated tones began pulling up higher into a more audible mid-range, and I thought of Seurat's dotted people on the grass in the art book I'd kept from the library when I was drafted. Hazel, watching for my reaction, apparently decided the piece was acceptable because she gently closed the lid and sat on the couch. Clarinets, a harp entered the fray — the harp playing separate notes, not Tchaikovsky arpeggios. Then suddenly, strings in profusion, violins sliding up and down in a strange blur of harmonics. I was overwhelmed: "Wow, I never heard anything like this before!"

"Maybe you haven't been listening to the right stuff."

The individual pitches and timbres became more transparent until the entire living room was shimmering. I grasped the edge of the bench. "Wow... wow! Wow, I have to speak to your father, I mean, I mean...."

"Come, sit on the sofa."

I made my groggy way over and grasped the arm. "...My god, it's incredible — it's... it's... not like classical music at all! I mean... shh, we'll... we'll talk afterwards."

She was half standing now, her hand on my sleeve to steady me, "Sit." She guided me down. The notes were more audacious than Stan Kenton's! A ringing bell; I couldn't tell if it were coming from the loudspeaker.

"I'll have to turn it off for a minute." She stood again, clicked the gramophone lever; dead silence, pierced again by the bell, deafening. It was the telephone. "Hello, Stapleton house." A pause as she listened. "Er, why... who is this, who wants him?" A further pause, "Hold on a minute," then she covered the mouthpiece and whispered: "I don't know whether to say you're here, he said it's Garrick."

"Garrick! What's he... how did he...?"

"What should I tell him?"

"Give me the phone, I'll speak to him." She handed me the receiver. "Garrick, is this Garrick?"

"Yes it is. I'm glad I found you."

"Is anything the matter?"

"I hope not, but Uri and the old boy were over here half an hour ago talking to Pop. They wanted to know if you were here, then when we said no, they wanted to borrow the Austin right away."

"Really!"

"They both sounded... shall we say, excited."

"They were, they did?"

"I had a feeling something was up so I gave Pop a signal, and old reliable said the car had a puncture, it couldn't be driven 'til we got it fixed."

"Alright, er...."

"So the old weasel said in that case they'd run over to Moishe's and use his lorry, and they both rushed out. I've never seen Uri like that."

"Hmm."

"We just got a feeling maybe they're after you for something."

"Really? But I mean...."

"I got the number and rang up where your room is in Wapping."

"Oh, they don't want anybody ringing them up!"

"I found out! A man said, 'stop bladdy-well ringing us up, that's the second time in half an hour!'"

"The second time, I don't understand...."

"Neither do we, this happened about twenty minutes ago, and Liz and I have been sitting here wondering. Supposing Fannie was the one who rang them up earlier — for her daughter, to check up on where you were."

"Good god!"

"That's what we thought. Also, maybe the Bliss females dispatched their male warriors to your friend Hazel's house."

"Jesus christ!"

"They wouldn't necessarily bring Jesus with them, but that's always a possibility."

"Wow! Well, thanks, I'll.... How would they know Hazel's address?"

"Sophy came with when we got your bags, she knows their surname, she knows it's Mile End, they could've asked the operator for the number then asked for the exact address, pretend they're checking it's the right house."

"I s'pose you're right!"

"So, old buddy, a word to the wise."

"Thanks Garrick, wow, thanks for…."

"You better get ready. If the lads do show up, you'll just have to deliver your famous one-two knockout à la Golightley. Let me know what happens." A click and he was gone.

"Hazel, I think Sophy's father and brother may be coming here."

"What for?"

"I don't know, Garrick thinks they're on the warpath. Maybe they found out I came here and they're wild, I don't know, maybe Sophy guessed."

"So what do you want to do?"

"Perhaps I should go, I don't want to involve you in any commotion."

As I completed the sentence, from outside we heard a rattling, then squeaking brakes, and a motor engine which ran for a moment then cut off. Hazel rushed over to the door and switched off the light. Through the curtains we could see a lorry by the curb, its little lights on.

"Christ, I don't even have time to leave!"

"Go upstairs, go on, quick, go in the front bedroom, on the left, you remember, that's my one."

As I hesitated a vehicle door slammed, followed by a bang on the street door. "I can't leave you to face them," I whispered.

"I'll say you're not here, come on, upstairs, quick!"

I grabbed my jacket, ran up the stairs and heard Hazel open the street door. It was Uri's voice: "We want to see Zachary Grossman."

"Zachary Grossman?"

"That's right."

"He's not here."

"Dad," Uri called back to the lorry, "she says he's not here."

"I'm sure he's here, he was here on Monday." My heart plummeted as I recognized Sophy's voice.

I opened the bedroom door and crept into the room. I could just make out the shape of the bed, and beyond it the window. I pulled the door to, edged around the bed and moved the curtain aside. Another man's voice was talking by the street door; I leaned forward to see down and bumped my head on a basket that hung from the ceiling. But even with my forehead pressed against the glass the angle was still too steep, so I gingerly raised the window.

"We know he's here, tell him to come out." That hard unforgiving tone was Mr. Bliss.

"He's not here, I've already told you he's not here."

I eased the window open further to look down and see closer to the door, how many people were there.

"You're lying!" That was Mrs. Bliss! "We know he's here."

The basket swung back, grazing me lightly on the back of the head. Raising my hand to steady it I accidentally knocked it sideways; it spun, tipped, and the plant together with its clay pot fell out of the basket. I tried to catch it but it bounced down onto the window-ledge with a loud thump. Again I grabbed at it, but the whole thing slipped out of my hands — and then, right out of the window. Aghast, I froze as it smashed to smithereens on the pavement below.

A scream, followed by Uri's voice: "What was that, who's doing that?"

"What's this," shouted Mr. Bliss. "Now you've damn well gone too far!"

I backed away from the open window; if I'd injured someone it would be serious. Suddenly, another voice, a man's, a different voice: "What's going on here, Hazel?"

"Oh, Dad, Mum, they came banging on the door, they want Zachary, I told them he isn't here."

Mr. Stapleton's voice again: "I thought you were going to have supper with him at home here, you said…."

"See, I told you she's a liar!" That sounded like Mrs. Bliss again.

Uri: "Someone threw some big thing out the window at us."

"Hazel, what exactly is going on here?"

"Jim, don't get excited. My husband he has a heart condition, I can't let you get him upset like this. Please, everyone be quiet. Now, Hazel, what happened exactly?"

"Mum, Zachary was going to come for supper but he rang me up, he met his friend from before the war…" she caught her breath "…so we arranged he should come another time, another evening."

"I don't want him coming here for supper…" Sophy began, but Mrs. Bliss took over: "I won't have anyone going with my daughter spending evenings having supper with someone else, it's not right."

"Well I've known him longer than you have…."

"Hazel, stop it now!" It was Mr. Stapleton again. "Answer me one question: Is Zachary in our house or is he not in our house?"

A pause: "He's… not in our house."

"Then I'll ask all you people to leave immediately."

"Somebody threw a big plant pot or something," said Mr. Bliss. "Nobody's getting away with that one, I'll have somebody in court I will."

"Hazel, where did all this mess come from?"

"Jim, don't get upset, you know you mustn't get upset."

"Hazel said no one's in the house." It was Mr. Stapleton's voice. "I didn't bring my daughter up to tell lies. So Hazel, how did these broken pieces get on the pavement?"

"Jim, Jim please don't get excited!" Mrs. Stapleton sounded ready to cry. "My husband has a heart condition, I'm giving you all fair warning if anything happens to my husband every one of you'll end up in prison."

"I don't know how it happened, Dad, I was just telling them he isn't here and suddenly *bang!* something landed on the pavement. I don't know where it came from."

Mr. Bliss spoke: "What friend did he say he was seeing?"

"I don't know… I don't remember…."

Mrs. Stapleton interjected: "Was it Jack? They had a friend Jack didn't they?"

"Er, yes, maybe it was Jack."

Mr. Bliss drilled on: "Jack who, what's his second name?"

"I don't know his second name…."

Mr. Stapleton: "And don't you address my daughter in that tone of voice!"

"Jim, Jim, quiet, go inside, please, I'll handle everything."

"I'm going inside alright, I'm going inside to ring the police!"

Footsteps in the passageway, another light came on downstairs, then the whirr of a telephone dial.

From outside: "Where does this Jack live? What's his second name?"

"I already said I don't know his second name, I've never been to his house. It's somewhere in Mile End, I don't know the street."

Mrs. Bliss spoke, "You're lying, she's lying, she knows."

"Hazel!" Now it was Mrs. Stapleton. "Hazel come inside, these people are too rude. If your father didn't already, I'm calling the police myself. Who knows, they probably brought something and threw it on the pavement themselves." Footsteps, then the street door banged shut.

Again, I heard Mr. Stapleton's voice: "Yes, would you please send a police car right away... yes, a disturbance... a group of people outside, they came in a lorry. Yes, it's Litchfield Road in Mile End...."

Out the window an engine started and Mr. Bliss was shouting: "Come on, everybody get in." A lorry door slammed. "We'll handle it another way, I'll catch the barstard alright, you'll see, Fannie. I warned you from the beginning, didn't I."

Through the curtain I saw Uri jump up onto the back, and the vehicle lunged off into the night, thick smoke from its exhaust causing the red light to flicker as it roared off around the corner into Tredegar Terrace. There were footsteps on the stairs; in the darkness I quickly eased the window down, fell to the floor and rolled under the bed.

The doorknob turned, and whoever it was waited a few moments before pushing the door open to enter; that caution suggested it was Hazel. The light went on. Whew! Sling-heel flats, but it could be Mrs. Stapleton! Lying on my back amid the dust and fluff I moved my head a trifle to the side. A flowered skirt, it *was* Hazel. "Hazel!" I whispered.

The door closed quietly. "Where are you?" she whispered back.

"Under the bed."

"Oh!" She kneeled. "They're gone, my parents are home."

"I know."

"I told them you're not here."

"I know, I heard everything through the window. Will I be able to get out of the house?"

"Stay there for now. Can you stay under the bed?"

"Yes."

She went around and fully closed the window, then kneeled again on the other side of the bed. "What happened with my plant?"

"It was an accident, I'm sorry."

"I had a terrible fright, it could have messed everything up."

"I know, I assume it didn't hurt anybody. Shh..." Someone else was coming up the stairs. She stood up as the door opened. Brown women's shoes: Mrs. Stapleton.

"Young lady, I'm telling you not to have Zachary here again."

"Why not? He didn't do anything."

"Because I said so, that's why not. We're not having your father upset like that anymore. That whole family spells trouble!"

"They didn't do anything, they're all gone to America anyway, Zech is the only one here still."

"I'm sorry young lady, I'm laying down the law, I don't want Zachary in my house again, is that clear?"

"Yes, but he didn't do anything."

"I'm not asking you whether he did or he didn't."

"Well he didn't."

"It's always the same with that family, this is nothing new. Katya came to see you and then her husband calls your father a liar and is ready to punch him. You want him to end up in hospital?"

"No."

"Mr. Grossman chasing them along the street screaming obscenities all hours of the night! Civilized people don't behave that way."

"Well that was their dad, it wasn't their fault...."

"You think so, miss know-it-all? Did you know the older daughters were entertaining American servicemen? You may be eighteen but there's still a lot you have to learn." Downstairs the doorbell rang. "I'll get the door, I want your father to rest." She ran downstairs, but already Mr. Stapleton was opening the door.

"Mr. Stapleton, sir?"

"Yes, officer, they've left, but thank you for getting here so promptly."

"Sir, were you able to get the license number?"

"I... I didn't think of it, everything happened so quickly. Just a minute. Emma, did you happen to notice the license number?"

"No, I'll ask Hazel." Mrs. Stapleton called up from the bottom of the stairs: "Hazel come downstairs, the policeman's here."

"Stay under the bed," Hazel whispered as she switched off the light. She ran out of the room and pulled the door to. "Coming!"

"She was at home when they arrived, they were threatening her when my wife and I got home."

"Young lady, did you happen to notice the license number on the lorry?"

"No sir."

"That's unfortunate, miss. If you were able to remember that number it would be a great help in apprehending them."

"I'm sorry, I didn't think, I didn't see it."

"Do you have any idea who they might have been?"

"No, not really, well...."

"...Well, what?" the policeman coaxed.

"Well... er...."

"Hazel!" Mr. Stapleton sounded abrupt. "Is there something you haven't told us? You know I shall be very angry if...."

"No, just that they were asking for Zachary, maybe they...."

"Zachary, miss? Who's Zachary?"

"Zachary Grossman, he was supposed to come here this evening."

"Officer, why don't we all go inside," said Mr. Stapleton. "We can answer your questions more comfortably inside." Heavy footsteps in the passageway, and the street door closed.

"Hazel, why did you leave the piano lid open? It gets dust on the keys, you know your father likes it closed if you're not using it."

"I... I... I just tried a few notes, I was going to close it."

"Do you play the piano, miss?"

"I... a little bit, I just tried a few notes."

"And, who is this... this Zachary Grossman? Perhaps he can lead us to the culprits."

"I...I...."

"His family used to live around the corner," said Mr. Stapleton. "They went to America I understand, maybe a year ago, the parents, that is."

"Was that Abraham Grossman, Morgan Street, he had an accent?"

"Yes, Russian descent I believe, I understand the father was from Russia."

"So that's the one! We have a record of him at the station, driving without a license, assaulting passersby," the policeman's voice continued. "Last year defrauding a family out of several hundred pounds over furniture or some such thing."

"Quite a family," Mr. Stapleton said. "Their youngest daughter's husband tried to assault me one evening."

"You didn't report it?"

"No."

"And Zachary is the son?"

"Their only remaining son. Rumor has it the father murdered his youngest son in London Hospital."

"Well, I'm not familiar with that one! My goodness me! Anyway, might we assume that this Zachary is involved in some criminal activity, taken over his father's bailiwick, so to speak?"

"What?!" That was Hazel.

"That's how it works with these foreign families, miss, they tend to stick together. Clearly your visitors expected to lay hands on him this evening, that's why they were here."

"Hmm, I'd hardly be surprised," said Mr. Stapleton.

The policeman went on: "The Soviets particularly, I have to say, tend to settle accounts with violence. Look at Eastern Europe! Given the opportunity they'd subjugate the entire free world."

Again Mr. Stapleton's voice, "It's ironic; these people produced Prokofiev, Shostakovich, not to mention Chekhov, Tolstoy...."

"Hmm, yes indeed, I see your point sir." A cough. "Now miss, can you give us an address or telephone number where we might be able to speak with this Zachary?"

"No, I...I...."

"What is it, Hazel? You seem determined to protect him for some reason."

"I just don't think he was involved in anything, he just, he only just got out of the RAF last week."

"Miss, I hate to disillusion you but it wouldn't be the first time that criminal activities were conducted under camouflage of military service. Do you at least know where he was stationed?"

"Sandwich, yes, in Sandwich. His sister told me he was a radar operator."

"That should be a good lead to finding out his present whereabouts. They have to register for the reserve, you know, keep their particulars up to date. So where is this sister of his now, do you know?"

"Yes, she just went to America, four weeks ago. She left her husband, they lived in Aldgate."

"Indeed! Did her husband remain here in Britain?"

"Yes, he's...."

"Aha! A classic husband-and-wife gambit! And what is the husband's name, pray?"

"Benny, Benny Cohen."

"Is that his real name? There must be a hundred Benny Cohens in Aldgate, no disrespect intended."

"I never thought of that...."

"You see?" It was Mrs. Stapleton's voice. "You think you're grown up already. You've got a lot to learn, young lady!"

"I... I... well, I know his mother's name was Bessie, Katya told me, she hated her."

"Bessie, hmm! Well, that might narrow it down somewhat." Silence for a moment, then the policeman continued. "Well, that smashed implement outside on the pavement certainly indicates your visitors were up to no good."

I heard movement down there, then footsteps. The policeman's voice continued from the passageway. "I think you've all given us enough to begin our investigation. I'll be getting along now, you've all had a difficult evening. A detective will probably be in touch with you tomorrow." The street door opened. "Mr. and Mrs. Stapleton, I can't urge on you too strongly, if you see or hear anything suspicious, ring us up right away and we'll dispatch an officer immediately."

The street door closed and the car drove off. I stayed motionless under the bed as a minute later footsteps came up the stairs. The door opened, closed again and the light came on. "It's me, are you alright?" Hazel whispered.

"Yes, I suppose so, I hope I don't have to stay under here too much longer."

"I remembered the dishes in the kitchen, I had to shut the door and put the extra plates away before my mother went in."

"Christ, I forgot about that!"

"So did I, that was a close one! Now we'll have to wait 'til they both go up to bed before I can let you out."

"When do you think they might go?"

"I don't know, maybe half an hour. I'll tell them I'm going to bed, then you can at least put your head out."

"Okay, I've been breathing dust and fluff...."

"Hazel!" Her father's terse call came from downstairs.

"Just a minute," she responded, jumping up and opening her door. "What's the matter?"

"Who left this record on the gramophone?"

"Er, oh, yes, I did, I meant to...." And she flipped the light switch off again, closed the door and I heard her tripping down the stairs.

"You mean, you were listening to Stravinsky all of a sudden?"

"Er, well, yes...."

I strained to listen.

"You mean, by yourself you were listening to the *Firebird?*"

"Er.... Yes."

"Hazel, look at me!"

"Yes, I'm looking."

"Answer me, keep looking at me. Was Zachary in this house at all this evening?"

"No Dad, he wasn't in this house at all this evening."

"And you were listening to the Stravinsky all by yourself."

"Zachary doesn't know about Stravinsky, he only likes American stuff, like...."

"Stravinsky is American, now."

"Well I mean… like Stan Kenton, I know for sure he does… like… that music… he does."

"I've never seen you quite like this before. But since you've told me he wasn't here, then I have to accept he wasn't here."

"Yes, no he wasn't here."

"Hmm."

"Alright. Then can I go up to bed? I'm tired."

"Yes, you're sure you feel alright?"

"Yes."

"Run along upstairs then. If you're… if you don't seem any better tomorrow I may have your mother take you to see Rosenthal."

"No, I'm well, I'm alright."

"Hmm."

"So… I'm going up to bed then. See you in the morning, Dad."

"See you in the morning."

She padded up the stairs, again put the light on and closed the door. "Whew!" A fresh cloud of dust flew into my mouth and eyes as she collapsed on the bed. "Let me get ready and put the light out, then you can come out." She disappeared into the hallway lavatory for a few minutes, came back in and put out the light. I glimpsed the lacy hem of a white nightgown, and she climbed into bed. "It's alright to come out now," she whispered. I finally rolled part-way out, on the door side. "No, you'd better come out on the window side."

"Yes?"

"In case."

"In case what?"

"My mother comes in."

"Oh, god." I rolled back under, across and out the window side, dragging my jacket with me. "Do you think I can sit up?"

"Yes, you can even sit on the edge of the bed if you want, just be ready to duck if the door opens."

As I stood, dust and crumbs flew off my clothes and before I could control myself I sneezed twice in quick succession.

"Shh, oh god, Dad'll think I caught something."

But all was quiet outside. Lightly, I brushed my jacket. Heavier footsteps ascended the stairs. "Ssh, he won't come in without knocking." I crouched perfectly still in the darkness.

The other bedroom door opened, the lavatory flushed, and voices. "Goodnight," Mrs. Stapleton called out.

"Goodnight Mum."

Their door clicked closed. All was silent. "You can sit on the edge if you like."

I sat. "Thanks Hazel, I mean you saved me from everything tonight," I whispered.

"That's alright. Whew, what an evening!"

"I hope I don't miss the last bus back to Wapping."

"We'll have to wait 'til they're asleep for sure."

"I know."

"You can lie down and rest if you like for ten minutes."

"Yes?"

"If you like, you can."

The house was finally serene and still as I quietly lay on top of the covers. The dim light of the corner street lamp pierced the curtains and cast lace patterns on the walls. Under the covers she turned to face me. She seemed to smile. "Hello," she whispered.

My eyes were adjusting to the designs. "Hello," I whispered back.

"It was nice this evening, wasn't it?" she said. "Apart from all the other business."

"Yes, it really was. I can't get that Stravinsky music out of my mind."

"Oh. Then I'm glad I played it."

"Yes, thanks, Hazel, you don't realize how important it is for me to hear something like that."

"Really?"

"Well, it changes my whole opinion about classical music, you know what I mean? Like someone else thought similar things about the predictable chords, everything on the proper beat. It's like it's all boring to Stravinsky so he's smashing the rules, you know? It's inevitable, really."

"Okay, shh."

"Sorry! My god, I want to hear more!"

"My Dad writes about historical perspective."

"What do you mean, that piece of music?"

"Oh, nothing really." She leaned her face toward me in the low light, then kissed me delicately on my cheek. "What I mean is, I'm glad we played it."

"Yes, so am I, I'm really glad." She stayed with her head slightly raised, next to my face. I thought about the strange combinations of notes and timbres, of the thoughts that must have gone through his mind as he decided this note, that note at the same time, then this note following. "Yes, I'm really glad we played it."

She lowered her head gently back to the pillow. From somewhere in the house a hum, an electric motor. "That's the refrigerator."

"Okay." After a few minutes: "Do you think they're asleep?"

"Probably. I'll come down and let you out. We have to be very quiet."

"Yes."

Downstairs she opened the street door. "I won't be able to ask you round any more, except maybe if my parents are away for a few days or something."

"I know, I'll talk to you on the phone. Don't ring me up where I live, they don't like it. Here's the phone number where I work in Wapping, Bituminous Products." I wrote the number down for her. "You'd better go in, Hazel, you'll catch cold."

"Yes." A subdued click as the door slowly latched, and in the damp night-time mist I rounded the corner into Tredegar Terrace.

—o—O—o—

53

To combat the night mist's chill I walked briskly along Tredegar Terrace, my head full of Stravinsky's delicately ferocious rhythms. A lamppost cast a feeble glow, barely enough to read the time on my watch: five after eleven. I'd be in a pickle if I'd missed the last bus to Wapping.

Approaching our old house on the corner of Morgan Street, a dark bulky figure materialized, hunched over the little wall. Was it one person or two? Mr. Bliss and Uri — had they waited for me? No lorry was discernible in the fog, but they could have parked it anywhere. As I girded to cross to the other side, ready to run if necessary, the figure stood up: it was one person, a man in an overcoat, wearing a trilby hat.

He saw me coming. "Good evening," the deep voice boomed.

A false alarm, but my heart was thumping. "Good evening, I...." He half turned toward me, touched his hat, and in the dim light I recognized the face. "Mister, oh, it's you... er, Mr. Lunch-Box Nose. Good evening."

"I... beg your pardon?"

"I'm sorry, I had a fright, I know you."

"A fright? I'm sorry, I was simply tying my shoelace."

"Oh, I had a lot of things happen this evening, you used to be down the shelter."

"Down the shelter?"

"In the air-raids."

"Everybody used to be down the shelter during the air-raids."

"Well yes, I mean you used to walk past our house at eight-fifteen every morning."

"I...."

"I'm late, I don't want to miss the last bus."

"Then far be it for me to delay you."

Feeling completely foolish I said, "What I mean is I'm Zachary, you used to be down the shelter, I used to see you down the shelter."

"Zachary, perhaps you should hurry so you don't miss your bus."

"Yes, I'm sorry, good night."

"Good night, Zachary."

I did hurry, all wound up, glad to get away into the darkness. Breaking into a run, as I approached the end of Morgan Street the misty illuminations of a bus roared by along Grove Road, perhaps the last bus. I raced around the corner after it, and red lights showed it slowing down at the bus stop near Mile End Road. My "Wait, wait!" reverberated along the deserted street, and luckily the bus did wait as I staggered up onto the boarding platform.

The conductor pulled me aboard. "'S' alright matey, you made it!"

I sat in the empty bus and fished for the tuppence. "Is this the last bus?"

"Yerse, it's beddy-bye after this one, matey."

"Thanks." It was good to know when the last bus left, in case Hazel's parents ever moderated their objections to my visiting, or if I came to see Jack. Through the bus windows, damp with mist, the only light came from distorted lampposts or an occasional illuminated house.

What a family, the Blisses! Two thuggish men, the mother calling Hazel a liar, Sophy shouting — more like Petticoat Lane than Forest Gate! When Sophy served food with silver cutlery and cloth serviettes, when she wore gossamer dresses and whispered in my ear, I would never imagine she could also scream like that! A bus drifted by in the opposite direction, then a car's lights, everything sculpted by the drizzle. And Mr. Bliss shouting he'll get me; what might they cook up, something with my job? All I'd done was have supper at Hazel's. A lighted boat materialized, bobbing on the Thames; we were almost there.

It was close to midnight and all was silent when I let myself discreetly into the Stokes' house. A light was on, however, and a man's head looked around the opened kitchen door to nod acknowledgement. He stood and came toward me, his rather large frame backlit from the kitchen; again a tremor of alarm, even though the Blisses could hardly get into this house. "Grossman?"

"Yes, who are you?"

"Who am I? Mr. Stokes, I only live 'ere!"

"Oh!" I realized I hadn't met him yet.

"Who'd you expect, in me own kitchen middle of the night?"

"No, I just… yes hello."

"Welp, Grossman, you an' me we 'as to 'ave a little chat."

"We do? You mean, now?"

"Now, that's exactly what I does mean."

"Alright." I followed him into the kitchen.

"The missus told ya' right out as 'ow ya' don't get no telephone service in this 'ouse."

"Yes she did, I'm sorry about what happened, I…."

"What 'appened was a couple o' your mates rung us up again this evenin'."

"I found out, I told them both they mustn't…."

"Welp, seems like ya' didn't tell 'em strong enough. Eleven o'clock tonight that phone starts ringin' again. Woke us both up with a bladdy fright it did."

"Eleven o'clock? That's just an hour ago!"

"You're bladdy right it's just an hour ago! An' I gotta be on the bladdy job seven in the mornin'!"

"Oh, I'm so sorry! Did they say who it was?"

"I wasn't in no mood for chit-chat, I can tell ya'! I gave that bugger a piece of my mind 'e won't forget."

"I'm… I'm…."

"Welp, I'll make this short an' sweet like. We wants you out of 'ere, sharp. If it ain't your fault, it ain't our fault neither."

"Yes alright then, I'm sorry."

"Sorry ain't good enough when you 'as to get up six in the A.M."

"I know, I'm…."

"Welp, it's close on twelve, I s'pose as 'ow I can't put ya' out in the middle of the night. Ya' can stay 'ere tonight, but first thing, out."

"In the morning."

"Right. I'm tryin' not to be too 'ard on ya', Grossman. What time ya' got to be at work, the missus said you're at Bituminous, round the corner?"

"Yes, at nine."

"Nine o'clock! I'll 'a' bin on the job two hours already, but the missus'll be 'ere alright. Out with your bags an' all then, 'alf past eight, sharp."

"Yes yes, alright."

"An' don't ya' be givin' me missus no malarkey."

"Malarkey? No certainly not, no, I'll be out with my cases and everything."

"Righteo. So let's say you owes us two bob, close enough?"

"Two shillings, yes sure." I didn't have any change, so I took a five-pound-note from my wallet.

"Blimey, I ain't got change of a fiver! You ain't got two bob?"

Through the skin of the folded wallet I felt the raised circle, ignored through familiarity. "Just a minute." Fishing out the last remembrance of my counterfeiting project so long ago, I handed him a shiny florin. Nervous, I fumbled and it slipped from my fingers onto a china plate on the wooden table-top, where it rang out clear and true.

"Right, no malarkey in the mornin' now, that's all I'm tellin' ya'."

"Yes.... No."

"An' that bladdy phone better not ring no more tonight."

"No.... Yes."

·   ·   ·

Thursday morning, carrying my two suitcases, I made Mr. Stokes' deadline. Garrick would always let me sleep at his place, though it would be better not to get involved there again and risk further melée with the Blisses. I stopped at a breakfast place, stuffed the cases under the table and ordered eggs and tea.

Approaching Bituminous's gate I avoided the small pool of tar on the pavement outside, and a bit before nine I opened the laboratory door. Dr. Nicolas was already there in his little green wrap, and he frowned at the suitcases. "This isn't a storeroom, Grossman."

I too could be short and nasty. "That's right," I said, placing them against the wall.

"Then what do you plan to do with them?"

"Take them with me when I find a new place to live."

"You're moving?"

"Yes, I'm moving."

"But you only just moved, you said."

"That is correct."

He paused. "Then will you still be at Bituminous?"

I looked him in the eye. "I will."

"Hmm. Run outside and draw the samples then."

I drew samples, started the distillation, and at ten o'clock the door from the little office opened: "Grossman?" The inquisitor was pallid white, stooped though barely middle-aged, wearing a black business suit and black tie — a veritable undertaker.

"Yes?"

"You're wanted upstairs. I'm Mr. Haffner."

"Upstairs? I'm sorry, I haven't met you before."

"I'm Mr. Haffner," he repeated in a louder voice. "There's a telephone call for Grossman."

Dr. Nicolas paused to watch, and my heart sank as I followed Haffner up the stairs: it could only be the Blisses. By the time I spoke into the receiver I felt sick. "Who is this?"

"Sol Bliss, you slimey barstard you, you're gonna pay for this!"

"What? I didn't do anything, what did I do?"

"Think you can play games with me, you arsehole, I wasn't born yesterday! We take you into our house, treat you like family, you lousey barstard!"

"I didn't, I didn't do anything! I only...."

"Nobody," he shouted, "you hear me...? nobody treats my daughter like dirt. You're gonna pay for this, mark my word!" A bang, and the phone was dead.

Haffner scowled as he took back the receiver. Downstairs, Nicolas fixed me with cold eyes. "What was it?"

"What?"

"Obviously, the telephone call."

"Oh that!" There was nothing I could explain. "Nothing, really."

"Nothing really! So now you're receiving telephone calls during working hours about nothing really! Do you realize the distillation had finished while you were upstairs talking about nothing really? I turned the Bunsen off for you."

"Alright, I'll prepare the next run."

"Grossman, I don't care for your attitude."

"Dr. Nicolas I don't care for your attitude either."

"What!"

"Before I went in the RAF I handled this whole job very well by myself."

"And set the building on fire! No doubt you were on the telephone upstairs, talking about nothing really?"

I had to pacify Nicolas in order to concentrate on more pressing problems: how to handle the Blisses, where to sleep tonight. "Dr. Nicolas, I do a good job here, this is the first phone call I've ever received, it *was* important. Now with your permission I'll get on with the next distillation. Mr. Smith will need the numbers."

"I... I...." His face was beetroot red. "I'll speak to Mr. Richardson about this, I...."

"The law says I'm entitled to return to this job after completing my military obligation. I returned, and I'm trying to do my job properly."

"I'll wager the law doesn't sanction insolence!"

"I'm sorry."

"Or, incompetence!"

"Incompetence?" I was disconnecting the flask as I spoke, and placing it on the balance. "Who said I'm incompetent?"

"Well!" He picked up his heavy book and opened it. "You have no academic qualifications."

"That's true, but they wouldn't have kept me here running the whole lab by myself for almost a year if I weren't competent."

He placed the opened book on his desk and sat down. "Enough of this chatter! Continue with your work."

"Right."

Work proceeded in complete silence until about quarter to twelve when the office door opened again, and once more Haffner stood in the doorway. "Grossman!" he snapped.

"What?"

"Upstairs!"

So this was to be the tactic: Mr. Bliss would keep ringing me up at work until they gave me the sack! Nicolas stood frozen with a flask in his raised hand as I followed Haffner out the door and up the stairs.

"What do you want?" I shouted into the mouthpiece.

"Hello?" It was a girl's voice. "Can I speak to Zachary Grossman, please?"

"Hazel! What's...."

"Is this Zech?"

"Yes, I'm sorry I shouted, I'm... I thought it was Mr. Bliss or Sophy's brother."

Haffner was standing by the desk chair, his glance alternating impatiently between my face and the telephone base standing on his desk — the desk that until last Friday had been Mr. Bitwood's.

"Is it alright ringing you at work?" she asked.

"I don't know... what... what is it?"

"I thought you'd want to know right away, it's a letter from Katya, it just came, there's a sheet for a ticket."

"A ticket?"

Haffner's hand was inching toward the receiver cradle as if to disconnect the call: "You know no one gets telephone calls at work, especially on working hours," he interrupted.

"Hazel, hold on for a moment." Then to Haffner: "Haffner, who are you?"

"Who am I! I'm clerk here, I'm Bitwood's replacement, *that's* who I am. And it's *Mr.* Haffner to you I'll have you know!"

"Haffner, take your hand away from that telephone. I'll tell you when I'm ready." Some sort of noise issued from his face, the hand jerked back, and I returned to my conversation. "Hazel I'm sorry, what were you saying?"

"Another letter just came from Katya, and there's a thing in it for a ticket, for you, a Cunard ticket, to America!"

"What? Really, so soon?"

"Yes, it's a form, you know, a docket, it's got your name on it, it's marked *Paid in Full.*"

"Wow!"

"Yes, it says the Cunard White Star Steam-Ship Company will give you a tourist-class ticket when you present it at their office in London, that's what it says."

"Wow! Wow!" Haffner, still standing, was guardedly looking my way.

"I thought you'd want to know right away."

"Yes, Hazel, thanks, thanks, wow! How can I get it?"

"You mustn't come over my house, do you want me to post it to your address?"

"Er, I don't live there anymore."

"You don't?"

"I can't explain now. Hazel, could you meet me at Johnny Isaacs tonight?"

"Oh great! Dad made me stay home today, he said I was ill, I'll tell him I feel better, they'll let me go."

"Good. Don't forget to bring the form."

"I'll bring the whole letter."

"Okay, about six o'clock?"

"Six o'clock. See you tonight."

Haffner glared as I hung up the phone. I leaned over the desk toward his face and whispered confidentially, "Haffner."

"What?" He seemed perplexed.

I leaned closer and whispered more quietly, "Haffner, in this company..."

"Yes?" he responded in bewilderment.

"...in this company," I continued, leaning ever closer to his ear, in the empty office dropping my voice even further, "in this company, you have to be... very... very...."

"What?" he whispered back.

"Very... very..." I dragged it out, "care... ful...." I spun on my heel and walked toward the door.

"What? Why? What are you talking about?" he asked through almost closed lips.

I opened the door, exited, and looked back at him. "When it's too late, Haffner, don't say I didn't warn you." I closed the door and started down the stairs. If it really were a ticket, then, then... I couldn't contemplate all the implications before I found myself re-entering the laboratory. My watch now said twelve o'clock, dinner break. "Dr. Nicolas, I didn't bring anything with me today to eat. Can I go out?"

"I assume there would be no point in my asking what *that* phone call was about?"

"Er... yes."

His face was dark. "Grossman, you may go."

I rushed to the telephone kiosk around the corner near the bus stop and procured the Cunard number. "Yes, it's something, a sheet of paper from New York, it says it's paid for, I have to get the ticket at your office."

"What is the number? There'll be a docket number in red on the top of the page."

"I don't have it with me, I can bring it in."

"That's the best thing, bring it to the office. It's for one way, you say?"

"Yes, it's third-class."

"That'll be tourist. Do you have your passport and visa?"

"No."

"You'll need those before you can go, of course, but with immediate family in America that should pose no delay."

I stopped for another cup of tea. Supposing Hazel had made a mistake? And what about Sophy? Despite everything, for over a year it had been very very nice going with her, though she probably didn't want me now anyway. Would anybody else ever like me as much as she had?

Returning to the factory, outside the gate Haffner stood waiting opposite the tar puddle. "Mr. Grossman, do you have five minutes?"

"Well, yes."

"With your permission, sir, if you could clarify your... what you mentioned... earlier?" His demeanor had changed remarkably.

"Well certainly, Haffner."

"Could we... by my desk, would that be alright, or a cup of tea somewhere, maybe?"

"At your desk, yes." If this were some sort of a trap on his or Nicolas's part, at this juncture I didn't even mind. We bypassed the laboratory and I followed him upstairs. He pulled the side chair over for me and sat himself down.

"Confidentially, sir," he began, "if you don't mind my asking, why... why do I need to be careful?"

I looked about. In the wall opposite, beyond where Mr. Margolin's desk used to stand, were the office's two windows. The drop to the concrete below would probably be six yards.

At the time of the laboratory fire I recalled they had broken one window to release smoke and let in fresh air. "That window." I pointed.

"Yessir?"

"The putty is — shall we say — fairly new."

"Alright sir."

"Haffner, they replaced that glass after the... after the last... well, they called it an accident."

"Accident sir?"

"Well... that's what they *called* it."

He squinted at me: "Er... sir... what? I...."

"That *is* what they called it, Haffner, officially."

"I...." He gulped. "I... I'm not quite sure...."

I looked at my watch and stood up. "Why don't you think about it for a few days."

He gulped. Then: "Mr. Grossman, sir."

"What?"

"Mr. Grossman sir, I'm supposed to tell you you don't work here anymore."

"What!" I sat again. "What?"

Now it was he who was whispering. "Mr. Richardson called me over by his office, before."

"He did?"

"You know, he only puts his head out."

"Yes?"

"I'm sorry sir, he said he's giving you the sack."

"Really!"

"Sir, I asked him if he could inform you himself on such an unpleasant matter." He spoke even more quietly. "He told me, 'That's what *you* get paid for,' and shut his door."

"Very interesting!"

"It wasn't my fault sir, I got caught in the middle."

"I realize...."

"Sir, I'm sure you'll be able to find something right away, you'll do alright wherever you are, I can tell."

"Yes, yes."

"This is extremely difficult for me, Mr. Grossman sir, I have to tell you this is your last day. I have to pay you for three days, twenty four shillings."

"Yes, alright."

"I did my best, sir, but he...."

"That's alright."

He opened a desk drawer, lifted out a small black box, unbuttoned his jacket, snaked keys out of a trousers pocket on an endless keychain hooked to a belt loop, and unlocked the lid. He removed a one-pound note, counted four more shillings, then carefully locked the box and returned it to the drawer, handing me the cash. "I know you're going to do very well somewhere, you're one of those that'll be at the top in no time flat."

I stood up. "True, true."

"Then there's no hard feelings, sir?"

"No, no hard feelings. But Haffner, to be honest with you I would be derelict if I didn't tell you that in accepting employment in this company you may not have done the wisest thing in terms of your future — *any* kind of a future." He swallowed, trailed me out the door, and as I descended the stairs he waved mawkishly.

So, Nicolas must have gone up and spoken to Richardson when I went out for dinner. They'd paid me for the full day, and whether or not I was obligated to go back to the laboratory, my suitcases were there. Nicolas was speaking with Mr. Smith as I entered. He avoided my eyes and motioned me toward the sink. "Grossman, you might as well clean that glassware."

"I tells you I got it just right the way it is," said Smith, continuing some conversation with Nicolas. "It ain't like you just shoves in more steam."

"I'm talking in terms of a minute fraction, two kilos or less, we'll raise the temperature no more than one degree."

"Last time we tried that it boiled inside the still, ran right over the top. We was three days cleanin' up the mess."

"No, no, no...."

"Every barrel of turps got sent back, it did. Mr. Margolin'll tell you, ring 'im up, 'e'll tell you."

I stood at the sink, my back to them, cleaning a pair of beakers.

"But that's what we have viewing ports for," Nicolas went on. "You'll watch, and immediately something...."

"Dr. Nicolas, that's what I'm tryin' to tell ya, there ain't no such thing as immediate out there in the yard, it ain't like in 'ere! You shut that steam down all the way, 'undred percent like, an' it's close on one minute 'til there's any difference, an' nothin' ain't gonna wait one minute! It's whoosh, over the top!"

As the two paused for a moment, I intervened. "Dr. Nicolas, you asked Mr. Richardson to give me the sack?"

"What?" That was Smith.

"On the contrary, I never asked Mr. Richardson to do anything."

"Then why am I getting the sack?"

"The sack! Matey, who's givin' you the sack?"

"Smith, this is hardly any of your business," said Nicolas. "Grossman, I'll discuss it with you later."

"What do you mean, 'ardly my business, I known Grossman 'ere since... since forty-seven I known 'im, 'e's the best bloke what you got workin' 'ere, they can't sack 'im just like that!"

"Mr. Smith, if you please!"

Smith came over to the sink. "Matey, who's tryin' to give you the sack?"

I lowered the dirty beaker back into the sink. "I don't know if it's Richardson or... or Nick here, but they told me today's my last day."

"Your last day? Blimey, this 'ole place is goin' straight down the fuckin' drain it is."

"Watch the language, you're not out in the yard! And Grossman don't you *dare* call me Nick!"

"Nick!" said Smith, turning to face Nicolas. "If 'e goes, I goes also!"

For the third time, the door opened and there stood Haffner. "Mr. Grossman sir, you have another telephone call sir."

"What!"

"Yessir. What would you like me to do?"

"Grossman, this is preposterous! And Haffner, why are you behaving so... so... obsequiously? What's going on, exactly?"

"If 'e goes," repeated Smith, "I goes. Clear?"

"Smith, what are you talking about? You're, you're... the plant won't... it would take goodness knows how long to train somebody, no that's out of the question."

I walked over to Haffner, ignoring Nicolas completely. "I'll come up and see who it is." Upstairs, Haffner handed me the phone. "Hello?"

"Hello, is this Mr. Grossman?" It was a woman's voice, not anyone I recognized.

"Yes, who's this?" Haffner was looking discreetly away.

"Mrs. Stokes."

"Oh, Mrs. Stokes, did I leave something there in the room?"

"No, but two men was just 'ere for you. I told 'em you don't live 'ere no more, I told 'em where you works."

"You did, what did they look like?"

"Skinny little bloke, bald, mean-looking. The other was some young tough, fancied 'imself. They started cursin', said someone already told 'em you don't work there no more."

"Wow, you mean they were here?"

"Don't rightly know. Me 'ubby was 'ome 'aving 'is dinner, 'e come out, that shut 'em up quick when they seen 'im!"

"Then what happened?"

"They said someone's givin' 'em the runaround at the place. We told 'em far as we knows that's where you works."

"Mrs. Stokes, where are the men now?"

"Mr. Grossman, my 'ubby says if we gets bothered one more time, if these blokes don't do you in first, 'e's gonna come over there 'imself and do the job."

"He did?"

"'E ain't never done no one in before, far as I knows."

"Are the men still there?"

"They come in a lorry, I gotta tell 'em you're still there at the factory."

"Why do you have to tell them?"

"'Cause I don't want me 'ubby doin' *me* in, that's why. You understands, Mr. Grossman."

"Okay, thanks." I threw the phone down and ran down the stairs, raced along the passageway, out through the gate and around to the telephone kiosk. Out of breath, I dialed 999.

Immediately a male voice answered: "Police, emergency!"

"Yes, listen carefully. A lorry is coming around the front of Bituminous Products. You know Bituminous Products, in Wapping?"

"Yes sir, who is this?"

"Just listen, please. The Bow police are looking for this lorry."

"What is this all about, and who are you?"

"Please officer, just listen, we have to hurry. Just get a pencil."

"Alright sir, I'm ready."

"This lorry and the two men in it are wanted by the police station in Bow."

"What for?"

I had to be careful. "I... don't know."

"Can I ask who you are, why you're giving us this information?"

"Someone double-crossed someone, they were out looking for the wrong person last night."

"And who should they have been looking for?"

For a moment I was stumped. "Er, Benny."

"Benny? Benny who?"

Why should I let Benny get away with punching my sister? "Er, Benny Cohen."

"Sir, there are lots of Benny Cohens. Can you give us...?"

"Aldgate, he lives in Aldgate with his mother Bessie...." I had to get off; the police might be trying to trace where I was telephoning from, also the lorry would arrive any moment.

"Thank you sir, and can you give us any hint...."

"Haffner."

"Haffner?"

"Nick Haffner; I use Nicolas at work but my real name is Nick Haffner."

I clicked the receiver off and ran out of the kiosk. The best thing would be, if a bus came by to simply jump aboard and that would be that. Then I remembered — my suitcases! Christ, perhaps I had time! I sped back around and along by the tarry wall to the gate, leaped over the puddle and raced inside the laboratory. The two men looked surprised as I grabbed both suitcases. "Thanks Mr. Smith for sticking up for me, I don't want to stay here anyway. You don't have to leave on my account."

"That's alright, matey, I bin gettin' more an' more sick of this place anyway. Richardson locked up in 'is office there, y' needs a special invitation jus' to talk wiv 'im, and this 'ere Nick barstard breathin' down me neck twelve hours a day, ringin' me up at 'ome on Sunday! Who needs it?"

"Get out, get out, both of you!" Nicolas screamed.

Smith opened the door for me: "'Ere, gimme one of your bags."

Nicolas came toward us: "Mr. Smith, you can't leave, we, we, we're all... we're all working together here."

"I bin 'ere thirty-one years I 'ave, worked 'ard, give it me best. I should'a left when Mr. Margolin sold the place. It ain't pretty watchin' a decent company go down the 'ol-shit-'ole."

As the two of us exited, Nicolas stood in the passageway by the open door: "Smith, we have to talk further, wait a moment, I'm sure Mr. Richardson can suggest an arrangement to your satisfaction.... Mr. Smith!"

We kept walking. In the yard, Smith lowered my suitcase on a clean piece of ground and pondered for a moment. "Get me stuff.... Nah!" He picked up the bag again. "Gotta come back for me wages, anyway."

"I'm in a hurry," I said as we walked under the main gate's wrought iron arch. Just then the lorry came careening around the corner.

"That bloke'll 'ave 'is bladdy arse in a sling if 'e keeps drivin' like that!"

"Mr. Smith, I know who they are, they're after me!" I darted over the road and ducked behind the stacks of barrels as the lorry slid to a stop just before the gate.

Smith followed me across and asked in a loud whisper: "These blokes is after you?"

"Yes, it's a mistake, I didn't do anything, they're just bullies."

Uri and Mr. Bliss jumped out of the lorry's cab. They noticed Smith, who had remained in view. He stood my suitcase down and went back over as the two of them banged the lorry doors shut. From my hiding place I saw Uri come around the front of the vehicle; suddenly he threw up his arms as his feet began to slither. His father, coming around the other side, grabbed at him, but too late; Uri had stepped into that yard-wide patch of spilled tar Smith and I had so diligently avoided. The next instant, Uri lay flat on his back. Mr. Bliss leaned over from the edge to lend his son a hand, but Smith strode forward: "Don't try it mate, you'll only fall in y'self. Gimme a cloth or something to catch 'is 'and with."

Mr. Bliss handed over a large handkerchief; Smith wrapped it around his hand, grasped one of the lorry's headlights for support, and pulled Uri up out of the tar patch. "Whew!" Uri whistled, "Christ, Dad, look at this mess!" The back of his jacket, trousers and hair were matted with tar. Mr. Bliss helped him remove the jacket, and the two of them spread it over the lorry's bonnet. As Uri fumbled in one of the pockets for his comb, then tried to sift tar out of his hair, Mr. Bliss said: "We're looking for Grossman, he works here."

"Grossman don't work 'ere no more."

"Bull*shit*, we know he works here, everybody's giving us bullshit."

"I'm tellin' you he don't work 'ere. I just saved your mate there, least you can do is watch your mouth."

"You're lying, we know he works here!"

At that, Smith grasped Mr. Bliss's lapel and shoved him up against the tarry wall. "You better watch your mouth, ol' bugger!"

Uri attempted to come to his father's defense, but as he lunged forward his stockinged foot came out of a shoe that remained stuck to the pavement. He managed briefly to balance on the other foot, but the next moment the shoeless sock was planted in the tar. Smith relinquished his grip on the older Bliss, who slid down the wall, then grabbed the front of Uri's shirt and pushed him back over into the tar puddle again.

Now it could only be moments until a police car came around the corner. Carrying both suitcases I began creeping out from behind the barrels, back toward the roadway. Smith bent down and wiped his hands on Mr. Bliss's jacket. He came over, took a suitcase, and we both started walking. As we turned the corner, a black Wolseley police car, blue light flashing, bell ringing, turned off of Wapping High Street and sped past us, screeching around the corner toward Bituminous Products, Ltd. We peered back around and saw the vehicle slide to a stop alongside the lorry. Two policemen jumped out. One grabbed Mr. Bliss, who was just managing to stand up; the other reached out for Uri, now kneeling in the tar patch. The policeman caught at his shirtsleeve, then pulled his hand away quickly. "Ugh!" we clearly heard him say.

Smith and I resumed our way toward Wapping High Street. "Are you really leaving Bituminous, you've been there such a long time." I asked. "It was nice of you to take my side, but don't leave because of me."

"Nah, it ain't been no good since Margolin packed it in, these new blokes don't 'ave no respect for no one."

"Yes, I don't like Nicolas."

"And that other bloke Richardson, 'e don't never come out 'is office. Me missus tells me she wants a telephone put in our 'ouse cause all 'er mates is gettin' 'em, so last year we gets ourselves a telephone and what 'appens?"

"I... don't know...."

"Ol' Nick here starts ringin' us up on Sundays like. Pack the bladdy job in, me missus bin tellin' me, a year ago I should'a packed it in."

"Really!"

"So what's goin' on with them two blokes in the lorry?" he asked.

"Oh, my sister's in-laws, it's stupid, they're rotten to everyone in my family, I don't know why," I said, as we approached the bus stop. "You know, some people are just troublemakers. Thank you for helping out with them."

"That's what mates is for."

54

I awoke on the sofa in Jack's bedroom, the view through the window presaging a drizzly overcast day. "Good morning, Mr. Inveterate Pupil!"

"Good morning, Mr. World Traveler," he responded from the bed by the opposite wall.

"You're slightly premature, you haven't gotten rid of me yet."

Downstairs, Mrs. Pristein served tea, toast and jam, and I thanked her again for her hospitality. "Not at all, Zachary. We want you to have fond memories of us when you're in the New World."

"It's beginning to look like you're really serious about deserting the old ship," said Jack. "How do you expect Britannia to keep ruling the waves?"

"Look, they'll have to ask someone else, I've done my stint defending Queen and Empire. Next comes Truth, Justice and the American Way."

"From the story you told us last night," said Mrs. Pristein, "let's hope you get as far as Southampton in one piece."

"The only one who knows I'm here is Hazel, she's on my side."

"Mum, if anyone blows up the house before Zech buggers off, I'll design a very expensive new one."

After breakfast, Jack and I donned our mackintoshes and braved the rain to the Underground station. At Aldgate East, Jack continued on to school while I went up to the terminus for a bus to the City. My heart thumped as I presented the Paid-In-Full docket at the Cunard office, but the clerk acknowledged it as though people brought them in every day. "When would you want to depart, sir?"

Sir! "As soon as possible."

He went through papers. "We have a tourist berth Wednesday of next week."

"Wow! On…."

"The *Queen Mary.*"

"Wednesday, I'll take it!"

"Alright." He made entries on a form: "It's on E-deck, cabin E-eighty-seven, double berth, the other occupant… a Mr. Anthony Parker. You'll board at Southampton, there's a new terminal you know, Ocean Terminal."

"Oh, I see."

"The boat-train leaves Waterloo Station at eight A.M. Of course you'll need your passport, plus your visa from the American embassy."

"Of course, thank you very much."

A photographers next door to the passport office took my picture. I had a bite of dinner while the passport application was being processed, and by late afternoon I left the office carrying the precious blue leatherette-bound booklet in which they'd hand-written my name above a gold-embossed lion and unicorn nestled in a coat-of-arms and crown. Inside, the scroll-printed *His* had been overwritten in ink with *"Her* Brittanic Majesty's Principle Secretary of State for Foreign Affairs...." They must have printed them during King George's reign! On the following page my photo — looking like I was on the run from Wormwood Scrubbs — was embossed with a raised Foreign Office stamp.

Everything had gone smoothly so far, and I slid the coveted document into my inside pocket next to the envelope of Cunard papers. It was late afternoon, still time to get to the American embassy in Grosvenor Square to begin the visa application. There, I completed a form and was told to return Monday morning, prepared for the medical examination. On the bus ride back as we rolled past the Empire in Stepney I remembered ominously that everything had also gone smoothly the day after my demob, one week ago: I'd gotten my laboratory job back and promptly found a place to live. And that same evening, after the pictures with Sophy and Garrick and Elizabeth, then later treating everybody to fish and chips, my future had seemed so well charted. Yet now, just a few tumultuous days later, everything was unrecognizably changed.

I didn't care to get back to Mrs. Pristein's place before Jack returned — around five, he'd said — and I didn't want to look as if I hadn't eaten, so I meandered over to Altman's. A new, younger lady stood behind the counter, a relief from the grim and surly Mrs. Altman; I bought a couple of apples and half a pound of gooseberries. When an elderly man I was not quite certain was Mr. Altman brushed aside the curtain separating the living quarters, he didn't acknowledge me, though of course I also looked older now. He gave the new assistant a familiar hug as he crossed behind her; maybe she was his daughter. After he disappeared I asked her: "Is this still Altman's?"

"Oh yes," she smiled.

"Was that Mr. Altman?"

"Indeed it was."

"Are you his daughter, then?"

"Do I look like his daughter? I'll tell him."

"I... I just wondered." From the shop I strolled past Mrs. Berger's house and wondered how Reuben was doing in prison. I would like to have rung Hazel up, even had supper out with her again if she were home from work, but I couldn't risk causing problems if her parents answered the telephone. As I approached Tredegar Square Park, flimsy cross-hatched wire fencing around the perimeter exacerbated the loss of the stately old iron railings and gate, with their aura of dependable permanence. In the park, the once-carefully-edged beds of brilliant giant daffodils, of carved red and black roses were now lost to the incoherence of yellow, white and purple wildflowers crowding the grass. I poked my head inside the concrete and brick sloped entrance to the old air-raid shelter, now echoing and musty with disuse; it was hard to imagine the acrid taste of explosive, the crowds swarming down the steps. Kids skated by; yes, the quaint old slate paving stones on the diagonal crosspaths had been asphalted, eliminating the wide cracks that had caught Zilla's skate-wheels that afternoon she'd come home crying. When Abie had seen her bruised nose and black-and-blue face that evening, he'd deliberately taken her hard-earned skates and burned them in the fireplace. "Disgusting," he'd said as she screamed and cried, her arm locked in his vise-like grip as he forced her to watch the metal slowly warp and blacken, the leather straps turn to ash. "Like a tomboy she's skating there for everybody to see."

Asphalt! Asphalt was bitumen. That meant that in some measure I was culpable for the ugly blanket of black uniformity. I sat on the grass and finished the fruit, read for a while, almost hoping that Hazel might come by, then walked back to the Pristein's house, joining them both for a cup of tea after their supper. Jack showed me details of the drawing table he'd set up in his bedroom, its ninety-degree edges for the T-square, the set of protractors and other instruments. After watching him begin drawing a plan and elevation, I propped myself up on the sofa and read his architectural magazine, about a Frenchman named Le Corbusier who was designing an apartment complex in Marseilles. Le Corbusier hated school and left for good at thirteen years old; he loved reading lots of books and he was now world famous. Over the page the article continued: he actually wasn't French, he was Swiss; further along, that Le Corbusier wasn't even his real name, it was Charles Edouard Jeanneret! Maybe people had been after him also, and that's how he managed to get away. I lay down on the sofa and closed my eyes.

Saturday morning the weather was still overcast and drizzly, not a day to go out. I needed to arrange to reclaim Marius's belongings from Sophy's embrace, so I rang up Garrick.

"Well, I'm glad for you, old bean, I think you're doing the right thing and I'm certain Liz will agree."

"You guessed I'd be going to America."

"Didn't realize it'd be so soon. Naturally the whole of Forest Gate has been apprised of your negative standing *vis à vis* the Bliss tribe."

"I'm curious, whose version did you get, who told you?"

"Fannie told Pop — and apparently everybody else as well. Did you know your buddy Hazel's parents have taken out a summons against them?"

"Wow, they have?"

"Assault. Mrs. Stapleton formally charged them. The four of them have to appear in court."

"The whole family!"

"When you're safely ensconced with a Yankee address, I'll send you regular communiqués from the front."

"My goodness, I didn't think it would go that far! Garrick, this exacerbates a certain problem."

"Ahem, what's next on the agenda?"

"You remember about my brother, who died."

"Marius, yes, I'm sorry."

"Yes, well my mother saved some of his things in a suitcase, that was the one bag we left in your boot last weekend."

"Don't tell me… that's the one you helped Sophy take in their house!"

"Yes. And I'm the last one in the family here, I *have* to take it to America with me."

"My god! A capital G — with your permission."

"This time you're allowed."

"So where is it exactly?"

"I'm not sure, she had me take it up to Uri's room but I think she moved it into her bedroom."

"Well." He was silent for a while. "That one's a minefield."

"I know, I couldn't think of any way to get it back — assuming they haven't already dumped everything in the dustbin."

"Let me discuss this with my second in command. Or maybe Pop can help. Do you know yet when you're leaving?"

"Wednesday, early morning."

"So soon! Oh, Zech, we'll miss you! Alright, I'll have to work fast and ring you back."

"Garrick, I can't give you this phone number. Whenever I give the phone number where I am it ends up in a catastrophe."

"Alright, you spend the tuppence and ring me back then. Say, tomorrow, Sunday?"

"Okay."

"Give me 'til early afternoon."

"Okay. Garrick, I really appreciate your trying. Don't mention to anyone I'm going to America, please."

"That's right, they don't know! Will you be telling Sophy, though, sometime?"

"I have to, I couldn't just disappear, but don't mention it yet, she'll tell the others and who knows what they'll do."

"Righteo old chap, talk to you tomorrow then."

"Right."

After a cup of tea with Mrs. Pristein and Jack I rang up Uncle Harold; I ought to tell Lily's brother that she was alright, and that I was going to America also.

Aunt Vera answered: her husband wasn't home but she'd tell him. Auntie Zelda was standing there, she said, and she, Vera, wasn't talking to the sisters-in-law because they were gossips, always making up stories. "Did I want to tell Zelda myself," she asked, "so no one could say you rang up Uncle Harold to tell him you're going to America and Aunt Vera didn't even tell Zelda, she's so spiteful?"

"Er, well...."

"...That she stole their brother who wouldn't have married her if she hadn't tricked him, like a full-grown man he doesn't know how to make up his own mind, I need to trick him, what do you think of that!"

"Well... maybe... if I could just speak to Auntie Zelda for a minute...."

"Zachary, in a minute I'll put her on, listen, I'll tell you the best thing that could happen."

"Alright."

"The best, the very best thing for the whole family."

"Er, alright, Auntie Vera."

"If your Uncle Harold only realized what a pair of troublemakers he's got here under his own roof, his own sisters always making trouble, gossip-mongers, they got nothing better to do than make up stories, lies."

"Yes, Auntie Vera, I see."

"Like they should move out right away, this week even they should move out, believe me I'd even help them schlepp all their rubbish they got up there down, I'd scrub the walls with my own hands, the floors, everything."

"Yes, I'm sure Auntie Vera, right... could I speak to Auntie Zelda just for one minute?"

"Who?"

"Auntie Zelda."

"Yes I'm sorry I'm going on, Harold says I shouldn't keep going on, why wear myself out I ask you?"

"Yes."

"A wonderful man my husband. That's right" — her voice rising — "yes he's my husband, you don't like it you can lump it, as I'm talking she's mumbling there under her breath. Ugh!, pearls before swine, what's the good, here's... here she is."

Aunt Zelda came on. "Zachary, fah! I can't bear to be in the same room.... So why didn't you ring us up for a long time, where are you, you're in the air force, I got a letter from your mother in America."

"No Auntie Zelda, I'm demobbed already."

"You're demobbed, so where are you, you'll come round, I'll ask Harold when she'll be out and you'll come round, better you come when she's not here. Did they tell you about Auntie Rae?"

"No, what happened?"

"She's in hospital, for tests, they don't know what it is, it's from all the aggravation if you ask me."

"I see."

"Yes, we'll see what it is, what can you do, you hope for the best."

"Yes. Auntie Zelda, I wanted to tell you I'm going to America also."

"You?"

"Yes, on Wednesday."

"Well what can I say, tell your mother about Rae, don't frighten her, maybe it'll be alright you never know with these things."

"Yes, yes."

"So, did you go to the cemetery?"

"The cemetery?"

"To see Marius, you should go and see Maudy, is that his name, before you go to America, who knows?"

"Yes I... know, I...." I had to have everything together by Tuesday — morning, preferably. "Yes, I'm going to the cemetery on Tuesday... Tuesday afternoon, I expect."

"This Tuesday."

"About... three o'clock."

"Where is it?"

"West Ham. Plashett Cemetery in West Ham."

"I'll tell you what, they'll give me half a day from the office. My sister's boy's going to America, maybe I won't see him again, what can they say, I'll come to West Ham, I'll meet you there, let me write it down... Plashett Cemetery, West Ham."

"Alright."

"So I'll meet you there, three o'clock, what can they say?"

"Yes."

"Tuesday afternoon, this Tuesday, three o'clock."

"Yes."

•   •   •

Sunday morning Mrs. Pristein woke us, calling up the stairs that I had a telephone call. At least, today the sun was shining.

"Hazel, you shouldn't really ring me here in case something goes wrong."

"I didn't tell anybody where you are, your friend Garrick rang us up just now, I didn't tell him where you are."

"Oh, good."

"He said he needs to talk to you, he said it's urgent."

"Yes, I was going to call him, alright, I'll ring him up right away."

"Zachary?"

"Yes?"

"What happened, did you get a ticket?"

"Yes, I'm going on Wednesday."

"This Wednesday?"

"Yes, I just hope nothing goes wrong. I got the passport, I have to go for an exam at the American embassy Monday morning, tomorrow morning. I'm trying to get the visa tomorrow, or Tuesday morning at the very latest."

"Really, I didn't realize… no, I'm glad you got it, it's just… so quick!"

"Yes, I know. I wanted to ring you up yesterday."

"Really, you did?"

"Yes, to tell you what was happening."

"I suppose you're busy, getting ready and everything."

"I will be on Monday and Tuesday, getting everything settled, but…."

"I thought if you wanted to play the piano… I forgot I can't have you over. You busy today, do you have some time? It's nice out."

"I've got to get Maudy's suitcase, Garrick is going to help me, I don't know yet when I have to meet him."

"When you know, you could ring me up if you like."

"Suppose your parents answer?"

"If you're going to ring me back for sure I'll stay near the phone."

"Alright, I'll ring him up now, then as soon as I finish talking to him."

We hung up and I dialed Garrick's number. "Cadbury's wholesale. Who's speaking?"

"Mr. Sharansky, hello!"

"Oh, it's Zachary! Well well well, I understand you've been a bad boy."

"Christ, not really…."

"Well, Fannie says you're currently *persona non grata* in Blissville."

"I, I…."

"Anyway for what it's worth, I hear Sophy might take you back if you played your cards right."

"I can't believe, after all the commotion they caused…."

"It's a matter of psychology, the ladies need to wait until the lads simmer down a bit. It would help if you distanced yourself from that other family…."

"You mean the Stapletons?"

"I don't know the name, the ones taking them to court."

"Boy, how things get distorted!"

"Anyway, good luck, I'll see if I can tear Garrick away from his princess."

"Thank you."

Garrick came on. "What-o, old chap! Mission accomplished!"

"You did? You got the suitcase?"

"Almost. Let's say there's a string attached."

"What do you mean?" I asked.

"Can we meet you later?"

"Yes. You mean, with the case?"

"Absolutely, with the case."

"Oh great, where do you want to meet?"

"Neutral ground, no-man's land."

"Er..."

"Don't worry, everything'll be alright, I'll have the suitcase, it's just... let's meet somewhere sort of — neutral. This evening."

"How about Mile End Road somewhere, would that be alright?"

"That fish and chips shop we ate in last week?"

"Johnny Isaacs, good! You remember where it is?"

"Past the Empire, on the left."

"Okay, what time?"

"How does seven o'clock sound?"

"I'll be there seven o'clock tonight."

Hazel answered immediately when I rang her back. "Hazel, I'm meeting Garrick tonight, seven o'clock at Johnny Isaacs."

"Oh."

"It's nice out, I've got time 'til then and there's nothing more I can do 'til tomorrow. Jack'll be working on his school stuff here all day. Like to go for a walk or something?"

"Oh yes, you want to meet me in Tredegar Square?"

"Okay."

"Fifteen minutes?"

"Okay."

In Tredegar Square I sat on a bench, half an eye on twenty-seven Morgan Street but nobody came or went. Perhaps tomorrow or Tuesday I'd have time to knock and say 'hello' to the Archers, see if they'd let me take one last look around the old dump.

"Boo!" Hazel stood behind me. "You were daydreaming. Hope I didn't give you a fright."

I turned; she was wearing a belted flowered frock and sandals. "Hello." I stood. "So...."

"I thought we could go for a walk in Victoria Park." She smiled, and the gap between her front teeth was comforting.

"Okay, so long as I'm not late for Garrick. Let me carry your bag." She handed me a small canvas bag. Walking the length of Morgan Street to catch the trollybus on Grove Road for the brief ride, I thought how uncomplicated and nice she was — that this might be the last time I ever saw her, walked with her. Four... five years ago when I'd escorted her home after that party with Zilla's piano and the American airmen, we'd sat on the sofa in her front room and she'd let me touch her breast. She was eighteen now, so she must have been fourteen or fifteen. I wondered if she remembered, if I'd been the first one for her. I stole a glance down at the frizzy ginger curls as they bobbed along but she noticed me look, and my ears flooded with heat. I wished I could simply tell her what I was thinking about, but that would make her terribly uncomfortable. Nonetheless I wanted to say something, do something so she would know how special she was. "Would you like to go rowing?"

"Really? I don't know how to row."

"That's alright, I know how." Rowing couldn't be difficult, just a simple Newtonian action and reaction in two different viscosities: you moved the oar forward in the air and backward in the water; it should be a snap. It might cost two or three shillings, so I'd just have a bit less to spend on board the *Queen Mary* — that wasn't so important.

By the small dock on the boat pond in Victoria Park, I paid the attendant two shillings. With a long hook he grasped a boat and pulled it close, holding Hazel's arm as she stepped in and directing her to the rear bench. When I climbed in, the boat wobbled. "No, face the stern," he said. "Did you ever row before?"

"No, but I know about...."

He didn't give me time to expound my theory. "Here, let me show you." He hauled me out, stepped in and grasped the oars. "See? Vertical when you dip 'em, then feather 'em on the return so they skim, like this."

Rowing wasn't quite as instinctive as I'd figured, but we made it out into the middle of the pond. Hazel pointed out a grassy island with sloping banks and a clump of trees toward the center. "I've got sandwiches." She patted the bag. "We can have a picnic on the island."

"Oh, how wonderful, great!" The escalating pleasures of the day made me forget to feather the oar, and a sheet of water sliced the air, barely missing Hazel — "Sorry!" Finally we were close, and in a flurry of turbulence I tried propelling the boat's prow as high into the strip of sandy beach as possible — and found out rowboats don't accelerate as easily as bikes. My shoes filled with water when I jumped out, but I lugged the prow high enough that she and the bag stayed dry as I helped her. We climbed a short distance up the hill, I lay out my jacket on the grass, and she spread a little checkered cloth on which she arranged challah sandwiches, plus a couple of bottles of Tizer.

"Hazel, this is lovely, I've never done anything like this!" I removed my sodden shoes and socks.

"I wanted us to have a little picnic. Katya said you like this kind of bread."

I bit into a sandwich. "Ham and mustard on challah! Very ecumenical."

"Very what?"

"Just a stupid joke. It tastes really nice."

The sun peeked intermittently around the brilliant high-topped clouds. Boats bobbing on the water, some dotted with colored umbrella-like parasols, reminded me of the painting from the Impressionist book — Seurat's *A Sunday Afternoon on La Grande Jatte*. We lazed on the grass, munching sandwiches. Back to the bag once more for afters, and she brought out gooseberries.

"Wow, goosegogs are my absolute favorite!"

"I got them in Altman's this morning, they're nice and fresh."

"I stopped in Altman's yesterday, they had a new person serving."

"That's Mrs. Altman."

"No, this one smiled." I was rearranging my shoes and socks on the grass to dry faster.

"That's Mrs. Altman, the new Mrs. Altman."

"Really? What happened to the old one?"

"Nobody knows. He was serving by himself there for a few weeks, then all of a sudden a new Mrs. Altman showed up behind the counter."

"Good. The old one was a terrible sourpuss."

"If he bricked her up inside the cellar wall," she said, "I think the whole of Mile End would be on his side."

Savoring the gooseberries, I lay back with a hand behind my head; Hazel lay back too, and I moved closer so her head fit in the crook of my arm.

"I knew about this island," she said.

"Oh?"

"Katya told me about it, she came here once."

"Oh." The sun flickered behind wispy clouds. "Hazel."

"What?"

"Hazel, you're a good kid."

"You're a good kid also. A large good kid."

"It was so nice of you to think of bringing sandwiches and things."

"Thank you."

"It was. You're always so... well, nice."

"So are you."

"I didn't do anything, you thought of it, you did it all."

She eased her head back to smile up at me, her expression brushed with a minim of triste. "That's alright, I like to, Zech, I really do." There followed several minutes of absolute peacefulness — which she finally broke with: "Can an ordinary-sized good kid make a confession to a much bigger good kid?"

"You murdered Mrs. Altman."

"Well, yes... but apart from that."

I looked down at the ginger frizz. "What?"

"I'm sorry we waited 'til your last Sunday to have a picnic."

"I'm sorry, things have been so mixed up for me, such a strain. This is the loveliest day since I got my demob."

"That's what I mean, it's such a lovely day for me." And she began to cry.

"Hazel!" I didn't know what to say. "I mean, I'm so glad you thought of coming here today...."

"Yes I know." She wiped her eyes on the sleeve of her frock. "I wanted to do this — other times, also."

"You did? I... didn't Katya tell you I could only get off on some weekends?" The flush of evasion colored my cheeks.

"She told me you were going to Forest Gate whenever they let you out. Wow, now I feel really stupid."

"Oh I don't know, everything got kind of complicated, Katya told me you were going... with the... milkman."

"I only went with him a few weeks. It was nothing really."

"I know, you told me what happened, I...." I could feel my ears shining bright.

"I feel really stupid now."

"Hazel, knock it orf or pow right in the kisser! Here." I took out my handkerchief to dry her eyes.

"I shouldn't have opened my big trap."

"Knock it orf mate! Who knows, maybe you'll come to America some time."

"Now it's my best friend's brother going away also, but *really* this time." She sobbed. "And there's nobody left."

I found myself with my arms around her shoulders. "Who knows, maybe the ship'll hit an iceberg and you'll be glad you stayed."

"Don't... don't... I'm sorry."

The very last thing I wanted was to make Hazel sad, particularly today. "Hazel?"

"What?"

"Can I write to you from there?"

"Well, course you can."

"Alright, I will."

"Will you really then?"

"Absolutely. Will you answer?"

"Course I will. I'll get your address from Katya."

"You don't even need to, I'll write as soon as I get there. You never know, maybe you'll want to come also before long."

"I'll come and watch you get famous, then you'll be too important to talk to me."

"Famous? With what?"

"Singing. That party with the Yanks that time with your sister's piano, that's what I knew you should do, singing. I loved it."

"Really?'

"Yes, I did."

She laughed, her shoulders shaking, then immediately burst into tears again. "Oh, fuck! Pardon my French." She shoveled the leavings back into the bag. "We'd better get started back so you're not late for Garrick." She brushed her hair back and flicked grass and crumbs from her clothes. "Where did he get that stupid name Garrick?"

"His mother wanted it because it didn't have a diminutive. Ga... Ga... come here, Ga. Yes, I mustn't be late." I pulled on my still-wet socks.

"What happened to his mother?"

"She died when he was born." I looked at her face, and in a silence congested with the sudden strangeness of taking her fragile hand to help her back into the boat, I rowed us over to the dock.

"Didn't his dad want to get married again?"

"I don't know." The Mile End trollybus arrived quickly, and I took my seat next to her, not knowing what to say. I tried something neutral: "Do you ever talk to the new people in our house? Their name's Archer."

"Oh no, the Archers moved out."

"They did?"

"Yes, right away, didn't you know, Katya knew. There's someone else there, they keep to themselves, no kids. Why, did you want to...?"

"Sometimes I wonder what it's like inside there now."

"Let's knock then, maybe someone's home."

I helped her down off the boarding platform. Walking along Morgan Street, my awkward strides seemed unable to synchronize with hers. And to boot, it was already after six, less than an hour before my slated meeting with Garrick. I barely had a mind to stop at number twenty-seven, but the decision to knock seemed already coalesced. I stepped up the two high concrete steps and knocked.

"Oo is it?" came the call from inside, so gruff we both instinctively moved back.

"It's... I'm...."

The door was opened by a stocky fellow perhaps five feet eight, clean-shaven, wearing a tan striped shirt, no collar, and a cap that seemed a permanent part of his head. "Wha'cha lookin' for?"

"Mr. Archer."

"Archer, no 'e don't live 'ere no more, they ain't lived 'ere more 'an a year. Oo are you then as wants 'im?"

"Oh, I'm... I'm... well, I don't know if you know a Mr. Grossman?"

"Know 'im! You ain't one of them Grossmans, are ya? 'E owes me, 'e does."

"Er, well no, Mr. Grossman used to be my uncle when I was little, I'm not...." I took Hazel's hand to leave.

"Where's 'e livin' nah?"

"I don't know, we didn't speak to them for years and years, no one knows where he is now...."

"That bugger owes me dear, 'e does!"

"I don't know where they live."

"Slippery customer, I'd pay ya five quid to get me 'ands on 'im."

"Five quid... I mean, five pounds? My parents don't know where he is, he owes them money also."

"'E does?"

Hazel's eyes were locked on me, and I gulped, "Yes."

"Welp, I'll give ya me telephone number 'ere, you ring us up if you finds out anything, it'll be wuff it, five quid."

"Well certainly, if I find anything out."

"'Ang on a minute, I'll write it dahn for ya."

As he disappeared I looked through the street door to the living room. From street level all that was visible was the ragged arm of our old settee, and beyond, on the ceiling, the gas mantle, its horizontal arms and short pull-chains draped like some religious relic. He was handing me a piece of paper: "Give us a ring, mate."

"Right, can I ask your name, like when I ring, who to ask for?"

"There's only me an' the ol' trouble an' strife. Well..." He pulled the paper back, and wrote again. "Ask for Joe, that's good enough. Now, don't you tell 'im no one's lookin' for 'im."

"If I find out anything it'll be confidential."

"You know what else that blighter did?" he said.

I took Hazel's arm. "We have to leave, we're in a hurry."

"'E sold this 'ere place to them Archers, furniture and stuff."

"Uhuh."

"I comes 'round for me money, this job what I done for 'im, they says as 'ow 'e don't live 'ere no more, an' *they* don't want to stay 'ere neither."

"We really have to go." I pulled Hazel with me, but that didn't deter him.

"So I tells 'em I'll take the 'ouse orf their 'ands, one 'undred quid for it, ten quid right out me pocket."

"I'm sorry, we have to see someone, we're late, we really must go."

He kept talking after us as we started along Tredegar Terrace. "It's rainin', the cellar's like the bloody English Channel it is." Our distance increased, and he shouted: "All you needs is a boat down there."

Hazel hurried alongside me toward Litchfield Road.

"The fellow's cracked," I said and looked at my watch. "Twenty-five to seven, I can't risk missing Garrick."

"You know something?" she said.

"What?"

"Should I come with you to meet Garrick?"

"You want to? It's your whole day."

"You couldn't come in my house now anyway, there's no time and my parents'll be there. Can I come? Today's probably the last time...."

"Well yes, I'd be grateful if you came with."

"You would?"

"Well sure."

"Alright, I'll come." We swung around and retraced our steps.

"The truth is I'm nervous in case there's any problem getting Maudy's suitcase back. I never should have taken it from your house. I probably won't be seeing Garrick again either after tonight."

Joe was still standing at the open street door, and I nudged Hazel over the road so we could pass by on the far side. "It ain't never gone away," he was ranting, "you gotta wear bloody wellingtons down there, smells like a shit'ouse it do, sorry miss."

"I'll be ringing you up if I find anything out," I called across.

"Five quid for ya, mate."

Hurrying through Tredegar Square, the first isolated spatters of heavy raindrops deflected the leaves above our heads. We crossed Mile End Road and ran for the trollybus, hopping aboard just before a deluge rattled at the driver's windscreen. By the time the bus slowed at Johnny Isaacs and we jumped down, the downpour had diminished, leaving the evening air cleansed and refreshed. We ran across the wet pavement to the entrance. Three minutes to seven; the Austin hadn't yet arrived. "Let's dry off inside," I said. We commandeered a table by the big window, where Hazel placed her bag on a seat. "Tea?"

"Yes, please," she answered. I joined the perennial queue, and a minute later she was waving her arms, "Zachary!", and pointing out the window. As I peered into the rain-peppered twilight I saw the side lights of a car that had pulled up to the curb. As I looked, Garrick stepped out and came around onto the sparkling pavement.

"Hazel, take my place in the queue." I gave her a two-shilling piece. "Get three teas, I'll go get him." Outside, the rain fell in heavy widely-spaced drops that bunched together as the wind blustered. "Garrick, want to come inside?" I called across. "I ordered tea."

He waved, but remained standing in the rain over by the curb.

"Do you want to have tea? Do you have time?" He stood awkwardly alongside his car in the burst of pelting rain, lightly tapping the roof with one finger, so I came across the wide pavement. He held out his hand to me in greeting.

"Do you want...?" I continued.

"Well...." He looked ill at ease. "I had to sort of...." I glanced down into the car and realized the front passenger's seat was occupied. "Everything's alright," he continued quickly, "we've got the suitcase."

He edged me away as the passenger door began to open, its bottom edge scraping the pavement. "Hold it," he called, lifting the door by its handle so he could open it without damage. A figure — Sophy, wearing a black mackintosh — unfolded onto the sodden twilit pavement. "Hello, Zech."

I checked quickly to see if anybody was in the back seat. "No, no one else. Sorry Zech, I was caught in the middle. The only deal I could get was if I promised I wouldn't tell you."

"I see. Hello, Sophy."

Her mackintosh was becoming shiny as it caught the rain. "It's my fault," she said. "I wouldn't give him the case unless he let me come with."

"But I drove a hard bargain also, tell him," said Garrick. "No throwing anything heavier than half a pound."

"I had to see you Zech, I don't want us to argue," she said.

Garrick unlocked the boot. "Let's give him the suitcase first so at least we've completed the bargain."

"I'll give it to him." She followed Garrick around, the two of them in tandem lifting out the case. He relinquished his grip to close the boot, and with both hands she held the case toward me, "Here you are, Zech." She removed one hand, and in grasping the handle's loop my hand was around hers.

"I'll wait in the car while you two lovebirds chat." Garrick climbed in behind the wheel on the far side, closed the door and switched off the lights.

"I didn't really want to break up," she said. Together we lowered the suitcase slowly to the pavement. As she let the handle slide from her grip she rotated her palm to clasp my hand. "We could forget about everything that happened, if you wanted to."

"Forget? You mean, the commotion where I'm not allowed in Hazel's house anymore, or what your father and Uri did at my job?"

"Dad and Uri were very wild, you going over her house like that. You shouldn't have had supper there, you know I would have made you supper."

"Hazel's a friend, does going with you mean giving up my friends?"

"I don't know, Mum said be firm from the beginning so Dad and Uri don't have to get involved. I should have told you, it's my fault…."

"Uri and your Dad don't have to get involved! You know what they did, what happened?"

"I know Moishe's wild with them."

"Moishe?"

"Something about tar all over the inside of his lorry. Mum didn't let them in when they came back, she made them climb over the fence and take their clothes off outside in the yard."

"Did you know because of them they gave me the sack at my job?"

"But Zech, you don't need that job in Wapping, really."

"What do you mean, need?"

"They'll help me start my own place, our own salon, we can make five shillings profit on a customer, it'll be perfect."

"Sophy, you have to realize I just don't like hairdressing."

Abruptly she released my hand. "Why not?"

"I've got my own things I dream about."

"But you've got to wake up, you can't live on dreams."

"But I love dreams — I dream about relativity, where the universe comes from, why some notes sound like Stravinsky and others… make… well… Schubert."

"But… but…."

"Zachary!" From the doorway, Hazel was waving . "Tea's on the table."

"Who's that?"

"Alright, we'll just be a minute," I called back.

"Who is it?" Sophy scowled; then her tone became incredulous: "Is that her?"

"Her? Yes, it's Hazel."

"What!" she screamed. "You brought her with?"

"With? I mean, we were… out. I didn't know you were going to…."

"You… you rotten sod, you!" A slash of wind flung rain into our faces as she grabbed at the suitcase standing between us; simultaneously I grasped at the handle, and the lid pulled open. Immediately she was on her knees lunging at the clothes spilling onto the wet pavement, flinging them in all directions. "You rotten barstard you, Dad was right!" As fast as I could retrieve Marius's old favorite, a pair of grey cor-du-roi trousers, she grabbed at one of the legs, and to avoid tearing them I relinquished my grip, at which she tossed them away again into the downpour. A small group of onlookers had paused at Johnny Isaacs' door. Garrick now stood by the open driver's door, observing us over the car's roof, silent, neutral. Hazel had started toward us, just her frock and sandals in the rain, and as she approached, Sophy stood up and picked up the opened case strewing a pullover, socks, a shirt and Marius's old jacket in a wide semicircle. Holding the case by the handle she swung it at Hazel; centrifugal force flipped it fully open and more socks and another pullover were flung out as the suitcase's arc barely missed Hazel's face.

"Enough of this, get in the car!" I bellowed, surprised at my own voice. I grabbed Sophy's arm, my hand squeezing as hard as I could through the mackintosh.

"Ow!" she exclaimed, and dropped the case. I forced her over to the car and wrenched open the door. Garrick quickly climbed back in on his side and started the engine. With both hands I pushed her down toward the seat while she kicked at my shin repeatedly with a ferocity that made me gasp. I thrust her into the seat, lifted the door and slammed it shut, and as the car began immediately to pull away from the curb, her window was lowering: "You rotten barstard, you!" she cried out.

The car staggered, her door swung open again, a commotion issued from inside and Garrick's hand reached across and pulled the door shut; I heard his shout, "Stop it!" Luckily the glinting slick black surface of Whitechapel Road was empty of other vehicles as the car executed a hasty U-turn, its lights flickering on belatedly as it reached the opposite side of the road; the engine whined at high revolutions and the vehicle leaped ahead. Save for a distant crashing of gears, ten seconds later the Austin had dissolved into the elements.

I backed away and felt for my shinbone, if it were broken. A drenched Hazel kneeled in the middle of the pavement gathering the sodden garments, placing them tenderly back in the suitcase that lay open alongside. The onlookers by Johnny Isaacs' door watched as I kneeled too, retrieving the last remnants, folding the saturated trousers on top. Hazel was crying as we snapped closed the suitcase, "Poor Maudy, poor Maudy!"

"It's alright Hazel, it's just clothes, we'll…."

"Poor Maudy…."

"It's alright, let's take it inside." Someone among the witnesses held the door open for us. I placed the waterlogged case on a chair by our window table still earmarked as taken by Hazel's canvas bag, mackintosh and three untouched cups of tea. We caught our breath and wrung some of the rain from our clothes. As a thin stream of water began dribbling from the suitcase I stood it down to the floor on the less-obtrusive window side. "Let me get some fish and chips. Something to help us simmer down a bit." People moved aside, allowing me to go to the head of the line; I stood there, dripping, finally bringing our meal over to where Hazel sat guarding the suitcase, sipping cold tea. "Hazel, you're all wet, I hope you don't catch something."

"That's all right, I stuffed serviettes inside my dress, that's what all these bumps are." Her eyes were still tearful as she pushed a stack of serviettes toward me. "Zech, I'm going to wash and iron all Maudy's stuff myself," she whimpered, smiling bravely.

"No, no, it's alright...."

"I won't take no for an answer. You're here 'til Wednesday morning, you'll come over my place Tuesday night and everything will be washed and ironed. I hope that selfish cow doesn't come back now with the rest of her family. If she does I'm going to get Mrs. Isaacs to ring up 999 for the police. They think they can go around doing things like that to people!"

"I hope Garrick's all right driving her back, she doesn't cause an accident."

"When you take me home tonight I'm keeping the suitcase also, I'll make sure the case is all dried out."

"Hazel, can you believe all this?" I placed my hand over hers. "Thank you for coming with me, I'm sorry for all the trouble I caused you. You're such a dear, you really are."

She burst out crying afresh, and again people looked. She lowered her head and I reached for more serviettes from the next table. "Oh, fuck everybody," she announced not too discreetly, her words tangled amid a composite of laughter and crying. With wet glistening eyes smiling at me, she whispered: "Fuck 'em all."

"You're right," I said. "Fuck 'em all, let's enjoy the fish and chips."

55

Monday morning I again left the house with Jack. At Aldgate he continued on to school and I took the bus to the City, to the embassy at Grosvenor Square. A medical exam, a few more forms, and they told me if everything was 'square' I'd get the visa the next morning, so not to forget to bring my passport. A brief bite to eat, then early afternoon on to Thos. Cook & Son Ltd. in Gracechurch Street, where they gave me twenty exotic dollars for £5/2/6. Four dollars to the pound; the extra two and six, they said, was for 'service.' By four o'clock everything had been taken care of for the day. The only task remaining would be to bring my passport to the embassy the next morning, Tuesday, and I'd be all set.

I floated out of Thos. Cook's building. I'd eat supper back in the East End where it was cheaper, maybe buy some afters to bring back to Mrs. Pristein, to have with her and Jack. The bus sailed along effortlessly, and I opened the window wide for the fresh breeze to bestir any lingering anxieties. As we rode through Aldgate, then past London Hospital, I suddenly remembered Uncle Albert's cellar in the alley. It was early enough, this would be my last opportunity to see him, so quickly I jumped off the bus, crossed Whitechapel Road and walked along New Road. Turning the corner into the alley, the vertical wall at the end seemed higher than I remembered, and rubbish piles even more mountainous. I went back out to the street to check; it was the correct alley. Inside again and to the far end, the window Albert used as his entrance was now covered with boards. I bent down and called "Hello," but no response. The top board had been nailed into the window frame, so I pulled it away and yelled: "Uncle Albert!"

A voice barked: "'Ey, wha'cha think you're doin'?" Behind me stood a rough-looking muscular character — a watchman, I hoped.

"My uncle used to live in there, I came to see him."

"Your what?" He came closer, scrutinized me.

The brick wall was too high to scale; I'd have to run around him to get out to the street. "My Uncle Albert, he used to live down there, he went in and out through this window. I wanted to say hello."

"Hello, huh?"

"Yes."

"Sure you ain't 'ere to nick 'is stuff?"

"Nick his stuff? He's my uncle, he was injured in the war, the first war, World War I."

"When j' see 'im?"

"Last?"

"When j' last see 'im?"

"Well, it must have been… two or three, three years ago."

"Right." His demeanor had softened. "'E was your uncle?"

"Yes."

"No one told you?"

"Told me what?"

"'E's dead."

"Dead?"

"Bloke killed 'imself 'e did."

"Killed himself!"

"Shot 'imself 'e did, someone should'a told you."

"Christ!"

"Sorry mate. Six months ago must'a bin. We found 'im sittin' at the table down there, all 'unched up just like 'e was 'avin' 'is dinner like. Shot 'imself in the face, 'e did. Mess like you ain't never seen."

"Christ!"

"Like you don't never want to see, neither, 'e done it with some old rifle 'e fixed up wiv string."

"Fixed up with string?"

"Tied it up on them there shelves by the gas-stove, like pointin' at the table it was, a bit of string 'ooked round the trigger then back around the shelf. Tidy job 'e did."

"Christ, I…."

"'Ad 'is dinner then pulled the string. Sorry mate, someone should'a told you."

I sat down on a piece of wood.

"Sorry, mate." He backed away. At the end of the alley he turned, touched his cap respectfully and disappeared.

Uncle Albert, dead! What about Uncle Harold, bringing him money? Probably someone told him when he came that week, maybe the same watchman. I must have sat thinking for quite a while because when I finally tried again to pull the piece of nailed wood away from the window frame the day had already declined to dusk, and dark shapes were barely recognizable inside — the edge of the table, the back of a chair. So I simply pushed the wood back against the frame and left everything.

I realized I'd forgotten to buy something for afters when Mrs. Pristein told me to help myself from the saucepan and join them for supper. But I didn't feel like food. "I went to see my uncle in Whitechapel on the way back from the City. They told me he committed suicide six months ago." They both stopped eating. "No I'm sorry, I don't want to spoil everybody's supper."

"How did it happen?" asked Jack.

"With an old rifle he kept from World War I. He used to shake all the time, he spoke sort of … haltingly. He told me they tied him to a cannon because he didn't want to shoot anybody." They both were silent. "He said they sentenced him to the wheel for twenty-four hours, that's why he was like that." Mrs. Pristein stood up, holding her serviette to her mouth, and left the room. I realized my description had been too graphic. "Jack, I'm sorry, your dad, Normandy. I wasn't thinking, I shouldn't have said all that detail."

He was silently counting. "Two weeks four days ago it was six years already, June the sixth, 1944. It was a Tuesday."

"Tomorrow's Tuesday," I said. "I'm sorry, I… I don't know why I said that…."

"Mum told me he was missing when I got home from school the next day. He was on one of the first troop-carrying gliders in. After the war, other paratroops told us the Germans shot it down, and when it crashed they just kept machine-gunning everyone in the wreckage."

"My god! Jack, I'm so sorry, I shouldn't have...."

"They knew from reconnaissance we were coming, thousands of paratroops, you can't keep something like that secret. The Germans, they... killed nine thousand Allied soldiers on that single day, June the sixth."

"Jack, I'm...."

"Mum still can't bear to hear about dying and the war, any war."

"I'm... I shouldn't have said anything." I lifted my hand toward his shoulder; he brushed it away.

"The fucking barstard Germans, I'll hate every one of 'em for the rest of my life."

•   •   •

Next morning after walking Jack to the Underground station, I trotted over to Altman's to buy three pounds of gooseberries. As the new Mrs. Altman weighed them and placed them in a bag I took a closer look: she was slim with brown curly hair and one of those tortoiseshell combs on the side above her ear. Her teeth were white and perfectly shaped, which explained why she smiled so much. Hazel was probably right about him bricking up the first Mrs. Altman in the cellar. I ran the gooseberries back to the house. "Mrs. Pristein, you said you like making gooseberry pie, I bought some gooseberries."

"That's very nice of you, Zachary, you didn't need to do anything like that."

"But I really wanted to, though."

She lifted the bag. "My goodness, we'll have enough for a month. How about today I make a really big pie, and this evening we'll celebrate your last day in England. You can take some pie with you on the ship."

"Alright, thank you. I'm sorry for what I said last night, I was so stupid."

"Don't apologize Zachary, we bear our losses as best we can. What about your poor brother, such a young man."

"Thank you." It was terrible her husband was killed just as the Allies were about to win the war. What I felt ashamed to admit was that I rarely thought about Marius being dead, and when I did it was somehow analytical, distant. My only brother — but I never really knew who he was. "If everything's alright with my visa this morning, I'm going to the cemetery in the afternoon with my aunt, so it might be late by the time I get back."

"Certainly, I'm sure you'll be glad you went when you're in America."

"Yes."

At the American embassy a man they said was the Vice Consul asked me if I appreciated their giving me the visa in just three days. Because of his accent I couldn't tell if he were pleased or irritated; this interview was the final step and I couldn't afford to say anything wrong.

"Yes sir, I do appreciate it."

"You know how long it takes to get a United States visa in other countries?"

"No sir."

"Ten years. You got yours in three days."

"Yes sir, thank you very much, sir."

"You know why?"

"Er... no sir."

"Because Britain is the only country that never fills its quota, that's why."

"I see." I didn't know whether that reason was positive or negative.

"You're gonna have to learn to drive on the right side of the road, you know!" Suddenly he was smiling, stamping my passport in red with the immigration visa. "Think you can manage it?"

"Yes sir."

"Good luck in the United States." He got up from his seat and extended his hand.

"Thank you sir."

Delirium made me grasp the rail as I exited through the high doors and descended the steps to the street. Everything was completed, sewn up, and tomorrow morning — the boat-train! The bus, conversations among other passengers a pleasant blur, opening the window all the way for the sooty air to waft sweetly in my face. Hooters, traffic, a lady behind asking me to close the window again, please. Changing buses at Aldgate. Right on past Mile End, through Stratford — yes!, passing the building where Melissa lives! What happened with her, I never saw her again, maybe her husband is off his ship and lying drunk on their bed this very moment! Buildings more sparsely dotted, the countryside progressively expansive, and then cows, munching; cows must spend ninety-five percent of their lives eating.

Finally we reached West Ham, then the conductor announced, "Plashett Cemetery." I hopped off the boarding platform as two people, a red-eyed little boy and a mother in unrelieved black, climbed aboard. The bus chugged away and there I stood on the pavement, suddenly alone and facing the stillness of the cemetery entranceway across the road, its gate framed by crumbly brick pillars and a black iron archway. I crossed the road. Beyond the railings ran the endless grass patches, some capped with new markers and fresh flowers, others seemingly abandoned to ravaged concrete headstones. Here and there a plot lay quietly deserted within unkempt tall grasses. As I passed through the gateway a solitary red-breasted bird chirped on a tree branch, ruffling defiant feathers. The dirt and stone roadway crunched beneath my shoes — too loud; a fluttering and the bird flew off. A remote distance ahead of me stood the little stone building with small-paned windows and a slate roof. I climbed the step onto a concrete platform and pushed the vertical wood-planked door, which swung away into a black interior. After the sunlit outdoors the contrast was extreme: a darkness barely pierced by a shrouded green-glassed lamp on a counter-top. A voice said, "Zachary, you're here, I was wondering already," and as my eyes began to adjust, Aunt Zelda materialized on a bench by the wall.

"Hello, Auntie Zelda."

She stood up. "Where were you, I was wondering."

"What's the time, it's just three o'clock, isn't it?"

"I've been waiting and waiting, they let me out early from the office, what could they say?" Her face was falling into focus, and a worn, unrecognizable face it was. The meager light reflected off her smooth skull between scant wisps of hair. "So we'll go outside, then?"

I asked the man propped behind the counter for the location of the grave. In the darkness a chair creaked as he resuscitated himself to consult a ledger. His bony finger ran down and across several pages, each inked entry, I could now discern, in a different script, until: "Aha, righteo!" He pointed through the building's solid wall. "To the end of that road, then go right. You'll cross over another path on the diagonal, keep going straight, then it's…" he counted… "the fourth site on the right." He circled the location on a small map which he slid across the counter. "You can't miss it."

Zelda donned a little round hat that she pulled down firmly as we exited into the mid-afternoon brilliance. "So when are you leaving then?"

"Tomorrow, tomorrow morning." If she offered, I didn't want her coming with me to the boat. "Very early."

"So, another Yank we'll have in the family."

"Yes." Nobody else was in sight, and save another bird twittering among the leaves off to our left, the crunching of stones under our feet constituted the only disturbance. "I haven't been here since Maudy was buried."

"You haven't? You should have come. What about the stone setting? You came for the stone setting."

"I was in the RAF, I couldn't come home that weekend."

"They wouldn't let you out for a stone setting, terrible, a *broch* on them, your own brother, you should have told them they *had* to let you out." Why hadn't I gone? Was I preoccupied with Sophy? Sophy would have wanted me to go, she would have insisted on coming with. "Where's your *yarmulka*, you've got to wear something on your head."

"I... I don't have one." We'd reached the end of the road, and now veered right, onto the path.

"You don't have one!" She fished in her handbag. "What am I looking? I don't have anything. A handkerchief, you got a big handkerchief?" I took out my handkerchief. Now on each side we passed tended plots, engraved plaques: *Morris Levy, died 23rd October, 1943. Dear Dad, Forever in our loving memory. And the rest will be told in the books of the chronicles of Israel.* "Tie it, the corners tie, each corner, tie a knot." She checked that I'd tied them properly. "On your head, pull it down, that's right." *Hannah Bloom, 34, beloved wife and mother, passed away too young. 23rd November, 1947. Mordecai, Asha and Sheila will always miss you.*

Marius. He had lain in bizzare parallel silence with these unknowns for... for one and a half years. I had not come to his grave even one time since that day when Katya and I stood here, when a rabbi, a stranger who ten minutes earlier had never even heard the name Marius, recited with grave and sonorous mien: שִׁבְטְךָ וּמִשְׁעַנְתֶּךָ הֵמָּה יְנַחֲמֻנִי — he translated for us, *Thy rod and Thy staff, they comfort me.* Marius. When he choked I would slap his back until he could breathe again. But that was all. That was all: he was a stranger, his life was foreign to me, to all of us except Mum. And I'd not come here again since, this place, at most a half-hour from Forest Gate, even less in Garrick's father's car, fifteen, twenty minutes. I tried to breathe, "Poor Maudy."

Zelda followed me across the diagonal path and reached for my arm. "Where is it?"

"The fourth one now it's supposed to be, on our right, there. It looks different... they must have buried other... people." Tomorrow morning, after I departed England, nobody would visit this spot again. Except the strangers, people he didn't know. I pulled the handkerchief off my head to staunch the tears, to blow my nose. It was hard to breathe; that must have been what Maudy felt like every time it happened, but much worse, much much worse, desperate.

"No, no, you mustn't, quick!" She grabbed the handkerchief from my hands, spread it back over my head, snot and all, pulling down the corners. "Here, here's another hanky." From her bag she handed me a prim embroidered cream-colored thing.

The stone said: *Marius Grossman, aged 14, died 12th December, 1948.* That was all. No *always in our memory,* no *your family misses you,* only blank marble consigned to wait in eternal silence. The whine of an aeroplane engine reverberated among the grasses, the weeds, across the lifeless charted fields as above our heads a tiny biplane, a DeHaviland Moth, darted freely through ominous clouds suddenly menacing the blue sky. I kneeled and the trimmed grass was wet through my trousers legs, grass shaped, combed and fed by workmen so that some essence of living might permeate downward into the soil, maybe even penetrate the polished mahogany below. I found myself rocking forward and back like the davening rabbi: Maudy, Maudy. Everything in the world was tortuous chance, inexplicable.

Zelda stood there watching, watching me. "I'm worried about Rae."

"Not now, Auntie Zelda, this is, this is…." I was mumbling, wiping my nose. In the distance a blur of five or six people inched their way along another path.

Zelda found a pebble and placed its flat edge on the arched marble. "They let her go home for the time being, she can't work, how can she go to work, she's lost one and a half stone the hospital said, she's thin as a stick." A sudden spatter of rain darkened Marius's headstone as I stretched way over to my left to steal one yellow hollyhock from a cluster on the adjacent grave. "Don't, what are you doing, no no, it's not nice, somebody…."

I clawed a small hole where I thought Marius's chest would be and planted the stalk, squeezed earth around it, buttressed it to stand vertical. "It's alright."

"No, it's not nice," she said. A few more raindrops. "Ee, it's starting to rain,"

"Yes."

"So, do you want to go? There's nothing more we can do, what can we do anymore? Other people they'll wonder, a flower's missing, they'll see."

"I suppose there's nothing more, we might as well go."

"Yes, we'll go then, it's good you came before you went to America."

I brushed off my knees and backed away from the rectangle of damp earth, from the solitary upright bright yellow flower. We started along the pathway to the wider road. Several times I looked back; the yellow became a blur that homogenized with other yellows and browns, and soon there was nothing. At the stone building I asked her, "Did you have anything, did you leave anything in there?"

"Anything?"

"A coat?"

"A coat, in this weather?"

"An umbrella, I don't know, we might as well go then."

"Yes, we'll go."

Outside the gate we sat on the bench waiting for the bus. "Auntie Zelda, do you come here, might you come here sometimes?"

"Me?"

"I mean, where is Uncle Albert, did they bury him here in this cemetery?"

"Uncle who?"

"Uncle Albert. If Uncle Albert's here and you come sometimes, maybe you could just go where Marius is… to look, to see everything's alright…."

A bus on the horizon floated like a mirage, slowly drifting closer, its image and then its crunching wheels staying the completion of my question. I helped her aboard and followed along the aisle, stumbling into the empty seat beside her.

"Where to?" The lady conductor stood alongside. In a seat ahead of us a fourteen-year-old's hair bobbed with the bus's jiggling. He laughed to himself; he was reading a copy of *Hotspur*, the same comic book Manny used to lend me, that sometimes Marius would read.

Outside, a street, shops, already we were in a town. "I'd like a cup of tea," Zelda said.

To the conductor, "Just two three-halfpennies, please, we're getting off." She leaned across me, pulled the cord, the bus stopped.

A waitress with red hair done up in a bun poured two cups of tea.

"Auntie Zelda...."

"What?"

"Auntie Zelda, I hated leaving him there like that."

"Well what did you expect?"

"I... I don't really know, it's just...."

"That's what it is, how do you think we all felt with Cissie?"

"Auntie Zelda, I mean, if they buried Uncle Albert here and you come here sometimes...."

"Uncle Albert... who?"

"Your brother."

"My brother?"

"I'm sorry, I mean Uncle Harold's brother, Mum's brother." The tea was hot, my lips wouldn't form. "Yes, your brother, I'm getting mixed up. Uncle Albert."

Zelda covered her mouth with the white cloth serviette. "What are you talking about, what is it, your father's brother? No, they don't have an Albert."

"Em, I'm mixed up, no, it's not Dad's brother... who is it then? Yes, that's right, Mum's brother, the one from the war, Uncle Harold's brother.... Yes, your brother, he must have been your brother, then... you know...."

"What are you giving me a headache already! I don't know any Albert. Harold's my brother, your mother's brother, what's...?"

"Uncle Albert, tsk!, the one who lived in the alley off of New Road. The watchman there told me he committed suicide six months ago." My struggle to sculpt some request was slipping away.

"I don't know what you're talking about, I don't have a brother Albert." Her lips were narrow.

"Now you don't."

She began to cry into the serviette. "Stop giving me a headache already! Brother! I don't know any Albert."

"I... I.... He told me Uncle Harold used to come to see him every week, he used to bring him money and bread and things."

"Who..." she struggled to catch her breath, "...what's going on here?"

"Don't you remember? His hands used to shake, he couldn't speak properly. He couldn't work because of the war, what they did to him in the First World War. He told me."

"What, are you trying to drive me mad?" A man and woman at another table, the only other occupants of the teashop, shifted uncomfortably at our intensity. "You think I don't have enough aggravation looking after Rae, with that *broch* Vera downstairs, nag nag from morning til night? What do you think killed Cissie?" Her eyes were small and red, she blew her nose into the serviette. The waitress looked. "All the aggravation, that's what it was. You don't have heart failure for nothing, it's aggravation," she gasped. "If it's not this then it's that, always aggravation, you'll find out."

"I'm sorry Auntie Zelda, I didn't want to make aggravation."

"You don't want to make aggravation? Then stop it already!"

"Alright."

Zelda signaled: "Tea, more tea, a scone. You want a scone?"

"Er, no thank you, I...."

The waitress cut and buttered one scone, put the plate in front of Zelda. Obliquely from under an arm she lay a fresh serviette by Zelda's cup and with two fingers removed the old one. Next she returned with a teapot and refilled both our cups. "Marmalade? You want marmalade?"

"No, just plain, I like it plain."

The waitress retired. We drank our tea in silence. Zelda cut off a small end of the scone to eat.

"Auntie Zelda."

She swallowed. "What?"

"Can I tell you just one little thing?"

Again she swallowed. "Not if you're going to start making aggravation."

"It's about something that happened, a few years ago before I went in the RAF, when I used to work in a factory."

"Alright, so tell me then."

"One day I was coming home from work and someone called me, a man."

"So, already?"

"I told him I had to go home. At home, I told Mum and Maudy, and she said that's him, the one who came round Tredegar Square when we were little, from a long time ago, I shouldn't talk to him."

"She's right. You mustn't talk to a strange man in the street, you never know."

"Yes."

"So you're finished then?"

"Nearly, the next night or something I was going home the same way, along New Road, and the same person called me. He had trouble talking, I didn't know what to do so I went in his place, he lived in a cellar. His hands were shaking when he tried to make tea."

"You went in somebody's cellar?"

"It's just that he knew everybody's names, he told me Uncle Harold used to come round and give him things. He knew Mum's name, he told me never to go in the army."

"He was in a cellar, this one?"

"You know who I mean, then?"

"How do I know what you're talking about? A strange man, how do I know, it's danger-ous, you have to be careful, you never know."

"I... I don't know, I thought.... He knew everybody's names."

"Look...." She was quiet. After a few moments, she wiped her eyes then sat still, looking at the table. She took a sip of tea. "Look, you don't understand, you were all babies. That one, he didn't live anywhere."

"What do you mean?"

"I told him I'll take him to the baths to get a wash, I'd go with him, like a filthy tramp he walked around."

"When I saw this one he had a cellar, he slept in a cellar, he had a sink with water."

"In a cellar?"

"Yes, so was it maybe the same one? I thought I was getting everything mixed up. He said they made him go to France to fight the Germans. He said if he'd gone to America instead everything would have been different."

"Different! Disgusting the way he kept himself, a good-for-nothing there in the park with his head on one side sleeping, in the rain sleeping out in the open, like people looking.

Once I had to talk to him in the park, I was with Harold. Harold gave him five shillings."

"This one told me Harold gave him money."

"I told him leave him alone, what can anyone do, if that's what he wants good luck to him, you should worry! If Vera found out she would have killed him she would, giving away hard-earned money to a… a tramp. Harold said it's a shame, from the fighting there, you have to help your own flesh and blood. I tried, filthy dirty, a terrible smell, still I talked to him. Soft like a girl, Harold, he always was, why do you think he married Vera, he felt sorry for her." She was squeezing the scone. "We were desperate, the whole family, what could we do, he wouldn't even have a wash!" She put a hand to her mouth and spat out some of the scone, "Ugh!"

"I… I…. I don't know, I just felt sorry, what they did to him. He was shaking, he seemed frightened to talk to anyone because he sounded…."

"You think we didn't try?" Suddenly she was crying openly into the serviette. "I told him, you want to say something to somebody…" again she gasped, "think in your head, *think,* before you open your mouth, I told him. Put your hands in your pockets if you can't stop with the fidgeting there. His clothes they stank, he never washed, you think we all didn't try to help?"

"No, I… I…."

Chairs scraped; the other couple were standing and the woman was pulling her handbag off from around the back of the chair; the man put money on the table and pulled at her arm as they stumbled toward the door.

"What do you know," Zelda's sobs filled the room, "you weren't even born yet, nobody listened. Your mother, you think she listened? We told her not to marry him, your father, everybody knew he was mad, what's the good, I just wanted a respectable life without all the meshuggeners everywhere making aggravation so you have to be ashamed to go out the street door."

"I… I…."

"Don't talk to me anymore about it. You'll find out when you get older, when you have more experience you'll understand better. Suicide! A fancy name they got for it! He should have done something years ago, he waited and waited, driving us all mad with worry. Suppose one day he showed up by the street door, can you imagine? For the neighbors, can you imagine?"

—o—O—o—

–56–

When the bus arrived at Mile End, I bade Aunt Zelda goodbye and she continued on to Harold's and Vera's house alone. From the kiosk outside the Underground I dialed Hazel. "Hello, they gave me my visa this morning, so everything's settled."

"Oh, I see, okay, so you're definitely going."

"Yes."

"That's good then. Okay."

"Yes, tomorrow. I just got back from the cemetery now, I wondered about Marius's clothes and stuff."

"Can you come over?"

"To your house?"

"Yes, can you come over?"

"Now? What about your parents?"

"Just come on over."

In less than three minutes I was on her step ready to ring the doorbell, but the street door opened before my hand reached the button. There she stood, frizzy ginger curls and big toothy smile. Under an opened cardigan she again wore a white blouse, but this one was different: it had a lace-up front that ran from waist to neck. I wrenched my eyes upward past sections where the fabric edges scarcely seemed pulled together. The brass ends of the long ties from the bow at her neck dangled level with a stretch of bare skin which I was sure signified *no bra*. Back up to her face again, she smiled and her eyes were certainly darker, although it could have been the doorway's shadow. I gave her a peck hello, and tasted lipstick.

"Here's the suitcase." It stood on the floor behind her. She spoke quietly. "Everything washed, dried, ironed and folded. Neatly, I'll have you know." The eyes — not quite the heavy greenish shadowing that Zilly and Rivka used to painstakingly apply from eyelashes to all the way up to under-the-eyebrows, but darker nevertheless.

"Yes, thank you, I don't know how to thank you enough."

"You can't come in…" she whispered, "em… are you taking it back to Jack's house now?"

"Yes."

"Can I come?"

"Back to Jack's?"

"Yes, just for the walk."

"Alright, they may be eating supper."

"I don't have to go inside, I've already eaten."

"Mrs. Pristein will invite you in. Sure, come on."

She called back into the passageway: "Mum, I'm going out, be back in an hour or so."

Mrs. Stapleton's voice came from behind the kitchen door. "Take your mackintosh in case it rains, don't stay out too late."

We started along Tredegar Terrace. "It was weird this afternoon at the cemetery."

"Yes, I'm sorry."

"Not just seeing Maudy's... place, there, but my aunt I went with, she's a bit cracked."

"Was it your Aunt Zelda?"

"Yes. Did Katya ever mention her?"

"She said she's a bit prim and proper."

"She is. I just wanted to know if she'd be going back there ever because... I had an uncle, oh, it's a long story." As we walked alongside Tredegar Square we both held the suitcase handle between us. "Hazel, you look...."

"What?" She kept her face down.

"Well, you look... nice."

"Do I?"

"Yes, you look sort of... very grown up."

The mackintosh and purse moved across to the other hand and the suitcase swung with additional vim. "You must be so excited about going."

"Yes, it seems like a dream, like I'll wake up. Maybe when I'm actually on the ship I'll believe it." I took the suitcase in my other hand and put my arm around her shoulder.

She raised her face: "Does Katya know you're going this week?"

"No, I didn't know for sure 'til this afternoon. I need to send a letter for them to meet me there."

"I'll post it airmail for you, tomorrow."

The sky was cloudless and an early-risen moon floated above the rooftops, its surface blotched with varied reflections of mountain and lowlands clearly delineated in the fading daylight. "Look at the moon," I said, "isn't it beautiful!"

"That first time you came over my house, remember, when those American airmen were at your house, that one that was playing the piano?"

"Yes."

"There was a great big moon that night, lovely."

"There was? It was such a long time ago, how can you remember?"

"You sang *This Love Of Mine.*"

"You remember that, god, I'd forgotten which song it was. But I was so excited, someone who really knew how to play letting me sing."

"When I went to bed that night I could see the moon through the window."

"What a memory!"

"I can tell you the first two lines: *This love of mine goes on and on. Though life is empty since you are gone.*"

"That's right, you're right."

"I used to think about it all the time you were in the RAF."

"You did? Er... it's a lovely song." We were crossing Mile End Road. "Hazel, I don't know what to say...."

"Well this is your last night." She took a deep breath. "When else can I tell you?"

"Yes, I don't know...."

"Will you miss Sophy?"

"Miss her! I don't think so, after everything. I don't know what happened since I got my demob, she's been like a different person."

"She probably feels terrible you're going to America, so she's wild with you."

"You know something!"

"What?"

"I just realized, with all the goings on I never specifically told her I was going!"

She whistled through her teeth. "She doesn't know?"

"Unless maybe Garrick said something on the way home. That's right — she may not even know! Christ, that's terrible, isn't it?"

A pause, then: "Serves her right! You know, Katya hates her also."

"What do you mean, also?"

"I mean... Katya hates her... a bit, I think."

"Funny with Katya, she always kind of sizes people up pretty quickly."

"She didn't do too well with Benny, though."

"You're right. Anyway, here we are." We'd arrived, and to my disappointment she buttoned up the cardigan. "Hazel, it's the last night so I have to say it, your blouse is very nice."

"It is?" She reopened the cardigan. I tried to turn off my mind, putting down the suitcase, kissing her without worrying, slipping my arms inside the cardigan all the way around to the back. "A minute, you've got lipstick!" She dipped into her purse, wiped off my mouth with her handkerchief, then took a little mirror out and straightened her own lipstick. "Alright."

She buttoned the cardigan up again as I rang, and Jack opened the door. "Jack, you remember Hazel."

"Hazel! Oh certainly! It's been a long time, come on inside." He assisted her up the steps, and with the suitcase I followed them inside. "Mum, meet *The* Hazel. Hazel, my mother."

Mrs. Pristein stood up. On the table, serviettes were crumpled and the plates were soiled; they'd just finished supper. "Hello, come in, nice to meet you."

"Nice to meet you."

"Zachary, we didn't know how long you'd be at the cemetery so we ate. There's more in the saucepan if you're hungry, either of you."

"No, really thanks, my Aunt Zelda and I had something in West Ham."

"Hazel, join us please. Zachary always says such nice things about you."

"Thank you very much, we already had supper at home."

"Then let me add some more water, we'll all have tea." She filled the kettle. "So Zachary, from your beaming face I assume all went well at the embassy, you got your visa."

"Yes yes, there weren't any problems. I'm going to be catching the eight o'clock train from Waterloo in the morning. It's hard to believe it!"

Jack tilted his head and nodded a reluctant affirmation. "So, you're leaving tomorrow!" He pulled out a chair for Hazel. "I hope it wasn't too... much at the cemetery."

"Well ... I'm very glad I went there," I responded.

"Good, then," said Mrs. Pristein. "So, tomorrow you're off to a new life! And for tonight the biggest gooseberry pie in London is waiting patiently for us in the oven. Come on, everybody sit down. Don't you want to take your cardigan off?"

"No I'll keep it on thank you, I'm a bit chilly." Hazel lay down her mackintosh, and even buttoned an additional button as she took a seat.

Finally Mrs. Pristein sat down and poured tea. The delicious pie stayed conversation briefly; then she continued: "Hazel, we heard about the disturbance outside your house last week."

"Yes, my Mum's taken out a court summons against them, Sophy's parents and her brother."

Mrs. Pristein nodded. "From Zachary's account, I don't blame her at all."

"My Dad has a weak heart so we have to be careful. Mum wanted to take out a summons a few months ago, someone nearly punched him. Dad said no, but this time she did it anyway."

"Was that... that was Benny?" I interjected between stuffing my mouth.

"Well yes it was, that time. Katya's husband, he rang the bell one night. My Dad told him Katya wasn't there but he started pushing and shouting. He's a bully, that's why Katya left him."

"My goodness me!" Mrs. Pristein was doling out seconds. "Well Zachary, I've also got another pie for you to take on the ship. It's big enough you can live on it for the entire trip."

Jack had been silent, and now he spoke. "Zech, I'll take tomorrow morning off and come with you to Southampton."

"Oh Jack, you don't have to do that, I mean...."

"Old fellow, it's not to help with the luggage and stuff, I just want to make sure you get on the right ship so we don't have to jump every time *our* doorbell rings."

"We'd have to leave early, six thirty or so to be at Waterloo before eight."

"Unless you really wanted to go by yourself." He seemed wistful.

"Oh no, I'd like it if you can spare the time from school. Then, when they throw you out and you end up taking a job emptying dustbins every morning, you can thank me."

Mrs. Pristein smiled. "Thirds or fourths, anyone?"

We bantered for another half hour, then I stood up. "Well, it'll be an early morning. Hazel, let me walk you home before it gets really late."

Mrs. Pristein gave me a street door key. "You can let yourself in without waking us. What would you like for breakfast?"

"Oh no, you don't have to get up so early...."

"Tea, toast and jam, six A.M. please," said Jack.

"It'll be on the table, also I'll put the other gooseberry pie in a bag."

Holding Hazel's hand I jumped exuberantly down the front steps, and didn't let go all the way to Mile End Road, where I pulled her to a halt. "Hazel, can I kiss you?" In the moonlight, standing on the edge of the pavement, we kissed slowly just like in the pictures — except that under the cardigan I was easing the back of her blouse out from inside her belt.

She laughed, "Not now," and tucked it back in.

Feeling marvelously free, I took her hand again and led her across Mile End Road. "There's something else about that night I went home with you, after that party with the Americans," I said. "I've nearly said it a few times but I... I don't know.... Anyway, you're right, tonight is the last chance 'til you come to America also."

"I think I'm glad it's dark out."

"You know what I'm going to say?"

She squeezed my hand. "Say it first, then I'll tell you."

"Well, remember that night...." Silence. "Remember that night, I... I sort of...." Absolute silence. "Well, when I... sort of... you know, I wondered if...."

"You were the first one."

"Really?"

"The only one... well, yes, the only one. The milkman wanted to but he must have thought he was milking a cow, I've still got a bruise."

"You were the first girl I ever touched also."

"I know."

"How do you know?"

"Katya told me."

"How would she know?"

"She knows everything."

"But... I mean.... I see." I *didn't* see, but... anyway.

"It's my turn to ask you a question," she said.

"Sure."

"Well, I feel stupid, I'm glad it's dark."

"In that case I promise I won't listen."

"Well.... I'll say it fast, did you ever do it with Sophy? Sort of, like, well, you know, I feel stupid."

High spirits left me nowhere near as embarrassed as I ought to have been. "Well...."

"You don't have to answer if you don't want to, I just wondered, that's all."

"Well, we never really actually did... well... had... what do you call it, sort of.... I mean she was nervous about getting pregnant."

"Oh," she said.

"Yes."

"Alright."

"I would have.... I mean we did... other sort of stuff but we never actually did it."

"Alright." We were back at her house. "Want to come in maybe?"

"What about your parents?"

"The light's out downstairs, I'll see if they're in bed."

"I don't want to make problems, they already hate me."

Immediately she was gone, and like a silent waif reappeared a moment later. "They're asleep, you could come in for a little while," she whispered.

"You think it's safe?"

"We could creep upstairs... my Dad wouldn't come in my room."

"What about your Mum?"

She was hanging up her mackintosh. The cardigan was unbuttoned again. "My Mum doesn't like me to wear this blouse."

"Oh."

"We'll have to whisper. At the worst you'll go under the bed, then you'd go back to Jack's."

"Alright."

"Let's take our shoes off."

And we padded up the stairs. A small light left on in the kitchen showed the foot of the stairway, but the upstairs landing was dark. I held her elbow as she eased her bedroom door open, and we slithered inside. From beyond the other door came her mother's voice: "Hazel?"

"Yes Mum, it's me."

I quickly groped my way around the bed and dropped to my knees, prepared.

"You locked the street door?"

"Yes."

"Good night then, see you in the morning."

"See you in the morning."

I breathed; it was dangerous, but I was too elated to be cowed. "What should I do?"

"Stay there," she whispered. "Sit on the bed." She came around, removed the cardigan, and we sat on the edge of the bed. "You can take your jacket off if you like."

Already my eyes were adjusting to the dim light from the outside street lamp; I lay the jacket over the back of the chair.

"You better put it on the floor so you can push it under the bed. It's clean on the floor."

I dropped the jacket to the floor and immediately we were kissing, teetering backwards and down onto the mattress. Again I began to ease the blouse out and this time she did nothing to stop me, actually kissing me fiercely.

"Should I take it off?" she mouthed.

I was amazed. "Er, alright, really? Yes."

She sat upright and untied the knot. "You can pull this, if you like." She held out one cord; I tugged it and the blouse fell away. I'd been right: no bra. She was outlined against the dimly illuminated curtain, and beyond the silhouette of her bare left breast I noticed that the hanging flowerpot had been replaced. She stayed sitting in the same position, her arms tight to her sides and lap. I raised myself and gently kissed her on her bare back; she shuddered but didn't protest. After an awkward moment when neither of us moved, she said, "You can kiss me… there, if you like."

"I…." I wanted to, but my face was a long way from her front and I didn't want it to seem too obvious and contrived. "I would like to, yes I would," I said, hoping she would turn a bit toward me. But she didn't, and all I could manage to kiss was her shoulder.

Still she stayed facing forward. "Do you really want to?"

"Yes, I'm a bit shy I s'pose."

"Alright, you go over there then." With her forearms glued to her thighs she pointed a finger toward the window, "and I'll lay down, then you can."

I went over to the window alcove.

"Don't look for one minute."

I was faced away, looking through the curtain. From the bed came rustling sounds and the soft rearranging of elastic, then a whispered, "Alright." When I turned she was lying on the bed, on top of the covers, and in the near-darkness she seemed to be completely naked. It was such a surprise I didn't know if I'd turned too quickly, if I should have waited until she had time to put her bloomers on or get under the covers. I spun back quickly, accidently banging my head on the flowerpot.

"Be careful!" she said in a loud whisper.

The flowerpot was rotating and I reached out to steady it; as it slowed it tipped slightly between its supporting strings and, deafening in the night-time silence, earth rattled onto the wooden floor in the alcove. *Not again!* As I grasped at the pot with two hands I heard the bedsprings creak; was she getting under the covers?

"What are you doing?" The voice was right behind me, the sudden proximity so surprising that my head hit the pot a second time. "Careful!" she gasped, reaching up to stabilize it. But a muffled thump and a further scattering of dirt and little stones signified the new plant had fallen out of its pot. The empty flowerpot itself was outlined against the white lace curtains, tilted on its side within its knitted string web, swinging from the imbalance. She reached up with both hands to straighten it, and — her breasts sharply outlined at the raising of her arms — her naked silhouette was so utterly compelling I couldn't pull my eyes away. But somehow her fingers must have gotten entangled in the weave, and I could scarcely believe what followed: the empty clay container slipped from her hands and fell. Quickly I grabbed her for support, simultaneously sticking out my stockinged foot to prevent it from hitting the wooden floor. I managed to avert a direct impact, but couldn't stop it rolling away in a wide arc, bumping over stones. In the darkened room, the noise was thunderous.

"Oh my god!" She was kneeling on the floor groping for the pot, and quickly handed it up to me.

I grasped it tightly. "Alright, I've got it."

"Who is it, what's going on?" Mr. Stapleton's voice came from immediately outside her door.

"Nothing, Dad, nothing!" She turned and leaped into the bed, pulling the bedclothes up over her head.

"I heard a man's voice, someone's in the house."

Had I not been holding the empty pot I might have had presence of mind to drop to the floor and roll under the bed, but instead I found myself standing there, relieved that at least this time nothing had broken. And those crucial seconds were my undoing: the door opened, the electric light clicked on and in blinding light Mr. Stapleton stood in the doorway, holding closed his maroon robe.

"I'm sorry, I'm sorry, I er…" I said, "I er… the pot."

Only Hazel's hair, eyes and fingernails protruded over the rim of the covers. Her voice was muffled: "It's alright Dad, he was, he was, he was just, em, he was just fixing the pot, the er, flowerpot, it was…."

A second light switched on outside in the landing and Mrs. Stapleton, in a pink lace-necked nightgown, now stood behind her husband.

Mr. Stapleton spoke. "So I see it's Zachary."

"Yessir, yessir, it is, I am sir."

"Zachary, I thought you were going to America."

"Mr. Stapleton, I mean I am, I am going to America, I'm going tomorrow."

"And what, pray, are you doing up here now in my daughter's bedroom?"

"I'm fixing the… there was something wrong with the…."

"I asked him to fix the… thing, there, the earth was coming out," said Hazel, her eyes barely visible above the top of the sheet, her red curly frizz splayed over the white pillow-case.

"I see."

"Yessir."

He thought for a moment. "Zachary, let me ask you a question."

"Yessir Mr. Stapleton, yes definitely you can ask me anything."

"Just *when* are you going to America?"

"Tomorrow sir, Mr. Stapleton, in the morning, early, I'm definitely going to America tomorrow, I have to catch the boat-train early in the morning, my friend is coming with me."

I cleared my throat. "To make sure."

"He is," squeaked Hazel. "He's going early in the morning, his friend is going with him."

"Hazel, you don't have to echo whatever he says."

"It's not, I'm just, he is going in the morning, I know for sure."

"Alright, Hazel."

"Yes Dad he is, so I... thought... you wouldn't... mind... if he walked me home just once."

Mr. Stapleton had moved forward and now stood inside the room. "I see....." He drummed fingers on the doorframe. "Zachary, if I may ask, how could we be sure you're definitely leaving for America tomorrow?"

"Oh yes Mr. Stapleton, absolutely I am, definitely."

From behind, Mrs. Stapleton pushed her husband forward until she also stood just inside the room. She spoke for the first time: "Do you have a ticket or something?"

"Yes, oh yes, Mrs. Stapleton, absolutely, I'll show you." I stood the empty flowerpot on the chest-of-drawers, and both parents stretched forward as I bent down to retrieve my jacket from the floor alongside the bed. Under quizzical scrutiny I pulled my wallet from the inside pocket and rummaged around, then remembered that of course the papers were much too large — they were all in the envelope in the other inside pocket. I removed that package and with outstretched arm handed it around the bottom of the bed to Mr. Stapleton: "There you are sir, everything's there, passport, I just got the visa this morning, the ticket's there, it's all paid for, everything, you can look yourself."

Mr. Stapleton, however, held up the palm of his hand at my forthrightness. "No, that's alright, if you insist you really are going tomorrow...."

"Just a minute." Mrs. Stapleton's curiosity was not as easily assuaged, and she came around the end of the bed in front of her husband. "Jim if you'll excuse me I want to see for myself."

"Yes, sure, certainly." I handed her the envelope; I would be relieved at their seeing the ticket and the other things.

Mrs. Stapleton opened the flap. The room was hushed as she leafed through the various documents. Finally, "Alright then." She handed everything back to me. "And now I think it's time you left," she said, simultaneously glaring at Hazel.

Mr. Stapleton looked down at my feet. "Where are your shoes?"

"They're downstairs," Hazel began. "We left them by the street door so as not to wake you up, he was going to leave in one minute, as soon as he fixed the pot...."

"Hazel, Zachary seems quite capable of speaking for himself," said Mr. Stapleton.

Mrs. Stapleton still glared at her: "And you'll come up with a better damn explanation than that, young lady, the moment he's gone."

"Emma, calm down now," said Mr. Stapleton. "We'll give Hazel five minutes alone to say goodbye. And Zachary, what we'll do is I'll wait outside in the landing, then in five minutes I'll walk you downstairs myself and see you out."

"No, Jim...."

"Emma! I said we'll give our daughter five minutes of privacy to say goodbye."

"Jim, I'm not taking any chances, I don't want you ending up in hospital again, do you hear?"

"Emma, please! Come outside, I want to talk to you." They both stood within the doorframe in whispered discord. Gradually they retreated further outside, and slowly the door was pulled closed. "Five minutes," Mr. Stapleton called through the door, and the muted contention further diminished, then ceased.

"I have to put my nightgown on," whispered Hazel. "Don't look." Again I turned away, at which she said: "Oh, who cares." Though the light was on, quite naked she slid out from under the covers, opened a drawer, pulled out a pale yellow nightgown and began wriggling into it.

I didn't know if I should have looked away, but before I had time to ponder that choice she turned to me, and I kissed her mouth. "Hazel, I'm so sorry, it must be in my genes or something, to keep knocking over flowerpots...."

"Shut up and kiss me." Her head tilted to one side and I grabbed her hair and kissed her on the mouth, on the side of her face, on her neck, her ear and her earlobe. I no longer cared about anything, I felt so absolutely wild — so I sucked the other earlobe as well. "Will you write to me?" she gasped.

"Yes yes yes, absolutely, as soon as I get there I'll write."

"You promise?"

"Absolutely, I promise I'll write the same day I get off the ship."

"I'm going to write to Katya and tell her you promised."

"I promise, I definitely promise."

"Alright then." Her eyes were rimmed red within the smudged mascara, but she was smiling, and she poked the tip of her tongue and wiggled it through the gap between her front teeth. "Now kiss me, slow." I grabbed her and gave her such a big hug that she fell backward onto the bed, and I didn't even wonder about hurting her as I fell on top of her. For a moment I thought the whole bed might collapse. Luckily it didn't, but at the noise there came a polite knock and Mr. Stapleton's voice: "Hazel, Zachary, it's five minutes."

"Yessir, I'm coming right out." I climbed down, brushed myself off and got my jacket. "Hazel, I hope you'll come to America."

"Maybe, but in the meantime you make sure you write or I'll tell Katya to... to... well, I'll think of something."

I backed to the door. "'Bye, Hazel."

"'Bye, Zachary." She came forward with me, and as I reached behind to grasp the doorknob she gave me another quick kiss, then wiped lipstick off my face with the sleeve of her nightgown. She sobbed, "Ta-ra, I love you."

"Oh, Hazel...."

The knob was turning and the door began to open. "If you people are through I'll walk you downstairs and make sure the door's locked." Mr. Stapleton seemed very gentlemanly considering the turmoil I'd caused. As he finished speaking Mrs. Stapleton put her head around the half-open door of their bedroom: "Zachary, *bon voyage,* we wish you all success in America."

"That's very nice of you, I'm sorry for all the trouble I caused, I don't know how it all happened...."

"That's alright," she said. "Good night now, and have a good trip." I started down the stairs behind Mr. Stapleton.

"You're sure you have everything you brought with you — passport, documents, everything?"

I felt in the jacket pockets. "Yessir, thank you very much." I wanted to say something nice because they'd both been so decent. "Mr. Stapleton sir, thank you very, very much for showing me about Stravinsky."

"Stravinsky?"

"Well yes, I like music very much, it's terribly important and I'd never heard of him until...."

Upstairs in Hazel's bedroom Mrs. Stapleton was speaking in a tone of sharp admonishment, to which we heard Hazel reply: "Mum, I'm eighteen, I'm grown up and you can't keep telling me off like that, I'm not a baby."

"Young lady I gave you strict instructions not to even have him in the house, let alone in your bedroom after we're asleep!" Hazel's door swung to.

"Emma!" Mr. Stapleton had stopped on the stairs in front of me, and he half turned: "Emma, please wait 'til I come up!"

The door opened again. "I'm just talking to her."

"Please," he repeated, "I'm asking a small favor, just wait until I've seen Zachary out and I'll be right up. That'll be time enough to discuss whatever needs to be discussed."

"I'm really sorry," I said.

He continued down the stairs, grasping the banister rail with one hand and looking back at me. "That's alright; now tell me about Stravinsky — I don't recall mentioning him."

"Er... well, not directly, but once Hazel said you said...."

"Yes? Was it something I'd written perhaps?"

"I... don't... remember, she said you know a lot about music."

"A little, I review recordings for *Gramophone* magazine, you know it? And sometimes live performances for *The Evening Standard.*"

"Yes, that was it, she showed me something you'd written."

"So you like Stravinsky?"

"Oh yes, I mean, they used to play Stan Kenton in the RAF...."

"Kenton, really?" He seemed pleased. "He's quite imaginative for that type of music."

"Well I liked Kenton a lot when I first heard it because of all the different... the way the sections contrast, but still his stuff is always metered, so that aspect is predictable."

"You mean, in terms of the measures."

"Each downbeat, yes, you can tap your foot, you know when it's coming, but Stravinsky disguises that, I can't even hear where the barlines are."

"Remarkable, isn't he? You know how he accomplishes that?" He was paused on the bottom step, looking back up at me.

"No."

"He keeps changing metre — time signature — sometimes even every measure."

"Really? Then how does everyone keep up with everything, like how do they all stay together?"

He wore a pleased grin. "These people don't get to play in the B.B.C. Symphony for nothing! First rank musicianship, that's how! Boult really has to be on top of everything."

"But what I like mainly about Stravinsky is I've never heard such combinations of notes, almost as though it's in two keys at the same time."

"You have a good ear — that's exactly what he *does* like to play around with. It's called polytonality, more than one tonality at the same time."

"Really, at the same time? How can...?"

"Yes, exactly. What piece did you hear?"

"Er, it was about something fire...."

"Firebird? The Firebird?"

"Yes, that was it."

"Where did you hear it, a record?"

"Er, well, Hazel."

"Hazel?"

"Well I mean, Hazel told me about it, so my friend has a gramophone and I... er...."

His face was so animated! "But did you ever hear it live in the concert hall?"

"No, I've never been to a live concert."

"Zachary, wait 'til you hear it live in the concert hall, it's the most wonderful experience ever."

"Really, I can imagine!"

"No, you think you can but it's hard to imagine the impact. It's not just the frequency range that gets clipped on a record, it's the very scraping of the bows, it's, it's the audience...."

"Really!"

"But what you absolutely *have* to go hear is *Le Sacre.*"

"What's that?"

From upstairs, "Jim, are you alright?"

"Yes Emma, I'll be up in a moment." Then more quietly to me, "It's Stravinsky at his finest, *Le Sacre du Printemps, Rite of Spring,* the work is phenomenal!"

"Really?

"It's polytonal, polyrhythmic, ferocious, tender, everything... but you need to hear it in the concert hall to get the full measure. Not Bruno Walter, he's better with Mahler, Mozart, but this young American fellow, what's his name... yes, Bernstein, Leonard Bernstein, he has a good feel for it, he's got the youth, the dynamic grasp of the complexities."

"Alright...."

"New York Philharmonic, when you're there you'll be able to hear it live, Carnegie Hall it's called."

"Jim?" Mrs. Stapleton had come to the top of the steps. "Jim are you alright?"

"Emma I'm *perfectly* alright, we're having a discussion. Go to bed, I'll be up shortly."

"Go to bed? But what about...?"

"Tsk!, what about what? Can't you see...."

"Well, er, don't you think that...?"

"Emma, what I think is that this young man has a jolly good sense of music and I'm thoroughly enjoying our conversation. Go to bed, please, I'll be up shortly."

"Well!"

"Zachary, you're familiar of course with Beethoven, Tchaikovsky, Schubert, I assume. Vaughan Williams, Britten...."

"Well, I've heard them, I er... Tchaikovsky's a bit schmaltzy, isn't he?"

"You mean, sentimental?"

"Well yes, and Schubert, I don't know, it's boring, everything's so predictable."

"Ah, but you must hear him in historical context."

"Jim, I want you to come upstairs. Now!"

"Yes dear! Emma's right, I really should...."

"Yes, I'm keeping you talking so long. I'm leaving tomorrow, I'm so sorry I didn't have a chance to hear more about all this! I absolutely love music!"

"Well, I'm sorry too we didn't get to talk earlier, I had no idea you were so interested."

"Oh, I absolutely love it, I'd like to write music myself. I love to sing."

"You know, I think singing is an essential requisite to writing. What better way to know the beauty of a melodic line than to produce it with your own lungs?"

"I...I...."

"Zachary, if I'd known you had such a lively interest we could have gotten together for a chat, even had you come with us to a concert one evening. Anyhow, I'd better be getting back upstairs, work tomorrow, you know."

"Yes, I should be leaving too, I have to be up very early." I held out my hand. "Thank you very very much Mr. Stapleton, really, it's been wonderful talking to you." He stepped forward to open the street door, then looked down at my socks.

"Perhaps you should put your shoes on."

"Oh, my goodness, of course... I kind of got carried away."

"Yes, me too, frankly."

I lay my jacket over the banister and put on my shoes. "Well, good night, sir."

"Good night, Zachary. And don't give Schubert short shrift. The *Impromptu number three, B-flat,* beautiful, there's more there than you may realize."

"Yessir."

"The *Sonata, B-flat Sonata,* a bit repetitious. Stay away from the *C-major.*"

"Yessir."

"Maybe we'll be hearing from you."

"Oh yes, I'm definitely going to write to Hazel."

"I meant, hearing *about* you, in some musical context."

"I... really?"

"Good night."

Again we shook hands. I waved as I left, he doffed a polite salute to his temple, and the door clicked closed. In the heady late night air I donned my jacket and turned toward the corner of Tredegar Terrace, but tripped on an untied shoelace. As I kneeled to knot it I heard voices through Hazel's open bedroom window.

"Sorry Emma, I was carried away."

Mrs. Stapleton: "Yes, you're always getting carried away." Then, apparently addressing Hazel, "So, now I realize we can't trust you when we ask you not to let somebody in the house."

Mr. Stapleton's voice: "Remarkable."

"We've always brought you up to be trustworthy, and now this."

Again, Mr. Stapleton: "Simply remarkable."

"Isn't it? Who knows what else has been going on when we're not home."

Mr. Stapleton: "I'm sorry?"

Mrs. Stapleton: "I said, who knows what's been going on? Next thing we'll find she's pregnant."

"Emma, have you talked with him at all? Seriously, I mean."

"What are you talking about?"

"Unusually perceptive ear."

"Jim, are you alright?"

"Really nice chap, not like the rest of his family at all. Lively interest in good music. Wish I'd gotten to know him better. Hazel, why didn't you tell me?"

"Jim, what the blazes are you talking about?"

"Emma, he's a bright young man."

"So who cares?"

"Indeed, I do! I'm quite sorry I never had the opportunity to get to know him better."

"Jim, here we find someone upstairs in our daughter's bedroom in the black of night and you're talking about music?"

"That's *precisely* what I'm talking about."

"Are you feeling alright?"

"Hazel, I do wish you'd told me what a nice young man he is. I wouldn't be at all surprised if we hear something of him after he establishes himself in America."

—o—O—o—

Jack rode the boat-train with me to Southampton. "Well old fellow, I have to concede I might even miss you — when I think about it, which obviously won't be very often."

I was grateful to my best buddy for helping me assuage the strangeness at leaving. "You'll be too busy getting your new ladyfriend all mixed up so she doesn't get higher marks than you."

"Binnie's a sharp gal! I'm sorry... well, actually no, I'm *glad* you didn't meet her, she might get to be weird like your Forest Gate lady. It's probably something you give off, some secret radiation, like dandruff."

"Well, if she does trounce you in school, remember only six more years and you'll have Reuben to hang around with again."

"Yes, Reuben! Six years he's got to go?"

"Five or six. And if you can't wait you can always join him in Wormwood Scrubbs in the interim, of course." The clattering of the train's wheels billowed back from passing fields where cows, still chewing, turned their heads lazily toward the interruption.

"Well," Jack added, "at least Reuben's more interesting than Izzy."

"Yes, say ta-ra to Izzy for me, I'm sorry I didn't get around to seeing him before I went."

"I will. Izzy! He lends credence to the concept of negative quantities."

"True. Positively."

"You know, there are interesting people at school," Jack sighed, "but if I may wax philosophical at this parting juncture, friends you grow up with do fall into a special category."

"Is that good or bad?"

"Seriously, even if they include an Izzy — even a Reuben."

"In America after I become a famous Italian actor in the pictures, I'll come back to see all of you."

"You know they'll never allow known counterfeiters back into England."

"I'll tell them I only want to reconnoiter the empyrean fields of Mile End."

"Old fellow, don't knock Mile End."

"You're quite right, Forest Gate was certainly a bit of a mix up."

"Somehow I don't think hairdressing would have satisfied your deeper aspirations."

"Yes, I s'pose...."

"Just remember, with that British accent and a spattering of long words, whatever you say there they'll think you know what you're talking about."

"Jack, thanks for... well... I don't know, you can fill in the blanks."

"Think nothing of it."

"I don't, actually. Any chance you might bring Binnie to America, it'd save me the fare money coming back to meet her. It's the least you can do for a friend."

"Maybe for a holiday after I get my matric and I'm making thousands of pounds every week, but right now I s'pose I'm pretty content in England."

The train finally slowed at Southampton, coming to a final halt right inside the newly constructed wood-paneled Ocean Terminal. Between us we carried the luggage to the queue leading to the Cunard Line check-in gate.

"I'm getting ready to miss Mile End." I hoped the quaver in my voice was camouflaged by the general hubbub.

"Keep that stiff upper lip, old chap, and after a month you won't even know how to spell it."

"What, l-i-p?"

"If I know you, you'll be too busy infiltrating Oak Ridge for those atomic energy secrets."

"You're quite right, I'll tell them I just want the facts! All that bunk about quantum mechanics and the Copenhagen Interpretation! Einstein wouldn't give you tuppence for any of it." The line was moving ahead. "And another thing, I found out Schrödinger is allergic to cat hair."

"His wife shaved the cat first."

We'd reached the head of the queue, and the prospect of boarding the ship alone was making my stomach queasy. Documents, rubber stampings, questions: "Nothing. No, no, to stay. Yes, permanent, my family's there." My three suitcases were gathered about me. "Jack, they'd let you come on board for a while if you felt like it."

"Alright, just a short visit to lock you in your cabin."

"Good, okay." We grabbed the bags.

"Then when the telly says the *Queen Mary* struck an iceberg I'll be able to visualize you sawing through the door."

"Okay."

We tramped up the walkway toward the cavernous opening in the side of the ship. It was comforting to note that the natural laws holding minuscule rowboats afloat on the lake in Victoria Park would carry over into the new world, supporting this riveted steel wall looming infernally large up against the quay side. "Seriously," he said, "I mustn't stay long, I've got an afternoon class I absolutely can't miss."

"Yes, sure."

Through, then all the way down and into the muffled and already-thumping bowels of E-deck we searched out my cabin — tiny, windowless, double-decker bunks on either side. Fat asbestos-bound steam pipes, painted in garish yellow and blue, rose from the floor and ran along the ceiling above the dividing double set of drawer cabinets and closets with no doors. At the opposite bunks, a blonde-haired stranger was already unpacking his bags and hanging up clothes. In the small confines he turned toward us, blue-eyed, fair-skinned, cleft-chinned: "Hi there, Anthony, Anthony Parker." The tones were excessively modulated — *speech-trained* went through my mind.

"Hello, I'm Zachary Grossman."

"Jack Pristein," said Jack.

"You're both assigned?" The lantern-jaw jerked in studied consternation. "My goodness, they said this was...."

"No, just me. Jack's seeing me off."

"Well then, hello!"

"Hello."

"So," I said to Jack, "I can unpack later if you want a quick scoot around while you're here."

"Okay, then I'll hit the old terra firma."

"See you later." With a vault-like *clang,* the metal cabin door swung closed behind us. Along the narrow passageway we began climbing a metal staircase.

"Corkoid," said Jack.

"Who?"

"New material." He pointed at the treads. "Resiliency of cork, much longer-wearing."

On D-deck, just beyond the staircase, a rectangular grey and chrome metal box topped with a huge inverted bottle half-filled with water was attached to the wall. Next to it a chromed tube dispensed little cups of fluted paper. Jack pushed a spigot button in the front of the machine and out gurgled water.

"Does that mean a different cup every time someone takes a drink?" I asked.

"Must be! More hygienic than the British communal lead cup hanging on a rusty chain."

"But the paper, the waste!"

"Zachary the war's over, we don't have to save everything anymore." He filled a paper cup, took a sip and his face screwed up: "Try it."

I did. "Ugh!" It was icy cold, too cold to swallow. "I wonder why they do that?"

A motor began rumbling inside the box. "That's probably a refrigeration compressor," he said. "Cunard has to attract Americans if they're going to have enough passengers, so it follows that Americans must like their drinking water ice-cold."

"Christ, I'll have to heat it up every time!"

We ascended to higher reaches and the stairways became wider, resolving to carpeting and wooden banisters, the hallways with old-fashioned scroll-paneled wooden doors. "The decor is so incongruous," Jack said. "I suppose they want the implication to be the safety of your own living room."

"*My* living room! I still can't believe the floor there never collapsed."

"Keep in mind, adaptation will be the name of the game. Remember Darwin whenever you come up against something exotic."

"Yessir!"

Again he looked at his watch. "Well old fellow, I'd really better be getting along." We found our way back to the entrance area, and he stood within the hoop of the steeply sloping ramp and extended his hand: "Mile End's loss, the colonies' gain."

I grasped my old buddy's hand. "Don't do anything I wouldn't do. Except" — I felt in my pocket — "I forgot, please post this letter airmail for me, so someone meets me when I get there."

He stuffed into his pocket the letter I'd forgotten to give Hazel, then clasped my arm. Under the shading canopy he started down the ramp. "I'll send you sixpence worth of chips from Johnny Isaacs," he called back as I watched him descend. At the bottom he turned, and from the concrete pier waved a brisk salute — then was gone.

·   ·   ·

Back in the cabin I found myself alone. I slid Marius's suitcase under the bunk, and hung up my belongings for the voyage — my jacket, another pair of trousers plus a couple of shirts, and deposited a change of underwear and socks in the top drawer, then a Gillette, toothbrush and sundry items into the second. And in the bottom, a pair of library books undergoing transitional ownership, massive volumes entitled *The Schillinger System of Musical Composition* — along with the untouched gooseberry pie. My empty cases joined Marius's under the bunk, and I lay down to catch my breath and let everything sink in. More depleted than I realized, I must have drifted off. The deep rhythmic pulses from the engines were considerably more pronounced when I awoke, and the wall clock said two P.M. My cabin companion still had not returned.

I meandered along passageways, signed up for the second seating at mealtimes, and peered through the steamed windows of a deserted indoor swimming pool. From the prom-enade deck I watched the quay slipping away as diminutive tugs pulled and prodded our hull, a strange triste welling up at the sound of their klaxons' breathy *whooooo!* Soon the tugs had fallen behind as the ragged and angular shoreline became ever remote, its land-locked comings and goings overlain now with a blanket of quiet.

A young uniformed waiter served tea, and I sat awkwardly alone at one of several small tables on a shaded section of the deck. At the next table a knot of travelers buttressed themselves with conversation and laughter, but I could think of nothing to say to join in. Further away half a dozen young people had pulled together two tables, and this group's American accents were evident in audible snatches of conversation; one of the party, a slender animated girl with long blonde hair and very white teeth that flashed as she smiled, flounced around in a flowered frock as her friends playfully pulled her back down into her chair. Everybody was with somebody. Perhaps tonight there would be someone at the dinner table traveling alone.

But no; and for some reason I found it barely possible to go further than offer my name after one kindly man and woman initiated introductions. The menu was intimidating, the dishes' names enigmas. My random choice, roast beef, though confidently articulated, turned out to be a plate of red and bloody slices. So I ate the vegetables and drank the tea, and pretended I was full. Even the afters were horrible — a piece of powdery yellow pound cake held together with whipped cream. If these were American-style delicacies, acquiring a taste for them would not be easy.

Back again to my cabin, and Anthony Parker was already asleep, his shoes under his bunk. I fortified myself with a hunk of gooseberry pie, which tasted more delectably reassur-ing than should be asked of food, then propped myself up on my bunk and opened the first of Joseph Schillinger's music theory volumes. I read for an hour or so, and as I chanced to look up at the clock on the wall, before my eyes the small hand jumped ahead one full hour, from two to three A.M. So, all the ship's clocks were electrically governed from some central control room! That must be how they correlated them with the ship's sailing through longi-tudinal time zones.

I cut myself some more pie, and read on. My roommate snored and turned intermittently. Over the page the section was headed 'Pitch Scales.' The book described what Schillinger called *expansions* of a melodic scale — an idea I'd never thought of. First it showed an ordinary scale of adjacent tones, which he called *expansion zero;* I sang it to myself as I read it:

The book's next example showed those identical tones, but this time placed in alternating succession —what he described as *expansion one;* the sequence then became:

Humming this fragment made me realize right away that I was singing exactly the first line of Gershwin's *I Loves You Porgy:*

This was amazing! I ran through the second line, *Don't ever leave me,* a mixture of intervals which didn't fit his theory, but the third line, *Don't let him handle me with his hot hands* was, note for note, expansion one, again! I tried singing it with the lyric:

Incredible; it was the song, exactly! Was that how Gershwin composed that melody? Did he read these same books, or maybe even study with Schillinger?

"Can't sleep?"

"Oh, er, I'm sorry, er...."

He turned over to face my way.

"I'm sorry," I said, "I like to read, I hope the light isn't bothering you."

"The light isn't, but you were singing." He looked at the wall clock. "It is three-thirty A.M., you know."

"I'm sorry, I'm so sorry, I didn't realize, it's just something I was reading."

"You usually sing when you read?"

"No, no, I... I'll put the light out, I'll...."

"That's alright, I'm awake now." He propped his head. "What's your destination?"

"New York. Queens, my family just moved there from Manhattan."

"Well, I'm heading for Hollywood."

"Really? You mean, where they make pictures? For the cinema?"

"Yes indeed, my... china plate... is already out there. I met him at the Royal Academy, we both graduated last year."

Royal Academy probably explained the diction and the mellifluous intonations, if not the Cockney rhyming slang. "Really!"

"We'd hit a bit of a rough spot and he... like... went alone, then out of the blue a ticket arrives in the Post, can you jolly well imagine that? He says it's difficult there alone, he hates Californians and he misses me! So, here I am!"

"I... I see."

He turned onto his back. "We're planning on getting a flat together and joining the Screen Actors Guild."

"Yes... I see."

His eyes fixed on the ceiling as he pondered a new life. "That was our like... original dream and now it's coming true."

Perhaps *Anthony Parker* would soon be one of the names scrolling down a list of credits on the screen. Myself, I would start off by going to Leonetti's. Katherine would come with, maybe help me to meet Graham Forbes; he'd probably know about schools that taught you to write music for records or the cinema. "I hope to do some music in America."

"Really!"

"Yes, maybe in Hollywood one day."

"Score films, you mean?"

"Maybe."

"What school did you go to?"

"Well I didn't yet, but in America...."

"Oh, then what have you done in music?"

"Well, nothing really at the moment...."

He turned away, "Uhuh," and pulled the covers over his shoulder.

At dinner the next evening I managed a little conversation, and to the dismay of the waiter I insisted on the meat being well-done. Later, buoyed on the strength of that small victory, even feeling adventurous, I roamed. Perhaps there might be a piano in one of the rooms — that would be the best company. And just as that notion occurred to me I happened upon a bustling lounge, people drinking and talking. From the far side came the muffled sounds of a piano, its tones blurred by conversation and laughter.

I made my way through to where a blonde silken-haired young woman in a pale pink blouse and white shorts, with long tanned legs, sang:

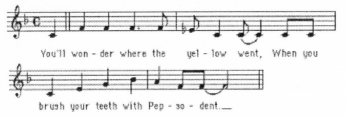

That's right, I'd read that on American wireless they set adverts to music to pay for the programs! I edged closer, and she was none other than the girl I'd seen cavorting on deck yesterday afternoon in the flowered frock. She looked lovely, but this evening my heart went out to the pianist because she sang so painfully out of tune. I watched, and after she'd massacred Pepsodent she stayed, encouraging the coterie of her friends to join her in slaughtering a couple more adverts. As they mustered a few halting phrases she coaxed them on, her Americanized *can't* rhyming with *Kant,* the laughter-filled asides to her companions so incredibly intruiging and provocative. However, her vocal abilities made even Vera Lynn sound good. Maybe terrible singing didn't matter; maybe being unaware gave you confidence, and that was more important. Perhaps automatic confidence was what Vera Lynn happened to have been born with, like this one with her blonde hair and pert nose. Though, standing there bathed in the spotlight above the microphone, she had more than enough to be confident about: the perfectly-arched eyebrows and glistening teeth made her more unassailably beautiful even than Joan Ingersall had seemed all those years ago in science class, lying helplessly on the floor beside that frog-stained bench at Coopers College.

She and her friends finally drifted away, and now the pianist, a heavy-set aging Negro man, came more clearly into view. As the crowd thinned, his feigned pleasure at accommodating their musical depredations resolved to relief. He took a deep breath and seguéd discreetly into a private performance of *Spring Can Really Hang You Up The Most*. Released from his obligations, his playing became a wonderful complex of melody and countermelody, the weaving combinations shaping the harmonies I knew so well from Joe Williams' singing it on the wireless. Williams had had an equally wonderful accompanist, and now these writhing lines were just as intoxicating as they implied joinings, touchings, implications fulfilled or delicately teased, analogous to what I imagined a sexual encounter would ideally be — romantic, playful, tender. His playing exemplified why Hazel had said that time she felt like her legs melted: this was love-making unequivocal, its transfiguration as music a transparent disguise allowing the audience to become consumed in its intimacy without violating any public decorum.

"Wow, I love the way you play."

"Y' play?" he asked, continuing to play. How could his brain, directing delicate contrary lines through his fingers, manage a simultaneous conversation through his mouth?

"I... I don't want to interrupt."

"'S' okay."

"Well no I don't play yet, I want to learn as soon as I get settled in America."

He played on. "Where y' gonna be? N' York?"

"I... I can't listen and talk at the same time, I miss bits."

He smiled, "Uhuh!"

"Queens, Jackson Heights or something... I want to listen...."

He continued playing as I savored each note. "Y' dig this, huh?" His concentration dissolved into another smile. "You come catch mah gig — Birdland, midtown." His heavy fingers wove spiraling threads. "Yeah, we startin' Aug'st, twenty-three Aug'st, two weeks, run through beginnin' Septemb'."

"When you finish this one, could I... sing something?"

A sudden closer glance at me, then he looked around hesitatingly — and quietly laughed to himself. A pause — then, "Sure!" *He must hate people who ask to sing!* "What'll it be?"

He was going to let me sing! "Can I try *Laura?*"

"Got it!" And as he meandered, "Y' know the key? Standard?"

I didn't know what *standard* meant. "Can you do it in C? Like, it starts on a D-minor nine?"

His eyebrows went up. "Sure," he drawled, as his hands reshaped their memory of the progression to a new, unfamiliar keyboard configuration. He rolled an arpeggio and banged the E, looking up to see if I'd catch it, not knowing I didn't need so blunt an invitation to the starting pitch.

Breath, *Lau-ra__* no-breath, *is the face in the mis-ty light,___*snatch-a-deep-breath-away-from-microphone, enough-to-carry-beyond-'hall,' *Foot-steps__* of-course-no-breath, *that you hear down the hall.___* His shoulders rocked from side to side with pleasure as I parlayed his playing into an easy rhythm. People looked across and started drifting back to the piano as I sang on, exhilarated, confident in prising out subtleties of text, intonation, breathing, of phrasing *primarily* to the lyric and *secondarily* to the melody, both he and I quickly entrancing every person standing within the glow of our small circle — *that's* what it was, what singing was about, music's *raison d'être*. I looked at him, his back hunched, eyebrows up, intent and nodding to the beat, his brief glance up at me from the keyboard carrying the easy recognition of our having known each other forever. As we completed the first chorus his soft brown face beamed a wordless invitation to continue at a light bounce, where I could feint and parry his largesse, by now both of us basking in — yet simultaneously oblivious to — the little circle of admiration in which our audience had framed us. He soloed the bridge, and after I'd completed the last chorus, with his encouragement I sustained a final tonic that he teased with impossible modulatory excursions before returning to earth. I'd taken a deep-enough breath to easily hold the note through all this to the very end, whereupon he jumped up and grabbed my arm with two mountainous hands, "Yeah, okay, okay!" His huge smile lit up the room. "Anytime, sing anytime, come every evenin' Ah'm heah!"

I sang, in front of complete strangers I sang, with a real jazz pianist! And until that moment I hadn't even been aware that the blonde goddess with the golden legs stood right up front, watching! *I'm going to love it in America — it's just like at the pictures!*

I wove through the crowd, past a seated Anthony Parker wielding an empty glass: "You chaps get yourself so stupefied singing about females!"

Stumbling across the lounge through to the passageway, on shaky, resolute knees I climbed the wide carpeted stairway. Against the resistance of a gusting wind I forced open a heavy door to the outside deck, and in the metallic moonlight plunged down the tilted floor to the perimeter, grasping at the rail. The seas were high and roaring, the stars had become stilettos of ferociously beautiful ice hung under a soft velvet parabola. A miraculous eternity passed as I strove to quell the clamor within and assess the magical tapestry of sky unfolded before me. The uncontrollable wind seared my face, insisting, whipping its way through jacket and shirt; I relinquished one handgrip to its driving sway, and thrilled to being swung around. Here we were aboard this ship racing at thirty miles an hour on an arc along the circumference of this earth, this chanced, mind-boggling sphere, itself hurtling around the sun at a thousand miles an hour in an ellipse so vast it would take twelve full months to return to where we'd started — except, we could never know if we *had* returned, Einstein had shown there are no absolute markers. And in fact, could we transcend relativity's constraints and indelibly mark this blessed moment, we still would not *quite* come back — a nostalgia only for the wilfully blind — because the sun was intent on its own prodigious quest around the Milky Way, a journey so immense that it had been privileged to complete only a few circuits; now was still early in the time of things, and all the dazzling creation accosting that frenzied deck was yet fresh and innocent. I was singing, shouting, shouting into the wind — *Laura is the face in the misty light* — loud, arrogant, drowning even the roaring seas.

"Hi," she called above the tumult. The Pepsodent girl, wrapped in a flapping coat that teased and tantalized the perfect skin.

"Hello." It was surprising to see someone out on deck. I probably had looked — and sounded — like a lunatic just now, but I didn't care.

She came closer. "I really liked the way you sang downstairs," she said.

"I liked the way you sang, also." A lie, musically, but love sanctions such generosities.

"Oh, I didn't really sing, just those stoopid commercials."

Styoopid, not *stoopid.* The spray reached up three stories.

"Gee, it's quite a wind."

"Yes, I like the elements. Really, I *love* them. There's something... elemental... about them," I said. "Like coming home." She looked so small, the wind whipping at her silken blonde moonlit hair. "I've never seen the stars quite as bright and still as this. They look unreal."

"Yeah." She hung on the ecstasy of the rail, next to me. "You sang great."

"Thank you, thank you." It was chilly on deck, and she was now close enough that I was able to venture an arm around her shoulder. The wind sang its encouragement in rapturous counterpoint. *I mustn't be nervous, I cannot be nervous, I mustn't slow down and allow myself to start thinking. Now, right now, commences the aeon of non-Boolean logic.*

"One night in London, during the war, it was late, way after midnight, they'd just sounded the *All Clear.* My friend, my best friend Jack and I were in the street outside my house..."

She listened, her face tilted up toward mine.

"...no more bombs, the bombers had flown off and the anti-aircraft guns were hushed, everything had settled into a sort of post-traumatic calm. There was a quarter moon; earlier that evening I'd watched the moon rise, and the stars..." I removed my hand momentarily from her shoulder to gesture toward the sky, "...the stars, they looked the way they are now, so peaceful, so eternal you felt... I felt privileged, it was worth everything, my life even, just to be there, to bear witness to the unspeakable beauty of the sky." I smiled down into the stunning portrait that was her face. "You know what I mean?"

"Beautiful...."

"Jack, he just saw me off at Southampton yesterday, Jack understood those things. And Manny, too, Manny had been our best friend, he'd been killed a few weeks earlier by a flying bomb, but his spirit was there with us, it felt so real it almost made me cry, I could hold his hand, I knew I was actually holding his hand."

She looked up into my face. "Beautiful," she repeated.

"Yes, it was... and I was in the middle of this... sort of celestial peace. I was... lucky enough to be there."

"You made it beautiful."

"Really? You mean because I saw it?"

"Yeah. Your words, the way you describe it — beautiful...."

The Copenhagen Interpretation. "You mean, the scene *itself* was beautiful, or my *description* of it just now was beautiful, or, my description of it *now, made* it beautiful then?"

"Yeah!" The wind howled. She laughed and threw back her head, and as in the pictures at the Empire she offered her lips, her soft and declining self. Now, standing side by side and facing the ocean, my arm around her shoulders, each of us with one hand grasping the rail, I bent my head and gently kissed her upturned lips. Her mouth flowed into mine. I eased her body closer, her softness accepting whatever shape my address demanded, holding her head, kissing her mouth, her cheeks, her temples, the silken hair. My hand slid beneath the flapping coat to her waist, to the delicate soft run of satined skin beneath the blouse. Her arms, now around my neck, pulled me down, down. Ferociously I kissed her large sparkling eyes, the tanned forehead, and then, a delicately carved ear; she gasped and I felt the shudder through her hips, her golden legs. I kissed her mouth, and her tongue was to my teeth, then behind my teeth pressing my own tongue. She pulled me forward and down, then fell sitting to the deck, pulling me over her. On my knees I eased off her wind-blown coat, held it beneath her as she reclined slowly back into its dark coiling folds. A sudden gust whipped at her hair, ballooning the coat and throwing me momentarily off balance; we each grabbed at the bottom rail, and thus supported I extended myself over her, kissing her neck, pulling down the blouse, kissing the perfumed aroma of her shoulder, unbuttoning, unhooking, my tongue running the burnished curve of her breast, circling the delicately noduled terrain of aureola, then, the firm raised nipple rolled slowly between my lips. My hand slid beneath her high arched back, and down, along the sweep of hip as we rolled onto our sides, the sequenced bursting of buttons from crisp white shorts that fell back and away, the small roundedness of her behind shining silver in the moonlight, the brown thighs, the dip of waist, the delicate rise of her abdomen.

I raised one of her knees to ease off the shorts.

"No, no, they'll blow over the side!"

Engulfed in an exotic mantle of serene confidence, I said: "We'll put them under the coat, we'll lie on them."

She acquiesced, and I slid them down around her little shoes, realizing she'd unbuttoned my shirt and was now fumbling with my belt. The wind caught her shorts and lifted them; with one knee I held them down then pulled off my own jacket and shirt and tied all in a loose knot around the rail, where they flapped and thundered in the wind.

Past the rail, beyond the small retaining lip that edged the deck, out into the moonlit expanse the waves crashed and fell. The wind climbed sonorously and tugged at our disarray. My fingers reached down the soft arc of her belly toward the moon-glistening thighs, slowly riding the incredible coming-together under a curlicued puff of transparent blonde hair, to lightly brush the innermost curvings — and she was all wet!

"You got... you know... any protection?"

"What?"

"A... rubber...?"

"Oh...er, one minute..." I took out my wallet and retrieved the unused package that had lain there for over a year. As I put the rubber on her hands were to my hips and thighs as she kissed my chest. She eased my torso square and courted me down. I lifted her slender waist and hips, and her neck became an inviting curve. In a slowed, deliberate frenzy I found myself embracing her high legs, her knees, arms, her waist, the deck reeling, the singing wind tugging my one hand clasped to the rail as she guided my audacious entry to the new world.

The wind fell, and chilled moonlight sparkled and danced onto the deck. I clasped her body in a mammoth shuddering embrace, kissed her forehead, and as she nested the side of her face to my chest I looked up once again to the stars: they were unmoved by our passion.

"So?" she asked from below, "you... you gonna say something?"

"It was wonderful. Wonderful."

Pause. "What you looking at?"

"The stars."

"Why don't you look at me?"

"I am," I said, and looked down at her.

"I'm Susan," she murmured.

"I'm Zachary."

"I'm cold."

The wind had again sprung up, and it whipped away the used condom. I pulled the side of her coat around us. The deck surface was hard to my forearms, and cold. I sat up, recovered her shoes lodged against the deck's lip and eased them onto her feet. She sat up too, and as she corrected their alignments I disentangled from the rail the rest of the flapping garments.

She searched among them. "Where's my panties? They're gone!"

"Perhaps... that's the price of love."

She eyed me as from a distance. We dressed, and I helped her up. "It's cold," she repeated.

"Yes, because of the latent heat of vaporization."

"You're... different." I held her coat around her shoulders and she grabbed at the collar to pull it tighter around herself. We climbed the tilting surface, pulled open the ringing metal door and stepped inside onto the carpet's welcome. The contours of ambient sound became again civilized as the door clanged itself shut. She surveyed my face: "What cabin you in?"

"E-eighty-seven."

"E-deck! You're down there!"

"Yes."

She drew a considered breath. "I gotta go back to my cabin, see you in the lounge," she said, and disappeared down the wide stairs.

Miraculously I found the old lounge; the pianist was gone, and now only two or three quiet groups were mustered in the parochial glow of low lamps. Across the tempering carpet I approached the piano and sat on the bench. I depressed one solitary key, and an anthem climbed up into the room's emptiness. Then another, and another, *C, E, G, B, D* — Schillinger's expansion one, and the opening line of *Porgy* — riches beyond belief. *Pianos cannot misinterpret because they bypass cognition; their sounds flood the ear and fall directly to the stomach, the seat of all useable knowledge, in divine concordance with each listener's compact.*

A half hour later, she still hadn't appeared. I wouldn't have known what to say, anyway, to a stranger. My lips were dry. The bar was dark, and a waiter cleaned off the counter as I walked over. "Could I have a Tizer?"

"Okay, s'pose I can get you one." He opened the bottle and inverted a glass over it.

"Thanks." I filled the glass.

"Bar's closed, y'know."

I took the drink to the piano and sat, careful to hold the liquid away from the keys, wondering at the waiter's grudging tone. Maybe his life consisted exclusively of serving drinks, wiping off counter-tops after other people's pleasures, sweeping up their crumbs; I smiled encouragingly as I returned the empty glass.

Making my way back along the passage, I came once more to the iron door. *So, I had sex for the very first time, and with an American, a stranger.* Again I pushed the door open and stepped outside. *She'd simply liked my singing; I hadn't needed to think, to calculate, estimate, ponder, die. America, America! I'm going to make love to every girl I meet, and I'm going to sing, sing, sing — for the rest of my life, I'm going to sing.*

A shooting star flashed across the night sky, and down, then was gone, gone to dust — after five billion years of icy hurtling stillness, for it to know the inconceivable ratio of three seconds of profligate radiance, then gone for all the rest of time. If I hadn't chanced to look would it still have staged its licentious show? Or was its exuberance a gift for me, just for me, because this is how the heavens requite love? Jack, ever the poet, was right; his science was sometimes a little beyond the pale and there was a fair chance any building he designed would collapse, but his intent was pure: to repose joyfully among the laws of the universe — quantum mechanics, relativity, the stunning mystery that manifests itself as the passage of time. Magic — the whole universe is hauntingly magical, and shooting stars are its poetic emissaries.

The passageway was deserted as the iron door clanged shut behind me. At the top of the stairway I poured myself a fluted paper cup of water from the machine on the wall. Cold, but not unbearably so — in fact, almost refreshing! Down the carpeted treads to B-deck, C-deck, then further down to where the wood veneers gave way to functional metal rails and the carpeting transmuted to corkoid, I reached E-deck and the narrow passageway that led to my cabin.

Ahead, a bulky figure approached, his dark brown face breaking into a golden-toothed smile as he recognized me.

"Late night, t'night!"

"Yes, I was out on deck, it's lovely, the stars and everything."

"Y' bunkin' down heah?"

"Yes, E-eighty-seven, just a bit along there, by the fan room where the noise comes from."

"Uhuh. Listen, Ah digs y' singin', man."

"Thank you, I love how you play."

"Keep singin' like that an' y' gonna be up there..." he nodded his head toward the ceiling, "...no time, with them rich folks."

I laughed. "I wouldn't know what to talk about...."

"Y' be in the lounge tomorrow?"

"Oh, yes, definitely."

"Good."

"Did you ever hear of a music theory person named Joseph Schillinger?"

"Schillinger? Ah sure did."

"Do you happen to know if Gershwin, George Gershwin...."

"George, huh? Word is Schillinger done help Georgie-boy w' *Porgy and Bess,* that's it!"

"Really! Do you know where this Schillinger is?"

"Sure do, Columbia, uptown. Hey, y' knows *Over The Rainbow?*"

"Judy Garland's one, yes, I love it."

"What key y' take it in?"

"Me? Wow, I'd sing it in... er..." I quickly ran through a silent stanza. "B-flat."

"B-flat, huh?" He continued on past me. "Okay, Ah'll be in the lounge tomorrow evenin'." He waved from the bottom of the stairway. "Soon's Ah done eatin' dinner Ah'll be there waitin' for y'."

"Do you like goosegogs?"

"Goosegogs? What's that?"

"Gooseberries, someone baked a pie for me. I'll bring you a nice big piece of gooseberry pie to the lounge, tomorrow."

—o—O—o—

Printed in the United States
20792LVS00006B/28-42